BAYONETS
& Lace

Barry Redmond

*I dedicate this book to James and Kitty and the people of Croghan,
Glenogue and Coolgreany. and Wexford County, who fell in the great
Battle of 1798.
May they find rest and peace eternal*

bayonetsandlace@gmail.com

Published by Barry Redmond
Publishing partner: Paragon Publishing, Rothersthorpe
First published 2014
© Barry Redmond 2014

ISBN 978-1-78222-194-4

Book design, layout and production management by Into Print
www.intoprint.net
01604 832149

Printed and bound in UK and USA by Lightning Source

Chapter one

The chestnut mare walked leisurely through the beech wood, the trees russet and gold in their autumnal colours. The rider, sitting sidesaddle, wore a blue riding habit that reflected the colour of the clear October sky. Her composure was confident and relaxed. In the distance, the clarion of the huntsman's horn carried on the light breeze, and pheasants protested loudly at being disturbed by the baying hounds. The old dog fox surveyed his pursuers from a rocky vantage point, planning his escape route.

Being forced to leave the hunting field annoyed Kitty. Her mare, Misty, had cast a shoe. It could have been worse. Early last spring a bad fall had put a premature ending to the whole hunting season for her. By comparison it was a minor mishap.

As horse and rider trotted in the stillness of the morning, Kitty felt a reluctance to turn towards home. The excitement of the build-up to the hunt still coursed through her veins. The days of anticipation could not be quenched in a matter of minutes. Her spirit had awaited liberation, and would not bow to circumstance.

The forge, she thought. Why not call there and have Misty's shoe replaced? The idea appealed as an adventure of sorts, such places being out of bounds to her. It was customary procedure for the groom to take care of her horse. 'Hang custom', a voice within her rebelled.

On approaching the forge, with its smoke emerging, she was hesitant yet fascinated. Her mount knew this noisy place well, and so ambled forward leisurely. 'What would father think of me?' she asked herself. She dismounted and addressed the shadowy doors, struggling to raise her voice above the rhythmic hammering.

"Can you please help me? My mare has lost one of her fore shoes."

The noise stopped, and a figure emerged as black as the entrance it walked through. Joe Gilltrap had worked the forge for almost twenty years, and this indeed was a rare sight. The Landlord's daughter in the flesh. Reading the curious expression written on the blacksmith's countenance Kitty explained her premature departure from the hunting field and reiterated her request.

"Certainly, my Lady. I will see to it right off," he responded.

His strong arm gently lifted the animal's foreleg to assess the hoof size, and reassuring Kitty of a replacement, Joe re-entered the forge and began to work instantly on the new shoe. Kitty was looking idly at the bees that clung to the ivy blossom climbing the adjacent building, when she thought she heard a second voice.

Her hearing proved correct as a figure emerged from the forge into the sunlight.

"Good afternoon, Miss Foldsworth."

Startled by the good looks and casual manner of the young man before her, Kitty replied rather haughtily.

"Good afternoon, and whom may I be addressing?"

"James de Lacey," came the reply. "Regrettable to see your hunting day coming to a sudden end, but sometimes these things seem meant, don't you think?"

"I think no such thing!" replied Kitty, surprised even more by this unusual sentiment from a stranger. Yet he was friendly and sincere, and his directness stirred something within her. She liked him almost instantly. She later reflected that this disturbed her more than his manner of address.

"I don't recall seeing you in the area before, Mr. de Lacey."

"Correct, Miss Foldsworth, I only arrived here last month. My uncle who is old and unwell bade me come, and so I'm here to be of whatever help I can to him. I find myself becoming very attached to this village and its people," he added with a broadening grin.

"I'm glad to hear it," Kitty replied, "and I hope the remainder of your visit will prove equally as pleasant."

"My hope is to stay here quite a while," responded James, somehow meaning it more than ever.

"In that case I'm sure we will meet again," replied Kitty, taking the reins from the blacksmith.

She mounted her mare with such liveliness that both men were a little taken aback. Sitting sidesaddle, with her long hair escaped from its netting, Kitty looked very much the lady in control of her life.

"I will send your fee, Mr. Gilltrap. Thank-you for your help this morning."

Kitty was aware of the gazes of both men.

"Regard it as a gift, Miss Foldsworth, no fee in question," said Joe, realising how Lord Foldsworth would probably react to his daughters stroll to the forge. Better to end it here.

"Goodbye Miss Foldsworth. It was pleasant speaking with you," said James, unable to take his gaze off Kitty.

"Goodbye, Mr. de Lacey."

Abrupt as her farewell, Kitty turned her mare and trotted homeward.

* * *

Her thoughts, however, remained at the forge. She liked this James de Lacey, whoever he was. She had enjoyed his easy familiarity, although propriety had not allowed her to respond in kind. Perhaps he was correct in his thinking – Misty losing her shoe may be part of destiny in some small way. 'How totally absurd,' she thought, and forced her mind to think of a nice hot bath and how welcome it would be.

Later that evening on entering the dining room Kitty was greeted casually by her mother, Lady Edwina Foldsworth, who stood rearranging a spray of late roses from the flower garden.

"Well, my dear how was the hunt today? I missed the outing dreadfully. This cold appears so reluctant to leave me."

Kitty looked at her mother, who did not look unwell despite her protest.

"I had to leave the field early Mamma. Misty cast a shoe," Kitty said, as she smelled a rose that still retained scents of the summer now gone.

"Oh dear, that was unfortunate," replied her mother. "By the way, your father will not be here for dinner this evening. He had to go to Dublin Castle. Some political issue or another.

Having rearranged the roses to her taste, Lady Edwina pulled the service bell, and they both sat down to dinner. Kitty wished her father was present. She never felt fully at ease in her mothers company.

"Were the Ryglies out today, my dear?" asked Lady Edwina.

"Yes they were Mamma, and Richard was very cordial and courteous. I sometimes wonder why he goes to such extremes to impress," said Kitty, sipping wine from her glass.

"I'm sure you do, Kitty. After all, he did appear so interested in you at the ball in Birch Hall last month. His background is excellent, you know, and his father's estate is one of the few remaining unencumbered properties in these parts."

"Yes, Mamma, and at what a price."

"And what does that mean?" Lady Edwina recoiled as if bitten by an insect.

"Exactly the truth Mamma. So many families made homeless through eviction, so many smallholdings gone with more and more herds of cattle grazing where once so many families lived. I don't agree with such policies, or prosperity at such a price."

"My dear, never express such radical views in your father's presence, or indeed for that matter in his friends either. The literature you have been reading on that dreadful revolution in France has seemingly turned your head right around. Hmmm, why next you will be sympathising with these groups of freedom fighters, as they call themselves. I trust that the meeting your father is attending in Dublin tonight will find a quick remedy. Our peace and our very lives hang on a thread these days, and never you forget that, Kitty."

Her meal unfinished, Lady Edwina left the table and swept out of the dining room, leaving her daughter amazed by her own assertiveness. Kitty was relieved to have expressed what she actually felt. As she lingered over her dessert she thought of what an unusual day it had been. Unpredictable, for a change.

While drifting to sleep that night, her mind happily entertained James de Lacey and their meeting that day.

* * *

Lord Foldsworth returned home later that week, tired and agitated. He paced the drawing room floor, waiting for his wife to join him. Lord and Lady Foldsworth still loved each other, and the sharing of all aspects of their lives was largely responsible for their healthy relationship. Today, Charles Foldsworth had decided to tell his wife the truth he had learned at Dublin Castle, despite the fact that the contents were alarming. He thought it better to speak to his wife directly, rather than her hearing it from one of her gossiping friends.

"Charles, I'm so sorry for delaying you, but there were..."

"Edwina, come and sit down, there are some issues I wish to discuss with you."

"Charles, can we not talk about the estate affairs this evening, perhaps after dinner. Why not come and enjoy a walk through the oaks. It's such a beautiful day."

Lady Edwina sensed the tension in her husband.

"I'm afraid not Edwina. It's not estate business I wish to speak of, but rather what poses a threat to the estate."

Curiosity, touched with fear, brought Lady Edwina to her husband's side. She noticed the increasingly worried expression on her husband's face, and her concern mounted.

"What is it Charles? You do seem serious."

"Edwina, throughout the country at present there is a lot of talk of rebellion. It would seem there isn't a village in the county that hasn't got a group together planning revolt. The Lord Lieutenant is anxious that we are at least aware of this, and alerted to the possibilities."

The pale face of his wife made Lord Charles wonder if he hadn't been unwise in revealing these facts, yet they had to be faced.

"Oddly enough Charles," she said, "the thought had occurred to me as to how long our happiness could last. Only last month, during Lady Ramsfield's Garden Fete, I heard such rumours, and preferred not to think of them. So they are true?"

"Yes my dear, all too true, I regret to say," replied her husband.

"Oh Charles, what are we to do? And then there is Kitty to think of. What of her safety?"

"Leave Kitty to me," replied Lord Foldsworth. "For the moment it is best not to worry her. Let her enjoy her life of hunting and parties for now. In the spring, perhaps, we could send her to John in Hampshire for a holiday."

"Yes. That is a good idea Charles. We will let the child enjoy her time, as it will change only too soon for us all I fear."

Anxious his wife would become too morose; Lord Foldsworth suggested they take that stroll she had mentioned. Lady Edwina was grateful. It was soothing to do something perfectly normal.

Later that evening, much to the curiosity of the servants, Lord Foldsworth gave orders that from now on all the shutters were to be closed securely throughout the house every evening.

* * *

"Perhaps he is feeling the draughts," remarked Hannah, head cook to the household for over forty years. "Seems to me his Lordship isn't the man he used to be. Of late he looks burdened, poor soul."

With that, she gave a sharp reminder to Lizzie to look lively and make sure the cauliflower was left steeping in fresh water. Hannah took great pride in her kitchen and staff, and her cooking abilities excelled. Tips her good friend at Birch Hall had passed on to her enhanced many of her recipes. After all, she had worked with a family in France, before the war there in 1789 had ruined all the great French families. Hannah presided over the kitchen of a content and happy household. Indeed, all the staff were fortunate to have a roof over their heads, good food and payment, unlike their counterparts outside who lived hand-to-mouth. This often served as a sharp reminder for Hannah to any member of the household who, as she termed it, 'dragged their feet'. It inevitably worked, as there was little future for anyone who was dismissed from service these days.

Just then Kitty walked into the kitchen, and Hannah went into a blaze of fuss. She loved this child, and what a beautiful lady she was growing up to be.

"Hannah, do you think you could prepare a picnic for me tomorrow? I intend taking Misty up by the Hill Fort. That is, if the weather is fine."

"Picnics in November, Miss Kitty? Whatever next!" responded Hannah teasingly, knowing how Her Ladyship was so fond of taking canters through the hills. The why of it evaded her, but to her mind the 'quality' did things most ordinary people wouldn't dream of doing. "Make sure the fairies aren't disturbed, Miss Kitty, or they might take you to their Fort altogether!"

This constant reminder of the 'good people' and what they might do never failed to make Kitty bubble with laughter.

"Oh, don't worry, Hannah. I will just be sitting by the Fort eating my lunch and the only ones disturbed will be the skylarks. There are so many of them up there."

'Sky larks and picnics,' thought Hannah, as Kitty left the kitchen. 'Time that young Miss had more serious things on her mind, like courtship and marriage'. Yet she loved Kitty's childlike enthusiasm for everyone and everything in general. Let her enjoy herself and her freedom. It wasn't going to last forever.

Suddenly, a sharp knock sounded from the kitchen door, followed by a loud groan. Startled from her thoughts, Hannah quickly opened the door. A total stranger collapsed onto the floor beside her.

"Williams, Williams, come quick!" cried a startled Hannah. The young mans arms were covered in blood. Williams came running in and went straight to the aid of the cook. Having lifted the almost corpse-like figure, they both managed to carry him to the big chair by the great fire. With short sips of whiskey, the stranger revived enough to groan, and eventually to speak.

"Please Ma'am, help me. It's my arm, hurted you see... in a fight at the market today. My head hurts."

A gash at the rear of his head was evident, despite the blood having dried and leaving a stain on the back of his coat.

Williams and Hannah looked at one another, and somehow this didn't make sense. To begin with, most victims of faction fights almost oozed of alcohol, but this stranger didn't, and he didn't appear to be the brawling type. Moreover, these wounds were some days old now. Not wishing to press the issue, they both sensed it best to help the stranger in whatever way they could, and send him on his way. If the master knew of this, he would be none to pleased.

"Hot broth, Hannah," said Williams. "That should help bring him back to himself."

Later, having eaten a plate of cold beef and some bread, the stranger was able to talk intelligibly.

"I'm here to find my brother Ma'am. He is in these parts having come to live with an uncle. I must find him before nightfall, or I'll have no place to stay tonight."

"Well, my young man," replied Hannah, "when you feel ready to go about your business, you'll need a place to stay alright. Where have you come from then?"

"Kilronan Ma'am, and lost my horse in the bargain. How far is the village from here?"

"Less than two miles," said Hannah, becoming even more curious.

With that, Williams came back into the kitchen and informed them the cart was going to the village, if the stranger wanted a carry in that direction. Only too glad of the opportunity, he stood immediately and thanked Hannah.

"I hope some day I can repay your kindness, Ma'am."

The sincerity of his remarked touched Hannah.

"What is your name, my lad?" she asked.

"Just John, Ma'am, just John."

Not wanting to impart further information, he left.

"So peculiar, Williams. His story makes little sense at all yet somehow there is a decent side to that fellow. Oh well, all's well that ends well."

Hannah returned her attention to the dinner menu and, realising time lost, sent the entire kitchen staff into a frenzy of activity.

"Don't ye forget what awaits ye should we all be dismissed... "

* * *

The morning dawned clear and mild, so Kitty decided to venture out directly after breakfast. Such days were a novelty as winter loomed. Dutifully, Hannah had made ample and varied provisions in the saddle pack for Kitty's lunch.

"Mind you keep warm, young Miss. Those hills hold a breeze even on the calmest of days," warned Hannah.

"Of course, Hannah. I'll be careful, and what a hamper you have prepared! Expect me home for dinner, as usual. Goodbye!"

Kitty mounted Misty, and with a sense of adventure, trotted briskly down the beech-lined avenue. Viewing the hills, Kitty was glad the day seemed to favour her. She travelled the old roads, smiling and exchanging a few words with those she met on their way to the village. Many had baskets of eggs and butter. Cartloads of freshly unearthed potatoes were being brought to the village, the sales of which guaranteed next months rent for their landlord, Lord Foldsworth. The people however, liked Kitty. She was always friendly and interested, and remembered their names.

Misty bounded over the neat walls of the small fields at the foot of the hills. A startled hare leapt from its set and ran uphill before stopping to look back at the intruder. Looking away from the little animal, Kitty noticed the silhouette of a man against the skyline. He seemed to be going in the direction of the hill fort also.

"It looks, Misty, as if someone other than ourselves likes the peace of the hill fort," she said to the mare, as she cantered briskly uphill.

She wondered who it could be. Perhaps someone looking for lost livestock. The walker had seen both horse and rider too. He was equally as curious.

Kitty reached the hill fort, dismounted, and tethered her mare. She looked down across the valley. It was so magnificent with autumn colours, and the coastline so clear, with the tall masts of sailing ships like toy boats on a blue pool.

"Beautiful, isn't it?" came a voice.

Kitty turned quickly to see the invader of her private thoughts.

"I'm sorry if I startled you," the young man said.

Instantly Kitty recognised him. The good-looking stranger from the forge.

"My goodness, Mr de Lacey, we meet again!"

"Yes, Miss Foldsworth, and what a surprise to see you here."

His gaze was fixed on the view before them. Kitty's gaze was on him. She noticed the firm jaw setting, the brown eyes, the smile, and the good white teeth.

"How did you happen to come upon my favourite place, Mr de Lacey?"

"Oh, quite simply. I have always enjoyed climbing the hill at home. Today was so clear and fresh I just decided on a whim... and if you like, you may call me James!"

"Well, I hope, James, you will enjoy the view every bit as much as I do. It clears my mind."

The ravens climbed the skies above them calling noisily at the intruders. Soon they would be nest building on the steeper slopes among the craggy rocks.

"You seem to have one thing in common with the ravens, Miss Foldsworth."

"And what would that be, James?"

"Your love of the fort."

"That is true. I love this place, and the ravens don't mind vacating to the sky for my visits. But please, my name is Catherine, or Kitty. Please call me Kitty. Formality and the wildness of this place somehow seem awkward companions."

Extending her hand, James took it in the polite manner intended. To himself, James thought, 'There's something different in this meeting. I am lucky to have come here today.'

"I have some lunch in my saddlebag. Perhaps you'd care to join me? Hannah, our cook, always packs enough food for a troop of cavalry!"

Finding a comfortable place to sit, they ate the cold chicken pie and ham slices, and drank the cold milk.

"This pie is delicious, Kitty. Hannah must be a very good cook."

"Yes. She's been with the family now for quite a long time and I can't imagine what we should do without her," replied Kitty.

Then, pointing across the hillside, she added.

"Over there, James. That is the valley where Hannah was born. Do you see the three white cottages? Well, her brother and sister live there still."

Her gaze then fell to following the flight of a hawk as it glided silently on the gentle breeze.

"How people make a living on these hilly slopes I'll never know," said James; aware that Kitty's attention was not quite with him.

He was relieved when his comment went unnoticed. It would be a pity to spoil this moment between the beautiful young woman and him. They rose and walked around the old hill fort, and Kitty began to tell him the folklore of the area. James responded with interest and an obvious love for the old stories. Kitty was surprised to find him so receptive and knowledgeable, so much her equal in the lore of the land. He might be one of the 'ordinary' folk, but he was definitely not ordinary.

Before they realised it, evening had begun to steal the light of the day, and the deep red and purple evening sky appeared over the hilltops.

"Kitty, this has been a beautiful day. We could... I mean... I will come here again. It's such a lovely place, is it not?"

James felt a tug at his heart that the day had to come to an end. That he must leave Kitty and the joy he had felt in her company. He wished time would stop, right now, and forever.

"Yes, James, truly lovely. I have no doubt I will venture here again should the season provide another day as agreeable as this one," Kitty replied, aware that she extended an invitation of sorts.

"Thank you for sharing your lunch with me, Kitty. And your company. Both delightful if you don't mind me saying so."

"Don't thank me, James. It was all Hannah's splendid doings," replied Kitty laughing, and trying to imagine Hannah's reaction had she known she had shared her lunch with a total stranger.

"I am told that Hannah makes a lovely broth. According to my brother, that is," James said, without really thinking.

"Why James, I wasn't aware your brother was working on the estate," responded Kitty, taken aback by this piece of information.

James realised he had said too much.

"Actually, he was over to visit me and a loss of direction seemingly brought him to call on the kitchen at Oak Hall. To enquire the way, from what I gather. He was treated to a bowl of broth... "

James knew better than to enter into further detail. He had said too much already. She was, after all, the Landlord's daughter. Meanwhile, Kitty tightened the girth on her horse.

"I must be off now. Father gets quite worried about my lone canters. Besides, it's almost time for dinner, which means I would have Hannah to contend with as well!"

Laughing, she mounted, holding her animal with great ease.

"Goodbye Kitty. Perhaps we will meet soon again," said James, hoping earnestly that they would.

"Perhaps we will," replied Kitty, and waving her gloved hand, trotted briskly across the breast of the hill. James waved back at her as he strode slowly away from the fort, where the ravens would now return to claim their homes again.

* * *

However lovely the afternoon had been, James was aware that there were more serious issues to be faced in the days ahead, with a meeting of a far different nature tomorrow. How contradictory to encourage a friendship with a beautiful young lady of the landlord class while he was part of a growing revolutionary movement planning the destruction of that very class.

The arrival of his brother John, and wounded at that, was something James had not anticipated. He knew he would have to arrange for him to live somewhere else. While it was credible that he himself had come to help his uncle, his brothers presence would be open to question after a while, as were natural amongst country folk. He could ask Joe Gilltrap would he know of someone needing a farm hand. Kitty apparently had not heard of the stranger going to the kitchen door for help, or of his wounded condition. Here he was thinking of Kitty again!

As he descended through the heather covered slope, he wrestled with the prospect of how one could tell the one they loved they were a part of a growing organisation planning to overthrow all of her class, and all it represented? He then chided himself with the common-sense fact that he had met the girl on two occasions, and here he was if needs be willing to expose himself, and so many more, to what could be treason against the government. Death by hanging!

"Seldom in war can love succeed," he reminded himself aloud.

* * *

Joe Gilltrap was tired to the very core of his bones. Providing for his wife Nell and their five children was hard work at the best of times. A good-natured man, he never refused to do a job for a customer short of money. He would gladly accept a bag of potatoes or a piece of bacon or ham instead. Today, as he washed himself at the barrel of rainwater collected from the roof of his cabin, his mind was on other things.

He had been asked to make one hundred pikes, and he was worried. Aware he was better off than most of his neighbours and friends, he had agreed. To date he had managed to make thirty, and had hidden them in a drain at the back of the forge, where they lay covered in two feet of silt. Although it was unlikely the military would ever suspect him of such activities, he would feel happier when they had been moved. This was to be next morning, concealed on the bottom of a cart, beneath a load of potatoes which himself and young James de Lacey were to take to town. From there they would be brought further South, and kept hidden until Father John Murphy decided it was time to arm the people.

Joe was only too aware that if discovered, he would be arrested and tried to a penalty of death by hanging. 'Eileen and the children,' he thought. 'Am I reckless and foolish to be part of such a plan?' He had told Eileen that his mother was unwell and that he had to leave on the morrow with James to go and see her. He detested himself for the lie, for she was loving and trusting and he knew that she would never question him. There was not alternative, he thought as he went into the house.

The children were in bed. Eileen stood at the table kneading the dough, making bread for the morrow. She glanced up at her husband and smiled.

"Your dinner is in the pot Joe. How did work go for you today?"

She wiped the perspiration from her forehead with the corner of her apron.

"Grand Nell, grand," he replied, as he sat at the other side of the table trying to conceal his anxiety. Nell was his pet name for his wife, and having married late in life he knew he was a lucky man to have found her. As he ate the potato and bacon he realised just how hungry he had been.

"You seem to be coming home later each evening Joe. Is the work building up on you?" she asked, with a frown of concern. "Why not take on young Brian Byrne? His mother tells me he cannot wait to start his apprenticeship with you."

"Not yet, Nell. The lad's barely twelve years old and not yet strong enough. I'll give him another year or so, and then we'll see."

"But Joe, another year... what difference is that going to make?"

"Nell, leave it up to me about young Brian," he replied, and Nell knew that her husbands mind was made up on the matter.

"I hope your poor mother will pull through this time, Joe. Why, this is her second illness this year, isn't it?" she asked.

"Well Nell, she is eighty-four years of age now, and what else can you expect at that age?"

He wondered what the outcome would be if Nell had found out he had not been to see his mother al all this year. He quickly turned the conversation to domestic matters about the children and her.

As he lay in bed that night he was restless. Nell slept by his side while he listened to the trees outside, and watched the flickering shades of light as the clouds raced over the face of the moon. Presently he slept, only to be awoken with a loud banging on the outside door. Nell woke with a start.

"Who in God's name could be at the door at this time of night Joe?"

A thousand thoughts ran through Joe's mind in seconds.

"Who else but a neighbour in trouble. You'll see," he said much more calmly than he felt. "Hold on, hold on. Have patience, coming to a man's door in the dead of the night."

* * *

Before him stood Lord Foldsworth.

"Lord Foldsworth, your honour..." his voice trailed off.

Raising a gloved hand, the landlord tried to convey his discomfort at disturbing the blacksmith.

"Gilltrap, I do regret the lateness of my calling, but my carriage axle has apparently snapped while coming from the ball. It needs repairing as soon as possible. Fortunately Brent was driving quite slowly, otherwise Lady Edwina and I would perhaps not have been so fortunate." Lord Foldsworths voice shook.

"Snapped, your lordship? 'Tis very rare a carriage axle snaps. Odd thing your honour."

"Well Gilltrap, examine it for yourself. The thought did occur to me that it was not a simple accident. There are some out there fit for any malign act."

Joe knew he referred to landlords being burnt out of their stately homes in retaliation for the relentless evictions being carried out. Was this 'accident' a gentle reminder to Lord Foldsworth that the grim hand of revenge was never far away? But no evictions had taken place in this area, so why target a seemingly fair-minded man? Watching the relief carriage pull away to take the late night callers to Oak Hall, Joe sighed. How different this night could have been? Nell, standing on the small landing, had heard the entire conversation.

"Her poor ladyship must have gotten an awful fright," she said tiredly, returning to bed. "But, haven't the quality a great life when you come to think of it, with their parties, hunts and balls, and all them servants to do their work. And then to think there are some people going to bed hungry. God, if I had someone to comb my hair for me and to do the cookin' and all the housework, I think I'd go foolish with idleness."

Joe laughed quietly.

"Well Nell, you can rest easy tonight with the thought that you'll never have to worry about going foolish then woman!"

Nell turned on her side and began to dream of being fitted for a ball gown. Joe lay awake thinking for the remainder of the night. Things were taking a turn to the serious side, even in this quiet village in the foothills.

Lord Foldsworth thought the same as he sipped his brandy by the fireside. He vowed to be more alert and aware of the activities in the area from now on.

* * *

James de Lacey had decided to get to the forge early, so he was surprised to see smoke rising while he was still some distance away. *Perhaps he has forgotten that we are going away today,* he thought. *What could he be doing? Shoeing a horse perhaps!*

The mare walked steadily with the cartload of potatoes, under which the bayonets were to be hidden and transported. It had been arranged that he would conceal the pikes while Joe made sure Nell didn't come out of the house. On approaching the forge James called out to Joe.

"You are working early this morning, Joe."

He sensed the tension from the blacksmith.

"Aye, Lord Foldsworth had an accident coming from the ball last night, axle trouble... seems it just snapped."

"Carriage axle's rarely snap, Joe, and you know that as well as I do. What way does it look to you?"

"Well, by the looks of this one, let's just say it was encouraged to do so. I don't relish the thought of telling them that up at the big house. 'Twill draw suspicion on the whole place. Where will that leave us then?"

Joe rubbed his hand across his face, and it left behind a black streak.

"Well, that's that job completed. I'll go wash while you load the cart, and for Gods sake be alert. Even at this time of the day. We can no longer take anything for granted."

James backed the cart to the rear of the house and began to load the pikes under the potatoes, placing wheaten straw around them to muffle any sounds they were likely to make.

Meanwhile Nell fried thick slices of bacon. She welcomed James warmly when he eventually came into the kitchen.

"Nice mornin', mam. Makes a man hungry bein' up so early," James said, only just realising how hungry he was.

"Eat up, young man, there's more there for you if you are able," replied Nell, as she stirred a big pot of porridge for the children. Both men ate hurriedly, saying little, anxious to be on the road.

"Here, Joe. Bring these eggs and cake to your mother. I'm sure she thinks it odd of me never to visit her, and she so out of sorts this past year, poor soul."

That Nell was a kind-hearted woman was evident to James, but he was also aware that she was no fool.

"Do you know, Nell, she will be delighted to hear from you," said Joe consolingly, "and 'tis well she knows that it is next to impossible for you to visit with a house full of small children."

This reassured Nell.

"Well, we'll be off now, and God willin' I'll be back before Friday. The carriage is ready for His Lordship when they call down from the big house."

He hurriedly hugged Nell and walked past James to the yard outside. James finished his tea in haste and thanked Nell for the fine breakfast.

"You're more than welcome, and I hope you get a good price for your potatoes," she replied.

James shut the door behind him and hoped she was right. With that both men braced themselves against the cool morning air and looked at the dark sky that lay like a blanket on the mountains.

"It won't be too long before we have snow, James. 'Tis in that wind coming from the mountains these past days."

James thought of the day he and Kitty had spent at the ring fort. It had been a pleasantly warm one for that time of year.

"You know, Joe, I love the wind. Funny isn't it? Since I was a child I remember my grandmother telling me stories about how the Tuatha De Danann always travelled on the wind with their horses. It was a story full of magic." For they were indeed a magical tribe.

Joe looked over at James who was gazing wistfully at the distant horizon, lost in a world that no one knew except himself, and Joe concluded there was no accounting for what some got into their hearts. The mare trotted happily forward while both men remained quiet in their own thoughts. After a few miles, Joe broke the silence.

"Let's hope Marcus Ryan will be here and ready, James. I hear the towns are crawling with military men. That attack and maiming of Lord Densby's cattle have them all on full alert. When word of last nights episode goes round about his Lordships carriage, it will only add fuel to the fire."

It was clear to James that Joe was nervous, and why wouldn't he be, he thought.

"Well Joe, we are selling potatoes, luckily enough."

Both men laughed heartily. They eased the pace of the mare as they began the uphill climb that led to the town, where the turf smoke of many houses rose blue against the overcast sky.

* * *

Marcus Ryan sampled a slice of apple tart as he stood idly by the pastry stall. He loved market day: the loud roar of cattle, the high-pitched neighing of nervous horses, the endless cackle of geese and fowl from all over the countryside.

It always made him wonder at the different lives people led. Already some men had been drinking too much, and their staggered walks and bawdy shouts were evidence that they had sold their animals. Drink always seemed to clinch the deal. Tinkers sold pots and kettles. Fortunetellers told of events, still held in the mists of time, to country girls who had heard all they hoped they would. From the food houses came the smell of boiled cabbage and bacon, roast beef and chicken. Ah yes, thought Marcus, the market is the place to see life going ahead.

He wondered if he would see Chrissie. Her mother usually brought her to help sell the butter she made. They always sold near the Bull's Nose, a public house that swelled to twice its capacity on market days. It was a landmark for many people, being renowned for its good food, stout and ale. The owner, Marjorie Bass, was a very good businesswoman. Kind, but equally firm. Her intolerance for those who couldn't hold their drink like men, as she termed it, was widely known. Her concern for the poor and unfortunate was also renowned. Marjorie seemed to have gained the trust of the local garrison stationed in the town, principally because of her tolerance of their late night drinking habits. She was aware that some suspected other reasons. But then she realised that life was so much bigger than small folks minds.

Marcus was firmly jolted back to reality by the slap of a big hand on his shoulder.

"God save ye, Marcus, and you're here on time, me lad," Joe boomed, relief noticeable in his voice. Lowering his tone, he proceeded to tell Marcus of the incident with the carriage axle, and that it was unlikely the military had been told as yet.

"How did your journey go?" asked Marcus, concerned at the news.

"The outpost just waved us on. They seemed to be more interested in the cattle on the road ahead of us than our cart load of potatoes," Joe replied.

"Good going that, Joe, but we'll have to be very alert, as the town is alive with spies. All hired for the day, and paid off with drink in the evening. No shortage of Judas men about the place," he concluded, and spat on the ground with the unpleasant taste of treachery.

Joe liked Marcus. He had a keen, alert mind and a sharp eye, and he came from a trustworthy family.

"Where's the cart load of spuds then, Joe?" Marcus enquired, anxious to be on the move and not to attract unnecessary attention.

"James will be back in a few minutes. He's gone to fetch a fresh horse. The old mare had a long pull here."

Joe scanned the crowd for a sign of James.

"Well, I'll meet him at the potato corner. I'll buy them off him, take over the load, and head south." Marcus was very confident. He knew fear was the greatest betrayer of all.

"Then we will ride ahead, as planned, and meet you at Slaney Castle. God speed you on your way," said Joe, as he began to move through the crowd.

He went to take up a position where he would have a clear view of both men. James with the cartload of potatoes, and Marcus, who would feign purchase and delivery of them. Shortly afterwards, James appeared, leading the fresh horse and load of potatoes through the thronged street. As he slowly made his way to the position he planned to stand by, he thought of the load of pikes underneath and tried to concentrate on his buyer, whom he had never even met before. Joe had told him to look out for a young man wearing a brown hat with pheasant feathers on the rim. Let's hope, he thought, that there is only one such hat!

Tethering the horse to a nearby cart shaft, he waited. There were some who enquired the price he expected for the load, but they soon lost interest when they heard the price demanded. James saw the brown-feathered hat bobbing in the crowd.

"This Marcus isn't tall anyway," he muttered under his breath with a grin.

The young man approached casually, looking at the potatoes and handling some of them.

"How much for the potatoes, me man," he enquired, without looking up.

"I'll give you the lot for fifty shillings," replied James, as casual as you like.

"No use to me," replied Marcus. "The fellow three carts down is only lookin' forty two and they are a better potato altogether."

'Well 'tis maybe three carts down you should be then rather than wasting my day here!"

Marcus looked directly at him, and James began to wonder if this was the right contact at all.

"Forty five shillings then," bargained Marcus, "and that is me final offer to ye man!"

Oh here, take them to the devil. How is a man supposed to keep a wife and childer at all, I'm askin' meself, and me givin' potatoes away like that!"

Marcus thought James was a better actor than seller, and handed his money over, counting it slowly.

"Mind you, I'll expect a bit of luck money back out of this."

And so the deal was done.

To the casual bystander it was an everyday bargaining deal, but, as both men were very aware, not everyone was a casual bystander. Some were paid to observe and report. It was the curse of Ireland, James thought, the way some would sell their brother for a pint of porter and others would not think twice of spilling their blood for strangers. Contrasts indeed.

Marcus mounted the cart and headed the horse out of town through the crowds of people. It all looked very ordinary and casual, with nothing that would draw attention. James made his way through the throng in the opposite direction, where he was to meet Joe at the Bull's Nose. The smell of food and drink reminded James how hungry he was, and he began to let the tension of the morning ebb slowly from his mind and body. He saw Joe standing at the bar counter exhaling large plumes of tobacco smoke and sipping slowly from a glass of frothy stout. Beside him was a woman laughing heartily.

"Come, James, and meet the very woman who would suit you down to the ground. A woman with a business at that!" Joe beckoned James with his arm.

James blushed with embarrassment as the booming voice attracted the attention of the bar and a large cheer arose.

"Sure he's only a lad Joe, for God's sake," laughed Marjorie. "Come over her son and don't pay too much attention to Joe. Sure he's been trying to marry me off for a long time. And I ask you, where would I be going at my age in life?"

James liked Marjorie instantly. There was no doubting she was a strong minded woman, well capable of looking after herself, and he felt she could sum up any man at a glance. They shook hands.

"Hello Marjorie, I'm pleased to meet you. Well, I see Joe is getting the dust from his throat at last."

"True lad, true. Coal dust at that. And seeing as it's your first visit here, allow me to treat you to a pint of the best."

With that, Marjorie went in behind the counter, knowing the two men needed to talk.

"Did you sell the potatoes, James?" Joe asked, with a gleam in his eye.

"I did indeed, Joe, and lucky I was to make a quick sale. The look on the sky out there and the chill in the air would make an man expect snow."

"We certainly don't need that bother, what with another fifteen miles ahead of us. Best drink up, and when you've eaten, meet me up at the top of the street. I'll have the horses ready."

With that, Joe left. Marjorie returned with a platter of roast beef and potatoes and another glass of stout.

"Now young man, get that into you, as no-one travels far on a stomach of wind. Especially the young."

"Thanks Marjorie, that's more than decent of you, and may God leave you your health."

"I hope he will James, and a full house to go with it. Now don't forget, whenever you are in town – come in, as any friend of Joe's is a friend of mine."

James sensed that Marjorie's feelings for Joe ran very deep. There seemed to be a strong bond there. Could she belong to the circle, he wondered? And if so, what was her role in it all? Money perhaps? Or... of course, he thought, the late night callers... the military... that was it! Marjorie would at all times be in earshot of their conversations and could pass information on to whoever her contact was. It all made sense now.

Before leaving he thanked Marjorie, and handed her the cake and eggs that Nell had intended for Joe's sick mother. Marjorie and James both realised that poor Nell would never be any the wiser.

"Goodbye Marjorie, and thanks for the great dinner, it was badly needed."

"Come any time, there will always be a dinner here for you. I'm just hoping the weather won't hold you both up. God speed."

Outside the Bull's Nose the air had filled with tiny snowflakes and the wind moaned through the overhead sign. James buttoned his coat up to his chin and shivered with the stark contrast from the roaring fire he had just left. He saw Joe waiting in the distance with the horse, which was restless with the chill wind that had swept over the town.

* * *

Many were making a swift departure now, in fear of an oncoming blizzard. Others just sat on in the pubs singing, oblivious to the weather or remarks on the sudden change. Market day was market day, and the monthly outing, so it mattered little. Women tried in vain to persuade their men folk to make a move. In the end they just drove their pony and cart into the rising wind, making their own way homewards.

Joe and James cantered out of town, and continued on the road south that would eventually lead them to the castle, the point of their rendezvous.

"Who exactly will be at this meeting Joe?"

"You'll see, you'll see," Joe replied, and added agitatedly, "and if we don't make a better pace we will miss it. Mind you, this unexpected snowfall will at least cover our tracks."

Then, as suddenly as the snow had commenced falling, it stopped. Around them was the silent countryside, all the softer a silence for the blanket of white snow.

"How far more is it Joe?" James asked, as he brushed the snow from his coat and the mane of his horse.

"Another couple of miles. From the top of this hill we will be able to see the castle turrets," Joe replied, settling his horse into a steady canter. "There it is James, with the turrets coming over the top of the trees. Two miles or less as the crow flies."

All of a sudden, Joe spurned his horse off the roadway and jumped a large ditch. James almost came unseated with the abrupt change of direction. They rode through the giant oak trees onto a small track. A pheasant flew up from the undergrowth protesting loudly at his intruders, and the wind moaned through the old trees, that had been standing for over two hundred winters. Wood pigeons, roosting early, looked down at the two horsemen as, arriving at the castle, they made their way through the ruins at a steady pace. From the shadows emerged a horseman. Joe stopped instantly.

"God save," he called, and the stranger saluted.

"Hello Joe, I see you have company," he responded in a thin voice.

"Indeed I have, and good company at that. This is James, and I may add only for him these pikes would never have been shifted."

Joe beamed in satisfaction, as if only now realising they were moved from the forge. James saluted Tim. He didn't like him, he thought. He didn't know why, other than the fact that there were people one liked instantly, and some one didn't, and Tim was one such man.

"Hello Tim. Are we finished with the snow do you think?" James tried to conceal his feelings.

"Hard to know, James," Tim replied, "but I think we'd better move ahead as you two are the last pair to arrive."

With that subtle rebuke, he turned his horse and both men followed him on the track that led to the castle. Tethering their horses in a sheltered place, they were led to a room at the base of one of the turrets, which was lit by two lamps perched on ledges. The dim light fell on the faces sitting around a table constructed of old ceiling timber roughly placed together. It served the purpose, James thought. A tall man all in black sat at the top of the table. He looked at James and smiled.

"So you are the man helping Joe. I'm glad you have an interest in our cause son. Murphy is my name. Father John Murphy."

James took the extended hand and shook it, liking him there and then.

"I too, Father, have heard a great deal about you, and the pleasure is mine at this meeting."

James was very happy at last to meet the priest who was renowned for his concern for the poor and oppressed. The other men at the meeting shook hands with James one by one. James felt that he was being accepted into the group without question.

Father John began to outline the plan for the making, collecting and storage of the pikes, and to sort out whatever monies they would need for their cause. James realised for the first time the seriousness of this movement and what the eventual aim of it was to be. The priest spoke with conviction and confidence, and conveyed to all present that victory and freedom would be theirs, despite all odds. It was just a question, he said, of organising enough men, arming them, and choosing the right time.

"Soon men, this government will be just a memory to us all, and this army will no longer walk our land. Our homes will once again be places of peace and plenty, and the crops we grow and the stock we keep will be our own. Ireland can finally take her place as a free land!"

James pondered deep on this vision, which he shared, and was the reason for his involvement. A vision a man would die for, he thought, if it meant freedom for the generation to come.

Then, into his thoughts came Kitty, and their outing at the hill fort. A feeling of warmth and love swept over him, despite the conflict that was beginning to take root in his mind. What would she think if she saw me here tonight, part of a movement which meant the end of her class and their authority forever? Can a man really be a lover and an enemy? It is said in the Bible that no man can serve two masters... he thought: I will try to keep it all in balance. Again he chided himself that this was a mere acquaintance and unlikely ever to be anything else. Imagine, the Lady Catherine Mary Foldsworth, to be the wife of James de Lacey, tenant. He smiled to himself at the unreality of it, and how foolish his thoughts were. Yet the uneasiness persisted. He decided to concentrate better on what the priest was saying. Startled, he jumped as a large white owl flew over his head, brushing his hair with its' wing tip. Joe, seeing what had happened, chuckled.

"Don't start jumping yet lad, because... "

Joe didn't get time to finish the sentence as the man on lookout called, "Disband, disband, someone approaches."

The tower was proving a great vantage point in over-looking the countryside, and sighting an intruder at such a distance gave all ample opportunities to escape in time.

"How many can you see Mick?" Father John asked.

Straining his eyes against the approaching dusk, Mick could count up to five horsemen.

"Five riders Father, maybe more," he replied, with rising anxiety in his tone.

"Put the lamps out men and go your own way. I'll send word of the next meeting, and God protect you all."

With the usual hasty blessing, the meeting ended.

"Have you secured the vault, Joe?" the priest asked.

"Indeed I have, Father. We have nearly 400 pikes there now."

"Well, at least the dead have no use for them, so they won't stir," Father John said, then smiling, added, "God rest them all."

An old family vault in the castle cemetery served as the hiding place for the arms, made by blacksmiths from around the county. With the remains of the deceased long since gone to dust it proved a great place for temporary storage.

Mounting their horses in haste, the men went their separate ways amidst the great oak and beech trees that swallowed them up in the thickening dusk.

The military patrol decided for some reason not to bother penetrating the forest, and their captain made a mental note to search it on the morrow, weather permitting.

Clear at the other side of the forest, James looked in awe at the full moon that bathed the white and silent countryside in a soft light. As they climbed higher on their path, both men were aware they would be visible as they rode the ridges of the hills.

"Marcus lives beyond the ridge, James. We will be staying with him for the night. Tomorrow we will go back into town and see what news Marjorie may have."

This was the first indication he had given to Marjorie's involvement in the movement, and James' curiosity mounted.

* * *

Marcus had a smallholding of five acres. His mother had died the previous winter, bequeathing him a loneliness to which he had never become accustomed. Consequently, he spent most evenings visiting with his neighbours. Or with Chrissie. He remembered how they had met, and how gradually their relationship had grown.

A sharp knock at the door jolted Marcus back to reality. On opening the door, he saw the two weary travellers.

"Joe. James. Come in. I wasn't sure what time you'd get here, but it's good to see you both."

"Marcus, we had to disband early from the meeting. I doubt if we have been followed, or even seen for that matter," said Joe with apprehension, then added reassuringly, "what's more, we came the long route, following the ridges of the hills."

Marcus heard the weariness in Joe's voice.

"Here," said Marcus, "go sit by the fire and I'll stable and feed the horses. We'll have some supper then."

In the frosty night air Marcus thought of the risk they were all taking by their involvement in the rebellion. Funny, really, how you get used to living with something so dangerous.

By the time he had stabled and fed the horses his thoughts were back to Chrissie. He knew she was expecting to see him tonight. Perhaps later on he could slip out.

Back at the house, James strained the potatoes in the big black skillet. Marcus portioned out the spuds along with some fowl pieces. Joe yawned, and smelled the food with relish. As they ate their simple meal, the three men became more relaxed. With the pikes delivered, the meeting over – even if a little prematurely – it was time to sit back and enjoy the great fire. The sparks hurled themselves up the big-throated chimney where they swirled in the night wind as if to meet the stars. Joe lit his pipe and sighed contentedly, then looked at Marcus.

"Tell me, Marcus, how many men do you think we can get to rally to the cause with Father Murphy?"

"I've often asked myself the same question Joe, and I think we will get a great many!"

James shared the note of confidence and optimism.

"My own feelings are that the people will be convinced by Father John's great sincerity and courage. The fact that he is a priest will inspire many too, I imagine."

All three men agreed with this.

"The pikes are growing in numbers daily, and by the spring we should have a great deal ready. Besides, men can bring their pitchforks and sprongs if they so wish, although I often think that only through sheer force of numbers will we have victory, when you think of the roar that will come from all those big cannon guns." Marcus added.

James agreed.

"We will also need a supply of guns and powder, and we may never have half enough if this battle lasts into weeks, or even months."

"There are plans to have a shipment in from France, James," said Marcus, "or had you not heard?"

James raised his eyebrows.

"I know of the plan, but shipments are uncertain between coast patrols and storms and what-not. God only knows the certainty of that!"

Joe cleared his throat.

"Well, men, we have our own end to take care of, and if everyone in the movement works as hard and as carefully as we do there should be no problems."

On this note of clear-mindedness, it seemed a good time for bed.

"Are you off on your rambles tonight, Marcus?" Joe asked, as he stretched his long legs.

"I'm going over to see Chrissie, even with the night that's in it."

"Thanks for the bed, Marcus, and don't let the rooster out too early in the morning if you can remember!" laughed James.

"Goodnight, men, and sleep well."

With that Marcus was gone. They could hear him whistle cheerily as he saddled his horse and rode slowly into the night.

Joe and James settled down to sleep. As the fire crackled, James thought of Kitty. He thought also of his brother, who had become involved in a riot in Carlow, and was lucky to be alive. A safe place still had to be found for him; somewhere he would not attract attention. He decided to ask Marcus in the morning if he knows of any such place. And Kitty. He wondered what she was doing now. Did she think of him? His thoughts drifted to the oncoming rebellion. There will inevitably be thousands killed and maimed on both sides. Men like him. Men like Joe, with wives and children. Freedom was always bought at a price. Always blood. Is there no other way at all? He preferred not to give it too much thought.

"Joe, are you awake?"

"What is it James?" Joe replied sleepily.

"Well, I just wondered. Do you worry over Nell and the children, knowing what lies ahead of us?"

"Sometimes I think of little else, but I've planned for them to move and live deeper in the hills. So at least they won't be on the marching line, and won't be reprisal targets. Our freedom may cost many lives, James."

"I know," replied James, "if only there was some other means of gaining freedom. If only we had some sort of reasonable livelihood, all this could be avoided. Sure, as it is, a lot of people are half hungry, and are not sure if they will have a roof over their heads from one winter to the next. Damn it, man, some would be better off dead than living the life they endure now!"

"What you say is true enough James, but tomorrow is another day, and 'tis best if we try to forget it for now and sleep."

Presently both men slept, and the red embers glowed as the wind gusted in the chimney. James dreamed of a beautiful young woman riding over the breast of a hill to an old fairy fort.

* * *

Lord Foldsworth relaxed before the fire in the drawing room sipping his port, savouring each mouthful. Lady Edwina sat opposite him engrossed in her crochet – a shawl for her niece. It was to be her Christmas gift to her. Her thoughts were on the coming season, and the many invitations they had received to parties and balls.

"Charles, I often think Kitty needs to be more involved with her own age group. She seems pale and withdrawn these past few days. I am worried about her, you know." Her brow creased with concern.

"What do you suggest, my dear?" he asked, not overly interested in his wife's reflections.

"I don't really know. But perhaps the coming festivities will bring more cheer into her life, and perhaps some new associates."

Lord Foldsworth noted that his wife had periodic bouts of anxiety about Kitty. Much unwarranted, in his opinion. A son would have been less of a worry, never mind knowing there was someone to take over the estate. Wishful thinking, indeed, he said to himself. He loved his daughter Kitty dearly.

"Charles, are you listening to me, or does your daughter's welfare not count for anything?" Lady Edwina became irritated when the attention she demanded was not forthcoming.

"Of course, darling, I am listening to you. I was just thinking, what if her cousin Florence were to come and stay for a while? Perhaps that would be of some help to her, do you think?"

This suggestion was in vain.

"I don't believe Kitty to be over fond of Florence. She apparently doesn't like outdoor pursuits. The only thing she bothers about is collecting wild flowers. Riding doesn't appeal to her at all, and I can't imagine Kitty strolling about collecting flowers, above all things. Can you, Charles?"

"No dear, it would bore Kitty to death. But remember, Florence is a city dweller, and unused to our rural lifestyle."

Lord Charles stroked his moustache pensively.

"Will you have a glass of sherry, my dear?" he asked, walking to the cabinet.

Lady Edwina knew that her husband had heard enough. This was his cue for a conclusion.

"No thank you, Charles. I am tired this evening. It was a tedious day, what with the ball gown fittings. You men are most fortunate when it comes to preparing for social events.'

"This may be true, Edwina, but you always look so stunning. You may believe it when I tell you that you will inevitably look dazzling when the time comes," he smiled, as his wife blushed.

"Goodnight, my dear." Lady Edwina rang the service bell to summon her personal maid.

Kitty had retired earlier with little fuss. As she lay awake, listening to the night sounds throughout the house, she thought of James de Lacey and his whereabouts. The candle flickered, and her mind drifted to the hill fort, where she believed her wishes to be granted if she were to name them. In the mists that arose in her dreams, James' face emerged, and then his whole form. He was dressed very smartly and he smiled broadly, extending both hands to her. Kitty felt a great pull within her to go to him. To be with James... upon the green... hill... forever... and... ever...

The candle gave a dying leap that filled her room with light for a brief instant, and then burned its last, as if to sanction the dreamers wish.

Chapter two

*I*n the spring of 1796, Parliament passed what is known as the 'Insurrection Act'. Scourging, burnings, tortures, hangings and half-hangings were the reality that many people were to face in their lives. It drove the people in many parts of the land to rebellion.

As Christmas 1796 approached, the people became aware of the overall change that was creeping into their lives and into the areas where they lived. An air of impending gloom and pessimism, mixed with wild hopes, filtered through to the poor; at the same time the army and military leaders became more and more anxious. Each night, around the fires of their homes, ideas were exchanged and thoughts freely expressed by men tired of poverty, hunger and death. The public houses became less busy, and the sight of drunken men became a rare one. No member of the United Irishmen was permitted to be either drunk or disorderly. This Organisation, founded in Belfast in 1791 by Wolfe Tone, Rowan Hamilton and Napper Tandy, was growing in strength. Its aim was straightforward: to unite all Irishmen, and to establish a National Parliament.

At this point, the government had opposed Catholic emancipation and National reform. This served only to fuel the air of revolution. The initial oath of the organisation had been legal and public. Now, however, a secret one had replaced it. Almost every village and town in Ireland had members, and the country began to organise itself on a military basis.

In the year 1795, on September 21st, and incident took place in Armagh which was to have far reaching effects. A skirmish broke out between rival groups, (Protestant and Catholic), and thirty people died as a result. This later became known as the 'Battle of the Black Diamond'. On that evening, the 'Orange Order' was founded, and its aims were to 'protect and maintain the peace, the law, the Protestant Constitution and the Protestant Ascendancy'. The Orange Order grew rapidly into many thousands of members.

In 1796, a local defence was established and titled the 'Yeomanry'. It was an armed force, whose purpose was to protect life and property in the local neighbourhood. Its members were Catholic and Protestant alike. Throughout the country the Yeomanry consisted mainly of Catholics, but with the Officers mainly Protestant. Harmony did not last. When the United Irishmen decided on a policy of armed force – driven to this measure by the relentless pressures of the government – large numbers of the Catholic Yeomanry joined its military ranks.

The alarm with which the Protestant Officers of the Yeomanry received this change was to be expected. To counteract this trend within its ranks, the Yeomanry insisted that all its members take an 'Oath of Allegiance'. Those already members of the United Irishmen resigned, and were consequently classified as deserters, and viewed with great suspicion. The training they had received as Yeomen they now utilised to full capacity within the United Irishmen organisation, and many became leaders in their locality.

Such were the forces that prevailed in Ireland that were to lead to the Insurrection, and the eventual battles of 1798.

* * *

Lord Foldsworth considered the main facts of this evolvement, and began to scrutinise his tenants more closely for signs of Insurrection preparation. He had to admit to himself that, apart from some who were not meeting their rent dates through inability or intent, there was little else that was obvious to him. There were certainly no indications of resistance or disorder. He maintained an open mind on the incident of the carriage axle. Village life had changed little, he thought, though the public houses were reported quieter – which was no harm! If anything, they were all too fond of alcohol. Who knows, he thought, perhaps they are getting their priorities right at last. He was aware that of his class, he was known to be a reasonable Landlord. Eviction would be a last resort, as it made little sense to him. His associates in this regard constantly ridiculed his attitude. This didn't deter him in his attitude. Nevertheless, the meetings at Dublin Castle had stamped firmly on his mind what seemed the inevitability of a rebellion. What was one to do about it all? Money always bought information, he knew. It spoke all languages. When the Christmas festivities were over, he would investigate further into local matters.

Having reasoned out all these thoughts, Lord Foldsworth felt a little more at ease. He considered taking his favourite mare out riding. A closer look at the December sky, that hung heavy with snow, and the huge flocks of birds seeking shelter, made the fire seem a more inviting place to be. Selecting a volume of his favourite poems, Lord Foldsworth relaxed into the evening.

* * *

Less than a mile away, May Ryan took the pot of boiling potatoes for the children from over the open fire. Taking it to the outside door, she strained the water from the pot. Her husband, Pat, lay by the fire with the racking cough that had persisted relentlessly for the past eight months. He had become frail and weakened from it. He knew he would not see another springtime, and cried in the night with despair as to what would become of his wife and their seven children. The bailiff had warned them the previous week that their long-overdue rent would have to be paid on the next rent day, otherwise they would by evicted. The neighbours had assured them, and consoled them, that this was only a mere threat. Sitting by their turf fire that evening, May felt in her bones that the bailiff had meant what he had said.

"Musha woman, why worry so, you're only meeting the devil halfway," Pat assured her, his body wracked with a bout of coughing.

His pale forehead showed a multitude of tiny beads of sweat, and his pallor a bluish tinge. He tried to control the fear he felt rising within him. May wiped his forehead with a damp cloth, and comforted him in her thin arms.

"We will have to get you well again, Pat. Put all else out of your mind, do you hear? The doctor promised he would call again tomorrow, so rest love and try to sleep."

The fear subsided somewhat.

"Rest, May, seems beyond me just now. Will you light my pipe for me? It helps content my mind."

May filled the pipe with turf dust and finely ground gorse bush. She lit it and handed it to her husband.

"You should know, Pat, that you only cough more when you light that pipe," she told him firmly, feeling guilty for doing so.

Spreading fresh straw on the floor beside her husband, May lay down to try and sleep. Each night the same thoughts haunted her. What am I to do for rent money? Will Pat ever get better? The children look so thin... Oh God and His Holy Mother, please help me...

As she slept fitfully, her husband prayed the same prayers, and the only other sound he heard that night were the mice rooting in the thatch roof.

Across the fields at Oak Hall, Lord Foldsworth was ordering his bath filled, and fresh towels were being laid out for him. He looked in the mirror, and felt satisfied with life. Later he would enjoy a nice brandy and port. He hummed a tune as he ascended the great stairway.

* * *

Pat Ryan was aware of his wife stirring restlessly beside him. He felt hot and clammy, and the deep pull of something stronger than sleep. He could no longer resist, and felt himself sinking, without pain, into a great light that seemed to engulf him. His body cooled slowly as death settled over him, and May would sleep some hours more before she would awaken to find he had left her quietly in the night.

The neighbours came to her aid the next morning as the news of Pats death reached them. The priest, Father Doyle, came and anointed the stiff cold body that looked twenty years older than the forty-two it had only known. May was numbed with disbelief and shock. She was incapable of thinking clearly or speaking coherently. She just sat on a chair and stared at the body of her dead husband who lay on the wooden table, hands joined. His face was as white as the fresh fallen snow. A Rosary beads lay entwined about his fingers, and the clay pipe he loved so well was beside his head.

Nell Gilltrap tried to coax her to the fire to drink some tea. Joe had heard the sad news at the forge early that morning, and Nell had set out instantly to the aid of the young widow. The house was full of people, women making endless pots of tea and snuff being passed from hand to hand. Local gossip was exchanged and acquaintances updated.

"What will become of the family, Nell, do you think?" Father Doyle asked, when they were out of earshot.

"Only God knows that, Father. The gossips say that May and the children are to be evicted, and her a widow, with seven children to provide for. How she will manage doesn't bear to think on, does it Father?" She looked at the priest with the question before their eyes.

"Never, Nell. It's unimaginable that Lord Foldsworth would order her eviction. It has never been his policy, as far as I know. Besides, God is merciful," he concluded.

Nell searched her mind as to how God might stop the Bailiff when he came to make the young widow homeless. He didn't leave her husband with her, so was it likely that He would intervene to stop an eviction? She rebuked herself then for what her mother would have called, 'flying in the face of God'. Father Doyle loved his people, she knew. But she doubted if he could be of any practical help. He could pray alright, but sometimes prayers took a long time to come true.

"There are very strange times you know, Father," she continued, "Jerome Hennessy, the bailiff, has had a grudge against poor Pat these ten years or more."

Her gaze fell to the corpse, and she thought of how final death really was.

"Grudges are a great burden to carry, Nell, for any man." Father Doyle replied. "I hope it won't end up pulling the bailiff down!" He looked back at her and added quietly, "If there are any problems, Nell, I'll depend on you and Joe to let me know as quickly as possible."

He then went over to May and talked quietly to her, blessed the mourners, and left. As he mounted his horse, he sensed trouble in the making. If necessary he would, without hesitation, approach Lord Foldsworth personally, and have him change the eviction order on the grounds of compassion. He prayed the need would not arise.

As Father Doyle approached the turn on the laneway, he noticed an approaching horsewoman, and soon recognised Lord Foldsworths daughter.

"Good morning, Father Doyle."

The greeting was friendly and pleasant.

"Good morning to you, Lady Foldsworth," he replied, as he brought his horse alongside.

"I was sorry to hear of the death of Mr Ryan. How very unfortunate indeed."

Kitty liked the priest and was aware of his keen interest in his people.

"Yes," he answered, "and a very great loss to his wife and children."

He knew Kitty to be a kind-hearted young woman, and had heard his parishioners speak of her kindness from time to time.

"I have some things here from Hannah at the kitchen. Only this morning I learned that herself and May are cousins. Her concern for her is great. With such a young family to take care of alone." Kitties own concern was obvious.

Father Doyle knew that the fate of this family lay in the hands of the Landlord, and doubted if his daughter, now before him, was aware of that fact. He considered for a moment voicing his concern to her, but decided against it.

"It's very kind of you to visit Mrs Ryan and I'm sure it will console her," he said, with the sincerity he was so well known for.

"It's the least one could do in the circumstances, Father. I better not detain you, as I believe we are going to enjoy more snow and I imagine you have other calls to make."

"Yes, it is a busy time indeed. I bid you good morning, Lady Foldsworth, and I am glad to have met you this morning."

"Goodbye, Father."

With a gentle heel, her horse moved forward gracefully. Father Doyle admired the lovely qualities the young woman possessed. Despite the differences in their class and creed, they shared a mutual concern for people. The bond of this spirit was forged between them that day.

Kitty approached the two-roomed cabin. The thatch looked torn, and in need of repair. Some poultry scratched underneath a hedge. A small black dog barked furiously at the stranger. Inside, the commotion was heard above the din of conversation, and Nell looked out.

"Why, it's Miss Foldsworth come to visit," she exclaimed, and began to tidy the wisps of hair around her face. This was followed by a great deal of shifting in the small kitchen. As Kitty approached the door, she could hear the hum of voices, and a distinct voice asking, "What on earth could bring the Landlord's daughter here, disturbing the dead...?"

Kitty bit her lower lip in embarrassment. As she entered the kitchen, the men and women realised she had heard the remark, and felt equally embarrassed.

Approaching the table where the dead man lay, and where May sat her vigil, Kitty found her voice.

"I'm sorry, Mrs Ryan, to hear of the sad loss of your husband. I have come here to offer my condolences to you and your family. I hope you will accept them."

May stood up and curtseyed to Kitty.

"Thank you, your Ladyship, for your sympathy, and for taking time to come to see us. Please, take this chair by the fire."

Before realising it, Kitty found herself seated and a steaming cup of tea in her hand. Nobody spoke, until Nell broke the silence.

"Is the tea alright, Miss Foldsworth?" she asked.

"Lovely, thank you, and very welcome indeed. There is a chill out this morning, and Father Doyle seems to think it will snow."

The neighbours glanced at each other. Somehow all the tension seemed to melt away. Everyone began to talk again, but in low tones. Some whispered, 'what is it coming to, with her Ladyship at a wake.'

The sight of Kitty sitting there beneath the large open chimney, sipping tea in a black riding habit, seemed almost like a vision to them. The smell of her perfume was like the scent of white clover in a June meadow. Kitty enquired as to the whereabouts of the children.

"I sent them up to their Uncle in the hills this morning, Miss Foldsworth," said May, who had taken a liking to her visitor. "They were broken hearted to be sure, and it's sorely they'll miss their father... " May's voice trailed off, cracking with emotion as she stared into the fire.

Flames licked the bottom of the large skillet; wherein lay a meal of potatoes for the mourners. Kitty remembered the food Hannah had given her for the bereaved woman, and asked May if she would accompany her to the yard. Paying her final respects to the remains of Pat Ryan, she left the forlorn scene, and the mourners bade her goodbye. Kitty noticed how pale and thin they all were. She wondered, momentarily, what their future held...

Unpacking both saddlebags, she handed the contents to May.

"Hannah asked me if I would give these to you, Mrs Ryan. I personally would like to pay for the funeral expenses, and I'd prefer to keep this our own secret, if you wouldn't mind."

Both women looked at each other in total understanding.

"Thank you, your Ladyship. I am very grateful. Please thank Hannah for me." She extended her hand and shook Kitty's.

"Remember, Mrs Ryan, any food you need for the children you are to send word straight away to Hannah. Under no circumstances are they to ever be in need." Kitty felt this was the least she could do.

"How can I ever thank you? You have been kindness itself to us at this time," said May, quite overcome by this sudden flow of generosity.

May dabbed her eyes with a piece of red cotton, and her face seemed small and shrivelled from her grief.

"Goodbye, Mrs Ryan, and thank you for the kindness and hospitality of your home."

"Goodbye, your Ladyship, and God bless you."

May watched the young woman mount her horse, and settle her skirts to the sidesaddle. Just then a rider came up the laneway. It was James de Lacey. Conscious of May Ryan's presence, he saluted Kitty with customary respect.

"Good morning, Miss Foldsworth." He looked at Kitty with a steady gaze. She nodded in recognition.

"Good morning."

Then, as if unaware of his presence, looked back at May and smiled.

"Remember all I told you, Mrs Ryan."

With that, she cantered briskly out of the yard, conscious of James yet unable to relate to him on this chance meeting. James caught the quick wave she gave him, and then looked over at May. Her eyes were following the figure of the retreating horsewoman in the black habit.

"You know, James, she is different from the rest of them."

"I know full well, May, full well… "

Having dismounted, James helped May carry the food into the kitchen, where all eyes were upon her. They wondered what had passed between the two women.

That evening – when two barrels of stout were delivered and thick slices of ham cut, with neither shortage of tobacco nor snuff – most guessed that the Landlord's daughter had made sure there would be no shortage at Pat's wake. When the new coffin arrived, it was confirmed.

They buried Pat the next day, earlier than was customary, for fear of heavy snowfall. Otherwise the corpse would have to be held until a thaw, as had happened many a time before. In less than a week it would be Christmas Day, May thought. It meant little to her, as they shovelled the dark earth onto the coffin of her husband. May cried from depths within her she had never realised existed.

After the burial, Nell and Joe brought May and her family home. Some of the neighbours called in to say goodnight. When all the children were in bed, she found herself alone by the fire. She tried not to see Pat in the cold earth. Without his wracking cough and his gasps for air, the house seemed quiet and empty. His clay pipe lay abandoned on the shelf above the hearthstone. Apart from his tattered old clothes, there was little else left to remind her of him.

May thought of the visit from Kitty, and her assurance of food from Hannah. Oh God, she thought, how am I going to pay the rent? What am I to do? She wept afresh for Pat, for herself, and for the children. The future had always been bleak, but now it was empty also. The sounds of her children sleeping comforted her, and soon she too lay sleeping. She dreamed of herself and Pat as they had walked on the heather on the mountain, and the way he would hand her a spray of bog cotton blossoms, then kiss her. It was only ten summers past.

* * *

Jerome Hennessy woke early.

He was hungry. He looked at the ceiling in his room, and stretched his heavy body in the large comfortable bed. Feeling his forehead with his hands he tried to press the headache away. Whiskey and the after effects were not new to him. He felt his own anger, at himself, and at life. The eviction... I'll show them at last... They laugh at Jerome Hennessy... well, I'll show them... and their laughs will die in their throats, he thought. With that, he left the bed and called for his housekeeper, Tess.

"Are ye bloody deaf, or dead? Do ye hear me?" he bellowed.

Tess came into the room shivering. It wasn't the fresh fall of snow that made her do so, but her fear of this man. She detested him, but her life, and that of her children, depended on what he paid her for housekeeping.

"Sorry, sir. I was just boiling the water for your wash, and... "

"Get me a decent feed, and be quick. Today is the day I'm going to teach that crowd of cabin crawlers who's the real boss in these parts," he snarled, and Tess was sure he meant it.

She had heard the rumours of the threatened eviction. Her thoughts went to May and her seven children. Suddenly, a large boot came hurling across the room towards her, and in an attempt to avoid it she fell against a chair and to the ground.

"Get up ye stupid bitch!" he roared, "are ye getting too old for the job here, is that it?"

Hennessy delighted to see the look of fear and dread on her face each time he threatened her position as housekeeper.

"No sir, I'm sorry sir. I'm just a bit clumsy sir..." she replied timidly.

"Well, clumsy, get down there and cook and be quick about it, before I give you good reason to lose your balance!"

Tess fled, and as she fried the bacon and eggs – enough to feed four people – she wished she could show him what she really thought of him. He was, however, not a man to get on the wrong side of. The thought of the eviction had aroused such excitement in him that he seemed to look forward to it more than to Christmas.

Meanwhile, May heated some potatoes for her small children, the remains of last night's pot. Today she would have to see Hannah for some more food. The funeral visitors had eaten everything the day before. The rent money seemed almost insignificant as the question of the next bite to eat loomed.

Jerome Hennessy felt the chill morning air as he saddled his black horse. His first task was to secure the assistance of six local militia and two men who knew how to use the 'battering ram'. The notorious 'battering ram' was a mechanism that swung a large pole, to and fro. As it gathered momentum, the walls of a small cabin would crumble under its repeated blows. It lived up to its dreaded reputation.

On reaching the local barracks, Jerome Hennessy made his intentions known to the Officer in command. Colonel Walters looked at him amazed.

"Hennessy, you know it is not Lord Foldsworths policy to evict. Let alone evict a widow with children," he stated adamantly.

"Look here," replied Hennessy, his small eyes dancing in anger at the prospect of a threat to his plans, "it's my responsibility to collect the rents around here, and has been for the past twenty years. His Lordship knows well that I'm in the best position to know who's able to pay and who isn't. So I'll be the judge of that, as I've always been. The widow Ryan gave a great wake, with no shortage of beer or meat. A stylish coffin, as only befits the quality, was got for her husband. That alone cost three guineas. In other words – the rent money she has held back on me this many months. She had the bloody nerve to plead with me on the last rent day! No! I know what's to be done. Let her off the hook now, and everybody else around these parts will do the same. Where will that leave Jerome Hennessy then, Colonel? Well?"

Colonel Walters realised that this man before him had the makings of a tyrant, and to try to reason with him would be futile. The vengeance in the mean eyes told him so. Sighing heavily, he looked at him.

"Well, Hennessy, remember, this is your doing, and as you said, you are answerable to his Lordship."

Hennessy jumped up and stamped his feet in the true fashion of a bully, almost screaming in his frenzy.

"Where are my men? Where are they? I'm not paid to listen to you... hmmp... respect... responsibility... who pays your wages Walters... well? Who pays them?"

Hennessey's jowled jaws were now a purple-blue colour, and saliva spewed across the table at Colonel Walters, along with the stale smell of whiskey.

Walters stood up looking at the spectacle before him.

"Get out, Hennessy, NOW! My men will join you presently. I begrudge them to you for your despicable intention. Leave now while you are able, before I change my mind and take the law into my own hands to kill you where you stand."

The pale face and quiet tone of the Colonel took Hennessy by surprise, and he thought it best to leave as told, lest his plans were foiled.

* * *

As the battering ram was finally yoked to the horses, the people in the village looked on in horror and dread, afraid to imagine their destination. The drummer came next, beating in step for the six soldiers who walked before the mechanism of destruction. Hennessy sat on his horse and seemed to swell with pride and power. A voice shouted out from the public house, "Hennessy, we'll get you some day, and when we do you'll squeal like a trapped rat!" A loud cheer came from the dozen or so men who watched on as the small parade went by. Old hatreds rekindled rapidly, an uncontrollable hatred of this enemy of the people.

May Ryan swept the floor of the cabin. She had sent the older children to gather firewood for cooking the mid-day meal. The younger ones sat by the almost dead embers, a blanket covering them to keep them warm. 'When the children return, I'll go over and see Hannah and get some food,' she thought. She considered herself very fortunate that she could go to her Landlord's kitchen. God bless his Lordships family, she thought. While the neighbours were very good, they had no food to spare, and May understood that well enough. Times were hard for everyone. God grant that things will improve. Poor Pat must be praying for me. Her simple faith had always carried her through times of difficulty, as it had done for her parents before her. Prayer was rooted in the minds of the people, and it came to them as naturally as breathing the clear air from the mountains.

Her quiet thoughts were shattered by a piercing scream.

"Oh God, May, they're commin'!"

Betty Tompkins, her neighbour, came running down the lane, her hands covered in flour and her red hair flying in the December wind.

"Calm yourself, Betty. Who is coming that frightens you so?"

"Oh May, love, it's the Bailiff; and soldiers; and the cursed battering ram that comes!" Betty wailed in terror.

May swayed with a weakness that came over her. They wouldn't. They couldn't, she thought, as the infernal nightmare gripped its cold fingers around her heart.

"The children, May, where are they?" cried Betty, a she regained some of her composure.

May stood motionless as she watched her small yard fill with neighbours, all looking aghast at the spectacle that was about to unfold before them. Joe Gilltrap raced into the yard on horseback, and slid from the animal before it had even stopped. He grabbed May by the shoulders and shook her.

"Come now May, and gather your few things from the house... where are the children?" he gasped, breathless from the mad gallop to the cabin.

Realisation finally dawned on the woman's ashen face. In a quiet tone she replied, "The two eldest are in the woods gathering sticks, the rest are here by the fire trying to keep warm... " Her voice seemed to ebb away.

Joe beckoned to Betty to take the youngest children to her home, away from the forthcoming scene, and asked her to send her son to find the two in the woods. The sight of her small children being hurried through the small cabin door brought a scream from deep within May's body. She wept uncontrollably and was linked into the cabin by two women, who helped her gather the few remnants of clothing, shoes, Pat's clay pipe, some plates, mugs and cooking pots. All of her earthly possessions were taken clear of the cabin.

"Oh Pat," she cried, "'tis as well you're in the clay this day as all this would have sent you to the Almighty a bitter man."

Joe put his arm around her. They could all hear clearly the sound of the drums carrying on the wind. At this point the small yard was crowded with people: the young unable to understand, the old unable to forget. To forget that they could not own their own acre of land, or the roof above their heads, in their own country.

James came riding into the yard, his horse a lather of sweat having leapt the small walls of the fields. The chickens ran cackling, wings spread, amidst the confusion. Having dismounted, he stood on top of an old pony cart and addressed the crowd. A hushed silence spread amongst them.

"Good people. Today you see the oppressor in the yard of this widow woman. You see her house levelled before out very eyes, and then burned to the ground. Her fate? To live beneath the hedge with her small children, while her husband lies not yet cold in the grave. I know full well how you all feel. I know what you would like to do to Jerome Hennessy and his men. But I say to you, do nothing! Say nothing! Their day is coming to an end, and this reign of terror can now be numbered in seasons rather than years. I am asking you to stand firm. Without resistance. Without a word. In time, we will deal with them in our own way. Bloodshed here today would be blood shed in vain. But remember, time is ours, and like the land, it will wait for us."

A great loud cheer filled the air. As Jerome Hennessy came into view he heard the cheer and ordered his men to load their guns and prepare to fire if necessary.

By a quiet corner, in the hedge, Bartley Finnegan stood looking and listening to all. He noted James' opinions, and was also aware how Joe Gilltrap supported this newcomer to the area.

May Ryan stood at her cabin door alone, in front of the great crowd, of Hennessy, and of his men. The drummer rolled his drum, and then stopped abruptly. The battering ram stood, its rusted hinge creaking, as if impatient to fulfil its purpose. The militia stood with their guns in readiness. No one moved. No one spoke a word. Not even a cough was to be heard. Somewhere in the distance one cock was answered by another. Hennessy looked at the sea of faces that gazed at him, his eyes filled with hatred. He spurred his horse forward.

"Are you May Ryan?" he shouted.

"You know I am," she replied. She stood with feet apart, arms folded and her face ashen.

Her cool composure stirred the bailiff even more. 'We'll soon see how cool you'll remain,' he thought. His sickly smile did not go unnoticed by the crowd. Edging his horse ever more forward – until the animals muzzle was within inches of the widow's face – he began to shout almost hysterically...

"In the name of Lord Charles Foldsworth, you are now commanded to leave this house and land this day, never to return. You have failed to pay your rent, and you are hereby to be evicted by his lawful agent."

Turning to the crowd, he continued.

"Let it be known to all here present, that whoever gives this woman and her children shelter will suffer the same fate."

May still managed to stand, despite the fact that she was trembling to pieces. Hennessy noticed her fear mounting and it delighted him further. The crowd was amazed by her strength. For a woman not yet a widow one full week, they had great admiration for her.

"Front line advance!" shouted Hennessy. "Seize that woman and remove her to the roadside."

Two of the soldiers moved forward, in order to remove the woman as commanded. A loud piercing scream rose into the air. They stopped as if by threat of a cannon gun. The widow fell to her knees and pointed an outstretched hand to the bailiff on horseback. Her eyes seemed to penetrate his soul. Then calmly, she said:

"Hennessy, over the body of my dead husband I curse you this day for destroying the home of a widow, and leaving her children to die like dogs in a ditch. So may it be for you, Jerome Hennessy, that you will die in a ditch and be the food of foxes."

The crowd crossed themselves as the widows's curse found a resting place on the man before her. He paled, and she saw it.

"Bring on the ram," he shouted, in the same high-pitched voice that verged on hysterics.

May Ryan walked unaided from her home. The crowd made way for her, and as she walked down the laneway, she heard the slow thud of the battering ram. The cabin crumbled piece by piece. The thatched roof fell with a sickening thud that spoke the dying gasp of a house and home. Fire from the hearth within took hold, and when May turned around, all she saw was the only home she had ever known rise towards the dark December sky, a pall of thick black smoke. She cried silently. All sound in her seemed to have died.

"Oh Pat. Oh Pat," She wept over and over.

The cold stares from the crowd still rested on Jerome Hennessy. He began to wonder, as if coming out of a dream, what all this was going to achieve? These people were unbeatable, as the years had shown. Still, he reassured himself, 'They will respect Jerome Hennessey's' authority'. He turned his horse and trotted out of the yard, with the militia behind him. These men were frightened by the silence of the people. They were not without knowing that, if the crowd wished, they could overcome them in a matter of seconds. Hennessy included. They didn't, however. It was then that James de Lacey realised he held a quality of command with people. Leadership, as Joe Gilltrap later described it.

Slowly the yard emptied, and sparks flurried through the air as the wind gushed at the heap of ruins. A rat squealed as it ran from a sidewall, lucky to have escaped the inferno. The black dog caught it, and with a sudden jerk, broke its neck. Despite the threat from Hennessy, the neighbours took May and her children to their homes. It was part of their nature to help one another.

News of the brutal eviction carried out by the bailiff, Jerome Hennessy, on the Foldsworth estate travelled like wildfire to the surrounding counties.

That night it snowed heavily, and the last remaining fires of May Ryan's cabin were soon covered in a thick white blanket, as if in a burial shroud.

Chapter three

Dublin Castle was ablaze with light, and as the guests arrived, the merriment grew at the Vice Regal Ball. The splash of colour created by the women's gowns and the glitter of expensive jewellery, which adorned the slender, and not so slender necks and arms of the wearers overwhelmed Kitty.

Dashing young men, handsome in their uniforms of red and blue, bowed courteously to her upon being introduced. Some she recognised from previous social events, while others were completely new to her. Kitty was conscious of her mother's presence beside her, and the subtle protective hold she exercised. She felt somewhat smothered by it. Announcing to her mother that Lady Caroline Fitzwilliam was beckoning her, she floated across the room, busily trying to catch the eye of her friend.

"Why Kitty, how wonderful to see you!" cried the excited Caroline, embracing her. Standing back she looked at Kitty and with equal enthusiasm exclaimed, "You look stunning, and I see Colonel Wanewright thinks quite the same."

Kitty blushed as she looked into the handsome face of the young officer who stepped forward to take her hand in greeting.

"Lawrence, This is my long-standing friend, Catherine Foldsworth," she introduced gaily.

"Delighted to meet you, Colonel Wanewright," Kitty responded, solemnly.

Caroline interrupted with her well-known exuberance.

"Oh Kitty, please... Colonel Wanewright... Kitty is so formal, is she not?" and she laughed mischievously.

Stepping closer, Wanewright looked at Kitty, paying no attention to Caroline.

"Please call me Lawrence. Such formality from one so young and beautiful is quite unacceptable," he smiled shyly.

"Then you must call me Kitty, and pay no attention to Caroline. She simply loves to create dramatic scenes when we are out for the season. She simply thrives on it."

The three laughed before Caroline, prodding Kitty discreetly, announced that she had to leave them momentarily, promising to return. Looking at Lawrence, she stated emphatically.

"In your capable hands I am leaving my best friend. Should you neglect her, I will personally chide you."

With that, Caroline glided away, leaving him in no doubt as to his responsibilities.

"So, here you are Lawrence. Having scarcely arrived you've already been given a task by Caroline."

They both laughed, and felt at ease in each other's company.

"How do you come to know Caroline?" Kitty asked, curious that she had never heard her friend speak of him before.

"Caroline's brother, Christopher, is in the same regiment as I, and we are good friends. Occasionally I go to Castle Park House with him at the weekends, hunting and so forth. Hence my acquaintance with his sister. And you, Kitty. How do you know Caroline so well?" Lawrence asked, totally engrossed by the beauty of the young woman before him.

"Somewhat similar to you, in ways. We were both at finishing school together, and we had many wonderful times. She is a wonderful person. I am so fond of her." Kitty was aware of his intense gaze.

She wondered if, in fact, he was even listening to her.

"May I have the honour of the next dance, Kitty?"

"Of course, gallant sir," said Kitty, and curtseyed, much to his amusement.

The orchestra played a selection of waltzes, and they made a striking pair as they all but commanded the centre of the ballroom floor.

Lady Foldsworth wondered who was the handsome young man dancing superbly with Kitty. On discovering him to be the Viceroy's nephew, she all but swooned with excitement. The evening seemed to be one endless dance for Kitty, as Lawrence was reluctant to let this gem out of his sight. He found Kitty delightful company, and they both seemed content to spend the entire evening together.

"I notice, Lawrence, that you are taking your duty quite seriously," remarked Caroline loudly, meeting them both at the punch bowl. Then, discreetly, she asked Kitty if she desired a change of company.

"Of course not, Caroline. I find Lawrence quite entertaining," she whispered happily.

"So many ask about you Kitty, are you sure you are not doing yourself an injustice?"

Kitty knew that Caroline meant well.

"Caroline am I? Is Lawrence... your particular friend? I'd hate to think I was intruding... it escaped my mind to ask you," Kitty raised an eyebrow.

"Don't be silly, Kitty. Lawrence and I are just friends. Really. He's more like a brother to me in many ways. Not need to concern yourself, dear. Lawrence is quite unattached, and seems more than happy to be with you. I am so glad."

Caroline slipped away as quickly as she had appeared. Lawrence was immediately at Kitty's side with two glasses of champagne.

"Caroline seems very busy tonight, Kitty, don't you agree?" The broad smile said more than the words spoken.

"Indeed she is, and she will make a splendid hostess one day."

"I quite agree," he said.

"She has that rare quality of making everyone feel that they are on the verge of some new and exciting adventure. Rather like making the ordinary extraordinary."

"And you? Are you not extra-ordinary, Kitty?" Lawrence asked, taking her once more onto the dance floor.

Kitty was aware of an attachment developing over the few hours she had spent in the company of Lawrence. She kept telling herself to relax more and enjoy the evening. She noticed her mother's large flickering eyes appearing occasionally above her fan. They beamed with approval and delight.

Her father, meanwhile, stood with a group of officers. They were so interested in their discussions that little else seemed to distract them. Lawrence noticed her observation.

"They seem to think there is revolution in the air. All rather serious, apparently... Still, what a pity to allow such depressing conversation spoil such a splendid evening. Plots, places and such surmising."

"Do you not sense the unease in the people, Lawrence? And goodness knows how they survive, with disease, poverty and hunger their only inheritance." Kitty was allowing her true sentiments to surface, and was aware of it.

"Why, Kitty!" he exclaimed, "You sound almost sorry for them, and you apparently have an insight regarding them uncommon among young ladies of your class and position!"

Kitty stopped in the middle of the dance floor. His rebuff was apparent.

"Lawrence, young ladies of my class and position, as you so categorise me, do have eyes and ears. I am well aware of what takes place on our own estate, and indeed on may other estates. These people you frown upon, Lawrence are people of flesh and blood, just like you and I."

With a simple courtesy, she abandoned the dance floor and her dancing partner. Many, including her parents, noticed the departure. Lady Foldsworth went directly to her daughter's side. She was very embarrassed by the incident.

"Kitty... whatever is going on... leaving the floor and the young man so abruptly? Did he offend you, my dear? Or dare to insult you? My goodness, the entire ballroom is buzzing with it."

"Mother, please... stop fussing. I was neither insulted not offended. I was simply tired with the conversation. I have spent most of the evening with Colonel Wanewright and I do have other admirers, you know." Kitty was exasperated by her mother's reaction.

"Do you realise, my dear, that the young man you were with the entire evening is none other than the Vice Regals nephew? Your father seems quite shocked at your manners... " Lady Foldsworth was clearly beside herself with frustration at the turn of events. Kitty stood up, and as her mother continued reprimanding her, she1 walked away and left her standing open-mouthed.

Going directly to the ladies powder room, she stood with her back to the door and breathed deeply. 'Well,' she thought, 'viceroy or not, tenants are people too, and class and position do not alter that fact. Besides, I do not feel obliged to surrender my opinions. Perhaps I shouldn't have left Lawrence on the floor, but it is important to be true to ones beliefs.' As she was about to leave the powder room, Caroline came sweeping in.

"Oh Kitty, I have been looking for you all over the place," she gasped.

"Spare me another etiquette lecture, Caroline. Lawrence crowds my mind. I simply had to get away, and I'm sorry if I have left you in an embarrassing position." Her voice trailed off, and Kitty suddenly looked like a lost child.

"Kitty, don't be absurd. To tell you the truth, I am delighted with what you have done. I didn't like to tell you, but Lawrence Wanewright is a bit too pushy for my liking. It's the army, it does that to them all, you know. They expect us ladies to be,' yes dear, no dear!"

To see Caroline so highly strung made Kitty laugh heartily.

"Oh Caroline, you haven't changed at all since our days on the continent! You were always the one I could rely on to get me out of scrapes of one type or another!"

"Well then, let's go Kitty. There are many others waiting to dance with you, while Lawrence Wanewright can soak up the fact that you are an intelligent woman as well as a beautiful one."

Kitty was touched by the sincerity of her friend, and on that note, she re-entered the ballroom.

Lady Foldsworth decided it would be better policy to avoid her daughter. She felt a degree calmer about the incident, and had decided it was no harm at all if Kitty was able to assert herself. Abandoning ones partner on the floor, however, was not the desirable place for self assertion! She reflected on her own life. She had been so fortunate to meet Charles. How many of her friends had fallen prey to domineering husbands? Kitty was different. Lots of spirit, with a beauty that would always prove irresistible.

"My dear, you do look deep in thought," interrupted her husband.

"Yes, Charles. I was thinking of you in fact... "

She looked at the grey silken locks of her husband, and the still young-looking face she loved so dearly.

"So, let's dance, and I shall tell you my secret thoughts... "

They both laughed and, taking her hand, Lord Charles led his wife onto the floor. They looked so very happy. Their fidelity to each other was well known, and envied by some.

Kitty found, to her delight, that she was in great demand, and danced the evening away on a cloud of happiness. She did not see Lawrence for the remainder of the ball.

* * *

The following morning her maid woke her early.

"I am sorry to disturb you so early, madam, but these were delivered just now."

Kitty opened her eyes to a huge bouquet of red rose buds, and a note that read:

Deep and sincere apologies, for upsetting a rose bud last night.

Perhaps I may be allowed to make amends?

Signed: Repentant Lawrence.

Kitty laughed, and felt happier that the matter could come to such a pleasant conclusion.

"Will there be an answer, madam?" the maid asked, "There is a footman waiting downstairs."

"Yes, Melda, there is an answer. Would you please bring me a card and an envelope?"

She mused over an appropriate reply. Then she quickly penned:

'The rosebuds are delightful, and thank you.

Perhaps we may meet at the Hunt Ball next month?

Signed: Catherine Foldsworth.'

A little formality, she thought, never goes astray.

After breakfast her mother fussed greatly over the bouquet, with sighs and exclamations...

"What a gentleman, Kitty... the good breeding coming to the surface as only good breeding will... "

Kitty felt glad for her mother's sake. Tension with the Viceroy's family was not to be desired.

"Where is father this morning, mother?"

"Would you believe it? He is gone to a meeting at the Castle. He appeared to be most anxious to be on time. Even at Christmas time they place such importance on those national issues."

Kitty was aware that, underneath the mild protests, her mother was proud of her father's commitment to his duty, and his allegiance to the Government. Lady Edwina could not resist returning to the matter most occupying her thoughts.

"I am so glad that you have managed to come to a degree of reconciliation with Colonel Wanewright before we leave Dublin. It is important, dear, to carry oneself properly in society in Dublin... after all, it wouldn't do for them to consider you an 'upstart from the country'."

The direct gaze of her mother's eyes alerted Kitty to the sad fact that the statement she had made may contain a thread of truth.

"Oh, let them think as they will, mother. I will never be placating to any man where my true feelings are concerned, and, I may add, the same principal applies to you and father."

Her mother was freshly alarmed by this further display of revolt, and that was exactly what Lady Edwina considered it to be.

"Don't you understand, mother? It's time I stood up for the person I really am. What sense is there in being everyone's 'ideal girl', to the detriment of ones true self?"

"Such conflicting ideas you have, Kitty. Wherever did you get them from?" her mother asked.

Never having noticed such determination in her daughter before, she hoped it was just a phase she was going through. Whatever had transpired between herself and Colonel Wanewright, this was more of the same. And today is definitely not the day to enquire, she decided. Letting the issue drop, she turned her attention to other matters.

"We expect to be leaving at half-past-two today, Kitty. We have a great deal to do when we arrive home..."

Kitty appeared to be in another world. Had her mother known it was one where James de Lacey resided, she would indeed have thought her daughter to be totally deranged.

"Kitty, are you listening to me?"

"Yes mother, I'm sorry. I'm just a little tired after the ball last night. Dublin has much to offer, but there is something so lovely about home."

Lady Edwina, happy with this explanation, kissed her daughter as she left the room.

Looking at the rosebuds, Kitty thought of Lawrence Wanewright, and then of James, with whom she would rather be walking the hills anytime. Kitty wondered what her mother and father would think if they knew that the company of a tenant meant more to her than a Viceroy's nephew! She smiled to herself, thinking, and 'Is it not yet another truth?' Well, she thought, there are times and places for truth. Would there ever be a time and a place for this one? Something inside her seemed to say, 'When you are ready for it'.

* * *

Bartley Finnegan sat at the small table in the pub. Looking at his half glass of ale, he felt depressed. 'Will it ever be any different', he thought, 'always a bloody struggle from one week to the next'.

His job at the village pub barely paid enough to live on. Taking another mouthful of beer, he again made up his mind he was going to change all that. Perhaps go to a bigger town and get a better job there. He had heard of one such job going, at an establishment called, 'The Bulls Mouth'. He had been afraid to express interest in it. If his present employer caught wind of it, he could be out in the street in no time. Then all would be lost. 'I will do something to get more money, and if that means getting out of here, so be it', he concluded. But, town life might not be so easy either. Money or no money. He felt at home in the village. His attic room at the pub was house and home to him. Never having married, he comforted himself in beer and whiskey, and supposed life could be a lot worse.

Getting another drink, he sat down and filled his pipe. 'A smoke contents a mans mind', he thought, 'company in a way, as my mother used to say'. She had also been a lover of the clay pipe.

"God Bartley, you look a bit lost in yourself. Far away... " Joe Gilltrap stood towering above him, smiling benignly.

"Aye Gilltrap, and so I was," Bartley replied.

"Was what?" asked Joe, as he counted out the money for his glass of ale.

"Far away, far away, for Jesus sake. Isn't that what you asked me, well... wasn't it?" he snapped.

Bartley looked at Joe with frenzied eyes.

"Ah yes, Bartley. Sure me own mind isn't with me at all today... wool gathering." Joe laughed at his own remarks.

'Stupid lout, big stupid lout', thought Bartley, as he finished his ale, 'thinks he's somebody... that's his trouble. Some day I'll nail that bastard'. He nursed his grudge as if it was an investment of some type. Stubbing out his pipe, he put it in his pocket and walked out, ignoring Joe's farewell. Joe knew Bartley disliked him, but did not suspect to what great depth this hatred ran. It would have been beyond his understanding.

Outside, Bartley did not know what to do with his free afternoon. He always had a free half-day during Christmas week, before the rush. Soon he would be taxed to full capacity, kept on his feet. 'Cursed Christmas', he thought. He found himself walking through the fields, and decided to pluck some holly for his room back at the pub. There seemed to be lots of holly trees, but there were no red berries on them. 'Bastards of birds, they never leave a bit of berried holly'.

He decided to go up near Oak Hall. There was bound to be some there. They have everything else, why not berried holly? he thought. Turning around the corner of the large paddock to the rear of the house, a large holly tree, abundant with berries, stood before him. Four wood pigeons flew away from the tree. He picked up a piece of stick, and firing it at them, shouted, "Get away, ye thieving whores!"

Bartley snapped off the berry-laden branches nearest to the ground until he had as much as he could carry.

"Well, at least I got something off old Foldsworth," he shouted aloud, and began to walk back the way he had come.

The chill east wind began to rise, and his gripping hands were numb with the cold. Leaving down his large bundle, he blew noisily into his hands. Deciding to take the shorter route home, he picked up his bundle and hurried off. He rushed through a group of spruce trees, cursing them quietly as they stung his face and hands. Then he stepped out onto the avenue of the estate.

Before him was Lord Foldsworths carriage. Coming to a halt, Lord Foldsworth stepped out. Bartley felt as if he had been struck by lightening.

"Good-day your Honours worship," he gasped, his face white with fear.

"And where do you think you are going my man, and with my holly?" Lord Foldsworth demanded of him.

The landlord took an instant dislike to the man before him. It took Bartley a while to find his voice.

"Only gathering holly, yer Honour... ah... for Christmas... and I thought... "

Bartley didn't get a chance to finish his statement.

"You only thought?" queried the landlord, stamping his polished shoe on the gravelled driveway. "No, you forgot to think, didn't you? Do you know I can have you transported for theft, at the next court sitting? Well, do you?"

Bartley all but collapsed with fear, and the coachman looked on at the anger his master portrayed, trying to keep the horses still.

"Oh, no, your Honour, you wouldn't," he wailed piteously.

"And why would I not? What is your name and where do you live?" Lord Foldsworth demanded.

"Bartley Finnegan, yer Honour, and I work as a barman in the village pub. I live there as well," he replied, unable to take in what was happening to him.

"Bartley Finnegan, you will come to my house on the first Saturday in January, and then I will decide if it is best you are imprisoned or deported. Now get off my estate this instant!"

Bartley broke into a half run, amazed to be able to run at all, wailing bitterly.

"Holy mother of Christ, help me! Poor Bartley is either going to jail or across the ocean to the far side of hell!"

He tripped and fell; crashing down on the holly he had held onto throughout the whole ordeal. Looking back over his shoulder he saw the end of the carriage as it rounded the corner of the avenue.

"All over a bit of holly and me life is as good as ended, and that auld bastard can throw a widow out onto the side of the road and no-one can say a thing! God, this is a cruel world, and things are getting worse," he cried aloud.

Walking back to the village, he contemplated hanging himself. But that wouldn't do him either because the priest has always said you go to hell if you take your own life. 'Oh God', he thought, 'why didn't I go for that job in the town? Anywhere would be better than here!'

Going into the pub, several greeted him, but the voices seemed to be coming to him through a mist... he felt this must be worse than being dead... a living nightmare. Going to his room he threw the holly into the corner and fell onto his four-poster bed with the hollow in the mattress. He prayed to die... and soon. He fell into a fitful sleep, and awoke some time later. The room was dark and cold. Slowly, the afternoon's episode returned with fresh intensity. He leaped from the bed. People, company... I'll have to get downstairs where there's distraction, he thought.

The pub was crowded and thick with smoke. He ordered a whiskey and sat in the corner, where he began to mourn his fate. His employer, Brian Wolohan, looked over at him and wondered at the gloomy sight.

"Eh, Bartley. The missus left you a plate of cold meat on the table inside if you want it," he shouted at him.

"No. Nothing for me. Only fill this glass up again, to the top this time."

"You're hitting' it hard tonight, aren't you? Well, it is Christmas, and why not?" Brian filled the whiskey glass and laughed heartily.

"Aye, 'tis Christmas alright, and God only knows... may be me last... " Bartley swayed as he made his way from the bar counter.

"Don't say that, Bartley. Sure there's lots of life left in ye yet, auld boy!"

Brian looked at his barman more closely. Then Bartley began to wail loudly.

"Christmas is right! Poor Bartley is for the hangman or for the ship. 'Tis a good thing me poor mother never lived to see this day!"

A silence fell over the pub. The sight of the hardened barman in such great distress was a sight never conceived of. It even stirred the hearts of those who disliked him. Wiping his hands in his apron, Brian walked out from behind the counter.

"Now Bartley. Christmas is a sad time for us all, if we were to let it be, but what's all this talk of ships and hanging? Where have all these queer notions come out of?"

Gradually, with skill and patience, the afternoon's events emerged, and the ultimate date of Lord Foldsworths judgement in January. The crowd was dumbfounded, but the angry exclamations all round comforted Bartley little.

James de Lacey suddenly stood up. He had listened to the tale, and he called for order.

"Men," he began, "I believe what Bartley has said, and I think – since the eviction of May Ryan – we are facing a turning point. We cannot allow this to happen to Bartley."

A loud cheer rose from the full house, and Bartley's spirits were lifted. He felt a hero.

* * *

At Oak Hall, Kitty was dumbfounded by her father's reaction. She never remembered seeing him so angry, and all over a bunch of holly.

Her mother was equally taken aback, to the extent that she dared not discuss the event with her husband. Certainly not this evening, she decided, but I will find an opportune moment.

Lord Foldsworth sat through dinner calmly, as if the incident had never occurred. He was aware of the effect it had produced on his wife and daughter. It was regrettable, he thought, that they had been present for the encounter. Nevertheless, they were going to have to become accustomed to the change of attitude, which he was, of necessity, implementing on his estate and towards his tenants. The last meeting he had been to at the Castle had made the landlords conscious of just how dangerous their position was becoming. There had been reports of some of the great houses being burned to the ground; some of the occupants killed; livestock being maimed and killed. Fortunately, his wife and daughter were so far unaware of these events. Lord Foldsworth viewed the future grimly. Why does it have to lead to rebellion, he wondered. No answer came to mind.

Lady Foldsworth decided it was time to discuss the Christmas menu and catering plans with Hannah. Summoning her, she waited in the drawing room. After a polite knock, the door opened, and Hannah stood before her mistress. She did not look her usual self. Her mistress bade her be seated.

"Now Hannah, we have quite a lot to discuss, so I would like to commence immediately. Tomorrow bring Christmas Eve, we will have dinner at six o'clock instead of half-past-seven, as we must attend carol services. Reverend Watson always insists that we attend. To show example, as it were. Now, as to Christmas Day... "

Lady Foldsworth continued to outline the plans. With the skill of a great hostess, she chose dishes to be prepared, and the different sauces and wines to accompany them. Hannah dutifully noted all her mistress dictated to her, but throughout the interview she could only think of May Ryan and her children. They would be dead from hunger, if it were not for the food she was sending from the kitchen. She felt a lump rise in her throat as she tried hard to repress the emotions she was feeling. It was her employer who was responsible for it all, she couldn't help but think. Suddenly she felt the tears run down her face. At the sight of her housekeeper in such distress, Lady Edwina stopped talking abruptly.

"Hannah, what is it? You seem overwrought. Are all these Christmas arrangements too much for you? There, there... I'll have help brought in from the village for you... will that do?"

Hannah was unable to answer, and continued to wipe; her eyes with the corner of her apron.

"Come now," persisted Lady Edwina, "will that suffice?"

As Hannah failed yet again to respond, she realised the trouble lay deeper. Standing up, she looked at her housekeeper, whose loyalty and diligence she had never found fault with over all her years at Oak Hall.

"It is neither the kitchen not the Christmas arrangements, is it Hannah?"

Looking up at her mistress, Hannah at last found her voice, though barely audible.

"No your Ladyship, it is not... but, I can't... I have no right to speak to you about it... it isn't my business madam."

Lady Edwina stepped nearer to her.

"Now Hannah, you came to this house when I was a young bride, and we have known each other many years, surely you can trust me?

Hannah knew her mistress was genuine in wanting to help her. Slowly she began to tell the story of Pat Ryan's long illness, his eventual death, his wife and children and the climax of the eviction by Jerome Hennessy. The story, as it unfolded, shocked her mistress beyond words. As Lady Edwina paced the drawing room floor, her face ashen, Hannah felt remorse for having disclosed the information to her. What possible good would it serve?

"Why Hannah... this is dreadful news... simply devastating... and tomorrow Christmas Eve... what must our tenants think of us? ... Poor Mrs Ryan... "

Stopping near the fireplace, she looked at Hannah.

"Thank you for telling me, Hannah. I shall speak directly to my husband about it. You may go now."

Leaving the room slowly, Hannah glanced back.

"Thank you, you Ladyship."

She was about to open the door when her mistress called her back.

"Hannah... Hannah, I wish you to keep me informed as much as you possibly can of our tenants problems. Privately of course. I wish nobody to know of this arrangement, do you understand?"

"Yes, your Ladyship, I understand perfectly, and I am grateful to you for hearing me out madam," she replied, feeling relieved.

"It is the least I can do for the best cook in the country, Hannah!" Lady Edwina smiled, and it spoke volumes to Hannah. She left the room feeling as if a great weight had been lifted from her.

Lady Edwina rang the bell for Williams. When he eventually entered the room, she noticed the same look of gloom, as had graced Hannah's face.

"Williams, will you please ask Lord Foldsworth to join me as soon as possible?" she requested.

Williams guessed Hannah's protracted menu meeting had a bearing on this summons. Upon entering the library, he looked at his master, who was in a deep slumber by the fireside. The book he had been reading had slipped to the floor. He decided to clear his throat, by was of announcing his presence. His master woke with a start.

"Williams... what on earth are you thinking of sneaking about like a cat... what is it man?"

Williams noted that he did, indeed, look alarmed by the intrusion.

"Your Honour, Lady Foldsworth wishes you to join her in the drawing room," he imparted nervously, omitting the urgency of the summons, lest it would irritate his master further.

"Yes Williams. Goodnight." Lord Foldsworth sighed deeply.

As he rose from the comfortable chair by the fire, he wondered the reason for this unusual request, and why his wife was still up-and-about at this hour. On entering the drawing room, the sight of his wife pacing the floor, so obviously irate, was sufficient to alert him to the fact that she wasupset.

"Edwina, what in heavens name is the matter?" he asked, genuinely concerned.

"Charles, you will recall I come from a large, well run estate, where we had an excellent relationship with all our tenants. Do you also remember that when I married you, we made it our ambition to do likewise?"

"Of course I do, Edwina, but what is the relevance of all this... at this time of night?"

He did not get the opportunity to question her further. She clapped both her hands together in a gesture of despair.

"What is the relevance ?... I shall tell you what the relevance is. An eviction on this estate!" She glared at her husband.

"Eviction? What nonsense is this Edwina... ah, so that's it... the fellow we met on the avenue, with the holly. I am sorry for that incident... "

Again his wife interrupted. Turning round and walking towards him she exclaimed in anger.

"Holly? Drat for holly!"

The shock of his wife swearing shocked him. Continuing in anger, she almost shouted.

"Do you realise that your agent, or whatever you title him, evicted a widow and children while we were at the Vice Regal Ball in Dublin? Yes, evicted them, and her husband only having died three days prior. Irrespective of his death, I find this barbaric act beyond belief. I demand an explanation now, Charles, in spite of the hour. If it is not forthcoming, and of a satisfactory nature, I shall not be associated with this dreadful cruelty. While my father is ninety years old, I think he could be reconciled with both Kitty and I going to live at Castle Longwood."

Almost breathless, Lady Edwina fell into the fireside chair, her frustration and anger almost spent.

"My dear, I swear to you I know nothing of an eviction carried out on this estate. Much less did I authorise one. Do you think that I would go to such lengths with my tenants, and with a widow and her children?" he asked, totally horrified by this episode. "I shall summons Williams this instant."

With that, he pulled the service bell, straining the cord with an angry jerk. Williams arrived after several minutes.

"Williams, what do you know of an eviction taking place in my absence, and in my name, it would seem?"

"Well, your Lordship, Jerome Hennessy evicted Mrs Ryan and her children, because they were unable to pay their rent, and her husband had died just days prior. He told the crowds that it was your wishes sir, and there seems to have been a great number of people present. If I may say so, sir, news of this eviction has travelled all over the countryside. People are upset and very angry, if you don't mind me saying so."

The old butler stood almost aghast at his own proclamation, yet found himself continuing.

"And sir, the whole village is in uproar because the man you found taking holly is to be deported or hanged," Williams concluded.

Lady Edwina was aghast, and let a brief cry.

"Hanged! To hang a man for taking holly? Charles... what is happening?"

Williams began to tremble. In all his life of service to this household he had never witnessed a scene like it. His Lordship and Her Ladyship shouting like the scullery maids. Just then, Kitty came into the room smiling.

"Oh mother, there you are. I have just completed wrapping my Christmas presents, and I have so much..." Lady Edwina raised her hand.

"Please Kitty. Sit down and be silent."

The tone of her mothers voice alarmed her.

"Mother, what is it... father, what is the matter...?" Kitty was reminded of when they had received the news of her uncle Rogers's sudden death.

"Is there someone dead, father? What is wrong?" she asked, feeling fear and apprehension rise within her.

Lord Foldsworth addressed his daughter.

"Kitty, there has been a dreadful mistake made, and it may be too late to rectify it."

He explained the matter quickly but fully to her. Kitty looked at him as though he were a stranger.

"But father, how could this have happened?"

Unable to comprehend the implications this incident could create for her family, for herself, for their very lives, Kitty just sat still. 'James,' she eventually thought, 'If only I could see him and ask about May Ryan and her small children. How they are, and their whereabouts'. So many questions presented themselves to Kitty.

"Williams, I wish you to send a messenger this instant to summon Jerome Hennessy, and within the hour I might add!"

"Yes, your Lordship, I most certainly will," replied Williams, and departed with a speed quite uncommon to him.

Lord Foldsworth realised that his family was in a dangerous position, and the sooner this was dealt with the better. Descending the stairs, Williams wondered where the matter would end for his master and mistress. For them all, for that matter. Just then the service bell rang again, and he trudged wearily back up the stairs.

"You rang, madam?"

Looking at the butler's tired face, Lady Edwina admired how he was always so patient.

"I'm sorry Williams, but would you kindly ask Hannah to send up some tea. I fear it may be a long night!"

"Certainly, madam... will that be all?"

This subtle remark didn't go unnoticed by her.

"Of course Williams, and thank you once again."

She smiled, and her expression softened. Lord Foldsworth sat limply in his chair and looked at his wife and daughter.

"I am indeed so sorry for the way this matter is upsetting you both, and I promise I shall do all I can to ease things... my God, what was that fool of a crazed man Hennessy thinking of? I will deal with him this very night. Edwina, Kitty, I know how upsetting this matter is for you both. Please forgive me."

His wife saw his distraught face and felt pity.

"Charles, please forgive me also... but a widow and small children... However, we shall put things to right. Then let us hope for an end to the matter."

They both wondered if it would be so simple. Kitty excused herself and went to the kitchen to see if the tea was ready.

"Oh, Miss Kitty, what do you think will happen?" asked Hannah, as she noticeable shivered while placing the silver teapot on the tray.

"Happen?" asked Kitty, as she stared into the flames of the great fire. "Why Hannah, to begin with, father will speak to this despicable fellow who carried out the eviction, and then find a suitable home for that unfortunate woman and her children. We must pray, Hannah, that all will work out. For all our sakes." Kitty paused. "Now, let's bring up the tea, shall we?"

Obediently Hannah followed, feeling a bit more comforted.

* * *

Jerome Hennessy lay by his fire, full of whiskey, and snoring loudly. A large dribble hung from his chin. A half bottle of whiskey stood by his chair, with the cork beside it, waiting to be consumed when he awoke. Beside the fire the large ginger tabby cat groomed its coat and paws, having just eaten the remains of a chicken, which Tess had left out for her employer. The cat stood up and arched its back. A large rat moved under the stairs. It scented the cat. The flames of the crackling beech wood fire sent sparks up the chimney in abundance.

A loud pounding on the door shattered the stillness. The rat scurried away rapidly. Jerome Hennessy heard it as though it came from quite a distance. But the knocking persisted, getting louder, and his name was being called repeatedly. He opened his eyes and tried to focus on the door.

"Who's there, and what do you want?" he slurred, as he began to scratch his matted hair slowly.

The voice replied authoritively.

"Lord Foldsworth demands you at his home within this very hour," called the messenger.

"What the bloody hell does he want with me at this hour?" he grunted, as he stumbled to the doorway and took away the iron bar, which he always placed across the centre.

"Lord Foldsworth demands to see you now," the messenger repeated.

The cool night air through the opening door seemed to make the information clearer.

"Right so… right. I'll saddle up and be there after ye."

On re-entering the house, the cat was greeted by a familiar large boot to its rear, and made its escape through the open door. Taking another mouthful of whiskey, Hennessy put on his grey cloak and went to the stable to saddle his horse.

As he cantered towards his master's house, the reason for this late summons formed in his mind. 'Of course', he thought, 'Now I know… it's to congratulate me on the way I've been getting the rents up-to-date for him! That eviction let him know I mean business. Threats and curses don't work on Jerome Hennessy! Then he will want to give me the usual bottle of whiskey for Christmas. Why can't he wait until tomorrow? But then, they will be very busy with other quality visiting, I suppose. So what of the late hour! What's the matter with me at all, and me complainin' about collecting me Christmas present!' He chuckled to himself, and felt recklessly elated. The frosty air made him feel a little refreshed. He was more heady than he thought.

Kitty and her mother left the drawing room and went to the library when it was announced the land agent had arrived. They had no intention of being present when the interview took place. They did, however, leave the door slightly open, to glimpse the visitor. The sound of voices rose from below stairs. It was Hannah protesting.

"… The state of you… coming into this house in that condition… Have you no respect for your betters, Jerome Hennessy?"

Hannah sounded very authoritative downstairs. Kitty nudged her mother deeper into the shadows of the room as slow feet ascended and plodded towards the drawing room door. Lady Edwina placed a hand over her mouth as she caught sight of the visitor. Kitty felt an urge to race forward and deliver some well-aimed blows. Instead, they both stood motionless as they watched Jerome Hennessy as he drew his sleeve across his nose before knocking on the door. Lord Foldsworths voice boomed clear.

"Enter!"

As the bailiff entered he stumbled on a Persian rug and almost fell before his master.

"Beggin' your Honours pardon, 'tis the rug that tripped me… "

"Close the door and step forward." The ice-cold tone and rigid gaze of the landlord erased all expectations of the Christmas gift he had in mind.

"What obscene act did you carry out both in my name and in my absence, Hennessy?"

"Well, your honour, if it is the eviction ye mean, 'twas well comin' to them… they paid no rent this six months, so I says to meself, I'll put a stop to that, takin' advantage of your Honours decency, says I."

He felt very assured by this expression of the events.

The smell of whiskey coming from the man was sickening, and the blackened teeth, which seemed to nest in the grey stubble beard, did nothing but anger the master more. 'Imagine him to be an employee of mine, a representative', he thought. On closer examination he could well imagine the way this man would revel in his use of authority.

"How dare you, Hennessy, do such an act without consulting me. I should have you horse whipped, yes, even publicly, for your treatment of my tenant. A widow, I believe, with small children. As and from now you cease to be my agent, and you will leave my estate at first light. Should I ever find you on my lands again, or in fact, even see you... you will receive a public horsewhipping. And that, my man, is letting you off lightly! Now. Get out of this house, and send me the keys to your dwelling at dawn as you leave. Now go... while you still can...!"

Lord Foldsworths face was ashen and distorted with anger, and his finger shook as he pointed to the door. Jerome Hennessy told himself that this was a nightmare and expected himself to wake at any moment. Whiskey does strange things to a man. He stood as if rooted to the ground in total bewilderment. His employer interpreted this as defiance and slowly opened a drawer containing a small pistol. He fired a shot once into the air. Ceiling plaster came cascading down. Hennessy turned and ran, the reality finally registering with him.

He met Lady Edwina and Kitty screaming in the hall. The kitchen was in uproar. All the servants had gathered, and Williams was desperately trying to maintain calm and control.

Soon the dim figure of Jerome Hennessy could be seen galloping on horseback down the avenue, the sound of the hoof beats dimming into the distance.

"Charles, darling, I thought that man had killed you! Oh, how dreadful for you to even have been in this room with him."

"Edwina, I'm alright. Kitty, will you ask Williams to send someone after that vagabond to see that he goes to his own house and to maintain surveillance of him through the night."

"Certainly father."

Kitty went downstairs and delivered the message. All the staff were in shock. Nothing like this had ever happened in the house before. The quiet order and tranquillity had been badly shaken. Hannah was the first to speak.

"Good riddance to that scoundrel, and I hope we will never see him again!"

Her voice trembled and she tried to straighten her hair.

"Williams, will you please see to my parents with some brandy punch, and Hannah, will you please prepare food for all present. Perhaps a drink of something also. It has been a dreadful night for all I fear."

The household began to settle down as the fire was stoked and the smell of whiskey and cold roast meat filled the air. Hannah was a mother to all these people. Kitty left them, knowing her presence curtailed discussion on the events just passed.

* * *

The east wind began to rise gradually, and small flakes of snow fell slowly to the earth and rested on frozen ground. Jerome Hennessy walked into his house, a very sober and quiet man in contrast to the one who had left an hour ago. There were no choices. None. It was that simple. Revenge would mean certain death for hi, he reasoned.

"Well," he said to the still air, "I can go to my brother in Carlow. There are worse places. I'd better gather what's mine and leave this blasted place!"

'Money', he thought, "at least I'll have some to get a fresh start with'. Money was hidden in various places around the house. All the furniture belonged to the house. The thought occurred to him to burn house and all, his home for many years.

"No, I'd only end up worse than ever. Little else matters now but to leave before daybreak." Then, through gritted teeth, the house ringing with his voice, "I won't give anyone the pleasure of seeing me leave. But as for you Foldsworth, I'll be back for you. I'll kill you some dark night!"

It takes time to plan proper revenge. He knew there were many who were seeking an opportunity to harm the landlords. In time he figured he would meet up with them, and then he could 'finish off that bastard at Oak Hall'. To let some months pass would serve his purpose well.

Consoled at the thought of eventual revenge, he hastily stuffed money into a cotton bag, and tucked it inside his coat. He collected some good clothes, and packed them into the saddlebags. Bracing himself against the cold wind, he mounted his horse and quietly rode through the sleeping village. A thin layer of powdery snow lay around, and as the clouds parted, a Christmas moon shone through. The road ahead was empty, and the rims of the mountains stood out clearly. If the weather held, he should reach his brothers house by mid-morning.

Taking the half bottle of whiskey that remained; he drank several mouthfuls, hoping it would prevent the chill winds penetrating his body. Having passed through the village unseen, he waited to get to the outskirts before spurring his horse forward to a brisk canter. The animal sensed there was something wrong, and became increasingly more nervous with the jibes and shouts of its rider.

Deciding to take a shorter route through the foothills, he crossed an open field adjoining an oak wood. There was a trail that would lead him to the sheep tracks that spanned the foothills. The moon gave great light, which the snow covered ground only served to enhance. He was grateful, as it would shorten his journey considerably. The horse shied several times at the shadows cast by the trees, and he became more and more irritated with the animal, as with the journey itself. Leaping a large ditch safely, horse and rider trotted on the narrow trail.

Hennessy thought again of the frenzy in which his landlord had bade him leave, and of the eviction he had carried out.

"I'd do it all again. It was worth every minute of it to show them what I can do if I wish. Let May Ryan and her children remember that!" he shouted into the dark.

His voice startled an owl that lay ahead on the path, eating a mouse it had just caught. It flew suddenly into the path of the oncoming horse, and its broad wingspan lifted it barely out of reach of the thundering hooves. The startled horse reared up suddenly, and Hennessy, losing his balance in the saddle, fell heavily to the ground. He shouted out in fright. The last thing he felt was a searing pain at the base of his head that shot down his spine. He rolled over and fell into a ditch where he lay motionless.

As his eyes drifted to the moon as it made its way across the sky, life ebbed from Jerome Hennessey's body. The rider less horse would run some miles yet before its fear and panic would give way to fatigue.

* * *

Joe Gilltrap moved uneasily in his sleep, and his wife felt his restlessness.

In his attic room over the pub, Bartley Finnegan drank another glass of whiskey. He gazed at the flickering candle as it neared its end, and contemplated his fate.

Somewhere a cock crowed, announcing Christmas Eve 1796, with Bartley its only listener.

Lord Foldsworth arose early, after a very uneasy and fitful sleep. He was anxious to sort out this eviction problem and to rehouse the widow Ryan. 'Yes', he thought, 'Hennessey's house would be ideal. And there is a smaller cottage near it which the next land agent can use'. In the dining room, he was surprised to find his wife and daughter half way through their breakfast.

"Good morning, Charles. Did you manage to sleep darling?" His pallor told her that he had slept little.

"No, Edwina. How could I sleep after that dreadful episode last night? Let's hope that scoundrel is far away by now. I have decided to give his house to the widow Ryan, which reminds me, I must ring for Williams to check if he has left our property yet." Taking the top off his boiled egg, he continued, "I'd like this matter sorted out as soon as possible... after all, it is Christmas Eve, is it not?"

A faint smile appeared on his tired face, and the atmosphere of gloom lifted somewhat. Kitty, having finished her breakfast, asked to be excused.

"Father, I shall see Williams now and ask him to convey your request to Mrs Ryan."

"Yes Kitty, please do, and lest I forget to say it to both of you, thank you for your patience and understanding in this matter."

Kitty kissed her father on the forehead and went bounding to the kitchen. Her mother felt Kitty was rather too familiar with 'downstairs'. Still, it was a habit formed since she could first walk. Pointless to stop it now.

Kitty was breathless with excitement at the prospect of rehousing Mrs Ryan, and in such a solid house too. The children would have lots of space for sleeping, but the animals should not be allowed in. It would be father's task to outline that matter, she thought.

"Oh, Hannah, Williams. Father wishes you to see Mrs Ryan this morning, and guess for what...? Oh, I shall take you out of suspense. She is getting Hennessey's house! Oh, isn't it wonderful news!" Kitty clapped her hands in delight. "Isn't it wonderful? Oh, I am so thrilled. I intend going to see her myself. Don't tell father or mother though, as they wouldn't approve. Should they enquire of me, I have gone for a walk in the park."

With that, Kitty flew out the door in a whirl of excitement. Williams looked after her in disapproval, shaking his head slowly.

"That girl is going to be reprimanded by her father one of these days for not keeping her station. Humm, next thing we shall hear that she is gossiping in the village houses."

Hannah began to busy herself with the preparations of the day ahead, while Williams gave orders to the rest of the staff, delegating duties, which seemed endless this Christmas Eve.

Kitty cantered happily to the village, and wondered where she would find Mrs Ryan. She decided to go the forge. Joe Gilltrap was likely to know. Tethering her horse outside of his house, she politely knocked on the green door. She could hear the noise of the children playing within, all laughing happily. The door opened, and James stood before her quite taken aback by the visitor.

"Kitty... where have you come from?" His was surprised to see her.

"From home of course, James, where else?" She was delighted at the turn of events the morning was bringing. "And how have you been James?"

"Oh, busy as usual. You know the way it is for me," he replied, ill at ease now. "I hear you have been to Dublin Kitty. Did you enjoy it there?"

"Yes, it was lovely indeed. We attended the Vice Regal Ball at Dublin Castle. Delightful really. Now James, perhaps you can tell me where to find Mrs Ryan and her family. My father wishes to see her this morning, as soon as possible."

Noticing how his expression had changed, she hastily added,

"Nothing to worry about, I assure you, but rather the opposite."

She wondered why she tried to explain the nature of her visit to him. He was a comparative stranger in many ways. Kitty didn't have to wait for a reply, as Mrs Ryan herself appeared from behind James. On seeing her, Kitty exclaimed.

"Oh, there you are, Mrs Ryan. Isn't it fortunate to have found you so quickly."

She noticed the strained white face that still bore grief and shock.

"I have already heard you Miss. What is it your father wants with me?"

"My father wishes to speak to you concerning recent events, and it would be in your best interest to come as soon as possible."

May Ryan looked faint and sighed deeply.

"Alright miss, I will be there as soon as I can."

James turned and looked at the widow.

"May, I'll drive you in the pony and trap. So you ready yourself, and don't worry."

May disappeared, and James pulled the door closed behind him. He looked at Kitty, her authoritative voice still ringing in his ears. Putting his two hands up in the air he exclaimed...

"When the master calls... '

Kitty noted the mock tone in his voice and without thinking continued.

"Yes... it would be wise to come!" Then, mounting her horse she looked down at James. "Perhaps you should be getting the trap ready for Mrs Ryan. I am sure she is anxious to be going for her interview."

There it was again, James noted. That tone in her voice, 'do this" and, get that... bred into her'.

"As I've already said, Miss Foldsworth... we hasten when summoned... "

He bowed to her with a broad sweep of his hat.

"James, I don't quite know why you act like this. It doesn't suit you to act the gombeen man. I should have thought there were enough of them about!"

James was taken back by her comment and before he could think of a suitable reply, Kitty had cantered away.

"Why do I act like that? She is quite right, I suppose", he said aloud to himself, scratching his head.

"They say people that talk to themselves are either mad or in love, James," May Ryan stood beside him, smiling, "and James, I don't think you are going mad either!"

It was good to see May smile again.

"Into the trap with you, May, 'til we go see what his Lordship has on his mind at this early hour of the day."

They both shared a woollen rug across their knees and the pony took off in a brisk trot.

"I hope to God James that Joe will not get in trouble for taking us in. You know the penalty for giving a home to the evicted."

Fresh tears ran down her face as she tried to hide her growing fear. Where would they go if they were ordered to leave the Gilltraps? The idea of the poor house almost made her vomit with apprehension, but she managed to control it.

"You don't worry now May about seeing his Lordship. It could be almost anything other than what you expect."

While James tried to comfort her, he was aware that anything was possible, and nothing would surprise him anymore. Not after the encounter Lord Foldsworth had with Bartley Finnegan in relation to the holly incident. As he was driving the trap into the side entrance of the estate, May rubbed her ashen cheeks to try and bring some colour to them.

"Now May, just stay calm, and make your answers brief and to the point when his Lordship questions you. Remember, even though you were made homeless, he is a powerful man, and your future lies in his hands, like it or not."

"You needn't worry, James. I know my situation and how to respect the gentry!"

Hannah opened the back door, and was delighted to see May.

"May love, come in, and hurry! His Lordship has been asking if you had arrived yet."

Hannah was shocked at the widow's appearance; at how frail and thin she had gone.

"Hannah, thank you for the food you sent us. I am only shivering at the thoughts of meeting his Lordship."

She pulled the grey shawl about her thin shoulders.

"You needn't worry, May. 'Tis all good news for you. Now come and I'll show you the way."

The smell of roasting meat and freshly baked bread assailed May's senses as they passed through the kitchen and ascended the stairs. Knocking on the drawing room door, Hannah opened it, and in a clear voice announced May.

"Lord Foldsworth, this is May Ryan whom you wished to see. Will that be all sir?"

Hannah's matter-of-fact approach surprised May in a way she couldn't explain.

"Yes, Hannah, that will be all. Thank you," he replied, equally polite.

Hannah left and closed the door behind her. Charles Foldsworth looked at the frail woman before him, who, for one so young, bore all the marks of poverty and hardships. Yet he could also see the remains of what was once a beautiful woman.

"Mrs Ryan, please take a seat. I will not detain you any longer than is necessary."

He was aware that if his visitor did not sit down, she would probably fall down, as her trembling did not escape his eye.

"During my absence in Dublin, I heard of the dreadful way you were taken from your home and the manner in which it was destroyed before your very eyes. Perhaps you may know it was never my policy to evict, but rather to help sort out my tenant's rent problems?" He realised it was harder than anticipated to handle this meeting. "Jerome Hennessy did not have orders from me at any time to carry out this solution to a problem. I regret to say it was his own deliberate act. I have dismissed him from my service and from my estate for all time."

Standing up he went over to the table and picked up a pair of keys and handed them to her. The small thin hand accepted them with large questioning eyes.

"What are these for, my lord?"

"They are the keys to Jerome Hennessey's house. I wish you to accept this house for yourself and your children, as your new home for all time... rent free. Hennessy will never be back, so you can rest without worry again."

Tears spilled down May's cheeks, and her voice failed her.

"Now, now, Mrs Ryan. Just think of it as a Christmas gift from eh family here."

May stood up.

"I am very grateful, Lord Foldsworth, and surely there is a God in heaven, who has heard my prayers. I don't know how to thank you, and it is such a fine home too."

"Yes, Mrs Ryan, it is a solid house, and there are outhouses at the rear for stock. Now, thank you for coming so promptly, and I will let you go as I have much to do this Christmas Eve." He extended his hand to her, "I was sorry to hear of the death of your husband."

"Thank you, sir, and a very happy Christmas to you and to all your family."

Hannah seemed to appear at the door with remarkable timing, a habit her employer had noticed on many occasions, much to his amusement.

"Thank you, Hannah. Perhaps you would be kind enough to give Mrs Ryan some tea before she leaves."

"Of course, your Lordship." she replied, impatient to get May downstairs, where all the servants were waiting to hear the news from her own lips.

"Oh James, you'll never believe it. Not alone did his Lordship say he was sorry for Hennessey's brutality, but he has given me his house to keep for all time, look!" May held up the keys for all to see.

She beamed with happiness and delight, and everyone cheered her. Upstairs, their employers, who felt equally happy for her, heard the voices of jubilation. James was stunned by this amazing development.

"What of Hennessy, where is he gone?" he asked.

"Well, he must be gone for all time or else I wouldn't have the keys, would I?" said May. She looked younger already since her brief visit.

"There will be no need to worry about that rascal returning again May. He is gone from these parts, and if he shows his face here again, he is for the rope, so he is!" said Hannah, not disclosing any further information, but letting everyone know that she was aware of most of the masters decisions... if not all of them!

"Well, May, you have some work to do," said James, taking her arm, and after thanking Hannah and Williams for the tea, they left. When they had gone, Williams looked thoughtfully into the great fire.

"You know, Hannah, that fellow James looks remarkably like the fellow who came here one day wounded, or whatever it was had happened to him. Did you notice the resemblance?"

"Of course I did, Williams, but I didn't want to start talking about it in front of everyone else. What would the master think if he heard of that visit here? I'll tell you what... he'd soon ask why we didn't inform him, that's what! And where would that leave us, do you suppose?"

"You may be right Hannah. Still, there was something odd about it, wasn't there? I'll have to be more alert, as these are funny times. We'll have to be more careful."

* * *

On their way home in the pony and trap, May was silent, thinking how life can change so quickly. As she wiped a tear from her eye, James noticed her sigh.

"Come now, May, 'tis over, isn't it? Put the past behind you and think of the children and all the new house will mean to them."

"I know, James. It's Pat I'm thinking of, and what this might have done for him. A warm dry house would have helped him. It's as if you have to lose something to gain something in this world."

Trying to lift her spirits, James suggested they get a big fire going at Hennessey's and have it thoroughly cleaned out. May's spirits lifted greatly.

On that Christmas Eve night throughout the village, when children were sleeping and great fires crackled, the news of widow Ryan's new home was discussed in awe and wonder. The disappearance of Jerome Hennessy was the greatest Christmas present they could ever hope for. Lord Foldsworth was praised and blessed for hours for his generosity and fairness. Many considered it to be Kitty's influence, and the incident provoked a great rethink on views that were expressed earlier in the week. Most concluded that there was, after all, such a thing as a humane landlord, and a new respect and liking took root among the people.

* * *

Bartley Finnegan felt a flood of relief sweeping throughout his being, and as he filled the pints of stout and ale he even began humming a song to himself, thinking that things could likely go in his favour also.

"Maybe the season of goodwill will last until January," he said to James, who stood waiting for a drink to be served.

"My advice to you, Bartley, is not to be meeting the devil halfway," he replied.

'That James fellow', thought Bartley, 'is a natural leader of men, though he isn't from these parts. Where exactly does he come from? He had heard rumours of pikes being made at Gilltraps, and that James was an agent of some sort. None of my business, but pikes or no pikes, 'tis all dreams to the lot of them. A good barman hears everything and says nothing. This United Irishman stuff...', Bartley chuckled, 'hah... lookin' about here tonight there's not many that could free two dogs in a fight! Imagine anyone around here in a Government!"

Everyone in the pub celebrated May's good fortune. Spirits ran high in jubilation. Outside, snow fell heavily and silently, as Jerome Hennessey's horse found its way back to the village, tired and hungry. It was an object of curiosity to some, and it filled others with the fear that Hennessy had returned. Word was brought back to the pub, and many left its comfort to see the animal, as it stood motionless, its saddle hanging sideways on its back.

"That is his horse, isn't is Joe?" James queried.

"It is indeed, James, and if that's the case, he isn't very far away. He could be staying with someone in the village. Yet I'd imagine if that was the case he would have his horse stabled."

"I don't like the looks of it at all, Joe. Look at the saddle for a start. The girth is loosened," James said, as he listened to his instincts. "I think we should follow the road that leads to the wood and have a look about the place."

Joe looked at him.

"James, only I feel as you do, I would say the porter had got the better of you tonight! The moon is bright lad, and the night air crisp. I suppose we might as well."

They both walked out of the village, on the crisp hardening snow, following the clear tracks of the rider less horse.

"Look here, James. There are two sets of hoof prints under the tree. One going into the wood with its rider and the other ones lighter, as you can see."

"It doesn't make a lot of sense, Joe. A rider less horse... in the snow? But then again, nothing would surprise me about Jerome Hennessy."

"You know, when you think about it, that was the best days work he ever did, the eviction. In a way it got May her new house and was Hennessey's downfall. It got rid of him rightly."

"The way May had the place gleaming, all traces of Hennessy gone, and all in a few hours," James said, feeling glad for May each time he thought of it. "It's hard to beat a woman's touch about the place, isn't it Joe?"

"An when do you intend gettin' one for yer self?" Joe laughed.

"Get what, Joe?"

"A woman, of course! It's time you smartened yourself up a bit."

They both laughed, but James thought of Kitty.

"Oh, I could surprise you, Joe. I have notions too, you know!"

"Well, so long as they are not too high above your head... it's only a caution, 'tis all."

Joe sounded serious, and despite the casual discussion James was suddenly aware that he had an inkling of his liking of Kitty. He couldn't help feel a twinge of resentment at what seemed subtle interference, no matter how friendly, nor how well meant.

Looking intently at the tracks on the snow, which seemed to be in a confused direction, James changed the uncomfortable topic of conversation.

"How far more will we follow these tracks?"

"I'm beginning to ask myself that same question, James. It looks as if we might be on a fool's errand. I'll tell you what, we'll follow it to the stream and no further. I don't know why we are bothering, to tell you the truth... curiosity, I suppose. What do you think yourself?"

"Ok. Let's go as far as the stream, but no further."

The moon had begun her decent in the Christmas sky, and its light was fading; by the time they found a leg protruding from the snow. When they pulled it clear they beheld the dead and stiffened body of Jerome Hennessy. He had been lying head downward in the stream.

"Good God, what a death to get, drowned in a few inches of water," said Joe, aghast at the sight.

"Best leave the body till we get help and a horse and cart from the village to carry the body, and also to have more witnesses, just in case somebody thinks this was our doing," said James, trying to be practical and careful at the same time.

"Yes, you're right. Well, God have mercy on your soul, Jerome Hennessy."

As they walked back to the village, the snow began to fall again. It seemed a far shorter journey somehow. Arousing the neighbours, a number of men set out to retrieve the body of the drowned bailiff. Some remembered the curse put on him by May Ryan.

While they were bringing the body back, it was decided to arouse Father Doyle and to bury the body within hours. Father Doyle agreed to come and many others came to say a prayer for the soul of Hennessy. They hoped, as Father Doyle said, that he might find rest and peace. Some doubted if he ever could.

Early Christmas morning the body of the bailiff was lowered into a narrow grave. Lord Foldsworth, having been informed, had agreed to the hasty burial. Many were plainly relieved to see him dead and buried, and after the funeral, Joe wondered if a man like that could ever 'rest in peace'.

"You know, James, the old people always maintained that going to meet your Maker before you time wasn't the best of things... "

Busy cleaning the shovel on a sharp stone, James looked at him.

"Well, I can see the sense and meaning of that, because I believe he will be back Joe, and you'd better keep you wits about you."

"May God forgive ye, James, and never say that in front of the Missus. Every time the wind hits the rafters, Nell will have me out of the bed!"

Both men laughed heartily and began to relax. As they strolled home they felt the rays of the morning sun.

"Have you forgotten its Christmas Joe?" James asked his friend.

"No, I haven't, but I remember happier starts to it though."

* * *

May Ryan remembered how she, and her husband Pat, used to walk through the summer meadows. The death of Jerome Hennessy made her feel little sorrow. He was well gone, and she didn't care. She was only interested in getting her children into better health. Little else mattered to her now. It was going to be a new life, and she vowed to make it better than the pitiful one she was leaving behind.

* * *

James wondered how Kitty was spending Christmas day, and did she ever think of him? He felt disgruntled at having to spend the day with his elderly uncle, and wished that the day was over. His thoughts raced ahead to the evening, when they would go over to Joe's to play cards. 'Odd, but I never cared much for Christmas. Not a day for anything really: no one in the village, the shop and pub shut; only for the Lord's birthday you could live without it all'.

He piled up the open fire with sods of turf while his uncle dozed in the chair. He decided to go for a walk. He took his cloak from the fireside and felt its warmth on his back. Securing the pin under his throat he gently closed the door behind him. It was good to be out, despite the coldness of late afternoon. He walked towards the oak wood along the bridle path, and kicked the small drifts of snow that lay where the wind had blown it. Just then he heard the sound of a horse coming towards him. As it rounded the corner, he recognised Kit. She reined the horse up expertly.

"Why James, what a great surprise... you here of all days... " She was almost breathless with exertion.

"And you, Kitty, also... " He laughed. Their mutual surprise and delight was apparent.

"Well, James, there is nothing as lovely as a canter in the cold weather. Besides, one gets tired of sitting by the fire. Some of father's guests are quite elderly, and their time is spent telling old stories, which they thoroughly enjoy. So, here I am. What has you here?"

"Well, my uncle fell asleep after dinner and, rather than following his example I, like you, decided to make the best of it."

"Great. I'm delighted to meet for a chat. Will you hold the bridle while I dismount?"

Her heart was racing at this chance encounter. As she dismounted, her breath brushed his face. Tethering the animal, she looked at him. She extended her hand, amazed at her sudden impulsive action. James took it in his.

"Well, James, let's walk and enjoy what is left of the evening."

Unsure of themselves in this new honesty, they eased into pace, hand in hand. Close to each other, no words spoken. Suddenly he turned to face her. She met his gaze. He took her face in both hands. All around them seemed to spin as their lips met in a kiss. One kiss, then another, and another until the short breathless kisses led to a long unbroken kiss that seemed to penetrate their very souls. A kiss that seemed to last forever, yet end too soon.

"Oh God Kitty, what a Christmas present! I never thought it possible that we would... that I could express what I have been feeling for you this long while. I love you, Kitty. I love you very much."

"I know James, as I have fallen in love with you... ever since the day I met you at the forge... I have tried telling myself that it was my imaginings, but not now. This is real, isn't it? You and I here, and what we are feeling... is it not, James?"

The hood of her blue cloak fell back and he stroked her hair as her head lay against his chest. She felt him suddenly become tense.

"What is it James?"

"What if someone should see us? Or your father hears of this? He would lose his reason, Kitty."

And I my life, he thought. She looked at the serious face before her, and laughed.

"Don't be so dramatic, James. How could he possibly hear? Are we not in a safe place? Especially on Christmas evening!"

She sounded so sure that he laughed with her. They strolled on through the gathering dusk, savouring their new love.

"Kitty. It must be time to go back. It will soon be dark. You will be questioned if you are too late." James was torn between his fear and his passion. "Let us plan when and where we will meet again. My love, my love, what can I say to you! My Christmas blossom! That's what I'll call you." He smiled, and kissed her gently.

"James, I know exactly where we can meet. Why not Kilninor. You know the place? Where the old church ruins are. It is on the side of a small hill. It once had nine alters, hence the name."

"My goodness, Kitty, you are knowledgeable, are you not?" he teased. She laughed, and her beautiful lips parted revealing perfectly white teeth.

"When?" she asked.

"Maybe next Christmas day!"

"Oh James! In a week? From today? The evening would probably be best."

"Let it be so, Kitty. A week from today, at the church of the nine alters."

* * *

What a Christmas day it had been. James de Lacey falling in love with the landlord's daughter, and she with him. A surge of warmth filled James as he looked forward to their next meeting. How long can a week truly be? Still only half believing it to be true, he realised it must remain their secret. Even Joe must not suspect. How could he explain it alongside his work for the Insurrection?

Yet, in spite of the threats that reality posed to their love, he somehow felt safe in it.

Chapter four

*M*arjorie Bass opened her licensed premises early on Saint Stephen's morning and prepared for her customers. Christmas day had been monotonous. Far too quiet for her liking. When the hustle and bustle of business is interrupted, even by a single day, the reality of her own life hit her. It forced her to wrestle with the wisdom of never having married or having a family.

She had married her public house! And had never taken to the drink like so many had in her business. These thoughts consoled her greatly.

"Marjorie, if's and but's and maybe's will not run this business on Saint Stephen's day," she scolded herself aloud.

With that declaration, she once again laid to rest the old haunting doubts. In her busy kitchen the smells of roast goose and beef reminded her of just how much work lay ahead that day. Her few employees had great respect for her. They knew that, while she was ruthless in relation to running the business, she was also as fair a person one was ever likely to meet.

Satisfied with her visit to the kitchen, Marjorie went to her private sitting room where her morning tea was promptly brought to her. As she relaxed, she recalled Christmas Eve. The local militia had drunk heavily, and their tongues had loosened in the process. Their news exchanged, which she could clearly overhear, worried her. There were more police to be sent to the town, and the rural areas were to be observed even more closely. Additional money was also being made available for information which would lead to the arrest of anyone involved in, or part of, any group whose aims were suspect of revolution. 'Informing rats', she thought. 'There are those who would sell their families for six pence...'.

The reality was, however, that she must pass on the information to Marcus Ryan. She also realised her own vulnerable situation, and wondered if the militia suspected her role in the rising tide of unrest. The impending meeting of the Insurrection men was to be held in her back rooms soon. She calmed her fears with the thought that no one would ever suspect a meeting being held only doors away from the barracks!

The very daring of the venture added spice to it all for her. Sipping her hot tea – which was laced with whiskey – she thought of James, and the solid type of young man he appeared to be. She trusted Joe's judgement of him. The other too were solid enough, except Tim Flanagan, with whom she had never felt easy... a gut feeling, but nothing other than this. Resolving to think more about 'Shades Flanagan', which was her name for him, she finished her tea and went to the bar, where all the usual faces greeted her. The public face of Marjorie Bass took over again and listening to the many and varied descriptions of how they 'got over Christmas' amused her greatly. The relief to be able to sit and talk to their comrades made one imagine they had not seen each other in months rather than one day. Mick Brown, the shoemaker, came to the bar.

"Marjorie, can I have the usual rum please, when yer ready."

Pouring it for him from a measure to glass, he struck up conversation.

"Did you enjoy the Christmas, Madge?" This was his name for her. She smiled.

"To be sure Mick, I enjoyed it, and I had a great rest. How is Ellie and the family?"

"Thriven', thanks be to God!" He began to sip his rum slowly. "I heard a bit of queer talk goin' round the town this mornin'?"

He looked into his glass without expression. Wiping the counter with a damp cloth, Marjorie feigned disinterest.

"This town is full of queer talk, Mick. Some have little to do but gossip for hours."

He looked up wondering if she was referring to him, but dismissed the idea.

"Well, this is more than mere gossip! The bailiff of Lord Foldsworth estate was found dead. Did you not hear?" He fixed a gaze on her.

"No, Michael, I did not, God rest the poor man," she replied.

She was aware he had his sources. He repaired all the boots for the barracks men. It was well known that they were in the habit of spending a lot of time in the shoemakers shop. More time than a usual visit would merit. He was a paid informer.

"Mind you," she added, "now that I think of it, I remember hearing one day last week that the bailiff out there had begun to drink whiskey as if there was no tomorrow. But who knows what the poor unfortunate man had on his mind. You know the old saying yourself: whiskey makes you well when you're sick and sick when you're well." She looked at him with a feint smile.

"Oh, you'll find it wasn't the drink killed him. No!" He stood to fill his pipe. "Someone lay in for that poor unfortunate wretch when he was drunk. Aye, that was what happened I'd say. Then they knocked him off."

Then, with the finality of a verdict that was strictly his own, he walked out. Those who were standing nearby heard the opinion, and decided it must be the truth. Rapidly, opinion became fact in their minds, so that by mid-day the entire town heard how Lord Foldsworths bailiff had been murdered in cold blood on Christmas Eve.

Sergeant Cosgrave was very disturbed by the news, and decided to ride out and see Lord Foldsworth in order to recommend an increase in police presence in his area. It puzzled him as to how he had not been informed of this murder earlier, and concluded that the landlord hadn't wanted to disturb him over his Christmas break. Michael Brown was always the first with the news of the area, and for this reason he was indispensable. Nonetheless, the sergeant detested him. A weed of a man, in his opinion.

When Sergeant Cosgrave was gone off on his mission, talk in the pub turned to a 'rising'. Marjorie laughed loudly each time the suggestion was voiced, assuring everybody present that the only 'rising' about these parts was the rising of pints of beer. This was reassuring to the fearful and dulling to those who craved excitement. Marjorie realised the implications of this rumour, be it fact or fiction. Insurrection was unmentionable

* * *

Joe Gilltrap mopped the sweat from his brow when he noticed a horseman approaching the forge. His heart was gripped by fear. Sergeant Cosgrave reined his horse in, and his two companions did likewise.

"Well Gilltrap, what's been going on here?"

Joe had difficulty struggling with his fears.

"What do you mean sergeant?"

"Don't play games with me, man. Here in this village there has been something going on!"

Sergeant Cosgrave, with his trimmed moustache, his impeccable uniform, his sure seat on the tall chestnut horse, symbolised so much to Joe.

"Oh, just people getting over Christmas. You know the way it is about this place?" he replied, trying desperately to speak casually.

"Aye, and your bailiff murdered I hear. In cold blood on Christmas eve... probably a good enough reason to celebrate for the lot about this place." He looked at the man before him. Hard to understand these fellows, he thought.

"Oh indeed, poor Hennessy, God rest his soul... died just outside the village here. We found him in a drain, dead for some time." He wondered what would come next.

"You say 'we' found him in a drain, Gilltrap. Who is the 'we'?"

The question obviously disturbed Joe.

"Myself and another lad. We found the horse Hennessy generally rode, rider less and saddled, and thought it odd. So we followed the tracks in the snow and found him dead in the wood. Seems his horse threw him, Sergeant, and Hennessy must have fell and hit his head on a stone. The stone was blood stained." He waited for the next question.

"The question I asked, Gilltrap, which fell on your deaf ears and empty head, was 'who' was the other person with you. Damn it man, are you as stupid as you are big!" The temper of the questioner was becoming dangerous.

Miraculously, Joe later thought, they were interrupted.

"Good day, Mr Gilltrap."

Joe sighed with relief. Sergeant Cosgrave rounded his horse in the direction of the speaker.

"Who the devil...?" He shouted

His voice trailed off as he saw the beautiful young woman, in a blue riding habit, who seemed to have come from nowhere.

"I beg your pardon, or did I hear incorrectly? How dare you address me in that fashion. Now, step aside instantly."

Kitty, overhearing some of the conversation as she approached the forge, knew she had only arrived in the nick of time. She had seen how trapped and uncomfortable Joe was.

"Blacksmith, I would like my mounts shoes examined before I join the hunting party," she said haughtily, and gave Joe a wink from her left eye.

"Yes, your Ladyship. I'll attend to it this minute!" he said, helping her to dismount.

His relief was almost tangible. Revealing James' identity would inevitably have led to him also being questioned. Sergeant Cosgrave, having regained his composure, looked steadily at Kitty before he spoke.

"Who, madam, do you think you are, interrupting police business?" he demanded, with an icy tone in his voice. Kitty turned and looked at him.

"I am Lady Catherine Foldsworth, and you Sergeant are not just a man of ill-manners, but impertinent as well!" Her instant reprimand and the disclosure of her identity was more than the Sergeant could handle. "Furthermore, I suggest if you have any questions to ask in relation to events of the past week, you should go to my father. Now Sergeant, I am a busy woman, so you are dismissed!"

Giving a vague salute, he turned his horse just in time to notice the smirk on his companions' faces.

"Well, what are you both gaping at? Advance, I say, advance!" he shouted angrily.

They were not without noticing the small party of bystanders who had witnessed the whole scene. Joe looked at Kitty, realising how close to real trouble he had been.

"Thank you, lady Catherine! You helped me out of a rough situation just now. The Sergeant seems to think we here in the village killed Jerome Hennessy, and I am obliged to you."

"Never mind that base fellow. He is only looking to display his authority, or what he likes to consider authority," she smiled, then continued, "Well, he can get all the information from father. I'd rather not be there, for father has little time for anything today but hunting. How are the shoes? Are they secure?" she suddenly remembered the reason for her visit in the first place.

"Yes, they are well fitted, and I hope you have a good days hunting, Miss. Call in anytime you need help."

"Thank you, Mr Gilltrap. I shall keep you to that!" and she bade him goodbye.

Joe was relieved. He resolved that any more pikes were to be kept well away from the forge. After all, he had Nell and the children to think about. Had the police suspected his involvement and found the pikes on his property, he would have been jailed that day, and maybe even hung.

Sergeant Cosgrave rode up the tree-lined avenue that led to the imposing residence of Lord Charles Foldsworth. Assembled on the lawn were at least one hundred or more ladies and gentlemen of the hunting party, surrounded by baying hounds that were anxious to hunt their prey. The approach of the police on Saint Stephen's day caused quite a sensation for the gathering. Lord Foldsworth, busy talking to his old friend Viscount Harley was unaware of their approach.

"Since when, Charles, do the local police-force ride to hounds?" his friend asked.

"Whatever do you mean, Harley?"

"Just look behind you... "

"Let's go and see, shall we Harley."

Both men strode forward leading their horses. Sergeant Cosgrave made a slight bow.

"Lord Foldsworth, I regret to come to you as you are about to go off with your friends here," he said, looking at the hunting party with contempt in his eyes matching his cynical tone of voice.

"Well, Sergeant, what is the purpose of your visit? You can see we are quite late as it is."

The impatience of the landlord surprised the Sergeant and he decided to state the facts clearly. Standing as erect as he could manage, conscious of his duty and role in the maintenance of law and order, he began.

"Your Lordship, I am here to investigate the murder of your bailiff, Jerome Hennessy, which took place on Christmas ever or thereabouts. It is my duty to do so!"

The look of shock on the landlord's face gave the Sergeant a feeling of satisfaction.

"Murder of Hennessy... I was not aware he was murdered... " he replied, quite appalled at the revelation.

A murmur rippled through the gathering, and whispers of 'Bailiff murdered' brought looks of shock to all who were present. Just then Kitty arrived.

"Father, our guests are ready to leave on the chase, we are quite late as it is!"

Kitty looked at the Sergeant and sighed deeply with exasperation.

"Sergeant Cosgrave, Jerome Hennessy was dismissed from service here by my father because he carried out an unauthorised evictionr. I believe you actually assisted him in evicting a widow and her children into the snow, without my father's authority or permission. Is this not correct?"

She spoke in a loud clear voice. The gathering closed in to listen.

"Why, your Ladyship, I... "

Kitty did not allow him to finish.

"Is it not the case, Sergeant, that you assisted in this shocking brutality?"

Sergeant Cosgrave had lost his voice. He could not answer.

"Mr Hennessy left this estate heavily intoxicated, as can be bourn out by our staff who observed his departure. His horse apparently threw him some miles from here, where he subsequently fell and hit his head and lay in a dike of water. So you see, Sergeant, Jerome Hennessy died from drowning, as can be verified by Father Doyle who attended the brief wake. In fact, Father Doyle is on his way here now."

Looking at her father, who now seemed more than surprised as the tale unfolded, she added.

"And father, I was aware of all these happenings, and did not wish to upset you or mother for Christmas. However, if there had been foul play in question, you would have been told instantly."

A great murmur of approval went through the crowd. A horseman approached. It was Father Doyle. Dismounting, he looked first at the landlord, then at the Sergeant. He realised he had come upon a situation needing skilful handling.

"Good morning, Lord Foldsworth."

"Good morning Father, and I regret your morning has been disturbed," Lord Foldsworth began. "We are discussing the death of Jerome Hennessy, Father, and respectfully wish to hear your account of the matter. I believe you are of the opinion it was due to drowning, rather than violence."

"Yes, Lord Foldsworth, that is correct," he replied in clear voiced authority, "Mr Hennessy did have a gash to his forehead. The bloodstained stone was a very large boulder, wedged in the ditch. So it was quite impossible, due to its size and fixture, to even move it, let alone pick it up. The snow also held a lot of his blood." Then, turning to the Sergeant, "Furthermore, Sergeant, this question of Mr Hennessy being murdered is idle and malicious gossip. I suggest now that you return to the source of your information and ask them for proof of their allegation." Looking at Lord Foldsworth he added, "Now, your Lordship, you must excuse me. I have a sick call to make." Finally, looking at Kitty, he smiled, "Lady Catherine, should you need my help again, please ask."

"Thank you Father for taking the time to visit here this morning," she replied.

Addressing the gathering, Father Doyle wished them a pleasant days hunting, and departed.

"Well Sergeant, you have heard what the priest had to say, as have all here! I was not aware until now of your involvement in the eviction on my property. I will have to speak to the County Sheriff about your conduct in this affair. Now, you have detained us for too long as it is."

As Lord Foldsworth mounted, his friend Viscount Harley looked at him with raised eyebrows.

"By Jove, Charles, that daughter has more courage in her blood than any young man I know!"

"Yes, Harley," Lord Foldsworth smiled, "she can be persistent when she wants to be."

He felt very proud of his daughter, and the manner in which she handled the entire matter. He decided that when the hunt was over he would question her further on the details, and how she had so much information on the matter. 'Possibly servants gossip', he thought. Well, either way, only for her intervention with Sergeant Cosgrave, he would have appeared very out of touch on the matter. Would have looked foolish, in fact.

Taking a sip from his hip flask he shouted, "Hunt Ho!" and with that the meet soon took off at a brisk pace, anxious to make up for lost time. The hounds soon picked up the scent of a fox and bayed loudly. The excitement heightened and soon the dark cloud of the morning's events lifted from the mind of Charles Foldsworth. The morning mists cleared from the hilltops and exposed their snow-capped heights bleached white against a blue December sky.

Kitty felt the cold air against her forehead and face. She thought of the arrogance of Sergeant Cosgrave, and was satisfied with the way she had handled him. 'Put him in his place', she thought, using one of Hannah's favourite expressions. The thought of seeing James at the end of the week sent ripples of happiness through her being. She wondered what he was doing right now. Perhaps working with his uncle feeding cattle, or whatever! Should her father hear of their friendship, it would b devastating for them both! Not wishing to pursue the matter further, she dismissed it from her mind. Such anxiety was an unwelcome guest on a splendid day like this... or on any day, for that matter.

"Race you to the next ditch, Catherine!" The voice was her friend, Isobel Hurley, who was a horsewoman renowned for her daring – and not just confined to the hunting field.

"I will wager a sovereign, Isobel," said Kitty, quickly taking up the challenge.

As both women raced sidesaddle, Lord Foldsworth laughed at their youth and gaiety.

* * *

In the village, the pub was packed with men; all anxious to find out more about the police visit earlier that morning. Rumour had spread that Joe had been interviewed, and that Lady Catherine had insisted that Joe attend her, to the great annoyance of sergeant Cosgrave.

"Great girl that, not like the rest of the gentry... up in the sky in themselves... nature you see... it can't be bet... breedin' or no breedin'... " Mag mumbled to herself as she drank her ale. Her daily tonic, as she called it.

"What's that yer sayin', Mag?" asked Bartley Finnegan, who was so relieved he had not been the subject of the police visit.

"Oh Bartley, I was simply crooning to meself here as usual. That young Foldsworth is a good girl, her heart is with the poor people. Shure look at the way she fixed things up for May Ryan."

"Well, Mag, you could be right there, but wouldn't anyone do it for her?" he replied, with a hint of sarcasm.

Mag did not like the way Bartley's tone cast a shadow on her bright thoughts, and snapped back at him.

"Be quiet Bartley, there's too much gloom in yer head and too little good to say."

Pouring her ale into her glass Mag looked intently into his eyes.

"Who knows, Bartley Finnegan, you may need her good help yet! T'was the unlucky bit of holly... eh Bartley?"

Walking away from her with plummeting spirits, he wished he had said nothing to the old woman, the old witch! Feeling dejected, he wondered if she had put a spell on him, and a shiver ran down his spine at the thought of it. Mag laughed to herself in the corner as she took out her clay pipe, and thought how Bartley Finnegan would find it hard to admit the beauty of a summer's day! She thought of the summer, and silently hoped she would live to see another. She would collect her herbs and dry them, the way her mother had taught her. Cures for everything, and the people respected her for her craft. She helped them when they were wounded, and bruised. She gave them potions for fevers, and sweet smelling ointments for skin ailments. Some even tried to coax her to help them with their love affairs! But she would firmly tell them NO! Her skills were with their illnesses, not with their fortunes. So people trusted her.

"Not asleep Mag, I hope!" The strong voice brought her back to reality.

"Oh Joe, 'tis yourself. How are Nell and the little ones?"

"Great Mag, thanks. No complaints, and they enjoyed Christmas too," he answered. "I hope Mag that you'll have plenty of cough recipe ready for them to use when the cold comes upon them?" He sat down beside her.

Mag delighted in her gifts, and in being reminded of them. She chuckled happily between gushes of blue tobacco smoke, which seemed to hide her toothless gums.

"Be assured, Joe, I will look after them to the best, if God spares me through the winter."

With that, Bartley came to their table in the corner with Joe's usual stout, and another bottle of ale for Mag.

"Now Mag, let's raise our glasses to your good health and a Happy New Year to us all."

Looking at her friend, she smiled.

"And many more good years of health and happiness to you and yours."

Having left down her pipe, Mag swallowed deeply from her glass as if to affirm the wishes just expressed. They talked of old times, Joe's mother being a long-standing friend of Mags for more years than she could remember. Leaving Mag, now contented, he approached the bar counter. Bartley eyed him with great interest as he washed the drinking glasses, then said, with a gleam of mischief in his eye.

"Well now, Joe. I was just thinking, you are a man who must have gotten a fair fright this mornin'."

"And why would you say that Bartley?"

The other customers were listening intently, while Mag had begun to snore in the corner.

"No Bartley, all they did was ask me how did Hennessy die, which any man here tonight could have told them."

A murmur of agreement rippled through the packed bar, but making the most of his audience, Bartley continued.

"But Joe, 'twas you they went to... thought it was odd meself, mind you. As if you were the person to know most about it."

Joe was aware that Bartley was trying to put a different slant on Hennessey's death, and very little held him back from grabbing the little wizened barman by the throat. He took a long drink from his glass, and decided to give Bartley something a little more serious to think about for the evening. Leaning closer to him over the counter, he said in a lower tone , yet all around could still hear.

"Well, Bartley, seeing as you are so keen to hear the details, there was another question they did ask me."

"And what was that, Joe?" the barman asked, his curiosity mounting.

"Indeed, 'twas an odd question really, I thought. Then again, maybe you'd understand it better. 'Twas to know if a Bartley Finnegan worked in a bar around here?"

Bartley paled. The pitch of his voice rose.

"Me... asked about me... what did they want to know that for... or how do they know my name...?"

"Well, that's what I was wonderin' too. Like I said, you might have the answer to that!"

Joe lifted his glass and returned to his seat.

Mag had heard the end of the conversation. The rest of the customers resumed talking, but in lower tones. The only thought on Bartley's mind now was the stolen holly, and his impending visit to Lord Foldsworth at Oak Hall in the forthcoming days. The nightmare took fresh root in his mind. Mag chuckled and tipped Joes foot beneath the table.

"That will fuel that fellows fire for the night, the mischievous little stirring stick. I hope to God his Lordship will make him dance about the place."

Joe laughed at her innocent attitude, and concept of vengeance. The sparks from the fire spurted out at their feet, and the flames threw light on the faces around the bar. It was an evening of contentment for most there, with Christmas now over, and the New Year approaching.

"Do you know Joe, this coming year weighs heavily upon me. Why, I don't know. A bad omen I say, police here on a Holy Day, Hennessey's death, and the eviction. No, it's not good at all Joe... not good!" Mag sounded dismal, which was most unlike her.

"Well Mag, I will have to agree with you there," he replied.

"There is something else, Joe, I want to say to you," Mag looked him in the eye. "I only live across the fields from you, and all that hammering you spend your time at, I often ask myself, "What is it that Joe is making so late into the night?'"

Her observation jolted Joe more than the visit of the police earlier that day.

"A man has to work hard to rear a family, Mag, in the days we find ourselves in," he said, realising that the old woman suspected him to be making pikes. The dead of night being the safest time to do so.

"I held you as an infant, Joe Gilltrap, and gave you medicine for your coughs and colds before you could walk or talk. I am also your Godmother, so I have your best interests at heart. Your workings late into the night are safe with me, but there are others who would have different ideas. That barman over there, for one! Be careful, Joe. You must think of Nell and the children?"

Mag sipped from her glass, and Joe knew that she had said more than she had intended. He leaned his head towards her, and said in a whisper.

"Mag, we have to get ready to change things... sometime. I know my secret is safe with you, and you are right, 'tis pikes I am making!"

As the fire began to subside in the great hearth, its warm glow was a mass of pulsating embers. Mag dozed off to sleep again. Lighting his pipe, Joe sat back contentedly beside the old woman. Looking at her fragile frame, he wondered who else might have heard the hammering from the forge so late into the night, and if so, did they question it? He decided to put the days disturbing events from his mind. He looked up, and saw James coming in through the door, his cloak covered with a dusting of fine snow. James was in jovial and bouncing form.

"Why Joe, you look very happy and snug sitting there!" he said, as he proceeded to order drinks for them both.

"Sometimes, James, looks can be very deceiving," Joe replied, his agitation showing.

James chose to ignore Joe's gloomy response.

"Christmas went really well, you know. My uncle was delighted with the company. It did him good."

James sat close to the fire and took off his cloak. Shaking the snow from it, he hung it close to the fire to dry. Bartley brought their drinks over, with a scowl on his face. He then hurried back behind the bar as if seeking refuge.

"What's the matter with that fellow this night?" James asked curiously.

"Sit back and I will tell you all, James, and it's my regret if it makes you uneasy in yourself," said Joe quietly.

James sat back in the chair by the fire, making himself comfortable, ready now to listen to his friend. Joe told him of the day's events – the visit by the police, Lady Catherine's timely arrival – concluding with Mag's remarks and her advice minutes earlier.

Their tight conversation did not go unnoticed by Bartley, who suspected that it had to do with the police visit. Mag watched his careful observation with her left eye, which was barely open. Her eighty years of wisdom told her that Bartley Finnegan had all the makings of an informer. Resolving to tell Joe to be careful of the fellow, she nodded back to sleep, dreaming of picking herbs in the June summer sunshine; she could almost hear the call of the cuckoo in the valley.

Also observing Bartley's keen interest in their conversation, James felt uneasy. He told Joe that he was going to sit at the counter, and that they would discuss events properly on the morrow.

Mag slept on, and Joe finally nudged her, asking her if she intended going home at all that night!

"Indeed, 'tis well time an old woman was beneath her blankets," she replied merrily.

"Well, Mag, may I have the pleasure of seeing you home?" Joe asked.

They both laughed warmly, and bidding goodnight to all, left the smoky comfort of the pub. Outside the thin frosty air, and the lonely sound of a dog barking some fields away greeted them.

"Mag, you will come home for a mug of tea with me, and Nell will be delighted to see you," Joe insisted, not about to take 'no' for an answer.

Mag was pleased with the kind offer and as she held onto the strong arm of the blacksmith, her Godson, she almost glided over the frozen snow. She was happy to be alive, and to have such a good friend and neighbour.

"Life has been good to me, Joe. I've had me ups and downs you know, but as they say, 'too much sun causes drought'!"

Chapter five

The drawing room seemed quite crowded to Lady Foldsworth. Many had decided to stay for the night to celebrate, and there was tremendous merriment and revelry. Kitty loved such occasions. They brought such life to the house. All the guest rooms were full, and downstairs in the kitchen the staff worked efficiently under the direction of Hannah, and the supervision of Williams.

Dishes of fowl, beef and pork were being roasted for dinner. Fresh salmon cooked gently in the great fish pans, and bottles of chilled champagne, beady droplets on their sides, lay in the cold room ready to be consumed. Lady Foldsworth glided into the kitchen very excited and happy.

"Oh Hannah, the different smells are just wonderful. Is everything all right?" she asked her much-loved cook.

"Why, of course, your Ladyship," she replied, as she wiped her forehead with a white handkerchief, one of the presents her mistress had given her.

"We will commence dinner in twenty minutes Hannah, if that suits you?"

"Certainly, your Ladyship. Everything is laid out except the salmon. You know how I like to serve it directly from the pans. Otherwise it doesn't flake out to the fork as it should," Hannah explained proudly.

"Oh Hannah, you are such a treasure! I simply don't know what I would do without you," her mistress exclaimed as she left the kitchen to return to her guests.

Hannah, with renewed vigour, ordered the salmon to be lifted, and apportioned on plates for the first course. Williams returned to announce that the guests were seated, and so the silver cauldrons were filled with clear soup to follow, and the food proceeded from the kitchen in generous, sumptuous quantities.

Kitty, seated near her father, thought he looked tired and worn.

"How are you this evening, father?" she enquired.

"Why do you ask, my dear. I feel wonderfully well and happy, and ravenous I may add. Isn't this salmon simply delicious Kitty?" then, as he sipped his white wine, a thought occurred to him. "And you Kitty, how are you feeling after the hunt?"

"Tired, father, I must admit, but pleasantly so."

"Tell me, my dear, you who seem so in touch with the events of the past week. Who were the men who initially discovered that fellow Hennessy dead?"

The question took Kitty by surprise. She had assumed the matter well closed at this point.

"Eh, as far as I am aware, father, it was Mr Gilltrap and some friend, I think. Why do you ask?"

"Simply curious, my dear. I would like to meet them. Seems only fitting, don't you think? After all, it was upon my instructions that he left that fateful night. Hmmm, that salmon was simply superb."

"Yes," said Kitty, glad to change the subject, "Hannah's cooking is decidedly wonderful."

"Kitty," Lord Foldsworth resumed, "you still have not answered my question."

"What question was that father? Oh yes, I am sorry... the men who discovered the body... yes, it seems like a good idea to meet them. At least you could question them and learn of the incident at first hand." Her heart was pounding at the thought of James being in the same house as her, meeting her father.

"Kitty, do you not enjoy the soup?" her mother asked, noticing that she had not yet lifted her spoon.

"Just allowing it to cool, mother. The flavour is lost if taken too hot!" Trying to relax she asked her mother challengingly, "Mother, when do you intend hunting again? We do miss you."

Lady Edwina laughed loudly.

"I think my days on the field are well and truly over, darling. I don't seem to have as much energy as I used."

"Nonsense, Edwina. Too modest of you," interrupted Viscount Harley, "why, there is not one here this very evening who can jump the high wall as cleanly as you. Not one, I say."

The attention of the table now focussed on Lady Edwina. Having a full and captive audience, Viscount Harley jumped up and raised his glass.

"Why, let's toast... to Edwina, goddess of the hunting field!"

The entire table rose.

"To Edwina!"

"Oh Timothy, you are too kind." Wiping a tear from her eye, Edwina stood from her chair. "I promise then to take the field before the end of March." There followed loud applause.

As dinner came to a close, Lord Foldsworth stood to make his customary speech, and all listened attentively.

"My dear friends. My wife, daughter and I are very happy to have you as our guests this evening. It has been an excellent day; thoroughly enjoyable. We are delighted to round it off with such an excellent dinner, for which I must not forget to compliment the cook.

The times we are presently living in are indeed challenging times, as you are well aware. The country seems restless, though it would appear we in this part of Ireland are very fortunate. Those who carry responsibility for the larger estates and tennantry appear capable of handling them with firmness and caution. As we prepare to enter the year 1797, I would hope that these principals would continue to be the corner stones on which our society firmly rests. We must also be vigilant and fair-minded. We must continue in the tradition of our ancient family values. I would like to take this opportunity of wishing you and your families' health and prosperity in the coming year. The ballroom is now open for your continuing enjoyment! Thank you all for coming, and please enjoy yourselves thoroughly." Resuming his seat to loud applause, he smiled at the company happily.

Viscount Harley stood up. Taking a large pinch of snuff, most of which alighted on his cravat, he responded to his host on behalf of the guests.

"My honourable friend, Lady Edwina and Catherine. Coming to your home for many years now has always been one of the highlights of the Christmas season, and I know I speak for all here present when I say this. Perhaps the main reason I feel this way is the ever-wonderful welcome – the great hospitality we each receive on coming here. We wish you, in return, good health, peace and prosperity, and we most certainly do look forward to dancing the night away!"

With that, the Viscount resumed his seat and once again resorted to his snuffbox. Everyone clapped with enthusiasm. Slowly the guests began to move towards the ballroom.

Lord Foldsworth made his way to the kitchen to convey his customary thanks to the staff. It was the only time in the year when he would do so. The staff stood in line, and curtseyed as he entered. He smiled and greeted them in turn. Standing before them with clasped hands, he began.

"Hannah, Williams, and each and every one of you. I would like to thank you all for such an excellent and sumptuous dinner, and indeed for such service all the year round. I may add, Dublin Castle cannot boast of such an excellent staff, as we are so fortunate to have here. Indeed, their cooks would have to learn a great deal before they could even begin to compete with Hannah. I wish you to have a very happy evening, and Williams, please see to it that everyone is catered for from the cellar, oh, and lest I forget, your gifts are in my study. Williams, perhaps you would be kind enough to collect them and distribute them on my behalf. Again, our renewed thanks and appreciation."

The servants clapped and bowed courteously as their master left to join his guests in the ballroom.

Hannah was elated and kept reminding everyone how she had left the cooks at the Castle in the 'halfpenny' place. Each took their place about the great kitchen table in a happy and jovial mood. Kitchen rank did not matter on this one night of the year.

* * *

In her tiny cottage on the edge of the wood, Mag pulled the blankets over her tired body and soon drifted into a deep sleep. Bartley Finnegan drank black rum in the pub, and thanked God for closing time. James journeyed back to his uncle's house, his thoughts on all Joe had told him, with the chill night air on his face.

As James lifted the latch on his uncle's cottage door, the warm smell of turf smoke greeted him, and he was glad to be home. He was tired, and looked forward to a good nights sleep.

At Oak Hall, as Lord Foldsworth retired to his room. He was glad the day was ended. Much as he had enjoyed it, the memory of the visit of Sergeant Cosgrave still irked him. It had been the only unpleasant aspect to an otherwise perfect Saint Stephen's day. He decided that he would summon Gilltrap and the other man the next day. His uneasiness lifted with this decision, and soon he slept soundly.

* * *

After breakfast the next morning, he summoned Williams.

"Yes, my Lord?" Williams asked on entering the study.

"Williams, would you please send a servant to the village to summon Gilltrap the blacksmith and his companion, whoever he is, who discovered the bailiffs body. Ask them to come here this afternoon."

"Certainly, your Lordship."

When the messenger arrived at the forge, Joe and James were discussing the events of the previous day, which included the attitude and questions of the Sergeant to Joe and the timely arrival of Kitty. Recognising the employee of Oak Hall, they assumed it was in connection with the shoeing of a horse. Upon hearing the request to attend Lord Foldsworth for questioning, their fears mounted afresh.

"Whatever you do, James, don't let Nell get wind of this or she will get very upset. Besides, there's little point in meeting the devil halfway. It can only be about Hennessy and us finding him."

The very thought of being interviewed by Kitty's father repulsed James. Loving Kitty was one thing, but meeting her father was an entirely different issue. He could not accept what he represented, and never would. The French had revolted in 1789, and ended their oppression. Part of him was revolted by the bloodshed. Then he thought of the fear and deadness of spirit in Ireland, and how the vast majority accepted it all. So deep was it rooted in them, they could not envisage being free. He also realised that if Lord Foldsworth ever learned of his love for Kitty the consequences were unthinkable.

"Are you in dreamland, me boy, or in love?" Joe asked, irritably.

"Neither, Joe. Just thinking of the meeting at the big house and that all we can say is how we found Hennessy dead, and what happened after that."

"Hmm, if that's all he wants to know..." said Joe, filling his pipe.

"What does that mean? Shure what else could he want to know?" James asked uneasily.

"Well, to begin with, you are new in the area. You better have your answers ready, and good ones at that!" he looked sharply at James.

"You needn't worry, Joe. 'Tis a simple and well known fact in these parts about my uncle's health. Besides the only other person that suspects anything is Mag, from what you told me of last night. Is that not so?"

"Aye, that's the truth as it is. Now, there's little point in getting ourselves all worked up about it. After dinner we will hear it all, and that's that!" said Joe, adding, "and before I finish on the matter, remember that his Lordship is a very shrewd man, and if he sees us all jitters he will begin to think we had a hand in Hennessey's death. Whatever about being found guilty for making' bayonets, wouldn't it be a cruel thing to hang for our supposedly killing Hennessy? Imagine it!"

Joe roared with laughter, his big frame shaking. James felt the relief of the tension between them breaking. Just then Nell came across the yard, scattering oats from her apron to the fowl that crowded about her feet. Looking at both men, she shouted over to them.

"Would you two men ever wash and come in for your dinner as soon as you're finished talking."

As she walked back across the yard, she stopped and turned around.

"Joe, wasn't that young Matt I saw here some time ago, the servant from the big house?"

"Begor Nell your eyes are as sharp as that bantam cocks. It was to be sure. Haven't myself and James to go up and look at the carriage wheel that gave trouble the last time. We'll stroll up there after the dinner. Is it ready you said Nell?"

"Joe Gilltrap, are you deaf into the bargain, or did you hear me at all? Can you not smell that goose roastin?" and she skipped back to the house laughing.

"God, isn't she great too James. Always in good form, God bless her!"

They both walked in after Nell.

At the inn across the way, Bartley Finnegan stood back from his attic window where he had been watching them, his curiosity well aroused.

"I don't care what anyone says but there's something between those two there," he declared aloud, as he sat down on his old bed.

De Lacey is no length in this village, he thought, and he's forever in that forge. He was sure it wasn't for the work he got done there either. He recalled the events of the last night in the pub, with the two of them and old Mag sitting in the corner muttering between them. He decided to go and visit Mag that very day and see if he could learn anything. The rash on his feet provided him with the very excuse he needed.

Going downstairs, he ate his dinner of boiled mutton and vegetables, and drinking some ale went back to his room and slept for an hour. When he awoke, his curiosity was as ripe as ever.

* * *

Joe harnessed the pony and trap, and both men began their short journey to Oak Hall. The oak lined avenue, the tree branches naked against the weak afternoon sun, followed the gently curving route up to the house, which stood out as if in defiance to any intruder.

"A very fine looking place, Joe, and to think I was reared on a piece of ground the size of their croquet lawn! God, there's no understanding it at all, is there?"

Choosing to ignore this remark, Joe continued to whistle idly, the tune lacking any air whatsoever. He gently encouraged the sturdy mountain pony to the right-hand approach that led to the servant's entrance, and the rear door of the stately mansion. Tethering the horse to a holding ring, Joe looked steadily at James.

"Hold your tongue in here now young man. There's a great deal at stake. Let those thoughts of your remain unsaid."

The icy tone of the voice said it all! Looking towards the stable, James saw Kitty standing there, wind eyed in amazement. His heart thudded deep in his chest. She approached with a small nosebag for the pony, which she had conveniently found.

"Well, what a surprise, Misters Gilltrap and de Lacey. I have some oats here for your pony."

She was aware that she must retain her formality. The eye of scrutiny with which the blacksmith was viewing her made her very uneasy indeed.

"Thank you, Lady Catherine. Good of you to think of Sparky here. I'm sure he will be glad of the oats. If you'll excuse us now, my lady. Your father is expecting us." Joe was aware of the tension.

"By all means, go ahead. Hannah will direct you to father. I know he can be an impatient man." Kitty found herself struggling to find words.

James saw how pale she was, and as Joe turned his back and strode towards the door, he looked at Kitty and gave her a quick wink. She returned a very feint smile. James felt his heart lurch at the awkwardness of the situation. Following Joe into the kitchen, the smell of food assailed his senses.

"Well Joe, if it isn't yourself, and who is this handsome young man beside you?" asked Hannah, as she wiped dough from her hands.

"This is James, Hannah, and we are here on the command of his Lordship," replied Joe in a rather curt manner, not unnoticed by the cook.

"Hmm, for goodness sake, anyone would think you had committed a crime or something with that sour face you have on you Joe Gilltrap. Well, as you please... "

Calling Williams, she returned. She looked at James.

"Well, young man, it's good to see that you are not as cranky as our blacksmith is today. I'll have something nice for you both when you come back down."

"This way please," a voice said, and Williams stood there.

'Stiff as a coffin lid', thought James to himself.

As they made their way up the stone steps that led from the kitchen to the living quarters, James' attention was taken with all the colours about him: the velvet curtains, the crimson and light blue carpets. They were truly beautiful, James thought, and imagined Kitty as she made her way about this beautiful big house that was her home.

They found themselves standing with the butler before a large well-polished oaken door. Knocking with the usual three knocks, Williams entered and disappeared inside. Both men looked at each other. Joe winked, and James looked at the blacksmith's big hand as it gripped his cap firmly. Suddenly the large door seemed to spring open, and a voice behind it, Williams, announced them in a firm clear fashion.

"Joe Gilltrap and James de Lacey your Lordship."

Both men walked into the room. To their left sat a man behind a writing desk, looking at them with an unreadable expression.

"That will be all for now, Williams. I shall ring when I need you."

Williams bowed, and left the room, the click of the well-oiled handle falling precisely into place.

"Thank you both for coming here today. I hope our meeting can be as short as possible," the landlord began. His voice was well spoken and rang with centuries of authority. He looked directly at Joe.

"Joe Gilltrap, you I know. Your companion, I do not recognise... " His eyes, swift as a sparrowhawk's, rested on James.

The young man before him was sturdy, brown haired, green eyed. He seemed quite able-bodied. Certainly not ones average tenant, he calculated. He was clean-shaven, respectably dressed, and there was something oddly familiar about him.

"Your lordship, James de Lacey, your servant, Sir," James volunteered, and bowed slightly as he had seen Williams do.

Joe was quite amazed at this display of servitude. Lord Foldsworth became convinced he was not the usual sort. Not by any manner or means.

"Quite an unusual name for these parts. You are not on my tenant register. I would surely recall the name."

Unsure if this was a question or a statement, James decided to supply the information regardless.

"That is correct, your Lordship. My uncle is your tenant. He has been very unwell for some time now, so I have come to be of whatever help I can be to him. His rent was in arrears this past year, and now we have it updated." James felt a little more relaxed, and began to think Lord Foldsworth was perhaps a reasonable man. He tried to keep the fact of him being Kitty's father from his mind.

"So Gilltrap," Lord Foldsworth was obviously satisfied with James' credentials, "you both found my former bailiff dead, I am told. Would you like to tell me how that came about?"

The question posed, he sat back in his large comfortable red leather chair, and idly toyed with a wax tape used to seal his letters. James also noticed the small pistol on the desk, within easy reach of its regal owner. Joe proceeded to explain how they had noticed the rider less horse and retraced its trail, and so the story unfolded. Lord Foldsworth believed the blacksmith, who did not falter and whose delivery was slow and precise.

"I see," he replied. Then he looked directly at James. "Haven't I seen you somewhere before, young man?"

James was taken aback by the sudden change of subject, and the direct manner of the question.

"I do remember your passing by in the carriage one day. I was by the roadside, your Lordship."

The landlord remembered instantly. He also remembered the way his daughter had looked at the young man.

"Correct, indeed, yes, that was it… for a moment I thought my daughter knew you."

"Yes, your Lordship. I was at the forge one day and saw her there."

James' heart resumed its heavy pounding. Looking at Joe, Lord Foldsworth asked with a raised eyebrow.

"And was my daughter at the forge Gilltrap?"

"Yes, your Lordship, on Saint Stephen's morning to have the horses shoes checked out before the hunt." Joe felt the tension mounting.

"And you, what were you doing at the forge that morning, de Lacey?" the landlord asked.

"I was having a scythe fixed, your Lordship," James lied.

"Odd, is it not, having a scythe fixed in December. What did you require a scythe for that day?"

"It is very simple. My uncle's tools had all become very rusted and neglected. As and when I can afford to, I bring them to the forge for repair, your Lordship."

"How very diligent and industrious of you," replied Lord Foldsworth, impressed. "Your uncle is a very fortunate man to have such a conscientious nephew. Would the position of bailiff interest you?"

"Thank you for the offer, your Lordship, but my uncles small holding, like his tools, is not as trim as it used to be. It too needs improving or it will eventually become overgrown. I think it best to improve it and update it or otherwise... " James stopped in time before he made reference to the recent eviction, and his tact didn't go unnoticed by the landlord.

"Or otherwise what? Please continue."

"Or otherwise, your Lordship, it will become so out of hand that what little money is left will all have to be spent on paying someone to help me," James sighed inwardly, realising he had only barely redeemed himself.

"Very wise indeed. If all my tenants were so diligent, would I not be the fortunate landlord!"

He registered the quick mind and quicker tongue of the young man before him, and made a mental note to keep an eye on him. Then, opening a drawer with a jerk, he took out a box. Taking a half-sovereign for it, he tossed it in the air to Joe.

"I believe I am now no longer in your debt, Gilltrap. The axle on the carriage was excellent work, and I trust the work for my daughters is also covered in that." Standing up, he pulled the bell rope. "These are strange times we are living in, and now that I am satisfied as to the circumstances of my former bailiff's death, you may go."

Lord Foldsworth gave a cold half smile. Williams opened the great oaken door with his usual prime timing, which begged the question in his employers mind as to how one of his age ascended the stairs so quickly?

"Oh, before you go, Gilltrap. While you are not my employee or my messenger, will you tell that Finnegan fellow in the village to be here this evening... before nightfall."

In the kitchen, Hannah's face looked strained with the tension of curiosity.

"Hannah, there's no trouble, none at all, just a fair enquiry about how we found Hennessy, that's all." Joe said calmly, then, looking at James, "Time we were on our way."

Hannah tried in vain to have them stay for some tea, calling Joe back to the kitchen while James walked briskly to the stables. He noticed Kitty in the shadows of an archway.

"James... oh James. Is everything all right? I never knew that father was summoning you both!"

"Shhh, shhh... " he replied, and placed his hand across her mouth. "Now, now. There's no need to worry... your father was just asking about Hennessey's death... and if we are seen talking like this, there will be another interview! Will I see you at the oak wood then?"

"Of course, but we will have to be careful. So many things went through my mind when you were with father."

James heard Joe's firm footsteps approaching. Looking at Kitty, he put a finger to his lips. He walked over to untie the pony, which was eating the last of the oats from the nosebag. Kitty remained in the shadows until Joe had walked past. He held a bag in his hand. In it was a present of roast chicken from Hannah for Nell.

"Ready, Joe?" James asked, noticing the more relaxed face of his companion.

"Ready as I'll ever be, James."

As both men departed down the avenue, Kitty went back into the house. Her heart lurched as she began to realise the extent of her feelings for James. How she would willingly surrender her home, class and wealth just to be sitting with him in that pony and trap. Hannah noticed the troubled expression on her face as she entered the kitchen.

"My, my... you'd think the end of the world had come, Miss Kitty. Why so sad a face?"

Kitty attempted to smile, but knew that Hannah wasn't one to be fooled.

"Oh Hannah, I get so tired and bored here at times. Winter is so dismal... so dead."

"Hmmm. Winter indeed. Do you think I am so easily fooled? Now take that hot cup of tea and those mince pies and follow me to the 'room', Kitty," she commanded.

The 'room' was Hannah's private quarters where she would retreat in order to escape from the tension and heat of the kitchen. Patting a chair with her hand, she indicated to Kitty to sit down. She sat opposite her in her old armchair, having closed the door firmly.

"Now, child. I have known you from the first day you came into the world, and I also know when you are troubled about something. Tell Hannah, and we will both sort it all out."

The soothing tones of Hannah's voice brought back layer after layer of memories to Kitty. Hannah would take her here when she had been in trouble upstairs, or in fights with her visiting cousins or friends. For all the kindness and love her mother had given her, she had never been able to listen to her as Hannah did. She looked at Hannah, so good, so faithful, always there, expecting so little from life. Happy to please her parents with her good housekeeping...

"Hannah, I cannot possibly tell you this matter. There are times when I am too afraid to think of it myself," Kitty began, as tears welled up in her eyes.

Now, now, dear, dear," Hannah took her hands, "why be afraid to tell Hannah, love?"

Looking into the deep blue eyes of Hannah, her friend, Kitty knew she could trust her with everything. Yet she wondered how she would react when she knew her secret about James... yet, it would be good to talk to someone.

"Hannah, I think that I am in love."

Hannah's eyes lit up, and a big smile beamed over her face.

"Oh child, love, isn't that great news. And what in heaven's name is there then to be so upset about? Let me guess... it's some dark, tall Viscount you met at the Ball in Dublin Castle. Oh goodness, won't your mother be so thrilled! Why, only last week she remarked to me how all the young officers and lords were queuing up to dance with you." Hannah was jubilant.

"No Hannah," Kitty interrupted, deciding to be more explicit before Hannah's expectations instilled further fear into her. "He is tall and dark and handsome, without doubt Hannah, but he is neither Lord nor Viscount. He may not, in fact, even have a house to call his own, nor even five acres of land, for that matter."

"Now child, love, try to be calm. Start all over again, there's a dear," it was Hannah's turn to interrupt. "You are telling me that your are in love with someone who is neither titled, not even of your own class. He is poor like us and has nothing, so to speak?" Her voice cracked as though to ask, 'please tell me this isn't true'.

Kitty looked out the window. Slowly she began to tell Hannah of how she had met James, all quite innocent and unplanned, their picnic at the Fairy Fort, their many trips into the hills. Hannah was dumbfounded. This was unthinkable! What were her parents going to say? 'Mother of God...' she thought, 'All this going on, under their noses... and not a hint of it from anyone anywhere!'

"Who else knows about this Kitty," she asked as calmly as she could.

"No-one except you, Hannah," she replied.

"And how do you think, Miss Kitty, this secret of yours is going to remain a secret? If your father finds out you will be sent away... a marriage arranged for you within a month... and this young man exiled to some far off land. Oh child, love, get some sense! Forget him! For all our sakes, forget him! Not to mention your mother. Oh, the Lord look down on us all... What has taken your good sense child? I warned you often enough to keep away from that Fairy Fort... no good ever came out of them, so it didn't, and here's more of it!" Hannah wailed miserably, in total turmoil.

"Hannah, please stop that fairy fort nonsense, and stop being so upset," pleaded Kitty, also crying.

"Well, you have told me everything now, even his name, but who is he. I'm afraid even to ask, in case it's a footmen."

Kitty felt sorry now that she had told her, and in doing so placed a burden on the old cook's shoulders.

"He has just been here Hannah... " she began.

"Oh sweet Jesus, child... Joe Gilltrap... a married man... "

Kitty laughed softly.

"No Hannah, It's not Joe Gilltrap, don't be so silly... it's the man with him, James de Lacey... Oh Hannah, even to be able to say his name to someone is a relief to me," and she sat back in her chair, sighing with the relief that all had now been told.

"That fellow here with Joe?" Hannah began, as she recalled him to mind, "Yes. He is all you say he is, and also not a shirt on his back. If your father had known what he was up to, courting' you, well I'll tell you, he would have been carried out of here a corpse. Shot him dead, he would have."

Kitty protested by pouring out her feelings for James, while Hannah, though listening, was hoping this was just a phase the young girl was going through. She was also aware that it was something she could never, ever, speak of to a living soul. She decided she would never refer to it again, not even to Kitty, lest she should mistake her concern for approval. 'No', she thought. 'This is something I will have to put out of my mind or I'll never have a days peace'.

"Hannah, are you listening to me?" Kitty asked her when she noticed the distant look in her eyes.

"Yes child I am. Now you listen to me! And listen well! You are Lady Catherine Foldsworth, granddaughter to the Duke of Devonfort, and niece of Viscount Lundy, advisor to our present King. You are the sole heiress to this vast estate, and may I add that one day you will be responsible for all the wealth and all that goes with it, including the hundreds of tenants that live on the great estates. Just think of it! Think of it and choose. Choose well... " Hannah paused for breath.

"If you have any common sense you will remain faithful to your family, your class and your inheritance. On the other hand, if you don't, you will be denounced by them, disinherited, and your name the laughing stock throughout the country. At Dublin Castle, on every hunting field in Ireland, and every social gathering. It's not my place to tell you what to do, but remember this... Love can change. It can melt like the dew on the grass, or the mists on the mountains. You are young, and not well up on such things, and this James fellow could well leave you high and dry, when he tires of you! What then? Well? Where does that leave you? Kitty, I will neither aid nor hinder you. You can rest assured your secret is safe with me, but I am pleading with you to think where your real future lies. That's all, child, I'll say to you. Now, up with you and dry those eyes. I have still a dinner to prepare, and a lot to think on!"

Kitty threw her arms around Hannah, and hugged her tightly. Tears welled up in the old woman's eyes, and she remembered how Kitty had always done that as a child, when she was most afraid.

"Alright, Hannah. I will think of all you have said, but there is something about all this that gives me a peace in my soul, as foolish as you think me to be."

When Kitty left the security of Hannah's 'room', she decided to go for a short walk before facing dinner. She felt drained and tired, but lighter in some way, having spoken of her feelings.

Hannah sat and stared out of the window. She prayed that the young mistress would come to her senses. If she failed to do so, the consequences were completely unthinkable.

* * *

Arriving back at the village, Joe tethered the pony and trap to the holding ring at the pub. Taking out the half sovereign, he looked at it, and decided to have a drink with James to celebrate the successful conclusion of their meeting with the landlord. They both felt very relieved, and were glad the interview was over.

Bartley stood behind the counter with both hands resting on it. He looked at the two men as they entered. Joe sensed his curiosity, and decided to allow Bartley to question him at will. The barman rubbed his hands together.

"God men, me poor heart dropped when I heard that his Lordship had sent for the two of ye for to be questioned. How did ye's fare out? Not, mind you, that it's me business either ways!"

James looked at the face of the speaker, and thought how it resembled a ferrets.

"Shure don't I know well, Bartley, how worried you would be for us. Wouldn't anyone be?" Joe filled his pipe and ordered two drinks. "The best in the house, Bartley."

"The best today, is it Joe?" and his eyebrows lifted.

"Ye heard right, and while you're at it, get one for yourself," Joe added.

This gesture threw the barman into greater whelms of curiosity and confusion. Winking at Joe, James raised his glass.

"To his Lordship, and all his family. Long may they live and prosper."

"Yes. To his Lordship and family," Joe agreed.

They were both aware of the barman's lack of enthusiasm to the toast, but did not comment.

"And how are you Bartley?" asked Joe. "Glad I'm sure that Christmas is over, with all the rushing around here. But then once a man stops to think about it, here you are making your livin' in a dry warm place with neither chick nor child to worry about!"

Bartley always disliked people commenting about his life, or how he lived it.

"Hum," he replied. "I don't know so much about all that, Joe Gilltrap. You do get tired lookin' at the same auld faces, day in and day out... and havin' to wipe up their slops after them too!" with that poorly disguised insult, he went up the counter to serve other customers.

"Well Joe, you could say you asked for that one," quipped James, and they both laughed.

"Wait 'til we pay him. The half-sovereign will put the sparkle in his eye, and a shift on his tongue."

When Bartley returned, Joe handed him the money. He looked at it, quite amazed.

"Be hell aren't you the well off man Gilltrap. 'Tis not that I'm sayin' you don't work hard enough, but that's a rare sight, isn't it James?"

"Indeed it is, but there are lots more where that one came from," James replied casually, taking a sip of his drink.

Incensed by so little information, Bartley began to lose control.

"Oh the pair of ye would make a man up with news, and I'm not without knowin' your snig remarks, and the makin' of faces behind me back. And as to you, Mr James... whoever you are... don't think you can arrive into this village and rule the roost. I'm wonderin' what you're really here for, me man, and don't think that I'll be the one to believe that your uncle's few little acres is the purpose either!" he wiped his frothing mouth with his hand.

James leaped from his stool and caught Bartley by the shirt with his right hand to deliver a blow with the other. But the strong arm of the blacksmith caught it in time.

"Leave 'em be, James, leave 'em be." Joe was livid that the incident was catching the attention of the whole house.

James stood tall, his anger still apparent.

"I'll tell you this, Bartley Finnegan, if you ever... "

Joe interrupted him before any threat was delivered.

"Give me two more pints, Bartley, and as for you James, sit down and control yourself. Time you got some sense."

The bar was silent as anxious eyes and ears awaited further developments. Bartley slammed down the two drinks before them, spilling a lot of the ale on the counter. Joe looked at him.

"I asked for two pints, not two half-pints. Now fill them up please!"

Joe was known as a quiet man, and not one easily provoked. The drinks were reluctantly refilled. As Joe handed over the money, he leaned over to Bartley.

"Finnegan, as you well know, I don't normally drink in the daytime. So I'm going to tell you why I'm here. I was at Oak Hall with James. I had to look at a carriage wheel, and his Lordship also asked James to be your new bailiff. Now, when we were leaving, he politely asked me to tell you to present yourself up there before nightfall. Here's to your good health!"

A wild hum buzzed rapidly through the premises, and Bartley felt a weakness sweep over him.

"The devil blast you... and your Lordship... and you sittin' there like a trumped up turkey cock," Bartley hissed, with as much venom as he could muster.

Joe jumped up and pounded the counter with his big fist.

"One more word from you, and I'll put you beside Jerome Hennessy this very night. Now if I were you, I'd be gone to Oak Hall, as his Lordship isn't a man to be kept waiting, and your chances are better with him than with me... "

Backing away slowly, Bartley removed his apron. He realised that his life was at a crossroads. He vowed never to set foot behind that counter again. As he trudged up the road leading to Oak Hall, he spat tobacco from his mouth with a promise of revenge.

* * *

Lord Foldsworth looked at the man before him, and found very little about him he could like!

"So you are Bartley Finnegan whom I found stealing my holly and trespassing on my grounds," he began.

"Yes, your Honours worship. 'Twas only a few sprigs, and you'd hardly miss it... " He replied, in the weak and whining voice he had decided to employ as the best approach to his own defence. The desired effect was lost on Lord Foldsworth. In fact, it had the opposite effect.

"Few sprigs or not you were stealing, and I could have you tried at the next court for it if I so desired. But as it is still Christmas tide, I will have clemency.

Instead, you will leave the village and not return. Do you hear me? Have I made myself clear?"

Bartley felt so relieved he could have floated through the door.

"Well?" the landlord asked impatiently, "What are you waiting for? Is there something else?"

"Of course, your Honours worship, that's perfectly clear. I'll take me leave now."

With that he bowed and shuffled to the door, which opened instantly as Williams appeared with the usual precise timing. Lord Foldsworth looked at the ceiling. 'It's the best policy, getting rid of the trouble makers from the area', he thought.

"Thank you Williams. Show this man to the door now please."

"Yes sir," Williams replied, quite surprised at the brevity of the meeting.

On his way back to the village Bartley felt relieved. It was not the emotion he intended sharing in the village He would announce to all that he had been banished from the area. 'A martyr so I am, God help me', and he knew he would have the sympathy of the village to support him. That leaving suited him, especially after the scene with Joe and James, was beside the point.

As freezing fog tumbled down from the hills wrapping the fields and woods in its icy shroud, crows noisily winged their way to the oak woods. Somewhere a robin chirped dismally in a bare hedgerow, and flakes of snow whirled to the ground.

May Ryan noticed the small frame of the barman pass by her home, and she guessed where he had come from. She felt secure and safe in her new house, where her children slept warm and safe. 'Still, fortune smiled on me with the odd turn of events', she thought, as she observed the darkening sky and prayed that Pat was happy in heaven. Looking at her children as they sat around the table for their dinner, she noticed how much better they looked in less than a week. Lighting a candle, she hummed a tune, in a happier frame of mind than she had been for some time. The wind gusted in the chimney and the fire leaped in response. It was a happy home.

Brian Wholohan was just wondering about the fate of his barman, when Bartley swooped through the pub door with a clatter and came straight over to him.

"Well Bartley, how did you ... " Brian began.

"He has banished me from here, from this village, just as he banished Hennessy before me, and I've to be gone by tomorrow evening. All because I robbed a bit of holly and walked on his land," he announced, aware that all eyes were on him.

"Banished ye?" Brian repeated, shocked.

"Oh that's me fate, and ye may get yourselves another barman. I've to take to the roads of Ireland now, a tramp and a beggar, without house nor home nor a crust of bread. Wouldn't a man be better dead, aye... danglin' from the end of a rope?"

Out from the dark corner by the fire came the old voice of Mag, where she sat drinking her punch.

"Musha, Bartley Finnegan. You'll neither dangle, die, starve nor be found in a ditch, and 'tis well you know it me man."

Springing around like a startled fox, Bartley looked at the old woman.

"Who the hell asked you to tell me fortune? Drink up yer punch and keep yer dotin' notions to yourself."

His fury at Mag was obvious. In one sentence she had dispelled the dark picture he had painted of himself and his plight. Brian interrupted his anger.

"Bartley, I'm just thinking. There's a job at the Bull's Nose. I'll ask Marjorie if it's still to be had for you." Then he added appropriately, "I'll miss you for here for sure, after all these years."

Some around the bar expressed sorrow at his ill fortune. Some were glad to see him go. Mag was glad he was leaving the village for good. Another worry less.

Suddenly, the door clattered open again, and in rushed James. All attention fell from Bartley. James looked pale and upset, and was visibly trembling. He went straight to Brian and spoke to him in an urgent whisper that none could hear.

"Brian. The uncle has died, and I'm in a spin trying to do all the necessary. I'll need snuff, tobacco and drink up at the cottage. I'd also appreciate if you waited 'til I'm gone before you said it to the customers."

Offering his condolences discreetly, Brian filled a sack with more than enough goods for a wake. With sincere thanks, James left as suddenly as he had appeared. Brian went over and sat beside Mag.

"James' uncle has just died, God rest him... he was a great man."

The company assembled heard the news.

"Well, Brian," said Mag, "like myself, he has seen a great many summers, and was weary maybe, as folks can sometimes become at a great age!"

"Aye, 'tis too true. The grim reaper will visit us all sometime I'm afraid."

Bartley's plight was completely forgotten. He left the bar, unnoticed by anyone.

Going to his room he looked about it, as if seeing it for the first time. The small window overlooking the street, where he could see the dim light of candles in the small windows opposite. It was all so familiar to him... the chest of drawers where he kept some of his clothes... the hook where he hung up his grey cloak... the two pairs of boots beside the washstand. Stooping down, he pulled up a floorboard and took out a small leather pouch. Wiping off the cobwebs he opened it and spilled the contents onto the bed. He had fourteen shillings. Better than nothing. He lay down on the deep hollowed bed and gazed idly at a spider that couldn't make up its mind whether to stay on the ceiling or descend onto the chest of drawers. 'Well', he thought, 'tomorrow I'll no longer live here'.

While the idea frightened him, he also felt a sense of freedom, and that surprised him. He fell into a short fitful sleep. When he woke up he went down to the kitchen, where he helped himself to a thick slice of meat pie. He brought it into the bar, where he sat alone to eat. Many who were leaving came over to him to say goodbye, and wish him well. Others ignored him, and he pretended not to notice them leaving. When he had finished eating, Brian called him over to the counter.

" Bartley, I'll give you a letter in the morning for Marjorie in the town. She owes me a favour or two. I'll ask her to give you a start, and if you suit the place, I'm sure she'll keep you."

Brian felt sorry for Bartley. He realised that he was a very changeable and temperamental man, and that many people found it hard to like him. He had no real friends of his own and Brian saw his isolation at a time like this.

"If she'll keep me on is it? Well, 'tis like this. If I like it I'll stop, and if I don't 'tis the bigger town of Wexford I'll be goin' to, and that's that!" Bartley declared ungratefully.

Brian threw his eyes heavenward.

"Only tryin' to help you, that's all me man. No need to growl at me like a terrier." Brian didn't wait for his response and went over to put more wood on the fire.

Sparks flew out in profusion and old Mag exclaimed with intoxicated glee,

"Oh, money, money, money. The sparks are the sign of it comin'," and she chuckled merrily.

Bartley looked at her and thought of how she had lived all her life in this village, collecting herbs to cure other people's ills, and how 'twas no wonder she'd gone queer doin' the likes of it, God help her.

As he left the bar to go to bed early, he bid no-one goodnight, and kicked at the large tomcat that came onto his path. The cat shrieked in pain. Mag saw it happen.

"Aye, Bartley Finnegan, you should be ashamed of yourself and ye kicking a poor dumb animal. Wouldn't you think at your stage in life you'd have more decency in ye!"

He looked at her with a cynical grin.

"Like I said to you old woman, drink yer punch and stop yer doting."

"Indeed I will do that Bartley, but isn't it the pity you'll never know the pleasures of old age."

She then stood up, and taking her walking stick in her hand went slowly towards the door, bidding all goodnight.

"Nothing but a bloody auld witch..." Bartley muttered, but Brian interrupted.

"Now Bartley, don't be mindin' poor old Mag. Wouldn't it be the better thing for you to go and have an early night? Tomorrow will be an early start for you. God knows I'll miss you a lot. How am I going to get on here without you?"

On hearing this, Bartley felt sad. 'In all me lifetime no one ever said that to me', he thought, 'even if it was only for working in a public house'. He wiped a tear from his eye with his coat sleeve.

"Yes Brian, 'tis time I was in bed before I go soft in meself," he replied, as he made his way up the stairs for the last time.

Lying in bed he heard the old familiar sounds of the dogs barking, and the ivy branch scraping against the windowpane with the groan of the wind that seemed to be rising.

It snowed afresh during the night as the village slept soundly. The dogs didn't even notice it, so silently and swiftly it came down from the hills. Morning dawned clear and the last of the remaining clouds drifted southwestward. Birds fluttered, helplessly attempting to alight in an effort to find some food. The village pump stood transformed, defiant in its icy dress.

Bartley woke with the brightness pervading his room, and he knew from winters past that it was the brightness of the snow and the strong sunlight reflecting on his otherwise smoke stained ceiling. On looking out he saw that four to five inches of it lay on the ground. He could hear Brian walking about downstairs, and the smell of frying bacon assailed his nostrils. He felt cheery for some reason, despite the fact he had to leave the village today, and forever. Brian called from the kitchen.

"Bartley, are you up yet? The tea is already made."

Placing his belongings in a trunk, he carried it downstairs. A plate of bacon, eggs and his favourite black pigs puddings lay before him. The letter for Marjorie lay propped up beside his tea mug. It reminded him fully of the day that lay before him.

"Now Bartley, get that breakfast into you, and meanwhile I'll put the trunk into the brougham. We'd better get started before another fall of snow comes," Brian said, and he lifted the trunk and laid it across his shoulders.

Outside, he placed it in the back of the brougham, and then yoked the two horses onto it, ready to leave when his passenger was. After a while Bartley emerged in his grey cloak and black hat.

"Eh... here Bartley... a gift for you." Some coins were placed onto his hand.

"God, Brian... 'Tis decent of you," Bartley said as he put the money into the small leather pouch which he kept in his breast pocket.

Brian drove the horses out through the archway of his yard, and they slowly picked their steps through the snow, until they felt more surefooted. Curtains were pulled back slightly in some of the small houses, as the occupants peeped discreetly at the sight of Bartley as he left the village for the last time. 'Banished forever by Lord Foldsworth', was the way some people put it. Many could understand why he banished the bailiff; hand over his fine house to a widow that had been evicted. But exiling the village barman for simply taking a few branches of holly? The overall feeling was that Lord Foldsworth was a man to be respected but not trifled with. He could do anything at the drop of a hat!

The blacksmith watched the departure, with Bartley sitting erect. He felt only relief at his departure. Deciding it best to remain out of view, Bartley did not see Joe's observation of him. Soon the brougham had left the village and all onlookers behind. For most of the journey, both men were silent. The horses, though slipping occasionally, made good progress. They arrived in town earlier than they had expected to.

Brian reined in the horses in the town square.

"Well Bartley, this is goodbye, for now I suppose. I wish you plenty of luck."

Bartley took down his trunk.

"Yes Brian, and luck I'll need," he said, and abruptly walked away.

Brian was yet again mystified at the peculiarity of his former employee. 'Always was a dark side to that fellow, and I'd say the bar will do better trade with him gone too'. As to who would replace him, Brian had no idea.

Journeying back to the village, he decided to call to see James, and make an appearance at the wake of his deceased uncle. Turning the horses into the by-road that led to the house, Mag stood on the road before him.

"Well God be praised Brian, for you to come at this time. I was just wonderin' if me poor bones would take me the rest of the way," she cackled shrilly.

Brian helped her into the brougham. Looking at her he admired her great love of life.

"Do you know, Mag, God himself isn't up at this hour of the mornin', and you trottin' to a wake and you no length in the bed! Do you ever sleep at all?" They both laughed.

Cleaning out her clay pipe, she looked up at him.

"'Tis a good mornin's work you've done Brian, riddin' the place of that fellow, with his black rats eyes... never cared for him at all... " Mag volunteered.

Brian was taken somewhat aback by the unexpected admission of the old woman, whom he respected and liked.

"Well, I'd never have thought of it like that, to tell you the truth. He was a good barman."

"Good... hmmm... I'll be swearin' 'til the day I die that he always over watered my punch, savin' the whiskey for himself... blast the little weasel... good riddance is what I say."

By her tone of voice Brian concluded that the topic was now closed. Bartley Finnegan was history as far as the village was concerned. When they arrived at the house, the wake room was crowded, despite the early hour. The corpse lay in a coffin resting on two chairs in a side room. When Mag entered the room she blessed herself, then sprinkled the corpse with holy water.

"God rest ye," she sighed, "and may ye rest in peace forever."

She couldn't help but think that her own death would be sooner rather than later. She was not afraid to die, for life had been long, full, and good. Brian meanwhile conveyed his sympathies to James, and told him of his early morning mission to town.

"Bartley banished?" he asked, astonished. "Well, to tell you the truth, I can't say I'm sorry, but at the same time it sounds a bit harsh to make a man leave the area all over a bit of holly."

"Well James, perhaps his Lordship knew what he was doing. Perhaps he knew more...?"

"What could there be to know, Brian?" James asked, his eyebrows rose in curiosity.

"Well, I don't now what to say James, but I often think that Bartley knew more than his prayers," Brian replied, looking directly at James. Then he added, scratching his head, "And it leaves me with the big question of trying to find someone to replace him."

The wake progressed. James saw to it that Mag was well catered for. The old woman went and sat by the fire where she talked to the other old women and men. They talked of past times, the present, and the recent events at Oak Hall.

Early the next morning the remains of James' uncle were laid to rest. The women who were invited to keen and lament his passing wailed shrilly. As the house of the deceased was too far from the graveyard, the company went instead to the pub after the burial. Brian fund that he was totally unable to cope with the large crowd, and missed his barman already. Spotting James alone and lost looking in the throng, he shouted for him to come and help him.

"For God's sake James, will you hop over that counter and give me a hand before I lose me patience with the whole lot of em!"

James served with the skill and patience which made a few ask themselves if he had done this work before. As the rush subsided, most people now sitting in small groups happily talking, Brian looked at James. He wiped his brow with the side of his apron.

"Do you know something James, I could do with you here. You're one of the best I've seen. Would you ever think about taking over from Bartley? You could even try it out for a couple of weeks. See if you like it or not?"

"Well Brian," James laughed, "I will think about it, I promise. Give me a few days 'til I see what's what, with the uncle now dead. There are things to be sorted out."

Brian was delighted with the spark of interest expressed.

"And James, the wages are fair, the food is good, and there's the room upstairs if ever you need to use it."

"As I said Brian, I will sort things out first. 'Tis good of you to offer it to me."

James thought the offer a good one. The small holding only offered a scant and frugal living once the rent due to the landlord was paid. His brother could perhaps do with it... James groaned inwardly: another problem facing him. Nobody had commented on his brother's presence at the wake. It was only natural for ones family to be present at such times. To date he had not frequented the village, and spent most of his time trapping rabbits. Resolving to sort out the matter with his brother in the days ahead, he joined the rest of the company.

After a time, James felt tired and decided to go for a short walk. He gulped in the fresh air, and Kitty came floating into his mind. This only added to his confusion. He thought about the job offer. It would be convenient to be near the forge and Joe, for the movement of pikes. The job would also enable him to learn more of what was happening in the area.

He decided to mention it to Joe and get his opinion. The excuse for his living in the area had been his uncle. With him now dead, there was no legitimate reason for staying. The job would provide one. Feeling less muddled, he returned to the noise and heat of the small pub. He went directly over to Joe and sat beside him and told him of Brian's proposition.

"Eh, well to tell you the truth James... and I hope you don't mind, but 'twas myself who recommended you for it... and I hope your not offended... " Joe confessed.

"So 'twas your idea! What do you think I should do?" James asked.

"If 'twas my idea, need you ask, James," Joe threw his eyes up to heaven. "Wouldn't it make very good sense in every way!"

His mind now made up, James went to the bar counter and told Brian of his decision to accept.

"Would next week be alright to start with you Brian?"

Brian was jubilant. He asked for hush in the bar.

"Listen now everyone... as and from next week, James here is your new barman," he announced, "and the next drink is on the house to welcome him in!"

Funeral or no funeral, cheers filled the pub, and James was happy to have made the decision.

Bartley was now just a memory to them. So much had happened in so short a time in the small village. It was almost as though a gust of wind had blown through it and altered the pattern of things.

Chapter six

Springtime 1797

*D*affodils were in profusion in the park at Oak Hall, and the willows were bursting into bloom. Crocus had taken the place of the snowdrops that had gracefully run their course. Honeybees once again danced on the landing boards of their hives, jubilant that winter had finally passed and their imprisonment ended.

Hubert was a familiar sight to them as he prepared the vegetable beds for their usual task of producing only the most succulent flavours. He loved his work at the 'big house', as year after year the cycle repeated itself. Beginning his employment on the Foldsworth estate in 1751, he thought today of how quickly those forty-six years had passed as head gardener.

Each morning Hannah would ask him to bring up the vegetables fresh, and Hubert prided himself on the firm good quality produce, from 'his garden'. As he sat watching the bees leaving their hives to inspect the day, he smoked his pipe contentedly. It was a relief that winter had finally lost its icy grip, and he could now finally plan out where the carrots, parsnips, onions and cabbages would be planted for the year. The herb garden, however, was his favourite patch. It took up the least space, he thought, and produced the loveliest flavours. Hubert's son, Billy, was the gamekeeper. His task was to prevent poaching, if possible, and to provide pheasant, venison, snipe, fresh trout and salmon – depending on the season – for the table at Oak Hall.

On this particularly splendid morning, Hubert felt good to be alive. He lived contentedly with his wife, Mary, in the small house provided on the estate. Now that their family was reared, there was not as much to worry about.

"An ideal day for barrowing dung!" he said aloud, as he placed his pipe back in his jacket pocket.

Before going to the stables, where a mature dung-pile awaited him, it was time to go to the kitchen for his morning mug of tea. Hannah was pleased to see him as always.

"There you are Hubert, and isn't it such a lovely day, at long last."

"It is to be sure, Hannah. So, what do you need today, or have you decided yet?" he asked.

"Well, the usual amount of potatoes, and carrots, onions, also some parsley. And ask Billy to leave me in some venison, and two seasoned hares. Her Ladyship has a cold, and some hare soup would do her the world of good," she replied matter of factly.

Hubert admired the way she had everything so well planned to the last detail. Her cooking also was without compare, which his own wife would always become quarrelsome about if he persisted in his praise for too long. A service bell rang, and Williams, looking at the wall box, saw it was the library.

"Must be for you, Hannah. Her Ladyships usual timing," he said, as he resumed his seat at the big kitchen table, grateful to rest and enjoy his morning tea.

Hannah, tidying her hair, ascended the stairs. She knocked gently on the library door. This ritual seldom varied.

"Good morning Hannah. So, what have you planned for lunch and dinner today?"

Lady Foldsworth sat by the large fire, with a rug over her knees. Hannah discussed her menu plan for the day, and seeing her mistress nod of approval, ventured to ask her how she was feeling.

"Oh, I am afraid, Hannah, this cold I have is very reluctant to leave me. The doctor tells me on no account to go outdoors, lest it might develop into pneumonia. So, here I am… sitting by the fire, when I should be down on the lawn collecting some daffodils for the drawing room. I have seldom seen them so abundant!"

Hannah was alarmed at the pale complexion of her mistress, and the fact that this cold was now lingering into its second week. Settling the rug afresh on her knees, her mistress continued.

"To think I shall have to miss the Castle Ball on Saint Patrick's night in Dublin! It does not bear thinking on, Hannah. I am hoping Lord Foldsworth and Catherine will attend, and not be foolish enough to miss it on my account!"

Hannah stroked the fire vigorously.

"I'm sure his Lordship will do what's best, your Ladyship," and she smiled reassuringly at her mistress.

Lady Edwina loved her morning chat with her cook, whose quaint habits and mannerisms she found so endearing.

Their peace was suddenly shattered as a loud smash startled both women. A large stone crashed onto the mahogany table, while broken glass from the window scattered everywhere. Hannah screamed. Her mistress stumbled and fell when her feet become caught in the rug as she tried to flee the room. They both reached the landing, where they stood trembling. As Hannah began to cry in distress, her mistress struggled to regain some composure.

"Come, come, now Hannah, we are both unharmed. What a dreadful thing to happen... "

On hearing the commotion Williams came rushing to the scene and found the women comforting each other.

"Oh Williams... a large stone came crashing into the room... glass everywhere... we have both been very fortunate not to have been injured. Do find Lord Foldsworth... please hurry Williams, please hurry," Lady Edwina pleaded.

She was now becoming very distressed, and when her husband arrived he was baffled at the scene.

"My God... what has happened both of you... Hannah... all those pieces of glass in your hair?" He was freshly alarmed when he noticed the snow-white face of his wife. "Edwina, has a chandelier chain snapped or what on earth has happened? I heard a loud crash but didn't... "

He was quite out of breath having rushed to the scene. Raising her hand, his wife gestured silence.

"Charles, a large stone came crashing through the window in the library, with the obvious intention of trying to maim, or even kill. Go and see for yourself, my dear."

On entering the library the draught from the window blew the heavy velvet curtain, which in turn caught a large ornamental pot and sent it crashing to the ground. This, in turn, evoked a further scream from the already frightened women, who visualised a further attack in progress. Lord Foldsworth called for calm.

"It's alright, only that blessed big pot smashed. No need for alarm."

He saw the large stone on the mahogany table, which was bejewelled with splinters of glass. On closer examination, he found the stone to be stained with dried blood, which added to the sinister and horrid gesture. It became obvious to him that this was a planned and deliberate attack, and done in broad daylight. A sickening feeling crept into the pit of his stomach.

"So finally," he thought, "my home and family has become the target of some militant person or persons."

Regaining his composure, he told both women to go to the drawing room, and asked Williams to go instantly and arrange to have the grounds thoroughly searched. The kitchen was in an uproar and Williams had to muster all his authority to restore calm, and to reassure the staff that the house wasn't under siege.

"Who knows, it may have just been a loose stone from the westerly turret. After all," he continued, "it is the oldest part of the house, and what with the storms of winter... "

The kitchen staff were unconvinced. A large party of men were assembled, and the search for the perpetrators of the crime commenced.

Lord Foldsworth looked at his wife.

"Are you sure you are alright, my darling?"

"I have just a little bump on my head, Charles, nothing else. I imagine I shall be fine. It's nothing to worry about," she reassured him.

Leaving the drawing room, he went to the kitchen, where the staff were totally taken by surprise at his unexpected visit. Lizzie was standing peeling carrots.

"What is your name?" he asked her.

Leaving her task she curtseyed, but was unable to answer her master from shock and shyness.

"Well, young woman, what is your name?" he wondered was she genuinely deaf.

"Lizzie, your honour," she replied shakily.

"Well Lizzie, go to the village this instant and ask Doctor Peele to come here as soon as he possibly can."

"Yes sir, I'll go this minute," she replied, and taking off her apron was out the kitchen door in seconds.

Returning to the drawing room, Charles Foldsworth pondered on how little he knew of how his house actually functioned, the names of his employees, their background, and so much more besides!

In the drawing room both women seemed to have recovered from the shock of the incident. Hannah stood up and addressed her master.

"Sir, if you don't mind, I would like to return to the kitchen and prepare lunch. It has been delayed long enough as it is. And madam, if you need me, ring, and I'll come up to you."

"By all means Hannah, you do now as you think fit," replied her mistress.

Hannah was glad to leave the room and the event behind her. The familiarity of the kitchen comforted her and, with only the skeleton staff remaining, she proceeded to have lunch prepared.

Exhaustive searching of the grounds proved of little value in finding the offenders, or any evidence other than the trampled shrubs underneath the library window. Williams reported these facts regretfully to his master, and announced that Doctor Peel was ready to see Lady Foldsworth.

"Oh yes Williams, do ask him to come up, and please thank everybody for their help this morning."

The doctor examined Lady Edwina thoroughly. Other than the bruise on the side of her head, and another on her knee, there was no evidence of any serious damage.

"No, Lady Foldsworth, I can see no problem other than the bruising. However, should you feel any lightness of the head, do not delay in sending for me. I shall call again in the morning. Meanwhile, continue to rest, and let's hope that cold you have will soon leave you."

Closing his bag with a brisk snap, he bid them farewell, and Williams escorted him out of the room.

"I sometimes wonder about Doctor Peel, my dear. He seldom has much to say, does he?" Lord Foldsworth commented.

"Oh Charles, for goodness sake, don't be irritated by him. Let's just be grateful there isn't any damage done. The question remains, however, as to what sort of deranged person would do such a vile act?" She was more worried about this than her minor injuries.

Her husband could not answer her question.

"No, my dear, I very much fear we have no idea, other than some crank who was fortunate not to be discovered!"

"Charles, let's be honest with each other, this type of incident has never happened before, has it? Isn't it what the Castle has warned us to expect with the increasing restlessness of some people?"

His wife had expressed without hesitation what he had been afraid to entertain; the connection with the incident and the Castle warnings.

"It is a definite possibility, Edwina, while very unpleasant to think on," he replied hesitantly.

"Charles! Where is Kitty?" she asked, suddenly remembering her daughter's absence, and fearing for her safety.

"Oh, I forget to mention it... gone riding since early morning. Don't worry; she is safe enough and more than capable of looking after herself. So, don't fret, my dear. In many ways it is just as well she was absent for the incident."

"I hope you are right, Charles, but there are times when I do worry about her outings to those hills where she seems to spend so much of her time. You do realise we will have to give some serious thought to her future in the coming year."

Rising from her chair, she looked at the taut and pale face of her husband. He seemed at least ten years older at that moment.

"Charles," she continued, "I think we all need a holiday. It would give us the opportunity to discuss things, as a family."

She hoped he might consider Dublin or Hampshire for a month. Her husband began to laugh.

"Edwina, you really love Dublin, don't you? Well, I will tell you what we could possibly do. When things settle down somewhat, we will take a well earned rest" Reading her heart, he could deny her nothing.

* * *

The wind blew gently through Kitty's hair as she lay in James' arms. They were meeting weekly, and their love had grown at a pace they themselves were in awe of.

"James, do you really like serving people ale and all of that in that wretched public house?" she asked, unable to reconcile him with his job in the village.

James laughed, and running his finger along the outline of her face, looked deep into her eyes.

"I do love it, but not as much as I love you, Kitty."

She threw her arms around him and they both laughed and rolled on the soft heather in the March sunshine.

"But seriously, James, you can't possibly remain there all your life, now can you?" then added, "What about farming, or whatever?"

The wide-eyed expression on her face told him she was quite serious, and waiting for an answer. Sitting up and resting his back against one of the tall stones that formed the old Celtic circle, he gestured for her to sit alongside him.

"Kitty, love, I think it's time we looked at the real facts. Today is as good a day as any."

"This sounds all quite serious indeed James. Almost as if you think that us being here together is not one of your 'real facts.'" Kitty was apprehensive.

"Of course us being here is a reality, Kitty. Could we ever deny what we feel?"

She felt the deep sincerity in his voice and sighed deeply.

"Kitty, I am talking of who we are. Who I am. Who you are. You belong to the ascendancy, the ruling class of Ireland... I am a tenant. Yes, that's right, a tenant... a servant of that class, if you like. When did you ever hear of the daughter of a Lord marrying a tenant from the estate? Well, did you? And did you ever think of the consequences of such a notion?"

The reality hit Kitty, and her conversation with Hannah came back to haunt her. James looked at her, and the wisps of hair that blew over the lovely well defined features.

"It's true, James. All you have said is true. But that is not the way I see you. You are very different from the rest of them. You are intelligent. You have qualities I have never seen among the tenants. Why, you even speak better than they do, and you know so much about the affairs of the country. You are also kind and loving," she concluded the list of his qualities, her face becoming more and more clouded.

"My father was a teacher, Kitty. That is where my learning comes from. I also know that this very place where we sit, these big stones behind us in a circle, was an ancient site used by the Celts over two thousand years ago. It is where they came to worship the sun and the moon. Yes, and most people in this area strongly believe they belong to the fairies, isn't that so? But all this is only knowledge, Kitty, and knowledge isn't enough to bridge the great social divide that exists between us. Another fact is your faith. We belong to two very different Christian traditions. To me it matters little, as it's the same God we worship, but to most it's a barrier too great to even imagine crossing."

As James continued to outline the issues that separated them socially, Kitty felt a sinking feeling in the pit of her stomach, and began to seriously question their relationship for the first time. When he finished speaking, she looked at him, and saw a similar look of hopelessness in his eyes. Tears spilled down her face, and she clung to him, as if trying to hide from the fact that fate had allotted the inheritance from which both had emerged. Stroking her hair gently, James gazed over the gently sloping hills, and felt his own deep sadness.

"If only, Kitty, I could buy a place far away from all of this, where there was no division... Oh God, if it were only possible for us to leave it all, just go and be happy forever... how I wish... " He stammered, knowing the futility of such thoughts.

He suddenly jumped up. He was sure he had heard something. Looking about, he saw no one.

"Did you hear that noise, Kitty?" he asked, ears still alert.

"Yes James. I heard it, and I've heard that noise twice before in my life... Oh God! Oh James, let me tell you something... " Kitty was very excited.

She stood up, and looked slowly around at all the stones in the circle.

"What do you mean, my love... twice before? What on earth is it?"

Walking closer to him, she entwined her arms tightly around his neck and looked deep into his blue eyes.

"Hush James. You will probably laugh at this. Many years ago, when I was a little girl, I had a pony I really loved who became very ill. My father took me to the stable one day, and taking me on his knee told me gently that my pony, Rody, was not going to live for very long. I ran from him, sobbing and very upset, and went to Hannah in the kitchen. She took me up in her arms and I told her all about Rody. She hugged me until I had cried all my tears dry, and then told me she was going to take me to a secret and magic place. She said I could make a wish there that Rody might get better. I can still recall, James, how she went out to fetch her big grey cloak, and taking me by the hand brought me to this very place. I did not understand what these big stones were when I was eight years old, but Hannah said it was where the king of the fairies lived, and you could make three wishes. They all had to be very good wishes, as only those type were granted...So, as a little girl, I stood here and wished with all my heart for Rody to get better. Oddly enough, he did.

"The second wish I made here was about five years ago when Mamma was very ill, and she too recovered. The noise you heard just now, I heard on both occasions. You too made your wish, and you too heard that noise, as did I. It is the wind rushing around through the stones. We can rest assured that we are going to be together. I just know it!"

Breathless with excitement, Kitty looked at James with shining eyes. He laughed, throwing back his head and then looking again at Kitty.

"Kitty, you can't expect me to believe all that fairytale nonsense. Wishes... and noises... come now my darling... " He wiped the tears of laughter from his eyes.

Kitty was annoyed by his casual dismissal of her story and the significance.

"No James, I don't believe in fairies, if that's what you mean. But I shall tell you what I do believe in, and that's simple truth and goodness. I also believe that the wish you have made for us to be away from all this division will be granted somehow."

James knew she was genuinely convinced.

"I know, Kitty, what you say, but don't you see how very unlikely it all is?" He looked at the beautiful young face before him so full of hope.

"No matter what you say, James, it will happen. You heard the wind sound, and so did I. Well, now it is all quite clear to me. As you feel our union is so impossible, I now realise that somehow it is going to happen! And nothing will convince me otherwise."

"Kitty, if anyone else were to hear us talking like this, they would consider us quite mad. Probably laugh themselves silly." He felt equally amused, yet the story had touched his heart.

"Well," she continued, "This I do know, and this too will sound every bit as foolish to you. That the wind is our friend, in some way too great to explain." She looked at the man she loved so deeply, and kissed him with a new passion.

Leaving the stone circle as evening drew close, they realised that their relationship was now different in some way, strengthened by a force they didn't quite understand. As their horses followed the old sheep track, they were happy in their silence together. Bringing her horse to a standstill, Kitty turned round and looked back at the old stone circle. The ravens had resumed their noisy gathering there.

"James. I am just thinking we should meet in future at the old ruin, as we did before," she said in a low voice.

"Why do you say that, Kitty?"

"For obvious reasons. It is too easy to see us coming and going from the hilltop. Besides, we like the old ruin, do we not?" She smiled to herself.

"Why do you smile at the idea?" James asked curiously.

"Oh, it seems such an odd place for passionate young lovers. Imagine what people would think! Besides, it's such a draughty place, is it not?" and she laughed mischievously at him.

As they galloped across the rolling countryside, the sheep scattered before the thundering hooves. On parting, they agreed to meet in future at the old church ruin. Their mutual sense of anticipation was obvious.

"'Til then, my love, go carefully," said James, and he blew a kiss towards her.

Kitty reached into the air and caught it.

"Don't worry, James, I shall be alright."

They parted and went their separate ways, both thinking of their strange experience on the hill.

As Kitty reached the stables, the groom rushed out anxiously to meet her.

"Your father has been enquiring as to your whereabouts," he told her breathlessly. "Let me look after your horse..."

"Is there anything wrong, Tom?" she asked, wondering at the unusual behaviour of her father having come to the yard in search of herf.

"Just a little trouble, your Ladyship, and 'tis best you go in now and see your parents."

He gently led the horse into its stable, leaving Kitty still looking at him. Not taking time to stop to speak to Hannah, Kitty went directly to the drawing room and stood before her parents, her riding crop still in hand.

"Father, what is it... what's wrong? One of the grooms told me you were looking for me! Mother, is it you? Are you alright?" Her anxiety was obvious.

"Calm down, Kitty. Sit down beside your mother, and I shall explain." He gestured towards the large red velvet chair.

"To begin with, Kitty, we are worried about your prolonged rides, and the fact that you go unaccompanied. In the light of this mornings' events, perhaps you will be able to understand our anxieties better."

Sitting in his usual high backed chair before the blazing fire, he explained what had taken place in the library earlier that day. Kitty was horrified.

"Oh mother, are you sure you are all right," she asked, with tears in her eyes.

"Yes, my dear, I am all right, and Hannah also," replied Lady Edwina.

Looking directly at her father, Kitty continued.

"Father, why on earth would that villain try to harm us?"

"I don't understand it, child, but it was a deliberate act, and a violent one also. Quite planned, and daring too when one thinks of it!" His expression clearly bore the marks of a worried man.

Looking at her daughter, Lady Edwina took her hand.

"Kitty, more than likely it was someone with a nasty grudge, and happily there was no harm done. It's also highly unlikely that whoever it was will ever return here, so we are all quite safe. However, darling, the point your father made earlier in relation to your riding out alone, and so often, will have to be viewed in the light of what has happened. Now can you understand our concern?"

Kitty realised that what her parents asked was not unreasonable. It was uncanny, in a way, how just today James and she had arranged for a much nearer rendezvous.

"Well, father, you are quite right. In future I shall restrict my riding to the village outskirts, and leave it at that until you both feel otherwise."

She realised that this was a compromise, as her parents had hoped that, for a while at least, she would leave off riding altogether.

* * *

News of the stone being hurled through the window at Oak Hall reached the village by evening. It was the topic of conversation throughout the bar all that night. James was very concerned. Nobody condoned the act, he noticed, as he listened to the different comments and views expressed. The overall opinion was that the Foldsworth family were, in fact, decent. The re-housing of May Ryan and the expulsion of Jerome Hennessy were the main reasons given in their favour.

Joe Gilltrap listened intently, and was genuinely puzzled over the incident. It served no purpose of any type. He was reminded, however, that the second lot of pikes that he had made throughout the winter were almost ready for moving down the county. He was hoping to meet Marcus at the 'Bull's Nose' in town soon again to plan the movement of them. Calling James to one side, he told him of his plans.

"Well Joe, needless to say, I will be with you. But it will have to be on one of my days off," he said, as he began to realise how his job as a barman was confining at times.

Later that night as James lay in bed he felt restless. Again, his thoughts turned to his relationship with Kitty, and her solid conviction that they were to be together. This idea, when viewed in the light of his involvement with the planning of an uprising, began to confuse him. His thoughts seemed to chase each other round his mind, with no place to stop for clarity. Unable to sleep, he sat upright in bed. Reaching out to the table beside him, he lit a candle. It flickered uncertainly at first, before the flame took hold and threw its soft golden light throughout the room. This calmed him somewhat. His mind began to relax, and the restlessness subsided.

"My first cause is the rising," he stated out loud, "and that is what brought me to this village. Yet I do love Kitty, which is another reality in my life."

The conflict was obvious. He considered the possibility of telling Kitty his real purpose in the area, but the risk was too high. If she reacted to the idea, which was very much a possibility, the whole movement in the north of the Wexford would be totally crushed. If he weren't executed with everyone else involved, he would be blacklisted as a traitor forever. He would also lose the love of the only woman he had ever cared for.

He ran his fingers through his hair in desperation and anger. The contradiction, he thought, existed only in principal. 'Outside of me, in a way', he thought. The fact remained, however, that he loved his country, and desired to see it free of oppression and poverty. Loving Kitty was second to that. Yet love seemed more real. You could feel it, and touch it. Tiredness returned in gentle waves, and blowing the candle out, he lay down to sleep.

All that he could see was the blue sky, and the fleecy clouds, and thought he could hear the voice of Kitty saying: 'Your wish is granted James, did you not hear the wind?'. He fell asleep feeling safe and secure. His worries seemed to slip away from him and vanish into the mists covering his dreams.

* * *

Business at the 'Bull's Nose' was very brisk, and Marjorie looked at Bartley Finnegan as he swept out the floors vigorously, humming a tune as he did so.

She recalled the January morning he had come to see her, looking miserable. Having read the letter from Brian, she had taken pity on him and given him the month's trial. So far, he had proved honest and hard working, and so his position had taken on a more permanent role. The fact that at times he was cantankerous, she tended to overlook. Overall, he seemed a good employee. He did not fall prey to meddling with the customers business, and had a respect for the local militia who ate and drank at her premises. He even referred to Joe Gilltrap from time to time, as if they were friends, or even confidants. Marjorie felt happy enough.

Sipping her morning tea, she had to also admit to herself that she did not trust Bartley completely. There was something about him that told her instinctively to be careful. Having his lodgings at the other side of the town meant that he left her premises each evening at half past ten. This suited Marjorie well. It was how she had planned it to be. She could listen intently to the police talking and have her friends from the movement come and go as she pleased. But recent events worried her. News of Lord Foldsworths house being the target of some vagabond had started gossip in the town. Some of her customers were convinced that there was a plan afoot to burn down Oak Hall at some future date. Each time Bartley told his story of exile, it served only to reinforce their views. Yet Bartley always ended his story by saying, 'Shure may God leave him his health, anyhow', which seemed to indicate that his malice had been short lived. Hence, there seemed little grounds to suspect him of the attack. Still, she felt in her bones that there was some link. While she detested the Landlord System, and hoped for a general uprising, the idea of a vendetta against a single landlord did not interest her in any respect. War was one thing, she thought, but cowardly bullying a totally different matter. The police seemed more alert of late, and were asking her at regular intervals if there were any strangers staying as guests. As there were none whatever, the reply never varied. Her thoughts again returned to Bartley. In one sense she regretted allowing him to remain on. She resolved that in future her heart must not rule her head!

Leaving the table, and taking her cup in hand, she walked towards the kitchen. At the end of the bar she heard the familiar voice of Joe Gilltrap.

"So here you are, Bartley! And didn't you land on your feet," he said in a tone of surprise as he saw the barman lifting chairs, then replacing them around small oval tables. Bartley was equally surprised.

"Well... if it's not the blacksmith himself... come to the big town then? How are you Joe?" he said, as he extended his hand to the very surprised visitor.

Marjorie stood watching both men. She assumed by their manner of greeting that Bartley knew Joe as well as he had maintained.

"Isn't it great when old friends meet," she said upon entering the bar.

"Well, Marjorie, let's look at you... hmmm... you look bloomin' so you do. 'Tis the Spring is in the air," Joe said, laughing.

"Enough of your smart remarks now Joe. You can't fool me that easily now, you know," she replied, with large round smiling eyes.

"Marjorie, I'm famished," said Joe, as he rubbed both hands together. "What has the kitchen to offer a man that's ready to eat down the house?"

"Well," replied Marjorie enthusiastically, "There's boiled fowl, roast lamb... " Joe interrupted her.

"Chicken, Marjorie, and whatever else the plate will hold," and he sat down at the bar.

"You'll have to wait a half and hour or so Joe. We're not quite ready for the dinners yet. It's barely eleven o'clock yet, you know," she added teasingly.

"Oh well, Marjorie, so be it. Another half-hour will only improve the appetite. Sure meanwhile, can't I enjoy a good pint of ale?" He decided to move over to a quiet corner of the room and stretch out his legs.

Marjorie went to the kitchen and placed his order. She returned as Bartley was putting the pint of ale before Joe.

"Well, Joe, any news from the village?" he asked, as he wiped the table with a damp cloth.

"Not a bit, Bartley, very same as you left it," Joe replied, as he wiped the froth from his mouth.

"Never changes, Joe, that village of yours. Almost asleep, I'd say," said Marjorie, as she pulled out a chair beside him.

Bartley stood as if waiting for an invitation to join them. Marjorie skilfully observed the empty mugs of two customers at the counter.

"Bartley, I think you are needed at the counter. Customers waiting to be served."

Reluctantly he walked away, muttering under his breath.

"Marjorie," Joe began, speaking in a low voice.

"What is it, Joe?" she asked, with eyebrows raised curiously.

"How in the name of all that's sane in this world did you let that fellow in here to work? I nearly died when I walked in and saw him, wearing the white apron on him," he concluded, with obvious disapproval.

"Now, now, Joe, don't be telling me how to run my business or select my staff. Besides, he is good at his work. No, it wasn't his personality or looks, I'll grant you Joe, but he is a very good worker."

"Well, Marjorie, let me tell you now. If he even gets a hint of your interest in the movement, he will sell you for two pints of porter. That's whom you are dealing with there. He's a very dangerous man... God, will you ever get a bit of sense," he said irritably.

His annoyance worried her. It was out of character.

"He can't be all that bad, Joe?" she asked; now seeking some reassurance from him.

"Well, it's up to you to judge, Marjorie, as you so rightly said. It's not my place to tell you how to run your business."

Giving Joe a friendly slap on the arm she looked at him.

"For goodness sake, that was only a jibe Joe. It's odd I should hear all this now, as only this morning I was feeling uneasy about him. What should I do?" she asked.

"Get rid of him as soon as you can, or else we will all end up at the end of a rope."

She knew by the tone of his voice that he meant what he said.

"I can't just go up to him and tell him to get out. Give me a week to make up a reasonable excuse. Besides, I don't want him as an enemy in the town. I think I could live without that," she said, with a worried look on her face.

While their conversation was held in low tones, Bartley observed them and was surprised by their easy familiarity. He wondered if Marjorie was Joe's 'fancy woman', as he termed it.

Joe ate his dinner eagerly when it arrived. Between mouthfuls, he asked Marjorie to tell Marcus that the next consignment of pikes was ready, and that they would meet him as usual on the next market day, when James would be with him.

"I'll tell him indeed, Joe. He'll be here tomorrow night, so leave it with me. Anyhow Joe, how is young James keeping?"

Oh, just great Marjorie. Didn't he land himself the job that Bartley lost in the village? With the uncle dead, it left him as free as a bird to take it up. Otherwise he would have looked very odd hanging about the village." He wiped his mouth with the back of his hand and sighed with contentment.

"And Joe, what of the breaking of the window at Oak Hall. What do you make of that? Or, better again, who do you think it could have been?" She placed both elbows on the table in anticipation of her friend's response.

"I don't know, Marjorie, but I'd hazard a guess," he replied, and looked at her intently.

"Well then, who is it?" she asked.

"Who else but your new employee," he said, as he casually picked up a piece of apple pie.

"No, Joe, he was here all that day. I'd already thought of that, but that's him off the hook," she said.

"Marjorie, be sensible. There is no one else with sufficient reason to do a thing like that. Hannah, the cook up at Oak Hall, told Nell that had her Ladyship been sitting nearer the window, her head would have been split asunder. Don't you know that money in the right hands here in the town would buy anything these days." He looked at her. There seemed little else to say.

Marjorie moved uneasily, realising what he had said was a distinct possibility. A cold shiver ran across her back.

"I wouldn't like to think that's what I have beside me all day. A cold-blooded villain?" She looked over at Bartley, who was leaning over the counter talking quietly to a customer.

"It's entirely up to you Marjorie to take that risk, but it's a pity you ever employed him in the first place. However, that's enough about him for now. The main reason for me being here is to ask you to tell Marcus about the pikes. I also want to find out about the next meeting, and where it's to be held. Will you get all the details for me?"

"To be sure, Joe, I will. Now, would you like a cup of tea to finish?" She smiled, looking more her usual self.

"No thanks, Marjorie. Nell will be waiting for me," he replied.

"Oh, you never mentioned she was in town, Joe," she said surprised.

"Indeed she is in town. To get the best price for the eggs, as usual. A great woman to bargain is Nell... a bit like you, Marjorie," and he boomed a loud laugh.

Having paid for his dinner, Joe walked towards the door, bidding Bartley a cheery goodbye. Bartley did not acknowledge it. Marjorie watched unnoticed from the side door, and the expression on Bartley face convinced her that what Joe had said was true. She sighed heavily. 'He must go, and that's that', she thought, 'but I need a good reason. Hard as it will be to find one, find one I must'.

* * *

The following evening, Marcus came into the premises as expected. He sat talking amicably to those whom he knew there. Marjorie was aware of Bartley watching Marcus, and so did not approach him. She decided to wait until he had gone home. The very nature of their business demanded great caution, and the minimum of risk. The hope of finding a good and valid reason to dismiss Bartley from her employment still worried her. His work was good, and he kept the place clean. While his manner with some of the customers was curt at times, he was generally as pleasant as on might expect.

She liked keeping busy, and the customers liked it when she moved among them. She smiled to herself at the thought of herself as 'Marjorie the Revolutionary'. It sounded funny to her, yet the oppression of the people always reaffirmed her in her cause. She looked at the great-grandfather clock, which seemed to labour heavily as it struck ten. At this time Bartley generally made himself a cup of tea before going home, having checked beforehand that the shelves were well stocked. Marjorie walked over to him.

"Musha Bartley, seeing as it's not such a busy night you can go ahead a bit earlier. I'll be well able to manage," she said, trying to sound as casual as she could.

"Right Marjorie, 'tis you is the boss."

Taking off his apron, he hung it up behind the door. Putting on hi cloak, he seemed delighted to be finishing work early .Not lingering for to chat, he left the pub. Marjorie walked over to Marcus casually.

"Well, Marcus, one would expect you to be out courting tonight, instead of out on the town!" she joked.

"Too cold a night for that Marjorie. In fact, I'm thinking of going over to that fire there. I'm chilled to the bone, whatever has gotten into me." As he spoke, he moved over to the big fire blazing in the grate.

Seeing first to the needs of other customers, she joined him some time later.

"How is business, Marjorie?" he asked, sensing the tension in her.

"Oh, can't complain. Why do you ask?" She looked at him, wondering was there more to it.

"Just thought you were very on edge all evening, and the place doesn't seem too busy, that's all." He sipped at his drink slowly.

"Well, there's no point in trying to hide it from you, lad. Joe was here today, and told me in no uncertain terms to get rid of Bartley, that he is a dangerous man. If he's here much longer, I fear he might prove to be just that," she explained, sighing aloud.

"Why is Joe so convinced about him, Marjorie?" Marcus asked.

"That business at Oak Hall," she replied, looking intently at him.

"You know Joe is seldom wrong, don't you?" Marcus asked, with concern.

"Indeed that's what worries me... and I'm stuck for the first time in my life for a good reason to show him the door," she replied, and for the hundredth time that day wrestled with the problem.

"What I'm going to tell you next will give you plenty of reason. The next meeting is to be held here, and all the main leaders will be present. Now Marjorie, it's up to you after that. You know what will happen if we are discovered. The rope for us all, no other ending."

Marjorie gazed into the fire and knew she would have to get rid of Bartley, sooner, rather than later.

"Don't worry, Marcus. He'll be gone by then. What date is it set for anyway?" She decided to concentrate on the matter at hand.

"On Saint Patrick's night. We'll meet here at about ten o'clock or so, if that suits you Marjorie. There will be about ten of us, as far as I know. Will the back room be alright to use do you think?"

"Indeed it will. I'll get Lizzie Toole to work for me that night. That will leave me free. She's reliable, and that's what I need." She leaned over and prodded the fire with the great long poker.

Marcus looked at her. He had great admiration and affection for her, and her courage was remarkable. Her skill in gathering information from the military, and never being uneasy in their company, amazed him. Almost like a rabbit sleeping outside a fox's den, he thought! Her information had proved invaluable to-date, and extremely accurate.

"We purposefully chose that evening because there are always strangers coming and going then, so our men will pass without drawing too much attention," Marcus continued.

"A very clever idea, if I may say so Marcus. Now, what are the plans for the removal of this next load of pikes? Joe says they will be here as usual, hidden beneath the load of potatoes." Marjorie's mind was clear and alert despite the lateness of the hour.

"Tell them I will be there, and go through the motions of buying the potatoes as usual. We could perhaps leave them in one of the old coach houses Marjorie, out the back?"

"That will be alright, but how long do you intend leaving them there? It is risky enough," Marjorie replied, realising that there was very little choice in the matter.

"At first light I will depart with them," he said reassuringly, and she knew that his word was his bond.

He yawned and stretched his legs wearily. He realised how tired he actually felt.

"Is there anything else to discuss now, Marjorie?" he asked, running his fingers through his hair in an attempt to fight off the fatigue.

"No Marcus, we have covered everything, and now I will make some tea, or would you prefer another drink?" She stood up and was aware that she too was weary after the long day.

"Tea will be fine, Marjorie, and then I will be on my way."

The pub was now empty. Only the dim light of the lamp glowed on the mantelpiece, and the fire was a glow of pulsing embers. Presently Marjorie returned with a tray of cold chicken, buttered bread and tea.

"Now, eat up like a good man, Marcus. You can't ride back that distance on an empty stomach!"

"God bless your big-heartedness Marjorie, I will do justice to that!"

Marjorie went off to close the shutters. The chill of the early March night came through in cold draughts. Bolting the doors, and the three rear windows, she then proceeded to the front of the house, bolting a further four windows. From habit, she opened the front door to look down the street. The shadow of a man disappeared with a scuffle around the corner. She would recognise that scuffle anywhere. She felt sure it was the outline of Bartley Finnegan. She closed the door again and told Marcus what she had seen.

"Are you sure, Marjorie? It could have been anyone. Is not Bartley too much on your mind?" He knew she was seldom wrong in her conclusions.

"I only wish I was wrong, Marcus. I'd know the drooped shoulders and the shape of him any place. I see him every day of the week. The only good thing is he couldn't have been able to hear a word we were saying. And seeing us together this late? Well what of it. Nothing so awful in that, is there Marcus?"

They both laughed at the innuendo.

"Oh, for heaven's sake Marcus, go home to your bed before I am scandalised in the town!"

Letting him out through the back door, he went to the stable and saddled his horse. As he rode out, he waved to her in the moonlight. She watched the figure become dim in the distance; the only sounds being the hoof beats and a dog howling at the rising moon. She sighed deeply.

"If I were only twenty years younger, Marcus, I would be gone with you!" She smiled afresh to herself.

Going to bed at the other side of the town, Bartley was thinking of Marjorie and her late night familiarity with Marcus.

"Mad for a man, that one. I always knew it," he said aloud, as he unbuttoned his boots. "And I'd bet me life on it that it's a toss-up between that lad there tonight and Joe Gilltrap."

Well, he thought, tomorrow I'll throw me own cap in the ring. I could do worse. She's no picture, as me poor mother used to say, but wouldn't it be the greatest thing that could happen to me? Imagine it! Bartley Finnegan, landlord of the 'Bull's Nose'.

Bartley slept blissfully, having blessed Lord Foldsworth for sending him away to meet such a good future!

* * *

March, unpredictable as ever, when a morning of warm sunshine can change in minutes; to heavy showers of hailstones, even light snowflakes.

Lord Foldsworth sat by the fire in his study, thinking how excited Kitty was in anticipation of the forthcoming Ball at Dublin Castle. He knew only too well how little opportunity she had for socialising with her friends. It would be a pity for her to miss the chance, he thought. He was also aware of the meeting he had to attend, where other landlords and magistrates would be present to discuss the levels of unrest in various parts of the country. Thankfully, Lady Edwina had recovered from her long cold, and also from the 'incident of the stone', as it was now referred to. A gentle knock on the door broke into his reverie. Kitty came in, smiling.

"Good morning, father. I hope I am not disturbing you?"

"Certainly not, my dear. Come and sit down, and tell me to what do I owe this rare honour of your visiting me in my study?" He was teasing her, laughing softly and clearly delighted to see her.

"Well father, what compliments! I think you would have made an excellent detective. Isn't that what they call people who suspect when something is up? Well, the truth is father, with mother deciding to stay on here and rest; I do not expect you to come to Dublin solely on my account. I would be more than content to remain here." Her sincerity was apparent.

He looked at her in surprise.

"Not at all, darling. We leave here in the morning as planned. I hope you have told your maid to pack your ball-gown, and all the other items you ladies endow yourselves with." Then, changing the subject, he continued. "Where is your mother at present? I must speak to her on some matters, lest I forget them.

I am getting older, I am afraid! Do you ever think, Kitty, how some day you will inherit all of this, and the property in England as well?" His tone of voice conveyed to her the responsibility of such a fortune.

"Yes father. I think of my future a lot, and I realise what your ambitions are for me. But if I ever choose to live elsewhere, will that be alright, do you think?" She was amazed how freely the words came from within her. She realised that her love for James was the driving force behind her question.

Charles Foldsworth felt a knot in his stomach, as he looked at his beautiful young daughter, very much a determined woman now. He realised that there was nothing immediate about the question, and relaxed just as quickly.

"Of course, my dear, you could live anywhere you choose to. A lot of families who own estates here in Ireland have their real homes in England these days. You could, in years to come, do likewise, and appoint someone dependable and responsible to run the estate here. But why such a question now, Kitty? Are you no longer content here, or have you grown tired of country life?" He looked closely at his daughter.

"Of course, father, I am content here. Remember, it was you who prompted the question. But it's nice to know, none the less, that I do have a choice in the matter. As to the present, father, do you think that mother will be all right here when we are away in Dublin?" she asked, concerned.

"Rest assured, she will be safe enough. I have arranged for the grounds to be guarded vigilantly, and it's most unlikely we will ever have that trouble again." His assurance pacified her.

Aware that she had arranged to meet James soon at the old ruin, she did not want to be late.

"So father, we leave as planned tomorrow then?" she asked, smiling at him.

"Yes, my darling, and I suggest if you have things to do in preparation you best see to them, eh?" He walked towards her and kissed her lightly on the forehead.

"Yes father, and I shall see you at dinner tonight as usual." She looked at the lawn through the window, and the sunshine breaking through the clouds. "I think I shall go first for a quick canter. I shall miss it when I am in Dublin."

"Yes, you do just that, and go carefully my dear." He watched her as she glided happily from the room.

Putting on her riding habit, Kitty was almost breathless in anticipation of seeing James.

As she rode across the small fields, the shorter route to the old monastic ruins, Kitty wished that James, by some miracle or other, could be part of the Dublin social whirl. While this was a total impossibility, she none-the-less allowed free rein to her imagination. She envisaged him in a dark blue uniform, with a red collar and yellow stripes along the arms of his jacket. He would look so well, she thought. On the other hand, then he would most likely meet some other beautiful young woman. She then imagined him dancing with this stranger underneath the huge chandeliers, and she almost began to feel jealousy. She smiled at her vivid imagination. On approaching the old ruin, Kitty wondered if James was already there. The thick grove of evergreen yew trees and the wild laurel obscured the ruined church. As she dismounted and led her horse gently through the grove, the blackbirds sang their shrill song. Tethering her horse, Kitty looked at the ancient ivy covered building, its roof long since gone. The walls were high, and the tall narrow windows were intact. There were nine alcoves where once the nine altars had stood, and where prayer had been unceasing.

A deep sense of peace and tranquillity still lingered in the air, she thought, and the chorus of birdsong gave an added sense of timeless magic. The hills in the background, towering to the sky, gave her a feeling of security. Where better to meet the person one loves, she thought.

Walking freely around the ruins, she could see no sign of James, and wondered what could be delaying him. Perhaps something had happened in the village to detain him? Finding a small sheltered alcove that trapped the sunlight, Kitty sat down to wait for the man she loved so much, to arrive. A blackbird flew from one of the laurel trees, shrilly protesting at being disturbed. Kitty, expecting it was James, stood up and walked through one of the granite-posted doorways. To her surprise, a small boy stood there, with two rabbits tied to a stick that hung over his shoulder. It was obvious he was frightened by Kitty's sudden appearance.

"Hello… and what's your name?" she asked, bending down to try to allay any fears the boy might have.

But he remained silent and looked anxiously about him, unable to speak, much less run. Just then, a dog appeared and barked excitedly, first at its young master, then at Kitty.

"What a lovely little dog you have! Does he have a name?" she enquired, hoping the dog's presence might calm his fears.

"Patch," he replied, and then turning around he ran through the trees, disappearing as quickly as he had come, his dog in pursuit.

Understanding the child's fear, Kitty wasn't surprised. She realised the very clothes she wore would be alien to the child; so different from the clothes of the women he would know. It was unlikely he would ever return here again, she thought, and wondered what he would say to his family when he got home.

A hand suddenly rested on her shoulder. She spun around to meet the warm embrace of James, who was laughing at having startled her.

"My mother always told us, Kitty, that those who frighten others get the bigger fright themselves," he said, and saw a smile come to her face.

"So, you were spying on me," she said, her eyebrows arched, her head held at a slant to avoid the strong rays of the sun.

"Well, I couldn't help it. I stayed in the trees. There was every chance that the youngster would recognise me. When he goes home now and says he saw a beautiful woman in the old church, God himself only knows what people will say!"

Taking Kitty by the hand, they both walked into the old ruin. They found a warm and sheltered nave, and sat down.

"James," Kitty began, "Tomorrow I am going to Dublin with father to attend the Ball at Dublin Castle. It should be fun, I suppose..."

"I see. And meeting some gallant young officer, no doubt, whom you will fall hopelessly in love with, and then marry. But I will still come here when I am old and grey and tired from life and remember the lovely Lady Catherine whom I was so in love with," he drawled teasingly, and then sighed, thinking how perhaps that would, in fact, be the inevitable course of events.

"Don't be absurd, James! At the last Ball I met a fellow by the name of Colonel Wanewright, whom I left standing on the ballroom floor. He recovered his embarrassment, and was to come down for the Saint Stephen's Day hunt, but never arrived. Why, I don't know. That aside, riding here this evening I was wishing with all my heart that you could be part of the Castle party. Oh James, imagine it. We would ;have no problems then, only to marry and be happy."

They kissed passionately, with the intensity and urgency of deepening love. Suddenly Kitty pulled back and stood up.

"What's wrong, Kitty, what is it?" James asked surprised.

"Oh, it's just me, James. I am sorry. It would be so easy to get carried away, and besides, if by chance anything should happen... we must try and think of the consequences... " she felt embarrassed and foolish.

"Anything happen?" James looked at her. "What does that mean? Will you tell me what you are thinking?"

"Yes, I will tell you what I am thinking James. I would love to bear your child, and it would be so easy for it all to take place. But not here, not in this way... " And she cried silently.

James held her hand tightly, as her tears flowed and deep sobs rocked her body.

"Kitty, my love, forgive me, but I didn't know your feelings ran so deep. Come now, try and be calm."

As Kitty regained her composure, James looked at the tear stained face.

"You are right, Kitty. We could so easily be swept away by our feelings, and that would be a fatal mistake. Let's walk for a while."

Taking her hand, they strolled through the grove in silence, content now just to be together.

"Some day, James, when things are clearer, there will be a time we can love in the deepest sense possible. I feel it in my bones, and I only wish it were now," said Kitty as she looked at his weather-tanned face and the deep-set eyes above a firm jaw line.

"I am happy to wait for that day too, Kitty. The thought of you bearing my child is more than I ever dreamed of. I love you so much, Kitty... will you ever be able to know it fully... " Taking her face in his hands he kissed her with deep emotion.

They melted onto the soft ground below them, their kisses and entwining limbs expressing their pent up passion for each other. Both longed with all their hearts and all their desire to unite completely, to consume each other. It was only the change in the light that brought their senses to bear on the real world again.

"I must be going, James. If I am too late, Father will question me," Kitty said, brushing the dry mosses for her riding habit.

The sun cast long shadows outside the old ruin, as woodpigeons flew into the trees and prepared to settle comfortably for the night.

"Well then," James' voice was hoarse, his passion still aroused, "when will I see you again Kitty. Next week, is it then?"

"It will be about eight days from now James, as we may well be detained in Dublin, goodness only knows."

Taking the reins of her horse, she mounted. James looked at the woman on horseback, so beautiful, so lovely, and knew in his heart that if she had said eight months, he would still have waited.

"I shall count the days, darling," he replied, and smiled up at her.

Reaching down from her sidesaddle, she kissed him once more.

"Goodbye, my love," she whispered, and rode quietly from the grove.

James walked to the other side of the grove to collect his horse. Again, the question arose in his mind about his involvement with the revolutionary group. So complicated, he thought, but decided not to wrestle with it for now. As he rode briskly back through the woodland, he smiled as he remembered Kitty's words... 'Trust the wind'... and he remembered the day when they had lain in the old Celtic fort. How convinced Kitty had been of their inevitable future together ever since that time. He too had come to believe it. Why, he did not know, but that was how he felt.

That night, James called to see Joe, who was working late at the forge. The hot coals threw a warm glow, their heat welcome as the night air of March still held its chill. Joe was not surprised to see him.

"'Tis you are the late traveller, James," he said, as he continued to hammer at the anvil, in his usual cheerful way.

"Indeed, and 'tis you are the late worker, Joe," James retorted, chuckling.

Changing to lower tones, the two men planned the moving of the pikes. How to pack the straw thickly above and beneath them, thus preventing the clammer of metal on the rutted roads. With the potatoes piled high on top of them, they planned to leave at dusk on Saint Patrick's evening.

"This will be a big meeting by the sounds of it, with the Wexford leaders present. God only knows what we will hear?" James said, as he looked at the firm expression on his friend's face.

"It will indeed be a big meeting," Joe replied, as he poured cold water on the molten metal. It billowed in a gush of raging steam, obscuring James for a few seconds.

"We will probably hear of the total amount of arms ready, and maybe even the date of the rising, Joe. I wonder what will it be like for us to actually know the day and the month when it will all begin. Where we are to gather, and all the other details."

Both men remained silent. Joe wiped the beads of sweat from his forehead. He looked up at James with gravity.

"I know what we'll think, and so do you James... of those we love and their safety, first of all."

James didn't want to dwell too much on that aspect.

"You will have Nell and the children to think of. You said before that they would be going up to the hills. Is that still your plan?" James asked him.

"Still the same plan for them, up to the relations there. I'll have to get old Mag to go also. How I'm going to manage to shift her, I still don't know. If my guess is correct, James, this village will be directly in the path of the advancing forces from our side. By the time we will have reached here, the army will be heading for a direct confrontation. Oak Hall will most likely be levelled by some of our troops as well." He looked at James as he said this.

"But surely they won't kill the Foldsworths, Joe, will they? Why, they have been decent landlords all down the ages. I couldn't see the sense in that whatsoever," he protested, the torment in his voice quite obvious.

"It is true they have been decent landlords James, and never ill-treated their tenants. You see, it's not so much them, but what they stand for, that is the real trouble. In years to come, old Foldsworth will be dead and the some new fellow will come along and marry Lady Catherine. Then the real trouble will start.

No, I'm afraid it's unfortunate. It will, in all likelihood, be even burned to the ground; and if the family are there at the time, they will without doubt be killed by the army." Joe concluded the macabre scene with a sigh.

James felt dumbfounded. The reality of the future events loomed large before him, and he felt sickened at the prospect of Kitty being in such imminent danger. Her home, her parents, and the servants. They were all such an innocent lot when one thought it out.

Joe was aware of his silence. Again he asked himself if what old Mag had told him was the truth? He remembered the evening she had come to the forge almost breathless. She had been up in the hills collecting heather roots, and had lain against an old stonewall to rest herself. The sound of galloping horses alerted her, she had said. Looking through the large stone gaps in the wall, to her amazement she had seen them. Young James, and he embracing the Lady Catherine from the Big House.

Having told Joe her extraordinary story, they had both made a pact never to repeat it to anyone else, ever. 'But tonight it's time I did', he thought. I must talk to James about it all, or I'll have neither rest nor ease, he told himself firmly.

"Do you know what we'll do, James. We will go and get ourselves a drink and then we'll be able to talk more about things. Nell is too close here for my comfort anyhow."

Without waiting for James to answer, he took his old coat from off the nail in the corner. James walked slowly ahead of him. He was aware that Joe had noticed his reaction to the inevitable destruction of Oak Hall and the Foldsworths. 'The rebellion is almost upon us', he thought, 'and I day-dreaming of love and romance'. He relaxed, however, with the thought that Joe knew nothing of his relationship with Kitty.

"What's your guess on the weather, Joe?" he asked him, finding it to be perhaps the safest topic for now.

"A change in the wind, lad. Look at the ring around the moon... could even be another bit of snow," he replied as they walked into the dimly lit bar.

It proved a quiet night. Brian, who sat by the fire alone, stood up.

"Well men, I was beginning to think that everyone around these parts was dead, or else lost their taste for porter!" He went behind the counter to serve his two customers.

"Well James, did you do anything worthwhile with your free day?" he asked, as he placed the ale before them.

"No, Brian. I had a nice quiet day. Did a little about the uncle's place, and went for a bit of a canter. Must say it turned out a better day than an evening."

He sipped his drink slowly.

"No need ever to ask our blacksmith what he was at," Brian added good-humouredly, "I can hear you from here hammering day and night. Do you never stop?"

Joe felt a bit uneasy, but replied casually.

"With the rush of the spring, Brian, you have lads coming day and night getting tools fixed, the usual things. I often ask myself, why do they all leave it until the last minute to get repairs done? But isn't that life for ye!"

"Bar work is a never ending job too," continued Brian, and he began sweeping up behind the counter.

Both men decided to move over and sit beside the fire to have their chat.

"Well Joe, what's on your mind," James asked, sensing the blacksmith's tension.

"I suppose it's similar to what's on yours James," Joe said honestly, looking into his glass and then up at James.

"The meeting in Marjorie's, is it?" James asked, in a quiet voice.

"Not exactly James. To be honest with you, I feel it's time I asked you something. It's none of my business on one level, but important for many other reasons. It's like this. Are you courting Lady Catherine Foldsworth?" He sat back in his chair, relieved that he had finally asked the question.

James was hit with a mixture of fear and relief.

"Yes Joe. I am. I am, to be true, and we are very much in love."

The frank and unhesitating admission staggered Joe in his thinking. So old Mag was right after all.

"We meet every week," continued James, "even this evening before I came to the forge."

He looked at the blank expression on the blacksmiths face. James remained silent. There was nothing else to say, he thought. Joe took out his pipe and cleaned the bowl of it with a twig picked up from the hearth.

"How did you know Joe? Who else knows," James asked, suddenly realising there was more to it all.

"Mag told me a few weeks ago. She was up in the hills collecting roots for her remedies. She saw you both there one evening and how fond of each other you obviously are. We decided there and then that no-one else should ever know, at least from our lips anyway." He proceeded to light his pipe.

The blue clouds of tobacco smoke filled the corner where they sat, until the draught from the fireplace caught it and sucked it skywards.

"I see," said James, as he thought of the many implications that this news had for them. "I won't stop meeting her. She simply means too much to me, and we both love one another and before you ask me, no, she knows nothing of the movement, or the rebellion plan. Rest assured, she never will. I don't get that carried away you know."

He stood up and went to the counter to order another drink for them both. On his return, Joe looked at him.

"I'd just like to say this much before I finish. Your secret is safe with me, and Mag also for that matter. But there are two more serious threats. First of all, there is Lord Foldsworth. If he ever finds out about this, he will not rest until he hounds you out of the area, and I'll go even further James: if he could banish Bartley for taking a bit of holly for Christmas, what do you think he would do to someone like you trying to take his daughter? I'll spare you the trouble of thinking it out James... he will kill you. Do you understand James? Kill you. Besides that aspect of it all, if the movement hear of it, you will be equally dealt with. Not killed, no, but branded as a traitor to the cause and to your country."

Joe sat back in his seat, his statement finished. James was surprised at the anger Joe displayed towards him. He also knew that he was genuinely concerned. For very good reason too, he realised.

"Look Joe, don't think I haven't already thought of all you have said. God knows it has given me sleepless nights. Place yourself in my boots for a while," he asked, trying to reason the matter further.

"The simple answer to that James is that I wouldn't. What bothers me most about it all is, how could you have let yourself into such a situation in the first place? I've asked myself a few times have you an ounce of sense at all?" Joe's frustration seemed to be mounting.

"Joe, Kitty and I often talk of the huge problems that lie between us, and somehow we believe there is a life for us together, as foolish as it may all sound to you. It's our only hope, Joe. To try and believe it will somehow work out for us." His feelings of desperation were evident to his friend.

Joe took the pipe out of his mouth.

"James, did you ever think that Lord Foldsworth has already someone in mind for his daughter? The landlord class consider these things when their children are born. Yes, even before they can walk or talk! They don't think like the rest of us. There are the vast estates to consider, titles, money; ancestry... love has little, if anything to do with it all. It's their way of life." Joe nodded his head in defeat. "I can well see how I'm wasting my breath. I can see that you love her Ladyship. It's as plain as day. There's no reasoning with you, is there?"

James just nodded.

"No, there isn't Joe. Live or die, I will be with Kitty, and the rebellion," and there were tears in his eyes and it embarrassed Joe to see them.

"Very well James, I know you are to be trusted, and I'll stand by you with the movement. But as for you and her Ladyship being together... God help us, what a dream! Maybe you'll both grow out of it... it's as unlikely a union as... " Words failed him.

The fire flashed a sudden flame as a log fell into the glowing embers.

"Aye, I know how you think Joe, and it is unlikely a union as bayonets and lace."

They decided to talk no more about it, and began to discuss the forthcoming meeting. With the heat of the argument now subsided, they dreamed and wove their dream of freedom for their people and country into the night.

* * *

March the seventeenth, 1797, blew cold and overcast, but dry.

After mass people gathered outside the church to chat, gossip and exchange news. May Ryan walked quietly to the old graveyard to visit the grave of her husband, Pat. She placed some early spring flowers on the sods, which were beginning to sink. She sat down on a stone nearby, and looked at all the signs of spring about her. Dew lay heavily on the grass and matched the tears that lay in her eyes unable to spill forth.

"I miss you Pat," she whispered lowly to the quiet earth, "more than ever," and so do the children. They are well, and love the new house. I miss the old one, for there we lived our life together. The new one is dry and warm and all their coughs have left them. There is not a day but I think of you, and miss you something terrible, and the long nights when I wish you were there to hold me. I'll always love you Pat Ryan, and someday I'll lie there beside you for all time." She patted the hard cold earth, and her tears flowed freely.

Wiping them away, she stood up. Nell Gilltrap came up behind her.

"Are you alright, May," she asked, concern on her face.

"Yes Nell, I am okay. It's just I miss him so much, and what I'd only give to have him back for a single day." She wept afresh, her heart near breaking.

"I know. It must be very hard, May. If 'twas my Joe who lay there, I can't imagine how I'd ever be able to go on living myself." She shivered at the thought of life without him. "I was wondering, May, if you and the children would come down and have your dinner with us today? Joe and young James have to go to town with a load of potatoes, and God only knows when the pair of them will get back," she said good-humouredly.

May accepted the invitation gladly, as she felt very lonely on this special day.

"Did you ever know, Nell, that it was at a Saint Patrick's night dance that Pat asked me to marry him?" She smiled as she recalled the night. "We were at a house dance in Foley's, and 'twas as he walked me home he asked me. Imagine it's only twelve years ago, just twelve summers ago, and here I am so alone after all the love I had for him. God Nell, life can go so very wrong, can't it?"

"Yes May, 'tis true enough. But you are young, and you have a lovely snug home, and God will take care of you. Who knows what the future will bring?"

As May smiled in hope, both women linked one another and walked slowly from the old graveyard to join the other neighbours walking back to the village.

* * *

Bartley decided that on such a great and prominent day he would speak to Marjorie about his feelings for her. He was convinced he was the only man for her, and was determined that Marcus would never take his place as spouse! He had dressed meticulously that morning, and combed his hair in fresh rainwater. His mother always said it would never fail to make it curl. 'Why am I nervous?', he thought, 'Amn't I a great catch for her! A great man for the business and I'd keep her happy for many a year to come.' He chuckled. Still, his mouth was dry. He attributed it to the fact he hadn't eaten any breakfast.

Rubbing his hands together, he approached the door of his employer's public house. He visualised that next year he would be well established as landlord. He walked through the door, whistling a lively tune. There before him, at one of the front tables, sat Marjorie, having her morning cup of tea.

She looked up at Bartley with her usual smile, and greeted him in her usual way, aware of the fact that she was going to have to get rid of him, somehow or other, from the place. In his amorous frame of mind he misinterpreted her greeting and smile, and with renewed vigour and conviction he approached her.

"And good morning to you Margaret," he said, smiling broadly, revealing his front upper teeth with three distinct gaps.

Taking a spray of shamrock from the collar of his cloak, he placed it on the table before her, and made a sweeping bow. Marjorie paled visibly, and a peculiar feeling swept over her.

"What's this for Bartley, and all the bowing and scraping?" she asked in a voice she hardly recognised as her own.

"For you, Princess, and I am prepared to give you much more."

Before she had time to hazard a reply, he had gone down the bar singing to himself.

"Mother of sweet divine Jesus," she thought, "help me, but if that lad isn't half drunk my poor mind is going queer."

She looked at the shamrock on the table, and it was real enough all right! 'Calling me Margaret, and princess... the very nerve of him'. She decided to finish her tea, and say nothing. As she walked back towards the kitchen with her tea tray, Bartley seemed to appear out of nowhere.

"Stop right there, and give me that tray. You shouldn't be carrying anything Margaret," he said to her in a singsong tone.

'No, this is real', she thought, 'something very badly amiss with him. If he continues this much longer I will have to check him. God help me, but if any of the customers were here to see his antics, there's no accounting for the gossip it would cause. Oh my God... '. The very thought of being intimate with Bartley sent a shiver through her entire system. She stood before the bar mirror to adjust a pin in her hair, and tied up the loose strands that had escaped the green bow at the back. In the mirror she could see Bartley standing behind her, smiling again. She thought she was going to faint.

"Bartley, have you been celebrating into the early hours?" she asked him, turning to face him.

"No Margaret, I have not. But I soon shall be, and you along with me," he replied, still smiling.

"What, may I ask Bartley, will we be celebrating do you think?" She was totally bewildered at the transformation in the man.

Bartley made a sweeping gesture towards a table quite close to where they were standing.

"Margaret, I have something to say to you, and I think we should sit down first of all."

Taking Marjorie gently by the arm, he led her to the chair he had pulled out from beneath the table. She felt as if she were in a dream state, unable to take control.

"What is this celebration you are talking about Bartley?" she asked, more perplexed than ever.

"A wedding Margaret, my Princess," he replied.

"A wedding Bartley. And who is it that's getting married then?" she asked, still unaware of his intentions.

"I hope it will be ours, Margaret," he said, and sighed heavily, relieved at having made his proposal.

Marjorie froze. 'Definitely gone a bit mental', she thought, 'all that princess stuff and Margaret this-and-that. God save me, but I mustn't panic now. Lunatics can kill if resisted, she'd heard that somewhere. I must stay calm and hope someone will come into the place soon. Please God, soon'. Her thoughts became a prayer for help.

"Well, what have you to say, Margaret?" he asked her, the smile still stuck to his face.

"Oh Bartley, it's all so sudden," she gasped, full sure he had completely lost his mind. "I never expected you to ask me to marry you. I will... I will... er, have to think about it... er... lady's privilege, isn't that it?" In her head, her prayer continued, 'God come between me and all harm...'.

"I knew it. I knew it all along... you would never say no," Bartley squeaked out loud, then, leaning over the table closer to her, whispered, "and I know you need the company, just like meself."

Marjorie thought for a moment she felt something on her leg beneath the table, and then realised that it was Bartleys hand gripping her thigh. She lost all self-control, and jumped up with a scream. The table toppled over and caught Bartley unawares. While he fell back off his chair onto the ground Marjorie ran to the drawer behind the counter where she kept a small pistol wrapped in an old rag.

"Easy now, easy now," called Bartley, in a soothing voice. He stood up and began to edge his way towards the bar counter. "Don't get excited now Margaret, 'tis well I know you're mad for a man. I watch it all here you know, the way you're keen on the married lads as well as the single ones, eh? Gilltrap, and then young Marcus."

Marjorie could not believe that no one had come into the premises on this morning of all mornings. Where were her early customers when she needed them? Realising that it would be a grave mistake to shoot Bartley, she fired a shot up at the ceiling. The noise was heard on the street and brought passers-by running in her door. They were confronted with the sight of Bartley grappling with Marjorie on the floor behind the counter. She was shrieking wildly, in terror of her assailant. She fainted.

The taste of brandy brought her back to reality, by which time the place was crowded with people. Sergeant Cosgrave helped her up, and brought her to sit by the fire.

"Well Marjorie," began the sergeant, "and what happened here this morning?" His tone was official and demanding.

"It's very simple sergeant. That fiend I was foolish enough to give a job to went raving mad here and then assaulted me. What's more, if I ever find him in here again, it's his corpse you'll be taking out." She had rapidly gained some composure.

Sergeant Cosgrave didn't like Marjorie's attitude towards him in front of the crowd. She wasn't respecting the 'law' in their midst.

"Did you discharge a firearm on this premises, Marjorie Bass," he asked in very official tones and with as much authority as he could muster.

"Sergeant Cosgrave, are you deaf?" she asked defiantly, in no mood for displays of any type.

Again he tried to act out his official role.

"There was a disturbance here this morning... "

He didn't get time to finish his sentence. Marjorie sprang from her chair by the fire in a fury. Standing directly in front of him, she looked at him coldly. The crowd hushed into a silence of increasing curiosity.

"I have already told you what happened here this morning, and I will state it clearly again, so listen well, Sergeant. If any man comes in here and tries to take advantage of me again, I will take out that pistol and fire without hesitation. Do you really think that Judge Fossett would find me guilty?"

With her hands on her hips and shaking with temper she awaited the sergeants reply. None came. He knew that the Judge and Marjorie were old friends.

"Now Sergeant, take this scoundrel out of here now, and do as you please with him. And let this crowd be my witness: if ever he comes into this premises again, he will be dead within minutes. And the next time I will hold you personally responsible for negligence of the criminals in your charge." Marjorie swept out of the crowded bar and went into her private kitchen.

The crowd cheered her courage and her stand on the matter. They thrived on the fact that the authoritarian Sergeant had been publicly rebuked, and little he could do about it!

Two policemen escorted Bartley out of the premises. He was unable to speak with the fright of the gun being discharged, not to mention the unexpected response to his dream that now lay in tatters. A deflated Sergeant Cosgrave followed, realising that his handling of the matter had been out of order. Locking Bartley in a cell, where he pleaded pitifully for mercy, the Sergeant assured him that he would have plenty of time to explain it all to Judge Fossett when he arrived.

"And when will that be?" he asked, unable to control the quivering of fear in his voice.

"Next week," the Sergeant replied, "and until then you are a guest of the government. Tell me this," he continued, "now that I think of it. Didn't you get into trouble in the last place you worked for stealing Holly or whatever it was from Lord Foldsworth? I think I heard something about that, did I not?"

He fingered his moustache as he looked at Bartley.

"Oh, a little sprig of holly was all I took, and he banished me from the place, so he did." Bartley's voice had become a plaintive cry.

"Well, stealing is a criminal offence. You better hope and pray that the Judge has heard nothing of it, or that will be the end of you my man!" The Sergeant was in no mood for mercy, and Bartley a sitting target. He walked away, pulling a second door closed, and left Bartley in total fear and a dreadful sense of isolation.

By dinnertime, business at the 'Bull's Nose' had resumed, and the news of the assault on Marjorie was on everybody's lips. Many came into the tavern just to see how she was.

"Very well, thanks," was her stern reply. Then, in her usual cheery manner, "and how are you?"

Upset though she still was, she had managed to get rid of Bartley Finnegan!! 'God works in mysterious ways', she thought, not unamused.

* * *

The village was quiet in the afternoon. Nell and May took their children walking through the fields to visit Mag. Their absence provided the opportunity for Joe and James to load the pikes. The straw padding in place, they piled potatoes over the cache and made sure all was secure. Satisfied that the concealment was flawless, they yoked up the horses and left the village in their usual quiet way. The late afternoon sun was warm on their faces, and a gentle breeze arose. Despite the gravity of their conversation of the previous night, both men were in good form.

"About last night, Joe," James began, feeling the need to talk about the matter, " I'm grateful for the way you had the courage to talk about Kitty and myself, and for respecting my feelings for her."

"That's alright James," Joe replied. "You know the danger you are in. It's up to you to be cautious."

Joe drove the horses forward and both men were silent for a while, each thinking what would happen if the relationship ever came to light.

"She's in Dublin Castle tonight for the Ball. She'll be back tomorrow night, as far as I know," James said, smiling happily at the thought.

Joe made no reply. He felt too awkward about the whole affair and had no desire to even discuss it.

"Well James, all that is your business and I'd prefer to remain ignorant of what you both do, or where you go. I am far too uneasy as it is! I'd be glad if you'd remember that. No offence meant. I'm just telling you the truth." He looked at James with a wrinkled brow that expressed his anxiety better than any words.

"Alright Joe, I'll discuss it no more. What time do you think the meeting will be at?"

"I suppose it will be ten o'clock, or soon after. Depending on what time Marjorie can clear the house at. You know well yourself how slow a job that can be sometimes," Joe replied good-humouredly.

James looked at the dark clouds that were gathering on the horizon to the east.

"What do you think of those gathering?" he asked Joe, pointing.

"The wind has gone east this two hours or more, and it has gone a bit cooler.

Little point in worrying about the weather at this stage. As long as we get these pikes as far as Marjorie's coach house, I don't mind."

Gaining sight of the town, Joe's anxiety increased. The main street was busy with people coming and going, having spent the day visiting friends and relatives. Joe drove the horses gently forward, and sighed with relief as the 'Bull's Nose' came into view.

"We're nearly there and I won't be sorry," Joe said tensely.

Looking to the side, James noticed Sergeant Cosgrave walking close to them.

"We have the law, Joe. Just beside us. And he is looking at the cart as if it was a new invention or something," James said out of the side of his mouth, trying to remain casual.

Joe continued whistling a tune that had no particular air.

"You pair are very busy today, are you not?" The voice of the Sergeant sounded in their ears like the roar from a cannon.

"Well Sergeant, you can't stop people from eating, and as this is the only free day I have, I decided to make use of it and deliver the potatoes," Joe answered.

The Sergeant continued to walk beside them.

"Where are you delivering to?" he asked them in a toneless voice.

"We're on our way to the 'Bull's Nose' with them Sergeant."

He looked directly at him as he answered. 'An upstart in uniform', he thought, with carefully concealed dislike.

"Is there a law Sergeant about delivering potatoes on a rest day?" James asked, deciding to challenge him.

The Sergeant did not like to be questioned.

"Mind your tongue, young man, or I'll take you to the station for interfering with the law," he replied icily.

They had reached the side entrance of the tavern, and Marjorie herself appeared out of the door. Summing up the situation rapidly, she strode forward.

"Back again Sergeant Cosgrave? Is there further trouble, or can I interest you in buying some of the potatoes from my load?" Turning from the Sergeant she looked up at the men on the cart and winked an eye at them. "God bless the pair of ye for taking the trouble of coming this day. Believe it or not, I have hardly a decent potato left in the place."

As they entered the old courtyard, Marjorie stood at the gate and looked at Sergeant Cosgrave.

"Isn't it great Sergeant to see conscientious people left? And that reminds me! I hope you have that criminal behind bars since the episode this morning. Just imagine what Judge Fossett would say if the likes of that villain was on the loose again!"

The reminder to where his duty lay did not go amiss on the Sergeant, and as Marjorie heaved the heavy doors closed, he turned and walked away without comment. As the great doors slammed behind Marjorie, she put her back against them and sighed with relief.

"Thank God that lad is out of the way," she said, as she looked at the anxious faces of both men in front of her.

"You're not half as glad as I am Marjorie. And glad this is the last load I'll be doing!" Joe replied as he backed the cart into the coach house. "James, hold the team 'til I get down, and Marjorie, you go back inside just in case that fellow decides he wants to interfere any more!"

Joe found he was perspiring, despite the cool evening air. When the cart was safely inside, James unhitched the horses and brought them to the stables. Locking the coach house securely, both men went into the tavern. They were glad to sit and relax in the atmosphere of revellery.

"I don't see any sign of Bartley, James. It's hardly likely that he has the evening off, being so busy and all," Joe remarked as he looked around the packed tavern.

"Marjorie may have him in the cellar getting kegs or something or other," James replied casually.

His mind was on Kitty as he imagined her dancing under the blaze of chandeliers at Dublin Castle. He wished for the hundredth time that he could, by magic, be a part of that world. Sometimes he would allow his imagination to wander, and visualise himself as a young and prosperous landlord, owner of a vast and well run estate, a palatial home, and inviting Kitty to dine with him. Then to hold her close to him before a blazing fire, asking her to marry him and...

"You look as if you're in a trance James. If I didn't know you better, I'd say you were in love." The voice of Marjorie entered his mind as though through a thick haze.

"And maybe I am," he replied, irritated at having to remove himself from his fantasy.

Marjorie raised an eyebrow in surprise, and looked at Joe to try and discern if perhaps her words of jest might indeed contain some grain of truth. The blacksmith's eyes avoided hers. He stared into the fire instead, and his silence spoke louder to her than any words might have. She prodded Joe jokingly under the arm.

"Hmm, you're a mine of information too, sitting there lost in yourself. Drink up that whiskey, and maybe it will jolt a bit of sense back into the two of you." She walked away through her customers, with a jovial word to all whom she knew there.

"A very sharp woman, Marjorie. Able to read anyone like a book," Joe said, looking at his companion.

James swirled the gold liquid around the side of his glass.

"She is indeed, Joe, I'll grant her that. I hope she will be as sharp tonight for the meeting. Do you know something," James continued, "that Tim Flanagan, Joe. I don't like him. Something about the fellow... can't quite figure it out... " James wished he could express what he felt, but words failed him.

Marjorie returned and sat down beside them.

"God, I'd give anything to shift this lot out of here early. I feel worn to the bones lads." She looked at the faces of her customers and sighed wearily. "I suppose 'tis not often they have reason to celebrate, to have a bit of a laugh and get away from the grind of life. Poor devils. Anyhow, isn't it a night to be happy," and she smiled more contentedly.

"Marjorie, I meant to ask you earlier. Where have you put Bartley for the night?" James asked.

"Well! Don't tell me you haven't heard? I thought the whole country knew about it by now." She was genuinely surprised.

"Heard what?" Joe asked, taking the pipe from his mouth and tipping it against the heel of his boot.

"Oh indeed. Didn't he arrive in here this morning in a trance? That's the only way to describe him. He began bowing to me, and sweeping the ground with his hat, and it was all 'Margaret this' and Margaret that', and full up of the strangest notions. Then out it all comes... 'Will you marry me Margaret', says he... now where did he get that notion from, I ask you?"

Both men rocked with laughter until the tears came from their eyes.

"I fail to see the humour in it," she said, getting embarrassed. "Indeed, it didn't end there either, I'm afraid."

She knew that sooner or later they would hear of the subsequent event, so better to tell it all herself. The more she spoke, however, the more it seemed to add to the hilarity for them both. She stood up disgusted.

"Mmm, indeed, the pair of ye and ye enjoying it all. Hmm, should have expected it from the two of you. And not a mention of what could have happened to me."

She walked briskly away, thoroughly disgusted with them both. 'A pair of ganders', she said to herself. 'A little sip of whiskey and it goes to their heads. Oh, where are the men who could hold their drink and feel sorry for the plight of a woman'. She proceeded to collect empty glasses in preparation for closing the tavern. 'Still no sign of the rest of the group', she thought, hoping nothing had happened to them. She looked over at Joe and James in mock disdain, and noted with amusement their awkward glances towards her. She loved them both in a simple sort of way, she thought.

"I wonder what Marjorie would say if I told her about Kitty, Joe?"

There was a sudden change of expression on his friends face.

"Wouldn't advise it James. The less people who know the better is my feeling on it all."

"Do you have any idea what it's like loving someone against such odds, Joe? It's bad enough her being one of the ascendancy, but to have to never speak of it is so hard to bear."

Prodding the fire with a long poker, Joe continued as though he hadn't noticed the obvious pain in James' voice.

"I have told you before, James, and this is the last time I will say it to you. This... courtship. It's not the girl in question as such. I know she is a lovely lass, and granted, is different from the rest of them. But in all reality, it's not, well... not workable, is it James? Look at you tonight, for talk sake. Here you are drinking with the local blacksmith in a smoky noisy tavern, and the girl you say you love so much is in Dublin Castle with the Viceroy, Earl Camden, and all those who serve. Those who are unflinchingly loyal to the government! You, on the other hand, are going to a meeting soon, a meeting about plans to revolt against all they stand for... " Joe became quite exasperated, and rubbed his hair with his right hand, a gesture that always spoke of his agitation in a situation.

"There's no point in talking about all this, is there Joe? No one understands, and I'll have to continue to dream that it's possible someway or other. Is it so wrong to dream? Being a nobody, Joe, doesn't mean I can't dream of a better life, does it?" His voice trailed away when he realised that Joe was unable to fathom the depth of his feelings.

Over at the door a great fuss arose, and a hum of talk rippled through the crowd. Marjorie came running over to them, very excited.

"You'll never guess who's coming in here now," she gasped, hardly able to contain her excitement.

She hurriedly tried to tidy her hair, looking towards the door anxiously.

"Who Marjorie? Is it the King himself."

"Well, you are not too far wrong. It's Lord Foldsworth and his daughter. Now, behave like gentlemen. I'll have to seat them over here beside the two of you at the fire."

She proceeded to dust two chairs and the small table until they gleamed. The fire glowed warmly, and looked very inviting indeed. James was dumbfounded.

"What on earth are they doing here?" he asked, feeling his mouth going dry.

He peered over the heads of the crowded tavern. He saw Kitty first, and her father standing behind her. Marjorie was walking briskly towards them.

"Goodnight, your Lordship, and Lady Catherine. Please come this way."

Marjorie walked ahead of them through the crowd, who made way for them. James began to think he was dreaming.

Lord Foldsworth opened his dark brown cloak and stood before the fire rubbing his hands vigorously and sneezing frequently. Kitty stared at James, overcome at seeing him there. They nodded briefly at each other, careful not to allow her father notice the glances of familiarity. Joe noticed instantly, and it added to his discomfort.

"Now father, you must have a warm drink while we are here." She looked at Marjorie directly. "Landlady, may we have two hot whiskey punches please, and is there any way we could have the carriage fixed, even temporarily, do you think?"

Marjorie looked at the beautiful young lady before her, and the lovely face, with glittering eyes that seemed so clear and innocent. Joe stood up, knowing he could help.

"If you wish my Lady I well look and see what the difficulty may be." For the first time he too realised how beautiful she actually was.

Lord Foldsworth looked around suddenly from the fire where he had been engrossed trying to heat himself.

"Why Gilltrap, it's you! What splendid good fortune to find you here. Yes, it would be very good of you to have a look at the carriage for us. It's the left back wheel come loose, I'm afraid. I had to leave Dublin with this dreadful cold you see, and here we find ourselves!"

There was no doubt he looked very unwell. The deep cough seemed to rattle his chest. Kitty was very concerned, and wished for her father's sake that they were home and he in a warm bed, before he got pneumonia. He had already collapsed twice while they were in Dublin, which is why she had insisted on their immediate return to Oak Hall. She was grateful they had reached the town before the carriage had broken down under them.

Marjorie returned with the steaming whiskey, and Lord Foldsworth took a seat.

"Thank you, madam," he said, looking at Marjorie, who nodded her head and smiled.

"You are welcome sir, and I am sure we will be able to have the carriage fixed for you in no time at all."

Looking over at James she noted the expression of sheer delight at the esteemed company he now found himself in, and she also noticed the warm glances he seemed to be directing at Lady Catherine. Or was it her imagination?

"James, can I get you another drink?" she asked, as though to break a spell.

"No thank you, Marjorie," he replied, "I have not yet finished my ale."

Lord Foldsworth turned from the fire and looked at James.

"Yes," he said, "I thought I had met you before... that voice... now where was it? Let me see?" With knitted brows, he tried to remember.

"Yes, Lord Foldsworth, you have indeed met me before. At Oak Hall with Joe Gilltrap, if you recall?" James was trying desperately to maintain a relaxed attitude.

"Ah yes, now I remember... we met in relation to that nasty eviction affair... what was his name... Hennessy. Yes indeed... "

He was then seized by a coughing bout, and his hands trembled as he raised the glass to his lips. The rasping pain seemed to tear through his chest before it would subside.

"Father, are you alright?" Kitty's concern was mounting as she noticed the beads of perspiration on her father's forehead and face.

"Yes, my dear. It's just a nasty cold, that's all. And how are you? Can you forgive me for making such a faux pas of your ball? I am really sorry Kitty. It is old, I fear, I am getting!" He smiled at her weakly.

"Nonsense, father. It was only a Ball I missed. Besides, your health is far more important, and Mamma will be so surprised to see you back!" Kitty looked fleetingly at James, who was fascinated by the easy relationship she shared with her father.

"Your Ladyship," he interrupted, "I'm afraid you have an uninvited spark on your cloak."

James reached out and took the hem of her cloak between his fingers, then shook it vigorously until the spark fell away.

"Oh, thank you, eh... I hadn't noticed it... thank you." Kitty's voice sounded unfamiliar to James.

Lord Foldsworth laughed.

"You know, you aunt Lady Annabel firmly believed that such things were a sign of good fortune!"

Kitty smiled. It was good to see his sense of humour emerge. It helped to ease her mounting tension. James, relaxing more, wished that he could just stand up and speak to Lord Foldsworth about his love and devotion to Kitty. 'What would his reaction be, I wonder... possibly empty the remains of his glass into my face', he thought. 'Madness", he said to himself, 'nothing but pure madness'.

Joe meanwhile fixed the loose wheel, and instructed the coachman to drive slowly back to Oak Hall. Returning to the warmth of the tavern, he resumed his seat opposite Lord Foldsworth.

"Well, your Lordship, the coach will bring you home safely. It would be wise to have it seen to as soon as possible, as the wheel pin is wearing down very quickly."

Marjorie walked over with two more glasses of punch for her unexpected guests.

"How very kind of you, Landlady. This is too good of you altogether," Kitty said, handing one of the steaming glasses to her father.

"Don't mention it, your Ladyship," Marjorie said proudly, "It's on the house." She was thrilled with the impromptu visit of the 'quality', as she termed it.

"On what house?" asked Kitty, puzzled.

James laughed at the bewildered look on Kitty's face.

"If you don't mind, your Ladyship, my interrupting... but it's an expression we use when a drink is a gift from the Landlady to her visitors!" James looked unflinchingly into Kitty's eyes.

Marjorie noticed instantly the way they both looked at each other, and again a curious suspicion began to form in her mind. 'Could it be... could it be remotely possible?'? she wondered, half fearing the truth emerging in her mind. The familiarity developing made Lord Foldsworth uneasy, and he moved restlessly in his seat. Joe sensed the tension, and fumbled in his pocket for his pipe.

"Well Kitty, I believe it is time we were on our way," He stood up and fastened the buckle on his cloak, waiting for his daughter to do likewise. "Our grateful thanks to you all for your help and kindness tonight."

Joe and James stood up as their landlord prepared to leave. He looked at them in their simplicity and kindness. Leaving adequate payment on the small table, he stepped forward, bidding all 'goodnight'. Kitty smiled, and turned to follow her father.

Marjorie turned to James and smiled.

"Your eyes certainly have sparks in them tonight, or do I imagine things?" she asked him.

"That could be the case Marjorie, and why not?" he replied, half in jest.

She did not answer him, but looked at Joe, whose expression said even less! 'There'll be no straight answers out of those two', she thought, and went back to work.

Tim Flanagan was the first to arrive for the meeting, and he walked directly over to Marjorie who hadn't noticed him come in. He looked at her across the bar with anger in his face.

"What was that bastard doing in here? Well?" he asked her, his voice filled with contempt.

"Who are you talking about?" she asked, taken aback by the sudden onslaught.

"Bloody Foldsworth, who else? What next!" he exclaimed, "It's a wonder you didn't invite him to come to the meeting." Then he walked away, muttering, "Bloody women as usual... "

Marjorie took off her apron, folded it, and placed it beneath the counter. She followed Tim over to the table where he had sat down with Father Michael, Joe and James.

"Marjorie, it's good to see you... " Father Michael began pleasantly. He was a well-built man with an open face and a subtle strength that defied description.

"Father, I will speak to you in a moment. I need to talk to someone else just now." She turned to Tim Flanagan, who was sat poking idly at the fire. Tapping him on the back with her finger, she got his attention. "Tim Flanagan, if you ever come in here again and tell me who should or should not be in my tavern, I will ban you forever from this place. I simply will not have it. Do you understand? Furthermore, you should realise that it's from the local militia that I get my information for this cause, which we are supposed to be meeting about. Remember it's me, and me alone, who decides who comes under this roof, and that includes you also! Now, do you understand?"

Tim looked at the three men present. All appeared to support the mistress of the house.

"Well, now you listen to me Marjorie Bass. It's only the rebellion I am interested in, and that alone. There is no way I'll take that sort of guff from any woman, tavern or no tavern. Rebellion is all that keeps me here, and that's final." He stood up and walked to the bar abruptly.

Joe looked at the ceiling.

"Give him a bit of time and he'll cool off. Always a bit hot in the head, poor Tim," he said resignedly.

"What in heaven's name, Marjorie, was that all about?" Father Michael asked, perplexed by it all.

"Oh, just that he stormed over to me and asked why Lord Foldsworth was allowed into the place. Their carriage had broken down, Father. Joe here fixed it for them. Nothing more or nothing less," Marjorie explained, her annoyance abating.

"Well, that's quite proper Marjorie, is it not? It is a public meeting place. I think that poor Tim gets very heated, with personal vendetta a priority." A troubled shadow covered his countenance.

James suddenly spoke, breaking his long silence.

"We would be better off without that fellow. I just don't trust him, and it's a mistake having him at these meetings at all. Or am I alone in these thoughts?" He looked at Joe and then at Father Michael. Father Michael spoke first.

"Pray God you are wrong, young man, otherwise none of us will see the summer, let alone the Rebellion." He sighed deeply. Then, looking at Joe, asked him his feelings on the matter.

"Well father, there are times when I do think there might be something in what James says. But there is little we can do if he proves treacherous. He knows our meeting places, our men, and our arms; who makes them and where they are hidden. He does not know the dates that will be suggested tonight, no more than I do. He could be waiting for that information before he goes to the authorities."

There was silence between them.

"But why, then, is he so against the ascendancy? Or is it a cover-up he uses? It's hard indeed to fathom him," Father Michael added.

Marjorie knew that they had to consider all aspects of their suspicion carefully.

"All we can do is be vigilant with Tim Flanagan, and if we get the slightest reason or evidence of betrayal, his future will have to be considered, and that's that," James said firmly.

Marjorie felt uneasy about what this 'future' could be. Surely not to kill him, she hoped. Being of a direct nature, she asked.

"Would killing him be part of the plan, Father?"

"Lord no, Marjorie," Father Michael replied firmly, "we could send him to France to arrange an arms shipment. Have him detained there. That would solve our problem, should the need arise. In a decent way. Perhaps a lot more decent than what he may have in mind for us! Anyway, there will be enough death without us adding to it. But, let's hope and pray that we are all indeed jumping to conclusions, and none of this dreadful suspicion is true. It is, after all, only a sense of uneasiness we are talking about. There is nothing to support it as yet. Nonetheless, there is no harm in being vigilant. Now, Marjorie, when I mentioned France a thought occurred to me."

"And what would that be, Father?" she asked.

"Some of their Brandy, if possible," he replied, laughing.

"Well, I'll have to hand it to you, Father," said James, laughing with him, "you can't beat keeping the mind on matters of the here and now!"

"James, it is always important not to let things get out of hand with anxiety. This rebellion will be the first great effort by the people to free themselves, and if we, as their leaders, can't find it among ourselves to keep a united front, how can we ever hope to direct them?"

"Father, that is wise thinking, but it is important for us also to keep in mind that unity within the leadership is based on trust. I still maintain that vigilance with Tim Flanagan must be maintained." James was adamant that his suspicions were kept in mind.

The remainder of the group were unusually late, and James expressed his irritation.

"What in the name of heaven is keeping them? Let's hope nothing has happened," he said, looking at the dwindling crowd.

Tim walked over to them with the brandy Marjorie had poured for them.

"Now men, here we are. Help yourselves. Good brandy that Father, by the looks of it. Mind you, I wouldn't say no to some food though. I didn't have time to eat much before I cam here. It makes a man irritable, so it does, and we don't want that now, do we?"

It was Tim's way of trying to excuse his poor form earlier in the evening, James thought.

"We all get like that from time to time, Tim," Joe said, trying to rid the atmosphere of all bad feeling before the meeting began.

He knew that the bottle of Brandy was Marjorie's way of trying to restore calm. They toasted the feast day and sat back in a more gentle and relaxed atmosphere. Joe told them of Marjorie's earlier encounter with Bartley, and the subsequent fracas. It somehow became funnier in the telling, and they roared with innocent laughter.

"Great to see men in good form."

They looked up to see Marcus standing there, taking off his cloak and shaking the fine mist from it. He sat down beside James, and then Joe poured him a drink.

"Here you are Marcus, down this and get the fog out of your lungs!"

"I'll be singing at this meeting tonight lads," Marcus replied, and joined in the festive mood.

Father Michael looked over to the door to see the remainder of the men coming in.

"Finally, here they come, and good to see them."

They made room for them around the fire. They all sat together exchanging small talk, and eventually the mood of the men settled as they realised that they were the last occupants of the tavern. Those who had left before them were too merry to notice anything odd about the group who sat at the fire.

Marjorie closed the large oaken door, and placed the iron bar across the centre of it. Going to each window, she closed the shutters, and then dimmed the lamps one by one, quenching those that were not necessary. The fire threw a warm glow, as it hungrily gripped the firewood with flames that seemed to play with the air around them. It cast long shadows on the walls too, of the men who sat around it, and lit their faces. Faces that reflected determination in preparing a people to strike for their freedom. Being together gave them a sense of unity, strength and hope. They discussed the numbers of pikes in storage, and those still to be collected. It was a considerable amount. Father Michael spoke firmly for the need for great care to be taken in their activities generally in order not to arouse suspicion. They all knew only too well that a life was cheap to some. Money bought all information, they realised.

James admired Father Michael. He was one of the few priests, he thought, that do not pander to the authorities. A man that saw and lived with the pain of his people, and was determined to change it.

Marjorie settled down at the meeting, glad that all her customers had finally left. She felt tired and exhausted. Flashes of the events of the early morning with Bartley flitted through her mind. She tried unsuccessfully to concentrate on Father Michael's words, but was unable to. 'Maybe I should have a chat with him later', she pondered. Having decided to do so, the troublesome memories were dispelled.

Joe felt on edge as he listened to the priest. He had decided that he would finally state that he would not be making any more pikes. Somehow, in front of all the men, he found himself reluctant. However, he was jolted into reality quickly by the voice of the priest addressing him.

"Joe, how many more pikes do you think you can supply? Could you manage two or three hundred more do you think?"

Joe looked at the group and rubbed his hands together, aware that he was sweating. He looked at Father Michael directly.

"Well Father, I am glad you've raised the matter," said Joe, clearing his throat. "You see, Father, I've decided to stop making them for the time being. I am a bit uneasy about events around the village lately."

He proceeded to outline the recent events, beginning with the eviction of May Ryan and the death of Jerome Hennessy. Then from the incident of the axle on Lord Foldsworths carriage to the exile of Bartley Finnegan. Everyone listened intently and with respect. They knew that the blacksmith was a man of courage, but also a man of wisdom.

"I see," replied Father Michael pensively. "I can see your concern, Joe, and I know you have a wife and a young family to think of. Yes, there seems to be tension around the village. While I know that Lord Foldsworth is by present standards a good landlord, he is nevertheless a vigilant one. He seldom if ever misses a meeting at Dublin Castle, so he has been well warned to be on the lookout for signs of the movement. Hmm, I think given the circumstances, perhaps you are wise to cease making pikes, for the present at least. Maybe if things settle down again you will continue for us Joe," he concluded.

"Yes Father, to be sure I will, but for now 'tis better I leave them be."

Joe was very relieved at the priest's decision. Tim Flanagan looked at Joe through narrowing eyes, and James noticed. He tried to read the expression but was unable to. It left him with a feeling of greater unease. Marcus looked at Marjorie, who seemed ready to give her information. Instead, she left the meeting mumbling about making some tea for them all. Father Michael noticed her silence.

"Is Marjorie unwell?" he asked anxiously.

"No Father. It's that unpleasant experience she had this morning with Bartley Finnegan." James continued to outline what had happened earlier that morning, with the eventual arrival of Sergeant Cosgrave and Marjorie's abrupt dismissal of him. Nobody was laughing this time, their concern for Marjorie paramount.

"She was bloody right," Tim Flanagan said, pounding the table, "the poor woman... God knows that lad should be put in place by someone." He was referring to the Sergeant.

The priest looked at him alarmed.

"No Tim... Marjorie can't afford, in more ways than one, to lose the trust of the local police. After all, look what information she gleans from them while they drink here!"

It made sound sense, and Tim's thoughtless intolerance of people became clearer. Marjorie walked in through the door carrying a tray laden with meat sandwiches and tea.

"God leave you your health Marjorie," said Joe, as he made way for her to get to a side table, where she placed the heavy tray with a sigh.

"Marjorie, I am sorry to hear of what happened to you this morning. The man is clearly out of his mind, and you're fortunate to be rid of him. So don't fret anymore about it."

The priest placed his hand on her arm. Tears filled Marjorie's eyes.

"Thank you Father. You will never know what a comfort it is to hear those words." Taking a handkerchief from her pocket, she dried her eyes. "And now, like good men, eat up those sandwiches."

She poured out the tea. The priest drank his slowly, pondering deeply. Eventually he spoke to the silent men who were busy eating.

"This time next year men, we will be within weeks of our bid for freedom. By then our stocks of arms will be ready. Furthermore, I have learned that the French are willing to aid our cause and they will send ships and men-at-arms to Ireland's rescue. Let us continue to hope and pray that all will go according to plan, and do all in our power to see that it does."

The men were dumbfounded. James spoke first.

"French ships... soldiers... why that's more than we ever hoped for... dreamed of. It's just... well; it's just such a surprise. With such support how could we possibly lose?"

The priest looked at them all, so young and so full of trust and courage.

"Well men, I can't say where they will land around the coast... not just yet, because there are a number of possible sites. But we must wait for the French Generals to decide all that. They are very skilled in the art of war, on land and on sea, so the decision will be up to them. But they know our plans and will therefore select the best vantage points. On that note, I think it best we disband before it gets too late. Our horses could attract attention at this late hour, so we will leave two-by-two. It would be safest. Marcus, we will leave first, if that's all right with you?"

Not waiting for an answer, he stood up and put on his black cloak. Everyone was disappointed the meeting ended so suddenly. James' mind raced with a thousand questions still unanswered. The air was full of excitement and awe. Marjorie thought of the dashing French Generals in blue uniforms and felt palpitations with the excitement of it. Marcus reluctantly stood up, anxious to know more.

"When is our next meeting, Father?" he asked, trying hard to conceal his curiosity.

"I will let you know, Marcus, and then you can tell the rest of the group here. But for now, remain alert and vigilant for changes, and above all... no loose talk of any type. Marjorie, I will be relying on you as usual to keep the upper circle informed of any developments and anything you hear from the barracks. God bless you all!"

Suddenly, he was gone. Marcus bid all goodnight and followed the priest into the cold dark night. The slow walk of their horses clopped over the cobblestones in the rear courtyard and faded away. The remainder of the group sat by the dying fire in silence. Somewhere a dog barked.

"Well, well," Joe said, as he again took out his pipe and methodically cleaned out the bowl of it, to fill it once again.

"Indeed," said Tim Flanagan, "I hope these Frenchmen are all they are cocked up to be, that's all I'll say on the matter. Now, I have to go ahead on my own as the rest of you live in the other direction. I'll see you all again, and thanks for the supper, Marjorie."

He left then, muttering to himself. As they heard his horse leave the yard, Marjorie looked across at James.

"I know James, I know! Is her ever satisfied, I ask myself?" she chuckled good-naturedly.

"No Marjorie," James replied, as he sat back in his chair. "My question is, Marjorie, can he be trusted? The priest is no fool either, the way he refused to say where the French armies would land. He knows the full details to be sure but he is waiting for Flanagan to show his true colours."

They all sensed the truth in this.

"What will really happen to him James if he is found to be leaking information to the authorities?" Marjorie asked, and sat back waiting for an answer.

"He'll be silenced, Marjorie... silenced. Never to talk again," Joe replied, holding his pipe in his hand.

Marjorie paled; realising a 'holiday' in France was probably only priest's talk.

"But let's hope," Joe continued, "let's just hope for all our sakes that we are wrong about him."

Slowly the group dispersed. As James and Joe stood in the cold night wind, Marjorie held the lantern in readiness to bolt the big gate after they had departed.

"Marjorie, will you be alright tonight? You aren't nervous about Bartley Finnegan are you?" Joe asked her with concern.

"Not a bit, Joe. Where he is tonight there is little fear of him roving abroad. If Judge Fossett sets him free, that will be time enough to worry. I sincerely hope he won't." Her expression was one of tiredness rather than worry. "Who knows," she added reflectively, "someday I may have a dashing French General to mind me here for the rest of my days, calling me Madam Marguerite," and she curtseyed with the lantern in hand and laughed merrily.

Both men laughed with her. They parted on this happy note, with Marjorie sending the bolt on the double gates home firmly.

"Safe home lads," she called softly, and was gone.

They rode through the town slowly. Their horses, fresh from being rested, were anxious to go faster, the chill wind making them restless. Dim lights shone through the windows of some of the low thatched cottages, and as they came to the outskirts of the town, they began to canter the horses steadily without conversation. They were aware that even in the ditches there could be some who were sleeping from the effects of too much beer. Prudence was in order, James thought, and while darkness hid their faces, voices could be recognised. As the dim lights of the town faded behind them a half moon rose in the east and cast shadows on the road before them. It seemed less cold, now that the blood of man and horse began to beat. A lone owl flew across their path, intent on hunting its prey. The blacksmith yawned, his breath steamy on the cold frosty air.

"God, I'll sleep tonight James," he said wearily, "I'm as tired as an old dog."

"Well, it has been a long hard day, you know, and it is well past two o'clock in the morning. Why wouldn't a man be tired?" James remarked, then added dreamily, "and to think of French ships coming to our aid! The greatest thing I have ever heard or even dreamed of. Can you just imagine it all? I wonder will they land on the Wexford coast or where do you think it will be?"

Joe looked at the vision James had placed before his eyes.

"I doubt it," he replied, "or for that matter anywhere on the east coast. It would mean that they would have to come up through the channel, and if I know anything, French Generals won't take the risk of being hemmed in. No James. The south or west coasts would make more sense. For that matter, it could even be the north coast," he said, with an air of knowledge on the matter.

"You know, Joe, I have never seen the north or western coastline of this country of ours. Have you?"

"No. The furthest I have been south was to Cork and west was to Roscommon, and, I might add, I'd have no desire to march on Dublin from either place!" He laughed at the idea of it.

They rode quietly into the village which lay sleeping in the foothills. Even the dogs slept. The only sound greeting them was the noise of the river as it ran under the bridge, the twin arches that divided it being the only obstacle as it trundled from the mountain slopes.

"Will you come in for tea James, or something to heat your heart before you go home?" Joe whispered as he dismounted from his horse quietly.

"No thanks, Joe. I'll go on ahead and try to get to bed. I have another half-hours ride still ahead of me, and the morrow is not far off. Goodnight Joe."

"Good luck and safe home James," Joe replied, but James had already gone quietly into the night, while the moon began her descent over the rims of the mountains.

Joe thought of Lady Catherine's visit into Marjorie's. No doubt she was a lovely lady. He found himself wondering how she might feel about James. He had little to offer her in terms of money or property. She must really be fond of him. Love, I suppose, he mused, and for the first time ever he found it in his heart to wish them well.

Yet what future was in it, love or no love? He brushed down his horse, and then gave it a generous feed of oats. Where could they go or where would they live? Question upon question came to mind in relation to James and Kitty until he had to stop trying to imagine it at all. He yawned again, went quietly into the house and made himself some hot punch. The children slept cosily. He heard Nell moving quietly in the upper room on her way down to see him.

"Where did you get to, Joe, and it almost time to be up lighting the breakfast fire?" she asked sleepily.

"Marjorie had a terrible tale of woe to tell us, Nell, about what happened there to her this morn," Joe offered by way of explanation for his late arrival home.

Nell sat down opposite him.

"Well, what happened Joe, or do I have to coax it out of you or what?" Nell asked, becoming a little irritable.

Joe marvelled how women never tired of talking no matter what the hour of the day or night it was. He related the tale to her as he had heard it, and by the time he was finished Nell was awake and wide-eyed. She was shocked by Marjorie's ordeal.

"Well God help poor Marjorie... and I always said that Bartley Finnegan was never right in the mind. Wasn't it the luck of life that no harm came to her Joe? I hope Judge Fossett gives him his deserved punishment, and that will cool his heels. The nerve of him to think he could ever be a match for Marjorie, not to think of her fate had she been foolish enough to weaken to his proposal, like some women might!" she declared, thinking how she herself had suffered at the hands of her cruel stepfather.

She shuddered at the memories that emerged from the depths of her past when she least expected them to. Joe sensed her unease.

"Well, Nell... what is worrying you now? You may as well tell me."

"Ah, 'tis just some of my own memories from the early days at home, Joe, with my stepfather, and how he treated me. I have forgiven my mother for the way she never defended me. I supposed she was just afraid that he would walk out and leave her with the seven of us. Then, she never got over the way he died at the Mill, when the big wheel caught him. He died as violently as he lived, poor soul. Yet she really loved him, Joe. Strange, isn't it... love, when you think of it? The surprise you get with some couples," she concluded, as she stared into the soft glow of the lamp that seemed to fill the room with peace.

Joe looked at her big round eyes, which he loved, and her hair, which fell loosely about her shoulders. Thinking of what she had just said, he couldn't help but think of James and Kitty. What better example could there be of two such people? He wondered should he tell her. He would love to, but thought it better to leave it for another time. He wanted to reach his own conclusions first. But was not all love good, despite faith, position or class? Was it not all much bigger than that?

"Let's go to bed, Nell. 'Tis time we slept."

Silently they left the room, taking the lamp with them. They slept deeply as the dawn sent shafts of light and turned the mountains crimson. The great black ravens rose and wheeled in circles above the great circle of stones, celebrating life once again. They eyed the sleepy village from their lofty heights, only to plummet earthwards in their elaborate courtship display.

James slept fitfully, dreaming of great sailing ships, storm-tossed on the deep blue ocean. He saw himself standing alone on the sand dunes with a lantern in his hand, beckoning. Somehow they didn't seem to notice him. 'Why? Why? Why?' he screamed, and woke up sweating.

Chapter seven

Oak Hall was a hum of activity. It was the last hunt of the season. Soon the land would be sown and the crops sprouting. It had always been that way from time immemorial. Lord Foldsworth viewed the great fields that lay ploughe across the west side of the estate. He could hear the guests that filled the house, on their way to the dining room for breakfast. Their voices were full of excitement for the days hunting awaiting them. Some would eat heartily, others not.

He smiled to himself. People are similar to horses that way, he thought. Some very calm and some extremely excitable. Still, the mixture made the blend of a great day ahead. He was thrilled that Lady Edwina had finally decided to join him on the field for the last meet of the season. The sky was clear and blue, though the mists on the turquoise horizon still waited for the sun to rise above it and burn it away; to dispel the glittering white frost in a glistening death.

From the stables came the shrill neighing of some of the hunters, who were highly excited as they sensed the days hunting ahead. They would eat their oats and mash eagerly. Foxhounds barked hungrily, eager also to scent the earth for their prey, running ahead of thundering hooves.

The dining room was full of people, who greeted their host cheerily. Lord Foldsworth looked at the happy faces of his many friends: -

Lord Atherby, now in his eightieth year. Lively and eating heartily. He boasted never having missed a hunt since he was eighteen years old. His wife, Constance, five years his junior, sat beside him laughing shrilly at some comment he had made; Lady Julia Fairbrass and her two daughters sat opposite him. Judy, as her friends called her, never missed an opportunity to display her two daughters, ever hopeful of marrying them off to land and money; The Earl of Ashton sat a safe distance from them, talking about some Inn he had stopped over at in Meath where he had eaten some venison which simply melted on the tongue. Lady Julia found him enthralling, irrespective of his topic, and in her widowhood fantasised about him to a great extent. He, however, seemed quite oblivious to her rapt attentions.

Viscount Stewart, or Timothy, as his friends knew him, found Lord Atherby's boasting too much to cope with at such an early hour of the day, and decided to turn his attention to Lady Joanna Winters, who had come once again unaccompanied. He recalled that rumour had it that she was very unhappy with her husband, Samuel, who preferred dogs and horses! He seemed quite unconcerned where his wife went or to whom she gave her attentions. She was beautiful, Viscount Stewart thought, her simplicity so appealing. Her black ringlets framed a face of great beauty. She looked over at him directly, their eyes meeting.

"Well Timothy, are you ready for the day ahead?" she asked him, gazing steadily into his green unblinking eyes.

"Without question, Joanna, and I truly believe we are all going to have an exhilarating days sport. It must be some months now since we last hunted together, is it not?" he asked.

"Indeed yes. It was the second meet in November. I remember it well," she answered assuredly.

"Why, you truly have a splendid memory," he commented in admiration.

"Well, I should think I would remember, Timothy, since it was my first and hopefully my last fall of the season," she laughed.

He loved her honesty and humour. A rare quality. Further down the table sat the young bloods: the Gillanders and Boylans, the Wrights and the Cunningham's.

"Are you having breakfast, father?"

The voice of Kitty brought Lord Foldsworth back to reality.

"Of course, my darling. Let me see now. Yes, some scrambled eggs and kidneys would be good I think, with a little fresh parsley lightly sprinkled over it?" he smiled at her teasingly.

"Well father, be seated and I shall serve you myself," she chuckled in response, and kissed him lightly on the cheek.

The hum of conversation subsided as Lady Edwina entered the dining room. She looked beautiful, radiant and happy.

"Good morning my dear." Her husband stood up to greet her, as did the other male guests seated at the great table.

"And good morning to you, Charles," she replied, gesturing for all to resume their seats and continue breakfast.

"What will you have my dear? There is a long day ahead of us." He was pleased to see his wife's obvious eager anticipation of the day's hunt.

One of the servants brought her the usual lightly boiled egg. It seldom varied.

"Edwina dear, are you sure that is enough for you?"

"Charles, you know how I abhor large breakfasts. This will absolutely suffice," she replied, smiling at him.

Kitty arrived with her father's breakfast of scrambled eggs with kidney. She greeted her mother with a kiss on the cheek.

"Good morning, mother."

"Good morning, Kitty. Did you sleep well my darling?"

"Very well, mother. You know, I can hardly wait to see you back hunting once again. It seems so long since we had you out with us," she replied gleefully, as she sat beside her mother.

The guests were aware of the close and happy family who sat at the head of the table, and loved them for it. As they finished their breakfasts, they proceeded to the yard, where the grooms stood holding their mounts in pristine readiness. Charles Foldsworth looked over at his wife who sat sidesaddle, striking to behold in her dark plum riding habit. She waved at him from a distance, and then cantered over to join him.

The sun shone through the cloudless sky as the frost melted rapidly. The horse's breath came in steamy clouds from their nostrils. Almost seventy in number, Lady Edwina estimated. The riders called cheerily to each other.

Lord Atherby and his wife joined Lord Foldsworth and Lady Edwina and waited patiently for the group to fully assemble before moving off. The hounds came bounding from the courtyard baying loudly, and were called to heel by the whipper-in.

"Well Charles, it seems we can go ahead. Things are as ready as they ever will be, I should think."

Lord Atherby croaked hoarsely as he produced a hip flask of brandy.

"Why really, William!" his wife protested. "Why on earth do you have to take that so early on in the day? You will be seeing two ditches ahead instead of one." She laughed regardless.

Lady Edwina loved their company. They were so full of life and had such a tremendous bond of natural affection between them after almost fifty years of marriage. Their appetite for life and its challenges was totally undimmed with the passing years.

The hunting horn resounded about the courtyard, and horses and riders began to move slowly to the front of the great house. The servants stood there waiting, dressed in plumb coloured velvet and holding trays proffering the stirrup cup. Hannah stood in the dining room discreetly eyeing the group. 'How well her Ladyship looks', she thought, 'so straight and so lovely. Hasn't changed a bit from the first time she rode to hounds from here'. She saw Kitty, laughing happily as she raised her glass to some handsome young man. A cloud crossed Hannah's mind at the thought of her recent discussion with Kitty about this young man she had apparently fallen in love with. Hannah prayed that she would strike up a friendship with one of the young men today. A friendship that might, perhaps, blossom into something more. Would anyone ever believe that it was possible for her to be in love this day, with a fellow from the village that had neither name nor seat, she mused alarmingly.

Gradually the meet went down the long tree lined avenue and out of sight. Hannah clapped her hands loudly at all the staff.

"Come now! They will be back here in no time at all, and we here with almost one hundred dinners to get ready," she announced, with a determination that spoke of her desire to have her kitchen ticking over like a well tuned grandfather clock.

* * *

The hounds were slow to pick up the scent of the fox, but now, in a small thicket nearby, they began to bay excitedly. The horses pricked their ears in anticipation of the chase. At the shrill call of 'Tally-Ho' and the clear call of the hunting horn, all began to gallop ahead for what promised to be a very exciting chase.

Lord Atherby, red-faced with excitement, remained up front calling out in his usual croaking voice. His wife was in hot pursuit, trying to caution him, aware of the effects of the brandy! Lady Edwina felt exhilarated with the chase. She took the jumps masterfully as they came, and the merriment ran high.

At a distance James watched, unnoticed by all as he stood behind a large stone. His eyes were on Kitty, who looked a striking figure as she rode behind her mother, both expert horsewomen. Behind them rode Timothy Viscount Stewart, pursued avidly by Lady Julia Fairbrass, who strove gallantly to impress the Earl of Ashton whom she knew to be directly behind her.

The fox ran uphill ahead of the hounds, where he paused momentarily to assess his position. He saw James behind the great rock and realised that he posed no threat. The advancing hounds brought the fox back to reality. He decided to run downhill, bounding over a stonewall, and then into a stream to lose his scent. He knew that if he could reach the wooded hillside he was safe. He would then be able to outrun his pursuers.

Lord Foldsworth rode up beside his wife.

"Edwina, do be careful at the next stone wall, will you?"

She waved her gloved hand at him, signifying that his concerns for her were unwarranted. Lord Atherby rode on; eyes fixed firmly on the jump ahead, and began to pace his hunter. Up front the riders cleared the stonewall with ease.

However, the cock pheasant that had lain still in the heather with the passing thundering hooves became frightened at the loud croaking voice of Lord Atherby, and rose in protest from its hiding place. Lord Atherby's horse shied violently in fright, moving across the direct path of Lord Foldsworths hunter, and inevitably both horses collided. It was all that Charles Foldsworth remembered before he crashed to the ground, his horse stumbling also and falling heavily. Kitty and her mother reeled in horror at the sight before them, and tried frantically to avoid the unseated rider. Bringing their horses under control, they dismounted. The figure of Lord Foldsworth lay still amidst the heather and grass tufts, and seeing his lifeless form, Lady Edwina fainted. Not in much better condition, her friend Lady Constance came to her aid.

"Oh father, father," Kitty cried as she went to lift his head.

Viscount Stewart instantly prevented her.

"Do not attempt to do any such thing, Lady Catherine. Heaven only knows what additional damage you could do to him," he said firmly. Then, looking about desperately, he called out, "Will somebody go quickly for a doctor and get some help. We need a flat cart here, filled with straw."

Lady Joanna Winters volunteered instantly. Her thoroughbred was renowned for its speed and its rider for her skill. She dashed away with great and urgent determination.

"He is still breathing," Kitty cried helplessly.

Lord Atherby staggered over in a daze having finally gained control of his terrified animal.

"Oh dear, Lady Catherine, I am so dreadfully sorry... my entire fault" he sobbed piteously.

Viscount Stewart jumped to his feet.

"So well you should be sorry, you clumsy old fool, with your reckless charging about the place. This is a hunt, Atherby... not a blasted battlefield!" He stamped his riding boot angrily on the ground, shouting loudly.

"Gentlemen. Please. That is quite enough."

Both men turned around to see Lady Edwina, quite recovered from her fainting spell.

"It wasn't Lord Atherby's fault," she continued, "I saw the entire thing. The culprit, gentlemen, was a startled pheasant that upset Lord Atherby's horse. Now, if you are both quite finished, I would like to see my husband!"

They stood aside.

"Oh Mamma, what a dreadful thing to happen," Kitty sobbed.

Looking at the helpless body of her husband, Lady Edwina sobbed quietly.

"Oh dearest Charles, please don't leave us ."

She wiped blood from the side of his head, using her silk scarf. The remainder of the hunting party had by now returned to the scene of the accident and were standing about in small groups, shocked.

Meanwhile, Lady Winters reached Oak Hall with the news, and consternation broke all round.

"Here. Quickly... get a flat cart deeply piled with straw and go immediately to Primrose Hill. Come now. Quickly, I say!" she shouted, and then rode on to the village for the doctor.

Upon arrival, she was relieved to find him at home.

"Doctor, you must come quickly. Lord Foldsworth has taken quite a bad fall during the hunt at Primrose Hill. Here, take my horse. He will have you there at twice the speed. No offence meant, but time is of the essence."

She proceeded to remove the sidesaddle and waited impatiently for the doctor to mount. She whispered a quiet prayer that he would be able to manage Connary. The doctor, with medical bag in hand, surprised her with his skill and confidence. Without a word, he galloped away from her. She placed her sidesaddle on the doctors surprised looking mare, and followed.

Having witnessed the entire accident, James saw the flat cart coming in the distance. He mounted his horse and joined the young groom, who was travelling hard to the scene where his master lay unconscious.

"Slow down, lad. Slow down or you will never arrive alive to help your master," he shouted.

The groom noticed the steep decline that lay ahead of him almost too late. Riding ahead, James caught the pair of horses and slowed them just in time to prevent a further tragedy. The doctor arrived just behind them, and leaped with bag in hand from the thoroughbred, which stood shaking in a lather of sweat.

"Make way," called Viscount Stewart.

The doctor knelt down beside the unconscious man.

"Is he dying doctor?" Kitty asked.

The doctor did not hear her. A lark soared high above the heathery hillside, singing its tuneless song. Kitty then noticed James in the background with the straw filled cart. Without thought or hesitation, she called out to him.

"Oh James, thank God you're here. Father has had a dreadful accident and I... " She stopped abruptly as she noticed the strange expression on her mother's face.

Others standing by thought her familiarity peculiar, but were too preoccupied to give it significance. Her mother, however, looked directly at her.

"And whom, may I ask, is this James fellow? Why, to listen to you one would think he was more important than the doctor. Really Kitty, whatever will you come out with next!"

Kitty, blushing scarlet, ignored her mother's remarks. She asked the doctor once again about her father's condition. He stood up and stroked his grey beard thoughtfully.

"Concussion, I'm afraid, and some broken bones. Fairly bad bruising. He should recover, thank goodness, though when he will regain consciousness, I can't say."

"Oh what a relief doctor," exclaimed Lord Atherby, with tears spilling down his cheeks. He suddenly looked his fourscore years and more. His wife put her arms around him consolingly.

"Now to work," the doctor continued, "some strong young men to lift the patient into the cart. Very gently, mind you, very gently!"

Slowly they lifted their host into the deep piled straw. James stood at the horses' heads holding them and soothing them gently, lest any jerking movement upset the operation. He felt deeply embarrassed by the comments of Lady Edwina to Kitty in relation to him. He tried desperately to avoid looking at Kitty. It would only serve to embarrass him further. Kitty looked at her father lying in the straw filled cart, her mother now sitting beside him. She wiped perspiration gently from his forehead.

"Please do try to go gently with the cart," the doctor asked of James, who now sat ready to drive away. The groom was glad to have a more experienced helper under the circumstances. Slowly the procession made its way back to Oak Hall. Gloomy though they were, all realised that things could indeed have turned out a lot worse.

At Oak Hall, Hannah and Williams stood on the great steps to the front of the house, anxiously searching the horizon for the return of their master. The sick room had been prepared for him, the bed made warm and a large fire burning hungrily in the grate. The sun had begun its descent into the March evening sky when Williams sighted the slow cavalcade.

"Here they come, Hannah. Quickly, inside, before they catch us gaping," he quipped.

Four servants came to wait at the door of the house bearing a stretcher, and they carried their master into the room, where only the doctor and Lady Edwina were allowed to follow. Kitty spoke to the group, asking them to proceed to the stable with their horses and then to prepare for dinner as planned.

Examining his patient more thoroughly, the doctor discovered that Charles Foldsworth had a broken leg and a collarbone. He looked at Lady Edwina.

"We are most fortunate he has no ribs broken. Miraculous indeed. His spine also appears undamaged. However, Lady Edwina, there is the slight chance that he may have some brain damage. Now hopefully I am wrong. Only time will tell. He is very fortunate to be alive, may I add. We have a lot to be thankful for." He sat back in the chair exhausted, more as a result of anxiety over his patient than the journey in the cart.

"Thank you, doctor, for being so thorough and so kind. When do you think Charles will regain consciousness?" she asked anxiously.

"I don't honestly know. Perhaps in a few hours from now there will be some response. If it takes longer than that, I would be afraid of damage, as I have said..." Pausing to contemplate the reality of the situation, he added more cheerfully, "... well, let's just hope for the best. I would like if you could arrange for him to be watched round the clock."

He looked at his pocket watch.

"My word, it's time for me to be on my rounds, Lady Edwina. I shall call later on this evening. As for you, my dear, I suggest you have a warm bath and a good dinner. Your guests await you, and I am sure they are anxious to know the condition of their host. There is little you can do here for the moment." He smiled and shook his head kindly at her, hoping she would do as he asked.

"Yes indeed, doctor," she sighed, "I am quite exhausted. I shall arrange for someone to remain with Charles, if you would be kind enough to wait a further few moments."

She went to the drawing room where the guests stood about, awaiting news.

"Well mother, how is father?" Kitty asked, nervously fidgeting with her hands.

"The doctor says he will be alright with time and care." she replied quietly, "Now, I must inform our dear friends."

She proceeded to the centre of the room, and all went silent to hear her speak.

"My dear friends, while my husband still remains unconscious, he is nonetheless going to be alright. He has a broken leg and collarbone. Hopefully in a couple of weeks he will be up and about again."

A loud cheer went up all round. Waving her hand in a gesture commanding silence, she continued.

"Now, please do rest yourselves and enjoy the rest of the evening, and, for that matter, your stay here at Oak Hall. It is what Charles would wish and we do have a lot to be grateful for. In an odd way, a lot to celebrate!"

There was prolonged applause. Lady Edwina returned to speak to Kitty who was seated beside Viscount Stewart.

"Kitty, would you mind staying with your father during dinner. The doctor wishes him to be watched at all times. I think it only right that I should join our guests."

"Of course mother. I shall be only too delighted to do so."

"Kitty, I would dearly love to join you. If Lady Edwina has no objection, that is?" Viscount Stewart looked at his hostess.

"Why, that would be more than kind of you, Viscount Stewart," she replied, surprised at the warm gesture from her guest. "I am sure Kitty would be only too pleased with the company."

She smiled at her daughter through tired eyes. The thought that this young man would make a wonderful son-in-law flitted through her mind. That familiarity she had with farm workers was something she would enquire into later.

On entering the sick room again she found the doctor smiling.

"Good news even now, my Lady. Your husband seems to be coming round a little. He is beginning to say a couple of words. Mind you, mostly calling a lady by the name of Glencora. Is it some close relative or friend, your Ladyship, or was it his mothers name perhaps? It is not uncommon, you know, for those who have been injured to revert back to a former time of life. The brain is such an extraordinary thing, one never knows really."

He continued to monitor his patient's pulse at the wrist. Lady Edwina looked puzzled.

"Glencora? Glencora? No... can't say I have heard the name before. It certainly isn't a family name, wherever else it may have derived from," she answered, perplexed. "Well, it's wonderful news nonetheless that Charles is beginning to come round. Has he opened his eyes yet, doctor?"

"Yes, he has, though ever so slightly. Just as I was resetting his leg bones, if you will pardon me not sparing you detail. Now, Lord Foldsworth must be kept very still and calm for the moment. When he is more alert, explain to him what happened. It is possible he will be unable to recall the details of what took place." Picking up his medical bag, he walked slowly to the door. "I shall call later as I said, Lady Edwina. Goodbye for the present. I shall see myself out."

"But surely, doctor, you must have some refreshments before you go. Please do. It will be no trouble whatsoever."

"No thank you. Time will not permit it. Perhaps later on I may avail of your hospitality," he added, by way of compromise.

Outside the door Kitty and Viscount Stewart sat patiently. The doctor walked past them, nodding recognition. Lady Edwina almost passed them by.

"Oh! My goodness! I had almost forgotten you both. How good of you, Viscount Stewart, to assist Kitty and keep her company."

"No need for thanks, Lady Edwina, and please, do call me Timothy. I would so much prefer if you would," he smiled broadly at her.

"Why most certainly. Timothy it shall be.

"And that applies to you also Kitty," he added with raised eyebrows.

Kitty suddenly felt relaxed in the presence of this man, comforted by his strength and kindness.

Inside the room the atmosphere hung heavy, with only the dim light of one lamp and the leaping flames of the fire casting long shadows.

"He does look somewhat improved, does he not Kitty?" Timothy said, as he peered closely at his host.

"Yes, but why is he so restless? I hope the poor darling is not in any pain," she replied, taking her fathers hand and caressing it lovingly. He appeared to be wrestling with something deep inside himself. Tears welled up in Kitty's eyes.

Charles Foldsworths pain, however, was not of the body. His mind was tossing and turning in a most tormented fashion. Surrounded on the one hand by familiar voices he couldn't place, on the other by his uncle's great house in Hampshire, memories gathering as though they were more of the present moment... his mind wove in and out, from one reality to the other. At length, the twilight world deepened. Hampshire became very clear to him.

Thoroughbred mares with foals at foot grazed leisurely in the March sunshine; the shrill call of peacocks echoed throughout the great park. It was a beautiful day and the year was 1767. He permitted his mind to return completely to that time, when he was still such a young man. It was lovely to come to stay with uncle Jeremy... and tonight there was going to be a great ball. He walked towards the great house, which resembled a castle with its great turrets on the wings, a relic of bygone days. Most of their friends throughout the County were coming, and above all he felt a deep delight that Glencora, Lady Camden, would be there.

His mind then seemed to lose the picture. He tossed restlessly, as if to try and grasp it again, but to no avail. He almost cried out in desperation when suddenly it appeared again, as if through a fog at first, than with greater clarity than before: the great ballroom... ablaze with light... laughing faces... cheery greetings... all so exquisitely dressed... then, she was there... Glencora... in the distance.

Slowly, she walked towards him through the crowd.

"Oh Glencora. Glencora... my darling... " He murmured, over and over again.

Kitty and Timothy looked at each other, startled. A moment later, Lord Foldsworth became calm and still. An expression of great serenity spread across his face.

Again, memories came unbidden to his mind: he reached out and took Glencora's arm and guided her through the crowded ballroom. They went into the magnificent gardens, heavily scented by the flowers of early spring. They walked close together, so much in love, and went to an old summerhouse some distance through the trees. There, he held her in his arms.

"I love you so much," he murmured. "Will you not come to Ireland with me, my darling?" Silence followed.

Kitty now realised that her father was reliving some part of his past. A past that neither she, not most likely her mother, knew existed. A past never spoken of.

Charles Foldsworth recalled their passionate lovemaking... so many times they had melted from a chaste embrace into each others flesh, trembling with the need to touch, taste, kiss... to consume each other. He could recall every detail of her body, her beautiful rounded form, so soft, so smooth. The feel of her skin set him on fire, his hands cupping her breasts, moving to her waist, her hips... every part of her was familiar to all his senses.

Suddenly, his expression changed. Another day... A July evening, when he met her as usual at their rendezvous in the beech woods. She could scarcely dismount from her horse, such was her distress.

"Glencora... what is it? What is it, my dearest? Why are you so upset?"

A long silence followed as she tried to compose herself. She looked at him directly.

"Charles, I am expecting our baby... "

The man lying on the bed struggled violently.

"What... our child... but you can't be... how long have you known Glencora...?"

Kitty looked at her father in disbelief. Viscount Stewart felt like an intruder. He thought of leaving the room, but decided against it. Tears streamed from Kitty's eyes as she sat quietly beside him.

"Kitty," he whispered, "don't be upset. You know your father is not himself, not in his right senses. Delirious... yes... that's what they call it, I think. Just talking plain nonsense."

"Oh Timothy, thank you for being so kind and understanding, but I know in my heart he speaks truth. I have always sensed something troubling father deep down. You have heard him... It doesn't take a lot to piece it together."

Slowly she let go of her father's hand and he continued to call out, 'Glencora... my child... our child... it cannot happen... I cannot marry... '. Deep sobs were now coming from the chest of her father, beyond comfort in his sorrow. It was too long ago and too late to alter. Kitty sat beside the fire, numbed by the revelation. Timothy sat beside her, unable to offer any words of consolation. After a long silence she spoke.

"So Timothy Stewart, I have a half brother or sister somewhere in Hampshire, whose mother's name is Glencora, and my father is its father too. Thank heavens mother did not hear it all."

"I know it sounds like that, Kitty, but how do we know that it lived, or was even born for that matter. Why, anything could have happened... anything," he added, trying desperately to change her trend of thought and lift her spirits. It was to no avail.

"Listen to him sob, Timothy. Is it not the cry of guilt and remorse; of pain so long hidden; of a child denied; his own flesh and blood; and then love unrequited. Well? Is it not?"

He realised that what she said was true. Somewhere there was now a young man or woman, the illegitimate child of Charles Foldsworth, in Hampshire. Taking his hand Kitty looked beseechingly into Timothy's eyes.

"Timothy, you must promise me that you will never disclose what you have heard here tonight. It is not for my sake that I ask this of you, but rather for my mother. Should she ever find out she would die from grief... I know she would. How many times have I heard her say so proudly that she was father's first love? You must promise, Timothy, you must!"

"You need never worry, Kitty. Nobody will ever know what has transpired here tonight, ever. I give you my word," he replied, feeling desperately sorry for her.

The deep sobbing had now ceased from the man lying near them, and a contented breathing ensued. He slept peacefully. Timothy smiled.

"They tell me that confession is good for the soul," he said.

Kitty knew that her father's revelation was safe with him. Timothy was known to be an honourable man among their friends, not one who engaged in idle talk and speculation. A gently knock on the door brought her mother into the room. Kitty stood up.

"He seems much more settled now mother. Don't you think?" she remarked, looking at her father.

"Yes indeed Kitty, and sleeping like a child too, thank heavens. Did he... well, did he say anything Kitty? You know, anything unusual or strange?" her mother asked her, looking down at her husband.

"No mother, nothing at all," Kitty lied. "Why do you ask?"

"Oh, it's not important, my dear... It's just that before I went to dinner your father kept repeating the name Glencora... that's all. Such a strange name."

Viscount Stewart stepped forward.

"No, Lady Edwina, as you see he is sleeping soundly. Not a word left his lips; only an odd sigh. Understandable, don't you think, when one considers what he has been through today?" He hoped to change the conversation onto other lines.

"Yes, we have been so fortunate. It could have been so different.... Now. You two go and have dinner. I have asked Hannah to serve you in the library. Cosier there, you know. I am expecting the doctor back at any moment, so off you go. And Timothy, lest I forget, thank you so very much for all your help and kindness to us today. You have been a splendid fellow."

As they left the room, Lady Edwina couldn't help but think what a fine young man he would be to have as a son-in-law. She sat by the bedside of her husband, and knew how much she loved him.

Seated cosily in the library, Kitty and Timothy ate their dinner, having forgotten how hungry they actually were.

"Mother is quite right, Timothy. You were wonderful today. With all that has happened, I don't want to forget to thank you."

"For nothing Kitty. I would be delighted to help you out at any time. Preferably under happier circumstances, needless to add." He thought to himself how much he would love to see more of her if given the opportunity.

"There is, however, one more thing which I must do, Timothy," Kitty said, as she stood up.

"What on earth could it be at this hour? Why, you must be thoroughly exhausted," he said.

"No, not now. It's out of the question until father is better. But I must go to Hampshire and find this child, or should I say, adult, and do it I shall!"

"But for what purpose? What could it possibly achieve, only to upset people?" he asked, quite taken aback by the determination in her voice.

"I must. I simply must, Timothy. I shall ask father when he is well again to arrange for me to visit uncle John. Fortunately, he is constantly asking me to go there for a holiday, so it will not seem such a strange request. But, for now, I am going directly to fathers study to look through his old letters. Perhaps I may learn something there. Who knows?"

Timothy looked shocked at such an intrusive idea.

"Why, you wouldn't dare Kitty! Search through your father's papers and private things?" He looked at her open-mouthed.

"Yes Timothy, I shall. I think I have every right to do so, and if I don't do it tonight, I may never get the opportunity again. Now, will you help me this last time, or shall I go alone?" she asked with raised eyebrows.

Seeing how determined she was, Timothy decided there was little point in arguing.

"Oh, very well then. I don't agree with what you are doing, but I can understand your need to find out. I suppose I would do the same if I was in your predicament," he added, resignedly.

They crept silently upstairs to the study, and closing the door gently behind them, lit a candle. Kitty then locked the door. She found the key to her father's safe in its customary hiding place, in an old disused riding boot which he kept for sentimental reasons. She opened the safe very quietly. There were bundles of old documents before her. Deeds and land and property titles. Kitty searched meticulously through the papers for over an hour, but to no avail. There was nothing remotely resembling correspondence from England.

"This is useless, Timothy. There is nothing here. I feel so utterly foolish now. What on earth did I expect to find. Stooping down to pick up a piece of paper from the floor, something caught her attention. It was a long piece of faded pink ribbon. It seemed to be coming from the corner of the safe. On closer examination, she found that it was attached to an old letter, yellowed with age and sealed with wax.

"What on earth is this, Timothy?" she exclaimed.

"Be careful for goodness sake Kitty not to break the old seal too clumsily, lest you can't replace it properly," he cautioned.

Gently Kitty opened the old, carefully folded, yellow paper. She caught her breath. She knew in her bones it was significant. It read:

Ravens Wood Castle
Hampshire
England
The Fourth Day of May 1768

My dearest Charles,

I write to tell you that I have given birth to a baby boy. Yes. Our son.
He is now one month old and he has your dark hair and clear blue eyes. I know you would love him. My family have finally accepted him, and indeed me, back into the fold. It has not been easy, Charles. However, they now dote on him and love him dearly.
Each day father and mother have beseeched me to name the child's father, but I never shall. It would create too great a feud between our families who have been such friends for, indeed, centuries. There would be little point in allowing that to happen.
Should you ever find it in your heart to love me again or recognise your son, I should think I would have reached heaven. Oh Charles, we could still be happy, and all would understand and forgive. Please do change your mind.
I am going to call our son Henry William. I do hope you like it.
Please do write to me at least, as I have not heard from you since your return to Ireland. You did promise to write that last evening we met in the beech woods. Yet, somehow, as I watched you ride away, I sensed you never would.
I love and cherish you still, and our times together. I regret not a single day of it all.

Yours ever faithfully,

Glencora

Kitty handed the letter to Timothy and cried silently. Poor father, she thought. He never did write to her or accept his son. He has carried this secret around in his heart all these years. What a burden to live with. Glencora seems never to have written to him again. Nor, obviously, did she ever name him as the father of the child. So all this meant that the baby was now a young man of twenty-nine or thirty years of age... Henry William... my half brother!

|Timothy handed her back the letter.

"Kitty, we must replace this letter now, and join the other guests. It confirms all that we have heard. It is a lot to have to accept, I know, but what choice do you have? Your father must have had very good reasons for not going to Glencora or the baby at that time, and we may never know what those reasons were. You know your father to be a good and honourable man, and his fidelity to your mother is so well known, unlike so many who have at least one mistress. You also know that he loves you and always has. So you must judge him on what you know of him in your own lifetime. After that, trust that his reasons for not returning to his first love were extremely valid at the time."

"I know what you are saying is true Timothy. At least I now know the name of who I am looking for, which is a good start. I shall find him... I know I shall!"

Timothy Viscount Stewart didn't doubt her for a minute. They carefully replaced the letter, resealing the old wax and placing it in the niche where it had lain undisturbed for almost thirty summers. They walked back to the great hall and the sound of happy voices.

"It's odd, Timothy, when one thinks of it. This morning I sat with father at breakfast, so excited about the days hunt ahead. Tonight I feel as if I have discovered a totally different man, a part of my father that I would have never dreamt existed... and he, himself, unknowingly revealed it to me. It reminds me of one Sunday at service, sitting as a little girl beside my mother. The parson said something that always remained with me... 'There is nothing hidden that shall not be revealed'. I thought a lot about that, and trembled at the prospect of mother finding out that I had stolen some of her chocolates and hoping she would blame one of the servants for doing so. But surely this night proves the saying true."

As they sat with their friends relaxing in the great room, Kitty realised that the parson's maxim was also true of her relationship with James, that it was bound to come to light. She wondered if her love would prove strong enough to withstand the rejection that Hannah had warned her about, or if she would crumble beneath it. A wave of dizziness swept over her, and she felt a heavy tiredness come upon her. 'No. I must remain strong', she thought, 'I do love James and nothing will ever change that. Life changes, and look what just one day can bring! I must meet Henry William. I must see him... sometime... even talk to him'.

"You look tired, darling, and deep in thought," her mother interrupted as she sat down beside her. "Let me guess now? You are thinking of Timothy perhaps? He is such a good young man, is he not?"

"Yes mother, he is all you say. How is father now?" Kitty asked, tired of her mother's subtle hints about Timothy's marital suitability.

"He is sleeping like a baby. The doctor says he is doing very well."

"That's wonderful news. We all got such a dreadful fright on the field. I hope you remembered to thank Lady Winters for her gallant work today," Kitty added.

"Yes. Joanna was so good, and really brave in her dash for the doctor. Thinking so little for her personal safety. I meant to ask you earlier, Kitty. Who was that farmhand you seemed to know so well? The fellow who drove the cart... James... I think you called him. You appeared far too familiar with him. Who exactly is he anyway?" Lady Edwina asked.

Kitty's tired mind raced for an answer.

"Oh, he is just a fellow who replaced a shoe on my mare one day when I had to leave the field. Very kind, I may add," she replied, totally taken aback by the turn in the conversation.

"Kind? How do you mean, kind?" her mother asked, looking perplexed.

"Just that, mother. Like you, I always acknowledge kindness. Just like you did with Viscount Stewart. The only difference being, titles or not, I will still thank people for their help. Is that such a breach of etiquette... to call people by their name and thank them?"

Kitty stood up and walked away. Lady Edwina decided her daughter was quite overwrought by the events of the day. There could be no other possible explanation for such a rude and indeed impertinent reply.

Kitty felt very ill at ease with her mother's questioning. She felt the old feeling of being trapped and hemmed in with her life and wished she could break free of it all. Convention and title forbade it. After struggling for some minutes, she regained her composure. Viscount Stewart came towards her with a glass of wine.

"Now, you look as if you could do with a little of this, Kitty. Come now, it will only serve to relax you if you sip it slowly. It has been a harrowing day all round."

"Yes Timothy... I shan't forget it in a hurry."

"I have just been talking with Lord Atherby. I must confess I was rather rude to him on the field to say the least... blaming him and so forth before everybody," he admitted repentantly.

"What did he say to you? Was he still offended?" Kitty asked.

"No Kitty. A perfect gentleman. He just dismissed it all, saying it was understandable considering the shock we all got. He then toasted the courage and skill of Lady Winters. He was in high praise of her, as indeed we all are. She is a gallant lady, Kitty, is she not? That marriage of hers is such an unfortunate business. I imagine she would be the dream of so many men with her beauty and manner. Whatever happened to me... still looking for a lady to share my dreams with?

Kitty thought she detected a tinge of despair in the voice.

"Come now, Timothy. Cheer up. Life isn't all that bad for you really. One of these fine days I am sure you will find someone you really love. Why not?" she added happily.

"To tell you the truth, Kitty... I think I may have found her," he said, shyly. He knew it would be unwise to say more.

"Well, at least that's a start, and let's hope whoever she is she will have the good sense to see how fortunate she is to receive the attentions of such a promising young man."

She tapped his arm in a gesture of encouragement and reassurance before standing up and bidding him goodnight. Timothy Viscount Stewart knew in his heart that he had fallen in love with her, and had the good sense to realise that to even mention it to her would be most unwise at this present time. The past, as revealed by her father and the letter, had all proved quite extraordinary. It would take Kitty some time to adjust to it. Perhaps tomorrow, if the day proved fine, he would invite her to ride out with him. It could only do her good. With that happy thought, he decided to go to bed. The wine had made him very relaxed and he felt wrapped in the warm glow of his newfound love.

Lady Edwina sat beside her husband's bedside before retiring herself. She had hoped he would wake up, even for a short time. He had not since mentioned the strange woman's name, but she decided that when he was better she would ask him about it. It both intrigued her and disturbed her that he should call out the name of a perfect stranger in the throes of illness. The doctor had repeatedly told her, almost to the point of irritation, that it was quite common for people to become fanciful with all sorts of imaginings while concussed. She felt this was not the case. She knew when there was desperation in her husband's voice.

Kitty also wondered about her father's past and tossed endlessly in bed, unable to find rest. The same question remained unanswered in her mind. Why... why... why did he not marry her? Why did he never write to her and acknowledge the child of their love? No. He had instead closed the door on the matter with a grim finality. She knew there was no way she could ever ask him about Glencora, but her resolve to go to Hampshire to find her half-brother was adamant. With this decision embedded in her mind, peace finally came as the grey light of dawn crept over the hills and vigilant blackbirds heralded the birth of another day.

Charles Foldsworth awoke feeling the pain of his broken leg and collarbone and wondered what on earth had happened. His mind, still numbed, slowly recalled the hunt and then his rearing horse. He could recall nothing else. He concluded that he had taken quite a bad fall. The ache in his head came in repeated throbs, and he sighed with relief as they became less frequent. Quite suddenly he remembered somehow seeing Glencora, but realised that it was absurd. How could I possibly have, he wondered? She is living in Hampshire in England... with... my son. There! He had finally managed to admit it to himself. Conscious of the fact that he had never permitted himself to dwell on this truth, living in denial had been a great strain indeed. He wondered how Glencora was, and their son... Henry. He tried to imagine what his son might look like but failed to place a face on the name. Keeping the secret for thirty years had not been difficult when one had refused to even acknowledge it to oneself. He sighed.

The house was still and silent, the servants not yet up and about. Outside, he could see the grey light of dawn and eventually the rose tinted clouds. Blackbirds and thrushes hopped across the front lawn collecting worms, and from the great spruce trees, wood pigeons cooed happily.

The bedroom door opened gently to reveal Lady Edwina holding a lighting candle aloft.

"Come in, my dear," her husband whispered.

"Oh Charles, darling, ho do you feel?" she exclaimed with relief, seeing him awake and so alert.

"Sore and stiff, my dear. Do come and tell me whatever happened."

He gestured to a chair nearby, and his wife sat down, only too happy to relate the events of the previous day. She left nothing out, except his delirious references to the mysterious lady called Glencora. She had decided not to mention it at all. It might only serve to embarrass him and was probably only some childhood memory or such like.

"You were very lucky, Charles. The doctor said it could have been so much worse you know."

"I fully appreciate that, Edwina. Now, tell me, how are our unfortunate guests, Atherby and so forth?"

"Oh, they are fine now Charles. I must say they all got such a dreadful fright. I imagine they will be a lot more careful on the hunting field in future. But, as Lady Winters so rightly said, the most experienced rider cannot possibly see pheasants crouching in the undergrowth."

Her husband sighed and smiled weakly. His mind seemed to drift off again.

Lady Edwina found her curiosity as to whom Glencora may be suddenly return. The instinct that led her to the question was the same instinct that told her not to ask.

Downstairs, the servants were moving about. Another day had begun. The great fires were rekindled to life and Lady Edwina rang the bell. Presently Williams came into the room and was visibly cheered to see his master sitting up.

"Good morning, Williams," his master said weakly.

"Good morning, your Lordship, and if I may say so it is wonderful to see you so much better this morning."

"Thank you, Williams," he replied.

"An what may I get your Lordship for breakfast," Williams enquired, looking more to Lady Edwina for the answer.

"Some weak tea, Williams, and perhaps, Charles, you would eat some lightly toasted bread?" she asked of her husband coaxingly.

"Yes, that would be lovely indeed," he answered, while lying back deeper into the pillows.

Williams left the room quietly, and hastened to tell Hannah in the kitchen how much their master's condition had improved. The tray of steaming weak tea and hot buttered toast was ready in minutes.

"Thank you Williams," said Lady Edwina, taking the tray from him, "and please tell Hannah that I shall meet her as usual to discuss the menu for today. I shall have to check among the guests discreetly to see how many are remaining on with us."

The aged butler admired her constant efficiency and clarity of mind in all circumstances.

"Very well, my Lady. Will that be all?" he asked with eyebrows raised.

"Yes Williams, and thank you," she smiled in acknowledgment.

Going downstairs, Williams looked forward to his customary boiled eggs. His breakfast choice never varied.

Calling in to see her father before breakfast, Kitty was delighted to find him so alert and having morning tea.

"Why father, you look so much better today," she said, her relief obvious.

"Yes Kitty, and only for the wretched pain in my leg and shoulder, why... I think I would be off with you for a canter. It looks as if it is going to be a splendid day," he replied, looking at the clear blue sky through the windowpanes.

"Charles, I actually believe you would, you dare devil!" said Lady Edwina. "And now, I must leave you to join our guests for breakfast. They will be so cheered to hear how well you are. Oh yes, Charles, should any of them wish to visit you, what shall I say?"

"Let me see," Lord Foldsworth considered how he was feeling. "Perhaps after lunch. One's duties as host still prevail Kitty, sick or well." He looked up at the ceiling and shrugged his shoulders in a humorous way, before wincing in pain.

"Father, you must rest now. Let me take your tray, and I shall be back presently. Perhaps you would like me to read to you then?"

"How kind of you to suggest it, but maybe you would rather go for a morning canter with your friends. It is an ideal morning to do so, Kitty."

"Why goodness, father, I almost forget. Viscount Stewart did ask me if I would ride out with him this morning. I would gladly remain here to read to you father if you so wished?" she felt a little guilty and undecided.

"No. I insist. You must not disappoint Timothy Stewart. He seems a good fellow, from what I know of him. By all accounts he did gallant work yesterday in keeping me intact in the back of the cart after my accident. I am truly in his debt. Anyway, you'll have plenty of time to read to me in the days to come. The doctor has ordered me to rest for the next six weeks. Heaven alone knows how I shall endure it!"

"Very well then, father. I shall see you in the late afternoon then," and kissing her father, she left the room in a flurry of excitement.

He smiled to himself. Youth has no hesitation, he thought. Once again he found his mind drifting back to Hampshire. Again, when he slept, Glencora entered his dreams. She seemed to be waving him goodbye as she rode through the beech woods. Somehow his horse was unable to keep up with her, and she eventually disappeared from view.

"Glencora! Glencora!" he shouted, but she had gone.

The voice of Lady Edwina woke him from his sleep.

"Charles, wake up darling."

He awoke to a look of astonishment on Edwina's face. He remembered his dream clearly... the sense of loss... Glencora...

"Charles, the doctor is on his way to see you. Let me comb your hair and have you looking more presentable."

She hastened to comb the black hair, now greying at the sides. She was acutely agitated on hearing him again call out the name of this mysterious lady. Her curiosity could no longer contain itself.

"Charles, who is Glencora?" she asked suddenly.

He was taken aback by her direct question.

"Glencora? Why, my dear, I... I don't really know. Why do you ask?" He avoided her eyes.

"I am very curious, Charles, because last night you called out for her on numerous occasions in your delirium, and again just now as I was entering the room. Who is she?"

"Edwina, I told you, I do not know. Or at least if I do, I can't remember. Perhaps a childhood friend. I don't recall..."

His wife accepted his simple explanation, but he had lied, and he disliked lying to her. Just then, Williams announced the doctor.

"Good morning, Lord Foldsworth." His tone was sombre.

"Yes, and good morning to you doctor," returned Lord Foldsworth, very relieved at the timing of this interruption.

"And how are you today, your Lordship?" the doctor continued, as he raised the bedclothes to examine his patient's leg injury.

"Oh, stiff and sore, you know. But I am alive, and lucky to be so, from what I have been told."

"Indeed yes, very lucky," muttered the doctor, as he continued to examine the casing around his patients leg. "As I have told your wife, Lord Foldsworth, I recommend at least six weeks rest for this leg injury, so that it may set back properly. We don't want you going about with a limp for the remainder of your life now, do we?"

It was a very sobering thought, and his patient was aghast at such a possibility.

"Are you serious, doctor? I mean, a limp?" he enquired almost sheepishly.

"Most certainly. But it will be avoided if you give your leg the rest it requires to heal properly. Bones knit slowly, it is simply nature's way, your Lordship. Now, you will have to be assisted whenever you wish to leave your bed for washing purposes and so forth. This limb must be given every opportunity to heal correctly, or I shall not be responsible. On a brighter side," and here the doctor smiled, "you could consider taking a holiday. You could both do with a tonic, and I can recommend nothing better than a complete change of scene and routine. Good for the spirit, you know!"

"Oh doctor, what an utterly splendid idea. Charles, we simply must. Yes! To England. We must write to your brother in Hampshire this very day and tell them our plans. Goodness knows they are tired inviting us over!" his wife exclaimed happily.

When the doctor and Lady Edwina had left the room, Charles Foldsworth thought how ironic life could be. Glencora was a ghost he had long run from. Now it seemed it was time to meet her again, and his son. He realised that he could not expect Edwina and Kitty to understand this aspect of his past. He trusted, even after all the intervening years, that Glencora would never have divulged their secret. He had never told her the reason for his disappearance, for not marrying her. She could have no idea of the pain it had caused him. He resolved to tell her on meeting, and hoped she could understand. He felt it was time to take that risk.

It was with a measure of anger and sadness that he recalled his father's attitude to one of a different religious persuasion. Marrying one such as Glencora, regardless of her rank and title, would have been insupportable to him. His father had been a bitter old man, and had Charles gone against his wishes, he would have been disowned, perhaps even publicly. He would have been disinherited and left penniless. To marry Glencora would have left her an outcast in society. Religion, an accident of birth, caused more turmoil and bitterness, Papist and Protestant fighting each other in the defence of the One God. How futile and how dreadful, and where more than here in Ireland. He had loved Glencora, but not enough to pay the ultimate price. It was with sadness alone that he admitted this to himself.

Tears filled his eyes. Regret? Relief? A sense of peace slowly filled him; a peace that only truth can bring.

A sharp knock jolted him back to the present. Williams entered.

"Lady Edwina informs me, your Lordship, that you will be meeting some of the guests after lunch. Are you still of the same mind, Sir?" he asked, in his usual crisp manner.

"Yes, Williams. Do you have any idea who wishes to visit?"

"Well, my Lord, Lady Winters, Lord and Lady Atherby, and Viscount Stewart, to name but a few."

William gave a subtle smile, knowing that his master' favourite friends would cheer him.

"Of course! Tell them it would be great to chat with them for a while, Williams," he replied.

"I thought so, my Lord. Lunch will be served quite soon, and I am very pleased to inform your lordship that Hannah has prepared your favourite soup."

"How very kind of Hannah, trying to cheer me up with her culinary delights. Do convey my thanks Williams, and thank you, also."

"It is our pleasure, Sir," said Williams, and left to convey the master's compliments to Hannah, knowing it would thrill her.

Charles Foldsworth appreciated his staff. They were loyal and kind and earnestly sought to please the household. Invaluable, he thought, as his thoughts began to drift again to Hampshire. It would be lovely in June... birdsong in the English countryside... mares with foals at foot grazing leisurely. He drifted into sleep, where he once more saw Glencora ride through bluebell strewn pathways. She seemed now to be laughing happily and calling back to him. Again he urged his horse forward and found to his delight that he was riding abreast of her. She looked lovelier than ever. All else forgotten, they again made love amidst the tall green ferns as their horses grazed, swishing summer flies from their flanks with long finely combed tails.

* * *

Kitty and Timothy sat by the racing torrent. The countryside about them seemed poised to launch into the exuberance of spring once again. Lambs ran fitfully, exploring the rocky crevices. Overhead, crows flew tirelessly with twig-laden beaks repairing old nests after the ravages of winter. Young members of the flock built nests for the first time, listening to the silent instructions nature issued to them.

"Lovely, isn't it Timothy? The surge of life constantly renewing itself?" Kitty's eyes were closely following a robin that appeared quite undecided as to where it would build a home for its mate.

"Yes, incredible really, when one thinks of it," Timothy replied as he gazed at the clouds casting long shadows over the gently rolling countryside.

"You know, I often think we don't make the most of life. When it's almost over we seem to awaken to it," Kitty remarked philosophically.

"Oh come now, Kitty... you sound such a sage... really. Why, look at the choices that lie before us. Is choosing not fun?" he asked.

"I am not really sure. Do you realise, Timothy, that choice by its nature means exclusions?"

"Yes, you are quite correct, though I freely admit I have never thought about it that way before. Sad, I suppose, that to choose one path or direction, one must surrender God knows what in the other. But then, do they not say, Kitty, that what one has never had, one will never miss?" He laughed as he stood up, brushing the blades of dried grass from his tweed jacket.

"That is very true, Timothy. But isn't there a security in choice, a sense of, 'this is me and what I want from life'... stepping into ones own destiny."

Kitty spoke with such conviction that Timothy believed she was somehow about to do just that.

"I must admit, Kitty, that it is very refreshing to meet a young lady who actually thinks more on life than a piece of silk or the latest gossip at the Castle."

"Timothy, of course I think about life! Good heavens, life is full of mystery and surprise. When one turns up a stone, for example, and finds a myriad of ants all scurrying about their business, it teaches us that there is far more to it than the eye can see."

Engrossed in their philosophising, they failed to notice the horseman approaching them on the bridle path that emerged from the small grove. It was James taking the shorter route to the village. He approached quietly.

"Good afternoon, Lady Catherine," he said, in a gentlemanly tone.

"Oh, for heaven's sake James, don't surprise us so," Kitty, exclaimed.

"My apologies. I never intended to," James replied.

Timothy looked at the man and tried to remember where he had seen the face before. Reading his expression, Kitty decided she had better introduce them.

"Timothy, this is James de Lacey. If you recall he drove the cart yesterday when father received his injury." She felt nervous and awkward.

"Yes, now I remember. Good day to you." Then, looking back at Kitty, he continued, "I do believe it is almost lunch time, Lady Catherine. We must return to Oak Hall without delay."

His dismissal of James was obvious. Kitty decided it best not to aggravate the situation any further, but disliked the rudeness Timothy so blatantly displayed.

"Yes, it has gone late in the morning."

Timothy ignored her remark and mounted his horse.

"James, would you be a gentleman and assist me to mount," Kitty asked, ignoring Timothy's further display of bad manners.

"Certainly, my Lady. I would only be too delighted."

Taking her horse firmly by the bridle, he held it until Kitty was comfortably seated in the sidesaddle.

"Thank you, James. You certainly do seem to have the happy practice of appearing when help is needed," she smiled at him warmly.

"Always a pleasure, my Lady," James replied, and winked at her discreetly.

Not bothering to address Viscount Stewart he rode away briskly, his heart racing from the chance encounter.

"Hmm... I see you know that fellow quite well, Kitty?" Timothy snapped.

"As a matter of fact I do. He isn't one of our tenants, but I have met him occasionally in the course of my outings. Coincidence really. As I said earlier, we each decide how to live our own lives. I have always made it my practice to be courteous to everyone. Your disdain of the ordinary people, Timothy, is quite apparent."

"How very observant of you, Kitty. It is quite extraordinary for you to address them by a first name. I find it odd for a lady in your position," he said with agitation.

"Indeed Timothy! Furthermore, had you not forgotten your manners, I would not have had to ask for assistance with mounting. So, we learn something about ourselves every day, do we not?"

Without further banter, they both rode downhill, and James became a distant figure on the horizon. Still in silence, they entered the stable yard, Timothy distinctly uncomfortable at the tension that prevailed.

"Kitty... please do forgive me... my lack of thought. I realise I have no right whatever in questioning you about your lifestyle," he said by way of apology.

"Dear Timothy," Kitty laughed, "think nothing of it. You do however remind me of Mamma... always looking out for my good."

He resented the comment, but thought it better to ignore it. He remarked to himself, and not for the first time, that Lady Catherine Foldsworth was a very strong-minded woman. Certainly not one to be told what to do. Then he realised that was the very reason he loved her. She was different.

* * *

James walked into the forge and found Joe hammering out a horseshoe, shaping the molten iron with an age-old skill. So intent was he upon his work that for some moments he was totally unaware of James, who stood amidst the smoke and steam.

"God bless the work Joe," said James eventually.

"Huh," said Joe, surprised to see him, "and 'tis well for those who have little to do only stand back and watch. Have you the day off or something James?"

"No such luck, I'm afraid. That brother of mine had to go to Mentens farm, and I had to show him where it was. So, it's back to the Inn now. Brian is decent enough giving me the time. Not a mean man," said James, aware how much he liked his job there.

Joe was also aware that James was a great worker and that Brian appreciated him.

"What is he gone to Mentens for? Your brother, that is." Joe asked.

"They're getting the ground ready for sowing potatoes. To tell the truth, I'm glad to have him from under my feet. He's been very dead in himself, no great interest in anything, and that's not good for a man so young. Sometimes he sits for hours just staring at the fire, then maybe go for a walk in the evening. A bit morose, he is. Do you know, Joe, I never got an explanation from him about the condition he arrived here in, all bruised and gashed and the like. Must have been serious enough for him to run and hide."

Joe looked up at him.

"I hope he knows nothing of our doings with the movement," he said matter of factly.

"No need to worry over that Joe. I wouldn't be so foolish. I haven't even told him about Kitty. Neither is for idle discussion. Too close to the heart, if you know what I mean."

"Well James, I don't even want to hear about the love in your life. You know my feeling on that, don't you, or need I remind you again?"

"No Joe, you need not bother."

Joe began to blow the bellows vigorously under the dying coals. The reference to the Rebellion brought up his uneasiness in being a part of it, the risk to himself and his family. His knowledge of James' acquaintance with Lady Catherine was another worry he didn't need.

James, on the other hand, found it extremely hard not to mention her to the only person beside himself who knew.

"I met her today on my way here," he said, deliberately not using Kitty's name. "That fellow Viscount Stewart was with her, out riding. He's been staying up there for the past week or so. Do you know him Joe?"

"Aye. I've heard of him but never seen him. Supposed to be a genius with the Law, they tell me. Studied it in London. His ambition is to be a criminal Judge, and that's all I know or care to know I might as well tell you. Now hand me over that bucket of water like a good man."

"A Judge of criminals, no less! Seems very young to be one of those Joe?"

Joe sighed in exasperation.

"Have you still not gotten it into that thick head of yours that it's who you know in this world that counts. What has his age got to do with it, tell me? The great grey wigs they wear will give him to look of a seventy year old. Make him look wise as well, God save us. 'Tis a strange old costume in my opinion."

As both men laughed at the strange ways of the educated, Nell walked into the forge, lilting a tune as usual.

"'Tis well for the two of you, standing' about the place laughing. The work must be slack, and ye idling away the day," she remarked with a smile.

"Well Nell, wouldn't it be worse if we couldn't have a laugh," James replied, as he watched Joe resume his blowing of the bellows.

"You are so right, James. There's enough sadness in the world as it is. Now, are the two of you going to come in for dinner? 'Twill be ready in no time."

"Not for me, Nell," said James. "I have to be back at the Inn or else Brian will think I've taken a job here at the forge! Thanks for asking all the same."

"Don't mention it, James, I'm only glad I can. I remember too many days of hunger from my young life. Aye. A memory too common in Ireland."

They stood in silence, each with their own thoughts. It was all oppression, hunger, fear and homelessness. It had never changed, Nell thought. With the passing of Pat Ryan still fresh in the minds of the people, they knew deep down that lack of food was partly responsible for his early death.

"Well Nell, I'm famished and will do justice to your good cooking," Joe said, rubbing his hands together in anticipation.

"Well, I better be off to the Inn. I'll see you later tonight Joe, I suppose!"

"Aye James, I'll be over there later on if I get all the work completed for tomorrow," Joe replied, thinking of the load still to be completed for different people.

James led his horse up the village and into the stables at the back of the Inn. He hummed a tune as he prepared the feed for his hungry animal, and thought of Kitty and Viscount Stewart. Could she be growing fond of him, he wondered? He had a lot to offer: title, money, a vast estate in Kildare. He had everything, and to boot becoming a Judge. Suddenly a thought struck him with force. Was it possible that the authorities had become aware that a Rebellion was forthcoming and as a result were increasing the number of Judges? The thought chilled him to the bone, yet it went some way to explaining the appointment of one so young. He then thought of how obvious it was that Viscount Stewart has resented Kitty speaking to him. It might have been wiser, he now sensed, to avoid meeting them. He had made an enemy in Viscount Timothy Stewart, and decided there and then it would be prudent in future to avoid him.

With that resolved, he went into the Inn to begin work for the remainder of the day.

* * *

At Oak Hall the guests gradually began to depart. They expressed their appreciation to their hosts and wished Lord Foldsworth a speedy recovery and a happy holiday with his family in Hampshire.

His health improved greatly as his injuries began to heal. To the delight of his wife and daughter he announced that his brother John had written that very day to say he was looking forward to their arrival in June.

Kitty continued to meet James at regular intervals, and told him of the planned visit to Hampshire. She did not disclose to him the fact that she had discovered that she had a half brother.

She realised that her father was likely to meet Glencora. She saw it in his face as he read his brother's letter, how his spirits lifted greatly. Poor Mamma. If ever she discovered the truth she would never be able to cope with it. Kitty prepared herself to feign indifference should she be introduced to Lady Glencora in company.

No, she decided not to bother James with any of these family details, and to enjoy their time together for what it was; time stolen to love.

"How long will you be on holiday?"

"Two weeks, or perhaps three. I am not at all sure of father's intentions. I will write to you. I promise."

"No Kitty. It would be better not to. The risk of others finding out about us is too great."

"I wish it were a different world, James," said Kitty, kissing him tenderly, "where you could come with me. Oh, what are we going to do about our future? There are times when I despair. Don't you?"

"Of course I do. But we will work something out. It will mean living in England or France, or even America. I hope you will be able to take such a step, Kitty. It is a very big decision to leave behind all we have ever known. Particularly for you. You are renouncing so much, Kitty."

"But it is all worth nothing without you, James. I don't fancy the prospect of ending up with the likes of Timothy Stewart, even if he is going to be a Judge. I should hate to be married to someone who sentences people to death... my God, what a dreadful prospect!"

"He is going to be a Judge then. I had heard as much in the village, but was not aware that it had been sanctioned in Dublin."

"Why James, you sound almost shocked! What does it matter to us what office he has been given. The only irritating fact as far as I am concerned is that he will be presiding over the Wexford courts. Far too close Oak Hall. I am sure he will want to spend every free day visiting. My mother received a letter from his mother only yesterday, and she was absolutely thrilled with the appointment."

She sensed his tension around the subject. He had become very subdued.

"James, do you not think you are becoming overly sensitive regarding Timothy. Are you afraid of him?'

"Don't be silly, Kitty. Why should I have anything to fear from him other than he might steal your heart away from me.'

"James, I tolerate him because he is a guest at the house. That is all. If it were a matter of choice I would seldom, if ever, see him."

He believed her. But it was at times like this that he wished he had never become involved in the planning of the rebellion. Then he would be free to leave the country with her in a matter of months. As thing stood, he was going to have to explain a lot of things to her. He hoped she would be able to understand.

"You know, James, I miss our outings to the Hill Fort. One feels closed in here in this old ruin, as lovely as it is in its seclusion.'

"I know. I feel the same myself. But it is safe here. The only company we have here are the ones residing in the graveyard. Have you ever seen it Kitty?"

"No. I was not even aware there was one here. Can we go and see it?' she asked, her interest aroused.

Taking her by the hand, he led her through the grove of laurels, which suddenly opened out into the secluded burial ground.

"Goodness, did you ever see such a carpet of beautiful bluebells? There must be millions of them."

The massive blue carpet covered the sacred place, with only the odd flat headstone visible amidst the hue. A hare, startled by the intruders, raced erratically through the maze of flowers. Tall yew trees stood sentinel to the sleeping souls.

"As peculiar as it may sound, Kitty, it is a beautiful sight. So cut off from the world one could not help but rest here in peace. When we are old, Kitty, and coming to the end of life, I think we should rest here."

She clung to him dreamily.

"Why not James? Why ever not? As morbid as this sounds, we will have to leave this life sometime. I can think of no lovelier place for us than to be side by side here amidst the bluebells. Over there, James, where that tallest of yew trees stand."

"Settled then, my darling," he smiled, and taking her in his arms looked at her beautiful eyes and loved her. "Meanwhile, Kitty, we must live. I look forward to spending life with you first, and loving you every day of it."

Walking back to their horses they were silent. Happy and content. As they rode down the narrow, overgrown laneway, they heard the approach of a galloping horse. The loud hoof-beats rhythmically flogging the earth.

"Who could this possibly be, James?" Kitty asked, alarmed.

James did not wait to answer but turned his horse about and retreated rapidly back up the laneway. Before disappearing into the trees, he called softly, "Till we meet again," and blew her a kiss.

Kitty rode down the laneway, the approaching horse and its rider finally coming into view. It was Viscount Stewart, quite out of breath.

"Why, there you are! They were not quite sure at the stables in what direction you rode. Luckily I met a small boy, who said he saw a lady riding out in this direction."

Kitty tried to conceal both her shock and annoyance. He was the last person she had expected or wanted to see.

"Timothy, what a surprise. I thought you were back home in Kildare."

Their voices rang out clearly in the evening breeze, and James, standing rigid amidst the trees, hoped his horse would not betray his whereabouts. Kitty was also aware of that possibility. Her primary aim was to get Timothy Stewart away from the place as quickly as possible.

"You seem quite out of breath, Timothy. I always thought you to be a fit gentleman," she teased.

"So I am, Kitty. So I am. I shall race you to the side of the hill."

With that, he galloped away. She immediately followed him, tears obstructing her view at having to leave James in such a fashion. She realised that their place of meeting was no longer safe. James, having heard all of their conversation, also realised this fact.

Having galloped a full mile, they slowed on approaching the breast of the hillside.

"My goodness, you are the expert horsewoman," he laughed, as he looked at her flushed features. She was lovelier than ever, he thought.

"When did you arrive?" she asked, choosing to ignore his comment.

"Late this morning. I was travelling to Wexford when the coachman fell ill, so the journey had to be abandoned. Hence my impromptu arrival at Oak Hall. Your mother was as hospitable as ever and bade me stay until the coachman was replaced, or whatever. She told me you had gone on your usual ride out. I was very lucky to find you."

Kitty remembered the small boy. No doubt the boy she had previously met at the old ruin with his dog. 'How well he remembered me,' she thought.

"So, you have become a Judge, Timothy, since I last saw you. I suppose I must congratulate you, though for one so young it is rather a serious position, do you not think?" she asked him curiously.

"Thank you. Perhaps I am one of the youngest Judges in the country, but you know I have grown fond of the idea, and I must confess I think I shall quite like it. The number of those initiating disturbance is growing weekly, so the judicial system must be upgraded to deal with the troublemakers," he explained in a very authoritive voice.

"My goodness, Timothy, you make it sound as if there is going to be a revolution or some such like catastrophe. It all sounds quite dramatic."

They walked their horses, allowing them to cool down after the strenuous gallop.

"Well, to be quite honest with you, Kitty, there is a lot of unrest in other parts of the country. There is the real possibility of it spreading, you know! The Lord Lieutenant is actually of the opinion that there could indeed be a revolution, believe it or not. So the Castle is preparing in every respect should it come to pass."

"Oh, I don't know, Timothy. Ireland has always been on the verge of rebellion, yet all I ever see are people going about their daily work in the fields or whatever," she said matter of factly.

"That is the way it was in France, Kitty, when suddenly the people rose to seize power. As you know, they then proceeded to execute the royal family. Barbaric, I say. Now they are looking to Ireland. There is a new society started here called the United Irishmen. Have you ever heard of it?"

"No, I must say I never have. One hears little living in this quiet area," she replied truthfully.

"Well, they have actually asked for assistance from France with an uprising here. Guns and men. Can you possibly imagine the turmoil that would create? All that we have ever known would disappear overnight. Wholesale slaughter would result. A terrible prospect."

"It all sounds a little unreal, Timothy. I am aware that father does attend a lot of meeting at Dublin Castle. He has mentioned the possibility of there being some trouble, but nothing of the landing of French troops, or such like."

"Yes, I realise it all sounds a bit dramatic, but we do know from our intelligence services that this Society is growing in numbers, and such revolutionary groups use surprise as their best form of attack,"

"Timothy, calm yourself," said Kitty, alarmed by his intensity. "One would think we were going to meet them at any moment. Life here, you know, goes at a very gentle pace, and we have never had any problems with our tenants, even in grandfather's time. We have always been very fair, and have never known the slightest hostility from any of them. I simply cannot imagine them marching on Oak Hall. What an absurd notion. All they do about these parts is work and go to the inn, and the fairs, the market day in town and their churches. So, you see how difficult it is to visualise such a rebellion and bloodshed," she said convincingly.

"You seem to know a lot about your tenants and their doings, Kitty," he exclaimed.

"Yes, I do. It is my business to know. I have always found them to be friendly and pleasant. Why should I possibly have grounds to believe they are planning to murder us in our beds?"

He failed to find argument with what she stated so matter of factly. He did, however, remark to himself that she was far too familiar with the people and their daily lives. In Kildare, they raised their hats to his family on the roadside, and he could never imagine a tenant assisting his mother to mount!"

On reaching the stables, the grooms took their horses. They were both tired and hungry, and Kitty felt disturbed by what she had heard. Her sense of the predictability of life was threatened.

"Thank you, Timothy, for the company. What I need now more than anything is a nice warm bath. Shall I see you at dinner then?"

"Yes. It was lovely to have the unexpected pleasure of being with you today. What a pity it cannot be more often," he ventured.

"Yes, but the prospect of discussing bloody revolutions more often is not so pleasant! Life could become very grim dwelling on such prospects, I am afraid," she said earnestly.

"Possibly, but then, that is the world we live in today."

Tapping his riding boot with his crop, he proceeded up the stairs, muttering,

"She lives far too sheltered a life, far too sheltered indeed!"

Only then did he notice Williams nearby.

"Viscount Stewart," Williams began, noting the oddness of the man talking to himself, "Lord Foldsworth has expressed a wish to speak to you upon your return. Shall I tell him you will call in to see him in perhaps half an hour, Sir?"

"Certainly not. You shall tell him no such thing, my man. You assume far too much," Viscount Stewart replied rudely.

Williams was dumbfounded by the attitude of the guest and stood almost transfixed with shock.

"Is there something else, Williams?" Viscount Stewart continued.

"Eh, no Sir, nothing else," Williams replied falteringly.

"Well then, I suggest you return to your duties. Come now, look lively, my man." Then, muttering to himself again, "Hmm... one would imagine Lord Foldsworth would have you out to grass and a livelier young buck here instead!"

Williams knew it was intend that he should hear this insult. He decided that he would not accept such blatant impudence, guest or not guest. Looking directly into the angry face of the young Viscount, he said in a tone none too friendly.

"I will remind you, Sir, that you are a guest here in this house, without authority of any nature while under this roof. At this point in your life one would imagine you would have learned what common manners are. Further, as to you comments on my retirement, or 'out to grass' as you term it, I suggest you go and have a roll in it yourself. When horses do so it seems to have a calming effect on them."

Williams walked away briskly without waiting for a response. Viscount Stewart was dumbfounded. He stamped his foot angrily.

"I shall see to you, my man. The very cheek of you... " He shouted, on finding his voice again.

He lashed the banisters with his riding crop, unaware that Kitty was standing at the top of the landing. She looked at him with utter contempt, and it was some time before he noticed her.

"Kitty... are you not having your bath?" he asked, his voice choked with suppressed anger.

"Do I appear as if I am, Justice Stewart?"

The chill in her tone of voice threw his mind into confusion.

"No, of course not. How silly of me. That chap Williams ought to be..." he began.

"Ought to be what?" interrupted Kitty, her anger rising. "I'll have you know that Williams has served this family with loyalty and goodness all his life. Should

I ever hear you speak to him, or in fact any of the servants, in that incredibly rude manner again I shall insist you leave this house instantly. As Williams so rightly stated, your rank here is that of a guest. It is embarrassing to find it necessary to remind you of that myself, never mind your needing the reminder from a servant. Furthermore, I greatly question the judgement of the Lord Lieutenant, placing one as discourteous as you in such a position of responsibility!" With this, she walked swiftly down the stairs past him, forcing him against the wall in order to let her by. Timothy Stewart sighed dejectedly, and went to his room.

Down in the kitchens, Hannah was aghast when Williams told her of the behaviour of the young Viscount. In an effort to calm him, she made some brandy punch and put a glass in his hand.

"An absolute scamp. Spoilt and ill mannered", Williams continued, with a rare display of emotion.

On entering the kitchen, Kitty could heard his words.

"Williams, I happened to overhear what took place between yourself and Viscount Stewart just now. I am very pleased you reminded him of his status here in this house. He had no right whatsoever to speak to you like that. Should he report to father, you can rest assured I shall tell him the whole truth. I fear his new appointment as Judge for Wexford County may have placed a great strain on him, for he is quite the changed man since his last visit. Now! Hannah. I need to take a bath. Would you be so kind as to have the hot water sent up as soon as it is ready?"

"Yes, milady," Hannah answered with a beaming smile. She looked at Williams triumphantly.

"And that, Williams, is what you call real breeding. That other upstart has little of it. I dread to think what life must be like in the house where he comes from".

As she poured the hot water into the containers to be brought upstairs, she continued to mumble to herself, "...out to grass... I know the grass I'd give him...".

Williams, having sufficiently recovered his composure, looked at Hannah.

"You know Hannah, the Lord help me if ever I have to stand before Justice Stewart. Think of the pleasure he would have to see me dangle at the end of a rope."

"Not at all Williams," chuckled Hannah, "your type would be sent to the quarry to break stones for life!"

As Hannah laughed out loud at her own cleverness, the ringing of the bell from Lord Foldsworths room distracted Williams. He stood quickly, and went directly to his master.

"Williams, have you seen Viscount Stewart yet to deliver my message?" asked Lord Foldsworth.

"Yes, my lord, but he appeared rather indifferent when I told him," answered Williams.

"Whatever do you mean Williams?"

"Well, my lord, his exact words were that he would 'go in his own time', and that I should be 'out to grass'. Yes, that was the term he used."

Lord Foldsworth was somewhat taken aback by the straightforward attitude of his butler.

"To grass... eh... retired? What utter folly. Whatever prompted him to be so rude Williams?"

Deciding to speak his mind to his master, Williams continued.

"His upbringing, my lord. Simply that."

"I see. Indeed." Lord Foldsworth paused for thought. "I can't reproach him Williams, as you well know, but please inform me if he is ever abusive to you, or indeed any member of staff, again. If any guest is, for that matter. Thank you Williams."

On returning to the kitchen, Williams told Hannah what had transpired.

"His Lordship is no fool at all. I still say, Viscount or no Viscount, you won't find flour in a coal bin, as my old grandmother used to say."

It seemed that Oak Hall had decidedly taken a turn against Timothy Stewart. Even the portraits that hung on the great walls seemed to frown upon him, Kitty thought as she prepared for dinner. She decided she would manage to see as little of him as possible, and was glad his stay would be a brief one. She placed a necklace of fine pearls around her throat and admired them. They were last years Christmas gift from her father. Thinking of her father now, her mind went to the scene in his study when he spoke of Glencora, and to how Timothy had been party to this unwitting intrusion. She regretted he had any part in it. However, she also realised he would never be foolish enough to disclose the information they had come upon. He thought too much of his new post as Judge and he was not unaware of her fathers influence at Dublin Castle. Enough of that, she thought, time to join the others for dinner.

Meeting her mother on the great stairway, she couldn't help but admire how lovely she looked.

"You always manage to look beautiful mother," she said, as she kissed her lightly on the cheek.

"Thank you, my dear, and may I say the same for you. Did you meet up with Timothy today? He left here in a great hurry to find you. I think, Kitty my dear, that he has fallen in love with you."

"Mother, your sense of humour is wonderful this evening," Kitty replied dismissively.

"Ah but Kitty, he is now a Judge of the County. A very prominent position. He has a great deal to offer any young lady. I don't expect you to fall in love with him straight away, but in time do you not feel things might change?"

"Mother you do not seem to realise that I tolerate him in this house only because he is a guest of you and father. Otherwise I would scarcely bid him the time of day."

"My dear Kitty," continued her mother, "when one is so young one is sometimes confused. Just watch how you feel over the passing of time. You will realise then that you are only fighting a losing battle, and you will admit he is irresistible."

Kitty walked away exasperated, thinking how utterly misled her mother was in her anticipations. She then pondered if it were possible her mother was entering an early dotage. One heard of such things after a bang on the head!

Meanwhile, Timothy Stewart was finally honouring his hosts bidding. He knocked on the door of Lord Foldsworths study, wondering at the purpose of the summons.

"Ah, do come in Timothy. Take a seat. Will you join me in a drink before dinner?"

"No thank you, Sir. I shall abstain until later if you don't mind."

"Very well. As you wish. So, you are now a Judge for the County I am told, and what an honour for one so young. I drink to your success, and I you assure of my support." Charles Foldsworth sipped from his glass ceremoniously and smiled at his guest.

"Thank you Sir. Your kind wishes are much appreciated. We live in changing times, do we not?"

"Indeed we do, Timothy, indeed very much so. The old ways seem to be on the verge of breaking up before our very eyes. It seems there is a gathering of tensions in many place around the country. Fortunately we here seem to be quite unaffected so far."

"While that may be the case Sir, one needs to be constantly vigilant. I have heard that in some of the great houses in other parts of the country that the servants were found to be members of this growing organisation that calls itself the "United Irishman"."

"Really? How dreadful."

"Yes, and plotting the assasination of their masters. The very ones who give them a roof over their heads. Such people should be arrested upon suspicion and brought to justice and hanged forthwith, Lord Foldsworth. That would put a quick end to all others entertaining such notions. Treasonous behaviour. We need to make a couple of examples of some, and then that will be that!"

"Hanged Timothy!" Lord Foldsworth was shocked by these extreme measures being proposed. "Hanging servants for being suspected members of an organisation! An organisation that does little but speaks rhetoric of a free Ireland! These are dreams, Timothy, simply dreams my good man. Surely a Justice of the Peace does not want to begin his career with such bloodshed? I doubt if the Lord Lieutenant would be impressed with such measures. Common sense tells one it would do little but ignite the torch of open rebellion Timothy, rather than serve to quench any possible revolution.

"But Sir, the Lord Lieutenant cannot possibly be consulted at every Court sitting, or approached at the passing of every sentence. He has given me adequate room to decide what measures best to employ to quell any disturbances", stated Viscount Stewart most earnestly.

"I will give you some sound advice, Timothy. Do not be foolish enough to express those views outside this house. As you are aware, Judges have been found shot in the ditches for saying less. That would be a colossal price to pay for such unwise ideology."

The study door opened with a gentle knock. Williams announced that dinner would be served soon.

"Thank you Williams," said Lord Foldsworth, not missing an expression of distaste appearing on the face of Timothy Stewart.

"I am afraid you butler seems to have no difficulty in entering unannounced, Sir, if I may say so," remarked Stewart.

"Oh really? I do believe Williams knocked Timothy. He never fails to knock as a matter of fact. You need not worry. He did not overhear you, if that is what is disturbing you. Regardless, Williams can be trusted with ones life. Now, shall we join the ladies?"

Timothy realised why he had been summoned. It was to impress upon him one thing and one thing only; not to upset the rhythm of life in Lord Foldsworths County. Or in his home, for that matter. He admired how direct his host could be without causing offence. A subtlety his daughter lacked, thought Timothy.

Lord Foldsworth found himself chuckling silently at the suggestion of Williams leading a military attack. A very amusing thought indeed. He imagined poor Williams would faint at the very sound of a bugle to battle, never mind brandishing a gun or sword himself!

Williams, however, had indeed overheard the end of the conversation between his master and his new foe, and he was not in the slightest amused. He shuddered at the idea of hangings at the whim of such an upstart. He made up his mind to speak to all the staff about the matter at the first available opportunity, lest any were foolish enough to consider joining the United Irishman. At least then they would be well aware of the fate that awaits them at the hands of our illustrious new Judge. That should put a stop to any romantic notions, he decided.

The following day provided him with the opportunity he sought. With the family departed for the afternoon visiting friends, it was an ideal time to call a staff meeting. Between grooms, gardeners, grounds men, labourers, maids and so forth, the staff numbered about thirty in all. Williams sat at the head of the great wooden table in the kitchen, while Hannah sat beside him. Clearing his throat, he began.

"This meeting has been called because I wish to make you all aware of some facts. As you know, or should know, a lot of the great houses around Ireland are at this time experiencing problems from the tenants on their estates. Many of these tenants have decided to join a new society that calls itself the 'United Irishman' and this society plans to have a revolution. They hope to rout the landlords off their estates. Some even plot to kill their landlords in their own houses. They are also foolish enough to think that they can overthrow the Government here. Then they hope to run the country no less! Any fool can clearly see that this will never succeed. How can a pitchfork stop the roar of a cannon gun? If they do attempt a rebellion I can tell you that thousands of troops will come.

"Now, I have heard for an absolute fact that anyone found to be a member of this group, or even suspected of being a party to it, is going to be brought to Wexford Goal and after a short trial will be hanged by the neck until dead."

With that, a communal gasp filled the kitchen. Hannah nodded her head solemnly as if to affirm every word. Williams continued.

"Should I hear of any of you being foolish enough to be involved in this society, you will leave the service of this house that very hour. Think well, is my advice to you. This rebellion is doomed before it even begins. Why die for such a cause" Williams lowered his head. No one was left in any doubt as to the truth of the matter.

The staff was alarmed to hear Williams speak so directly to them. As a rule, he would only summon them in relation to matters to do with the house. Preparations for great events such as garden parties, hunt balls or for Christmas and so forth. For him to speak to them in such a forthright manner left them full sure he had heard the news from its source. Each felt a shadow loom large into their lives. Hannah was first to break the stunned silence.

"You know, as matters stand even now, neither the house, nor the family, nor even ourselves are safe from this air of rebellion. That matter of the brick coming into the upstairs room... we never found out where it came from. No one was ever caught in the grounds either, were they?"

Williams took advantage of the still captive audience.

"Very true Hannah, very true. But if the family were in any way threatened, it would leave his Lordship little choice but to dismiss most of us and move to live in England. Many families are doing that at the present time. So again I advise you all to stay well away from all foolish gossip or meetings on rebellion, and let our constant loyalty be to our master and mistress. Their welfare is our duty, and our loyalties lie with them in all circumstances.

Speaking of which, they will be home at any moment! So I suggest everyone return to their duties, I trust much the wiser!"

Forewarned is forearmed, thought Williams, as he watched them leave.

Returning to the great fire with Hannah, he realised that the arrival of Viscount Stewart heralded a new era. A new reality. He wished with all his heart that it were otherwise.

* * *

Lady Edwina was astonished when her guest announced his sudden decision to depart the following morning.

"Why Timothy, we had truly hoped to have your company for some further days yet," she said in genuine disappointment.

"So good of you Lady Edwina. However, I must attend a meeting in Wicklow, and I have some papers to review beforehand in relation to national security. Unpleasant table talk for such lovely ladies, who should anyway be preparing for their holiday in Hampshire." Then, looking at Kitty he added, "I am quite sure it will prove a memorable holiday".

Kitty detected the subtle sarcasm in his voice.

"Isn't it such a pity Timothy that you are unable to join us," she said directly, "but 'then one must look to the security of Ireland, and we are fortunate to have one as considerate as you to take care of it for us!"

The tone between the two left Lady Edwina in no further doubt as to the presence of tension between them. Choosing to ignore Kitty's remark, she looked at Timothy.

"I do hope you will come and stay soon again, Timothy."

"Indeed that would be delightful Lady Edwina, and I shall look forward to hearing all the details about Hampshire upon your return."

Though he spoke to Lady Edwina, his smile was turned on Kitty as though to say 'I am after all your parent's guest'.

"Yes Timothy," Kitty responded, "and you will be able to reveal your plans on how to deal with this revolution you so obviously expect."

Lady Edwina shot Kitty a disapproving look, which Kitty dismissed with a haughty smile.

Shortly afterwards, as Viscount Stewart made his way on horseback down the avenue, Lord Foldsworth entered the room where the women still sat. He looked out the window and sighed.

"There goes a young man who will be responsible for more unrest in this country than a hundred evictions could cause. I regret to say that his type is decidedly dangerous. I hope you are not upset by my saying so, Kitty. He so obviously admires you."

Lady Edwina threw her eyes to the ceiling and decided to say nothing. Her husband continued.

"I would rather he was not encouraged to visit again, Edwina."

"Why ever not, Charles?" she asked, almost faint at him going to this extreme.

"It is quite simple, my dear. During this stay at our home he has not only treated our butler with contempt, but in my own study told me quite distinctly that any person who came before his court whom he so much as suspects of involvement in plans for rebellion would be hanged forthwith. Without even the benefit of a proper trial, Edwina, but rather at his whim! No, my dear, Oak Hall has had its share of odd and peculiar people over the years, but never have I entertained one so full of hate and suspicion.

"Now! Tell me... have you both packed your choicest ball gowns? Don't forget the mid-summer ball in Hampshire." On that lighter note, he left the room to take his morning walk.

Charles Foldsworth wandered around the garden for a while admiring the roses, then eventually made his way to the seat beneath the giant copper beech tree. His thoughts turned to Glencora; how to meet her without arousing suspicion of any kind. He had written to her two weeks previous. He remembered agonising late into the night over the wording of the letter. Now he could recall the words exactly, and for the hundredth time re-read it as if it lay before him. She will have received it by now, he thought, and wondered what her reaction to it had been. He realised the dice was cast.

Dear Glencora,
You will without doubt be very surprised to receive this letter, which is many years overdue. I hope you and Henry are well. Of late you have both come into my mind constantly.
I hope to be in Hampshire soon. I had a riding accident in March, and the doctor advises a holiday, so I am taking my wife and daughter to John's place for a few weeks. If during that time I could call on you, I would be delighted. If you do not wish for me to do so, I shall understand perfectly. I hope, however, you can find it in your heart to meet, however briefly that meeting may be.
I remain,
Yours sincerely,
Charles Foldsworth.

The letter was short and to the point. In the event of it being lost or mislaid it revealed little. Yet he felt uncertain about the forthcoming meeting, should Glencora agree to it. Did Henry know that he was his father? If not, would she tell him? The questions were many, and for the first time in his life Charles Foldsworth was at a loss for answers.

The June breeze rustled through the beech leaves above him while the bees moved leisurely from flower to flower. He wished his life could have been a simpler one, but then was life not full of 'only'. In the distance he saw Kitty ride down the avenue for her regular afternoon canter. He smiled to himself. She was without doubt learning a lot about life and people of late. It should serve her well in the years to come.

* * *

Kitty rode to meet James at the old ruin. She was going to miss him while away in Hampshire, she thought, wishing not for the first time that she didn't have to leave Ireland. That she didn't have to leave James, she realised, and her heart skipped a beat at the truth in this.

James helped Kitty to dismount, and while still holding her hand, swept her into a strong embrace.

"My darling Kitty," he said with choking emotion, burying his head in her hair, "how can I bear to be parted from you?"

The two stood for some time in silence, wrapped in each other's arms. Finally Kitty broke away. Sitting on the soft grass, she patted the ground for James to join her. Looking out at the view, the two spoke in hushed voices, sometimes laughing, sometimes serious, their hands intertwined all the while. Nobody spying them would have had any doubt at all but that here were two young people very much in love. James was relieved to hear that Viscount Stewart has made his departure. Relief turned to alarm when Kitty told him of the new Judge's proposals to deal with 'troublemakers', as she put it.

"Imagine being that merciless, James! One shudders to think of any misfortunate person coming before him if a mere accusation of involvement is considered grounds enough for hanging."

"I know Kitty," responded James, trying to keep the shock out of his voice, "he seems determined to make a name for himself. However, enough of gloom and death! Will you miss me, Kitty?"

Kitty looked into James' eyes as her mouth found his. He needed no further answer.

Reluctantly, the two lovers prepared to depart. They did not linger, as though by an unspoken mutual consent. It was too painful for them.

As James rode back over the hillside, he could no longer avoid the thoughts waiting for attention in his head. Kitty's revelations regarding Viscount Stewart were deeply disturbing. He knew he must make no delay before informing the group of this development. Death upon suspicion, he thought. That is what it amounted to. I suppose what is new about that, he pondered cynically. Who ever had a fair trial?

His mind turned to Kitty again. While she was away, he must take the opportunity to think more clearly about everything; their future together; the rebellion; how they would escape to England or France. He felt the hands of time turning rapidly. He also had a strong sense of foreboding about events to come. He was determined, however dangerous these events, to have Kitty by his side. No matter what the cost.

Chapter eight

Hampshire, England

Eunice Gainsforth looked out through the window at the rain. So unpleasant for the roses, she thought. She was bored. Being a vicar's wife was quite dull at times, and with Bradley away visiting the workhouse so often, she was alone quite a lot. She looked at the distant horizon where sunlight had begun to filter through the clouds onto the Hampshire countryside. As the suns rays found their way towards the vicarage, the rain stopped just as suddenly as it had begun, and birdsong resumed even though it was now late morning. A familiar rush of melancholy swept over Eunice; the beautiful garden, and no children. After fifteen years of marriage, the gift of children seemed highly unlikely.

Her husband Bradley said it was 'God's Will', but Eunice had never been able to believe this 'God' of his. Too harsh, too judgmental. "A biological problem", the physician had stated, and that to her seemed much more realistic. The idea of a God somewhere up in the sky that boomed 'No family for the Gainsforths' was an absurd concept to her. Poor Bradley, she thought. Life was so black and white for him. No compromise or lighter shades of colour. But he worked hard for his people, and they loved him in return.

In the upstairs rooms she could hear Emily her housemaid busy cleaning and dusting. Emily took such pride in the vicarage. Each day she would scrub, clean, mend clothes and all the while humming a happy tune. Emily had never married. She lived with her brother in a fairytale cottage, where flowers bloomed in abundance between rows of vegetables and climbing roses clung securely to the whitened walls. Each morning Emily would arrive at the vicarage before seven o'clock, and served breakfast at seven-thirty without fail. Bradley loved her cooking and her pleasant disposition, which he attributed to hard work and a pure lifestyle. Eunice found this idea amusing, though she would never dare to say as much. Bradley believed his pronouncements absolutely. Eunice was intrigued at how readily some people seemed to find contentment.

She heard Emily singing as she came down the stairs.

"Will you be in for lunch today, Madam?" she enquired.

"Yes I shall, Emily. It is a little damp out. I am hoping the day will rise." Eunice replied, standing up from her reveries. She may as well go to the drawing room and resume her painting now that the sun had returned.

Painting was a favourite hobby, especially when the light was favourable. Her present work was a pastoral scent, the sheep and cattle quietly grazing by the river on a summers evening. Today she would work on the cloud formation, the hues of colour in a summer's sky. The challenge invigorated her. It always did.

Within what seemed a very short period of time Emily returned to announce lunch. With reluctance, Eunice left her work on the easel, reminding herself it would always be there to return to!

Eunice was quite used to eating alone. She too loved Emily's cooking, particularly her mushroom omelettes with fresh garden peas. She preferred her own company, and it was only on the rare occasion that she might invite a friend to join her.

In the kitchen, Emily sat and ate her lunch in the company of Tweed, the large tomcat. Eunice could hear her talking to the cat from time to time and found it very amusing, noting that Emily was quite happy to tell the cat all her problems! She imagined that somehow it must lift the burden for Emily, and wished she could so easily displace her own problems.

After her lunch, Eunice noticed that sunlight was now streaming through the windows, and she decided that it would be an ideal time to do some weeding in the garden. The soil was rain soaked and would make her task so much the easier. She loved the garden, and going to the small garden shed at the far side of the lawn, took out the tools required to accomplish the task. Carefully putting on her gardening gloves, she decided to work between the African Marigolds, and then to plant out some blue lobelia. They would be exquisite when they were in full bloom, their deep blue not to be found even in a summer's sky. The Lupins and Night-scented Stock, both lovely, not alone provided beautiful scents but also shelter for the less vigorous plants. Honeysuckle hung from the garden walls and exuded a perfume that pervaded the warm afternoon air. Soon she was lost in thought amidst the gentle hum of bees and the twittering swallows, which nested under the eaves of the vicarage each summer.

Emily came out carrying the tray with afternoon tea, and laying it on the garden table underneath the old ash tree, returned silently to the kitchen. Eunice removed her gardening gloves and sat down, grateful for both the shade and the refreshing tea. She admired the lavender. Its scent filled the quiet corner. She made a mental note to gather it in small bundles when the weather had completely dried it out. Emily would then place it in drawers and wardrobes, linen presses, and other strategic places prone to musty smells. This simple ritual marked each year.

As she finished her tea, the sound of horse's hooves approaching drew her attention. She instantly recognised the rider as being from the castle. He went directly to the vicarage door. Soon Emily arrived in the garden with a small white envelope in her hand.

"A letter from the castle, madam," she said, adding hastily, "The messenger has been instructed to await your reply".

Without ado, Eunice opened the letter.

It simply read:

Ravenswood Castle

My Dear Eunice,

Could you possibly come to see me this afternoon?
It is of the greatest importance.
If you can oblige, I shall send the carriage to convey you here at half past three this afternoon.
With love,

Glencora.

Folding the letter, she placed it in her pocket.

"Thank you Emily. Tell the messenger to await my reply.

Going directly to her room she wrote a note to the effect that she would expect the carriage at the time stated. Emily gave the small envelope to the messenger and he quickly departed. Eunice looked at the clock and realised that the coach would arrive for her in thirty-five minutes. Changing her clothes she decided to wear her lemon coloured dress. It was a summer favourite with her.

Whatever could the matter be? I hope Glencora is not unwell. I shall bring her some roses and lavender, she thought, and collecting the rose basket in the hall returned to the garden to select the choicest blooms. In the distance she could hear the coach as it rumbled towards the vicarage. Flowers ready, she collected her parasol.

"Emily, I am going to the castle and shall be home by six o'clock. If I am delayed, please tell Reverend Gainsforth of my whereabouts."

"Certainly madam. I shall take care of everything. You just go and enjoy yourself. It is such a beautiful summers afternoon," Emily chattered on in her usual cheerful way.

"Yes I shall, thank you Emily. Good bye."

Thomas the coachman raised his hat respectfully.

"Good afternoon, Mrs. Gainsforth," he greeted her, looking directly ahead. Eunice found it quite odd the way he never looked at her.

As Eunice sat in the coach alone, she thought about the unexpected invitation to the castle. Her last visit to Glencora had been only two days previous, and certainly there were no problems then. They had talked and laughed and exchanged news; had tea and then walked leisurely through the grounds. Eunice and Glencora had been friends since childhood. More like sisters really, Eunice thought. They had shared so much over the years that it had bonded them solidly, and they trusted each other implicitly.

The countryside looked fresh and lovely with lush crops growing in the fields. Amidst the distant trees, the turrets of the ancient castle appeared. Ravenswood Castle rested on a low hill, the only vantage point for many miles around. It had stood against the onslaught of its enemies over many centuries, and the lash of many English winters. It was one of the few castles that belonged to a catholic family. To Eunice, that mattered little. She was acutely aware that the history of England and many other countries had more than its fair share of bloodshed in the name of religion. Although a vicar's wife, religion for Eunice was not a yardstick of status, nor any kind of yardstick at all. Eunice took people as she met them. Glencora was known to be generous to all her tenants irrespective of their creeds, and indeed gave Reverend Bradley Gainsforth constant financial support for renovations he needed to make on his church. Eunice felt privileged to have such a friend.

Cattle grazed knee deep in the lush grass, while some stood in the river swishing their tails at the flies. Nearer the castle entrance, swans flew over the lake, majestic and serene. A small island in the centre of the lake was a crowded nesting site for the many wild duck that proudly displayed their trail of ducklings across its surface.

The horses slowed their pace as they drew the coach gently uphill. Thomas was a careful and considerate driver, who took pride in never having had an accident in his forty years serving as castle coachman. Approaching the broad gravelled sweep that lay to the forefront of the castle, Eunice could see Lady Glencora standing on the great steps awaiting her arrival. As the coach came to a steady halt, Glencora walked down the stone steps. She looked magnificent in her long sweeping blue dress, yet her face belied a tension that Eunice knew had not been there two days previous.

"Thank you, Thomas," she said, looking at her driver. The footman opened the door, and Eunice alighted. "So very kind of you Eunice my dear to come at such short notice." Eunice embraced her friend warmly.

"It is always lovely to see you Glencora. Here's a little gift for your." Eunice handed her the basket of beautiful roses and lavender.

"Eunice, how do you manage to have the best blossoms in all of Hampshire.

These are simply breathtaking. I shall have them placed in my room... no, I shan't... they would look delightful displayed in the front hall where everyone can admire them. They are too splendid to place out of sight."

As the coach moved away, Glencora took her friends arm.

"Shall we walk in the garden, my dear? I have the most important news to tell you, and I would rather discuss it away from the ears of the servants."

They walked across the lawn and sat on a marble garden seat. A sundial stood nearby, the gold roman numerals shining brilliantly in the afternoon sun. When they were seated, Glencora sighed.

"What I am about to discuss with you, Eunice, came as a complete and total shock to me. I received a letter yesterday. It is almost thirty years since I mentioned his name to you, and you are the only person I have ever discussed it with..."

Eunice looked at Glencora with total disbelief. It couldn't be? Yet who else?

Yes, Eunice. Charles. Charles Foldsworth. I was unable to sleep all night. I paced my room trying to come to terms with the contents of his letter. He is coming to Hampshire early next week, and he wishes to see me, and Henry Charles also. Whatever am I to do?" Her voice was almost a whisper at this stage, trembling with a multiplicity of emotions.

Eunice stood and walked over to the sundial. She traced the golden numerals with her finger slowly, desperately clearing her thoughts in order to advise her friend.

"What a shock for you Glencora. You told me he never answered your letter all those years ago. Is that correct?"

"Yes, Eunice. He never answered my letter despite the weeks and months I hoped and prayed that he might. He openly admits that fact in his letter, and somehow now wishes to reveal all to me."

"I see," Eunice replied with raised eyebrows, "Well, then you must ask yourself if you truly wish to meet him and hear him out. Why is he coming here to see you after all these years? It must bother him greatly, one must imagine."

"Yes, I expect you are right as usual, Eunice my dear. He apparently had an accident lately while out hunting, and his recuperation obviously gave him opportunity to reflect on his life. Oh Eunice, all these feelings rising within me after all these years. I just can't bear it." Tears tumbled unchecked down her face.

"Tell me, Glencora. Do you still love him? Is that what bothers you most?" Eunice asked her friend gently.

"Oh, I simply don't know! Feelings of love and hate, of rejection and of disappointment... so many feelings all together..." Glencora continued to sob quietly, dabbing her eyes with her blue lace handkerchief.

Eunice allowed her to weep her tears, and stood quietly at the sundial thinking. Glencora looked up at her with tear strained eyes.

"Silly really, isn't it? And I now almost fifty years old. One would think me seventeen, pining an admirer who failed to accompany me to a ball!"

"It has been a great shock for you, Glencora, yet I can't help but feel that somewhere deep within your heart you need to hear what he as to say. There are some things in life we need to hear, almost as if we owe it to our hearts."

"Your wisdom is so good to hear, Eunice. I suppose I am afraid. Meeting truth is sometimes difficult."

"I know Glencora. Not a day passes but I think how fortunate you are to have such a fine son. I have not been given that blessing."

Glencora was the only person in Eunice's life who totally understood the emptiness a childless marriage created for Eunice. Having regained her composure somewhat, she stood up and went over to Eunice at the sundial.

"Now, Eunice, we shall walk a little."

They walked down the gravelled pathway to the lakeshore. The waters danced with sunlight, and the swans looked curiously at them as they protected their signets, only weeks old yet. The two women sat on a nearby seat and gazed at the lovely view before them, both lost in thoughts of the unexpected letter.

Glencora thought about her son, now so handsome. She was so very proud of him. He had shown great interest in the running of the castle estate. It had prospered under his supervision. The tenants loved him. She had never told him the truth about his father. As a small child he had accepted without question that his father went missing during a war on the continent. As he got older, he had not questioned further.

"What shall I tell my son, Eunice? Should I tell him the truth?"

Eunice gave a few moments to the question before replying.

"What can I say to you, Glencora? There are many aspects to consider. Should Henry discover the truth, and that you denied him the opportunity of ever meeting his father, well, would he ever forgive you? On the other hand one must also consider what his attitude to Charles might be now. He may feel great anger, or rejection, for example. Then, what of Charles himself? Would he agree to meet him and explain his long denial of him?"

"I don't know, Eunice. I think it unlikely that Charles would wish to run the risk of allowing the real truth to emerge. He has a wife and daughter who are obviously unaware of us here. Think of the shattering affect it would have on their lives also."

"I know Glencora, but was not your relationship with Charles the best kept secret in all of England? Is it not still? Why not keep it that way?"

"The only person I ever told was you, Eunice, and I always knew it was safe with you. Yet I shall never forget the last weeks of my confinement. Those agonising days and nights. The endless questions from my family as to the identity of the father. My God, the strength my silence stole from me. There were times I prayed I would miscarry, but it was not to be so. I remained inside the castle all those months, apart from society and the social calendar, waiting my time of delivery. I prayed each day that Charles would come and claim his part of the responsibility, but he never did. Only now does he respond to my letter of all those years ago. Thirty summers, Eunice, and now he comes! Shall I even be strong enough to meet him? Will words fail me when I actually look into his eyes again?"

"I think God will strengthen you, Glencora, and give you the wisdom when the time comes. You are, after all, a woman of remarkable faith. You must simply trust. That will be sufficient you will find."

Eunice held her friend's hand comfortingly, just as she had done all those years ago.

"Shall we go and take tea, my dear Eunice? Heaven knows it is French Brandy I should be offering you after all that!" Glencora managed to smile.

"Really Glencora! Can you just imagine Bradley's expression if I returned to the vicarage tipsy! Why, I think there is every possibility you would have me back here by nightfall, and permanently!"

Glencora laughed, not least with the relief of having unburdened herself to Eunice.

The peacocks called shrilly to each other across the lawns, their usual evening ritual. They looked magnificent, some with their long tails sweeping the ground behind them, others with their tails displayed.

"Thank you again, Eunice, for coming up here today. How can I ever repay your kindness my dear"?

"Glencora, you will meet Charles and listen to him, as indeed he will listen to you. That, to me, will be fitting reward for my visit here today."

The evening light streamed through the large windows, enhancing the colours of the drawing room as the two women walked in. Portraits of Glencora's family seemed to gaze upon them. All had such noble and kindly expressions, the only exception being Lady Lydia, Glencora's grandmother, who wore an expression of deep sadness.

"I see my grandmother's portrait manages to hold your attention again today, Eunice. Why do you always seem so drawn to her?" Glencora asked, genuinely curious.

"It is the great sadness in her eyes. She seems so mournful, Glencora. Do you remember her, or know much about her life?"

"I remember her only vaguely. Mamma told me that she was full of exuberance for life until her second daughter, Elizabeth, drowned in a boating accident in the lake. She was only seventeen years old when she died in that tragedy. From that day until my grandmother died she never came fully to terms with her loss. My mother often told me the story. It all happened on a July evening when there was a great party held here. Somebody suggested taking the boat out on the lake, and Elizabeth was among the four who were in it.

"Nobody paid much attention to them as they laughed happily out on the lake. It seems that Elizabeth wished, at one point, to demonstrate her skill with the oars, and when they tried to exchange places for her to row, the boat became unbalanced and overturned. The others managed to swim into the shallows, but Elizabeth, while an excellent swimmer, caught her tresses in a piece of wood beneath the surface. She struggled in vain and to the horror of the guests on the lawn was simply submerged. All that evening they dredged the lake, and only at nightfall did they find her. My poor grandmother, refusing to accept her death, forbade her burial in the family vault for five days. In the end, she had to be sedated before the family could lay Elizabeth to rest. Only when grandmother awoke to hear the burial had taken place did the horror of what had happened finally come home to her. She wept bitterly for weeks on end, prayed to die herself, but she lived to be a very old woman. An old woman who had grown more silent and sad with each passing year. So you see my dear Eunice, that accounts for the great sadness you detect in her portrait."

"Oh Glencora, what a very distressing story. The poor dear, what a dreadful loss to suffer. Was she not wonderful to retain her sanity at all."

"Quite right," Glencora answered, as she studied the portrait as if for the first time, "I think her life teaches me that endurance is essential. When one considers her loss, it places ones own life very much into perspective. Perhaps I should reflect upon it a little more often."

They drank their tea slowly, and chatted into the evening, until finally it was time for Eunice to take her leave. As they walked to the main door, they were silent. Once outside, Eunice stopped and held Glencora's arm.

"Glencora, you will let me know when your visitor arrives, if I can be of any assistance to you in any way. I shall be only too glad to oblige."

"Yes, I know that Eunice. Please tell Reverend Bradley that I send him my fondest wishes, and also that he is not to overwork in the poor house," she said with genuine concern.

Outside, Thomas sat in his usual erect manner on the coach seat, while a footman held the door open for the passenger. The women embraced.

"Goodbye, Glencora. Some day you must come and see my garden, before the summer wanes."

"I shall, my dear. I shall," she replied, almost envying the simple life her friend seemed to have.

As the coach made its way slowly down the long avenue, Glencora turned around and looked at the great castle where she had spent all her life. Its vastness and grace never ceased to fascinate her, and her love for her ancestral home had only grown with the years. Its walls had held visiting Kings and countless members of royal families. Ravenswood, while renowned for its grace and beauty, was above all loved for its warm hospitality. It was worth the effort and all the pain she had endured over her lifetime here, she thought. She knew that Henry would continue the traditions. Thank God for Henry. He made her life worthwhile, and supplied the very means by which Ravenswood Castle would prevail. Going inside, Glencora arranged the roses and lavender in a large blue vase in the hallway.

At the vicarage, Eunice prepared to greet Bradley, who was rather late coming home. Emily sat in the kitchen and admired the strawberry tart she had made for dessert. The aroma filled the house. Eunice looked out at the evening sky. It seemed exactly the shade of colour she had tried in vain to perfect earlier in the day. Without further delay she returned to the easel and began work on the painting again, while the light was still holding good.

Emily knocked on the door and entered the room.

"Excuse me, Madam. May I go now? I have left all in readiness for dinner, and the whipped cream is in the cooling room."

"Of course, Emily. Thank you for all the trouble you have gone to. That tart smells absolutely delicious. You have Reverend Gainsforth and I thoroughly spoiled I'm afraid!"

Emily left feeling elated. She enjoyed her work, and wondered what on earth she would do if she had not got her job to go to at the vicarage. But there was no reason for concern. Reverend Gainsforth was such a young man, and would be their shepherd for a long time to come. Beneath her shawl she carried some slices of roast lamb, which she knew her brother would enjoy, and a smaller strawberry tart for their own evening tea.

By half past seven, Eunice became concerned that Bradley was still not home. Where on earth could he be, she wondered. Dinner will be thoroughly ruined if he is not home soon. It is so unlike him to be so late.

A sharp knock on the door startled her from her thoughts. It was a messenger from the castle. He handed her a note:

Ravenswood Castle

Eunice,

Again I need your help urgently. It is Henry. He has had an accident. Please come quickly.

Reverend Gainsforth is here.

In haste,

Glencora.

Running to the kitchen, she quickly removed the pots from the range, and then ran to fetch her evening cloak. Already heavy rain was falling. The carriage awaited her outside, the driver ready with reins in hand.

"Please hurry," Eunice called out. "I am not afraid of fast travelling."

The carriage jerked forward and was soon travelling at great speed. Despite it being a very well sprung carriage, it was a bumpy ride as the horses travelled at full gallop. Eunice hardly noticed, so distracted was she with concern for the young Master Henry. Several people stood by the roadside, well clear of the castle carriage as it sped relentlessly on. Many had already heard news of the accident. They hoped and prayed that young master Henry would live. While it is true that they cared for him, they also knew their futures depended on him.

The castle was aglow, with light from almost every room. Halting at the doorway the sweating horses panted heavily. Eunice alighted from the carriage without delay or ceremony. She ran up the great steps and Glencora met her at the doorway with a tear stained face and almost deathly pallor.

"Whatever has happened to Henry?" Eunice asked, brushing aside all formalities.

"Oh Eunice, the doctor is with him still. He fell from the loft in the grain store, and he is bleeding from both ears. What if he is going to die! Oh Eunice, I could never accept it..." and she continued to cry bitterly, almost on the verge of hysteria.

Eunice clapped her hands together sharply to get Glencora's attention.

"That's quite enough, Glencora. I shall not listen to such morbid notions."

Glencora was shocked into silence by her friend's tone of voice.

"Now, be seated Glencora and compose yourself. Have you been speaking with the doctor? How long has he been here?"

"He is not long here. He forbade me stay in the room. Bradley is with him also. He was on his way home to the vicarage when he met one of the workmen who told him of Henry's accident, and so he came directly here. Oh Eunice, my whole world is falling apart. Whatever shall I do if he dies?"

Just then, the door opened. Doctor Wilson walked in looking perplexed. He bowed slightly.

"Lady Bratton," he began, "your son is quite ill. I cannot say what the outcome will be, it entirely depends on the amount of damage he has sustained in the fall."

He said no more, and looked at the two women helplessly. Eunice spoke first.

"Doctor Wilson, has the bleeding stopped yet?"

"No madam. But it has subsided a little. I must be honest and say ,as much as it distresses us all, the bleeding is no indication as to the outcome."

"Well how on earth then are we supposed to know?"

"Time, Madam. We shall know before dawn, and that is all I can tell you because that is all I know. However, he is young and strong. I suppose the matter now rests in the hands of God himself."

Glencora was unable to speak. She sat on the blue velvet chair, completely stunned by the events of the past hour. Doctor Wilson prepared to leave the room.

"I shall remain with Henry overnight, Lady Bratton, and do all in my power to save him. I can promise no more." He closed the door gently behind him.

Both women walked up the great stairway slowly, following the doctor to the bedroom. The great four-poster bed at the end of the room was barely visible. Dim candlelight was thought best for the sick man. By the bedside sat Reverend Bradley Gainsforth, with Abbot William Hendron opposite him. Both men were praying life back into the young Lord Bratton. His mother stood by the end of the bed, pale as death herself, with Eunice standing behind her. The pillow was blood stained on both sides of Henry's head, and Doctor Wilson checked his patient heartbeat and breathing pattern constantly. No one spoke. The great clock by the wall ticked slowly and heavily, each second pregnant with uncertainty.

"I think, Lady Bratton, that you should sit by the fire and rest," the doctor advised her, gesturing to the chairs by the blazing log fire.

Despite the June evening, the room seemed dark and cold. Outside, a blackbird sang its piping song as the last glimpse of evening gave way to the rising moon. The women sat in silence by the fire, while the doctor worked with his patient from minute to minute. Looking at the young man before him, who was sweating profusely, he thought how fragile life could be. A maid brought in some tea, and Eunice poured it into the fine china cups. The abbot and the vicar joined them on the doctor's recommendation.

"Abbot, will Henry live? Reverend Gainsforth, will God hear our prayers?" Glencora asked, pleading for hope. Abbot Williams took her hand.

"My dearest Lady Glencora, while I have no doubt but that God is listening to Reverend Gainsforth and I, I think it is the prayer from the mother's heart He will answer more readily!"

The vicar nodded to her in agreement.

"Then I must sit with him awhile," she replied, and she walked toward the bedside as if in a trance.

The doctor stood behind her. She looked at the handsome face of her only son, the coal black hair and the noble features, eyes closed, and the beads of perspiration flowing gently from his forehead down the sides of his face, mingling with the small trickle of blood from his right ear. She bowed her head in a desperate effort to concentrate on praying for the life of her son. Slowly the words came to mind.

"Lord, please give Henry back full life and health again. He is all I have and I need him. Please remember me at this time of great peril and hear all our prayers this night." She then continued to hold her sons hand, and thought of the anguish her grandmother must have felt upon the death of Elizabeth in the lake. Then she remembered the arrival of Charles Foldsworth in a few days time. All that seemed so insignificant now, she thought. I shall tell Henry the truth... all of it... I owe him that at least. The years of Henry growing up in the castle flooded through her mind. His first words, his first steps, and his first time on horseback on a pony called Bramble. "Lord," she prayed again, "you must let him live."

"Come to the fire now, Glencora," said Eunice, who had come to stand near her friend. "There is fresh tea coming up. Come now, my dear."

Slowly Glencora left her son's bedside and sat by the fire, drained and weary beyond words. The abbot and vicar resumed their vigil. The doctor felt the temperature of his patient, now warming up a little, which was an encouraging sign. Eunice was aware that she had not as yet had an opportunity to speak with Bradley. There was little to be said under the circumstances. When tea was served, the doctor sat beside the two women and yawned in exhaustion.

"Hmmmm. Three o'clock in the morning! Lady Bratton, would you and Mrs. Gainsforth not go and rest for a short while. You both look utterly worn out. I shall summon you should there be any change in Lord Henry."

"Thank you doctor," whispered Glencora faintly, "but I would rather be at Henry's side. Perhaps Eunice would like to rest."

"Not in the least, my dear. I shall survive a little tiredness. My place is here with everyone else just now."

Abbot William suddenly stood up, and called the doctor. Doctor Wilson walked briskly to the bedside, followed by the two women.

"There seems to be some change, doctor. The bleeding has ceased," he exclaimed.

"It has indeed," added Reverend Gainsforth, "and the profuse sweating also."

The doctor looked closely at Henry and checked his patients pulse rate. He then looked over at Glencora with a smile.

"It would seem that the Reverend gentlemen are correct. God hears the prayers of mothers! The crisis has passed, thank heavens."

Everyone sighed with relief and exhaustion. Glencora sobbed loudly as the tension left her body.

"Oh thank you Lord!" she cried, "and all of you here with me. I shall be eternally grateful. You shall never know how much."

She wept on, taking her son's hand in her own. It was warm to the touch. Gone was the limp and sweaty feeling of just an hour ago.

"Oh Henry, Henry," she whispered, as the tears flowed freely down her face.

The doctor stood up.

"As it is almost dawn, I suggest you all have something to eat and some rest. I shall remain here until seven o'clock. So please, go and partake of something nourishing. It has been a very long night."

Outside the dawn of a June morning was breaking with a flood of birdsong across the park. The mist slowly lifted its veil from the lake and the first rays of summer sun lit up the battlements of Ravenswood Castle. Lord Henry Bratton, its sole heir, opened his eyes slowly as sunlight streamed through the large windows of his room. The portrait of his grandfather seemed to smile upon him, and somewhere in the park a cuckoo called.

"Good morning, Lord Henry," the doctor greeted him cheerily, concealing his anxiety as he awaited a response. He hoped the young man could hear him and see him, and that he had complete limb movement. Henry turned his head towards the voice and after a brief pause replied to the doctors greeting.

"Oh, good morning doctor. What on earth are you doing in my room?"

No sooner had Henry asked the question, than the answer came flooding to him. No wonder, he thought, he had such a searing pain in his head.

"You have had an accident, Lord Henry. You fell in the granary. Tell me, can you move your arms?" asked the doctor, trying to conceal his fear that Henry might be left suffering from paralysis. Henry lifted both arms. "And now your legs, my lord." Henry moved them up and down.

"Wonderful, my boy," the doctor jubilantly exclaimed, "you are miraculously intact."

"But my head doctor..." Henry smiled, "it feels as if a cartwheel went over it."

The doctor laughed.

"That, my dear boy, will clear up soon. Now I should like you to rest, and sleep if you can. You have given us all a dreadful fright. Your poor mother has just left the room having sat by your bedside all night with her friend Mrs. Gainsforth.

Abbot Williams and Reverend Gainsforth too. Why, they stormed heaven all night for you! I have just sent them for what must be one of the earliest breakfasts of their lives!" he chuckled merrily, "but now I can tell them you are in excellent health, the only exception being a pain in your head. My young man, I bet you have had worse after a night of merriment!"

Henry smiled, his eyes already drooping with tiredness. Soon he was sleeping gently, and Dr. Wilson went downstairs to relate the good news. Everyone in the dining room was jubilant, their fatigue forgotten.

"It is simply a miracle," said Glencora, with tears of joy, "and now I feel as if I could sleep for a month!"

"And I would thoroughly advise all of you to do just that!" laughed the doctor, adding, "or a few good hours of rest at any rate!"

"You are absolutely correct, doctor," said Glencora, remembering her duties as hostess, "I have some guest rooms prepared. You must all rest until lunchtime at least. I shall not take 'no' for an answer."

As the heavy drapes were pulled across the guest rooms in the west wing of the castle, everyone was only too happy to retire. Eunice combed her long hair as she sat by the dressing table mirror.

"Bradley, you must be so exhausted my darling," she began, but then saw that he was already asleep.

Soon she was asleep beside him, and as the sun climbed higher in the morning sky, Glencora sat by her son's bedside watching him sleep and offered a prayer of thanks. She was now determined in her course to tell him the truth about his father's identity. In her very bones, she felt it the only right thing to do.

* * *

Lady Edwina was exhausted. The journey, both by land and sea, was long and arduous. Her husband looked at her with concern. As much as he disliked the thought, he realised that the years were taking their toll on her. The increased visits by the doctor to Oak Hall also indicated that all was not well with her.

As the final miles passed by the coach window, Kitty became more excited. It was only her second visit to her uncle's home, and she struggled with memories of her childhood visit, trying to differentiate between the facts and the fantasies she had built about it. She looked at her father, and could see the hidden strain. He was trying so hard to conceal it. She knew he was planning to visit Glencora. Common sense told her so. How distressing that might prove to be for him. She was very keen to see this woman whom her father had chosen to ignore for so many years, and the son she had borne him, Henry.

Her mother sat opposite her in the coach, and Kitty noticed how pale and ill she looked. She prayed she need never know about Glencora or Henry. Lady

Edwina sat with eyes half closed, indifferent to the magnificent Hampshire countryside. Hopefully, thought Kitty, a few days rest would restore her to her usual buoyant self. The sea crossing had been, from Kitty's point of view, relatively calm and pleasant, and their quarters quite comfortable. But her mother had never been a good traveller. Her head pain seldom if ever abated. Hopefully the holiday would serve to restore her mother's health and heal her father's haunted memories. Deciding to put all of this out of her mind, Kitty looked instead at the passing scenery and allowed herself to enjoy it all.

She thought of her cousins, Mark and George. While they were somewhat older than she, she wondered how they would relate as adults. Her memories of them were happy ones. As children, they would ride their ponies together, and go on picnics and fishing trips to the lakeshore. Yes, she thought, they were blissfully happy times indeed. Both were now married and had small children of their own, and she was looking forward to meeting them again.

As the coach entered the village, the final stopping point, the trumpet sounded to announce its arrival. Lady Edwina awoke with a start, followed quickly by relief that they were almost at their journey's end.

"At last, Charles. My goodness, I shan't be sorry to reach John's. The thought of resting in a decent bed is pure delight," she sighed wearily.

"I know, my dear. I share your sentiments completely. Now, we must go to the Inn and see if he has remembered to send the carriage," her husband replied, feeling a little apprehensive.

Kitty was glad to be out in the fresh air. There was great life and excitement about the village inn. The innkeeper welcomed them, and ushered them to a quiet corner table in the large room. Outside the window a lilac tree dropped its flowers in profusion. When tea arrived, they were grateful for the refreshment, and Lady Edwina cheered considerably.

"I am glad to see you feeling better, my dear. Has your head pain cleared yet?"

"Oh, it is much better Charles, now that all the ceaseless rattling has stopped. I will be so glad when we reach John's."

"Well, I must go and see if the carriage has arrived yet". He left them both, and went outside rather anxiously.

Kitty looked about at the people in the large room. Some were eating a hearty meal, while others were drinking light ale to quench the thirst of the warm afternoon. A dog lay near the door, basking in the cool draught. Everyone seemed preoccupied, either eating or drinking, as they awaited relatives or prepared to journey further.

Outside, horses could be heard neighing shrilly, while dogs barked and men called to one another. Lord Foldsworth had almost despaired of finding his brothers carriage when he finally saw it approaching the inn. He felt relief and excitement all at once. Waving his hand, the coachman recognised him and drew alongside.

"Sorry to be late, your lordship. Sheep on the road, as usual, coming from having been shorn," he said, in good spirits.

"Why Ganley! It is you. My word, but you still look as fresh as ever," Lord Foldsworth exclaimed as he looked at the elderly driver.

"Good of your lordship to say so, but come winter, milord, I assure you I am never so fit," and Ganley laughed heartily.

"I shall go and summon my wife and daughter, Ganley. Will you see that our trunks are loaded carefully?"

"With pleasure, sir. You need not worry. I am well used to supervising these lads here," he said, in a tone that left one convinced that this was undoubtedly the case.

Lord Foldsworth was happy to see the old coachman once again. Somehow, it made him feel as if time had stood still, or that little had changed in Hampshire.

"Its here, Edwina. Kitty, the carriage," called Lord Foldsworth, as he approached the two women, "Would you believe, Ganley is still sitting atop! He is as cheery as ever. I was just thinking that when one sees him still, one could actually believe that time has been suspended!"

Kitty was glad to see him so happy, almost boyishly excited. The way she remembered him being some years back.

Having paid the innkeeper, Lord Foldsworth escorted his wife and daughter to the door. The innkeeper walked briskly ahead of them, giving the dog a sharp kick as it lay slumbering beside the doorway. The disapproving eye of Lady Edwina did not escape him.

"Well, we wouldn't like your ladyship to trip now, would we?" he said.

"I am not blind, innkeeper, you know," Lady Edwina informed him, her tone of voice reprimand enough.

The innkeeper bowed slightly and bade them a safe journey, deciding to ignore the rebuke. Ganley took off his hat and bowed to Kitty and her mother.

"My dear Ganley, how wonderful to see you again," said Lady Edwina, smiling broadly to the coachman.

"And you also, my lady. And if I may say so, how lovely indeed the lady Catherine has grown to be."

"Thank you, Ganley," responded Kitty, adding, "and you as handsome as ever, from what I recall of my last visit."

Ganley was delighted with the compliment. For a man almost in his seventieth year, he did look remarkably well and fit.

The horses trotted briskly through the small town. The local people recognised Sir John's coach, with its striking coat of arms against a background of deep purple on the doors gleaming in the early summer sunshine. The familiar sights evoked memories for Lord Foldsworth of his younger days. He looked at his wife sitting opposite him and smiled. She was looking better already, he thought, as he listened to her telling Kitty an account of her first visit to Stagheath Hall; how she had loved it at first sight. While they chatted, his own thoughts turned to Ravenswood Castle and Glencora, and of course, their son. It cast a gloom of anxiety to enter his mind on what was considered by the others to be a happy and carefree holiday. But he realised he had denied that side of his life for too long now, and could no longer do so. He knew that it was fear more than guilt that had been responsible for the years of total separation.

He would have to make sure Edwina was suitably occupied when he visited Glencora. He would simply say he was riding out over boyhood haunts. Looking at the happy faces of his wife and daughter, his raw nerves found some solace.

"Look father, we are almost there," Kitty cried excitedly, as she pointed out the massive structure of Stagheath Hall, bathed in the warm light of summer.

"It always looks so lovely," Lady Edwina added happily, "so inviting and welcoming."

The fatigue of the long journey was almost forgotten as the coach slowed down at the gate lodge, where an elderly man slowly opened the huge crested gates. The long gravelled avenue, with giant beech and oak trees either side, wound gently towards the house itself. From atop the coach, Ganley could be heard calling, "Welcome home Lord Charles!"

Tears filled Lord Foldsworths eyes as he took in the familiar trees of his childhood. Trees where he has searched tirelessly in their ancient hollows for owls nests. In the distance he could see his brother John and his wife, Lady Alice, standing at the top of the great steps that led to the massive oaken door of Stagheath Hall.

Lady Alice was hardly able to contain her emotions.

"You have finally arrived my dears," she cried out, as she dabbed her cheeks with her lace handkerchief. As each alighted from the coach, long and warm embraces were exchanged. Ganley was very touched by this scene of reunion, witnessed from his seat up high. As the footman closed the door of the coach, he raised his hat in salute and gently drove the coach towards the rear of the house, quite unnoticed by the family.

* * *

Lady Alice's joy knew no bounds upon seeing her much-awaited visitors.

"Wonderful, wonderful to see you all again. I told John just this morning that we simply see so little of you that it is of paramount importance that you move back here to England to live. Isn't that so, John? Yes, that is just the solution. And now you must all have a bath and a rest before dinner."

Gasping for breath she continued.

"Edwina! What a journey from Ireland! You may as well be living in one of our outermost colonies when one considers how long it has been since your last visit."

Lady Alice's husband looked at her in good-humoured resignation, knowing full well that to try and interrupt, even in the most gracious of ways, would be utterly futile. He would wait until the tornado of excitement abated.

"Kitty, darling," Lady Alice moved her attention to her niece, "why, just look at you. So lovely! I have a good mind to keep you here with us, and I think it highly unlikely your father and mother will leave Ireland. We would have a wonderful time! You must remind me to take this matter up again."

She embraced her niece once more. Kitty, at this stage, was totally in awe of her vivacious aunt. So unlike her own mother.

Stagheath Hall had been the preferred home of the Foldsworth family in the previous generation. Their estate in Ireland, which provided considerable revenue, had been occupied only in the winter months. Each April the family would move with the main staff to Hampshire, leaving only a skeleton staff at Oak Hall to maintain it. Upon his fathers death the Irish estate had been bequeathed to Lord Charles, who was deemed to be of more robust constitution than his brother John who had been given Stagheath Hall, where the demands were considerably less in every respect. Both had been happy to accept their fathers plan for their lives without question. But the best memories both men had were of Stagheath, where their summers had seemed endlessly happy.

As Kitty lay in the bath she considered her aunt's suggestion of living in Hampshire. It was quite unimaginable. Already she was missing James more than she had ever expected, and living here without him she thought would be unbearable. But on the other hand, she reasoned, if her parents could be persuaded to retire here, then she would be quite happy to run the estate in Ireland. It was a pipe dream she knew. Her father would never deem a woman capable of such an undertaking. She imagined James with her at Oak Hall, as her husband and manager. If only it were possible, she sighed, while knowing in her heart that it could never be. It was very unusual for a woman to be left running such a large estate, and yet she knew that Lady Marjorie Lockwood had done so in South County Dublin for almost fifty years. Single-handedly at that! Then, in her case, both of her parents had died relatively young, and not being interested in marriage she dedicated her whole life to the estate and to being mistress of hounds. Kitty smiled as she recalled a meet where Lady Marjorie had led the chase at breakneck speed through the small fields at the bottom of the Great Sugar Loaf Mountain in County Wicklow. People still talked about it with awe and delight. No, she thought, I simply would not be the Lady Marjorie type!

During dinner, which proved to be a happy and lengthy affair, the families talked of the times, the changes, and their ideas for the future. Eventually the sun cast long shadows on the front lawns, calling an end to another glorious day, and the chandeliers were lit, reflecting their myriad colours on the crystals that hung majestically from the high ceiling. Kitty suddenly thought of James. What would he be doing now, she wondered. Is he missing me as much as I do him? Again, her mind pondered the possibility of him running the estate at Oak Hall, and wished with all her heart that such fantasies were possible in reality.

Lady Edwina retired early with her husband. They both felt content, but tired.

"Charles, it is lovely to be here. Thank you for such a lovely holiday. I couldn't help but notice at dinner how well you are looking. I think you worry far too much about Oak Hall, my dear!

He looked at his wife and considered how overly simplified her views of life really were. But her calmness of spirit, which some misunderstood as lacking liveliness, always helped him to free himself of anxiety.

Sitting at the mirror combing out her hair, a talk she would never allow a personal maid to do, she continued.

"Wouldn't it be wonderful, Charles, if we could find Kitty a suitable husband, and you and I could then retire here? Oh Charles, it would be simply divine. We would have the season in London, mix through society again. You would have the theatre and a good club. We would have such a different life, darling."

She twirled on the bedroom floor like a ballerina, much to his delight. He admitted to himself that he had not seen her so happy in a very long time.

"You know, Edwina, I promise to give it some thought. All that you say is true. It would be lovely to be part of England again. We live such retiring lives in Ireland indeed, with only Dublin Castle functions and evenings at other country houses. The problem," he sighed before continuing, "is finding Kitty someone reliable and steady! Should that not prove difficult, then we will be free to do as we choose, and to live a little ourselves."

"Oh Charles, let us give it a lot of thought. Serious thought. After all, it is high time that our high spirited daughter considered her future, or she may well end up all alone in life."

But her husband's thoughts had already drifted to his forthcoming meeting with Lady Glencora. He decided to ride over to Ravenswood Castle at the first available opportunity. To await an invitation under the present circumstances would be quite absurd. There was little point in speculating on the outcome of the visit at this point. It would only serve to frustrate and annoy him further.

Four miles off, Ravenswood Castle stood on its hill, aloof and enduring as it had been all through the centuries. Lord Foldsworth tried to visualise Glencora. Was she asleep now, he wondered? Or was she too equally anxious in anticipation of the visit?

* * *

Neither was the case, in fact.

Lady Glencora sat before her son, very calm and collected, as she prepared to tell him the truth that she had hidden from him for so long. Earlier that day she had visited Eunice and discussed her intention of disclosing all to Master Henry. They both agreed that it was the right thing to do. Eunice hoped that he would be able to cope with the information, known only to both women and the young man's father.

Henry sat at the fire opposite his mother feeling much improved since his accident. After dinner that evening Glencora had told him that she had something very important that she wished to discuss with him in the drawing room. It was the room where they always discussed the important issues in relation to the running of the estate, but he nonetheless was very curious as to what his mother wished to discuss so late in the evening.

"Henry, I have something to tell you this evening that I have withheld from you for many years. The accident you had some days ago was the deciding factor that has brought it to a head. It is the truth in relation to your father."

Henry sat very still as he looked at his mother before him. He waited for her to continue.

"Your father is not dead, as I have told you since you were a boy. He did not die as a general at war for England. He is alive and well and he has been living in Ireland. We were unable to marry when I discovered I was expecting you. There were many reasons, I suppose, that prevented it being possible. However, the main reason was the Charles - for that is your father's name - well, he would have been disinherited for marrying a catholic. This may sound shallow to you, but he is Sir Charles Foldsworth, brother of Sir John at Stagheath Hall. No one, not even Sir John, is aware of this fact. The only other person who knows of your fathers true identity is Eunice Gainsforth, who has been a true and loyal friend all these years."

Again, Henry remained quiet as his mother fought to continue her revelations.

"As it would happen, Henry, your father wrote to me only a few short weeks ago from Ireland. After all this time, he expressed a great desire to see me and to meet you, his son. Upon receiving his letter I felt confused and very upset. It was difficult for me, Henry, after so many years of silence. But I have decided that I shall meet him. He is presently at Stagheath Hall with his wife and daughter and I expect him to call here at any time. Two issues I place before you this night, Henry. Firstly, to forgive me for concealing this from you for so long, and secondly, to give you the choice of whether or not you wish to meet him."

Glencora sat back in her chair, and looked at her son through tear filled eyes. Henry looked into the dying embers of the fire, and was suddenly aware of the silence throughout the great castle. It seemed that the very walls and the portraits of some of his ancestors awaited his reply. The silence continued and his mother had no wish to disturb it, for it was not the silence of fear or anger. Henry looked at his mother with eyes of understanding and great love. He stood up and walked to her chair, sat down by her knees and took her hand in his own. It was a habit he had acquired as a child when he would sense his mothers occasional sadness. Now and only now did he fully realise what the cause had been.

"Oh mother, it is you I worry for now. As for myself, why yes, it is a great shock to suddenly learn that I can actually see my own father at any time. But you! What of you? Carrying this secret for so long and the heartache of it all and your helplessness in it. Mother, did you love him... love... father?" he asked, acutely aware that the word 'father' was so new to their conversation.

She looked thoughtful for a few moments before answering.

"Yes, Henry, I loved him dearly. We grew up together, in that he and John would come from Ireland every summer, and I would count the weeks until their arrival. As we grew older and began to understand life more, it became clear that to marry would mean making great sacrifices, and that just as clearly, duty came first also. It was very hard being pregMagt alone. So many questions were asked and so many judgements were made, but I withstood it all. And I am so glad, so very glad. Just look at the wonderful son I now have! When you were lying there so very ill Henry, suspended between life and death, I resolved before God that should you recover I would tell you the truth. I am so glad that I finally have."

There was no hesitation in Henry.

"Mother, I shall meet father. I must. You need not worry, for I shall be gentlemanly and civil and do you proud. So, now I learn that I have a father in Ireland who is visiting my new uncle, and a half sister also!"

Much to Glencora's surprise, he laughed out loud.

"Mother, thank you for telling me the truth. To carry such a secret for so long must have been a great burden, but its disclosure must have taken even greater courage. I am so very, very proud of you mother," and standing up, he hugged her tightly.

She cried with relief, and with sadness and joy, and scarcely believed that she had finally opened her heart to him on the matter. Glencora knew that she would sleep well and allow the morrow to take care of itself. Somehow the prospect of meeting Charles was far less threatening than it had been for the past few weeks. It was time to rest.

The summer breeze of the June night seemed to caress the walls of the great castle with a sign of approval and by the lakeshore the waterfowl called in the distance to each other through the thin veil of mist. All seemed peaceful at last.

* * *

Morning came early at Stagheath Hall. Lady Edwina breakfasted in bed while her husband joined the family. He was agitated and anxious, and pondering as to how he would find a simple excuse to leave the house to go riding alone without offending whoever wished to join him. Conversation was lively, including Sir John conveying his regrets that he would be unable to spend time with his brother that morning, on account of some business with the estate, which had arisen. Lord Foldsworth feigned disappointment to cover his relief.

He decided to ride over to Ravenswood Castle within the hour. Kitty chatted happily with her aunt Alice, who was insisting that she must look at some gowns, which had recently arrived from London. Kitty could not help but marvel at the exhilaration and vibrancy of this household. Life at Oak Hall was dull, if not dead, by comparison.

Yet there was James. Only for him, she would have no qualms about staying with her aunt and uncle. Life held little else for her in Ireland. Why was it such a sad country, she asked herself? So much poverty, and the conditions the vast majority lived in were dire. There seemed little chance of change. But that argument or assumption made little sense, for the majority of the people could both read and write. They were a proud people too, she reasoned, but their spirit seemed almost dead. Thinking of May Ryan, and the manner in which she was evicted by Jerome Hennessy, showed just a small fraction of what prevailed throughout the land. It was reason enough for any people to die within; when they could not be sure of retaining the cottage they called home.

After breakfast, Charles Foldsworth went directly to his wife's room and announced, without hesitation, his intention of taking a morning ride. Lady Edwina was delighted to hear it.

"Why you must, Charles. I am sure you can't wait to revisit all your old boyhood haunts. Be careful of the bridle paths. They do change you know over the years."

"I shall my dear, don't worry," he reassured her, adding, "and if I am not home at lunchtime, don't worry. Be assured that I am enjoying myself."

He tried to conceal his growing unease and impatience to be off. He kissed his wife lightly on the forehead.

Bluebells were in a haze of abundance throughout the forest as far as the eye could see. The bridle path drowned in their nodding heads that seemed to resent the intruding hooves. Blackbird song echoed shrilly on the June morning as the sun tried to penetrate the brilliant bright canopy above him, succeeding only in odd patches. It was a morning heavenly to behold. The route he had chosen to Ravenswood Castle was the least conspicuous, with the giant oak and beech trees providing the privacy he craved for his journey, away from the prying eyes of fieldworkers. Steele, the grey mount he rode, trotted on briskly, pleased with the pace the rider had set.

Charles Foldsworth thought about his life, about Oak Hall, about his wife and daughter. He thought also of the impending rebellion, which the authorities at Dublin Castle had forewarned of as inevitable. It was indeed a very fragmented life. Nothing but uncertainty lay ahead. Life seemed to have somehow worked in reverse for him. If he had had a legitimate heir he could retire in England now, but that was not possible the way things stood. Instead he had a daughter who must soon find a husband, and a wife whose health was uncertain. Somehow he resented it all. He wished he could live in the peace and security of England, alongside tradition and close family ties. In many ways he regretted he had not married Glencora. It was the first time he actually acknowledged it to himself, even if it had meant disinheritance and public disapproval. Time, he felt, should have redeemed him in it all.

A stag leaped across his pathway, startling the horse momentarily. Despite the bad hunting accident, he had not lost his nerve in horsemanship as had happened to so many he knew. He soothed the frightened animal, which then resumed its pace once more, and finally in the distance the outline of Ravenswood Castle could be glimpsed through the trees. Suddenly he felt tense and fearful. A tree trunk lay across the pathway ahead of him and urging Steele forward, the animal jumped it with grace and ease. He patted him gently and slowed the animal to walking pace. He decided to ride across the main park once outside the forest, and approach the front of the castle.

The grounds looked magnificent. The tall rhododendrons, scarlet in the morning sunlight; the great ash trees, graceful beside the stately chestnuts where horses sought their shade from the flies. Charles trotted briskly to the main steps. As though out of nowhere, a footman appeared and offered to lead his horse away to the stables. Charles climbed up the great steps. The doors opened and the elderly butler led him to the morning room that was full of sunlight.

"Whom shall I say is calling, Sir?" he enquired.

"Please tell Lady Glencora that an old friend has called by," Lord Foldsworth announced firmly.

The footman nodded and left the room, closing the great doors gently. Alone in the room he felt like a child awaiting a scolding from its mother, of which he had clear memories. Upstairs, Lady Glencora's maid conveyed the message of the guest's arrival, and stood looking at her mistress with great wide eyes.

"I shall be down presently, Tilly."

When her maid had left, she tried to compose herself once again. She had watched Charles ride across the part, and dismount before the house. He certainly appeared fit and agile for one who had such a recent accident. She looked across at the lake, the swans almost hypnotised by their own reflections on the smooth clear surface. The sunlight danced on the waters, creating an image of a bed of sapphires. How very beautiful, she thought. Sipping from a glass of water, Glencora breathed deeply and realised that this was the moment that she had awaited for so long. If only it was all those years ago, she sighed. Walking down the massive stairway, she looked beautiful, and her calm demeanour belied the strong fear within her. She opened the door of the morning room, and he stood there before her.

"Good morning, Charles," she said casually, as if it had only been some weeks since their last meeting. He walked towards her and stopped some short distance before her.

"Glencora... it is wonderful to see you at last. It has been so very long... too long." he continued to gaze at her awhile. "Will you, or, should I say... can you... ever forgive me? For that is why I had to come here. To ask you if you could find it in your heart... if you ever can..." his eyes filled with tears as he stood erect and noble before her.

Glencora sat down and was glad of the support of the blue velvet chaise lounge. She indicated for him to do likewise.

"Forgiveness, is it Charles? It is a very long journey to come to ask for forgiveness," she said while gazing through the window.

"Yes it is, Glencora. But I have been unable to face you, or indeed our son, for so many years. I feel shame and disappointment within myself for abandoning you and the baby all those years ago, and for ignoring the fact of both you lives here as if neither of you ever existed. I have almost been afraid to contemplate what it must have been like for you when you discovered that you were with child, and got my indifferent response. It was unspeakable of me... I beg your forgiveness."

He sat now, limp and worn looking. She noticed that his side locks were showing the first signs of greying hair. He still retained his good looks. All she could feel for him was pity.

"Yes Charles. I do forgive you. I too have thought over my past, and I must say it was cruel of you, and unmanly, but yes, I do forgive you. When you did not answer the letter I wrote to tell you of our son's birth, I resolved to live my life for him. To give him my everything to compensate for your absence. I have never regretted that decision. Every day I look at him and I feel a tremendous sense of pride and love. Henry is greatly respected and liked in these parts, and runs the estate without fault. Only last night, Charles, I told him the truth of who his father really is. You see, for years I lied to him, out of necessity in a sense. I told him all those years that you had died while serving in the army for England overseas. Ironically, Henry too had a near fatal accident of late when he fell from a grain loft, and as he lay unconscious for a long time, I had time to think. I resolved that should he recover, I would tell him the truth. So, Henry now knows your identity, and where you live. He knows also that you are married with one daughter. He wishes to meet you, Charles, and will be here presently. Of course, if you wish to, you may leave without doing so. It is your choice."

She looked at him and at the changes of expression as her story unfolded. He sat there speechless, almost in shock. He had not expected a woman of such strength. No. He thought she would be timid, weak and fearful. But it was, in fact, the total opposite. She was composed, confident and beautiful. As for meeting his son... well, somehow it all seemed unreal for him.

"What is it, Charles? Do you not wish to meet our son?" she asked calmly.

"Of course I wish to meet him, Glencora, only I did not expect it would be today. Or perhaps it is the unexpected news that he knows who I am. This is hard for me Glencora... I just... well... meeting with you and then to meet with my son, a young man I have never seen before and all that I have missed in his growing to manhood."

His voice seemed to trail off in the distance somehow. It was obvious he was very upset with the encounter, and it gave her a little satisfaction. The long years she had dreamed of this meeting were suddenly a reality, and not the one she had expected either, she thought. He was here, she reminded herself, and had indeed spoken the very words her soul had need of hearing.

"Charles, tell me about Ireland, and of course, about your daughter. I have heard that she is indeed beautiful!"

She hoped the new line of conversation would help relax him a little.

"Ireland," he began, It is truly a beautiful country. Its people many and quite poor in many respects. I worry about my wife and daughter, and there are times when I curse the day when I took up my responsibilities there. But you see, it is my lot. My daughter, Kitty? Why yes, Glencora, she is beautiful, and spirited. But not in the least interested in ever finding her a husband, it would seem. Edwina is becoming increasingly anxious about it, but I expect she will succumb in time."

He was calmer now, as the tension visibly lifted.

"Shall I send for Henry now?" Glencora asked, with a feint smile.

"Yes, I think so Glencora," he replied, standing up suddenly.

Glencora left him alone while she went to summon her son, and in the distance he could hear voices approach. The door opened after a gentle knock, and then, a moment later, the young man stood before him. His estranged son, with his mother standing behind him.

"Henry, this is your father, Lord Charles Foldsworth," she began.

"How do you do, Sir?" Henry said, as he walked over to the stranger before him with hand outstretched. His father shook hands with him, looking at him intently.

"So Henry, I finally meet you after all these years," he said in a tone of audible relief.

"Yes Sir, you do. My mother has explained the circumstances of my birth. I hastily add it was a surprise and a shock. I marvel how she survived it all, but then as you can plainly see, she is a very competent lady." Henry would have liked to add, 'in contrast to your irresponsibility', but did not wish to create an unpleasant scene for his mother.

"Well Henry, I can see that she has every reason to be proud of you. There is little I can say to you but one thing alone. I do regret having abandoned you both and I have felt shame beyond words. I must ask you also, Henry, to forgive me!"

He looked at his estranged father before him and felt a surge of anger, but repressed it.

"I will forgive you, Sir, but do not expect me to call you father. I believe you have a daughter, and it remains her sole right to address you so. For her sake and hers alone I will not speak publicly of this matter. You have not earned that title in my case. I suppose one must admire your courage in coming here, sir, but you must excuse me... I have an estate to run."

Henry concluded at this, and kissing his mother on the forehead, left the room without a second glance at the visitor.

"Well, Glencora, he is a fine young man. He has your air of confidence and self assurance."

He smiled for the first time. They were both feeling more at ease now, and as tea was served, they said little until the servant had left.

"Indeed he is confident Charles, but like your daughter, quite unhurried in relation to marriage. Perhaps they are right. Let them enjoy their youth, for responsibility, when it comes, comes to stay." Glencora said, with the experience of the past behind her.

They talked at length of their youth together and the memories they shared. They laughed when recalling their exploits together in the summers that were seemingly endless. As noon approached, Charles stood up to take his leave.

"Glencora, how can I ever thank you for receiving me so kindly, and Henry also. I am very proud of him. I would love to see you again during my stay."

She looked at him, and realised that she still loved him.

"Perhaps we will ride out some morning, Charles," and she felt a surge of excitement run through her. He was delighted.

"Well, Glencora, if you wish we could go on Saturday... that is if you have no other engagements that day."

"No, there is nothing I would like more, and I shall be ready early, Charles. Now, I must meet your wife and daughter at some point. After all, I am an old childhood friend. I doubt if they would ever suspect our old relationship, Charles, would they?"

"No, never. Why should they? I think they would love to meet you and Henry," and he then took her hand and kissed it gently.

Their eyes met and then they both realised that their old love was rekindled despite the years of pain and separation.

"Until Saturday, Glencora..."

"Indeed. Until Saturday, Charles."

He left the room feeling an elation he never thought he'd find again in his life. He rode back through the forest, which shimmered in the heat of the summer afternoon sun. His mount sensed his happiness and it leaped the tree trunk with its rider hardly aware of it. He was joyously happy in his old love.

Glencora ate little of her lunch. I never stopped loving him, she thought, and I never shall. Her face was flushed and she looked at her hand that held the fork full of salmon. It was shaking. She ate alone, and was glad to savour these moments by herself. Who could possibly understand? Oh Saturday, come soon, she sighed. She considered telling Eunice of the meeting. I must, she thought, but not of how I feel. I could never tell her that I still love him. Why, she would deem it foolish and very imprudent. The heart knew only love, not the years of sadness.

Leaving her lunch almost untouched, she walked to the lakeshore and sat beneath the welcome shade of the trees. Eunice would arrive soon to hear the news of how the meeting went between Charles, Henry and her. How fortunate I am to have such a friend, she thought. Perhaps it is unkind of me to fail to disclose my feelings for Charles. Just then she heard the familiar voice as Eunice walked over the manicured lawns wearing a long yellow dress and a white sunbonnet.

"Oh what a golden afternoon, Glencora," she called out happily, and sat down almost breathless beside her friend, "and how did your meeting of this morning result?"

"My dear Eunice," Glencora laughed, "are you breathless from exertion or curiosity?"

"Both, I'm afraid," she replied, noting the glow on Glencora's face.

"Well," began Glencora, taking her friends hand, "Charles met Henry, and it was amicable enough, though while Henry contained himself admirably he left Charles under no illusion to the fact that there was little love between them, certainly not on his part. It was the moment of truth that mattered. The acknowledgment of the facts to Henry."

"And?" Eunice asked, with eyebrows raised awaiting further information.

"And, my dear, between Charles and I, well, it was very civil, honest and open, I think. He spoke of his life briefly since we last met, and about his wife and daughter whom I hope to meet. He looks well, and not quite as aged as I thought he might look."

"I see," replied Eunice, sensing there was a little more but saying nothing.

"Charles is worried about a rebellion in Ireland, Eunice. He is concerned about his family, quite naturally. It is such a troubled country, and dangerous for those who must maintain law and order there. Unsafe, it would seem, from what little Charles told me."

"Are you concerned for him, Glencora?" Eunice asked gently.

"Why, yes I am, and for his wife and daughter, Eunice. It would be unthinkable if anything were to happen to them. Why in heavens name he doesn't come back here to live and employ an agent to take care of matters in Ireland I shall never understand. So many do, you know."

"Yes. The Irish call them absentee landlords. It is a known fact that such landlords do suffer a gradual dwindling of income when they are not there to oversee matters themselves. It is possible that Charles' financial position is not as secure as that of his brother," Eunice added thoughtfully.

A brief silence ensued and Eunice looked directly at her.

"You are worried about him, Glencora. It is quite obvious you are my dear."

"You are correct, as usual. I am worried, and what is more Eunice... I find I still care for him."

She had said it without almost realising it.

"Oh dear, Glencora, please be wise and careful. A heart can only break so many times you know. Answer me one question. Why are you choosing a road that will only lead to loneliness and longing unfulfilled once again?" Eunice was most upset at this disclosure.

"I do not know. It is either destiny or folly. He is happily married, and I am not fool enough to believe that he is in love with me. But there are the empty years inside of me and if he could only be mine for one whole day, then perhaps it would be enough time to allow my dreams to evaporate into common sense or... it is hard to know what I feel, Eunice," and she began to weep quietly.

"As long as you know that it is a dream you are pursuing, my dear, all is well. But should you fail to be discreet, your lifelong secret will no longer remain so. That is quite self evident, is it not?"

Glencora valued her friend's insight and knew that she must not be swept away on a tide of emotion. To be suspected of being Lord Charles Foldsworths old love, or even worse, mistress, would be a scandal beyond her comprehension.

"I must keep a calm head, Eunice. You are correct indeed. It would be the undoing of all my years of careful discretion. I do plan to go riding with him on Saturday. After all, we are old childhood friends, and that should scandalise no one. What could they say?" she asked, feeling defensive already.

"Oh, very little Glencora. Friends are friends, are they not? I do not mean to spoil or dampen your time together, but I have always had to be your guide, and the role does not come so easily. But perhaps on this occasion I may be overstepping it a little," and she continued to gaze out across the surface of the lake, knowing that Glencora understood her subtle remark. At least she hoped she did. The message was simple: don't make the same mistake again!

* * *

The days passed happily at Stagheath Hall. Lady Edwina was relaxed and looked much better for the change already. Kitty was aware, however, that her father had visited Glencora. She had seen him ride out of the clearing across the part to the castle, and also realised the visit had been far from a disappointment for him, as he seemed to exude a dreamlike banality. She knew he still loved Glencora, and that he had probably never stopped loving her. Poor mamma, she thought. If she ever came to the knowledge of this secret she would surely die. Kitty wrestled with her feelings on the entire matter. For him to face the truth in coming here was admirable, but any further association between them was totally unthinkable. The very idea of it all was revolting to her. But she knew that her father would never betray her mother. Never. The mistake he made in his early life was excusable, but to repeat it would be intolerable for her to endure.

Yet to anticipate such events was, as Hannah would say, 'meeting the devil halfway'. Poor Hannah, she thought, and all the servants at Oak Hall. They lived lives of such mundane simplicity. Kitty wondered how they kept their sanity. Oddly enough, they seemed happy. Most of them had never been as far as Dublin, let alone England. The prospect of sailing in a ship would terrify them. No, their lives revolved around serving her family and rearing their own children. She wondered how May Ryan was settling in her new home. She hoped she was happier. And James... oh James... she sighed, longing to see him and hold him close. Father had failed to follow his heart with Glencora because tradition and loyalty had forbidden it. She resolved not to make the same mistake. Real love existed. She knew it did.

I will not have an arranged marriage, she thought. its only purpose is to maintain wealth and privilege in a society that mainly ignores the poor. I will not sacrifice myself for tradition. No, I never shall, she thought.

Just then her aunt Alice came flouncing into the room.

"My darling, I have great news! I have decided that we shall have our midsummer ball next week," and her voice peaked to a crescendo of excitement. She was breathless as she continued, "and who knows, my darling, perhaps you may meet some dashing young man and fall hopelessly in love with him. Oh, to think of it! And then we would have your wedding to plan for!"

Kitty couldn't help but laugh at her aunt's intentions.

"If only life were so simple, aunt Alice," she remarked happily.

"And my dear why not? Tell me one good reason why it could not be so? At present I can name at least five young men, all well founded too, who would duel for you at sunrise without any hesitation. Oh, romance and young love!" and with that she seemed to float from the room in ecstatic fervour.

The mid-summer days passed quickly. The hazy days of heat gave way to nights of mists, while summer peaked. Lady Edwina's health had never been better. Her days were spent strolling through the gardens, resting constantly and listening to her sister-in-laws plans for the forthcoming ball.

The two brothers talked long into the nights about Ireland, and what Lord Foldsworth should or should not do there. Charles' brother tried to persuade him to return to England, and to the security it could offer himself and his family, but he realised that Charles would be forever indecisive.

Kitty managed to keep busy and happy, with afternoons spent mostly out riding cross-country. As a rule, one of the grooms would accompany her, showing the places of interest and beauty, for there were many. Generally it was Bentley who went with her. He was known as 'Foxy' in the yard, which to Kitty seemed quite appropriate when one looked at his red hair. He liked her to call him by that name. He was quite flattered, as none of the household had bothered to ever recognise him before, let alone address him by his yard name. He seemed to know everything about both horses and the area. Riding by Ravenswood Castle one afternoon, Kitty decided to ask him who lived there.

"Why everyone knows its Lady Glencora and her son Master Henry's place, your Ladyship. Far too big a place to live I think, but their lands are very well farmed. Master Henry is very good at managing it all, and very decent too may I say to all his workers and tenants."

That was a great trait in Foxy's mind, she could see.

"Tell me, Foxy, is her husband dead or whatever? You did say only the lady and her son lived there." She was curious about what the servant's gossip on the matter.

"Don't know that, you're Ladyship. Dead, I suppose. One never hears mention of him, now that I think about it," he replied, with an air of the truth, she realised.

He is an honest fellow, she thought, and quite at ease in my company. It was a pleasant change when one considered the servants in Ireland, who were so full of fear, which many of her class interpreted as respect. But then England was so very different, she knew, even having been there for such a short time. As they cantered towards a junction on the bridle path, they both saw a lone rider approach.

"I see we have a fellow traveller, Foxy," she remarked casually.

"We have, your Ladyship, and if I am not mistaken it is Master Henry. You know, him we were just speaking of," and he slowed his horse and reined in behind Kitty, which was expected of him at such meetings.

Henry raised his hat to her.

"Good afternoon," he began, as he looked at the beautiful young woman whom he did not recognise as his half-sister.

"And to you also, Master Henry my good groom informs me. How do you do?" and she extended her gloved hand, which trembled on meeting her half-brother for the first time.

"Catherine Foldsworth. I am Sir John's niece," she stated simply.

They stared at each other, startled by the suddenness of the unexpected encounter. Henry wished with all his heart that he could call her his sister. He tried to continue the conversation.

"Yes, Sir John's niece from Ireland?"

"Yes, from Ireland," Kitty answered, feeling suddenly hot and awkward.

"I see," he replied, aware of her tension. "Well, you do seem to be enjoying the day and I hope the rest of your stay will be equally pleasant," he added, feeling almost unable to speak to her.

The question burned in both their minds, 'Are we supposed to know who we both really are?' but neither dared speak of it. Kitty thought it very sad and painful a meeting. Again she tried to converse with him.

"It is magnificent countryside, Henry, with its rolling pastures. In Ireland where we live it is a little mountainous, rather more rugged is the description I am looking for."

"Yes. I have heard that it is. But then I have also heard of the hunting. Why, it is the envy of all England!" and he laughed for the first time.

"Most certainly it would be. We do have compensations there, I suppose. Lots of fogs and mists too, in autumn especially."

"Well, none of us have the perfect world, I'm afraid," he added hastily, and somehow it spoke volumes to her. "It does sound magical though. Fogs and mists. Lovely I should think Kitty."

It was the first time he had called her by name. Not Catherine, as one would expect by a relative stranger or neighbour. Somehow a deep void was being filled in his life that he could not altogether understand.

"Well Henry, we simply must persuade uncle John to bring you over sometime. Why not?"

It was as close as she could come to claiming their mutual relative as was possible. Henry then realised that she was aware of his identity and the blood tie between them. He felt almost ecstatic with happiness and relief, and in those moments they bonded as brother and sister. Both realised that a time would come when they would be able to speak freely to each other of their respective lives and feelings for their mutual father.

"I do hope we will meet again, Henry," Kitty said almost shyly.

"Why ever not. Would you like to come over to us some evening? You could look over the old place and I would love to show you our foals of recent weeks. What do you say Kitty?"

"A delightful idea. Would tomorrow be too soon?" she asked excitedly.

"Not at all. I shall look forward to it immensely. Goodbye for the present then," and he rode on smiling broadly.

He was so handsome, she thought. His eyes were definitely a replica of her fathers, and his dark hair too.

Henry rode as if in a dream. He decided, forthwith, that Kitty was his sister, and dispensed with the almost crude term of 'half-sister'. It sounded absurd anyway, he thought. She is beautiful, and has spirit too by heavens! I can't wait to tell mother, he thought to himself. She will be delighted to meet her.

But upon hearing of the chance meeting, his mother instead became quite alarmed. He then decided to omit the veiled reference that was made to their mutual uncle. It would definitely not encourage his mother to meeting Kitty. He tried to reassure her that his discretion was paramount.

"You need not worry, mother. I was as polite as ever, and would never dream of is closing my identity or the relationship tie between us."

He was aware that it was an untruth, but he consoled himself that it was Kitty who had referred to it, not he.

"You do realise, Henry, that this planned visit by Kitty will alarm her father. I do not know how he will view it," she stated matter of factly.

"It's quite simple, mother. I met her while out riding quite by chance, and as a neighbourly gesture invited her over. Where is the harm in that?" he asked with raised eyebrow.

"Oh, none really I suppose. But it is somehow… awkward or something," she said flatly.

"Oh mother, you will really like her. She is indeed lovely and only for the fact that she is my sister I would not have a second thought of courting her!"

His mother smiled.

"Is she really beautiful, Henry?"

"Yes, she is. I am very proud of her and to have her as a sister, for that is the way I see her."

Henry felt no guilt in stating his relationship on his terms. It felt somehow good to have deleted the 'half' sister reference. The fact that there was an 'understanding' between Kitty and himself, unknown to his mother, reminded him of the time when he used to conceal mince pies under a cushion from Magny Adams probing eyes. He always recalled his boyhood days as happy and endlessly carefree. He thought of how lonely his mother must have been all those years ago, her days and nights guarding her sad secret, shared only with Eunice Gainsforth. He admired Eunice, whom he always addressed as Mrs. Gainsforth. After all, she was the Reverend's wife! He decided that he would talk to her some day to thank her for all the support she had given to his mother all through the years. It would be good to have someone outside the situation with whom he could share his thoughts on the whole matter.

* * *

Kitty awoke with a sense of excitement and expectation at the prospect of riding to Ravenswood Castle. Meeting her father's first love intrigued her a great deal. Questions abounded in her mind as she hummed while taking her morning bath. She was aware that she must not appear too curious, or ask any questions that might arouse suspicion with Glencora. She decided to let Lady Glencora do most of the talking. It would be the wisest thing to do. Anyway, she reasoned, most of the visit would take place out of doors, or with the walk through the castle.

Breakfast was the usual lively affair, with her uncle, aunt and father present. Lady Edwina continued her habit of breakfasting in bed, which convinced Lady Alice that such a habit was without question the sole reason why the headaches had disappeared.

"You must insist Charles that she continues to do so in Ireland. Such a simple solution for good heal the when one thinks of it. But I for one could never lie in bed. Isn't that so, John? No, I must be up and about supervising and so forth. But then, life in Ireland is so casual, Charles. At least that is what we are led to believe." Lady Alice stopped briefly for fear of her scrambled eggs cooling.

"You are quite right, Alice," Lord Foldsworth agreed, "I shall insist that your recommendations are carried out." He hoped that would put an end to that topic of conversation. Directing his attention to Kitty, he asked, "and what are your plans for the day, my dear?"

"I have been invited to visit Ravenswood Castle father, by Henry. I happened to meet him simply by chance while out riding yesterday. We talked for a short while, and upon learning that I was uncle John's niece, he insisted that I visit and look at some of his bloodstock."

It sounded casual. Simple and straightforward enough. Nonetheless, the colour drained from her father's face.

"I see... what a... what a lovely idea. It is a very enchanting place. You will love it there, I am sure."

Lady Alice was hardly able to contain her excitement.

"My dear, what an exciting time you are going to have! And young Henry is so handsome!"

Kitty looked at her father, who was finding it a great struggle to contain himself.

For his part, he felt helpless. If Kitty were younger, he could forbid it, but to do so now was totally out of the question. There were no grounds to do so, and it would appear very odd indeed. An insult to his brother's neighbour. Charles' brother sensed the tension, and was puzzled.

"Charles, relax. Kitty will be in excellent company with young Henry. A perfect gentleman, and may I add, much sought after." He dried his lips with his linen napkin.

"Yes, I have no doubt John that he is all you say. Enjoy your outing, Kitty, and I look forward to hearing all about it at dinner this evening."

With that, he rose from the table, excusing himself somewhat hurriedly.

His fear was obvious to Kitty.

* * *

After his breakfast, Henry decided to ride over to Sir John's and escort Kitty to the castle. It would be a surprise for her, and would give him some extra time to talk with her. He walked briskly towards the stables with purposeful strides. He was delighted at the prospect of spending time with her. As he cantered leisurely through the park, he wondered exactly how much Kitty knew about his blood bond with her father. It would be such a relief if he could talk to her about it, but for him to approach the matter with her in a direct fashion would be cruel. No, he thought, I must hold my counsel and wait patiently to see what emerges.

Arriving at Stagheath Hall, he was announced by the butler. After some moments, Kitty walked into the drawing room looking splendid in a plum-coloured riding habit. She was very surprised by him visit.

"Why Henry! How very kind of you to come over to ride with me," she said, smiling happily.

"My pleasure indeed, I assure you," he grinned, continuing, "and would life not be dull without the occasional surprise?"

"Yes, and life is sometimes full of them, Henry. I have the strangest feeling that this day will yield its fair share of them too. Meeting your mother, seeing your home, not to mention the bloodstock... why Henry, the day stretches before us endlessly, does it not?" and Kitty laughed merrily.

He looked at her in admiration, noting the lovely smile and the small white teeth perfectly set.

"Well, let's not delay," he said, extending his hand towards her, while she placed her small gloved one in his.

Kitty looked at him as they left the room.

"You actually seem taller today, Henry, and that's without your hat."

They laughed together and almost ran through the main hallway, where they then suddenly stopped abruptly. Lord Foldsworth stood before them, and he appeared to be attempting a smile.

"My word, but you both seem in a jolly mood," he began, as he stood uneasily before them. He looked at his two children with a mixture of emotions he had never experienced before.

"Father, this is Lady Glencora's son Henry. He has very kindly come, and unexpectedly too, to escort me to Ravenswood Castle." Her delight and surprise was evident.

"Yes, your paths crossed yesterday Henry, did they not?" Lord Foldsworth stated matter of factly.

"Yes, they did. Actually Kitty, I have met your father before. Good morning Sir," Henry added.

Kitty sensed the tension between them. She kissed her father on the cheek.

"Well then, father, we can dispense with the introductions and be on our way with you kind leave."

"Yes of course, darling, and I hope you both have a lovely day together. Ride carefully mind you, and Henry, I know that Kitty is in capable hands."

He then kissed Kitty, and she felt a slight chill run through her body. She was aware of his visit to Ravenswood Castle and now felt with certainty that he had, at last, acknowledged his son. She felt it deep in her heart. Outside, their horses awaited them, a stable lad patiently standing holding them. With Kitty comfortably seated, they both rode on at a slow pace.

"So Henry, you met father before. He did not mention it, oddly enough," Kitty stated simply, not wishing to appear overly curious.

"Yes, I met your father. He is quite a likable man. He looks very like your uncle John. A striking resemblance seldom seen between brothers. It is their eyes, I think. They share the same expression. It is hard to describe."

"They actually do, Henry, and when I walked into the drawing room just minutes go and saw you standing there, the same similarity struck me... but perhaps it was a trick of the light," she added tactfully, wishing to approach the truth with gentleness.

Henry laughed out loud, but she knew it was not from his heart. He was nervous.

"I shall race you to the chestnut tree at the far side of the park," and he pointed out the great tree, majestic and far-reaching.

"Why not," Kitty agreed, and raced ahead almost on the instant.

Henry, quite taken by surprise, followed some paces behind steadily gaining ground. He held his mount back purposely, simply to admire the daring horsewoman ahead of him. She knows no fear, he thought, absolutely none. He allowed her to win the race, and she was aware of the fact.

"Your are in generous mood today, Henry. You could have left me strides behind," she said breathlessly. He laughed heartily this time.

"You are as clever as a little vixen, Kitty, are you not? There is very little escapes your attention I am afraid. Is that not so?" he asked with eyebrows raised and head tilted at an angle almost mischievously.

"Absolutely correct, Henry, and you must also have noticed how tactful I am."

They smiled one to the other, realising that the inevitable was unavoidable. They rode on at a slower pace now, allowing their horses to cool down after their gallop. The June day grew warmer, and the silence seemed to surround them like a gently mist, save for the soft lowing of cattle by the distant river.

Kitty spoke first, in a tone almost inaudible above the rhythmic hoof beats of the horses.

"May I ask you something, Henry?"

"You may, and I promise I shall answer honestly."

He brought his animal to a halt and looked at Kitty directly opposite him.

"Was father at your house the other day?" She continued to look directly ahead.

"Yes he was, Kitty, and I think that you know that already somehow. Now, may I ask you a question?"

Now she looked at him.

"Yes you may, Henry."

"Are you aware of the purpose of his visit to mother and I?"

He could see the tears welling up in her eyes beneath her veil. He dismounted and lifted her to the ground gently. They both walked over and sat down on the massive roots which protruded around the base of the great tree. Lifting her veil slowly, he wiped her tear stained face.

"Yes Henry. I know the reason why father visited your home, but what I think is more important still is that I know you are my half brother. If you have no objection, I would like to consider that means you are my brother."

Now the tears welled up in Henry's eyes. He sobbed almost uncontrollably, and putting her arms about him, she held him gently.

"Oh gosh, I am making quite the fool of myself," he uttered apologetically, and looked at her attempting a smile, "but then, it is not every day that a chap discovers he has such a beautiful sister."

The tears of relief flowed freely from them both then as they held each other beneath the great branches. The bees hummed lazily in the luxuriant blossoms hanging in abundance above their heads.

"At last Henry we both know that we are not alone in the world for the years ahead. We now have each other."

Kitty sighed as one who has just been released from a great burden.

"It is something wonderful to know, Kitty. You are the greatest present I have ever received!" and Henry stood up, helping Kitty to her feet also.

She smiled as she looked at him.

"I have such a brother! Tall, handsome, and so very honourable," and she reached over to him, pushing a dark lock of hair from across his brow.

"How did you first discover this news, Kitty?" he asked, genuinely curious.

Kitty told him of her fathers hunting accident, and the subsequent unconsciousness and delirium. How the almost unintelligible murmurings slowly made some sense to her, and then the actual discovery in her father's study of Glencora's letter informing him of the birth of Henry.

"And you Henry, how did you learn of him? Or did you always know?"

"No, not in the least. I would have never dreamt of it, Kitty. It was odd really, but I too had an accident some weeks ago, and upon recovery my mother told me the truth. For many years she had told me that father had died in battle while serving in France. I just accepted it and never questioned it. Then your father came and spoke to me, and told me face to face that I was his son. I stood there listening to him. Somehow I felt it was more important for my mother and him rather than for myself. You see, it was a burden mother carried for so long. I think I wanted her to be acknowledged, after so many years of silence. It will take some time for me to realise the truth of it. But Kitty, I think the most wonderful thing of all is that we can speak of it to each other. I don't think I could bear to see you and not feel free to talk with you like this."

Again he embraced her warmly.

"Henry, mother must never know, and I am sure you will understand it from her point of view. It would kill her, and her health is delicate at the best of times, though only in recent years. Equally, your mother must remain unaware of my knowledge of it all, as she would I fear eventually tell father. He would never rest should he suspect that I know that you are my half brother."

"Yes Kitty, you are right in all you say. It must remain our secret alone," he added.

This having been agreed, they mounted their horses and continued towards Ravenswood Castle. As they rounded a clump of scarlet rhododendrons, the castle came into view.

"What an exquisite home my brother lives in," she exclaimed.

They both laughed joyously in their newfound freedom. They galloped across the broad parklands and the horses in the paddocks nearby snorted, equally excited, and kept pace behind their oaken palings.

Lady Glencora looked at them both approaching from where she stood, unseen, in the great turret. They appeared delightfully happy together, she thought, calling on to the other as they jumped the fallen beech tree trunk. To be young was wonderful.

Chapter nine

Hampshire, England

Lady Glencora met them both on the steps of the castle. She looked at the daughter of Charles Foldsworth. How very lovely she is, she thought. Tales of her beauty were definitely not unfounded.

"Mother, I would like you to meet Catherine, Sir John's niece over on holiday from Ireland," he beamed, noticing his mothers approving glances.

"Good morning, my dear, it is lovely to meet you," Glencora said sincerely.

"And you also, Lady Glencora. What a wonderful castle this is. I have seldom if ever seen its equal," Kitty stated as she looked at the great walls and turrets.

Lady Glencora looked from her son to Kitty, and could see the resemblance between the two young people. It was quite startling, she thought. Taking Kitty by the hand, they walked through the great doors.

"Would you like Henry to take you around the castle, Catherine, while I order some tea?"

"Yes, I would love to see it all, Lady Glencora," Kitty replied, as she gazed at the beautiful ceilings above her, and the magnificent artwork upon them.

"Now Catherine, you must call me Glencora my dear. No time for formalities," her hostess said, smiling at her.

"I shall, and you must call me Kitty." Then they both embraced fondly.

It was an instant acceptance, each of the o other, and Henry was delighted. The atmosphere seemed charged with life and possibility. Henry brought Kitty from one room to the next. The tapestries and portraits were magnificently arrayed, and the crystal chandeliers reflected the morning light, which streamed through the great south-facing window.

"Who is that portrait of?" Kitty asked, pointing to a canvas hanging above the fireplace in the dining room. The painting showed a young man, standing beside a huge garden urn, with two spaniels sitting by his feet.

"Grandfather," replied Henry, looking at the strange expression on the face before them. "I often ask myself, did he ever smile? He seems so dour, or something. Portraits seldom look cheerful, do they?"

Kitty studied the picture closely.

"Well, maybe he didn't much like the portrait painter!" she chuckled, "or perhaps he had gout! One never knows the story behind it all. He was certainly handsome, and the dogs look lovely."

Just then Glencora joined them.

"Ah, I see you are looking at father. That was painted just months before mamma died. He was so depressed then. One can always see it, I fear," Glencora said, with compassion in her voice.

Kitty glanced at Henry, her question now answered.

"Now you two, come along and have some tea. Cook has prepared some delightful French pastries. I know you will love them."

As they followed Lady Glencora back through the main hallway, the warmth she felt for her hostess moved Kitty.

They spent the remainder of the morning looking at the bloodstock, and the late foals, discussing the breeding and history of the mares and stallions. Than after a delicious lunch, Kitty and Henry went to sit by the lake. They talked of many things. Kitty told Henry of her life in Ireland, socially and domestically. He seemed fascinated by it all, not once interrupting her. She explained to him the political unease, and the real fear of rebellion amongst the people. Henry finally spoke.

"Does it not worry you sometimes, Kitty, the fact that there might be a rebellion, just like the rebellion in France? Upturning of everything, killing anybody who remotely represents the authorities?"

"No, not really Henry. The people on our estate and in the locality are really quite pleasant. Friendly. It would be quite impossible to imagine them killing anybody, or harming anyone. We are fortunate, perhaps," she concluded, as she threw small pebbles into the lake, gazing at the ripples they made. Henry sighed.

"The thought of you there, Kitty, amidst such possible danger, worries me. I shall keep myself informed, and mark you, should I ever fear for your safety, I shall come over immediately and take you all away from there."

She laughed at his brave and gallant declaration.

"Oh Henry, you are so funny at times," she said, trying to imagine him walking into Oak Hall and ordering them all to leave.

"Kitty, I am quite serious. I genuinely mean it. I would not rest knowing that your life was in danger, or your fathers either, not to mention your mother," he said, pausing briefly, "I shall study the map of Ireland and pinpoint Oak Hall. Just you remember I said it."

Kitty knew that he meant it. For an instant she was tempted to tell him about James, and her love for him. Oh James, James, she thought for the hundredth time. He was constantly in her thoughts. However, she was wise enough to know that Henry would be shocked at her association with a man of no standing. To him, it would be unthinkable. He might even walk away from her in disgust. Nobody would accept it; she knew this for a fact. Hannah was so right. She would be shunned and excluded from her friends company, and lose her rank in society for all time. Such things were spoken of in whispers and tones of shock and horror. It had always been so, and would never change.

"What are you thinking of, Kitty? I do hope I have not depressed or alarmed you."

"No Henry. I know you mean well, and you are gallant in your thoughts and concern for us. With you as an older brother, I have little to fear."

* * *

At dinner that night in Stagheath Hall, Kitty delivered a glowing account of her visit that day to Ravenswood Castle. Her father was both relieved and happy that it had gone so well, and her mother was intrigued by descriptions of the castle interior. Her aunt Alice was in total rapture at the possibility of a budding romance, which she openly expressed. This, of course, annoyed Lord Foldsworth considerably, and he barely managed to conceal his irritation.

At length, Lady Alice changed the subject in order to pontificate on her plans for the forthcoming ball. Invitations had already been issued, to one hundred and fifty people in all.

"My dears, you will simply love it. I promise it will be the social event of the year in Hampshire, and I shall have the greatest pleasure introducing all the young men of the county to my wonderful and beautiful niece. Oh John, I am so looking forward to it all. And you, Edwina. Just this morning I found a tiara of rubies which will look wonderful with your new russet ball gown."

Lady Edwina had never looked so lovely as that evening, and Kitty could not remember her mother being so excited about a ball before. Aunt Alice's excitement is indeed contagious, she thought. Lady Edwina's excitement, however, was now mingling with a growing feeling of expectation. Perhaps this young man from Ravenswood Castle might one day become her son-in-law! She went so far as to imagine that if Kitty did actually marry him, they could happily leave Ireland and come to live here. It would be sheer bliss. The very thought of Oak Hall depressed her. Stagheath was so full of life, and her health had improved dramatically. It was obvious to everybody. When she later told her husband of her secret hopes, he was totally indifferent to them.

"But Charles, we did discuss moving here at some future date. Why, only last night, was it not?"

"That is true, my darling, but we can't possibly plan who Kitty will or will not marry. She may seem fascinated by young Henry, but as for marrying him..."

He shuddered at the very idea of it. He had never considered such a development. As he lay in bed that night, he decided to discuss his anxiety with Glencora. They must discourage any growing intimacy between Henry and Kitty. They simply had to, he thought, and that was final.

Lady Edwina was puzzled by her husband's strange attitude. Had they not often talked of finding a suitable husband for their daughter, and who better than Henry? Why did Charles dismiss him so? The question grew in her mind. Perhaps he was aware of some skeleton in the Ravenswood Castle cupboard. Madness, for example. It was in some families she knew of, and castles were no respecters of it either. Yes, it must be something along those lines. He is too much of a gentleman to refer to it, she thought. He is such a dear, really, and would hate to say anything unpleasant about anybody. With this consoling explanation, she slept easily.

The night of the ball eventually arrived, and everybody was in wonderful form. Laughter, vibrant colours, and an easy companionship rippled through the guests. They all knew each other, and were catching up on family news and recent engagements. Occasional whispered scandals were uttered behind rapidly moving fans. It was their life, and their loyalty to each other in it all was unquestionable. Each guest was announced upon arrival, and Lady Alice anticipated the arrival of Lady Glencora with remarkable patience. As for young Henry, she was determined that a match should be struck between her niece and the heir to Ravenswood Castle. It would make the county simply dizzy with excitement, she thought, just as her long awaited guests arrived.

Rising rapidly, Lady Alice moved with single-minded determination towards them. Lord Foldsworth watched her, and knowing her motive felt very irritated. This whole affair was pushing his endurance too far, yet he could appreciate his sister-in-law's good intentions. It was customary, and quite the done thing in society. His eyes met Glencoras, and her gaze moved to Lady Edwina, who was standing beside him. It was the first time she had ever had the opportunity to see his wife. Glencora looked towards him again, with a lovely smile and a subtle nod that seemed to convey both approval and admiration. He felt joy and relief all at the same moment. He would have loved to walk over to Glencora and spend the entire evening with her, had he the choice. He was also more than aware of the inappropriateness of such an emotion.

Kitty and Henry danced together for many of the wonderful waltzes. It seemed quite natural to all, and they looked lovely together. The only two who could not agree were Charles Foldsworth and Glencora.

Lady Alice all but swooned with ecstatic delight at the sight of Kitty and

Henry together, and there remained little doubt in her mind that her next major task would be to draw up their wedding guest list. She told Lady Edwina as much, and they both agreed that the match was definitely a good one. It was obvious to all at the ball that there was a great bond between the two young people. Kitty and Henry were aware of these misrepresentations, and both laughed innocently that their bluff was the only way sister and brother could have a conversation of any worthy duration.

The evening was a magnificent success, and all the guests enjoyed it immensely, some becoming quite merry, others exhausted but happy. The summer's night eventually gave way to the gold of dawn, and the rapture of birdsong rippled across the great lawns.

"We are returning to Ireland very soon, Henry," Kitty announced somewhat hesitantly.

Really? And when was all this decided?" he asked apprehensively.

"Only this evening. Father thinks it is time we returned. I believe the turmoil in Ireland seldom allows him relax."

Henry was dumbfounded. He had not anticipated so soon a departure.

"Time has really passed so quickly here. It has been wonderful Henry. So much has happened. I have met you, and that has been one of the greatest events of my life."

"Yes, for me also," he sighed, "but I promise that I shall write to you, Kitty. Perhaps even come over to see you. Though that might be awkward, don't you think?"

"Oh, cheer up Henry. Who knows, we may even come back for Christmas. I will try to persuade father."

With that, they both felt less upset, and they arranged to meet the following afternoon at the far side of the great lake. Kitty thought of James with a deep longing. Knowing that she would be in his arms within days now consoled her.

* * *

Kitty was not the only member of her family who was wrestling with thoughts of forbidden love. Lord Foldsworth knew when he arranged to meet Glencora in the beech wood, miles away from their respective families that he was stepping outside the binds of his marriage vows. His longing for her on the night of the ball had grown into a veritable ache, and like a man possessed, possess her must.

It is entirely possible, he allowed as he rode along the way, that this longing is purely one sided. That their tryst would merely serve to allow them a private talk. To discuss their long held secret, and the evident bond between Kitty and Henry, and what they might do to discourage it.

Charles arrived first, as was his intention. So deep was he in thought, that he did not hear Glencora's arrival until she was almost upon him. Their eyes met, and as he helped Glencora to dismount, they held each other's gaze without speaking a word. Charles did not let go of her hand. Instead he found himself taking her other hand in his own, and continuing to gaze at her. Around them, the air became charged as years of suppressed feelings and desires made their way to the surface, exploding into the open like a flash of lightening.

All responsibilities, all thoughts of others, all fears of consequences, fled as Charles held his lover tightly against his trembling body. His hold on Glencora was the only support that prevented her legs from folding beneath her. Years and years of emptiness cried out in her to be filled. She was no longer a captive of her mind. Her heart was in control now, pumping blood through her body so that the surface of her skin tingled, her ears roared, her head spun and her mouth... her neglected lips...sought out the lips of this man, the father of her child. It was as though she had no choice in the matter.

Charles felt in himself a passion he had forgotten, a passion that had died within him the day he had shunned his duties to Glencora for the sake of propriety. Forsaking propriety again was to be the price of fulfilling this raging passion, but like Glencora, it was gone past the point where he felt he had a choice. Their bodies sought out each other as though their very lives depended upon it. In a way Charles would have hitherto found embarrassing, even with his wife of many years, they abandoned themselves to each other in a frenzy of love and lust, the one firing the other to yet greater heights as each moment passed.

When they were naked, neither could have said how this came about, so great was their desire to touch and be touched, skin to skin. Charles did not need to look at Glencora, only to see her with his hands as they boldly caressed every inch of her body. He knelt, and nestled his head against her belly as she stood and stroked his hair, his hands all the time moving up and down her silken skin from her legs, to her back, to her breasts, full and arching to his touch. Then Glencora too dropped to her knees, and taking his head between her hands, kissed him deeply and for a very long time.

They made love not once, but twice, the second time more slowly and gently than the first. It was only then, as they lay in each other's arms still naked, their bodies glowing in the aftermath, that they spoke their first words to each other.

"Will you come back, Charles? I mean, soon?" Glencora asked, her eyes now brimming with tears.

He turned to look at her, and nodded his head slowly, unable to answer her through chocking emotions.

"Christmas, my love. We must wait until then."

As they parted company shortly afterwards, both were acutely aware of the love they had deprived themselves of so many years earlier. Life had taught them that a love such as theirs is a rare thing indeed, and their unexpected reunion had let it be known that it was no less than a tragedy that this knowledge should come to them late. So while the happiness of their recently expressed love held them in thrall as they parted company, it was mixed with sadness for all the love lost to time and tide.

* * *

At Stag heath Hall that evening, Lord Foldsworth announced, after dinner, his hope of being reunited with his brother and family for the forthcoming Christmas. All were overjoyed. Lady Alice felt certain that the engagement between Kitty and Henry would be announced at the New Year's Ball, and her husband believed somewhat the same.

Kitty alone knew the truth of it all. It was now clear to her that her father had fallen in love, all over again, with his first love, Glencora. She never remembered seeing such light in his face, and she knew that meant only one thing. First love seldom dies, she remembered hearing once. Would I not be the same should James and I be forced to part? I would wait forever for him, she sighed to herself. Nothing would stop me, neither convention, class, religion or time itself.

All glasses were raised to a toast, which rang throughout the great dining room.

"To a joyous reunion!"

Looking about the table, it seemed that no power on earth or in heaven could prevent it happening. The memory of this moment was to remain with Lord Foldsworth for a long time to come.

Chapter ten

The Return From Hampshire

James scanned the winding road that led to the village from his vantage point on the hill. He stood holding his horse beside a large group of giant rocks that seemed to spiral towards the sky like some ancient cathedral. He was aware that, only for their great protection, he would be visible for miles. He knew the Foldsworth coach was due at any time, and he waited patiently to see the spiral of dust that would announce its approach. The late afternoon sun was hot, and the only sound was that of the skylarks and bleating sheep. The horse champed at the dry summer grasses, and shook its head from time to time to disperse the flies buzzing curiously about him.

For the hundredth time James asked himself if Kitty would have changed. It was two months now since she had left him to go to England. A lot can happen in that space of time, he thought. He had missed her so much that at times he had been tempted to follow her, simply to catch a glimpse of her. He would just as quickly dismiss such a plan of action for the folly it was. The separation had, however, served to convince him completely that life without her would be beyond endurance.

In her absence, he had thrown himself fully into the movement of pikes and arms, attempting to fill the emptiness inside his heart and soul. Both Joe and Marjorie had noticed his low spirits and his lack of enthusiasm for life. It was clear as day to them that James' love for Kitty had far outgrown his love of country. While they trusted him implicitly with the secret rendezvous and meetings, they realised that his relationship with the honourable Kitty Foldsworth was doomed. Their pain lay in the fact that James seemed totally blind to that reality. To attempt to point it out to him would be fruitless. They were concerned for his personal safety, and hoped that Kitty might end it all by falling in love with one of her own class.

Hannah at Oak Hall had also silently prayed the same. Marrying out of ones own class was a recipe for disaster. It simply never worked. Should his Lordship ever come to the knowledge... well, God help her Ladyship. Not to mention the fate that would lie in store for that James fellow. She shuddered at the prospect. Well, she thought, they were due home today, and that will be a happy event.

Williams, who was quite calm about his master's return, was none the less anxious that all should run as smoothly as possible. He had already dispatched a stable lad to watch for the approach of the family coach. On peril of his life he had been warned not to be lax in his observations, or he would be dismissed that very day. All the servants would have to present themselves in front of the great house to welcome the family home. It was a time-honoured tradition at Oak Hall for generations.

James continued his lonely vigil on the hillside. He looked at the ripening fields of crops that formed a great patchwork quilt on the lands beneath him. In the distance the sea was a deep summer blue. The sailing ship that he had watched on the horizon was now making steady progress, its sails held in the grip of the summer wind, well on its journey down the south coast from Dublin Port. Looking north again, he saw a spiral of dust, and his heart seemed to skip a few beats. Was it them? The coach disappeared momentarily as it made its way through a wooded glen, only to reappear some moments later.

Yes, yes, he thought, my Kitty is home again at last. He felt like shouting it to the high heavens. He could see the flashing brasses in the sunlight, and hear the trundle of the horses hooves and the steady whirr of the coach wheels. The trunks were piled high on the rear of the coach, while up front, the driver sat erect and perfectly in control of the chestnut team of horses in his charge. James wished he could dash down the hillside and ride alongside the coach. He cursed the class system that divided their love for each other. He consoled himself with he thought that the insurrection would end such distinctions forever.

The coach now entered the village, and went almost out of sight. James mounted his horse and rode silently up to the old ring fort. He was tired. He dismounted and tethered his horse, lay against a large stone, and slept in the cool air with a heart full of his love's return.

At Oak Hall, the stable lad rode into the yard yelling at a high pitch.

"His honour is coming! His honour is coming! He's nearly here!"

With that, the entire household staff hastened through the front hall and stood waiting on the great steps. There were fifteen staff in all, and Williams walked the long line with an air of gravitas, solemnly inspecting each and all. Satisfied that everyone looked impeccable, from black polished boots to stiffly starched linen collars, he strained his eyes against the evening sun for a glimpse of the coach. Just then, it rounded the corner that led to the approach to the front of the house.

The family were assisted from the coach, and it was evident immediately to Williams and Hannah how well their mistress looked. Williams cleared his throat and stepped forward.

"On behalf of the staff, your Lordship, we bid Lady Foldsworth, Your Honour and mistress Catherine a fond welcome home."

Then, turning to the staff, Williams called out in a clear voice.

"Hip! Hip!" to the resounding reply of, "Hooray!"

Hannah then stepped forward with a spray of many coloured roses to present to Lady Edwina.

"Oh Hannah, how very lovely, and what a splendid welcome." Turning to the rest of the staff, she added, "Thank you one and all."

They bowed and courtside, then, standing to one side, made way for the family to walk through the great doors. Williams was already standing in the hallway.

"I trust, Sir, you all had a most enjoyable holiday," he said to his master in his usual solemn tone.

"Indeed Williams, we had a truly wonderful time. How have matters been in my absence?"

"Everything has gone smoothly, my Lord."

It was not the time or place to inform his master of the rumours among people of increased military activity. That, he reasoned, could wait until tomorrow.

"Dinner will be at the usual time of half-past eight, if that suits my Lady?" said Williams, addressing his mistress.

"Excellent Williams. We need a few hours to rest and bathe after our journey. Oh, it is always good to come home." She turned to Kitty for confirmation of her sentiments, and smiled, "Are you tired, my darling?"

"Not in the least, mother. In fact, I am longing to ride out now to get some clear air into my lungs," Kitty laughed, trying to hide her impatience to be free of this homecoming and to go in search of her lover.

"The energy of youth is wonderful. Well, why not. Only don't overdo it Kitty, and be on time for dinner this once!" her mother chided her with humour.

* * *

James woke with cramps from sleeping against the stone. The sun was a blaze of fire, and on the western horizon the sky was a blaze of colour. Overhead, swallows, not long on the wing from their nursery nests, played on the summer breeze with their tender wings. James knew their journey to distant shores lay ahead of them, and he marvelled at the miracle of it all. He wondered what changes would come to pass before their return next spring. His horse whinnied. He stood up and looked about. In the distance he was sure he saw a woman approach on horseback. 'It could only be...' he thought with a racing heart. Soon it became clear that it was Kitty. Her horse, fresh after the summer rest, galloped uphill with vigour. He stood in admiration of horse and rider. Kitty waved at him, and he waved back. 'Love of my life...' he murmured to himself.

Suddenly she was beside him, soft in his arms. They held each other for a long time.

"I just hoped, James, that you would be here. Oh how I've missed you! Every day," she blurted out breathlessly, overcome by their reunion.

"Shhh, my love," James tried to calm her, "I too, Kitty, have thought only of you. I am on this hill since early afternoon, just to see the coach come home, but never in my wildest dreams did I imagine I would hold you in my arms so soon."

He kissed her with a passion and urgency new to them both. They held each other and talked of their love. Each statement led to more kisses, the closeness of their warm bodies causing them to tremble with desire. James told her of how he had passed the summer months missing her. She countered with her own missing of him, deciding to tell him about her meeting with Henry another time. The truth of their great love surrounded them, and their need for each other. Aware of having to be on time for dinner, Kitty reluctantly parted from his embraces.

"I shall see you in two days time, James. At the old ruin in the grove."

He looked deeply into her eyes.

"Yes, my true love. I will be waiting for you."

She leaned down from the saddle and kissed him one last time. Only the swallows overhead could see the onlooker who lay hidden in the deep heather. He had watched the two lovers in complete amazement. He was unable to hear them, and he cursed the breeze silently. Yet he knew he was the holder of information that would astound the entire country. Just imagine, he thought, the Right Honourable Catherine Foldsworth being tossed in the heather by that James fellow from the village! God, he gasped to himself, is it possible my eyes tell me lies? But Bartley Finnegan, who had been strolling and taking advantage of the absence of the landlord, was all too well aware of what he had witnessed.

So now your honour, he hissed to himself, did you know your daughter is a commoners mistress? He gloated maliciously to himself, and thought how he would get fat on seeing yer honours face the day this secret was divulged. He remained lying motionless, knowing that should he be discovered his life and newfound power would be in jeopardy. Watching the lovers go their separate ways, he chuckled deep in his greying stubble throat, air hissing through his decaying and blackened teeth.

As Kitty and James disappeared down opposite sides of the hiss, Bartley slowly stood up, rubbing his grubby hands together. All that remained for him now was to bide his time, and pick the most opportune moment to confront Lord Foldsworth with the news that his daughter was a woman of easy virtue for a village lad. The thought of revenge made him dizzy. Who knows, he thought, he may even pay me to keep my mouth shut. His chest swelled with the notion that he might even buy some land if he got money enough. He scratched his matted hair and told himself that God was good! His mother had always said that he'd be all right in the end.

"Bartley, you are as lucky as a cat. You'll always land on your feet."

He prayed earnestly that she would always have great influence on his welfare from her place up in heaven.

* * *

Williams felt uneasy about the fact that he had no alternative but to speak to his master about the current rumours of insurrection. He had seldom known his master look so well, or, indeed, for him to hum a song in his study for that matter. The holiday in Hampshire had been very beneficial for her ladyship also, he thought. What a great pity to have to cast such a shadow across it all.

He sat with Hannah in their own parlour and sipped tea. Hannah sensed his apprehension, and knew he was troubled about the current rumours.

"Well, when do you intend to speak to his lordship, Mr Williams?" she asked.

Whenever there was something important to discuss she would always address him formally.

"Today, Hannah. It must be today I am afraid. I do not relish the prospect, I may add, but the safety of the family and the servants cannot be taken for granted. Why, any night that band of murderers could assail the place!" he rubbed the side of his face in agitation.

"The last night it happened, her ladyship was very fortunate not to have split her head wide open with the fall she got, poor soul," Hannah declared sternly, as she sewed the apron upon her lap.

"Very true, Hannah. The next time they might try to burn down the house, or, God save us, shoot us through the windows. No. I must speak to his lordship today."

After lunch, Williams went to his master's study. Knocking gently, he was bidden enter.

"Why Williams, this is unexpected."

Seldom, if ever, did the elderly butler seek him out in his study.

"Forgive the intrusion, your Lordship, but I must speak to you on important matters of which your Lordship is unaware."

Lord Foldsworth sighed, and hoped it wasn't a matter of a squabble amongst the domestics, as that was clearly his wife's domain. On closer scrutiny, he could see by William's face that it was far more serious indeed.

"Well, Williams, I suggest you divulge this troublesome matter immediately, what?"

"Yes Sir. Well, while you were away, there have been a great many rumours. Rumours to the effect that the great family houses may be attacked, Sir."

"I see," his master replied, wondering if his butler had any more definite reports to go on other than rumour. "Williams, why are you so convinced of these rumours, or has someone told you something more definite?"

"In a manner of speaking, Sir, yes. On five different occasions, two strangers were seen at dusk, quite close to the drawing room windows. Furthermore, I regret to add that two very fine cattle were found maimed on the estate, Sir."

Lord Foldsworth paled visibly. Williams felt saddened by this threat posed to his employer, and of the wider implications.

"What exactly happened to the cattle, Williams?"

"One of the farmhands found them, Sir. Both had deep slashes in their necks and backs. Quite savage Sir, if I may say so. They were bleeding to death, Sir, so I ordered them slaughtered lest we lose the carcass also, Sir."

"Very sensible, Williams. And the intruders at the windows? Were they local people?" his master asked, his agitation mounting.

"We don't know, Sir. They escaped on horses tethered to the rear of the walled garden, Sir. They then rode south, and across country to the town, where they became lost in the crowds, Sir, as you can appreciate."

"Whatever are we to do now, Williams? I thought the last attack was the end of the wretched business. I was quite wrong, it seems." Lord Foldsworths anger began to mount. "These wretched insurgents. Savages the lot of them in my opinion."

"Yes Sir, it appears that the last attack may not be the end of it. I suggest, Sir, we continue as before. Closing the shutters before sunset and patrolling the grounds as well. The men can take it in turns, Sir."

"Yes, that must be done. We can't afford to take our safety for granted ever again, can we?"

Charles Foldsworth realised that their carefree days and nights at Oak Hall were over. Maiming the cattle was savage enough, but he guessed the reason the intruding men has done no more was because their targets, his family, were not in residence. For the first time in his life he felt real fear. Not for himself, but for his beautiful wife and his precious daughter. People who could act so savagely towards a dumb animal would not hesitate to harm a human being.

Williams stood quietly awaiting instruction.

"So be it, Williams. See to the security arrangements. I want all basement windows barred up tomorrow. Completely and permanently. With a house this size we can't presume to be aware of every window each day. For the ground floor, the same applies. In all rooms not used, secure the shutters day and night. Select some trustworthy men for nightime patrol-duty, and see to it Williams that they begin their duty an hour before sunset."

"Yes Sir, I shall. I think, Sir, that it is a very wise decision, if your Lordship does not mind my saying so."

"Wise it may be, Williams, but we can't rest assured. The safety of the stock or the horses is another issue. Make sure the cattle are moved closer to the house pastures, and that the stable lads keep a vigil on the bloodstock. We must remain on the alert for these murderous men."

Williams left his master's study very disturbed, and hastened to tell Hannah of the decisions that had just been made. In his study, the landlord sat mute as he considered the fact that Oak Hall was now as good as under siege. He considered sending Kitty and his wife back to Hampshire at once. However, the reality was that he knew his wife would never consider leaving him at a time like this. Also, he dared not allow Kitty to return, lest she become too familiar with Henry. It would not be fair to Glencora to expect her to handle the situation alone.

He opened the drawer, and slowly reviewed the half-written letter to Glencora, which he had hastily hidden upon hearing the knock on the study door earlier. A warm glow filled his being as he re-entered the spirit of the letter to Glencora. He read over the letter so far. It was filled with love and warmth. For Charles Foldsworth, the threat to Oak Hall receded as he became lost in the world he and his beloved Glencora now shared. He felt neither guilt nor deceit at the thought of his wife. He had given her the best years of his life and never once taken a mistress. No, he thought. I love Glencora. Perhaps I always have. I certainly never felt like this before.

He completed the letter, signing it, 'My love to you forever, Charles'. He would dispatch it to England when he attended the Castle meeting the forthcoming week. He sealed it, and hid it in the secret compartment of his desk.

Deciding to tell his wife and daughter of the unpleasant security arrangements, he arranged to meet them in the comfortable sitting room. He told them about the intruders, allowing this to be explanation enough without introducing them to the gruesome details of the cattle being maimed. Nonetheless, Lady Edwina paled. Kitty felt numbness come over her, a foreboding of sorts.

"Charles, could we not just close the house and go back to Hampshire?" Lady Edwina almost pleaded.

"I have considered that idea already, my darling. Would yourself and Kitty go? I would have to remain here, Edwina, but I would be so relieved if you would both agree to return to Stagheath."

"Never, Charles! Not I! I insist on remaining beside you. But Kitty, you shall go, you simply must," she urged with great sadness in her voice.

"No mother. I would never know rest worrying about you both. We shall stand together. Besides, it will not be too long before we return for Christmas."

"I see I have two very determined ladies on my hands," Lord Foldsworth said, not without humour. "Very well, until Christmas then. But mark my words, when we do return to Hampshire, you will both remain there until this evil threat no longer lies over our lives. Is that understood?"

Looking at the smiling faces of mother and daughter, he could feel the tension in the room subside.

* * *

The thought of leaving James so soon again gave rise to momentary panic within Kitty. She knew that if the threats persisted, there was little doubt but that her father's plans for them to return to Hampshire would materialise immediately. The situation must be serious, she thought, when he had given their safety such deep consideration. Hopefully it will all change, she prayed silently. The prospect of separation again was more than she could endure. Gloom spread over her like a fog. Only time alone would tell their fate. For the remainder of the day Kitty wrestled with her predicament, and her feeling towards these people who so threatened her family.

"Villains and murderers," she fumed aloud in exasperation, "God, they should all be rounded up and sent to the gallows."

As the weeks passed from glorious September to mellow October, there was no return of the dreaded intruders. The tension at Oak Hall eased somewhat, but the security arrangements prevailed. Kitty met James each week in the old church ruins, in the secluded grove. She had told him of how the household lived in fear. Oddly enough, he did not appear to be alarmed. He dismissed the sightings of the two men as mere thieves.

"And the cattle, James. Who could have done such a thing?" asked Kitty, who missed little that was spoken of between the servants.

"Probably some villains trying to slaughter them then sell them in the towns, I would imagine," he said casually.

"Do you really think so?" she asked, beginning to think that perhaps the servants had alarmed them unduly.

"Kitty, look here. Be sensible about all of this for heavens sake. Should anyone, God forbid, wish to harm your family, do they really need to sneak about in the night to do so?" Your parents drive to see their friends, to church. They walk about their estate. You ride out. Well? Has anything else occurred to raise fresh fear or suspicion?" He asked her.

"No James. Nothing else has happened. Nothing at all."

Sighing deeply, she put her arms around him, and hugged him warmly.

"What would I ever do without you, my darling?"

Chapter eleven

With the arrival of November, the hunting season was due to begin. There was mounting excitement in the neighbourhood for all the families who pursued the sport.

Joe was kept busy at the forge, shoeing horses for the first meet. There were to be three meets at Oak Hall, which meant that Lady Edwina was resuming her place beside her husband on the field. Since her return from Hampshire, she had maintained the good health she had enjoyed there. Lord Foldsworth was delighted when she announced her plans to ride to hounds again. He was happy for her. Yet he could not help thinking of Glencora wishing things were different. He wished that she could ride at his side.

The truth was clear to him. He was in love with her all over again, and nothing could change that. When the present unrest was over, he planned to return to Hampshire more often. His sole desire was to be with her. Edwina's health was no longer the source of anxiety to him that it had been previously. She could remain at Oak Hall and entertain her friends. Of course, he would invite her to accompany him to Hampshire, but he knew she would soon tire of it. It wasn't he reasoned, that he had rejected Edwina. It was, rather, that Glencora needed him more somehow. Or, perhaps his need of her? He would write to her tonight in the privacy of his study. He considered the many things he would say to her, pouring his love onto paper. He glowed within thinking of her, and how she would read these words of true love. This time I shall not run, he resolved. No. Never again would he desert that for which his heart yearned so. With these thoughts firmly in mind, he decided to inspect the stables and yard. A task he enjoyed thoroughly, though seldom took the time to do.

* * *

James awoke earlier than usual. He felt agitated and uneasy. Washing himself in the cold spring water served only to make him feel worse. He cut some slices of brown bread from the large loaf that Joe's wife had given him the previous evening. Placing two eggs in the small pot, he lit the fire on the great hearth, and watched the water heat, then boil and bubble around the eggs.

He thought of Kitty. He was worried about her, and their relationship. He had tried to avoid thinking about it for some weeks now, yet the facts were clear to him. He had lied to her, and hated himself for doing so. There was little choice.

He was fortunate at the last meeting to have the support of Marcus and Joe in having the attacks on Oak Hall stopped, and it had only been after lengthy and heated argument that he had succeeded. He knew that it was only temporary. He knew it could resume without warning, and he was powerless to prevent this happening. His dilemma was simple. He must warn her. Would she ever be able to accept his involvement in the rising? A political movement that was planning the destruction of her family and home? How many times had he had this argument with himself, the same-knotted conflict? This time it was different. Danger loomed ahead and he knew it. It was inevitable now. What if anything happened to her during the night attack?

He looked at the eggs in the pot, with the water almost boiled from them. He took them out and placing them on the table, felt little relish for them. He looked out of the small window at the early morning sunlight. It did little to raise his spirits. The cat mewed for its morning milk outside the cottage door, but he scarcely heard her. He ate without tasting a thing, and then fed the cat, who had brought a dead rabbit to the doorstep. He stroked the ginger tabby and smiled for the first time that day. If only all our lives were as simple as the cat's, he thought. The cat drank the milk eagerly, and then began to groom itself thoroughly. He decided to ride out to clear his mind. It always helped him to think more clearly. Dampening down the fire for safety, he went outside and fed his horse with oats and some bran. While the horse ate eagerly, he decided to clean the saddle. It was a good saddle, one worth taking care of. It had been a present from his father, and he had treasured it for that reason. Taking the stirrups off, he washed them, and rubbed a light coating of grease on them to prevent rust taking hold. They shone now in the sunlight, and by the time he had saddled his horse, he felt better. Riding down the narrow laneway, he looked at the frost-covered fields that lay in their winter death.

Blackbirds fed hungrily on the scarlet red-berried holly, vying with mistle thrushes. A robin sang shrilly and James spotted it, with its red breast thrust against the chill of the early morning. The laneway came to an abrupt end, and met the corner of the small road, spotted with small pools of frozen water. The horse's hooves crunched through them. Cantering off the road, James decided to ride across a small hill covered in gorse, petrified with frost. His horse followed the cow trail that led between the prickly bushes and ascended the hill at a slow pace. At the top of the hill, both horse and rider looked at the vast expanse beneath them. To the right was the hill with the ring fort, and in the distance the tree-lined avenue to Oak Hall stood out clearly, with its mansion standing boldly as if in defiance of all that lay around it. Suddenly, out of the silence, came the shrill clarion of he hunting horn. He had forgotten it was the first meet of the season. How he longed to be part of the chase, but he realised that this could never be. He watched the long line of riders file down the avenue, able to hear their shrill voices, as they called to each other in high spirits. His horse pricked its ears on hearing the baying foxhounds, and deep in its equine spirit longed for the company of its equine friends.

James decided to ride to higher ground to view the hunt. The red-coated hunt servants followed the hounds as they picked up the fox scent. There must be forty to fifty followers, he thought, none distinguishable from that distance. The fox suddenly turned in its course, as James knew it would, the vixen now headed for higher ground. She ran through the river trying to lose her scent. The riders were now coming closer into view. James searched with eager eyes for Kitty, and had little problem sighting the horsewoman in the dark green riding habit. He decided to ride into a thicket to avoid being seen. His horse stirred uneasily, wanting to join the thundering hooves of its companions. As the cavalcade came closer, James looked in admiration at the glamorous spectacle. He forgot for that moment that the majority of these people held most of the land and the power of the counties of Wicklow and Wexford. Just now they were simple men and women out having a very happy time with their families and friends. He almost felt part of their lives, with no resentments or revolutionary ideals. He admired how Lady Edwina took the jumps, to the delight of Kitty, who exclaimed, "Mamma, you are showing us all up today!"

Slowly the troop of riders melted into the distant landscape. James rode home feeling hopelessly dejected and depressed. Even knowing that he would meet Kitty at the old ruin later failed to raise his spirits.

Not having to work at the tavern that day gave him the free time to clean and tidy his cottage. The task did not bother him unduly. He liked to live in an ordered and clean fashion, a quality instilled by his mother, who, unlike her neighbours, refused to allow a dog in her home. He recalled how she would sing as she baked bread. She had been happy with her life and the man she had married. They had been lucky with their live's together, and they died within a month of each other, inseparable even in death. He wondered how they had ever met.

He remembered how he had first met Kitty at the forge. How then he had loved her at first sight. It had been a wonderful, though difficult, courtship, of necessity clandestine, and he resented this each time he thought of it. The sense of foreboding returned to him as she sat by his open fire, boiling potatoes and roasting some meat. He went outside to feed his horse a generous helping of oats and it was then he heard the distant rumble of hooves. He jumped onto the stonewall to get a glimpse of who the riders might be. He saw four men cantering towards the village silently. Perhaps they were going to see a dying relative, as was often the case with such small parties of riders. Dismissing the event, he ate a hearty dinner while his cat chewed hungrily on the scraps of fat he threw to it by the fireside.

It was now mid-afternoon as the sun moved through the November sky, with the promise of a further night of clear skies and heavy white frost. Soon it would be time to meet Kitty, he thought, and longed to hold her in his arms. He would not easily forget his sense of loss while she had been in Hampshire for the summer. Only for his work in the tavern he would have lost his sanity. He had thought of her every hour and had secretly worried that she might be forced into an arranged marriage, as was often the case among the ascendancy. But nothing like that had happened. In fact, it was the opposite really, in that she too had longed for his love and presence. He knew they were meant for each other, of that there was no doubt, unlike their future, clouded in obscurity.

Meanwhile, Kitty had dallied to the rear of the hunting party.

Unnoticed, she had taken the laneway that would lead her down the gentle brow to the old ruin. She tethered her horse among the ancient yew trees and walked into the old ruin to the alcove. James stood up and walked towards her. She looked so beautifully dishevelled, her complexion glowing from hours of riding in the hunt. Small beads of sweat graced her forehead, and James passed his lips across them, savouring the taste and smell of this woman whose presence set him on fire. With one hand he pulled back tendrils of damp hair clinging to her cheeks, while he passed the other over her closed eyelids, her nose, then with one finger, drew the shape of her lips. He longed to touch and taste every part of her, as though to lay claim to his rights as her lover, each kiss a flag of discovery. Her lips parted and she took his finger into her mouth. He could feel her teeth gently gripping, while her tongue slowly explored the fingertip. In his wildest dreams James had never imagined a passion such as he felt right now. In one swift movement he pulled his hand away and pressed his own lips over her still open mouth. They seemed to drink each other, as though the alternative were to die of thirst. It was Kitty who broke the spell, staring back and laughing, unable to suppress a long moan of pleasure, he kissed her to her very core.

"Oh, look at me, James, mud-splattered and hair all about the place, quite unbecoming for a courting young lady, don't you think?"

"Unbecoming you may be, but beautiful."

He lifted her up and carried her to the alcove where he sat with his arm about her waist.

"Did the hunt make a kill today?"

"No, I'm afraid the fox made good his escape. I delight when that happens to be perfectly honest, though I dare not say so. There was a lot of disappointment. Lady Emelia Thomson was due to be blooded. Some people derive an old satisfaction from splattering fox's blood on the face of new riders. It's an old tradition, you know, James.' She looked into his face. "Are you listening to me James?"

"Yes, of course I am. I was just thinking to myself what an odd custom it is for civilised people, that's all."

"I suppose it is, when one thinks of it. The look of horror on the face of the person is what most people enjoy. It's innocent, in a way," Kitty chuckled.

"No lady would like that. Can't say I'd blame her either. Rouge and vixen's blood don't match." They both laughed.

"James... hold me one more time. I must return home before it gets dark."

"You are beautiful, Kitty Foldsworth, and I will never tire telling you," he said, kissing her while murmuring, "Some day, my love... some day, I will fill you with my love."

"Soon, James... let it be soon... I yearn for you... want you... more than anything... I will always want you... always... always." Tears poured down Kitty's face, melting any doubts that may have lingered.

* * *

Kitty rode on to Oak Hall, her horse, now cooled, needed heating. She felt empty in one way, yet loved, so deeply loved, in another. She tried to turn her mind to the evening that lay ahead of her. There would be a large dinner party, and dancing afterwards. It was something her mother had been looking forward to, and every effort had been made to provide her guests with a wonderful time. The start of the hunting season was always celebrated. An act of defiance in the face of winter!

On reaching home, the great house was aglow with light and excitement. Laughter filled the rooms and, running down to the kitchen, Kitty embraced Hannah.

"Oh, I am just ravenous Hannah," she said breathlessly.

"Young ladies, Miss, are not and never should be, ravenous," Hannah scolded.

Kitty laughed heartily. "Don't be so silly, Hannah, of course they do... they are simply never honest enough to admit it!"

"Very well," Hannah conceded, "have this slice of chicken pie, and mind you, that's all you are having. I want you to eat all your dinner tonight," Hannah bustled about the kitchen. Kitty kissed her on the cheek.

"You are a darling, Hannah, and I must dash for my bath. Lovely pie!" With that, Kitty ran up the stairs, holding up her riding habit.

Dinner was a great success. As each course was served, all expressed praise for the cuisine. Lady Edwina looked beautiful. She wore a yellow silk gown and a necklace of emeralds shone on her graceful throat. Her eyes glistened with tears of laughter as one of her guests related an amusing story to her. Kitty had never seen her mother look so happy and so beautiful.

Her father was oblivious to his wife's beauty, unable to think of anything but his letter of love to Glencora in England. In the distance one could hear the musicians tuning their instruments, a promise of revelry until the early hours of the winter morning. Slowly, the gathering moved to the ballroom where a huge fire burned in the hearth sending out a warm glow. It was a very colourful ballroom with a happy atmosphere that would take the chill from a shy heart. Lord and Lady Foldsworth led the first dance to the applause and delight of their guests. Many were amazed how well they still both looked for their years.

The orchestra began with a lively selection of waltzes, then slowed the pace, knowing their dancers had already had a demanding day's hunting. The hours passed quickly and the punch bowl had to be constantly refilled – much to the pride of Williams who held tightly to his recipe despite many an offered bribe for it! Downstairs all the staff were enjoying a hearty dinner, happy that their efforts had been so successful for their master and mistress upstairs. Williams, having instructed the under-butler to remain beside the punch bowl, now sat down to enjoy a much deserved dinner. Very soon the men in the orchestra would be brought down for late super during the interval. The guests would be offered savouries and champagne, and then the entertainment would resume once again. As the night hours gave way to early dawn the party continued with great revelry. The elderly members sat down to rest with a look of contentment, grateful for the comfort of their chairs.

Lady Edwina felt tired now, her head a trifle dizzy, which she attributed to the champagne. She smiled; reminding herself that temperance was called for! But as the time passed, the dizziness did not ease as expected, despite swapping champagne for hot tea. Some of the guests were now retiring, mostly the elderly members of the party. It had been a long and lovely day, she thought. I am lucky to have so many great friends. She looked about the ballroom, smiling at some waving at others as they left to retire to their rooms for the night. Her duty as hostess for the evening was complete. She called her husband.

"Charles, darling... I think I shall retire. I'm feeling a little dizzy."

"Are you alright, Edwina," he asked anxiously, noting how very tired she suddenly looked.

"Oh, it's just a little too much champagne, my dear. It's nothing that a restful night will not remedy. Goodnight, my darling. And do enjoy the company of your friends." She kissed him lightly on the forehead.

"Goodnight, my dear. Yet again, you have made me so very proud of our home and hospitality. Thank you."

Slowly she left the great room, as her guests all stood and bid her a fond goodnight.

* * *

Outside Oak Hall, amidst the shadows of the giant trees, four horsemen had tethered their horses as each moved to a different position around the great house. Their plan was simple, and their orders direct. Oak Hall was to be burned to the ground.

So many guests being present at the time was the main motive for the act of terror. The message was intended to be a strong one and news of it to spread far and wide. It would clearly illustrate the determination of the planners of the rebellion, without apology. Slowly and silently they threw animal fat against the great wooden window frames of the ground floor. The torches would only be lit at the last moment, for fear of being seen. Music and shrill laughter pealed from the ballroom.

Lady Edwina sat before her dressing table as her personal maid helped her to prepare for bed. The maid chatted endlessly, she thought, irritated by the idle chatter. She realised that her headache was making her tetchy, and she felt the need for some fresh air. Deciding to wait until her maid departed, she would then open the shutter, and window herself. Suddenly, a loud scream rent the air. The maid jumped in terror.

"What's that, your ladyship?" she asked in a high-pitched voice.

"Oh, some guest having a bad dream, I should think," her mistress replied, anxious that the servants had as little as possible to gossip about.

"Now, Eileen, I am ready to retire. I shall need you at eight o'clock in the morning. Thank you."

The maid curtsied and left the room.

As Lady Edwina wondered herself about the scream, another rent the air. She quickly put on her dressing gown to investigate. She opened her shutter and saw, to her horror, a hooded figure carrying a torch, running across the front lawn. Panic and terror filled her, as she smelled the fumes and smoke. The whole front of the house seemed to be engulfed. She was not alone in her fear. Other guests were coming out of their rooms shouting "Fire! Fire! Fire! We are all going to be roasted..."

Screams of terror filled Oak hall. Lady Edwina realised that she must take some control before all was lost due to panic. Her mind raced. The servants must be alerted... water carried outside...

"Charles... Kitty... where are they? She ran up the great stairs to alert all the guests, many of whom were now running frantically past her, blind in their fear and confusion. The upper rooms were all vacated, so she turned and quickly made her way down the first flight of the great stairs. The house seemed full of smoke, but not fire, she thought. Please God, she prayed, let it all be outside... Those murderous people... How could they think of doing such a vile act with a house full of guests?

Reaching the last flight of stairs, she could hear her husband call out to her frantically. Then she saw him and some others waiting for her to come down.

"Quickly, Edwina, quickly! Everybody is out on the lawn."

As she descended, Lady Edwina did not see where the carpet rail on the stairs had come away from its secure bracket. It caught her slippered foot, and she fell heavily forward down the remaining seven steps. She lay motionless at the feet of her husband as her daughter and some of the guests stood, momentarily petrified. Quickly, they lifted her gently down on a piece of carpet. They covered her with a cloak and looked on in helpless desperation as the small trickle of blood flowed from Lady Edwina's ear.

"Quickly! A doctor! Get her a doctor!" someone shouted.

"Oh, Edwina, speak to me, speak to me," her husband cried out helplessly, but the only audible sound was a low moan from his beloved wife.

Kitty was hysterical with fear and bewilderment. Servants were running with pitchers of water to extinguish the burning windows. Soon the hallway was filled as the guests deemed it safe to re-enter. Gently their hostess was carried into the ballroom and laid on the sofa. The low moaning continued as life slowly began to ebb from her. The doctor arrived, with sleep-filled eyes. One glance at Lady Edwina told him that there was little he could do. He shook his head hopelessly. Nothing could be done to stem the flow of blood. Oddly enough, the gash on the side of her head was small, but he knew that the damage was done. He patted Lord Foldsworth on the shoulder.

"I am sorry, but there is nothing I can possibly do. Make her last moments as comfortable as possible."

Kitty held her mother's hand and cried the helpless cry of a child.

"Oh, Mamma, please... please don't leave me... Please. Please don't..."

The colour faded rapidly from her mother's face and her breathing came at short and shallow intervals. Kitty knew that her mother was dying. Her father cried quietly, unable to speak. The guests stood around in shocked silence. At the edge of the group, Hannah stood weeping, wiping her eyes with her apron.

They all felt so helpless and powerless. Lady Edwina gasped, and then lay perfectly still. Her husband and daughter knew she had left them forever. The household and its guests found it hard to grasp the reality of what was happening in their midst. The image of the dashing huntswoman and charming hostess now dead in front of them, in the hallway of her own home, was more than they could absorb.

Lord Foldsworth, stunned utterly, could no longer weep. His grief slowly gave way to anger at what had taken place, and, above all, those who had been responsible.

Later, as he sat in his study, where only hours earlier he had planned to write of his love for another woman, his guilt was compounded. In the large bedroom upstairs, his dead wife was being prepared for the ritual that would follow. Kitty sat in her room with Hannah beside her. Neither could speak. Only the odd murmured word passed their lips. The guests assembled in the drawing room, and it was reminiscent of the evening of Lord Foldworth's hunting accident, when his life had lain in the balance. On this occasion, however, there was no return from the finality of death.

Morning light began to seep across the November sky, and the servants, who had remained at their stations, began their morning chores. Continuity was vital. Numb still with shock, Williams managed to order the servants to their stations, but on this occasion with gentleness he had never known he possessed. His sense of loss was great. He knew that to stop and think over this tragic death of his mistress was a luxury he could not afford. The smooth running of the house was his sole responsibility, and he intended to do just that.

News of the death of Lady Edwina Foldsworth spread rapidly. While the villagers were shocked and saddened, some inevitably found the justice of God in it. It was a twisted concept, James thought, listening to the opinions of the customers in the tavern that day. With a chill running through him he realised who the four horsemen had been. The vengeance of the movement he belonged to only now began to dawn on him. Revolution was indeed a cruel but necessary step. He shuddered at what had happened at Oak Hall and the fact that Kitty could have just as easily been the victim made him feel almost physically ill. The entire episode was like a dark nightmare to him, which he could only look at in brief glimpses. He no longer knew how he felt about Kitty, and this alarmed him even further. The realisation that he had concealed so much from her summoned a guilt within him that now rent him asunder. He knew he should have told her, and taken the risk of either losing her or expulsion from the movement, labelled a traitor. It would have been easier to live with, he thought, rather than being a traitor to his heart. Making small talk with the customers was unbearable. He did not want to be there. What he wanted to do was to go to Oak Hall and rid himself of the terrible guilt, open his heart to Kitty. But he knew that was impossible. Joe and old Mag alone knew of this terrible suffering that engulfed him.

Mag sat in her usual corner. She could sense his struggle. Love, she knew, placed strain and bliss on a heart. Her body, old and tired, sat still before the fire, betraying the agile mind she possessed. Had he lost Kitty in the fire? How would freeing Ireland ever replace her? She looked up at him and their gaze met. With her long, bony and aged hand she beckoned him to come to her. James nodded to her, then, making sure all the customers at the bar were content, he joined the old woman by the fireside. She looked deep into his eyes and sighed.

"Young James... you are walking a very dangerous path and I think you realise it. Now, listen to what I say to you this night. It is time for you to stop and listen to your heart. I know it holds two loves. One is Ireland and the other... Ms. Foldsworth. You need not look so surprised. I gather herbs in the oddest places. Yes... even in old ruins! But lad, learn one thing and learn it soon. Ireland will always be here, but love will not. So make up your mind. If it were I, I'd let them fight their battles. The sword has no mercy... not even for the heart."

James sat dumbfounded. He knew many disregarded and ignored the old woman, dismissing her as odd and strange. But he had always known different. Her direct manner tonight jerked him into a fresh realisation. He knew she was right. He must choose Kitty above all else, for she was his greatest love, not Ireland. She was his all. The wisdom of old Mag had made it crystal clear to him. The gloom that had bound him slowly began to loosen its grip.

Later that night as he rode home, he wondered when he would next see Kitty. At the funeral, perhaps, if only at a distance. He decided that at the next committee meeting that he would declare himself a sympathiser, rather than an active soldier in the revolution.

There would be no need then to tell Kitty of his involvement with the United Irishmen Movement. Instead, he would persuade her to go to America, or France, and begin a new life together. A new beginning for both of them. With that, he slept peacefully.

* * *

Morning came with a heavy mist and the mountains were shrouded in fog. Tenants gathered at the front of Oak Hall in order to pay respects to the wife of their landlord. The family burial vaults lay some distance to the east of the estate, where a small church stood almost hidden amidst the tall yew trees.

The house was full of family, friends and relatives. In the library, the coffin containing the remains of Edwina – Lady Foldsworth – lay on two trestles. Kitty looked down at the beautiful face of her mother, like marble in death. Her grief was almost unbearable. She could feel herself drift in and out of weakness. She kissed her mother a final farewell, tears spilling gently onto her mother's forehead.

A small, red rose lay in Lady Edwina's white hands, clasped firmly in death. Kitty stood back to allow her father say goodbye to his wife. He stood, shaking his head slowly in disbelief. It was hard to accept the finality of the sight before him. Soon they will close this coffin, he thought, and I shall never again see her face. He felt a rising sense of panic and desperation, his body shaking almost uncontrollably. Then he remembered Glencora. Calmness descended on his mind, quickly to be followed by a deep sadness again. Realising that his life with Edwina was at an end. The tears trickled down his face and Kitty wondered if they were from sadness or guilt. He caught her glance and his heart warmed. And there is Kitty too, he thought...

The coffin was carried down the great steps and gently placed in the death coach, as it was known. Drawn by four black plumed horses, the funeral procession gently moved forward to begin its slow journey to the church. James could see Kitty. She sat beside her father in the family carriage, a black veil covering her face. How lovely she is, he thought, even in sadness...

Guests, people who had been close to the Foldsworths for years, thronged the front of the house, joining the procession according to rank. The small church could only accommodate one hundred people or thereabouts, so the remaining crowd stood about the church grounds, while the tenantry stood at a respectful distance. Thick cloud cover refused sunlight, and only a robin sang somewhere from a yew tree. Everyone had memories of Lady Edwina. Hannah, Williams and the staff had been accommodated in the church and they sat huddled together in their grief.

Kitty looked at the coffin being laid in the family vault and was comforted that at least her mother was not to be put in the cold, damp earth. Her tears seemed to know no bound as she saw her mother's lovely face that would never see the sky again, or ever pluck a rose or kiss her grandchildren. Looking at the tenants heading for home, a hate began to grow in her heart. In their midst are the murderers, she thought, and those who know them. She scolded herself for the sympathy she had felt for them in the past; the countless times she had helped so many of them. How she would have almost abandoned her heritage for them. The silly ideals of youth.

And James... I have been quite silly, have I not, to imagine a life with you? You too, for all your grace and charm, are also one of them... born, bred and think like them. You too are part of this violence, this hunger, this sadness and beauty that is Ireland. And I am not! The chasm is too great between us... far too great. How could I possibly be part of a people who were collectively responsible for the death of my beloved mother? Never. Oh never!

The days passed slowly for Kitty and her father. Autumn rains lashed the countryside relentlessly, as persistent as they're grief, and the grief of the staff. The grandness of Oak Hall appeared to wilt in the shroud that penetrated all around.

Lord Foldsworth seldom left his study. At mealtimes he emerged, looking ghastly. Kitty watched him play with his food.

"Father, you must eat or you will become ill," she spoke matter-of-factly, in an effort to be strong for him.

"It all seems so pointless, Kitty, without your mother. I never dreamed that she could leave us so suddenly."

"Nor I, father... nor I," she replied, fresh tears in her eyes, adding, "We must try to be sensible and plan our future. The question still remains: Do we leave Ireland or decide to remain here, despite the threat to our lives?"

He looked at his daughter as if waking from a dream.

"Yes, I had almost forgotten your future, my darling. What would you like to do?"

She did not need to consider the matter deeply. She had already made her decision the previous night while tossing, unable to sleep.

"I should like to go to Hampshire, father. To Uncle John. To live there. But I shall stay here until after Christmas, and leave perhaps in early January. Imagine father... it will be 1798. The years seem to have wings, do they not?"

"Yes, my darling. Wings indeed. I think you are very wise in your choice. Nothing but rebellion looms ahead for Ireland, or at least parts of it. I shall remain here to the bitter end... If I am able to do so. I shall have to let all the staff go with the exception of Hannah and Williams. It will mean closing down the house, selling off our stock, including the horses. But there is little choice, I am afraid."

Kitty was relieved to see that her father had a firm grasp of the reality that Oak Hall was doomed.

"It is so sad to think of our lovely home, and all the years of happiness we have known here, coming to an end, Father. Yet I realise that there is little future here for me." She considered how quickly her views had changed.

She recalled the eviction of May Ryan. Her father giving May the bailiff's house. The many acts of kindness she herself had performed. All for what? She asked herself for the hundredth time. Sure, there were some good people, but the evil-minded among them tainted them all for her now.

And James... the endless rain made it impossible for her to ride out to meet him. Besides, she felt little interest in meeting him, except to tell him her future plans. It was the end of their relationship. This did not unduly upset her. There was no choice.

Three day later, the heavy November skies cleared and the sun shone from the winter sky. At breakfast, Lord Foldsworth announced that he was leaving for a meeting at Dublin Castle. There was urgent need to address the growing tensions. There were numerous intelligence reports of a possible French invasion to assist the oncoming rebellion. This information he found startling, as did the authorities at Dublin Castle. It was unthinkable that Napoleon would actually dare to assist a rebellion in his Majesty's colony of Ireland. An absurd idea! Yet the French were skilled in war, as the past ten years had clearly demonstrated. The execution of the French monarch had chilled the blood in many veins. He did not, however, disclose this information to Kitty. She was shocked and frightened enough as it was. He tried to make light of the forthcoming meeting at the castle.

"And what will you do today, Kitty? Any plans?"

"I shall go and visit Mamma's resting place, father, with some of the roses she particularly loved. Then, perhaps, I shall ride out for some air."

He looked sadly at his beautiful daughter. She seemed so lost and so lonely, and it was somehow so very moving. England should change all that.

"I hope you will be alright Kitty... I mean, alone in the house. I shall be away for four days, you know. Will you not consider coming with me?"

"No, father. I need time alone. Can you understand that?"

He took her hand and held it.

"Yes, my dear. There are things I do understand, you know. But should you change your mind, do come to Dublin and join me. It would be good for you."

It was only then that Kitty realised what being alone meant. Later, going to her father's study to bid him farewell, she found the door open. He was not at his desk. She noticed a sealed letter on top of the polished mahogany writing desk. It was addressed to Lady Glencora. She didn't feel anger or betrayal, only a new reality of her mother's absence. If Glencora could help her father at this time of sadness and loss, it would be good for him. Walking down the great stairs, she found her father speaking to Williams, telling him to take good care of her in his absence.

As he entered the carriage outside she kissed him on the cheek and smiled faintly, then waved goodbye to him as he disappeared down the long avenue. She then went directly to the stables and asked for her horse to be saddled. Hurrying upstairs, she changed into a grey riding habit, and felt a small spark of her old enthusiasm rekindle a little. Then, gathering the roses for her mother's tomb, she was saddened afresh. Entering the small church – where her mother lay beneath the great marble slab – she felt all her emotions combine into a great sense of peace. About her lay the Foldsworth ancestors; Lords and Ladies of stone, she thought, as she sat in the silence broken only by the robin singing outside. The calm atmosphere gave her time to think, and naturally James came to mind. She considered how she would tell him that their relationship was over. Her feelings were numb as she tried to picture him, and what his reaction would be. The creaking of the door opening broke the quiet of the church. Kitty sat still and waited to see who was intruding on her privacy. She gasped as she saw James standing before her. She was unable to speak. Words refused to come and she looked down at the roses on the tomb.

"I saw your horse tethered outside, Kitty. I hope I am not disturbing you."

He walked over and sat opposite her. She had never looked so lovely.

"I have missed you terribly, Kitty, and I have felt so helpless seeing you suffer so much. I... I have waited for you... but you never came... even in the rain... over at the old ruin... but... it was the only place that I could be... for you... in case you needed me..."

For a moment Kitty said nothing. Then she stood up and put on her riding gloves slowly. She looked down at him where he remained sitting.

"My mother lies here, James, as you can see. Murdered is a more accurate description, I'm sure you would agree. She is dead because some fanatics tried to burn our home down or, to be more precise, its occupants. My whole life has been changed, James, by this single event."

"Yes, I'm sure it has, Kitty," he said, standing up, now feeling very uneasy by her cold stare and icy tone.

"You have no idea, James, not really. I am glad you are here... I came out riding today hoping I would meet you."

His heart soared in delight on hearing this, and he smiled.

"No, James, I need to explain to you that I am going back to England to live. I can no longer meet you. I am ending our relationship. It can only bring us both pain. There is no point in us living in a dream world. No, not any more."

He sat down again, and looked aghast at her standing calmly before him.

"Kitty, I know you don't mean it. You are very shocked and suffering great grief. But you will recover. I know you will. This will all pass and we will plan our future. You see, I too have had a lot of time to think. I couldn't wait to see you, to ask if you would come away with me to America. We could live there happily and free all our lives. Away from all this sadness and impending misery. Oh Kitty... say you will... please think..."

But she raised her hand to stop him speaking further.

"America, James! Do you think for one minute that I would abandon my life, the memory of my mother, to go away with you now? Yes, there was a time I would have thought nothing of doing so. But not now, not ever."

He sat dumbfounded; unable to think clearly, his mind refusing to accept what he had just heard coming from the lips of the only woman he had ever loved or cared for. Yet she stood before him looking down at the roses on the marble-faced tomb.

"No, James, my duty now lies with my father and the other members of our family in Hampshire. I am sorry, but my days of dreams of love are gone, simply gone forever. There is nothing there anymore James. My ability to love lies dead with my mother. I am sorry."

She walked by him without waiting for him to respond. He heard the church door close, and the hoof beats of her horse as she cantered away in the distance. He knew it would be futile to follow her. He sat there for a long time; tears running freely, wrapped in helplessness and despair. He looked at the other crypts, the generations of Foldsworths who lay at rest within the old church, and felt his anger rise. He began to shout, to shout out his rejection, to shout his pain at the silent sleepers within.

"Yes, I know. I know. It's the way things are! Is that what you will all say to me? Laughing at me, I suppose, to think that I even dreamed of marrying one of you! Yes, me. A nobody... fit only to groom your horses. You would perhaps have me flogged for such an assumption that I should love Kitty! But you see, I do love her." He continued pouring out his despair. "I do. I do. I do..."

He slumped onto the seat, weeping in desperation. He could not accept the Kitty who had spoken to him just now. She seemed like another person, changed beyond recognition. He stood up and looked at Lady Edwina's tomb, wiping the tears from his face.

"You," he began, gazing down, "were kind, good and beautiful and never deserved such a death. I am very sorry it ever happened... so very sorry, for with you died the only one I ever have loved, or ever will love. With that, he walked down the quiet church. Stopping, he looked back, and added, "I wish you gentle rest, Lady Edwina. I will always love your daughter, always and forever."

He rode home, unable to feel anything other than a great emptiness and despair. He went to bed and slept from exhaustion. He woke in the evening feeling lost and abandoned. He washed and prepared to go to the inn to work for the evening.

Kitty slept well, despite the events of the day. Next morning, she sat alone in the drawing room. Hannah took the rare liberty of coming upstairs to speak with her.

"Good morning, Miss Kitty," Hannah began timidly, not knowing what manner of approach to adopt. She had noticed such sudden change in the girl that it alarmed her. She never visited the kitchen now, and gone was any vestige of the once happy, bouncing, young lady.

"Yes, Hannah. About lunch, is it? Well, I shall be in all day, here for all meals. Is that what you wished to speak to me about?

Hannah had never felt such coldness from her and she was chilled by it.

"Not exactly... what I mean is... well, I came up to see how you were, really."

"I am very well, Hannah. In fact, I have come to my senses quite a bit; you will be very pleased to hear. Sit down Hannah. I would like to tell you something."

The housekeeper sat down and waited to hear what was about to be said by this young lady, who was clearly far from being herself.

"You will recall, no doubt, I once told you about my ridiculous association with James de Lacey. Well, I also recall your stern warning to me that day. You told me that I would be betraying my family, my class and all we stood for! Yes, those were your words if I am not mistaken, are they not?

Hannah felt almost weak from this stern approach.

"Yes, words like that... Miss Kitty," she replied meekly.

"Well then, I am sure you will be very glad to know this: I met him yesterday, quite by accident, in the church – of all places. I told him I had come to a decision that I no longer wished to ever see him again. Are you happy now, Hannah?"

The housekeeper looked at the girl before her and calmly stood up, a new strength rising within her.

"No, Miss Kitty. I am not happy at all. But that matters little to you at present. I stand here looking at a young lady who is very angry because her mother died so tragically. That is very natural. What I don't like is the way you seem to want to punish everyone else who love you. Say what you like about James de Lacey, you do love him, more than ever, in fact. But your hate is blinding you. Good day, Lady Catherine."

Curtsying, Hannah left the room with a dignity that astonished Kitty.

The title, the courtesy, the delivery of her truth, left Kitty feeling more confused than ever. Hannah's words came back to her. "You love him, more than ever..."

Opening the door, she ran downstairs after Hannah, calling her name, almost on the verge of hysteria.

Hannah stood and waited on the great landing. Kitty threw her arms about the old woman and wept uncontrollably.

"Oh Hannah, please forgive me. I am so unable to see things properly anymore." She sobbed from the depth of her being, expressing all the sadness and pain that had filled her for the past weeks.

"There now, child, my little pet. It will be alright."

She comforted Kitty as she had done a thousand times over when she had been a little girl. They walked down the stairs and Hannah brought the distraught Kitty into her own parlour, the scene of so many confidential exchanges in the past. A bright fire burned in the small hearth casting a warm glow into the room. It felt safe and secure. Hannah disappeared, returning with a pot of tea. Both women sat in silence for a few minutes, and then Kitty spoke softly, almost in a whisper.

"I cannot ignore the love I have for him, Hannah. Whatever am I to do?"

"At this point, Kitty, all I can say to you is follow your heart. God alone knows where it will all lead to, but you must remember that it can't remain a secret forever. In time it will come to light, my darling, and then you must be brave enough to stand by what you treasure most – the inheritance you were born into, or the love that guides you. But know this too – Lord Foldsworth will take it very badly and I tremble to think what he might do."

Hannah pulled her woollen shawl closer about her shoulders as coldness crossed her back.

"Yes, Hannah, father will feel betrayed. I wish it could be different for him." She thought privately that her father had not been very honest himself, and his relationship with Glencora.

"I must go and see James, Hannah, to talk to him, be with him. You may tell Williams, should he ask, that I am gone to town."

Both women embraced and Kitty left the small room, careful not to be noticed by any of the staff.

* * *

She knew where James lived, although she had only seen it at a distance. Her mind was clear, as she felt much lighter in spirit as she rode cross-country. When she reached the small cottage, it was deserted. No smoke came from the chimney and, on checking the stable; she found it to be empty. She stood, not knowing what to do next. The cottage was very neat and clean, and the yard, though small, was spotless. She realised that going to the village inn was out of the question for her. As she walked her horse to the gate, the sight of a very old woman standing nearby suddenly startled her. The woman carried a small basked of leaves and roots. Kitty thought it a very odd sight.

"Good day, your ladyship," said Mag, curtsying slightly.

"Hello!" Kitty replied, still in awe of the woman before her.

"If I may be so bold to ask, my lady, is it James you seek here?" Mag's tone was gentle and unthreatening.

"Yes, it is. Why do you ask?" Kitty gripped her mare tightly, not knowing exactly what to make of the old woman.

"I am very glad you are here, my lady, for James is in a very bad way, I am told. He is in the town, my lady, staying at the Bull's Nose. He will be the better for seeing you," Mag added, smiling.

Kitty liked the old woman. Her face seemed to exude kindness, not criticism.

"Thank you so much." Kitty walked towards her. "What, may I ask, is your name?"

"Mag, my lady. I live on the edge of Oak Wood. I gather herbs here and yonder."

"I see. Well, I am pleased to meet you, and thank you for your help." Kitty walked impulsively up to the old woman and kissed her on the cheek, to Mag's utter astonishment. Her eyes misted over at this gesture from the beautiful, young woman before her, who smelled of wild violets.

"Before you go, my lady. Some day... some day, come to my cottage. You will always be welcome there." Mag said this with genuine warmth.

"Yes, Mag, I should love to. Goodbye."

Kitty smiled at the old woman, who curtsied slightly as Kitty rode away towards the town.

The town was a hive of activity. Kitty wasted no time in going to the inn where Mag told her she would find James. When she entered, the buzz of conversation ceased at the sight of the young Lady Foldsworth. Marjorie Bass looked at her and silently admired her loveliness. Sensing Kitty's embarrassment, she walked over to her, extending her hand in welcome.

"I believe I have the pleasure once again."

"Yes, I recall being here the night our carriage wheel let us down. I remember your kindness that night to my father and I. I am sorry, but I cannot recall your name."

"Marjorie Bass, your ladyship."

"Oh yes, now I remember. May I speak with you privately, Miss Bass. It is rather important."

Without any further ado, Marjorie led Kitty through the crowded inn and through a large, green door that opened into a charming sitting room.

"Please, do take a seat Lady Foldsworth. May I offer you some refreshment?"

Kitty declined the kind offer.

"No, thank you. I have come to see James de Lacey. I believe he may be staying here with you."

"Yes, he is, your ladyship. He is upstairs in bed. Not quite himself, if I may say so." She could see the pain in the eyes of the beautiful woman before her.

"Shall I tell him you are here to see him?"

"Would you please? If he would be kind enough to see me," Kitty was almost on the verge of tears.

As Marjorie ascended the stairs, she muttered... kind enough to see me... it's coming to something when the aristocracy of the country sit in Marjorie Bass' sitting room sending for a fellow upstairs as if he were the Lord Lieutenant's son. She smiled, and thought that there was no accounting for affairs of the heart. Knocking on James' door, she heard the muttered response and entered. He lay on the bed, dishevelled, unshaved and pale.

"You are a picture alright," she chided. "You're a sight to behold, James. I'd certainly not appear like that in front of Lady Catherine." She smiled at him and sat down on the bed beside him.

"No fear of that, Marjorie. She never wants to see me again. You have probably guessed as much, the way I have been drowning my sorrows of late."

"Well, that's all very odd, for at this moment she is sitting down in my parlour looking as lovely as a picture and asking for you as if for the king himself."

James sat bolt upright in bed.

"Downstairs... looking for me, Marjorie? Go down quickly and tell her I will be with her in five minutes."

Marjorie went downstairs humming a song.

When James walked into the room, Kitty was shocked to see him look so ghastly. She tried not to show it.

"James, so kind of you to see me. I... I have no right to be here... but I simply had to think things over... and..." She began to stammer and tears welled up in her eyes.

He walked over to her and held her.

"Oh, Kitty... Kitty, my love. It has been hell without you – unbearable, so unbearable. How on earth did you find me?

"I went to your cottage and luckily met a woman there carrying a basket of leaves. Her name was Mag ."

"Oh, Mag... how fortunate. She knew about us, Kitty. It was on her advice that I went to the church that day..." His voice began to falter.

"We must forget that chance meeting ever happened James. To think I could have lost you forever."

"Kitty, I need to talk to you. I must. There are things I have never told you, and I now realise I should have done so long ago. After you have heard what I say, then you can make up your mind if you still want me. I will understand, this time, should you decide to go."

James told her all. He told her of his involvement with the revolutionary movement; how he had become involved from the beginning. She listened attentively and without interruption. The hours passed slowly as she heard of the plans and the hopes of a long-repressed people attempting to throw off their oppression. Finally, James told her of his plan to renounce his part in it all. Unburdened, he then sat waiting for her response. He felt almost naked before her. Kitty remained silent, gazing into the fire for what seemed like an eternity. She raised her head at last, and looked at him, at the man she loved.

She understood his involvement, his position. She also understood the terrible strain it inevitably placed on their relationship.

"James, you must realise that this rebellion is doomed. The Government is aware of its organisers, and a lot more besides. Thousands are going to die needlessly, and for what? A dream that is far too premature! It is your life that concerns me now. You must say nothing to these organisers. You know too much and they would never allow you to live. No, we must plan to leave the country some months prior to the rebellion itself. You must continue as if nothing has happened. I will, of course, continue to be discreet, as you too must be. Then we shall go to America. Oh, James, to think that we shall be free at last to be together. I simply cannot believe it.

He held her tightly and kissed her with the urgency she had become used to.

"You are the only person worth living for, Kitty. It took old Mag to make me realise it, and we must never lose each other again, never."

It was evening when Marjorie tapped on the door and entered carrying a tray of warm food.

"Now, your ladyship, would you do me the honour of partaking of the hospitality of the house?"

"Yes, I would be delighted to, Miss Bass," Kitty said and she turned to James, the man she loved, and smiled. The sadness and loss of the past weeks were like a bad dream. They ate together, the first meal they had ever shared and laughed innocently in the company of their rekindled love. Once again, Marjorie knocked gently on the door to remind Kitty of the impending dusk.

"Thank you, Miss Bass. How can I ever repay you for all your kindness today."

"Not at all, Lady Foldsworth. It is simply my pleasure. I can see you are both very happy and that makes my heart sing." Marjorie wiped her eye with the corner of her apron.

"I shall prepare your horse, Kitty, at the rear stables and see you off," James said, standing up. "In fact," he added, "I shall ride behind you at a discreet distance, until we are well out of town."

James kissed her as he lifted her onto her horse.

"See you in twenty minutes, my love," and he ran back to the inn to fetch his black cloak.

"So, James... that is the future Mrs de Lacey," Marjorie quipped boldly.

He looked at her and smiled.

"You know, Marjorie, I never quite thought of the Right. Honourable Lady Catherine Foldsworth as Mrs. de Lacey!"

"I did, James. From the first night I saw you both at the fire. Rest assured, your secret is safe with me. Your life would be worth little if the truth were to be told."

He was under no illusion about that fact.

"Thank you, Marjorie. I know we can trust you."

She kissed him on the cheek.

"Enjoy your young love, James, and take her far away – soon, my young man."

"I shall, don't you worry!"

Closing the door, James entered the twilight of early December. Outside the town, he could see Kitty riding ahead. She slowed her horse and waited for him to join her. In the distance, the mountains stood starkly against the blaze of the sun just sinking behind them. The evening star shone brilliantly in the southern horizon.

"Isn't it lovely, James... the evening star?"

"Yes, it is beautiful, Kitty. Beautiful also that we are free to admire it together."

"Miss Bass is a charming hostess. I would never have believed that she could be so warm and so welcoming."

"Marjorie thinks she is our fairy godmother at this stage, and nothing will ever convince her otherwise."

They rode forward together, allowing their horses to take a leisurely pace. Then, out of the growing dusk emerged the figure of a man. He seemed to stagger rather than walk.

"That poor man seems ill, James," Kitty said as he drew closer.

"Drunk, more than likely," James replied. He tried to discern the man who seemed oblivious to their approach. When he was right in front of their path, he stopped, swaying before them and laughed. It was the bitter laugh of a vengeful man.

The man was Bartley Finnegan.

"Well, if it isn't the Right. Honourable. Lady Foldsworth with her lover," he yelled at the top of his voice.

Kitty and James were aghast at both his attitude and his words. James rode forward.

"Get out of the way, Finnegan, and allow the lady to pass and watch that nasty tongue of yours," James ordered.

"Allow the lady to pass, is it?" Finnegan threw back in a provocative tone. "No lady worth the title would be seen with you, Master Lacey."

James began to dismount, but not before Kitty shot forward, much to the shock of Bartley Finnegan.

"Clear the road, you nasty little man!" Then, her tone changing to almost casual, "One would think that you might have learned your lesson about insolence since my father was decent enough to show you clemency. I can plainly see the lesson was completely wasted on you. Perhaps you need to be reminded again by the magistrate. Now, clear the road or I shall have to resort to behaviour that is quite unsuited to a lady." With that, Kitty took up her whip and spanked it against her riding boot sharply. Instantly, Bartley Finnegan stood aside and made a mock bow before her.

"Yes, your ladyship, I'll clear the road alright, but I've no fear of yer father. I heard he got his comeuppance lately..." He grinned, displaying his decaying teeth.

Kitty lashed out with her whip, anger infusing her to the very bone.

"How dare you... How dare you refer to my mother's death? You common vagabond," she screamed.

Her horse, unaccustomed to the violence of its rider, pranced about, frightened. Bartley had fallen to the ground with the impact of the sudden assault. Kitty rode on. Bartley got shakily to his feet again and watched them both canter into the distance. He began shouting after them, vowing vengeance on the Foldsworth name and yelling:

"Aye, I'll not rest until ye are all dead or gone. Do you hear me?"

Kitty did hear him. She was white-faced with fear and shock. James caught her bridle and slowed her horse to a walking pace.

"My God, Kitty, that was a dreadful episode."

"The sooner we are away from this wretched place the better, James. The sooner, the better. My world seems to be turning upside-down of late."

"We will, Kitty. We will. Just try to calm yourself. I will have to leave you soon, as the village is in view. The last thing we need for you now is to arrive home so upset. Your father would surely be informed on his return."

"Yes, I know. I will put that ugly incident out of my mind. The very look of that man is enough for me to have him arrested this very night."

"Yes, you could have him arrested, but when the magistrate asks for an account of what happened, you would have to tell him that James de Lacey was escorting you home! What would your father think then?"

"You are right, James. It is quite impossible. Mamma would have said – if she were here – that the poor man is demented, and leave it at that. She always had a very calm attitude to distressing events."

They laughed, and at the turn of the road, parted without a word or gesture. Sometimes even the woods had eyes.

That night, for the first time since her mother's death, Kitty slept soundly. She felt at peace with herself. A peace that only truth can bring.

* * *

In Dublin Castle the mood was one of gloom at the impending revolution. Even the street traders talked of the feeling of unease abroad.

Many of Lord Foldsworth's friends and colleagues sympathised with him on the sudden and unfortunate circumstances of the death of Lady Edwina. The tragedy instilled a sense of urgency into the proceedings. The authorities felt helpless and many of their families were making arrangements to move to England, leaving their stately homes deserted. The government assured the Lord Lieutenant that additional troops would be sent to Ireland, and that the coasts would be under constant navel surveillance. The expectation of a French invasion was treated as a top priority, by no means to be taken lightly.

On a more practical level, plans were discussed to identify the 'United Irishmen' by name. Every parish in Ireland was to be scrutinised for members and they were to be imprisoned to await trial. The death of Lady Edwina Foldsworth was a stark reality of how local law and order was beginning to deteriorate. This resolution was passed unanimously. A renewed determination was afoot.

Most members at the Castle meeting had known Lady Edwina personally, and her death had made a deep and disturbing impression on them. It was a reality now, to be contended with, for fear the same fate lay in store for their own families and friends. Additional forces were to be made available in every town and village for the protection of homes and families. This step once taken was an irrevocable statement to all tenants. Naturally, it meant divisions would accelerate and hostilities increase. Yet Lord Foldsworth knew it was a necessary steep. Too late, as far as he was concerned. He was aware of his own hostility and anger. Until this meeting all he had done was sit in Oak hall and brood over events. Now, in the company of military-minded men, he felt it his duty to hunt down and condemn to death the perpetrators of his wife's murder.

That night in Dublin he drank until he could no longer retain consciousness. Members at the club could quietly sympathise when they looked at the prone figure, slumped in his chair. They knew it was not his usual form. Never. Charles Foldsworth would normally have a social drink with his friends and then retire early to his lodgings. But, as the days in Dublin passed, he was to be found drinking at the club more often than at Castle meetings. His associates understood this reaction, but were nonetheless concerned for him. Within the space of five days he appeared to have deteriorated, both physically and mentally.

On the final evening of the gathering, it was noted that Charles Foldsworth was absent. During the second course, however, the door crashed open. An embarrassed footman entered, trying to support a very intoxicated latecomer.

His clothes were shabby, and Charles Foldsworth's friends were aghast at the sight before them. Struggling to balance himself at the dining table, he looked about at the faces before him.

"Well," he began, "haven't you seen me before? Perhaps not like this. But then, why not like this?" He staggered back to a chair and his head dropped to one side. Saliva dripped from his mouth and down his chin.

"Good heavens, Foldsworth, pull you together, man," the voice behind him, urged.

It was his friend Lord Goran.

"Go away, Goran. My life... My life is almost over. No Edwina..."

He sobbed quietly then lost his balance and fell onto the floor. The tablecloth and plates went with him. Two footmen came to the rescue and carried him out. A carriage was brought to the door and one footman was ordered to accompany Lord Foldsworth to his lodgings. The dinner ended abruptly. Heads nodded in disbelief and dismay.

Early next morning, Lord Goran went to visit his friend. To his surprise, his friend was up and having breakfast.

"Charles, my man, how are you today?"

He cautiously waited to see if his friend had any recollection of the events of the previous night.

"Dreadful, Goran... I made a great fool of myself last night. Do apologise to them for me, like a good fellow. Some food now. Come sit with me and eat something."

His friend sat down to a plate of ham and eggs, feeling little appetite for the food.

"Look, Charles, perhaps you should not attend any more meetings until you have come to terms with Edwina's death..."

Charles Foldsworth banged the table, his fist clenched, and shouted...

"Her murder, Goran! Her murder!

The food from his mouth splattered the table.

"Good heavens, Charles, control yourself. Last night your behaviour was somehow excusable, bad as it was. But this outburst is totally uncalled for, man. No one knew Edwin as well as my family and I. We grew up together, played together, and hunted together. Her death saddened us all greatly. Acting like a street man does her memory little credit!"

He stood up and folded the linen table napkin. Lord Foldsworth was now shocked. He also stood up.

"Goran, forgive me. I am just not myself. I can't believe all that has happened to me..."

Lord Goran looked at him sadly.

"I know, Charles, but as Chairman of the Security Committee I will not allow you to attend any further meetings at the Castle until you have regained your composure. I am not prepared to sit by and see you, above all people – you, whose record is impeccable – act like a common fool. Yes, this sounds harsh I know but Charles, I advise you for your own good. Is it better that I tell you this than be summoned by the Lord Lieutenant and told so? Do you not agree?"

"Yes, Goran... I agree. I can only ask you to forgive me again, all of you. I shall do as you request until I have recovered sufficiently."

He resumed his place at table.

"Good. Now that's more like it Charles. I will have a copy of all the minutes of the meetings dispatched to you, so you will be kept abreast of all developments. Now, rest when you go home. Try some fishing or hunting, and get back to normality. I doubt if there will be any further trouble at Oak Hall. Most unlikely. Goodbye Charles, and do give my regards to your lovely daughter."

"Goodbye, Goran. And again my sincere apologies to you and all concerned.|

As Lord Goran walked into the street to his awaiting carriage he shook his head dismally.

"Oh dear," he murmured, "I'm afraid you may never recover your loss, Charles. Only time will tell if we will ever see you again."

* * *

Journeying home, Lord Foldsworth felt guilt and shame. He thought again of his great loss. He knew that Lord Goran was right. He must put it out of his mind and begin to concentrate on the job at hand – organising a local militia. Yes, I shall flush out the rebel rats... and make an example of them one by one. By God, I will... hang them in the town square on market day. That will soon quell their nationalist ardour.

As he approached the town, the idea of having a drink at the tavern suddenly struck him as an excellent idea. Why not? He tapped the roof and instructed the coachman to draw into the Bull's Nose. Obeying the unusual request of his master, he proceeded to stable the horses at the rear of the tavern.

As Lord Foldsworth entered the inn, a great silence fell upon the occupants. Definitely something afoot, they thought. His daughter here only yesterday, and now the Lord of the estate today!

Marjorie stood transfixed, unsure of what the nature of this visit might be. She hoped he had not heard that Kitty and James had spent most of the previous day there. She was reassured by his pleasant and friendly manner.

"Good evening, madam. Would you kindly bring me a large glass of brandy? I shall take it by the fireside," he said, without so much as a glance at her customers. It was as though they did not exist.

Marjorie poured a generous measure and brought it on a tray to her esteemed visitor.

"Now, Lord Foldsworth, I hope you enjoy your drink. Is there anything else you require!" she asked in a pleasant tone of voice.

He looked at her directly.

"Not at present. But I shall call when I need you. Thank you." The tone he used was usually saved for Williams.

Marjorie noticed the dismissal.

"Certainly, your Lordship."

She returned to the bar, her customers by now having resumed their conversations, but in more subdued tones, casting swift glances at the man at the fireside.

One brandy followed another, until Marjorie felt embarrassed at her visitor's gradual deterioration. The occupants were becoming amused as Lord Foldsworth began to mutter to himself. She knew she could not stop them. A sudden crash brought the entire inn to a silent hush as Lord Foldsworth fell heavily to the floor. He lay there, totally helpless, totally drunk. Marjorie rushed to his assistance and beckoned to some of the men for help. They lifted him up and sat him in a deeper armchair where there was less chance of him falling again. Charles Foldsworth, half-conscious, was humiliated by their assistance rather than gratified. He looked around at the crowd in the inn and smiled cynically at them.

"Enjoying the spectacle, eh? A Foldsworth of Oak Hall falling from his chair... Yes, and from grace also... Well, soon you shall all have greater spectacles to watch." He laughed a harsh and deep-throated laugh.

"Yes, you are all going to have lots of entertainment in the square. That's right, the square... For one by one I shall tar and feather them, and then hang them as they burn... My wife's murderers... They shall scream, aye, scream to the high heavens for my mercy."

Everyone sat dumbfounded and horrified at the vision the threat conjured up in their minds. They seemed paralysed on hearing this voice of authority that seemed to command them to pay attention. Lord Foldsworth now stood up and swayed unsteadily. He pointed a finger at one, then another, shouting:

"Is it you... or you... or even you two there?"

He attempted to walk forward, only to fall heavily against a table. Nobody moved to assist him. One by one, they walked out of the inn into the cold night air. Once outside, they ran hither and thither, knocking on doors, stopping other people on the street. Within minutes, the entire town had the news. Terror was instilled into folks that night as they went to bed.

Alone, Marjorie managed to lift him back into the chair. She went in search of the coachman, who was hastily harnessing the horses to the coach.

"My God, man... hurry," Marjorie urged, "Get him out of here before someone comes and murders him in cold blood."

She felt fear ripple through her whole body, only to be startled afresh by a worse nightmare. Bartley Finnegan stood before her. He began to grin and then to laugh the laugh of a madman.

"The quality seem to come a lot now to Marjorie's, do they not?" he hissed.

"Get out of here, you limb of the devil, or I'll have the sergeant here for you in no time, Finnegan," she said to him coolly, summoning all her strength in the confrontation.

"Will ye now, Miss Bass?" and he laughed the high-pitched laugh of one insane with hate. "Who, Miss Bass, will go for the sergeant?"

The coachman ignored them both, walked past, intent on assisting his master. Marjorie walked towards the despicable man.

"Get out of the way, Finnegan, or I'll..."

But Bartley Finnegan rushed towards her and grabbed her by the hair. She froze in fear as he gazed into her eyes, smacking his lips. She felt faint. Just then the coachman, bearing his burden of a heavily intoxicated master, came out of the inn. Bartley roughly let go of Marjorie's hair, and stood before Lord Foldsworth. He made a deep sweeping bow in brazen contempt.

"Your great honours worship, do you remember me?"

Lord Foldsworth looked at the man before him, confused and uncertain, and said nothing.

"Well, yer honour, I'm the man ye nearly had hanged for taking a miserable bunch of holly."

He resumed his high-pitched laughter. The coachman was unable to let go of his master to push the intruder out of the way, but told him to clear off. Bartley ignored him, as if he neither heard him nor saw him.

"Yes... now I remember you," Lord Foldsworth began.

"He remembers! He remembers!" Bartley screamed, as he jumped around now like a crazed monkey. Marjorie prayed he did not have a pistol.

Suddenly Bartley stood still.

"Well, yer honours bloody worship, let me tell you somethin' now that will leave the grabbin' of a bit of holly a small thing. Aye, a small thing. Did you know yer little ladyship is acting the huar with a lad out of the village? Aye, to be sure she is! For the past two year nearly."

The horrified look on Lord Foldsworth's face gave Bartley Finnegan the surge of revenge his miserable soul had been parched for. He gloated on his moment of triumph.

"Ask her, if ye dare. Go ahead; ask her where she goes on her afternoon canters. I've seen them, ye know. Lying in the heather, rolling in it, aye, did I!"

He yelled in wild delight as the expression on the face of the man before him changed from horror to sadness, to disbelief. Amidst his shock, Lord Foldsworth remembered the small pistol in his breast pocket. He clumsily reached for it. But Bartley Finnegan read the intention and began shouting as he backed away.

"Go on, ask her, yer gutless heap of grandeur."

The shot rang out in the night air as a flame emitted from the barrel of the small gun. Bartley slumped and fell. But he jumped up again, this time screaming in terror.

"Bloody, drunken auld bastard. Yer gone past it. Can't even shoot straight."

He ran, still shouting, but this time in fear, before disappearing from view down a dark laneway. Lord Foldsworth now stood erect and without assistance. He straightened his cloak and looked at Marjorie with tears in his eyes. The coachman opened the door and stood waiting for his master to step aboard.

Marjorie stood trembling and speechless, her face tear-stained, in a state of shock. With one foot on the carriage step, Lord Foldsworth looked at the sky.

"Could it be true? Could it really be true that my beloved daughter is what that half-crazed fool says she is?"

He then stepped into the coach, without looking at Marjorie again. Walking to the coach door, Marjorie said calmly, "Your Lordship would be equally as crazed if he believed it."

As the carriage went from view, Marjorie's mind began to work feverishly. She must get to see James tonight. Running inside, she locked up the tavern, not bothering to extinguish the lamps or candles. She pulled on her heavy, woollen, black cloak and went to harness her pony and trap. Many people, upon hearing gunfire, had come out of them homes and assembled in small groups. Marjorie ignored them.

It took her almost an hour to find the familiar landmarks being obscured by darkness. Seeing the dim light within, she thanked God he was at home. James was astonished to see her at this hour and assumed she had urgent news of the rebellion. As she sat by the fire, however, and related the events of the past few hours, he could only stare at her in complete disbelief.

"My God, Marjorie, what about Kitty? We have no way of warning her. He could be confronting her right now. Bartley Finnegan, above all people. He must have watched us time and again, Marjorie.

"He didn't name you, James. He was clever enough not to, for fear of his miserable life. But even in the crazed frenzy he was in, he left his Lordship very troubled. Somehow, James, I think Lord Foldsworth believes it all to be true. He had the look of one greatly hurt, which means he suspects some truth in the story, however wild it sounded to him."

Marjorie sat by the fire in the small cottage all that night talking with James. She was afraid to return to the inn lest Bartley Finnegan was lying in wait for her. James advised her to go again to the police and have him re-arrested for assault. But she decided it would be to no avail, only leading to a long-term conflict.

"It's more likely that Lord Foldsworth will handle the matter," James said, as he stood up to pile more wood on the fire.

Dawn was breaking in the December sky, and Charles Foldsworth still sat slumped in his chair in the study. He had not bothered going to bed, much less disturb Kitty. Having thought over the confrontation with that wretched man, he knew that he must have spoken some truth. He would scarcely be fool enough to make such a wild allegation unless there was a grain of truth in it all. Besides, the look of revenge and sheer exultation in the wild face convinced him yet further that something was afoot. Just thinking that it could be true almost drove him demented. He decided that he would say nothing to Kitty for the moment, as difficult as that would be. If the matter was true, he decided he would find out for himself. He would follow her on one of her outings. That way he could establish the facts for himself, and, more importantly, the identity of the fellow in question.

He walked slowly up the stairs to his room, lay on his bed and slept, still wearing the clothes of the previous day.

In a back alley in the town Bartley Finnegan clutched his arm where the gunshot had penetrated. The searing pain almost rendered him senseless and as he drank more from the now almost-empty whisky bottle, he began to drift into a drunken sleep.

His hour of glory had been worth it. He recalled the devastated look on the landlord's face. Yes... it had been one... great night's work.

Lord Foldsworth tossed in an uneasy sleep. At intervals of consciousness he vowed that whoever the fellow was that was meeting his daughter, he would undoubtedly hang! The difficulty would not be evidence of crime in the least, for a word in the ear of Justice Viscount Stewart would ensure the quick trial and execution of the fellow. After all, Viscount Stewart had been vehemently opposed to the tolerance of any form of suspicious behaviour and circumstances. It stood to reason that whoever this fellow was, he had somehow secured information of the family's movements, culminating in the fire, which resulted in the death of his beloved Edwina. No, it would be no great task to arrange a conviction. Then two problems would be solved with one stroke; the end of his daughter's elicit liaison and an example to the country of the fate that awaited anybody who was implicated in the planned rebellion. Finally he slept, revenge his companion.

By lunchtime the next day, Williams was greatly concerned that his master had not yet appeared from his room. Kitty had returned from the church, having placed the last of the late roses on her mother's tomb. Waves of fresh sadness mingled with dreams of a new life with James, now only weeks away. Her spirits lifted as her thoughts turned to the future. She did not plan to tell her father the truth. He would never agree. While she loved her father dearly, she was not willing to sacrifice the greatest love of her life simply to honour family expectations! Never! The very idea of living her life with Viscount Stewart, or indeed any of the other men she was acquainted with, left her feeling cold.

Having lunched alone, Kitty went to her father's study only to find it empty. Going directly to the kitchen she was surprised to learn that her father had not left his bedroom. Williams looked quite concerned and suggested that she might go and knock, since no service had as yet been requested. The coachman said it had been well past midnight when they had arrived home.

"It's most unlike father, Williams. It would be perhaps better if you went and knocked on his door. I hope he is not ill!"

But no such action was necessary, for, at that moment, the dining room bell rang clearly.

"Thank heavens for that," Williams whispered as he ascended the stairs.

Hannah called Kitty aside hastily and whispered in low tones.

"Your father had a very disagreeable experience in town last night, from what I gathered from Bill, the coachman. Something about him meeting a lad by the name of Bartley Finnegan who said that you were consorting with a fellow from the village. I'm afraid your secret remains no longer. Be prepared for your father's wrath, just as I warned you it would be."

Hannah was pale-faced with worry and Kitty felt a knot in her stomach with fear.

"Oh no, Hannah... not yet. I am not prepared, or ever will be, to tell him. Whatever shall I say?" she asked, almost imploringly.

"Deny it, of course," Hannah advised matter-of-factly. "What else can you do?"

"Yes, of course I shall. You are quite right. I shall say he is an evil-minded man, Hannah, that Finnegan fellow."

Her body was shaking nonetheless, and she tried to control it while going upstairs to greet her father. He sat at the dining-room table, sipping a glass of wine, awaiting his meal. Kitty walked in smiling and kissed him on the forehead.

"Father, it's delightful to see you home."

She thought he looked tired and ill.

"Yes, my darling, I am glad to be home and you... how have you been?" he asked, calmly.

"The same as usual, father. I did miss you and it was lonely sometimes."

She sad beside him and he noticed that the deep grief and sadness seemed to have left her. It was amazing, he thought. She looked bright and almost her usual cheerful self. Clearing his throat, her father continued.

"I am sure it has not been easy for you here without your mother. In fact, while I was in Dublin I felt very upset, hopeless at one point. But we must continue, must we not?"

She was aware he was not his usual self and felt very unsure of the direction the conversation was taking.

"Yes, father, life must continue for both of us. As a matter of fact, while you were away I thought of little else but Hampshire. It will be so refreshing to live there. For you, also, father, when you can come and join us."

She noticed his sudden change of expression into one of surprise and relief.

"Why, yes, Hampshire. John's place will be delightful for you, my dear. And you will have London to look forward to," he added cheerfully.

"I know, father, it will be like starting life all over again. I need so desperately to do so."

Kitty tried to sound convincing, but she felt fear grip her spirit as they thought, "He knows. He knows about James and I. Why else would he react like that?" Her hands trembled beneath the table, yet her face remained calm in expression.

"You look very tired, father. Are you feeling alright?"

"Perfectly, Kitty, and don't worry. I shall be fine when I rest a little more. But before I do that I intend to write to John and tell him you will arrive on January 1st instead of the 10th. I am not happy about the reports from the castle, and I will only rest easy when you have left this country."

She was aghast at the sudden change of plan.

"Are things really that bad, father? This is such a sudden change of plan that..." She didn't manage to finish her sentence.

"Why the anxiety, Kitty? It is only ten days earlier, that's all. Did you not just say how much you were looking forward to it all? Or is there something you are not telling me? Something you are not happy about?"

His gaze was intent, but her strength returned. Looking at him she said matter-of-factly, "Unhappy, father? Not in the least. It simply means I shall have to begin organising myself all the sooner that is all. A woman's concern, you might say," and she managed a smile.

"Good. I am happy to hear that. For a moment I thought I detected some hesitancy, and that would be quite a contradiction, would it not?" He avoided her eyes as she continued to stare at him. Suddenly, she stood up, tired of his innuendo. My father has changed, she realised.

"It's all quite simply, father, really. I may or I may not go to Hampshire."

He stood up and banged the table in anger.

"How dare you question my better judgement, Kitty? The matter is settled and go you shall!"

She remained seated, her hands now firmly on the table, all the fear gone.

"No, father. This time I intend to do what I feel is right for a change. I may go to Dublin or Kildare for that matter. Caroline Fitzwilliam or the Wanerights are constantly beseeching me to go and stay. I shall no longer be told what to do. I have done a great deal of thinking in the past five days and feel it is time I took some measure of control over my life. As you said, father, before you went to Dublin... I have grown up!"

Her look of calm and control angered him further. He tried desperately to cool his temper. He did not want right now to accuse her of anything. I will follow her and discover it for myself. Then I will speak my piece.

"May I remind you, young lady, that you will do as I say until you are married and gone from this house."

She could no longer contain herself. Images of Glencora and her father's long-hidden son, Henry, floated before her. But no. This was not the time. Standing up, she looked at the man before her who had lived all his life concealing the truth. Her respect for him was diminishing rapidly.

"No, father. I shall not jump to your commands or be addressed as one of the servants, much less be told what to do. Mamma has bequeathed to me sufficient money to live independently. I shall do as I please at this point in my life. You have changed father, a great deal. I am not sure I like it." With that, she left the room abruptly.

He stood up and looked blankly at the empty table before him. He poured himself another glass of wine and disregarded the lunch that Williams had served him some time earlier. He walked to the fireplace and stood by his faithful dogs.

"I have lost you, Kitty," he thought. "But not completely. I will rid your life of whoever has taken your heart and in time, my young lady, you will only thank me."

For the remainder of that day Kitty avoided her father, taking her meals in her room and only walking in the orchard for exercise. Her mind worked rapidly. The money her mother had left to her was accessible. It meant instant independence for both her and James, instant freedom. She decided that she would go and see him the following morning at the cottage. We must leave within days, or else it will be too late. I will not even mention my new plans to Hannah, as father would dismiss her instantly should she confess to him out of distress or guilt.

That night, Kitty walked discreetly to the luggage room where she found two bags to pack her travelling clothes. She placed her jewellery and precious pieces that had belonged to her mother in a metal box. She locked it securely. She wept as she thought of her mother and cried to her in great sadness. "Mother," she wept, "I know now that you would not be displeased with me or want me to surrender the love of my life." As she undressed for bed, she looked around the large familiar room, wondering what type of house James and herself would find in the new world of America.

Dawn came silently, as winter dawns do, the only sound being the crows in the rookery. Kitty looked at the clear blue sky and the crimson dawn to the east. She dressed hurriedly in her riding costume and walked quietly down the stairs. There was no sound from her father's room and she felt relieved on reaching the kitchen, where Hannah was surprised to see her.

"My goodness, Kitty, you are abroad early."

"Misty needs exercising, Hannah," she lied. "I have neglected her now for some days."

She drank the warm milk that the old housekeeper handed to her.

"I shall be back soon, Hannah. Will you keep breakfast for me? I shall have it in my room when I return."

Hannah was surprised, but said nothing. If the young mistress wished to tell her something, well and good. Hannah felt she knew too much for her own good as it was.

"Be careful, my love," she said, looking at the beautiful young lady in front of her.

"I shall, Hannah. Don't worry. All will be well."

Going to the stables, Kitty saddled her own horse as the grooms walked about carrying buckets of water and feed to their stabled idols.

In the grove of trees on the small brow overlooking the avenue, Lord Foldsworth soothed his horse, which scraped at the thick carpet of leaves with an impatient hoof. He covered the animal's muzzle with his gloved hand to muffle a possible whinny. He heard the hoof beats coming to the corner of the avenue where out of the large cluster of rhododendrons his daughter appeared, cantering briskly. Slowly mounting, he rode forward slowly, aware that he was well camouflaged among the evergreen spruce trees. his heart lurched in sadness and anger at what he was about to do. He prayed it would not be the truth; hoped against hope that what the drunken lunatic had said outside the inn was an entire malicious lie. Perhaps she was simply going for an early morning canter, only to return to join him in the dining room for breakfast. Then he could reason with her, if it wasn't too late. Her route-veered right of the village and across the small fields, where her horse jumped the small stonewalls with great ease. He followed at a safe distance, keeping her in view at all times. He descended the wooded hillside and then saw her change route onto a small winding road where a cottage was clearly visible. Chimney smoke drifted high into the morning sky. He rode no further. From his vantage point her destination would be clearly visible to him. His hearts pounded as he saw her dismount and tether her horse outside the cottage. His blood coursed through his veins and sweat formed on his forehead as the truth unfolded before him.

"I shall wait for her to leave, then wait and see what the occupant will do next. I will then follow him and make arrangements for him to be arrested. Time is on my side," he thought.

James was surprised to see Kitty. A thousand questions leaped to mind. She told him briefly of her encounter with her father the previous day, and the news, which the coachman had told Hannah. Bartley Finnegan had revealed their secret.

"It's all true, Kitty, all of it," he said slowly. "Marjorie called here late last night and told me so."

"James, we must leave. We must go now, before it is too late. He will shoot you, or even worse. I have all my clothes packed and..."

"Kitty, Kitty, don't be so upset. We don't need to run away like frightened children. Be calm, my love, and let us discuss this sensibly."

"Have you changed your mind, James?" she asked tearfully.

He embraced her and kissed her with the depth of love she had come to know in him.

"Never, my lovely. If I have to wait at the ends of the earth for you, I will. Now we must plan this calmly. I will meet you at Marjorie's this evening at six o'clock. We will go there separately and then ride this night to Dublin. We can stay there with a cousin of mine and then go to England the following day. Now, stop fretting Mrs. de Lacey, for tonight we will begin our new life together."

As he held her in his arms she felt the fear leave her tense body.

"That all makes sense, James. I will be able to withdraw the money that Mamma bequeathed to me from the bank in Dublin. James, I can scarcely believe that we are finally going to be together."

As he made fresh tea, she told him more about the ugly scene in the dining room with her father the previous day and how her father had changed so much.

"At one point, James, I thought he was actually going to strike me. He looked at me with such hate, such derision. He is planning something, James. I can feel it in my very bones and I am frightened."

He stroked her dark hair, soothing her.

"Now, Kitty, ride back and don't act in any way out of character. At dusk, go to the stables when the grooms and yardmen are having their dinner and ride to town. I shall be there, I promise my love. I shall be there."

They kissed again with intense passion until James withdrew from the embrace, chuckling.

"Mrs de Lacey, we will have all the time in the world to love! But for now, go. Your horse is in the yard for all to see. We can't afford to be discovered at this point. Go now, my lovely."

She kissed him again. Going in to the yard, he helped her mount.

From the hillside copse, Lord Foldsworth saw the figure of the man and he vowed vengeance and death upon him. He watched Kitty gallop across country towards Oak Hall and he realised that she would never be his little daughter again. Minutes later, the man emerged from his cottage and went to a stable. A few moments later he came out leading a horse, which he mounted quickly. He rode towards the village and emerging from the wooded thicket, Lord Foldsworth followed him. James was so excited that he was totally unaware of his pursuer. It would be difficult for him to act normally for the rest of the day, trying to subdue his rising sense of excitement. He felt saddened that he had to conceal his plans from both his employer and from Gilltrap. Both men had been loyal friends to him. He knew that Marjorie would tell them eventually. He hoped they would both understand.

Lord Foldsworth waited for some time outside the village inn, which the young man had entered. He had brought his horse to the rear, he noticed, which suggested that he must work there or have some other business afoot. Deciding to enter the inn, he tethered his horse to the ring outside on the wall and walked slowly to the door. He had never been inside this inn before, nor had any of his ancestors before him. It was dim inside, in contrast to the bright morning sunlight outside, and the air smelled of stale smoke and leftover beer. James was humming a tune, unaware of the early morning customer who stood looking at him from the shadows. Looking up from the glasses he was washing, he was suddenly aware of the identity of the customer now walking over to the counter. He waited to be addressed.

"You, you are just after riding in here, are you not?"

"Yes, I work here, your Lordship, as most people know."

"I see," Lord Foldsworth said, staring at the man his daughter was associating with. "You have been at Oak hall once, if I remember correctly, with that fellow Gilltrap from the forge. Is that not true?"

"Your memory serves you well, Lord Foldsworth. You summoned us there to discuss the death of Jerome Hennessy. T'was Joe and I who discovered his body," James made his reply as casually as he could.

"De Lacey, that's you name. De Lacey. We shall meet again, of that I am sure."

He left James with doubt in his mind that he had been followed to the inn and identified as Kitty's lover. The question now in his mind was how, and when, would Lord Foldsworth act?

He was not a man who would ignore his daughter's choice of companion; of this James was acutely aware. He regretted not having arranged to leave with Kitty before evening. A lot could happen in a day, as life had so often clearly shown.

"Perhaps I am over-anxious," he thought. "Besides, there was only six hours of work and then off to the cottage to pack and head to town by a discreet route." He tried, with difficulty, to concentrate on the work at hand. Gradually the tension and fear left him as the customers engaged in idle gossip in their usual way. Kitty came to mind constantly and his heart warmed to the thought of them together.

Sergeant. Cosgrave was more than surprised to see Lord Foldsworth walk into the barracks. The appearance of his visitor was in stark contrast to their last meeting. The man before him, once so composed and well turned out, looked unshaven. The eyes blazed with anger, or contempt, he couldn't be quite sure.

"Good afternoon, your Lordship," he said, raising his cap.

"Never mind the formalities, Cosgrave. This is not a social call, nor am I here for idle chatter. I will get to the point directly. I want you to proceed to the village instantly. Go to the inn where you will find a young man, James de Lacey by name. I want him arrested within the hour. I have excellent reason to believe that he was the instigator of the attempted burning down of Oak Hall. I trust I need not remind you of my wife's death."

He paced around the barrack, tapping the furniture with his riding crop, agitated in the extreme.

Sergeant. Cosgrave was dumbfounded.

"Well, man, what are you gaping at? Well? You have failed miserably in tracking down the perpetrators and now you stand here, staring open-mouthed. Look lively. Take six men with you, armed, mind. If there is any resistance, shoot to kill. I want these people taught a lesson, do you understand, man?"

"Yes, your Lordship," the sergeant replied timidly. He had a distinct dislike for the task before him. "And where, may I ask, did your Lordship get this information from?"

Lord Foldsworth looked at the policeman before him with scorn and derision.

"How dare you question me, man? You, who can't keep law and order in this town. Drunken louts almost assaulting me during the week alone! What answers have you for me, Cosgrave? About my home? Hmm? Well, answer me."

"We are still making enquiries, your Lordship."

With that, the table was overturned and the oil lamp upon it smashed in the pieces on the ground. Two policemen ran into the room on hearing the disturbance. Lord Foldsworth glared at them.

"Well? What do you pair of fools want? I shall personally see to it that Justice Stewart inspects your conduct and execution of the law and order of His Majesty, King George! Now, Cosgrave, assemble the men, armed and mounted. Now!"

The mention of Justice Stewart had the desired effect upon the men, who had a dread at the mention of the name. Everyone who appeared before him was transported to the Colonies, even for the pettiest of crimes. Cases that had come before his court had been for stealing or drunken behaviour. No mercy had been shown to those who had stood before him. Those who begged for leniency were ejected from the court, instantly. He was a merciless man, ruthless. This was widely known. People were surprised that no one had, as yet, been condemned to death. It was only a matter of time.

Sergeant. Cosgrave ordered the men to assemble in the room before him.

"His Lordship orders that we travel to the village to arrest a man whom he knew to be responsible for the fire at Oak Hall. Six of you are to accompany me, armed and mounted in the event of resistance. His Lordship's orders are to shoot to kill. We will leave in five minutes." It was seldom Sergeant. Cosgrave's men had seen him so disturbed and they assumed the shouting and overturned table was evidence of the seriousness of the situation.

"Move, you fools, quickly! If this man escapes arrest I will see that Justice Stewart deports each of you for neglect of duty," Lord Foldsworth shouted abusively.

Lord Foldsworth's mind, now in frenzy, was incapable of rational thought. Vengeance, no matter how ill conceived, possessed him entirely.

The six-armed policemen, led by their sergeant. And the landlord, rode through the town. The main street was busy with people buying and selling at the street stalls, and the angry landlord cleared the way for the cavalcade. The bullwhip he had brought with him cracked and hissed above the heads of those who were slow to move to one side. His arrogance angered the bystanders, who shouted, while others stood in silent disdain at the sight of the armed police, obviously on a mission of great urgency. Justice, they knew, would have little to do with the matter. It seldom, if ever, had.

There had been reports lately of floggings in the south of the county, and no one seemed to know what the victims were actually guilty of. It was a disturbing development. As the small troop of armed horsemen left the town, many realised that the once quiet and unperturbed Lord Foldsworth had become a figure to fear and despise. Bartley Finnegan had spread a story of how he had been flogged and escaped an almost fatal shooting by Lord Foldsworth. Everybody believed him. One had only to see the gash from the shot as proof. As there had been no witnesses to the incident, so Bartley was free to embellish the story at will. Besides, the sympathy of his listeners assured him of an almost endless supply of free whiskey.

The town hummed with speculative gossip as to the destination of the armed party. Bartley alone knew, but was also wise enough to say nothing on the matter. The crowd would be without mercy for an informer. The thought of being summoned as a witness had not as yet occurred to him. The armed police rode briskly toward the village, with Lord Foldsworth well ahead of them. His instructions to the police had been simple and clear. Sergeant. Cosgrave was to walk in with his men, arrest James de Lacey there and then, and imprison him within the hour. The sergeant dared not question the matter and his men understood the situation.

Common sense told Sergeant. Cosgrave that whoever attempted to burn down Oak Hall would never be foolish enough to work in the village tavern. It was also clear to him that Lord Foldsworth had a crazed look about him, and power in the hands of a madman knew no bounds. For that matter, neither his men nor himself were even assured of fair treatment should anything happen to foil the planned arrest.

Joe Gilltrap was outside the forge having shod old Mag's donkey. The old woman was standing beside him when they heard the hoof beats approach. Lord Foldsworth rode past first, his horse in a lather of sweat.

"My god, Mag, there's a madman if ever I saw one."

They watched as the landlord hurriedly tied his horse outside the tavern. He turned and looked with disdain at Mag and Joe. The old woman turned her back to him and placed the harness on her donkey. Joe lifted the small cast into the traces.

"'Tis poor James, I'm afraid." Tears came down her cheeks.

Joe looked up again and saw the seven-armed policemen ride into the village. His stomach heaved in fear as he thought of the remaining pikes hidden in the deep-water drain.

Lord Foldsworth stalked into the tavern. James was just placing fresh turf soda on the fire.

"Good at fires are you, eh?" said Lord Foldsworth calmly.

James turned around and looked at him. He had not heard him enter.

"It gets cold in the afternoons, your Lordship," he replied, missing the irony in the remark made to him.

Sergeant. Cosgrave walked in with his men, who by now had pistols drawn and stood behind the landlord. It was that James realised that his plans for that evening and any other evening were now doomed.

"What is your name?" this time he made no defence to the rank of the man before him. Fresh waves of anger swept over Charles Foldsworth. He drew his pistol and fired into the thatched roof overhead.

"Your name, man, or the next shot will be for you," he shouted.

James stood perfectly still. Escape was impossible. The policemen in front of him aimed their weapons in his direction.

"My name, as you well know, is James de Lacey, or is your memory failing?" James said in slow, deliberate tones.

The bullwhip seemed to come from nowhere as it lashed out and wrapped itself about James' neck and face. The pain seared through him as the blood flowed freely down his neck and chest. James gripped the whip, pulling the unsuspecting landlord towards him. He placed one arm in a tight grip about the landlord's neck and threw him to the floor shouting,

"How dare you take a whip to me, you half-crazed lunatic?" Then, looking up at the stunned policemen, he shouted, "Shoot! Go on! Shoot now and you will kill us both. You will get me either way, but not before I say what's on my mind first."

Lord Foldsworth's face was blue and grey with fear. As he lay powerless in the grip of James de Lacey, looking down at him, James asked...

"Come to arrest me, have ye sergeant?"

"Yes, that we have, or to shoot you here if you like."

Outside the tavern a great crowd had assembled, having heard the shot ring out. Brian Wolohan and his wife stood behind the counter terrified at the scene before them. People outside could hear everything plainly. Joe and old Mag stood nearest the double doors, which had been thrown wide open by the police. James continued in a strong voice, now for their benefit.

"And what are you arresting me for, sergeant? I am entitled to know."

Charles Foldsworth jumped on hearing the question, only to be gripped even tighter about the throat.

"Let him go, de Lacey," one of the police shouted.

But James only stared at the sergeant before him, awaiting his reply. Sergeant. Cosgrave cleared his throat.

"James de Lacey, in the name of King George I, I arrest you for the attempted burning of Oak Hall."

The crowd outside gasped. Some of the younger men from the village pressed closer to the tavern door.

"Close that blasted door," the sergeant shouted; but the men refused to move away. The police sensed the anger mounting in the crowd outside. The sergeant looked back at James, who was still holding the landlord in a tight grip.

"I was here working all night, sergeant, when that incident occurred. Is that not right, Brian?" he shouted as he looked at his employer.

"That's right, he was here, and fifty other men can testify to that if needs be," said Brian clearly.

"Well, Justice Stewart can judge the facts of the whole affair. But in any case, de Lacey, I am now arresting you for the assault of Lord Foldsworth."

Suddenly, four of the policemen rushed forward and hurled James back against a wall, releasing the grip on Lord Foldsworth. Sergeant. Cosgrave sprang to the assistance of the almost immobile man, who gasped heavily as he leaned against the counter for support.

"Brandy... give me brandy," he wheezed.

Brian Wolohan looked at him in open hatred, making no effort to provide the drink demanded.

"Are you bloody deaf, or what? Brandy!" the landlord shouted again.

But Brian remained standing where he was, staring defiantly at him.

"Get me brandy, you deaf bastard or..."

Brian smiled and said, "Or what? You'll have me arrested too? Now, you listen to me, Foldsworth. Get out of my tavern, now! Me and mine were in this village before a planter like you were ever heard of. The blasted cheek of you, arresting a man on a trumped-up charge. Get out, get out the lot of you, before I make this a day you'll never forget!"

With that, he put his hand under the counter and pulled out a slash hook. He slammed it on the counter top before Lord Foldsworth.

Sergeant. Cosgrave realised that the situation was now getting out of control and that if the crowd were whipped into frenzy they would be overpowered in a matter of seconds. Lord Foldsworth stood back, terrified at the sight of the slash hook. Pointing a finger at Brian, he shouted:

"Be careful tavern keeper. Be careful, I say, or your neck will grease the end of a rope sooner than you think!"

Brian's wife fell to the floor in a faint, and the crowd outside jumped back as two more shots were fired through the roof from the sergeant's gun.

"Clear the way," he ordered, and the crowd stood aside instantly to let them through.

The sight of James with his hands tied behind his back and a rope tied loosely about his neck shocked the crowd further. The dried blood on his face and neck made him almost unrecognisable to them. He was suddenly jerked forward and, losing his balance, fell heavily to the ground. His face and head bounced off the cobblestones, opening fresh wounds. The crowd jeered and booed at the cruelty taking place before them. Lord Foldsworth took out his bullwhip and lashed wildly into the crowd, ignoring the cries of those unfortunate to be near him.

Just then all attention was drawn to the thundering of the hoof beats of an approaching horse, its rider sidesaddle.

Kitty rode through the crowd expertly and stopped when she saw the horrific sight before her. She cried out in grief and rage.

"Let that man go this instant, you pack of brutes." Her horse pranced, frightened, unaccustomed to the fear that gripped the rider's body.

"Do you hear me, sergeant? I command you to release him." Kitty screamed in rage.

Lord Foldsworth walked up before her and took the bridle of her horse.

"My lady, it is I who command here! Go directly home this instant! Do you hear me? This instant."

But instead Kitty jerked her horse free and looked down at the man she scarcely recognised as her father. Hate and derision welled up within her.

"No, I shall not obey you. Not now, not ever. How dare you treat another human being like this? Release him now."

"No, my lady. He will not be released. He will stand trial before Justice Stewart... your close friend, if I remember correctly."

Kitty realised that her efforts were in vain. She looked at the crowd who stood mesmerised. She asked the sergeant what the charge against the man was. On being told that it was attempted arson, she laughed at him in scorn.

"Fire, my foot! It was not his doing. Never!"

She looked at her father and felt the hopelessness of the situation.

"Why have you arrested him, father?"

The crowd stood motionless, listening to every word.

"The sergeant has just told you, my lady," he replied.

She looked at him with contempt.

"No, father, that isn't the problem at all, is it?"

Then she turned the horse and faced the crowd, who looked at her in awed silence. James felt the sting of his salty tears, as he looked on at the woman he loved, so torn asunder by the scene. She, in turn, looked down at him, in shock. Regaining her composure, she addressed the crowd in a clear voice.

"All you people here have known me all my life. The true reason why James is being arrested is not because he tried to burn Oak Hall, not at all. For why should he try to burn down the home of the woman he loves?"

The crowd were stunned.

Lord Foldsworth raised his whip and this time aimed at his daughter. She skilfully avoided it, laughing hysterically, fear in her heart.

"Whip me, father, is that your next intention, to whip your own daughter before a crowd? You are despicable. It is as well that my beloved mother is at rest this day, not to see the monster you have become!"

"Go home, you raving woman," he shouted, "You bloody hypocrite, unworthy of my name. No, don't go home. You are no longer my daughter. I renounce you now and for all time."

Kitty felt a fresh surge of anger.

"Hypocrite, father? Is that what I now am? At least I had the courage to love, unlike you, abandoning your illegitimate son, Henry. Ah, I see, you thought I was unaware of that, your hidden life. No father, it is I who renounce you, for you no longer deserve the name father. Out of my way!" She rode past him as if he did not exist. Halting her horse beside James, she dismounted.

"Oh, my love," she whispered, and she clung to him in desperation and despair.

The crowd moved closer and a double line of men stood between them and the landlord. He stood almost shaking in shame and disbelief. Going over to her horse, Kitty removed the sidesaddle and returned to James, removing the rope from around his neck and hands. The police made no motion to prevent her doing so.

"If you must take him to prison, allow him at least the benefit of my horse. I am sure he will be well within reach of your loaded guns all the way."

The sergeant nodded at the courageous and beautiful woman before him and felt shame at his task, realising the true motive behind the arrest.

"Move out," he ordered, and the police rode, surrounding James, out of the village.

Lord Foldsworth stood alone now, his hate and anger spent with the dreadful realisation that had had lost his daughter forever, and the respect of his tenantry Kitty looked at the crowd about her.

"I would be grateful for a home among you. I have none, now, much less a family."

Her father turned and walked away slowly to his horse. After two attempts he managed to mount, and it carried him from the village as if it too had lost its spirit. Joe and old Mag walked over to Kitty.

"Come now, my lady. If you will, we would be happy to offer you some refreshment in my home."

The crowd, as if released from a spell, cheered wildly.

"Long live Lady Catherine!"

She turned about and looked at the sea of faces sobbing. Then, looking over their heads saw a last glimpse of James, who waved back to her before disappearing around the corner of the small road.

"Come now, my pet," Mag urged.

Slowly they walked to Joe's house, as the crowd stood aside for them. They loved her for her courage and truth, and above all for her love. She was now one of them and every man among them would have given his life for her that day.

The tavern filled to overflowing as the events of the past hour were relived over and over again.

* * *

Hannah heard the news from May Ryan's eldest child. She was beside herself with grief. Wrapping her shawl about her, she told Williams that her years of service to the house were over forever. He pleaded with her to see reason.

"No, Williams, we have no longer a kind master, only a fool and a madman," she said sadly, taking her savings from her years of service, she walked out cross the open fields. As the dusk of the winter sky enfolded the surrounding mountains, she did not look back.

Nell Gilltrap looked at Kitty with pity. She was sitting by the open fire shivering from the shock rather than the chill evening air. Mag had gone to her cottage for a herbal potion, which she assured Joe would settle the young lady's mind and spirit.

Joe was extremely agitated and worried, and knew that he also could be arrested at the whim of Lord Foldsworth. The additional worry about the pikes in the water drain made his heart pound. He knew he would have to dispose of them quickly. Even to bury them in the woods would be better than having them discovered in his possession. He decided to move them that night, taking no further chances.

When Mag returned with the potion, she mixed it in warm milk and honey and handed it to Kitty to drink.

"Now, little lamb, here you are. This will help your worried mind. Trust Mag now, won't you?"

Kitty, still numb with shock, took the drink from the old woman with the kind eyes. She drank it slowly. She watched Mag light her clay pipe with fascination and, as the old woman sat back into the corner, she began to hum a song, which Kitty had never heard before. It was a haunting melody, with a sadness that she knew was as old as the land they lived in. Its tones and ripples invited Kitty into a gentle sleep, where the nightmare of the day's events left her mind and heart.

* * *

James sat in the narrow stonewalled cell. He looked at the damp walls. Green slime spread across them in places and the smell of dank decay was all around. His heart sank within him. Desperation came in waves. Had their plans materialised, they would have been on their way to Dublin by now, their first night together. The lump in his throat refused to leave him and he prayed for darkness, that his tears might fall unseen. A damp cloth had been passed to him through the bars, to clean his face and neck of the congealed blood. His flesh still stung from the lash of the bullwhip. His thoughts went to Kitty, and how she had spoken fearlessly and in defiance of her father. Her love for him had been declared openly and without hesitation.

Charles Foldsworth was now a man without mercy, and a man who realised that he was despised. His act of ultimate revenge would be execution of his daughter's lover. James thought of death. He sighed as he lay on the wooden bench thinking: my life to end in its 29th year, when I am in love and denied all – yet he felt no fear, only sadness about what might have been. He thought the feeling was going to totally engulf him, and he jumped off the wooden bench, breathless.

Sergeant. Cosgrave came to the cell door with a metal plate of bread and cold meat, and a mug of water.

"Here, eat this or leave it if you like, it's your belly."

The undisguised animosity made James realise the gravity of his situation. He felt trapped like a bird in a cage and he wanted to shout and scream his pain, but no sounds would come from his throat.

"I'll take the water," he said, simply.

"Suit yourself, but if I were you I'd eat something. It will be a long, cold night, the first of many for you, I'd say," he said, handing James the cold water.

"Death awaits me, sergeant. I know you had to do your duty today."

Sergeant. Cosgrave was surprised by this statement, and looked again at the young man in the cell before walking away silently. James drank the water slowly, sip by sip. He sat down and wondered where Kitty was or with whom she was staying. He knew the people would take care of her, for they would remember her many acts of kindness to them over the years. He thought about Joe and Nell and Brian as the scenes of the day presented themselves once again. His head thumped in pain and he felt a great tiredness sweep over him. He lay down again on the wooden bench and pulling the damp, grey blanket over himself, fell asleep.

Sergeant. Cosgrave came back to check his prisoner and looked at the man asleep in the cell. One of the guards would stand outside the barracks. Should the prisoner escape, he was doomed himself for transportation. Lord Foldsworth had warned as much. He shuddered at the very idea of transportation.

An oil lamp burned on a shelf outside the cell, casting long shadows. He shook his head slowly, knowing that soon this young man would sleep the sleep of death. He believed that he had worked all that fateful night of the burning of Oak Hall. The real problem was that he had fallen in love with the wrong woman. Lady Catherine had made no secret of it either. He pitied them both, and was in many ways amazed t their innocence. Love is blind indeed, blind to the danger in this case. How could that young man court the daughter of such a renowned family? Foolish beyond words, me lad. And now look where it has landed you, he said to himself.

James stirred restlessly as the sergeant closed the passage door, which creaked on its rusty hinge. A rat scurried down the dank passageway before leaping into a crevice in the old stonewall.

Lord Foldsworth awoke early the next day, cramped from sleeping in the armchair by the now blackened fire grate. It was not yet daybreak, but he knew that Williams would be on call as usual. First he decided to write a letter to Justice Stewart, and have the trial arranged and the date set as soon as possible. He wrote the letter, simply stating that he had traced the organiser of the fire at Oak Hall, which led to the death of his wife. The criminal had been arrested and was presently in the town jail awaiting His Majesty's Justice. He then sealed the parchment and rang for Williams, who appeared promptly.

"Good morning, my lord," he began, noting the condition of his master.

"Have this letter delivered to Wexford this morning, Williams, and have the messenger await a reply. I shall now wash and then have breakfast. See that the messenger leaves this instant."

"Yes, my lord. This instant I shall see to it. I must report to you also, my lord, that Hannah the housekeeper has left your service."

"Have her replaced today. I wish to hear no more of the matter. Now man, don't waste my time."

"No, my lord. And Williams left the study that morning, knowing that his master had indeed changed beyond recognition.

He heard with disbelief the scenes from the village the previous day and felt shame. All the servants had heard the same reports. Hannah had seen it as her duty to follow her young mistress. Who knows, perhaps she will be able to convince her of the folly of her foolish heart.

The messenger left promptly, and two hours later stood in the servants' hallway of Justice Stewart's residence, on the banks of the River Slaney. On reading the surprising letter from Oak Hall, Timothy Stewart sat down. Finally it seemed that the answer to his prayer had arrived. An example must be made, and here it was from the very man who only months previous had all but dismissed him for his concept of ruling with austerity. He laughed out loud at the strangeness of life sometimes. Well, well, well… Foldsworth, so you want my judgement on the matter!

His reply was simple. The sergeant in question was to have the prisoner escorted under armed guard to Wexford prison to be brought to trial in two weeks from now. Simple as that, he thought.

The messenger arrived back at Oak Hall in the late evening with the anxiously awaited reply, and upon reading it, Lord Foldsworth sighed with satisfaction and relief. With her lover hanged within the month, Kitty will come to her sense rapidly, he thought, and see the foolishness of her ways. Life will resume as normal once again, and it will serve to teach the people to respect their landlord. They must be taught a lesson. The problem is that I treated them too well… far too well, he thought. And it has cost me the life of my wife and almost my home.

His face became contorted as he imagined Kitty in the arms of her rebel lover, and he swore quietly. By God, he will hang! He swore as he filled his brandy glass yet again. No-one will ever take my kindness for weakness again, he resolved, more intent and convinced than ever.

* * *

Joe decided that Kitty must go and live in the hills with his aged mother. Hannah would accompany her, for to separate her from Kitty would prove quite impossible.

Kitty decided the next day to go to the tavern, again quite unheard of for her to do. But life now was very different, she reasoned, irretrievably altered. Brian greeted her warmly.

"Good morning, Lady Catherine. How are you?" he asked, genuinely concerned.

"Not too well, I am afraid, Mr. Wolohan. How is your poor wife? I am told she had a weakness during that dreadful ordeal you were put through."

"Yes, she did, my lady, but she is now as well as ever. Your mare is stabled outside. One of the policemen returned her last night," and he stopped abruptly, aware that neither of them had referred to James or the arrest.

"I see. I shall saddle her now, and thank you once again for all your kindness. I am going to spend some time with Mr. Giltrap's family in the mountains. They very kindly invited me," and unable to express her deep distress, Kitty slumped in the nearest chair.

Mag was sitting in her usual place by the great hearth, quite unseen in the darkness of its corners. She stood up and came to Kitty's assistance with surprising agility.

"Now, now, my lovely, there, there. Don't weep. Somehow we will have to try and keep our spirits up. After all, James would expect it of us."

At the mention of his name Kitty stood up and dried her eyes with her lace handkerchief.

"Yes, how very true. Now Mr. Wolohan, if you would be kind enough to escort me to the stable, I shall saddle my mare."

Brian led Kitty to the stable where Kitty saddled her mare, talking to her in gentle tones.

Hannah tried in desperation to face her new situation of uncertainty, having for so many years lived a life of total predictability, and a measure of comfort unknown to most of the people she now found herself among. Mag's old donkey and cart was borrowed to convey Hannah's few belongings and those of Kitty's, which she had managed to remove discreetly from Oak Hall the previous night. The very idea of having to live in a four-roomed cottage with very few of the comforts or conveniences which they had both been accustomed to, left her feeling desolate and depressed. And yet they were fortunate to have been offered a home to go to, she reminded herself.

* * *

An emergency meeting of the committee had been called and Joe gave account of the arrest of James and the circumstances that had led to it. Father Murphy looked grave as he stared at the rough wooden table they sat around. It was a serious development; he stated firmly, that now placed them all in danger.

"Will he talk, Joe?" he asked anxiously.

"Never, father. James will never utter a word and I can assure you of that. Lord Foldsworth's anger and revenge hinges around the fact that James was too close to his daughter, nothing else. The man has almost gone insane since the death of his wife and he needs a scapegoat," he said assuredly.

"Unfortunate that his wife died so tragically," Father Murphy said and added resignedly, "but the plan was never intended to harm the occupants – frighten them, yes, and the rest of the landlord class – the message being simple. The suppression must stop. However, this unexpected development places our entire organisation in this part of the country under very serious threat. They have methods of torture not that would make a good man deny his very God. The pitch cap is now being used in many places, any man would faint with fear at the prospect of melting tar being set alight with gunpowder on the top of his head," he said angrily.

The air of gloom and fear spread over the group of nine men sitting at the table. Joe cleared his throat.

"Well, the way I see it is simple. Justice Stewart will have a quick trial, sentencing James to be hanged, to state the policy of the government."

All agreed.

"Is there any news of the trial date yet," Matt Ryan asked matter-of-factly.

"No, not yet. Sergeant. Cosgrave or one of the policemen would have said as much when drinking at the Bull's Nose. Marjorie would have said as much to one of us. Rest assured she will when she hears," Joe said, adding almost helplessly; "God knows there is little we can do to help poor James. He is allowed no visitors, none. We all know that it will only be a matter of days until he goes to Wexford prison."

Again Matt Ryan spoke. "Isn't that the only hope the lad has of a rescue? An ambush on the route on the day they move him?"

They wondered why they hadn't thought of it already.

"That's exactly what we will do, for that lad deserves his freedom. It's unlikely that they will torture him in the town, but once in Wexford they will show no mercy. That's when he might be forced into talking under their barbarous methods of torture."

They all agreed, for to be tarred and set alight was a dreadful thought in itself. So the meeting then turned to the careful planning, in great detail, of the ambush; the location and how they would execute their plan. All that remained for them was to find out the day of the planned escorting of their comrade.

There had been neither comment nor criticism of James' association with Kitty. Matters of the heart could be strange. They knew James to be a tireless worker, brave and trustworthy. Little else mattered to them.

"Joe, we will be depending entirely on you to pass on to us the date of the transfer to Wexford and hope that Marjorie can get that vital information for us. If not, well... James is as good as dead and we will then be the hunted," and... Father Murphy said in conclusion... "And none of you, or your family members, will ever be safe again."

They were too well aware of this reality, and the new plan gave them the opportunity of avoiding such a terrible prospect. It also gave them a sense of purpose that dispelled the helplessness that had held them in its grip before the meeting.

"France, of course, that's where they must go – out of the country for a while until we need him for the insurrection," Father Murphy state clearly, as he threw his great black riding cape about his shoulders.

"And what of the Lady Catherine?" Joe asked.

"Well, tell her nothing until we have him three days out to sea. Then she may do as she pleases," the priest added bluntly.

* * *

Kitty awoke in the tiny room to the sound of a cock crowing in the late December dawn. A thick fog surrounded the tiny cottage and the smell of the turf fire in the kitchen crept under her door. Old Mrs. Gilltrap, though no in her 83rd year, was agile and a joy to be with. Hannah had seemed more relaxed these past few days in the company of the old woman. Despite being asked repeatedly by Kitty to address her by her first name, her hostess refused to drop the formal title.

"No, Lady Catherine, you are and Lady Catherine you shall remain," she announced firmly, adding with a smile, "What would the neighbours think with old Mary Gilltrap cackling Kitty this and Kitty that... Well, they would say, my dear, that I had ideas above my station; and none of them would talk to me then, you see." And no more was said on the matter.

As Kitty lay awake listening to Hannah and old Mary talking, she thought of James. She had cried her heart out these past nights and no more tears would come.

"It's time I used my position and went into that prison myself and see James," she decided resolutely. Calling Hannah, she asked her to prepare one of her best riding habits for the journey into town. Hannah was frantic with worry, and pleaded with her not to go, but to no avail.

Within the hour Kitty was on her way and bystanders stood and looked on in admiration. The story of her love and devotion to James was the main talking point now at gatherings throughout the five counties. It was a story people loved, and some even prayed for them.

Sergeant. Cosgrave looked up in amazement as Kitty entered the barrack.

"Good day... hm... Lady Catherine," he said, almost sheepishly.

"Good day to you, Sergeant. Cosgrave. I am here to see my fiancé. Please escort me to where you have him incarcerated," she said with an air of authority that made the man before her jump to his feet.

"Does your father know you are here, my lady?" he asked.

"Of course he does, sergeant. Now, do not waste my time please, lead on." And she stood looking directly at him feeling very much in control of the situation.

Taking a large bundle of keys from a hook on the wall, he walked ahead of her. Silently the great door into the dark passageway creaked open. She tried to suppress her horror at the smell that filled the air. Coming to the end of the passageway, the sergeant stopped and pointed silently to the cell where James lay sleeping.

"I shall be back in a half-hour, my lady. That's all the time I can allow you," he said softly.

But Kitty did not hear him. She stood shocked at the sight of the prone figure on the bed before her.

"James," she called softly.

He slowly opened his eyes, thinking he was still in the dream of minutes before.

"Kitty? Is it you my love?"

He rushed from the wooden pallet and they clung together through the iron bars of the cell.

"Oh God... my love... my love," she wept and James held back his tears of relief upon seeing her.

"How are you feeling, James? You look ill and thin."

"No, Kitty, I feel alright. I can't sleep with the town noises all night," and he attempted to laugh but could not.

"I miss you so much, James... so very much, my love," and she kissed him tenderly as the iron bars stung their faces.

"Kitty, what has been happening to you and where are you living and what do you do all day? Oh, just to see you is heaven," he said with a broken voice.

Kitty gave him an account of all that had happened and how Joe brought her home and how Hannah had left Oak Hall to take care of her in Mrs. Giltrap's cottage. James smiled.

"And how is life in the cottage for you, my love?"

"They are all wonderful to me, James. It's so warm and cosy there and Hannah has the old woman chatted almost out of her senses." For the first time their laughter was spontaneous.

But shouting that came from the sergeant's room interrupted it.

"How dare you allow him such a visit?" the voice boomed.

The two lovers held each other in anguish and disbelief. Kitty knew it was the voice of Justice Stewart. The iron door at the top of the passage banged open as the sergeant ran ahead of the judge in open terror.

"She said her father approved," the sergeant wailed.

"Get out of my way, fool," he shouted, as the cowering figure of the sergeant failed to avoid the lash of the riding crop.

"So this is where the Honourable. Catherine Foldsworth socialises, I see, amidst the criminals of His Majesty's Crown, no less," and he stood some distance from her, disguising a strange admiration of the woman before him.

"Yes, Timothy, as you can see I am here with my fiancé," she said calmly.

"Please, don't make me utterly sick. Fiancé indeed. Your mother's murderer, according to your father's account, young lady," he hissed in open hostility.

"My father has gone quite insane, Timothy. The reason your man is in prison is quite simple. He loves me as I love him."

Timothy Stewart glared at her.

"Love? That? A rebel from the hills? No, my lady, I am afraid it is you who have gone insane. I dread to think of what your adorable mother would have to say if she were alive. Everyone in society is shocked beyond words at your behaviour. Perhaps horrified would be a better term, I should think." Then he looked at James with derision. "And you, you slime from the gutter, you would dare set alight one of the finest and noblest houses in the land and as if that were not enough, to then attempt to seduce a young lady of one of the greatest families in the land. By God, man, you will pay. Yes, you will." And he spat at James.

James refused to look at him; only at the woman he loved who stood before him. He wiped the saliva from his face.

"Go now, Kitty, go now, my love," James bade her quietly.

Kitty kissed him gently.

"Till we meet, my love."

Justice Stewart shouted.

"You both make me sick, very sick indeed."

Kitty looked at him.

"Really, Timothy, sick you say. No Timothy, it is I who feel ill. The very sight of you and your blood thirst reminds me of our bloodhounds at home Yes, for that is what you have been reduced to, Viscount Stewart, a common bloodhound. Now, out of my way!"

He looked at her in disbelief as she walked past him, her perfume coming in wafts through the dank air of the prison passage.

"Lady Foldsworth, one moment please. Look again at your gutter lover for the last time, for by this time tomorrow he will be in my safekeeping at Wexford jail, and you, madam, will not walk through those doors, ever," he said with an air of triumph, trying to hide his damaged pride.

His statement had its desired effect, for she almost fainted. Placing a hand against the wall, she stood with her back to him for a few seconds before walking away. The pain in her heart almost overcame her, yet she refused to allow him to see it.

"I shall go to see Marjorie," she decided as she left the barracks. Nausea swept over her as she mounted her horse.

She was soon sitting in Marjorie's parlour sobbing bitterly upon relating the events of the past hour to her supportive friend. Marjorie, however, sighed with deep relief upon hearing the vital information that she had prayed would come. The transportation of James to Wexford was now to take place within twenty-four hours. As she tried to comfort Kitty, her mind raced wondering how she would get the vital information to Matt Ryan. Kitty's voice seemed to be distant to her now as she decided to send someone to Marcus' home on the pretext of having potatoes delivered to her inn within hours. She left Kitty and walked hurriedly onto the street outside. On seeing a young lad who was taking care of Kitty's mare, she bade him mount and go quickly to Marcus' home, requesting potatoes within the hour. She wished with all her heart that she could disclose the planned ambush to Kitty, but her oath of secrecy was a sacred one. No, this young lady in her present frame of mind would be unable to retain such confidentiality.

Later, as Kitty rode back into the hills to her new home, her mind whirled like the evening mists about her. She had chosen the longer route home, afraid of meeting her father. However, she need not have worried, for at Oak Hall he reels in shock as Justice Stewart told him of his encounter with his daughter at the jail that day.

"With your consent, Charles, she informed that buffoon of a sergeant. My heavens, will we ever be rid of fools like him, I wonder?" he said, sipping his brandy slowly.

"Tomorrow evening, you say, the escorting to Wexford will take place?"

"Yes, that's right. I have arrange for a further four armed men to accompany the police from the station. Charles, have no fear, he has no chance of escape. More chance of a butterfly flying out of a barrel of tar."

But the following evening the ambush party lay in wait nine miles outside the town, their pistols loaded and men well placed. They watched the corner of the road as it entered the wooded pass. James sat well tied on the chestnut horse, which in turn was being led by Sergeant. Cosgrave himself, so determined was he to deliver his prized prisoner. The armed escort had by now relaxed, talking casually one to the other. Sergeant. Cosgrave looked at the road ahead of him for signs of life or movement, but all was calm in the falling dusk. Matt Ryan, upon sighting the approaching escort, gave the low whistle to signal its arrival. Suddenly, they were in full view of the ten men who lay waiting on the roadside thicket, pistols aimed at their targets. Four of the policemen rode in front of Sergeant. Cosgrave and four behind. It was as they had anticipated. Matt Ryan moved with stealth aiming the evergreen trees where the rope lay concealed as it stretched across the road beneath the clay. He aimed his gun at Sergeant. Cosgrave. They waited for the signal from their priest as each gun was aimed at its target.

"Now," came the shout.

A volley of shot assailed the evening stillness. As Sergeant. Cosgrave fell dead to the ground, James, amidst the shouting and confusion, fell from his horse and hit the ground heavily. A dead body then fell upon him, blood oozing from the chest rent asunder from shot, and three more lay close to him groaning in the pain of death. The sound of galloping horses told him a few had escaped. The surprise attack had succeeded, and as James extricated himself from beneath the dead man, the face of Joe Gilltrap jerked him into reality.

"Run, for Christ's sake, James."

He found himself running, as he had never done before. In the thicket the frightened horses pulled at their tethered reins.

"We lost not a man," Father Murphy shouted triumphantly, adding, "God is surely with us. Now, James, go to Dublin this very night. Here is money and the address you will go to in France. I assure you, you will be safe there. Now, go like the wind, my lad, across the hills. The police who escaped have ridden south, so word of your escape will not reach the authorities for another few hours. Now go, go go," Father Murphy shouted.

Before James realised it, he was riding across the breast of the hills, the wind blowing through his hair, reminding him of the joy of real freedom. His heart leaped in joy as he thought how happy Kitty would be on hearing the news of his escape. But France... Oh God, the distance, he thought. So far, so very far. But I am alive and I am going to live. The great horse beneath him travelled north towards the dark mountain mass, their peaks cloud covered. He knew the high tracks he would travel that would bring him west of the city of Dublin, and the port at the north of the great River Liffey.

That night, as Joe lay in bed, he felt victory and an excitement he had never experienced before. He told his wife that he had been visiting his mother all that day. The sight of Kitty's face when she heard news of the escape was one he would remember all his life. The risk had been great, but they had succeeded. He knew there would be repercussions for the deaths of six policemen.

In the early hours of the morning Williams was awoken from a deep sleep by one of the footmen, who said that a policeman was seeking Lord Foldsworth and Justice Stewart on a matter of grave urgency. Williams dressed quickly and went to his master's room, holding his night lamp aloft.

"Yes, who is it? What the devil... Williams, what is it, man?"

"A messenger seeking to speak with you and Justice Stewart, your Lordship."

"What? A policeman at this hour? What the hell is wrong now?" he shouted angrily. Going to his guest's bedroom, he knocked and entered.

"Sorry to awaken you Timothy, but there is a policeman here to see us. Odd hour, is it not?"

"Blast them at the castle, messengers at this hour," his guest muttered sleepily.

The policeman was led to the study where both men stood before him, agitated.

"Well, man, what the hell is it?" Justice Stewart demanded.

"An ambush, justice. Sergeant. Cosgrave is dead sir, and five more men also."

"What?" he shouted. "Dead?"

But Charles Foldsworth then leaped forward.

"The prisoner, man, what of the prisoner?"

"Escaped, your Lordship... five hours ago."

"No, no. It's not possible," the judge shouted.

"Escaped, never!" Lord Foldsworth declared.

They were both dumbfounded and now speechless in disbelief.

"I regret to say so, your honours. And Sergeant. Cosgrave dead," he repeated.

"To hell with Sergeant. Cosgrave," the judge roared, "and the rest of them too that died for that matter."

Lord Foldsworth slumped into the nearest chair.

"They always win, the rebels. And now I shall no longer be safe here, shall I?"

Justice Stewart looked at him with derision.

"Well, your policy of benevolence has reduced you to this, Foldsworth. On your head it must rest from now on," and turning to Williams he shouted, "You there, have my bags packed. I shall leave within the hour. And hurry, you dithering old fool."

Later, for the first time in his many long years of service, Williams broke with convention. As he sat by the fireside murmuring, "Up the rebels. Who can blame them wanting rid of the likes of that Justice Stewart?"

The people in both town and village greeted the news of the ambush with delight. It gave them a sense of power. The authorities took a grim view of the matter, for it was the most serious outrage against law and order that had occurred for many years. Nell Gilltrap went with haste to see Kitty, whose joy knew no bounds, and the women danced together in absolute delight.

At Oak Hall, however, the mood was one of rage with a sense of increasing need for revenge. Lord Foldsworth paced his study pondering these choices. He considered having Kitty's hideaway home located and then to take her home tied if necessary. But he knew this plan would never be effective and only a temporary measure. He knew now she would never accept him. There were too many now who would conceal her, and further confrontation with her would be futile. Nonetheless, he resolved, they will now learn not to trifle with me, he fumed. Dublin Castle will mount a huge manhunt, he assured himself. Perhaps if they were to arrest and question Kitty, that would bring her to her senses, he pondered. He dismissed the idea quickly, realising that such a last resort would have him branded a lunatic in society.

Sitting in his fireside chair he admitted to himself that it was her association with this man had almost driven him insane. Her betrayal of her family and all it represented pained him beyond words, for she would never be recognised within her class again. Gone for her would be the glitter of all social events, riding to hounds and so very much more.

"Oh, Edwina, Edwina," he sighed aloud, "if only you were here to speak with her, she would listen to your calm reasoning."

Williams could hear his master's voice as he stood outside the study. It only served to convince him that indeed staff gossip was correct for a change. He has indeed gone insane. It pained the old servant to listen to it. Knocking gently, he entered the study, announcing the arrival of a letter from Dublin Castle and a messenger awaiting a reply. Lord Foldsworth read the letter. It simply stated:

Lord Charles Foldsworth is requested to attend a meeting in relation to national security on the morrow.

The letter was brief and to the point, the summons worried him. He quickly wrote his reply confirming he would attend. He knew the meeting would prove a great embarrassment to him. It was inevitable that his daughter's name would be linked to the rebel whose escape had cost the lives of six policemen. He cringed each time the reality came to mind, and his sense of desperation mounted. Deciding to go that very instant to search for Kitty, he could then inform the council that she had come to her sense having been misled by the manipulating rebel. Yes, he thought, that's it. I will be able to then say she is willing to assist in tracing him. It would go a long way, he thought, in redeeming the situation. With this in mind he rode to the village and knocked sharply on the forge door. Joe was totally surprised to see Lord Foldsworth before him.

"Where is my daughter staying, Gilltrap? I need not remind you that trying to prevent the course of justice is a very grave crime! Punishable by death! Need I say more?" he said calmly.

"She is staying with my aged mother in the hills, your Lordship," he replied simply.

Lord Foldsworth nodded and replied, "I see."

He then mounted his horse and rode in the direction of the mountains. Joe spat on the ground in desperation, and hoped no harm would come to the women, but Lord Foldsworth made a mental note that Joe Gilltrap was to be arrested and brought to the barracks for questioning when things had quietened down in the area. One thing at a time, he reminded himself calmly. His approach to Kitty and his overall attitude to her would greatly influence the outcome of his plan. He decided that he would talk to her about his rash and impulsive behaviour, and then to beg her forgiveness. Should be a convincing performance, he thought. The afternoon was cold and dry as he rode towards the foothills. He did not recall ever before being on this part of his estate, perhaps once hunting, he thought. The hillsides were dotted with thatched cottages and small well-kept holdings. Blue turf smoke spiralled into the winter sky, and somewhere in the distance a donkey brayed, only to be answered by a chorus of others. He halted at a stream to allow his horse to drink, and watched two small boys who gathered wood.

"You two there," he shouted, and the two small faces looked up at the horseman dressed in the russet-coloured cloak. The older of the two, not quite eight years old, answered.

"Yes sir."

"Where does the old Gilltrap woman live?"

The boy looked up the hillside and pointed to a cottage that seemed larger than those around it.

"There sir, the one above the rest of 'em. See the one with the black door? Well, that's where she lives."

The little boy connected the visitor with the lovely lady who now lived with the old woman. They both turned and ran like frightened hares up the hillside. He admired their surefooted agility and, grinning to himself, muttered, "Another generation of rebels to be sure," and then rode on.

As he approached the cluster of cottages he noticed the closed doors and the absence of human life. Three dogs ran after his mare, snarling at her hind legs. A swift kick sent one of the small terriers onto its back, yelping piteously. He rode on regardless, eyes riveted on the cottage with the black door, which oddly enough he noticed was the only one open. It looked clean and well kept, the thatch well maintained. He halted the horse but did not dismount, calling out sharply.

"I am looking for the mother of Gilltrap, the blacksmith."

An old woman made her way slowly out through the cottage door, leaning heavily on a walking stick.

"Well, here she is sir, and who is it who asks for me?" she replied feigning innocence.

"Your Landlord asks for you. Now where is my daughter? I wish to see her this instant or else know her whereabouts."

He found it difficult to restrain himself.

"Well, now, your Lordship, she was here till noon today with her maid. But then she left with her maid. Going to Cork, they said, sir, wherever that might be," she replied sheepishly.

"Cork! What the hell is she gone to Cork for?" he asked, puzzled.

"Oh sir, tis not for the likes of me to question me betters. But that's what I heard the two of them talk about, and the maid, sir, was crying something terrible about the high seas, ships and all sorts. T'would have made a stone cry to have heard her, yer honour."

"I presume my daughter's maid was Hannah. Is that correct?"

"Yes, yer honour, like a mother to her she was, savin' your honours presence at the loss of his lovely wife, the Lady Edwina," old Mary said sympathetically.

"Yes, yes, alright. Cork you say? I see," Lord Foldsworth said in desperation.

"Yes, yer honour. Went to town to get the coach. Is your honour thinking of going with them?" she asked with such sincerity that her visitor could no longer contain himself.

"Oh, don't be so bloody ridiculous woman. What the blasted hell would I be doing going to Cork, you foolish old witch," he boomed.

The old woman winced at his rage but decided to continue with her charade.

"Tis, as you might say, yer honour, the notion of a foolish old witch," and she looked up at the stately figure before her.

"Damn you," he shouted, and turning his horse about, addressed the silent dwellings where he knew the occupants were listening to every word.

"Damn all of you," he shouted, and turning his horse about, addressed the silent dwellings where he knew the occupants were listening to every word.

"Damn all of you. Maybe the battering ram will liven you all up," and he spurred his horse forward into a sudden gallop.

"Cork," he fumed. "So that's where she is meeting him, to sail to America, no less. Well, I shall have them both," he swore.

The people of the tiny village gathered around old Mag as they watched the horseman ride down the hillside, blessing themselves in fear of him.

"When he is gone, we will be well rid of him, aye well rid, for the devil rides with the likes of him," Mary said, and they agreed.

"God speed Kitty and James," she croaked, as she waved her stick in the air to the cheers of her neighbours.

The following day in the city of Dublin Kitty met James on the quayside. In the crowded tavern they sat holding hands, ecstatic with their newfound freedom. Hannah sat with them, almost overcome by the noise of the crowds of departing travellers. She looked at James and Kitty, now unrecognisable in their respective disguises. Kitty wore the attire of a common peasant, while James on the other hand, was dressed like a gentleman. They had agreed to travel separately on the voyage to France, he in the upper deck and Kitty below deck. They cared little about the temporary separation; for all that mattered was being together again. Hannah planned to remain in Dublin with her brother and await the news of their eventual return from France. She had refused to sail the ocean adamantly, so the compromise had been reached. It was a sad parting for

Hannah and Kitty, and to the immediate bystander it looked like the parting of mother and daughter.

* * *

As the great ship hoisted its sails, the wind filled them, and slowly she moved with grace and elegance into Dublin bay. Hannah cried bitterly on the quayside, realising that a great chapter in their lives had now been closed forever. She felt fear at the times to come.

Kitty looked out through the small porthole at the Wicklow Mountains as the ship sailed south down the coast. Her tears flowed in profusion as she thought of her mother resting in the marble crypt in the quiet church, the father she had once adored, now reduced to a man of unsound mind, who had denied her forever. James looked at the mountains in the fading light from his stand on the deck, and was grateful to the great God who had spared his life. He vowed he would return and help rid Ireland of the scourge of landlordism forever.

In the city of Cork, soldiers searched relentlessly for them both, questioning every passenger bound for America and failing to find the fugitive lovers. Later, Justice Stewart laughed on meeting Lord Foldsworth at Dublin Castle.

"I see they outfoxed you again, Foldsworth! Perhaps this time you may learn that our ways are the best. Execute them first and ask the questions later!"

It was then that Lord Foldsworth finally resigned himself to the reality that Timothy Viscount Stewart was correct. It was the only way to handle Ireland, and he wondered why he had never realised it before. Now it was almost too late for him.

Chapter twelve

The Rebellion

In the months that passed, security throughout Wicklow and Wexford increased and tensions mounted on every side. The prisons were full of men, young and old, who had been arrested on suspicion alone. Court sessions were held at all hours of both day and night, and summary justice prevailed.

Soldiers patrolled the towns and cities, while the coasts were constantly under surveillance for sighting of the French invasion that was expected hourly. Nightly attacks took place on the lands of the ascendancy and their homes, but the majority of families had by now left rural Ireland and were living in the security of their Dublin homes, or had returned to the safety of England. The mood of the common people was one of seething hatred of all things foreign and rebellion filled the air in every county. The vast stockpiling of arms had now been completed. It had been accomplished before the authorities were aware of the enormity and disciplined organisation of the United Irishman.

Church leaders in Dublin called on their loyal flocks to renounce all plans of insurrection, and surrender their arms and any information to the government, while the opportunity for clemency remained to them. Landlords, bishops and priests were united in their appeal to the people to abstain from all plans that would lead to violence.

However, rumours then began to spread rapidly among the Catholic population that the Orangemen were plotting their extermination. Alarm and panic became rampant. In the village of Tinahealy, Co. Wicklow, a series of public floggings took place of men who were accused of being members of the United Irishmen. Their homes were burned and many fled the area.

The local magistrate demanded a response from Lord Foldsworth, whom he knew to be almost gone insane from the happenings to his family of late. Nineteen men from the estate had been imprisoned and tortured mercilessly.

Joe Gilltrap had neither been arrested nor imprisoned, but was nonetheless under constant surveillance, with random raids on the forge taking place. Joe had sent his wife and children by night to stay with his mother, in dread of harm coming to them. The once busy tavern had almost become deserted, its customers afraid to travel by night as had been their custom. Only old Mag and a few men, who lived close by, now went there in the evenings.

The constant raids on the forge had now reduced Joe to a nervous and irritable man. He visited his wife only once weekly and he missed her a great deal, but he knew they were safer where they were. Each night he would sit with old Mag by the fireside and talk of events as they were unfolding. In hushed tones they toasted the health of Kitty and James in France.

Nothing had been heard of them since they had fled, and no contact was expected. A reward of one hundred pounds was offered to whosoever provided information that would lead to the arrest of James de Lacey.

Bartley Finnegan dreamed of being the recipient, and it was with this thought in mind that he arrived at the tavern one February night. He walked in casually with the cheery greeting, "God save all here!" Everyone present, who knew of his treachery, ignored him. Dismissing them all her ordered a pint of ale.

Mag looked over at the man responsible for the arrest of James and suddenly she realised what she must do! She knew him to be the sort of man who, having once gotten the taste for revenge, would never stop. It was like a disease, she thought. Suddenly Bartley turned around and saw the old woman sitting by the fire with Joe. It was the opportunity he had been waiting for. He walked over and sat down opposite them, jingling the money in his pocket as he did so.

"Well now, look who it is," he began, "the very woman I have come here to see. Mag how are ye?"

Joe ignored his intrusion and looked into the fire, staring blankly at the flames as they threw their glow on the face of the man he would have gladly killed that night. Mag, to his utter amazement, put the hand of friendship to Bartley, who was delighted with the demonstration of acceptance from one so well respected.

"Musha Bartley, it does my tired heart good to see you in here again. God, when I think of the times you worked here. No-one could ever make a brandy punch like you," and she sighed, looking at him with eyes larger than life.

Bartley was overcome with elation, and shouted over to Brian who stood watching it all.

"Well now, Brian, did you hear that! No-one could do it like Bartley!" He shouted and slapped his thigh as he roared his usual high-pitched laughter.

Brian did not answer him, just shook his head as if in total agreement. He neither wanted fighting nor brawling in the tavern, as it would only serve to attract attention to it. He did not want another visit from Lord Foldsworth, as he was weary of the constant visits of the police and their questions relating to his customers and their conversations. So he had decided to simply serve beer and spirits and agree with all that was said in good humour, and plead deaf to what might resound of conspiracy. He knew that the very walls had ears and he had not desire to be either flogged publicly or serve a prison sentence.

Joe looked at Mag in dismay and said, "That's the sort of welcome, Mag, you would give a long lost cousin"

"Hold your tongue Joe, or do you think that poor old Mag has lost her mind completely? Not a bit of me!"

Reaching into the pocket of her old cloak she took out a tiny bundle wrapped in old red cloth. She looked about carefully to see if she was being observed, but all eyes were on the man making the brandy punch for her at the counter.

"What is that, Mag?" Joe asked, taking the pipe out of his mouth slowly. She grinned her toothless smile.

"Oh, just a little something to make sure that Bartley Finnegan has a long sleep. A very long sleep indeed," she whispered.

Joe felt a knot arise in his stomach.

"God in heaven! No Mag! You can't. You will be had for murder!" Joe whispered in alarm and desperation.

"Don't worry Joe. This will never be traced to old Mag at all! The doctor isn't born that could tell that! All that will happen to Bartley is that he will simply fall asleep in an hour or two and never see the light of day again! He will wake up where he deserves, with the devil himself, before he sends anyone else to the hanging noose, and that includes you too my good man!"

Quickly sprinkling the brown powder into Bartley's dark ale, she watched the flavourless potion mix through the drink as it sank down through the glass. She laughed lightly as she heard Joe whisper a prayer for mercy.

"Save them for yourself, Joe. The good God never meant the likes of that weasel to have the innocent murdered," and she then sat back and lit her clay pipe.

Bartley walked over and ceremoniously presented Mag with the brandy punch.

"For a great woman who knows a great barman when she sees one and doesn't forget a friend," he said for the hearing of all present.

Mag raised her glass of brandy punch.

"I toast to Ireland," she said, standing feebly to her feet and all raised their glasses towards her.

"To Ireland," they called out, and Bartley drank his glass of ale to the dregs and went to have it refilled.

The night passed painfully slow for Joe, who was expecting Bartley to collapse at his feet at any moment. But their unexpected visitor laughed and talked with Mag heartily, one drink following another. Mag drank several glasses of punch and then sang her usual laments for Ireland that the customers loved to hear. It was with great relief that Joe heard Brian announce the tavern was closing and began bidding everyone a hearty good night.

Bartley went down the village street singing loudly and out of tune, as Joe and Mag watched him disappear into the fog of the February night for the last time.

"The walking will do it Joe, aye. The poison will spread to every corner of that traitor's body and all that any doctor will say is that his heart gave way," she whispered.

"I hope so, Mag, or we will dangle at a rope's end for it," he replied. Mag laughed shrilly.

"Don't be so foolish, man! Did Mag eve make a mistake yet? Well, did she?" she asked, teasingly.

"No, not ever!" he agreed.

"He will die in his bed, Joe, in the late hours of the morning and it is more than the bad inclined traitor ever deserved. No, I have given him a painless end. Not for his sake mind you, but ours! For no-one will ever know," she said with a great sigh of finality.

"I hope to God you are right, Mag," he said faintly.

"I am, and what's more no-one will ever know that you are the pike and bayonet maker!"

Joe stopped suddenly.

"What?" he exclaimed in surprise.

"I said, Joe, that no-one will ever know that you made the pikes," she said in a whisper.

"How did he ever know?" Joe asked in amazement.

Old Mag looked at him.

"Very simple, Joe. For many was the night I came through this village at four o'clock in the morning, and there would be Bartley peeping into the forge window watching you. I stood in the shadows and watched him steal back to the tavern. All he was waiting for was the offer of the reward for such information, when it would pay him to tell all. The way things are now; he knew it was only a matter of time until the reward money was offered. You were to be his next victim. He would have been the richer for your neck, Joe!" And she began to wheeze with the effort of the conversation.

"Come home now, Mag, and sit by the fire for the night. It is too late and too far to travel to the woods. You have done a great night's work, my God you have!"

As old Mag slept by the fireside, Joe lay awake on his bed thinking about James and Kitty, wishing them well. Before he finally slept, he thought about just how near he had come to arrest and death, and he felt a wave of relief sweep over him. Outside, the wind moaned in the old ivy tree.

Bartley Finnegan felt weakness creep through his body as his breathing became rapid and laboured. He sat on the side of his bed sweating profusely and his head ached. He struggled to his feet and walked across the room to take a drink of water from the tin bucket. His thirst quenched, he walked across the room once again and lay on his bed, muttering unintelligibly. Just as Mag had predicted, Bartley Finnegan died without a struggle as the February night gave way to another cold dawn. Only when he did not appear for his early breakfast did his landlady become suspicious. Having knocked repeatedly, she finally entered the room to find the rigid corpse.

Those who had known him in the village tavern attended his funeral. The coffin finally lowered into the deep grave, Joe felt further relief as the clay sods thudded on the lid. Odd, he thought, what fear and oppression does to people. There was a time when the very thought of murder would have been horrific. Not any more, he thought, as he helped shovel the earth into the grave. It's now a matter of trying to stay alive as long as you can. It's the only thing now that matters, he decided.

Chapter thirteen

The mood of the meeting at Dublin Castle was one of impending doom and the authorities were forced to accept the reality that Ireland was on the verge of revolution. Lord Camden sat deep in thought as he pondered the possibility of a French invasion. Dublin city reeked with rumour of invasion. He was viceroy for the past three years and felt frustration with Prime Minister Pitt's attitude to the Irish question. The Irish parliament and its functioning had left him less than enthusiastic, and with very little authority when all was summed up. He smiled cynically as he thought of the futility of it all. He looked around at the men assembled before him in the great room. He was saddened to see how his friend Lord Foldsworth had aged, and how ill he appeared. News of how his daughter had eloped with an organiser of the rebellion had left Dublin society stunned. The more charitable among them concluded that the loss of her mother had totally deranged the lovely young girl. To Lord Foldsworth's relief nobody referred to the matter. Good taste forbade it.

The landlords present waited with interest to see what measures would be implemented in view of the cold-blooded murder of the six policemen in Wexford. It was common gossip among them that Charles Foldsworth had allowed the situation to go out of control, and some on that account consequently despised him. They waited now to see what measures he would finally take to restore law and order, if it was not already too late to do so.

Viceroy Camden cleared his throat and the assembly quietened to a hush to listen to his address.

"Gentlemen, Ireland at present is, as you are all aware, seething with plans for rebellion. The peasantry are arming themselves and have been dong so for over a year now according to our spy network. The situation is very grave. In addition to this we have the very real possibility of a French invasion to aid the rebels! The attacks on country homes and families increase, with only last week the very brutal hacking to death of ColoNell St. George, and the murder of his host and hostess that same hour. Then some months ago we had the attempted burning of Lord Foldsworth's home, which resulted in the tragic and untimely death of his lovely wife, the Lady Edwina, whom we had all known and loved. This was followed by the arrest of one of the notorious rebel organisers, who despite the great efforts of Lord Foldsworth, nonetheless escaped.

"Yes, six of His Majesty's policemen were murdered by a gang who succeeded in freeing the rebel in question. Appalling. Furthermore, this rebel organisation would seem to be gaining an unprecedented grip in Ireland, which depicts our governing as weak and ineffective! Last week a report came to my attention of a landlord who allowed the trees on his estate to be cut down for pike handles; or the consequences for him and his family were unthinkable. What more can one say, other than is this the level of complacency we have all reached? To date you have applied the time-honoured remedies of severe penalties in order to suppress these murderers. At this point in time you now must decide for yourselves what measures you must employ considering the circumstances you find yourselves in. Nightly these treasonous groups meet in your areas. They hide their pikes on your estates.

"It is your responsibility to organise and train men who will patrol day and night and for them to use what measures necessary to assist in the hunt and arrest of such murderers. You will be kept informed of all developments in relation to national security by dispatch as we deem it necessary. Good day gentlemen."

The viceroy left the room without further comment and silence reigned for some moments. There had been no mention of troops arriving from England, or the reinforcements that were needed desperately in the larger towns. Little wonder, Lord Foldsworth thought, that panic was spreading among the ascendancy. He left the meeting in sombre mood. The viceroy had made it abundantly clear: take what measures you deem necessary in your own locality; don't blame the government is what he was really saying, he thought, should further harm come to any of you...

He decided to recruit members of the Loyalist families to patrol the areas of his estate on a daily basis. All those suspected of the manufacture of pikes and bayonets and their concealment would be publicly flogged until a complete confession was forthcoming. Members of the United Irishmen would be imprisoned and executed without trial. "Ruthless," he murmured, "ruthless I shall be!"

Had I acted sooner, perhaps Edwina would be alive today and my daughter by my side. He cringed as he thought of Kitty following her rebel lover. There had been no trace of them leaving the ports, and he tried to console his tortured mind by hoping that one day Kitty would arrive at Oak Hall begging his forgiveness. It was the only thought that kept him sane in a world that had changed for him beyond all recognition.

* * *

One week later Lord Foldsworth had recruited twenty men and armed them. He addressed them calmly at Oak Hall, through their leader Nigel Snell..

"Master Snell," he began, "I shall expect you and your men to patrol the estate and the village each day, reporting to me nay suspicious behaviour that comes to your attention. I expect that in time your men will discover arms, and those who provide concealment for them. I also want the hills and mountains watched closely for unusual movement. You will all be adequately rewarded for your duty, and needless to say for those of you who bring to justice significant leaders and organisers, there will be a very substantial reward."

"Yes, my lord," Nigel Snell replied. "You may rely totally on me, and on the men here, to re-establish security and order. All will be done as you have commanded. My men will be only too delighted to draw out the main perpetrators of rebellion."

"Thank you, Master Snell. You will begin tomorrow," Lord Foldsworth stated calmly, dismissing the column of men.

He was impressed with Nigel Snell, who was ambitious and a Loyalist to the very marrow of his bones. Leadership suited him and he was keen to prove his worth, he thought, as he watched the men follow Snell who rode in front of them.

"Yes, I shall rest easier now and await results," he said aloud, waking to the dining room to lunch. Williams entered after his customary knock.

"A letter, my lord, arrived for you this morning," and handing the parchment to Lord Foldsworth saw the delighted expression on his face as he instantly recognised the seal of Ravenswood Castle in England. Oh Glencora, my beloved, he thought.

"Shall I serve lunch now, my lord?"

"No, Williams, I shall have it in twenty minutes' time. Now, you may go," and he dismissed Williams with a wave of his hand.

Impatiently he broke the waxen seal. The letter began:

My dearest Charles,

I do hope this letter finds you safe and albeit sorrowful beyond words at the loss of your wife. We were all horrified to hear of the unbelievable tragedy and the horrific circumstances leading to her death. And poor Kitty! How is she Charles? Please don't hesitate to send her directly to us, as we would only be too delighted to take care of her and happier too for her to be away from troubled Ireland.

Charles, we do worry about you both!

Would you not consider coming over? Your brother is poorly of late also, which I expect you know already.

Do give it some thought.

Meanwhile our love to you both and hoping it will not be too distant in the
future when we see you.
Yours faithfully as ever,
Glencora.

He was surprised to hear of his brother's illness. He had not been informed as Glencora assumed. Perhaps they did not wish him to be troubled further under the circumstances. He was worried now. John meant so much to him, yet he reasoned should he be in danger of death, they would certainly inform him. His heart warmed as he re-reads the letter. It was obvious that she cared a great deal for him. Now the opportunity he had secretly dared long for had come. They were free to marry now, if they so wished! No one would begrudge them happiness, he thought.

At that moment he longed to be with her and he sighed, realising the impossibility of it. He felt sadness when he thought of Kitty, and relieved that the families in Hampshire were still unaware of the truth. It had been difficult enough to bear the shame of it in Dublin. Oh Kitty... why... why... why? Of all the gallant young men you met, could you not have chosen one of them? They all adored you... would have given the world to have married you! But no! A peasant, a rebel to boot, is all you could rise to, and look at the shame of it all, the waste of it all," he whispered to the silent room and then he wept for the first time since she had addressed him in the village. It now seemed like a nightmare to him and guilt and shame almost overwhelmed him. The knock on the door made him jump nervously. Williams asked if he would now like luncheon.

"Yes, Williams, I shall, and thank you."

The tone of civility, long missing in his master's voice, did not go unnoticed to the faithful old servant.

"Williams, is there any news of Hannah? Have any of the servants heard from her or seen her of late?"

Williams realised that his master was asking a greater question than the welfare of the old housekeeper.

"No, my lord. There has been no news despite our enquiries. It would seem that Hannah has gone off with, er... well..."

"It's alright, Williams. You need not be afraid to say it. She is gone with my daughter, I know. Only to God knows where. She always loved that child – so good, so faithful. Yes, Hannah was so close to my wife also, so very faithful too. Oh dear, has not our world changed, gone upside-down Williams this past month and more. I fear it shall never be the same again."

"Come now, my lord, if I may be so bold to say so. Let us hope that reason will prevail and that peace and order will be back in this house once again."

He looked at the ageing butler and smiled at him.

"Yes, you were always an optimist, Williams. Yes, I shall have lunch now and thank you!"

Both men looked at each other, their brief moment of common ground dispelled by the roles that life had cast upon them.

* * *

The people in the village and those who lived in the mountains looked with hatred at Snell and his yeomen as they patrolled the lands far and wide. As he led his men he always looked directly ahead, never to the right or left, people said, adding that he was the sort who wouldn't show mercy to a dying old woman. People knew that gone now were the days when they could feel secure on their smallholdings. Fear filled their hearts to the extent that they no longer visited their neighbours by night, as had been the age-old custom. Isolation crept into their lives, and suspicion, where once a happy and simple trust prevailed.

The United Irishmen continued to grow in strength both in terms of numbers and the distribution of weapons, and as the early months of 1798 dragged slowly for the people, they nevertheless were well aware of the approaching climax that they knew would ultimately come into their lives. Their homes were now being searched at random by Snell and his men, their thatched roofs rent asunder in the search for pikes. They had no voice, no one to speak for them, no one to voice their protest as they felt their rights being slowly taken from them.

Depression gave way to desperation until anger began to flare in many hearts and minds. And so it was on a fair day in the town that an event took place that was to turn the tide of complacency into the fire of rebellion.

Lord Foldsworth and Captain Snell conspired to make an example of their newfound powers of arrest and punishment. The escape of James de Lacey was still fresh in the minds of the townspeople, and Captain Snell maintained that the majority of the population assumed that they were now beyond chastisement. And so he persuaded Lord Foldsworth to give his support and consent to his much-needed display of power.

Being market day, the town was thronged with people. It was a beautiful March day, a borrowed day, as some said cheerily to one another. Cattle, which had been fed and housed all winter now, stood in the streets in herds of between five and ten awaiting buyers. Their owners were anxious to sell, knowing that many would be keen to buy them and fatten them on the coming summer grass. The atmosphere was almost carnival-like, as people called out to each other and relatives met and exchanged news and gossip. The arrest and escape of James de Lacey was on every tongue. The flight of Lady Catherine from the country with him intrigued them all and, of course, was added to in the telling.

The public houses overflowed and at the Bull's Mouth Marjorie dabbed her forehead in the heat of the large kitchen as she carved tirelessly from the great joints of beef and pork. She sighed as she told herself for the hundredth time that she was far too old for the fuss of market days! Yet she loved the excitement of it all, in addition to meeting all her old and faithful customers. They came season after season. She took great pride in the food she prepared and knew that it was appreciated. Thick slices now, she reminded herself.

She thought of Kitty and James, her heart leaping with joy as she imagined them in France together. They were safe at least for now. And Joe. She was looking forward to seeing him. Marcus, Matt Ryan, and Father Murphy also. The success of the ambush, which she attributed to the prayers of the priest, made her heart race. The men had risen greatly in her esteem and her confidence in the movement was now unshakable. She had gleaned little information from the new police force, as the new sergeant did not like his men to drink beer. However, this did not worry her unduly. Sooner or later, she thought, they will come to my tavern. They always did! She swore quietly, wiping her hands in her apron. Getting carried away on the drink, already, she sighed.

The customers were all going out onto the street from where the tension originated. Someone shouted.

"It's Gilltrap. They have Joe Gilltrap..."

Her heart missed a beat. How unlike Joe to be in a street fight, she thought, not like him at all. She edged her way through the crowd and then stood silent in horror. She looked at the sight before her. Captain Snell was riding his horse, dragging the half-naked body of the blacksmith by his hands which were well-tied. Blood poured freely from Joe's head and chest and he seemed to have been dragged up and down the street already. All semblance of life seemed to have left the big man. Suddenly she found herself screaming out,

"Shame, shame, shame. You demon from hell," as she stood before Capt. Snell.

He laughed at her raucously.

Lord Foldsworth rode up and struck her with his riding crop.

"Out of the way, woman, or you too will meet the same fate."

Marjorie fell back with the force of the lash. Suddenly, a group of bystanders rushed up and grabbed hold of Lord Foldsworth's horse, which then reared, unseating its rider. They dragged him into the crowd, while others assisted Marjorie to her feet, where she swayed to and fro dizzily. She was bleeding from the face and neck, the soft flesh gashed from the lash.

Lord Foldsworth shouted and swore before a kick from a big boot rendered him breathless. Gunshot rent the air as the police prepared to open fire on the crowd. It was for Marjorie like a scene from hell when the second round of shot was discharged into the crowd. Six people fell to the ground. Five young men and one old woman. People fled in every direction. The shops were crammed with people and their doors bolted securely. Terror reigned, and abandoned cattle raced through the street bellowing in panic.

Marjorie found herself back in the inn, unable to recall how she got there. Someone handed her a glass of brandy, which she gulped down gratefully. A young woman bathed her face and neck. She struggled to her feet and went to the window looking out onto the street. Lord Foldsworth was no standing beside his horse attempting to mount, and Captain Smell had tied Joe to a strong post in the middle of the street in view of everybody. The street was deserted and silent, only some dogs remaining that ran after ducks and chickens that had fallen from abandoned carts.

The dogs killed and maimed the fowl, whose pathetic cacklings only added t the carnage of the six people who lay dying and gasping on the street. The silence deepened as the groans of the dying suddenly stopped, silent in death.

Lord Foldsworth shouted in his clear English voice.

"Will you ever learn?" he began, "No, it would seem not, I think! Well, perhaps this will serve to persuade you all to think twice before you make or hide pikes to be used against His Majesty's forces in Ireland! Go ahead Captain Snell..."

A thousand eyes peered through the shop windows at the sight of Joe Gilltrap tied securely against the large post. A bucket of water was thrown over him in an attempt to revive him. Suddenly he jerked and opened his gashed eyelids. He looked at the deserted street before him. Pain shot throughout his body like the thrust of a thousand pikes.

"Oh God... let me die," he groaned and as his eyes drifted towards the dead bodies he gave a cry of piercing grief that rent the air. Before him lay the dying body of his aged mother. She looked at him and cried out.

"Be strong, Joe... Be..." And then her head fell against the yellow clay of the road, where her old blood soaked and dried in the warm March sun.

"You accursed bastard, Foldsworth... Murderer of an old woman..." he cried, as his tears of grief now turned to rage and hate.

"Come now, Gilltrap, that's not very civil of you, is it, addressing your landlord so?" The mounted figure before him drooled.

"Captain Snell, are you deaf? Proceed now, I say!"

One of the yeomen carried a small bucket of tar and to the horror of the concealed onlookers, they watched it being poured over Joe's head and rubbed into his thick hair. No one had ever seen this done before and idle curiosity made them forget their shock and horror momentarily.

"Watching, eh, all of you?" Lord Foldsworth shouted. "Well, let me dispel your curiosity at what happens when one conspires against the King!"

Everyone wondered what would happen next.

"A sprinkle of gunpowder, Captain Snell! The landlord shouted. He then dismounted and walked up to Joe.

He stood to one side making sure the onlookers had a clear view. He lit a match and held it aloft. People reeled in horror at what was about to take place before them. As the gunpowder sparkled and hissed, the pitch caught fire and Joe's screams and pleas for mercy rang out across the wide street. His body slumped, unable to cope with the level of pain cast upon it. Suddenly Father Murphy was standing before the blacksmith whose head was still alight. He threw a bucket of water on his head and quenched the flames.

"How dare you obstruct the course of justice?" Lord Foldsworth screamed in temper, his spectacle having ended too soon. He had not noticed the priest's sudden approach.

"Justice, you call this," the priest shouted, adding, "You murderous thug, taking the law into your own hands."

Captain Snell ran forward and the priest turned and looked at him intently.

"Going to murder a priest now, are you Snell? Aye, English summary justice once again? Stand back from me, you vermin."

To the amazement of all, Captain Snell walked backwards as if about to be wiped from the face of the earth. Marjorie walked out onto the street with a large carving knife, and ignoring the police, began hacking at the thick ropes that held Joe bound. Father Murphy walked slowly towards Lord Foldsworth.

"You, Foldsworth, A disgrace to your forefathers. One can well understand a daughter's reluctance to give you the title of 'father'! Now, on your horse and get out of this town if you want to remain alive and don't come out of Oak Hall ever again. Aye, and for your murderous deeds to day, look at that old woman, the blacksmith's mother, and the other young men! You confounded murderer! And for this I tell you this day, before this year passes your great rooms at Oak Hall will only be fit for the nesting of owls and crows. As there is a God in heaven, I swear it! Now go," he shouted as he threw his hat on the ground, his fury rising. "Go," he shouted again, "before I end up accounting to the almighty for your murder myself!"

Lord Foldsworth looked about at the crows that encircled him and Captain Snell and the police. Their hate and rage was tangible. Slowly, they began to chant, "Go Foldsworth, go... Go Foldsworth, go."

He felt faint with fear at the prospect of being executed there and then, knowing all the priest had to do was give the command. He mounted his horse and looked down at the priest.

"Your Popish authority will not last, priest. I shall see to that," he said loudly, but Father Murphy, unable to contain himself further, caught him by the riding boot, and the reins with his other hand.

"Popish authority, Foldsworth? Is that what you call it? No Foldsworth, its Popish mercy that gives you your life today," and then he slapped the side of the horse, which, being already frightened bolted instantly. The crowd cheered in their brief moment of triumph.

The attention now was focused on Captain Snell, who stood with his men looking sheepish.

"You, Snell, don't ride abroad again! Never, I warn you. And furthermore, I'd stay awake at night if I were you. For these dead men beside us all have families and relatives and they will not forget your slaughter in a hurry." Then the priest walked away from them and knelt down beside the dead to give them the last rites of the church.

Their relatives and friends, only now realising their loss, cried out piteously to heaven for vengeance in their helplessness and despair.

'The market day slaughter', it came to be remembered as, and it was the turning point for the vast majority of the people. They now realised that death could come swiftly and without mercy. Justice for them no longer existed!

Three days later, the funerals of the victims were held. They were all from the one parish, and three of the men left families of small children, their widows inconsolable. They tried to come to terms with how a simple, happy family day could end in such a nightmare.

* * *

Joe Gilltrap lay unconscious, totally unaware that his mother had been laid to rest earlier that morning. His head had been severely burned and the left-hand side of his face, where the molten pitch had trickled down, was raw and festered. The doctor looked at the big man lying on the bed and shook his head doubtfully. What an act of brutality, he thought. Father Ryan had given Joe the last rites in the event that death should come.

"Will he live, doctor?" he asked.

"I don't know, father. The shock itself would have killed most men at this stage. We can only wait and see, I'm afraid." He looked at Nell Gilltrap and then left the room quietly.

Nell recalled the scene over and over again. She remembered Joe carrying his youngest daughter aloft on his shoulders promising to buy her a yellow ribbon for her long black hair. Suddenly, the yeomen had appeared and Captain Snell had pushed Joe forward shouting, "pike maker".

Father and child had fallen to the ground together. Joe had jumped up quickly to deal with the man on horseback, but had been quickly overpowered. Nell remembered screaming as she saw him being tied and then beaten savagely by the yeomen. She then remembered no more for she had fainted. Her children had screamed in terror at the sight of their father bleeding and beaten. The crowd had been held at bay by the armed forces. Captain Snell had laughed.

"See him, do you? Another rebel man! Well, watch and see what Lord Foldsworth has planned for all united Irishmen," and tying the long rope to the saddle of the horse, had dragged the beaten man up and down the street. Nell remembered regaining consciousness and crying out before a yeoman plunged the stock of his gun into her stomach. She had remembered no more, and nobody had told her of the pitch capping. They knew she had seen enough. But Nell realised as she looked at Joe lying on the bed that worse had happened than being dragged by a horse. For now it didn't matter, she reminded herself. All she wanted, all she prayed for, was that he would live. She had not moved from his bedside for four days now, eating little and waiting for signs of life returning.

Old Mag crept up to the bedside quietly and looked at the man she loved as if her were her son.

"Oh dear Joe, dear Joe, Mag will make you better, don't fear."

She gently took the big hand of the blacksmith and sang a lullaby, which she had sung a hundred times to him as a child. It was always soothed him, she told the bed-sitters. They took comfort from the strength of her wisdom and they prayed for his life to be returned. The following morning Mag came early to the house, and beneath her shawl she carried an old tin containing a substance similar to goose grease. It was a potion of herbs and roots and its pungent smell filled the room. The old woman rubbed it gently onto the side of Joe's face that had been so badly burned, humming her lullaby as she did so. Nell sat watching the movement of the old woman's fingers as she smoothed the ointment on the damaged skin. This task completed, she began her rosary, fingering each bead in faith and trust. She smiled over at Nell.

"Don't worry, Nell. He will open his eyes today alanna, and you make sure the first thing he sees is a pretty face! Now go, tidy yourself my love, and don't have that fine man of yours waking up to see a white-faced banshee!"

For the first time in almost a week, Nell smiled weakly.

"Thank you," she whispered faintly, and the old woman left the room that was now being lit by the bright March morning sun. Mag walked slowly back to her cottage in the woods.

She thought of Captain Snell and his men, and Lord Foldsworth, and pondered their eventual fate. She decided that she would take care of Captain

Snell herself in her own time and in her own way. Meanwhile she hoped that one of her hens had laid an egg for her breakfast, as she felt hungry after her long walk. She was aware that when Joe would awaken, he would need a potion to ease the pain that would sear through his head.

Later that evening Joe regained consciousness. Nell was overjoyed and the household with her. At the bedside Father Murphy and Father Ryan sat together. Opposite them sat Marjorie and Matt Ryan. Old Mag, having returned, sat sleeping by the great open fire. Slowly Joe opened his eyes. Pain shot through his body and his head ached unbelievably. He looked at the faces around his bedside, trying to focus clearly.

Nell soothed his forehead, whispering, "Shhh, my love. It's all over now, you are safe and with us all."

He nodded in response and lifted one had to his head, which now trembled in severe pain. He groaned loudly and old Mag came into the room like a ghostly shadow.

"Awake then are you, my lad! Remember the time you fell from the old apple tree? Old Mag remembers well. Lay in bed for five hours near enough, and they all thought you dead!" Again her shrill laughter filled the room. "And then you woke up and roared like an ass with your head pain. Well Joe, alanna, old Mag's here, tis time too. Five days now you are in that bed, and a bigger head pain you have, isn't that so?" She looked at him with large kind eyes and raised eyebrows.

Joe nodded resignedly.

"Well, there will be no spitting it out this time. No me lad. Not one drop," and she gently spooned the liquid between the dry and cracked lips saying, "There's Mag's boy, good as gold, that's what you are. Swallow it all and you will not have a pain in an hour. That's my lad." And she smiled at him.

Tears spilled from the blacksmith's face as he then remembered the face of his mother as she lay dying on the street before him. Nothing else came to mind for him and he sobbed.

"Now, get this man something soft to eat and then let him sleep, like good people," and Mag left the room to return to her fireside chair.

Marjorie trundled to the kitchen where, on the great table, several baskets of food lay. Relief and delight filled the cottage. Joe ate the bread soaked in chicken broth and gradually the pains left his body and he slept. Nell gently closed the room door and she sat beside Mag who had fallen asleep, tired by all the extra walking. The two priests sat deep in conversation as Marjorie heaped roast meat onto the plates for all present. Matt Ryan and Marcus talking of the forthcoming rebellion. They knew that Lord Foldsworth would not tolerate a second public humiliation. He would remain quiet for perhaps a few weeks and then regroup his yeomanry. Evictions would follow and there would be no mercy.

Marcus looked around the room of happy faces, flushed from merriment and good food. He felt sorry for them all, as he knew that it would be a short-lived celebration. He knew they were like rats trapped in a barrel.

"You are very quiet, Marcus," Matt remarked.

"Eating and thinking, Matt," he replied despondently.

"You would not need to be a wise man to guess, Marcus," Matt said, as he licked the fingers of the greasy chicken breast just eaten.

"I agree, when will it be do you think, Matt?" he asked anxiously. "We can't sit back much longer or we will be shot one by one. Look at them all here tonight. God help us. I don't begrudge them their celebration. But they will have to waken to the reality that they will need to protect themselves. Isn't it time the priests spoke out to tell them to arm themselves? A public meeting, that's what we need. A demonstration," Marcus said, now enthusiastically.

"Are you a mad man or what? That's all they are waiting for and every cottage in the area would be levelled to the ground. No, public meetings would be a grave mistake."

There entire room now was in a hush having heard the two men. Marjorie was the first to speak.

"I agree with Matt, for I will never forget what I saw last week. Never. If I had a gun at the time, Captain Snell would be cold in his grave by now." People nodded their heads in agreement. Father Murphy stood up rubbing his head in an agitated manner.

"My good people, I know that you are afraid and defenceless in the face of what we expect to happen, for there will be retaliation. I suggest that those of you who live in the village leave it, and move into the hills to the old abandoned cottages. At lest here you will have the advantage of seeing the troops coming from a distance. In the village, you will only be easy targets. However, we do have a proper and organised plan which, with the help of God, will awaken men everywhere to take a solid stand and begin to defend what is theirs."

"But when, Father, when?" a quiet voice asked. It was Nell Gilltrap. She looked thin and worn from the events of past days, and no one had a better right to ask the question.

"Soon, Nell. We dare not say the week or the month lest we be betrayed. But let me say this. When the cuckoo leaves our shores, I hope the troops will be gone also! Gone for good this time," he said grimly.

"Gone by July, father?" Marjorie asked.

"Yes, Marjorie, July," he said simply.

Old Mag was now awake and smoking her clay pipe with ease.

"Well, we will have the cuckoo here in little more than a week, so with God's help I'll live to see Ireland free," and the cottage erupted into a wild cheer, forgetting momentarily that Joe was sleeping. "Whist the lot of you, don't awaken Joe," Marjorie said sternly.

Mag's piercing cackle of laughter rose to what seemed a pitch higher. Nell felt her spirits rising. She thought of Joe sleeping soundly, and fatigue now began to overcome her. Marjorie, noticing Nell's weak state, helped her to bed. Nell lay down gratefully on the straw-filled mattress and soon fell into a deep sleep.

Marjorie felt exultant in the light of what Father Murphy had told them. Father Ryan stared into the flames of the fire. Battle did not appeal to him, but then neither did the brutal murders of the past week. He felt uneasy about his dichotomy. The verse from the Old Testament rang out clearly in his mind, 'Thus says the Lord, if they were hot or cold... but as they are lukewarm I will vomit them out of my mouth...' He knew he would have to make a choice, and wished his mind could be made up for him.

The crimson hue of the spring dawn spread over the mountains and the morning mists dispelled. The cottage emptied slowly of the well-wishers, each promising to call in the days ahead.

May Ryan, unable to come the previous day, met them as they made their way home and was delighted to hear of Joe's recovery. Visiting later that day she sat with Nell by the fireside, waiting for Joe to awaken again.

"God be praised, Nell, isn't it a miracle to have Joe recovering?" she said happily.

"Yes, it's wonderful May, but what future have we now? We can never return to the village where our home is and Joe's work," she said sadly.

"The simple answer to that problem, Nell, is to start another forge here, and why not?" May suggested.

"I never thought of that, May, and some of the men would bring Joe's implements from the forge. Why, it might work out for us," she smiled happily. "And what about you, May? Do you feel safe living so near Lord Foldsworth? He is the changed man as you well know."

May thought for a moment.

"I don't know, Nell. But I doubt if he would harm us having given us the cottage to live in." However, she did not sound convinced, Nell thought.

"May, when he gave you that cottage he was a very different man! A gentle man. His wife was alive, his daughter was at home, happy with him, their friends called, and they were hunting, having balls and what a life they had! Now look at him. Insane, the poor man. You should think more of the children, for he is fit for anything at this point in time."

May knew that Nell was right in much of what she was saying.

"But Nell, would any of us not be the same having gone through what that man has been through?"

Nell stood up angrily.

"No, I will never excuse him or forgive him. I hope he meets his fate and a cruel one! May, you have not seen the state that Joe is in yet. Parts of his skull are plain to be seen where the flesh was burned from it. He set Joe alight, May! Alight, that's right! He poured pitch and the gunpowder on my husband's head and then set it alight and you then sit there asking me to forgive that murderer. I now want rid of him and his kind forever. May, I want to go to my grave knowing that my children are free men and women. Not looking over their shoulder every day, not having to suffer hunger to pay a rent. Look at what happened to you, May! You're home levelled before your eyes, or have you forgotten so easily? Your husband dying ahead of his time from poverty?"

May wept at the memory of her past, which she had tried to forget, and both women embraced in mutual support. Just then Marjorie walked into the room with two steaming cups of tea.

"Come now, no more sadness Nell. Joe will be awake soon, according to Mag. She is at his bedside.

Joe awoke to see the two faces he loved most at his bedside. He smiled for the first time and whispered, "Am I not the lucky man to have two such fine women?" and Nell kissed him gently. During the course of that morning Joe slowly began to remember the horrific ordeal he had been through, and the pain of the memory was greater than that of his body. He recalled the expression on his mother's face as she lay dying, having been shot down, and he wept bitterly when alone. But he knew there was no herb that could numb that pain within him. Only time, he thought. And in time I will deal with Snell, he resolved, his hatred of the man frightening him. He had never felt a depth the like of it towards another human being. He didn't like the feeling! It was not the humiliation of being dragged almost naked through the street. It was his mother, a kind and simple soul. He decided that he must recover as quickly as nature would allow, for he had a score to settle.

The village slowly and quietly emptied of its people. Mostly they left it by night. It was now a ghost village. The wind blew unfastened doors too and fro, loosening their hinges. Some dogs had remained behind and they howled for their owners. Brian Wolohan and his wife packed their dray cart with beer and spirits and other utensils from their bar and moved to the hills to a deserted house belonging to a now-dead relative. They lived in dread of Lord Foldsworth, not knowing what to expect from his irrational mind next.

Their lives could end at a whim from the madman, Brian said.

Within two weeks, the entire population lived high in the mountains, from where they had a clear view of the surrounding countryside for many miles. While they felt a great deal safer, it was nonetheless a siege mentality they now had to live with. Nell and Joe sat in the early April sunshine looking down across the vast panorama.

To the left-hand side, six miles distant, lay Oak Hall, its tree-lined avenue, outhouses and stables clearly definable. Then further to the right, their village, with its cluster of houses, where no smoke rose from the now cold hearths. It was a very eerie sight. Some miles further south lay the town, where a pall of blue turf smoke lay over it. To the east lay the blue ocean and one could see at least 50 miles of the coastline. Several sailing ships moved on the silk like blue waters of this calm day, slowly making their way south. Nell thought of Kitty and James. So many miles of ocean between us. Nell had never been to the seashore, and she pondered so much water ends where the land begins! She wondered how so much water remained in the same place day after day. She was about to ask Joe when she noticed the figure of a woman slowly walking up the mountainside. The woman seemed advanced in years. Her gradual approach drew the attention of many from the village, their curiosity mounting.

"Not a complete stranger," Joe remarked, his eyes straining against the noon sunshine. "She seems to know the sheep tracks at least," Nell remarked.

The woman was now standing at a stonewall to rest and get her breath. It was a long climb on foot, taking almost an hour for one who was young and fit, and double that for the aged. Nell stood up and walked towards the slowly advancing figure, who was no waving to her in obvious recognition. Nell returned the gesture, still unaware of the identity of the person. But as she came closer she recognised Hannah, the cook from Oak Hall.

She ran to meet her, and they embraced happily. While Hannah was not a close friend of Nell's, she was relieved to see a familiar face. On the other hand, Nell was shocked to see how thin and gaunt Hannah now looked.

"Oh Nell Gilltrap, you have no idea how glad I am to see someone I recognise, and the village? For a while I thought the black fever had swept everyone away. Then luckily I met May Ryan who told me how very tragic things have become." Hannah was now gasping for breath.

"Hannah, sit awhile and get your breath back. Yes, I nearly lost poor Joe, as you have probably heard. Life has become a long nightmare for us, Hannah! Now, tell me, where have you been? We often wondered what became of you.

We thought you had gone to France or America!" Nell laughed and Hannah relaxed visibly.

"I'll tell you all, Nell, after a cup of tea," as Nell linked her arm for the remaining part of the climb to the top, where everyone stood waiting for them both.

Upon seeing Joe, Hannah was for a moment unable to recognise the once fine man, so scarred and worn had he become. She concealed her shock admirably.

"Well, Joe, it's happy I am to see you so fit and well considering all you have been through," she said in her usual calm, sincere tone.

"Lucky to be alive, Hannah, very lucky. But look at you! Springing up the mountain like a young hare!" and they laughed heartily.

"Did we ever dream, Joe, that his Lordship would lose his mind and become the cruel and brutal man he now is?" she said sadly. "I hear that even the servants at Oak Hall are dwindling down in numbers. Can't say I blame them either. One day he is calm and considerate, then he rants and raves like a lunatic. It's all so very different Joe, isn't it... life...?"

"It's as if the devil has entered the man, Hannah," Joe said, as he gazed out across the horizon.

"Joe and Nell, I have great news to tell you both," Hannah said in more cheerful tones, "but the news must remain secret. James and Kitty are coming home!"

"What?" exclaimed Joe in surprise. "Who told you that," he asked excitedly.

"Well, one evening at my brother's home in Dublin a young man came with a letter, aye, from Miss Kitty it was. Very brief it was too, saying that she would see me in May at the place we last parted, among our loved ones. Where else would that be but here?"

Nell was delighted.

"We are going to have to put the cottage into tip-top shape, Joe Gilltrap!" and he smiled to see her so happy again, more like the woman he knew.

Both women went into the cottage chatting happily together as they made their plans for the young couple's arrival.

Joe's thoughts, however, were of a more sombre nature, for he realised that James was obviously informed to return with the imminent rebellion. Plans must be at an advanced stage, but he knew little as he was excused from attending the meetings until his health improved. He knew that the pikes and bayonets were under armed guard day and night in the various hiding places. The orders were simple. Should the yeomanry approach the hiding places, they were to be shot on sight, for daily they scoured the countryside searching in vain. It was then quite by accident that Captain Snell and his men came upon old Mag's cottage deep within the woods. It looked a pretty sight as it sat in the clearing, a myriad of bluebells in front of it that exuded a rare perfume following the shower of May rain.

Mag lay asleep in the chair by the fire, where the blue turf and wood smoke wound its way slowly up through the chimney. A loud bang on the cottage door frightened her from her sleep. The cat on her lap leaped to the floor and crouched under a wooden table.

"So it's not a friend, Cinders?" she said, looking at the frightened animal.

The door was heavily pounded a second time.

"Oh, give an old woman time," she called out loudly, as she drew back the two bolts, annoyed now by the rudeness of whoever visitor it might be. However, she did not expect to see Captain Snell with a group of men on horseback with him.

"Well, old woman, what kept you? Hiding the pikes, eh?" he sneered, as he roughly cast her to one side where she staggered and fell against the wall, crying out now in fear. Captain Snell walked about the small cottage.

"Here somewhere I bet, a dozen or two maybe? Well?" he shouted.

Mag regained her composure quickly.

"No, Captain sir, tis only an old woman's house," she said fearfully.

Captain Snell called his men inside and told them to search. In doing so they upturned all Mag's herbal bottles and jars, breaking them in the process and laughing maliciously. Some of the herbal remedies had taken months and years to mature, and the old woman cried pitifully.

"Oh, Captain sir, tell them not to be breaking my jars. Oh, please tell them," she pleaded.

But as the search yielded nothing, he shouted at her in rage, "Blast you and your bloody bottles," and turning to his men shouted, "Burn it, burn it to the ground!"

May cried out in disbelief.

"Oh no, sir, not my little home! Have mercy on an old woman."

But he roared with laughter on seeing her terror. He then gripped her by the thin shoulder and cast her out through the door, shouting, "You are damn lucky I am not leaving you in it and bolting the door on you. I am merciful after all!"

Mag slowly got to her feet again, panting heavily. Her cat escaped through the window and fled to the woods in terror.

"What's this, old woman, eh? Poteen I suppose," he said as he thrust the bottle of clear liquid before her eyes. She recognised the bottle of lethal potion instantly, the brew of the yew tree.

"Yes sir, Captain, that's right. It's poteen indeed. Will you not let me even have that much to take with me?" she pleaded, aware that in his frenzy of hate and greed he would never concede.

"No! I shall not. But I will drink to your health instead, old woman," and he pulled the cork from it with his broken yellow teeth and drank the small bottle of its contents. He smacked his lips and belched loudly.

"By God! That's great stuff indeed! He then fired the empty bottle at Mag's feet where it smashed to pieces, shouting, "Now go, old woman, before I hang you from the nearest tree."

She did not need to be told a second time as she hurried into the woods to hide, knowing that the lethal brew would kill Captain Snell within the half hour. Then, she knew, they would search for her and shoot her mercilessly. She ran as quickly as she could, surprised at her own agility. She climbed the wooded brow knowing where she could conceal herself safely. The yeomen set the cottage alight, their shouts of glee reaching her ears. Smoke and sparks shot into the evening sky as the black smoke whirled up through the clearing in the woods.

Captain Snell fell from his horse almost unnoticed by his men. The excitement of the fire having distracted them, one of them eventually noticed their captain clutching his stomach as he rolled around the ground screaming in agony. Mag could hear him from her hiding place. But she cried as she watched her small cottage burn to the ground. Captain Snell died within minutes, lying on the ground in a contorted shape, blood oozing from his mouth. The yeomen looked at one another and without any further comment rode off in the direction the old woman had taken. She watched them approach, their horses panting heavily on their uphill gallop. Old Mag withdrew further into the hollow of the great tree, which was some twenty feet from the ground below. They galloped past following the woodland path where they expected to overtake her.

But Mag sat back, her tears spent, and she waited. She knew they would return one last time before abandoning their search. Her mind meanwhile went back through the long labyrinth of years to the time she first discovered the great hollow in the giant oak. She had been only a little girl and she had hidden in it many times simply to be alone, to think about life. She chuckled as she thought that despite the fact that she could no longer run, she could still climb. She felt triumphant! For here was her storehouse of herbal remedies, contrary to what Captain Snell had thought!

In the distance she could hear the yeomen shout and swear as they combed the woods in search of her, but soon their voices began to fade with the setting sun. They rode back, passing beneath the tree and tied the body of Captain Snell to his horse for the return journey to the town.

Mag still did not leave her safe retreat. There was no hurry now, she thought. She asked God to forgive her, and then reasoned that she had really done him a favour ridding the earth of another devil! She thought of her cat, Cinders. She also decided it was time to leave her burnt out shell of a home. The mountains beckoned to her. "I must get there tonight, for they will return at first light with an even bigger search party," she thought.

Finding her cat, she carried him through the great oaken wood that would eventually release her onto the wild mountainside. She walked at a steady pace and by the time she reached the edge of the wood, a full moon shone brilliantly from the May night sky. She blessed the light it gave her for her journey. Eventually, finding an old sheep track, she walked up the gradual incline talking gently to her cat. The cat purred, content at being carried in the warm, woollen shawl.

It then became tense as it felt the old woman's fear rising. Mag heard horses approach from behind, and she looked in desperation for somewhere to hide on the bare mountainside. Two large stones leaned one against the other and she ran the short distance across the heather to hide between them. The horses galloped uphill and she trembled lest they had noticed her. The two figures became clearer as they now approached her hiding place. When they were within a few yards of the giant stones, Cinders took flight at the sight of the horses that were now to him a symbol of terror. It screamed in contempt at the intruders, and Mag swore silently. The first rider stopped, beckoning his follower to do likewise, and neither spoke a word. As he edged his horse closer, Mag knew that her hiding was in vain. The voice summoned her authoritatively.

"Step out quietly," it said, in a tone unfamiliar to her ears.

Slowly she stood up and stepped forward into the moonlight, expecting to hear a pistol shot. Silence prevailed for moments and then the familiar voice spoke to her.

"Mag, what the hell are you doing hiding among the stones this late hour of the night?"

Mag cried out in joy and relief.

"Oh James, James, where did you come out of? Just when I began to think my days were at an end!"

"Mag, look who I have with me!" James said, pointing to the rider behind.

"Tis only the one in the wide world it could be," Mag exclaimed as she walked over to Kitty.

"Hello Mag. It's wonderful to see you again," and Kitty dismounted and kissed the old woman.

"Tis only the mercy of God I'm alive, your ladyship, and how lucky I am that you both found me!"

James dismounted and lifted Mag onto his horse and then mounted behind her.

"Let's get to the upper village, Mag, and there we can talk the night away," James said, aware of the fact that there were mountain patrols not far away. Slowly they ascended the steeper sides of the mountain, careful in the moonlight. Mag laughed.

"If only some young lad had swept me away on a horse sixty years ago, your ladyship," and Kitty tried to envisage the spectacle it would have made.

Kitty felt sheer elation at being home again. It had been a long voyage and then the ride from Waterford port had been fraught with worry for them both. She breathed in the soft night May wind, the familiar scents of blackthorn and bluebells wafting up on the warm night air from the valley beneath them. She looked at the sea in the distance shimmering like a lake in the moonlight. She was looking forward to seeing old Mrs. Gilltrap, and had brought her a small bottle of French perfume. She longed to sit and hear all the news of the area, and the thought of seeing Hannah again... she could barely contain her excitement. Away in the distance she could make out the outline of Oak Hall and she thought of her mother in the little church. However, the months away with James in France had given her a new strength and purpose. It had given her time to look at her life and the values that she considered dear to her. She laughed as she listened to Mag and James considering eloping into the night, as Mag's cackling laughter was carried on the breeze to the village above them. The dogs barked loudly, announcing the arrival of visitors in the night.

Hannah peered through the small window and saw the approaching riders. Her heart raced in fear as she told Joe and Nell. Lord Foldsworth sprang to mind. Blowing out the lamps, Joe bid Nell be still as he slowly opened the door to watch the approach of the riders. For a moment he thought he could hear the familiar laugh of old Mag and chided himself for his imaginings. How would Mag ride a horse he thought, much less sit on one? He smiled at the picture it conjured up in his mind. But there it was again, unmistakable this time! He called Nell and Hannah to the door.

"Listen carefully and tell me if that's not the laugh of Mag!"

Again they heard it.

"Well, praise be to God, Hannah. What are things coming to with Mag riding a horse in the middle of the night, and with a stranger to boot."

The horses stopped a little distance from the cottage and James shouted out, "Joe Gilltrap, what are you doing here?"

"Oh James," Hannah called, "is it possible that..."

But Kitty had already dismounted and ran to her dear friend who was almost delirious with excitement. James shook Joe's hand heartily and stopped abruptly as the moonlight shone on the face before him. Had it not been for the familiarity of the voice he would not have recognised him. The side of the face was scabbed and the head a mass of sores and raw flesh. It was a dreadful sight and Joe saw the growing horror in his friend's face.

"I know, James. It is a sorry sight and a long story. But come ye now inside, and Miss Kitty, you are so very welcome." Kitty also concealed her shock at the sight of the man before her.

"Joe, it is wonderful to see you again and you also, Mrs. Gilltrap. It's so good to be back. I can't wait to see your mother, Joe. I have a little gift I think she will love," Kitty said cheerfully.

"Well, Lady Catherine, my mother departed this life only some weeks ago now," he said sadly.

"Good heavens, Joe! Whatever happened? She was so full of life when I left here," Kitty stated plainly, now sensing that something serious had happened to them all in their absence. James' expression warned her not to pursue the matter any further.

"A lot has happened to us all," Joe said, looking at the young couple before him. "More of that later. For now you must be tired and hungry. Tomorrow we can talk long into the day."

Inside, Nell was busy preparing food and Hannah ran to and fro, excited beyond words with the return of the couple. In the bright light of the lamps Mag noticed how well the young couple looked. They were like a ray of bright sunshine in the cottage and as the kettle steamed on the hearth, Mag lifted its rattling lid. James tried not to look too closely at the scars on Joe's head and face.

"Was it sudden, old Mrs. Giltrap's death?" she asked.

She noticed the glances exchanged before Nell replied that it was very unexpected. Old Mag was unable to eat despite several attempts to chew the succulent meat. She sat, dejected-looking.

"Mag, what is it? Whatever is the matter?" Nell asked with alarm.

"Did none of you even think it odd, me rambling at this late hour so far from home?" She felt angry now.

They all looked at each other at odds to know what to say next, and felt quite baffled.

"Well?" Joe began, "tis true you don't ramble up this far for herbs, Mag, so is it you just took the notion to come and visit? Don't you know we are delighted to have you. Only for you, Mag, I'd never be here today. You know that, don't you?"

"Well, I will ease your minds," Mag said slowly. "The great Captain Snell came to my cottage today thinking I was hiding pikes and bayonets, and having turned the place upside-down he burned it to the ground."

Everyone felt a huge sympathy for the old woman who was visibly shaking now.

"Oh yes, they did," she continued, "but one thing is for sure and certain. Captain Snell will not be troubling us any further, for he drank a bottle of poison and he thinking it was poteen. Yes, I let him think it, and I haven't an ounce of regret either. We are all well rid of him. I ran and hid in the woods and when darkness fell I set out for here, and that's what happened to me."

"Who is this Captain Snell? I don't ever recall hearing of him," Kitty said, looking curiously at Joe.

"You may as well tell them the whole story, Joe," and, rising from her chair, Mag placed more turf on the fire. Kitty and James sensed Joe's discomfort as he looked at Kitty.

"Lady Catherine, I had hoped not to be the person from whom you were to hear this, but perhaps it's for the best."

And so Joe gave a detailed account of all that had happened since they had left Ireland. How Lord Foldsworth had organised the yeomanry, their intimidation of the local people, the market day massacre, and of how his mother had died. Finally he told them of how he had been flogged and pitch capped, having been dragged through the streets. Silence prevailed. Kitty paled and left the room going outside for some air, to be followed by Hannah. James looked at his friend, grateful that he had somehow survived the ordeal.

It also explained why Nell looked so ill. In his stupidity he'd thought that Joe had probably had an accident in the forge: How very stupid of me, he thought.

"And this is why you have left the village Joe, isn't it?" he asked.

"Aye. And who could blame us for that James. Look what happened to you. An easy target, were you not?"

"Indeed I was, Joe. Foldsworth must be gone insane. It's only a matter of time until he comes here, Joe, and levels this village too," James said grimly.

"It is his daughter I feel sorry for. She will have to learn to separate herself from her father's madness, James. She must!"

Outside, as Kitty looked down at the lands below clearly visible in the moonlight, she knew her life to be inseparable from the tenants of her family estate. In France she had come to value what freedom truly meant. A free Ireland appealed to her. She looked at the dozen or so small cottages perched on the mountain ledge and her heart sank. They housed almost a hundred people, she thought, who were willing to tolerate such squalid conditions just to be free of fear and intimidation. Tomorrow she decided she would visit them all and speak to them. She felt them to be 'her people' as and from now.

Hannah shivered beside her in the cold night air.

"Come now, Miss Catherine, inside to the fire. Besides, we have to comfort old Mag now on the loss of her home. 'Tis a wonder her old heart hasn't failed her with all she has had to endure."

"Rightly so, Hannah. It is no time for self-pity. Tell me Hannah, did you like Dublin?"

"Dublin, with its crowds and noise? No, not a place I'd like to spend the rest of my life. Give me fields, meadows and the mountains where I ran and played as a child. 'Tis home to me, Miss Catherine, despite all the changes."

"Do you think things would be any different were mamma alive, Hannah?"

"The answer is yes, my child. Very different indeed, for there was a time when your father was kind and gentle. Remember how he looked after May Ryan? And then got rid of that wretched bailiff who made her suffer so?" Hannah said reflectively.

"Odd how father became more brutal than Jerome Hennessy ever was. He no longer resembles the father I knew and loved. Instead, there is a monster there now," she said sadly.

One had only to look at Joe to realise the truth of it all.

Inside the cottage the atmosphere was warm and homely. Nell hummed a tune as her children slept soundly in the loft above them. Kitty produced the bottle of perfume and decided to give it to Mag as a present.

"Well I never," the old woman declared, "it smells like a mixture of wild violets and honeysuckle, Miss Catherine."

"I am so glad you like it, Mag," but Mag's attention was no elsewhere.

"Whist! What's that I hear? She whispered, as all eyes went to the door.

"'Tis only a cat, Mag," Joe said reassuringly.

"Only a cat is right, Joe," she clapped her hands in glee as she scurried to the door.

Cinders leaped into her arms and her joy knew no bounds. She stroked the cat lovingly. Joe was glad to see Mag's spirits rise. Even her simple life had been touched by the shadow that was creeping over the land.

Joe and James went to Brian Wolohan's new sheebeen where there was great celebration at the return of Kitty and James. The following days the morale of the people lifted noticeably. The sight of Kitty as she moved among them inspired them and her love and concern for their families touched them deeply. She organised the children for schoolwork and they sat in awe as she told them stories of a life they never dreamed existed.

Each day both James and Joe would await a message to announce details of the next meeting to be held. As they discussed the mass movement of the men across the country, armed and victorious, they felt both excitement and fear.

"Did you like France, James?"

"Bordeaux is a fine city, Joe. Kitty loved it, you know. The fashion, the shops, the theatre, so much to do. As for myself, every day I longed to be here. I found no peace there at all. Strange language and people. A young state, getting on its feet only now. And you can smell freedom there. The people are happy and there is prosperity too. But having Kitty with me meant everything. When you think that I was so close to death! Sometimes I had nightmares about it all. Seeing the face of Justice Stewart, sneering and full of spite. That face visited me in my dreams so many nights. I would wake up thinking I was on the scaffold! I vowed many times I'd see him dead first, Joe, and that's the truth."

Both men looked at the fields far beneath them with the bloom of the yellow gorse bush and white hawthorn blossom, splashes of colour amidst the green fields.

"Judge Stewart will live to be old and grey, James, so get the notion of killing him out of your head. He will always have a heavy escort when travelling. Common sense would tell anyone that much," Joe said sagely.

"I know. But Joe, will you promise me something? And I really mean what I am about to say, it's very important to me."

Joe looked at the young man beside him.

"What is it, James?"

"Two things I ask of you. First, if anything happens to me, see that Kitty is taken care of, and second, if ever they capture me, for if they ever do I will hang without a trial, I want you to shoot me on the gallows before they get the chance to put the rope around my neck."

Joe was shocked by the image that James conjured up before him.

"That's not a very happy picture you are looking at, is it James? You should be thinking of a free life here with that beautiful woman at your side, instead of gallows and ropes!"

"I know you are right Joe, but I am just saying should something happen to spoil all that, will you do as I ask?"

Joe was looking at a sparrow hawk hovering high in the deep blue sky as it eyed out its prey.

"I will, James, if that time ever comes and it's in my power to do so, you will have as you have asked," and Joe swallowed hard as he watched the hawk dive to the ground where an unsuspecting mouse never had the opportunity to realise its sudden fate.

The days passed pleasantly as the weather of that early summer month proved warmer than any they had ever known. The children helped weed the potatoes after the morning's schoolwork, which they loved, was complete. Joe's work at the new forge continued, and he was delighted to be busy once again. James assisted him and they laughed and talked of many things and sometimes allowed their hopes and dreams to be expressed fully.

Hannah resumed her role as cook, much to Nell's delight, and many delicious meals were prepared to the praise of this now unique household.

Mag would ramble occasionally to the edge of the valley for leaves and berries, and once again began to process her special remedies. It had been a great change for the old woman and she had adjusted very well. Being with people all day was in itself an ordeal for her in the beginning, as she tried to become accustomed to the constant chatter. As she travelled to collect her herbal materials she delighted in being alone.

At times she would sit on the mountainside and gaze in the direction of her old home, and as time passed it became less of an ordeal for her. She was now quite happy with her new life, and going to the sheebeen every night gave her something to look forward to. Kitty had Hannah made some new clothes for old Mag, and with the French perfume and colourful shawl, Mag felt elated.

On the warm, still evenings James and Kitty would stroll together across the mountainside to the smaller hill where the old stone fort stood. They would laugh and talk of their daily lives and all that happened to them throughout the day. They talked of their future life together, marriage, and a family that they would rear together.

"When Ireland is free, James, I doubt if father will remain here. We will buy some of the estate land when he decides to sell it. It will be wonderful, you know... a life to call our own."

"Farming life for Mrs de Lacey! I can indeed see you collecting eggs each morning, Kitty. That will be a sight to behold indeed!"

"And why not, James? I can actually bake bread now, you know, much to Hannah's disapproval. She stood back aghast the day I asked her to teach me how to bake! She said, 'I suppose the next thing you will want to do is learn how to sow potatoes!'. I did laugh James at the expression on her face."

"I am so very proud of you, Kitty," James said, as he drew her near and kissed her. "Do you miss me these nights?"

She smiled shyly as she remembered their long nights of loving in Bordeaux.

"A great deal, James, but knowing that I can be with you every day here makes me happy beyond words," she said dreamily.

"Me too, Kitty. Have you ever thought of what being a Catholic will be like?" he asked, as he propped himself up on one elbow looking at her seriously.

"Yes, I have thought about it a lot, James. I have even learned some of your prayers. I hear Nell say them with the children each night," she said with sincerity.

"A lot of division is all it ever brings as far as I can see Kitty."

She looked at the summer sky silently.

"What are you thinking, Kitty?"

"Oh, it's just the way father couldn't marry Lady Fitzmaurice in Hampshire all those years ago on account of her being Catholic. When you think of all the suffering and heartache it must have caused her. He would have had to forfeit everything for to be with her. Lands, title, everything!" she said seriously.

James looked at her and smiled.

"And yet, my love, you have done just that, have you not? Then for you to be renounced publicly by your father and I am sure by society! You have great courage, Kitty." She smiled and kissed him.

"No, James. It's not courage. It's conviction! You see I love you and I know you love me and that's the difference between father and me. Had he truly loved Lady Fitzmaurice, nothing would have stood in his way. It's a question of what one considers important and worth the sacrifice. I know if I had chosen any of the young men who were deemed suitable for me I would only serve to produce heirs for them, while a mistress would have loomed in the background. It has always been the way with society."

They gazed at the magnificent view before them, which was dominated by Oak Hall. She wondered what her father was doing now. Probably sitting in his study or entertaining someone in the drawing room.

"He has had a sad, secret life, really, father. You know James, he never took a mistress! He must have loved my mother in many ways."

* * *

Father Murphy knew only too well that the increasing brutality of recent times was gradually goading the people towards inevitable mass destruction. He prayed for deliverance for his people, but expected it was hopeless. Rebellion stars them in the face. He convened a meeting in the old castle ruins. It was miraculous how it still had not been detected as their rendezvous point. There were one hundred men huddled together in the once great dining hall. He looked at the sea of faces before him, men in their prime of life and others in their declining years. He knew they were tired of meetings. Those present were from all parts of counties Wicklow and Wexford.

Beside him stood James, Joe, Kitty, Marjorie, Marcus and Matt Ryan. The sight of the two women aroused great curiosity among the attendance, who were for the most part, unaware of their identities. Slowly the crowd of men grew silent as they looked at the group standing before them.

A slight drizzle of rain fell on the gathering.

Father Murphy gestured for the two women to be seated.

"Fellow countrymen," be began, "we are standing here tonight as if we were criminals, hiding away here in this old castle ruin. And indeed, in the eyes of King George's government, we are! We have not alone become slaves, but conspirators. Daily our fellow countrymen are being arrested, flogged, and some flogged to death. This man beside me here was pitch capped. It is not late in the day of Ireland's oppression and time this island rose up against the brutal hand of the enemy. We have been left little choice. None in fact! Women and children now live in the ditches and groves too terrified to return to their homes. They are afraid of being murdered in the night or else burned in their beds. It is time to get up and fight!"

A thunderous cheer rose from the crowd before him.

"For we can no longer stand and be butchered like senseless sheep. God does not expect us to stand awaiting execution. Never that! We must rise together once and for all and take the stand that has too long been deferred. I know many of you have young families and live in fear for their lives. Well, if we continue to stand defenceless then that is what will happen. So tonight I am telling you that when our men march through your parishes, join them! Yes, I say! Let every able-bodied man come forward and fight for his life and for his country. Arm yourselves with forks, pikes, bayonets and a musket if you have one! In every parish in the county there are supplies enough of arms for everyone, and when the time comes, step forward. Go now to your homes and prepare and spread the word, for the great battle is almost upon us, this battle that will decide all!"

A sense of relief settled on the crowd now that they knew the time was near. Father Murphy raised his hand in blessing. He prayed to the God of victory, and prayed that He would lead his men to victory and triumph over their enemy. Gradually most disbanded all in different directions. Some remained discussing the events and the times they now found themselves in. Marjorie looked at Kitty, smiling.

"Well, young lady, do you remember our last meeting? The one in the inn? I was bound to secrecy and as much as I wanted to tell you of the planned ambush, you realise now the importance of secrecy. But I did feel so bad not being able to lift the anguish of your heart. Tell me Kitty, did you like France? We have had no real time to discuss it."

"Bordeaux was heaven! To be able to walk freely about the city without fear or threat of death, or having to meet in secret. Wonderful it was for us both. And the lovely sunny days we had together are times I shall never forget. It was there James told me everything about the United Irishmen. Its hopes and its dreams. I never fully realised, Marjorie, how tragic the history of this land really has been. It was something we were never told or allowed to know. You see, Marjorie, most of the people I am descended from and have associated with all my life truly believe the vast majority of the people in this country are very happy with their lot. Their lives were never once discussed at any gathering I have ever been at. It's almost as if the people don't feel or think or exist in many ways. The episode of history relating to Oliver Cromwell, for example. We were always told he came over here to rid the land of paganism! The true facts, which James told me, are horrific. The confiscation of the people's lands was beyond my comprehension," she said with indignation.

"Yes, Cromwell did irreparable damage here. The slaughter of women and children was barbaric. You see a people like ours never can lose their spirit of rebellion, simply because the memories of brutality runs deep within us. We are never allowed to forget. So this time I hope to God we have victory, for I dread to think of the consequences if we fail."

Marjorie then stood up and fastened the clasp of her grey cloak. James sat with a group of men, looking at Kitty from time to time.

"You two are very much in love, Kitty, are you not?"

"Yes, Marjorie, I love James above all else, and to think I almost lost him! It doesn't bear thinking about, how my father tried to achieve his pathetic plans for him with death. Some nights I awaken still pondering how a human being can become so brutal and bloodthirsty. Poor Joe being pitch capped and seeing his poor mother shot dead. No, the father I knew died with my mother," and Kitty's face was white with fear and concern for them all.

"Don't worry, love, soon it will all be behind us and you and James can have the life you both want and deserve. Isn't it great to have it all to look forward to?"

Father Murphy approached both women, raising his hat in courtesy.

"Lady Catherine, Marjorie, very good of you both to come out on a night like this. So very damp, isn't it?" And then, looking at Marjorie, said, "Marjorie, I am not happy with you still living in that town. The authorities are aware of where your sympathies lie, and hence my concern for your safety!"

"Well, father, I am not in the least afraid of them, and I will remain there as I don't intend to abandon my premises. Who would take care of it all?"

"Marjorie," the priest persisted patiently, "we all know that you have remarkable courage and your help over the past few years has been invaluable to us. But I fear the authorities are well aware now of the extent of your involvement. See sense, my child, and go and live among your friends in the mountains. You will at least be safe there until the rebellion is over. Will you please do as I ask? Just this one last favour? For me... please?"

Marjorie looked at Kitty.

"Father is right, Marjorie. They will come some day or night and arrest you.

It is inevitable. Besides, we could do with a really good cook, as poor Hannah seems frail these past weeks," Kitty added.

"Well, if that's what you really feel is for the good, father, I will do as you advise. For you, mind you!" Marjorie said sadly.

"Good woman. I knew I could rely on you to see sense," he said sincerely, for he knew it was only a matter of time until she would be arrested and subjected to torture in order to extract information. Their methods revolved the priest. He was relieved by her compliance with his wishes.

So in the nights that followed, horses and carts transported vast supplies of flour, meat and drink from Marjorie's inn, slowly making its way up to the mountain village. The supplies were to be stored safely, for they knew there would inevitably be food shortages. Hannah supervised the unloading and storage of everything, a task Kitty knew she would enjoy. Surprisingly enough, Hannah did not take umbrage at Marjorie becoming head cook. Instead, she announced that it was high time she took up her proper duty as ladies' maid to Lady Catherine. So once again the growing household settled down into the routine of daily life. From time to time Marjorie took exception to old Mag, whose curiosity demonstrated by sampling every dish irritated her. The intrusion of Mag's cat was never tolerated, for Marjorie had an intense dislike for cats! So the daily confrontations, simple as they were, helped to dispel the greater tension of the forthcoming rebellion.

Marjorie sat outside the cottage every evening chatting with the other women. They all loved her easy manner and her great selection of stories she told them of life at the Bull's nose. Kitty would join them, much to Hannah's disapproval, which reminded her that it was "high time to draw the line somewhere and act like the lady she was reared to be". Kitty's reply was, a real ladies' maid would never dream to tell her mistress what to do"! It was a game they played and enjoyed.

Meanwhile, the men whom Lord Foldsworth had instructed to survey the old ring fort and monitor the frequency of James and Kitty's visits finally reported back to him. They informed him that on Wednesday and Sunday evenings they came without fail. He sat by the fire in his study and looked at Justice Stewart, who was sitting opposite him. They had just enjoyed a sumptuous meal and they sipped their port wine appreciatively, thinking of the recent news the spies had just given them.

"Fifty men, Charles, should be sufficient. I expect forty of those will then accompany the prisoner directly to Wexford jail. I am sure your daughter will be less resistant. Coming here, I expect, is she?"

"Why, yes, of course," his host snapped. "You hardly think that she is going to accompany him to prison, do you, Timothy?" Lord Foldsworth said irritably.

"Now, now, Foldsworth, no need for that! I know too well the embarrassment all this has brought upon you. I hope when she is finally at home, she will realise the folly of her ways. Somehow I think she will, and then in time take her place in society once again. We all expect it of her, Charles," he added sincerely.

"Yes, I realise that the poor girl became unhinged with the death of her mother. They were inseparable, you know. She lost all sense of propriety Timothy, didn't she?"

"Yes, I am afraid that is precisely what occurred, Foldsworth. Damn shame really," and Timothy Stewart remembered how close he had once been to her when her father had the hunting accident.

I loved here then, he thought, and then there was the letter she had found! He wished he could have told his host the discovery of that letter, and the facts it disclosed, was the commencement of the change that had occurred. However, he had given his word as a gentleman that he would never reveal her secret and he intended to keep it.

"You know, Charles, I really do care for her despite her present change of attitude. I often think that given time, she would learn to love me. I could not ask for a more lovely companion in my life," Justice Stewart said to the utter amazement of Lord Foldsworth.

"My God, Timothy... you and Kitty... married? Why I never realised that you had any feelings for her whatever!"

His guest felt a little embarrassed before replying.

"Well, I never bothered to tell you before. Only in recent months have I come to recognise my feelings for her. That is why the sooner the better that rebel, who has cast his spell upon her, is gone from her life permanently. I know that she will then come to her senses given time. I am a patient man, Charles."

Lord Foldsworth looked at him in shock as he listened to this declaration of intent.

"Why of course I would give my blessing to the marriage, Timothy. It would be my greatest wish to see Kitty happy and married finally. You would both be the toast of Dublin without question!"

Lord Foldsworth's spirits soared at the very prospect of such a union!

"I am sure you are right, Charles. And that is why it is so important that we make no mistakes in the capture and delivery of our prisoner on this occasion. I have no illusions but that Kitty will reject me for months. It would be only natural. But a young heart soon forgets and in time she will mellow. You will see Charles."

Lord Foldsworth nodded in agreement as he rang for Williams to serve the whiskey. What an amazing turns of events, he thought. Who would ever have expected it? The relationship between both men changed after those moments of truth. Lord Foldsworth began to see Timothy Stewart now in the light of his future son-in-law, and it tempered his attitude towards Kitty substantially, and felt his anger towards her abating. Her public denunciation of him in the village now paled to insignificance in the light of her becoming the wife of Viscount Stewart. Poor girl, he thought, I failed miserably all along to see the real effect that her mother's death had upon her. From now on I shall be the ideal father. I hope it's not too late."

It was the first night that he slept well for many months. In the guest room, Timothy Stewart sat at his bedside drinking what was left of his glass of whiskey, as he considered the vast inheritance that would be his with the eventual marriage to Lady Catherine Foldsworth. She must, and she will, agree to it, he thought decidedly. Patience is the key to it all he told himself as he blew out the candles.

At breakfast the following morning both men sat down to eat in jovial form.

"Tell me Charles, have you ever considered taking that village up there in the mountains by force?"

"Indeed yes, the thought has occurred to me many times. While I may succeed in getting my daughter back by force, her rebel friend would flee and go aground! As matters stand we now know where they both are, and both purposes will be served with the current plan. Besides, not until that fellow hangs on the end of a rope will she ever relinquish her fascination of him," he said casually.

He knew that it would be very unwise to speak of the intimacies he had witnessed at the old ring fort. It could easily jeopardise everything now, and that was something he could not risk.

"No, she is simply fascinated by that fellow. That's all there is to it and it will soon fade, as you in time will persuade her to look at greater things. Incidentally, are the kidneys to your liking? We have a new cook and she is extremely good, I am glad to say."

"Charles, the cuisine at Oak Hall is excellent, leaving nothing to be desired," he replied happily.

After breakfast both men rode out across the lands west of the estate. The outline of the village high on the mountain ledge stood out clearly, with the smoke from the cooking fires spiralling into the bright morning sky. The crowing of a cock descended onto the valley beneath where both horsemen had stopped to gaze up at the sight. It looked beautiful and the atmosphere was calm and peaceful.

"It is such a dreadful pity that this land of Ireland is so full of unrest, Charles. One wonders if it will ever be anything else!" Timothy Stewart remarked.

Lord Foldsworth looked at the scene about them. The cattle grazed knee-high in the lush May grass, and mares with foals at foot stood allowing their young drink the nourishing milk.

"Indeed, I think they will never change. But I remember when I first brought Edwina here she thought it heavenly. She saw no hidden dangers, nothing sinister. She constantly visited the poor, the sick, a practice long held by her own family. Then when Kitty was born, she dedicated her entire life to the child, refusing a nanny or governess for her. I sometimes asked myself and more so of late, if those happy and peaceful days were all a dream. With Edwina now dead, and an estranged daughter, and surrounded now by many who would willingly shoot me dead if they could... it's a nightmare to ponder," he said dismally.

"Not at all, Charles! You have just tried to defend your home by maintaining law and order as the government wishes. You can't possibly hold yourself personally responsible for the breakdown of these peasant people. One can be too kind, you know, Charles! These people always mistake kindness for weakness. Ignorance, you know, and nothing else." Timothy Stewart remarked with contempt.

"Can you see the outline of the stone fort, Timothy? It is on the summit of the first mountain shoulder," Lord Foldsworth pointed with his riding crop.

"Ah yes, now I see it. Pagan site is it?" he asked curiously.

"Something like that. The northern side is approachable without being seen from the village itself. Our plan will work perfectly and I am impatient for the day. That vagabond's days are now numbered. Soon my little girl will be home. She will be like a breath of fresh air in the house again."

He felt satisfied and certain of events now as they became clearer in his mind. Soon his house would be filled with guests again. They would only be too willing to come back to Oak Hall, for was it not one of the finest homes for entertaining in the southeast?

Timothy Stewart's mind considered how he was going to have to conceal his excitement. After I marry that rebellious young lady, her father will undoubtedly return to Hampshire and the arms of that Catholic Lady Fitzmaurice, he reasoned. His reasoning was indeed correct, for Lord Foldsworth had suddenly become very tired of living this estranged life of violence and fear. The prospect of further bloodshed on a major scale held no appeal for him. He now found himself suddenly free to plan a new life. Kitty and Timothy will live at Oak Hall and eventually he would make regular visits there to visit his grandchildren!

At lunch Williams noticed the radical changes in both men, who were now very amicable towards one another. He wondered what had brought about this change of atmosphere, for indeed it was welcome.

"We are on the verge of an uprising, are we not, Timothy? Lord Foldsworth looked at his guest directly.

"Yes we are, Charles, but one can't possibly imagine that it will be of any great significance. Possibly a few skirmishes, rioting or whatever. But when proper justice is meted out and when they see their so-called leaders kicking at the end of a rope on the gallows, rest assured the will scuttle to ground like frightened foxes," his guest said reassuringly.

"Hmm, I see. Nonetheless, I think you would agree with me when I say that it would be in Kitty's best interests for her to go directly to Hampshire. They may well attempt to burn down the house again. I would be greatly surprised if they didn't attempt it."

Timothy Stewart felt suddenly apprehensive at the very idea, but admitted it made sense nevertheless.

"Yes, Charles, though reluctantly, I agree to it. But as you rightly say they will come again some night with their torches. Particularly after the execution of that rebel fellow, they will strike out in any possible direction," he said noticeably agitated.

"I may then write instantly to John and inform him of our plans and the current state of affairs here. Now let me consider it all a moment. Next Wednesday the planned recapture will take place. Then I will allow Kitty one week here in the house to adjust somewhat, and then have her escorted to Hampshire. I am not fool enough to think it is going to be easy. But Timothy, you will assist me no doubt."

"Of course, Charles, in every way. We will wait until she has left the country before we execute him, telling her that he will be treated very fairly."

"Well, these few days, Timothy, have proved very worthwhile. I know you are anxious to return to Wexford, so I shall summon Williams and see if your escort has arrived.

Presently Williams arrived.

"Has Justice Stewart's escort arrived, Williams?" he asked curtly.

"Yes sir. They arrived an hour ago," Williams replied, avoiding all eye contact with Justice Stewart, for whom he had an intense dislike. Justice Stewart noticed the attitude towards him.

"Have my horse sent round, old boy, and be quick about it," he quipped at Williams. But Williams did not respond, only looked directly at his master.

"Well, Williams, what on earth are you waiting for?" Lord Foldsworth barked.

"Your instruction, sir," he replied.

"Oh, for heaven's sake, don't stand on ceremony, Williams. Justice Stewart has just issued them, which I may add is something you will have to become accustomed to. He will be your new master soon, Williams!" And the look of shock on Williams' face almost evoked a laugh from Justice Stewart who thought, "and on that day you will go down that avenue, you old goat".

Going downstairs Williams was in a state of shock. His world was coming to an unexpected end. The very idea of being butler to Justice Stewart was unthinkable. Titles do not procure breeding, he thought. He decided to write that very day to his brother in queen's county to inform him that he would be coming to live with him for his retirement soon. Life was becoming more unpredictable by the hour, he thought nervously.

* * *

Lord Foldsworth looked out at the escort of fifty men, mostly from Carlow. They had been handpicked, carefully selected from Loyalist families known for their allegiance to the King. They were totally trustworthy and beyond bribery. They too would be escorting de Lacey to prison and the gallows. He rubbed his hands together in satisfaction and poured himself a glass of brandy, for he was delighted with the sudden turn of events. Why! He thought... I never hoped for such a wonderful outcome to a visit. They way was finally opened for him to be with Glencora. Elation filled him.

Damn them and their rebellion! They will now be quietened down for the next hundred years or more. We need another Cromwell, he thought. They understand little else. Ringing for Williams, he decided to discuss the security of his great mansion. Williams, on entering the room, considered the wisdom of presenting his notice to quit, but then decided to wait until his mater was in a more cordial mood. He would use the excuse of back pain and failing sight. That should ease the way, he thought.

"Oh, there you are, Williams! For a moment I thought the bell was not working properly. However, I wish to know how our security arrangements for the house are coming along."

"The arrangements are as your Lordship ordered with all shutters secured below stairs and on the ground floor. The livestock are guarded every night. No intruders have been sighted since the last attack sir."

"Good, Williams, I am glad they are doing a good job. You may go now."

"Before I go sir, I would like to remind you that Lady Joanna Winters and Lord and Lady Attlee are coming to dinner next week, lest it escapes your Lordship's attention."

His employer had indeed forgotten.

"Yes, yes, Williams, I will remember," he replied distractedly.

Blast that old fool Attlee coming, with his collection of doting stories, he thought. "Well, I shall leave all the arrangements to you Williams, as usual! What day do they arrive?"

"Thursday evening of next week, sir," the butler reminded him.

"Thursday... hmm... I see. Well, that will be all Williams."

When Williams had left he paced the room anxiously.

That will be the evening following the capture and Kitty will be here! I shall have Joanna Winters speak to her, and perhaps she will succeed in making her see sense, he thought. Most of our friends now are aware of her elopement. It will be interesting to look at the expressions of his guests when they see Kitty at dinner. For the first time ever he blessed Constance Attlee, knowing she would carry the gossip the length and breadth of both counties. People would believe her as the Attlees were an old family and greatly respected. In addition to this, he would discreetly tell them of the forthcoming engagement of Justice Stewart to his daughter, and a forthcoming engagement party. Lady Attlee will be enthralled to be the first to know of the planned liaison! Lord Foldsworth took out his diary.

May 23rd, 1798.
Wednesday.
Arrest of rebel, James de Lacey. Kitty comes home...

May 24th, 1798.
Thursday,
Lady Joanna de Winters and Lord and Lady Attlee, to dinner

He looked at what he had written, and closing the brown leather diary of 1798, he replaced it in the drawer of his mahogany desk. He felt tired and decided to retire after dinner. It had been a long day. Or had it? he wondered, or am I simply getting old? He knew the strain of past months had taken its toll. His thoughts then drifted to Glencora. He decided impulsively to write to her telling her of Kitty going to Hampshire within the next few weeks, to remain there until he deemed it safe for her to return. He would also tell her of his forthcoming plans for her wedding to Timothy Stewart, which as far as he was concerned she would consent to, given time.

His second letter would be to his brother John, which would be a somewhat more frank disclosure of recent events and Kitty's subsequent nervous breakdown resulting from her mother's death. As he wrote the letters he found that his fatigue vanished as he reflected upon the grim realities, which had beset his once ordered, and happy life at Oak Hall.

* * *

Life at the mountain village began to take on the character of a miniature Oakfort. The renovated old stone house at the entrance of the village was now the forge, where Joe carried out his daily work. He was healing in body and spirit while May, Nell, Kitty, Marjorie and old Mag were a happy team.

James would sit all day examining old maps and the routes of old roads and byways of Wexford and Wicklow. Contingency plans for unforeseen events were now a priority to him, and escape routes essential to know in detail. He worried about Kitty and the other women. The fact that they were living so high up on the mountainside assured them safety from the main battle route. Looking at the vast expanse of the plains before him, it seemed a distance of almost fifty miles in both directions. He glanced over at the old ring fort. It was a magical sight, he thought, backed by the towering purple-coloured mountain range that seemed to beckon him. He remembered how he had met Kitty there and how their love had blossomed and grown with time. So deep, he thought...

Ravens wheeled and glided on the warm thermal current high above the fort that warm summer evening, as they had done from earliest times. It was close to their nesting sites and as they flew they surveyed the ground beneath them for intruders. But they saw no enemy and they did not cry out in any alarm. All was well.

No one around the hillside, James reflected.

"Daydreaming I see," Kitty said, smiling broadly.

"Of you, my love," and he reached out and took her hand as she sat on the great granite stone beside him.

"What exactly were you dreaming of, James? I'd love to know" she asked him quietly.

He placed his arm around her waist and drew her closer.

"Look up at it, Kitty, the old ring fort. Are those stones not like giants looking down across the countryside?"

"Yes, they are, and I often wonder about the ancient people who congregated there. It was a place of great significance for them, one imagines. A sacred and special place without doubt," she mused.

"Just like you, my love, sacred and special," he assured her as he kissed her tenderly. They strolled onto the hillside admiring the view as they usually did, trying to ignore the reality of the forthcoming rebellion that seldom now left their minds.

Joe watched them from his small forge. He felt both happiness and melancholy for them both. He had come to know Kitty very well and cared for her now as if she was his own daughter. He pondered for the hundredth time their future together. James had a price on his head. Lord Foldsworth would never relinquish his hopes for being reunited with his daughter. Their situation together was impossible, he thought, no matter what way one looks at it. They should have stayed in France, for it had been their only real chance of happiness together, away, far away, he sighed, as he threw the hammer down in anger.

He then thought of the next council meeting. It would the last one and the venue would be different, which they would be duly informed of only hours beforehand. The leadership were not going to take any chances, for the countryside was full of spies, and also men that would sell information and a life for a gold guinea. He spat in contempt at the reality of the treachery that prevailed in Ireland. He looked up the village at the children and the dogs who ran to and fro playing, the women standing as usual at evening time chatting. There was safety here, he thought, more so than in the low lands. In addition to this, Mag had found two old caves well concealed, which had been used by the shepherds of old. They had provided shelter for them from heavy snowfalls and storms. Supplies of barrelled water had now been stored there. In the event of an attack on the village the women and children would be safe there. Beds of dry heather had also been prepared there, and also all the food that had come from Marjorie's tavern was stored in an orderly fashion.

Joe pondered if he would ever see Nell and his children again, and he knew that thousands of men had the same thoughts! Many would never return, but there was little pint in living in fear, yet at times he felt it. Chiding himself for his gloomy mood, he walked home feeling hungry. He promised that he would do justice to the fine meal that awaited him. The novelty of the new way of life for the many people living there added a sense of adventure, and for many of them the idea of a bloody revolution was remote. The young men, however, were certain of victory. Being out of the mainstream of daily life and not hearing of floggings and hangings, their false sense of reality was easy to maintain. James and Joe were aware of this, but did not interfere with their hopes and dreams. For what time remained to them of relative peace and normality, they would not disturb. It would have been wrong to do so.

Father Doyle looked at the village high above him as his horse slowly picked its steps up the rocky incline. It was his first visit to the members of his flock. He himself had been unwell for many weeks, as his stomach gave him severe discomfort from time to time with severe pain. The doctor had advised him to eat less gruel and more potatoes, which he seldom found the time to cook. But on this particular evening he felt well and in good spirits. In a black leather saddlebag, frayed with age, he carried his sacred vessels and vestments; bread and wine which he would consecrate for his beloved people. They were unaware of his coming and he looked forward to surprising them and spending time with them. He would listen to their confessions on the morrow and then celebrate mass with them. Looking at the great mountain range before him, and the crimson sky behind them, he praised the great creator of heaven and earth. Stopping his horse to allow the aged animal to catch its breath, he could hear the laughter of the children from the distant village.

He smiled, remembering his own youth free of all worry and responsibility. He knew he had been fortunate to have had such a happy childhood, and a family who had never known hunger or want. He prayed then for his father and mother, and thought of the quiet graveyard where they both lay at rest.

He urged his horse forward now, feeling hungry and excited at meeting everybody. The cattle, though few in number, looked at him with large, curious eyes. They looked well he thought, feeding on the summer grass. The calves raced and frolicked, tails held high in excitement. Innocence prevails in all young things, he thought happily. Upon reaching the village, there were no signs of life. Everyone would be eating their evening meal, he knew. Routine seldom changed. A simple people and a frightened one too. It was not long ago when priests had to hide in these mountains also, ministering to their flocks from granite altars, a price on their heads.

A door opened and a woman emerged carrying a steaming pot of potatoes. She was in the act of straining them when she looked up and saw Father Doyle.

"Father Doyle," she cried out in amazement and delight.

"Busy as ever, Nell, I see," he replied, happy to see her again, and soon other families came out to welcome the priest with warm affection. Presently Nell ushered him into the cottage. Father Doyle looked at the table before him and those seated at it. All the familiar faces gladdened his heart. He was intrigued to see Kitty, but knew in time all would be made clear to him. Joe insisted that the priest be seated at the top of the table and soon plates were piled high.

"Good god, Marjorie, if I eat all that I will sleep for two days!" he exclaimed.

"Nonsense, father, I assure you the thin mountain air will keep you wide-awake and alert," Kitty assured him.

"On your word, Lady Catherine, I rest my case! And may the Lord bless the cooks, the food and the company," he said, to which there was a resounding 'Amen'.

As they ate, they told the priest of their new life and he in turn told them the news of the lowlands. He seemed to them as almost one from a different land rather than the seven miles that lay between the village and their old homes.

"And Mag, how are you keeping? I was very angry to hear what happened to your home in the woods," the priest said with palpable sincerity.

"It was an awful thing to happen, father, terrible to watch all that you ever owned go up in smoke. But then I have another home and a family too, which I've never had before," she replied.

Joe smiled.

"To tell you the truth, father, she is the boss about the place here, if the truth be known, and she is storing up the cough medicine for the children for the winter. So we are the ones who have gained in lots of ways."

Mag laughed as she stroked her cat, which sat on her lap contentedly.

"And you, Lady Catherine, how are you? Settling down?" the priest asked almost falteringly.

"Splendid, father. Why I even have my ladies' maid with me, who doesn't let me out of her sight!"

Hannah felt embarrassed, and dabbed her lips with her table napkin, but Father Doyle could discern a great bond between them all, which is all that matters, he thought. He could see that James and Kitty were very much in love and he decided that he would have a serious chat with them to see if he could be of any assistance to them.

When the meal was finished, the women busied themselves clearing up and old Mag built up the fire with sods of turf, her usual evening task that nobody dared interfere with. The children, now in their loft beds, peered down at the scene beneath them. Nell chided them from time to time, reminding them of school the following day.

"You have a school organised, Nell?" the priest asked, surprised.

"Yes father, all thanks to Miss Kitty. The children love it, you know, and you would imagine they were going on a picnic every day with the scramble every morning through the door."

"How very good of you, Lady Catherine, to take such an interest," the priest remarked, his regard for her increasing hourly.

"Not at all, father, I look forward to it myself, in fact. I think it must have been my true vocation," she said with a tone of conviction.

Hannah looked up at the ceiling with exasperation, wondering if Kitty would ever hold herself like the lady she was reared to be, and as usual blamed herself for allowing Kitty to be too familiar with the kitchen staff at Oak Hall. Noticing the frown Hannah wore, Kitty asked the reason.

"Nothing much, my lady, only that you haven't finished that piece of lace work yet. You seem to be taking ever so long to complete it," Hannah answered sharply.

Mag's piercing laughter filled the room and Hannah looked at her thinking how very sad old age can be. But Mag continued, "lace-making on the mountain," she exclaimed loudly, and the tears came to her eyes with merriment.

Hannah stood up and taking her shawl from the peg on the wall announced that she was going to visit more sensible company. The priest smiled at the simplicity of it all.

Lying in bed unable to sleep that night, Father Doyle thought about how very vulnerable his flock were. The bishop had issued instructions that all clergy were to insist that their flocks were to cooperate with the government and the law and order of their respective areas. The very idea revolted him, as he recalled the excruciating torture that Joe Gilltrap had to endure, as so many others now endured each day. Even Marjorie's tavern had now been turned into an interrogation centre and the military presence in the town had been increased greatly. She seemed to be unaware of the fact, and he decided not to mention it to her. She would learn of it sooner or later, he thought.

Neither shall I ask them to cooperate with the authorities. It was unthinkable to ask them to do such a thing. He would instead encourage them to remain at the village and try and continue life. At least they were safer here, but for how long, he wondered?

The following morning the people were happy and relaxed as the solemn ritual, which they had greatly missed, unfolded before them once again. Overhead, skylarks soared high above the congregation who bowed their heads in prayer. Kitty attended the mass, much to the astonishment of them all, but somehow it didn't surprise them. Father Doyle then addressed the people.

"My people, I know that you are afraid... afraid of what might happen to your families, and what remains of your homes. I have been told by my bishop to order you to surrender all pikes and muskets and bayonets that you have either hidden or are in your possession. Also that you are to obey the authorities in all that they demand of you!"

He paused as he looked at the helpless and the defenceless before him.

"However," he continued, "my conscience forbids me to tell you to do so! Recent events show me clearly that justice no longer exists. In the months that you have all been living here, very great injustices have been carried out the length and breadth of Leinster. Due to the fact that you are living up here, isolated, you have been spared a great deal so far, for many of you would have been flogged or half hanged or worse."

He paused again, but this time his gaze seemed to go beyond them, and the people waited for him to continue. They noticed how pale he had become and then he began to walk through the large group towards the ledge of the mountain, the reason soon becoming apparent. In the valley beneath them, on the outskirts of Oakfort, a tall spiral of black smoke drifted into the morning sky.

"My church, my church," he cried, as the people looked in shock. "My God, they have burned my church!"

"What an appalling act of villainy," Kitty declared. "Surely my father would not resort to such a base act," she said to James in trembling tones.

He looked at her sadly and shook his head.

"I don't know any more, Kitty. As Father Doyle says, we are out of touch. God alone only knows what's really going on down there."

Father Doyle, his composure now somewhat regained, took Kitty gently by the arm.

"Don't blame yourself, Lady Catherine. You could not have prevented it had you even been there, no more than I. We are very fortunate the church wasn't full as it normally would be this morning. Think then of the consequences."

The priest's words spread through the crowd and their realisation of what was about to take place in their lives became clearer to them.

"You must not go back down there, father," Joe said firmly. They all looked at him, fearful for his safety.

"No, father, you must not. Joe is absolutely correct," Kitty said emphatically.

The crowd pressed about the priest.

"Am I not duty bound, Lady Catherine, to investigate the perpetrators of this act of sacrilege?" he said angrily.

"Duty bound, father?" Kitty said with increasing agitation. "Don't be so ridiculous! The idea of burning the church is simply their method of locating you! Surely you can see that. For you will suffer the same fate. Look about you. Your duty is now here, not going down there risking your life for a heap of charred timbers."

A loud murmur of approval went through the crowd. In the distance the fire had subsided.

"I suppose you are right, Lady Catherine," he conceded.

"Yes I am, father, and it's a great pity your bishop is not here to witness the sight. Perhaps then he would reconsider his advice to his people! Is it not sad that these eminent men obey the crown instead of the truth before them?"

The crowd cheered her wildly. Before they dispersed, James announced that there would be a general meeting at noon and suggested that three men remain behind on lookout duty, while the remainder took their late breakfast.

"Do you think that they will come up here, James?" The priest asked as he looked at how little actual defence there was.

"They could, father, they could well do so. But somehow I think that if or when they do, it will more likely be some morning before sunrise, rather than daytime."

At noon the situation was discussed thoroughly by the entire village population. It was hot and dusty, as the sun shone brilliantly from the cloudless sky. James' address was simple and direct.

"From today we can no longer take our safety for granted. We will have to post men on lookout duty by day and by night. If the army decides to march on our village, the most likely time will be just before sunrise.

You all know what to do if the alarm is raised. Women and children to the caves, while the men will assemble armed, and wait till they are in sight of the enemy. At that point we will appear to be retreating from them further into the mountains. Naturally they will follow, the idea being to distract their attention from the caves. If we can entice them as far as the deer's pass, we will have the overall advantage." The plan met the approval of all present. James continued.

"Lady Catherine will be in charge of the women and children. When the time comes everyone will have to move quickly. Father Doyle will remain with you in the event of discovery."

The priest nodded his agreement, for it had been his own idea. In the event of discovery he would offer himself as a prisoner in exchange for fair treatment of the women and children. He knew he would be more highly prized in the present political climate... a rebel priest!

Those posted to reconnaissance duty reported nothing unusual. The lower slopes of the mountain range looked serene with sheep grazing placidly, no signs of disturbance. Tension in the village subsided gradually.

Mag sat smoking her clay pipe watching Marjorie who basted pork over the great cooking fire. Cinders, her cat, sat with ears pricked as fat spurted from the roasting joint.

"Cinders loves pork, don't you, my pet?" she crooned.

"Well Mag, rest assured she will get a large slice of the crackling when it is cooked," Marjorie assured her, her distaste for cats finding an exception in this case.

Hannah walked through the door with a bunch of wild flowers, which she placed at the centre of the table.

"Very grand all this, Cinders, isn't it?" Mag said to the cat, and Hannah decided that she wouldn't allow Mag's comments to irritate her.

"The quality love flowers on the table, isn't that right, Hannah?" Mag said pleasantly.

"Yes, Miss, it's what they are used to, colour and beauty on their table – sparkling glass and silver cutlery," Hannah replied.

"Did poor Lady Edwina like flowers?" Mag asked innocently, and Hannah then found herself talking about life at Oak Hall. Mag sat enraptured, listening to a way of life so vastly different from her own. She could almost see the ballgowns on the elegant, slim, young ladies, the glistening chandeliers ablaze with light. Marjorie was also intrigued, and became engrossed with the minute details which Hannah would discuss each morning with her former mistress. When Hannah completed her account of the regulated and opulent life at Oak Hall, Mag sighed and shook her head from side to side.

"Makes on think how Miss Kitty could turn her back on all that way of life for the love of James," Mag said to Hannah.

"Oh, she was always a single-minded young lady. She came to the kitchens from the time she was knee high, to tell me she would like three roasted potatoes instead of one and what vegetables she did not like! And the puddings she did like! As she grew older, I would hear the stable lads speak of her riding skills and they had great respect for her fearlessness with the horses. Very confident and with a mind of her own," Hannah said decidedly.

"But she is very compassionate too, Hannah," Marjorie added. "The time May Ryan's husband died there was nothing too much trouble for her to do for that family. I have often heard of many a kind deed she did and never spoke of either. Always had time for the poor and always will have if I know anything. There are very few like her, as we well know at this point!" and Marjorie stood up, taking the roasted joint from over the fire.

"Apple sauce! We must have apple sauce," Hannah announced, suddenly realising just how engrossed she had become in her reminiscing of her former life. Mag looked up at her, seeing Hannah with different eyes. She too had left if all behind for her devotion to her young mistress. And so at dinner Mag was noticeably more polite towards Hannah, and even complimented her on the delicious applesauce, though the smacking of her lips was quite exaggerated. But Hannah knew she meant well and a new bond grew between both women. A bond of tolerance and respect.

The following day was exceptionally warm for the first months of summer. Father Doyle was busy hearing the confession of some of the villagers. In the distance the rhythmic hammering at the forge continued as Joe shod a horse, and Kitty taught the children a short French song, which carried on the morning wind. Mag began her slow walk up the mountain to collect the herbs she wanted for the treatment of the ailments of the village. She looked up at the towering mountains that pierced the vaults of heaven, as she termed it. She now loved living with people and felt well and very happy. It was a stark contrast to her former way of life, which had been so solitary.

She decided to concentrate now on herbs that could be used for wounds received in battle. I will need cleansing ointments, solutions for infections, she murmured. I will give the men a potion each, for they will need it without doubt, she thought sadly. As she sat digging up the tender young roots required, her thoughts returned to Hannah and the stories of the years she spent in service at Oak Hall. She paused to look down at the great mansion, where the sun was reflecting on the large windows. The lawns even from this distance looked well cared for. She recalled as a young girl going there with her mother to the kitchen door to sell eggs. The cook of that time would bring them in and give them something to eat. She was a decent woman, Mag thought. I must ask Hannah about her this evening and whatever became of her! She looked at the fields, which crept to the base of the mountain, and then suddenly she stood up as she noticed a horseman riding along the path that led to the village. He was alone, she could see, and clutching her basket of roots she hurried back to the village with news of the approaching visitor.

She stood gasping at the forge leaning against a cartwheel and called out to Joe, breathless.

"What is it, Mag?" he asked in alarm.

"A man comes on horseback, Joe," she said falteringly.

"Alone or in the company of footmen?"

"Alone, Joe, quite alone," she replied.

Running to the nearest lookout post he found the youth sleeping and he pushed him roughly. The lad awoke with fright.

"Look down, lad. Well? What do you see? Well? Where were we all if that was a regiment?"

The young lad was red with guilt and shame. Joe called James and Father Doyle and they watched the approach of the visitor. Kitty now joined them and wondered if it was her father. The horse looked familiar and it was definitely from their stables. The half-bred chestnut with its rider came into full view. It was an elderly man.

"It couldn't possibly be!" Kitty exclaimed.

"Who?" asked James impatiently.

"Williams," she replied still unwilling to believe the evidence before her eyes. "Why, I never knew that he could even ride!" she said in total disbelief.

Without hesitation she ran down the hill towards Williams.

"Oh Williams, Williams," she cried openly shedding her tears at the familiar sight of the old butler.

"Oh dear Lady Catherine, how good it is to see you again," he wheezed, tired from the ride.

"It's Williams, Hannah!" Kitty called out. "What a wonderful surprise!"

Hannah clapped her hands in sheer happiness on seeing her dear old familiar friend. She embraced him warmly, much to the butler's embarrassment.

"But what on earth are you doing her, Williams? Is father ill?" Kitty asked.

"No, my lady, he is very well indeed."

"Come in Williams and have tea. You look as if you have been on that horse for two days," Hannah said with concern.

As Williams sat by the fire with a glass of punch, he looked at the faces about him. And he to them seemed quite odd, dressed as he was in his service uniform.

"Williams, I never knew you to ride," Kitty said, expressing her frank admiration of him.

"I must confess, my lady, that it is almost twenty years since I have done so. Brett assured me that Flossy would take me safely to town and back, for that is where I told them I was bound for."

Mag sat intrigued y the manner and tone in which he spoke to Kitty. Hannah fussed endlessly, preparing tea for him.

"Williams, these are all my friends, my new family if you like. May I present Nell, Joe, Marjorie, Mag, and of course, James," Kitty said.

"I see, my lady, I am pleased to meet you all, as friends of Lady Foldsworth," he replied in his usual tone of formality.

"It's like a dream to see you, Williams. Is it not, Hannah? I almost expect to awaken at any moment," Kitty said, still amazed by the visitation.

"No, I am not a dream my lady, not in the least. My back is aching badly I fear from the ride," he said, trying to sit more erect on his chair.

Mag seized the moment and going to her leather bag she rummaged and presently handed the butler a mixture shaped like a bar of soap.

"Just place that in your tub, Mr. Williams, and you will not have a pain or ache again," she told him assuredly.

"Oh, I see, yes, in the tub... How very kind of you, ma'am," he said kindly.

Looking at Kitty, Williams stood up.

"My lady, there are matters which I need to discuss with you privately if I may."

"Why of course, Williams. Shall we sit outside in the sunshine and Hannah shall serve tea by the stone wall."

As they both went out through the door, Mag looked at Hannah, thinking similar thoughts. Tea by the stonewall, Mag muttered, as she lit her pipe. No accounting for the fads of the quality!

Once outside Williams was again the formal butler of Oak Hall addressing a member of the family he faithfully served. Kitty was surprised how much she had actually missed him.

"It must be very important, Williams, for you to have risked coming here," she began, attempting to dispel his formal tones.

"Very important indeed, my lady. It is, I regret, unpleasant news, and a matter of great urgency as you will appreciate."

For a servant to speak of what he has overheard his master say in private conversation with a guest is not recommended, but in this instance I think it necessary. The guest in question is Viscount Stewart."

He paused, uncertain of how to continue.

"Speak freely, Williams," Kitty assured him. "I have always known your loyalty to the family, Williams. So don't be afraid to say what is troubling you."

Williams looked at the young face before him, now tanned by the mountain winds.

"My lady, while I do not support or agree with this cause that you have given your allegiance to, nevertheless my concern for your personal safety is uppermost in my mind. I am here to tell you that in a matter of a few days a regiment has been organised to capture both you and James de Lacey. The old fort I believe is where they anticipate finding you both." He paused and looked down at the view beneath them, avoiding his mistress' eye. "After that, your ladyship, he intends for you to marry Viscount Stewart."

"I see, Williams," she replied, aghast at how close danger loomed. "And why, Williams, if not having any belief in the cause of these people, have you taken such a risk in coming here to warn us?"

The old man thought for a moment, his grey hair now cast across his face by the rising breeze. It looked off to Kitty who had never seen his hair like that before. It was strange too, she thought, how this was the first time she ever had had a conversation with the butler, the first time she had seen him as a person. The realisation shocked her when she considered it.

"The reason, my lady, why I came to warn you is twofold. Firstly, I feel I owe it to Lady Edwina, whom I respected so much and secondly, your father's judgement and sense of reasoning appear to have left him. I am leaving his service... soon, and quietly I may add. I intend to go and live with my brother. I do not intend to announce my resignation either, my lady, if you understand. Your father would never accept it, I fear. So I ask your blessing, my lady, that I may go with a clear conscience and live out the rest of my days in peace."

His expression was one of pleading silently.

"Of course, Williams, of course you may go and live your life of retirement. You have been wonderful to us all through the years. My mother would have wanted it for you. Besides, these times are very different. You too must think of your safety."

Kitty took the old butler's hands in her own and tears filled her eyes. To her, Williams was the embodiment of Oak hall. He now suddenly seemed an old man, who was tired and afraid and confused.

"When do you plan to leave, Williams?"

"In two days' time, my lady. Your father is expected to attend the meeting with the regiment to finalise your capture that day. I will take advantage of his absence and leave soon after him that day. I will travel north to Dublin and then on to Meath to my brother the following day."

"Do you need someone to accompany you, Williams? I mean,..." she paused.

"Never fear, my lady. I will be all right. I shall wear old clothes and speak little to anyone on the way. I would not like to provoke your father, my lady, in his present state of mind. I am sorry to have to speak thus of him. He might interpret my going as an act of betrayal of sorts."

Kitty knew the deep struggle that was taking place in the man's heart. Everyone's lives seemed to be blighted in some way or another.

"So you must understand, my lady, that my purpose here is to warn you and then to say goodbye to you." They looked at each for a brief moment.

"My mother would have fully understood, Williams, and she would have supported you. I think that you already are aware of that. I, for my part, shall be ever grateful to you for so much," and she embraced him suddenly.

"Oh now, now, now, my lady. Don't fret so," was all he could say in deep sadness.

"Williams, I am sure you would like to spend some time with Hannah, who has a nice meal ready for you?

As Williams sat talking to Hannah, Kitty sought out James and told him of the impending ambush. He was very taken aback at how unguarded their movements had been in retrospect. They would have been easy targets.

"We must leave here Kitty, soon. They will not stop at the ring fort. Your father's rage will compel them to come to the village here. On this occasion he will not be deterred."

"What shall we do, or where shall we go, James?" she asked anxiously.

"I don't know right now. This is a surprise change. Sudden capture never entered my mind. One can become too complacent. There is nowhere safe now. Not here. Not anywhere, Kitty," he said sombrely.

"I shall go and see Williams off, James. And you see Joe and tell him the news. We must try and prevent alarm and panic at all costs."

James reached over and kissed her.

Hannah was heartbroken with the news of Williams' departure from Oak Hall. Their partnership had been a long and loyal one based on hard work, with many happy moments together. Memories of them both sitting in Hannah's parlour, chatting. For almost fifty years, she thought. Neither had ever married, for their work was their life. Kitty wondered if she should give Hannah the option of going back to Dublin to her brother or sisters there. She would be company for Williams for the greater part of the journey. Hannah felt helpless now in the face of what was coming upon the village.

Kitty joined Hannah and Williams at the table. It was obvious to her that Williams was uneasy with the familiarity of the situation.

"Hannah, i have been thinking about your future. And just now the thought occurred to me that this would be a heaven-sent opportunity for you to travel to your brother or sisters in Dublin, in the company of Williams."

"And why should I go there?" she asked curtly.

"Why Hannah," Williams interrupted, "her ladyship has only your best interests at heart. Would you not do as Lady Catherine suggests to you?"

Now look here, Seymour Williams, for over fifty years I have never questioned your judgement, but this once I do! I shall certainly not leave the side of my mistress, and that's an end to it now!" she said adamantly.

Williams sighed resignedly.

"Are you sure, Hannah? You do realise that there are very tough and violent times ahead of us all. Our lives are not our own anymore, and we could be massacred at a moment's notice when the battle begins. No-one may be spared, Hannah, so be very sure of what decision you are making, for this opportunity may never come again, and I do not want you to regret it," Kitty said firmly.

"I know my mind, mistress, just as Seymour Williams knows his," Hannah replied.

"Seymour," Kitty said slowly.

"Yes, your ladyship?" Williams replied.

"Your name, Williams. Imagine, I have never known your name."

He looked at her.

"There was never any need, Lady Catherine, for you to ever know it," he said softly.

Then Williams took out a red cloth from his pocket and slowly unwrapped that which lay carefully protected within it. Both women looked on in curiosity. Williams held up a glittering necklace of rubies and emeralds. It was exquisite silverwork with the jewels embedded in ornamental holly leaves of gold. He caressed it lovingly as he remembered its history.

"My mother was personal maid to Lady Claudia Leastone. Her eldest child, Johanna, contracted fever that threatened to swell the child's brain. The doctor told Lady Leastone that he had done all he possibly could, and that the child was beyond human aid. But my mother pleaded that she be given the chance of nursing the all-but-dead child, and reluctantly her mistress agreed. For a week the child lay close to death and then suddenly the fever subsided. Great rejoicing followed and as a token of unforgettable appreciation Lady Claudia presented my mother with this magnificent necklace. Never having had a daughter herself, she gave it to me so that when I had a daughter, I in turn could give it to her. Alas, not having married, this is not possible.

"So Hannah, I would like you to have it – a token to remember me by," he said sadly. He stood up and placed it about her neck while she sat overcome with emotion.

"Oh Seymour... thank you. It is magnificent," she cried, as she felt the beautiful necklace with her aged fingers.

"Yes, it looks so well on you Hannah! Need I say, no-one deserves it more." He then kissed her gently on the cheek.

Kitty now felt like an intruder, and sat silently wondering if things had been different would these two old friends have married and lived out their lives together. All our lives have been shattered aborted from their destined course. Oh God, she prayed, lead us to a peaceful harbour at this perilous time.

They watched Williams as he slowly rode down the mountain slopes where he would stop from time to time to wave many farewells. Hannah continued to wave back to her old friend, her red-cloaked figure dimming in Seymour Williams' eyes.

"I loved him once, you know. Oh yes... oh yes, I loved Seymour Williams. But I had the good sense to know that he could only see Oak hall and his duty. His real love, I think. At night I would dream of him, talk with him; love him, all in dreams. Then slowly I accepted the fact that all he saw in me was a friend, a housekeeper, someone to talk to on long winter nights as we sat in my parlour drinking tea or punch. It could have been all so very different for us."

Kitty took Hannah's hand and looked at her.

"I don't know, Hannah. I think Seymour loved you. I saw it in his eyes and his gift to you says as much. Are rubies not for love?"

Hannah looked at her necklace in deep thought.

"So they say, so they say, and he did kiss me, did he not?" and she looked into the distance but he was now gone from view, lost to her in the mountain slopes. James had suggested that route, lest his visit be observed by the patrols.

He is gone now also, Kitty thought. Piece by piece our lives are changing as my old world leaves me, she thought sadly. Marjorie interrupted their thoughts of Williams.

"Are you two going to come now and have your dinner? We are all waiting at table for you both, you know!" She was aware that they were both sad.

"Thank you, Marjorie. Hannah and I were just bidding Williams farewell, a long farewell to a great friend."

Hannah smiled and they both followed Marjorie into the house, where everyone was aware of their loss. Mag noticed the sparkling necklace instantly.

"Oh my, oh my, what a lovely lot of jewels, Hannah. Hmm, it tells a story... aye it does... and a story not finished yet, Hannah, I'll tell you this night!" old Mag added dreamily.

The atmosphere was sombre, as they all knew now the news that Williams had brought. When the meal was finished they sat around the great fire, as plans had to be made. Old Mag sat in the chimney corner and smoked her pipe, with Joe and Nell sitting beside her, while Hannah, James, Kitty and Marjorie sat in the centre. The door had been firmly bolted as they wanted no interruptions without warning. James spoke first.

"You are all aware of the true purpose of Williams' visit, which was to give us advance warning of a regiment being sent to capture Kitty and myself. Consequently, we must make new plans. The first thing that must be done is to remove the threat to you all here, which our being poses for everyone. So this is what I propose. Lord Foldsworth will be leaving Oak Hall early in the morning, two days hence. We have little option now but to blatantly encounter him – cross his path, in other words," James said plainly.

Hannah gasped. "Oh never, never. Why he could shoot you there and then, James," she exclaimed loudly.

"No, Hannah, he will not do that. It would be too simple, too straightforward if you like. What we have actually to do is to let him see us plainly, even address him if needs be. he must see us ride northward to Dublin. We will then circle the mountains and go back to Marcus' home. We would be safe there."

"Absolute madness," Marjorie said. "What if he has an escort, or, as Hannah says, shoots you there and then? Besides, how will you make ground enough to flee the military which will follow?"

"Very wise thinking," Mag added, having forgotten both pipe and cat momentarily. James stood up.

"It's all quite simple. Our only alternative would be t ride through the town and be openly seen by the military. There would be no escape in that situation for us, like a mouse going up to a cat in fact. What Lord Foldsworth wants is his daughter firstly, and my life secondly. He will not then bother with you all here if he has undeniable proof that we have fled."

Nell looked thoughtfully at Kitty.

"Could you not just ride twenty miles north, then come back to us?" she asked.

"I would dearly love to, Nell, but the risks are too great. The women, children, the priest, and Joe here a wanted man. No, it is a chance we cannot possibly take. I agree with James fully. It is our only hope. My father has, in effect, promised my hand in marriage to Justice Stewart. It is a social and political arrangement and nothing will deter him from it. Sadly, James is prime target. In his hate and fury he will think that we are fleeing to Dublin and consequently pursue us. Our hearts must not rule our minds at this point."

Marjorie knew that Kitty was right. It was their only chance, risky though it was. Mag felt afraid for them both.

"May God help you both somehow, and may we here have the good sense not to be taking our safety for granted in the future," she said wisely.

They were all agreed that it was fortunate the priest was not present to hear their plans for they would be afraid that he would divulge information under torture. He was a gentle soul and they respected him for it.

"Well, are we all agreed?" James asked with a faint smile.

They nodded in agreement aware of the chill reality that was coming towards them like some nightmare that would change everything for them forever. Nell shifted the black kettle over the flames, and Joe pulled back the bolt from the door and opened it quietly. He peered up and down the village that lay in the summer dusk, turf smoke pervading the air. A dog howled as it looked at the full moon rising out of the distant sea.

"A beautiful May night," he announced cheerily, as he rejoined the group who were eating scones that Hannah had made earlier.

"Never was a good cook, Lord help me. Now boiling rabbits or chickens or the like, now that was different altogether. But sweet cakes. Wouldn't know where to start with them," Mag said as she helped herself to yet another scone. Marjorie looked at the ceiling thinking of Mag plucking a chicken.

"But look at the wonderful talent that you have. All the remedies you make that have helped relieve the suffering of so many. You don't give yourself enough credit, Mag," Kitty assured her.

"You know, you are quite right, my lady. I never thought of it all that way. Now, I want to get some liniment for lame horses ready. We don't want your horses going down on a hoof now, do we? And perhaps a little something for their wind, as they will want lungs like potato sacks to carry you both swiftly and safely away," and she then left them to go to her herb chest, singing as she did so. Soon everyone was gone about their evening tasks, leaving Marjorie and Hannah alone at the fire.

"You will miss her, Hannah, I think."

"Yes I will, Marjorie. I will miss her a great deal. Even today with Williams here it felt as if everyone I ever have known is leaving me. But it's Lady Catherine I am most worried about, travelling with James. Why can't she be content to let him go alone? He would travel faster, and he too would have an easier mind knowing that she would be safe here."

Marjorie looked at her pondering.

"In one sense I agree with what you say, but as they said themselves, the purpose is to get the attention away from the village. Besides, if she were found here she would be brought back under force to Oak hall, a prisoner perhaps, and you with her. She is afraid of that father of hers, Hannah. Who could blame her? One can't reason with a madman, can they?"

"You are quite right. The man is gone beyond all reasoning, and would even charge me with something if he could do so. Oh poor Lady Edwina! When I think of the beautiful person she was, and he so happy then with her! And now he is a lunatic. But Kitty loves James and a year ago only I warned her of what might happen. Do you think she would listen to me?"

Marjorie laughed.

"When we were her age, did we ever listen to anyone, Hannah? I will never forget how that Bartley Finnegan made his advances towards me. God, I shiver when I look back on it. He was like some wild thing off the mountain, the look in his eyes still haunts me some nights."

It was now Hannah's turn to laugh, much to Marjorie's indignation.

"Thanks be to God he is dead, or I'd never have known a night's sleep. And poor Sergeant Cosgrave dead too. I was so glad the evening he arrested Finnegan. The relief I felt. 'Safe' is the word I'm looking for, Hannah."

So many are going to die, Hannah thought, and where will it ever end for me? She wondered would there ever be a future at Oak Hall again. Perhaps I should have gone to Dublin to end my days, but she was determined not to leave Kitty's side until the end, whatever that end might be. It didn't bear thinking about. Again she thought of Lady Edwina. She never once suspected where her daughter's afternoon rides took her, or to whom! A revolutionary, and that is what James is. She was now grateful to God that she had never told her former mistress anything. She then put her hand in her pocket and took out the beautiful necklace. She fingered the rubies and emeralds set amidst the holly leaves of gold.

"Beautiful, Marjorie, isn't it?" she said, caressing it.

"Yes, it is beautiful. You must have meant a great deal to Williams, Hannah," Marjorie said gently.

"Oh, I don't know, and then sometimes I think that perhaps I might have."

"May I take a look at it, Hannah?"

"Of course you can, and try it on also Marjorie and let me see what it looks like at a distance."

In handing over the necklace, it slipped from Marjorie's fingers.

"Oh my very clumsy hands, Hannah! She exclaimed as she picked it up from the floor and looked at it lest it had been damaged. As she turned it over carefully, she noticed Hannah's name engraved on the back of one of the gold holly leaves, then she read the remaining words.

– TO HANNAH WITH LOVE. 1770. –

"My goodness, Hannah, look at what I have discovered. The necklace is engraved. Here, read it for yourself, my dear."

Hannah read the inscription on each of the leaves and tears filled her eyes.

"Oh Seymour, 1770, almost thirty years ago now. With... love... Seymour..." she repeated.

"Well, Hannah, if that's not proof enough for you. He did love you after all and like yourself never found the words easy to say."

"Well, Seymour Williams, if God spares me out of this bloody conflict I will go and find you and tell you the same as you have told me," she said slowly.

"Now, that's what I call sense," Marjorie said, "and furthermore you should be going with him, never mind waiting to see if you will live through the rebellion."

Hannah knew she was speaking the truth, and her heart ached now with the conflict within it.

"No, I can't go yet. Something tells me that I am needed more here for the young mistress. When I know that she is safe, then I will go to Seymour."

Marjorie admired her loyalty and strength.

"Very well, Hannah. But rest assured I will give you no peace until you do go to Seymour. You both deserve happiness after a lifetime missing it.|

They embraced and laughed and Hannah decided that they both needed a cup of strong tea.

"And add some of that French brandy, Hannah," Marjorie insisted. "We must toast your love and a safe journey to Seymour."

* * *

Back at Oak Hall Williams locked the shutters. He was relieved to know that his long absence had not been noticed. The food trays were almost untouched, left outside the study door, and the air smelled of brandy. It told its own story.

Williams felt the effects of the long ride, for his body ached. Yet he prided himself in his accomplishment. It had been a daring mission. He was not without knowing that should Lord Foldsworth discover his activities of the day he would consider it treasonous. He calmed his anxious mind of such thoughts, and slowly made his way towards the kitchen to have something to eat. He felt hungry and had a generous helping of fresh salmon and cold potato. He thought back over his visit to the mountain village, and how unreal it had almost seemed. Finding Lady Catherine living amidst such poverty. The people were indeed pleasant, though some a trifle odd, he mused, recalling old Mag. However, her ladyship is very well respected and Hannah was taking great care of her also and one must be grateful for that at least!

And then there was James...

He stopped eating and gazed at the dying embers of the great fire. James de Lacey, he repeated to himself. Lady Edwina would have liked him, had he been of the correct rank. He was handsome, and had a quality of bearing that was quite impressive too. The wrong class and part of that revolutionary group. God knows it would drive any father out of his senses. His thoughts then drifted to Justice Stewart, and he somewhat reluctantly admitted to himself that her ladyship would be better off with the handsome rebel. Will they ever escape, or live through the rebellion?

Young love seldom, if ever, recognises reality. But he knew the determination of his master to regain his daughter. It was a dangerous issue, and he tried to keep his fears under control. He thought of Hannah and wished he had asked her to go with him. He admitted his lack of courage and then also knew that she would never have left the young mistress, for such was her dedication to her.

In the privacy of his bedroom, Williams double-checked his two saddlebags, packed in readiness for his silent departure. He felt excitement mount and then panic in case Lord Foldsworth would change his plans and not go away as expected. His responsibilities, held so dear over so many years, no longer made any sense to him, and lying in bed he prayed for the people of the mountain village. He prayed separately for his mistress who lay in the church vault.

Lord Foldsworth stumbled to his bedroom drunk and he threw himself upon the four-poster bed. He didn't bother undressing. He cried out in the night for his beloved Edwina, as the great silent mansion stood shrouded in the fog of the May night. It was dawn before he surrendered to sleep.

His dreams were a strange mixture of seeing Lady Edwina gather roses and offer them to him, and then seeing Kitty laughing at her mother's gesture. He awoke with a sudden jerk, the stale taste of brandy in his mouth and a raging fire of hate towards the man who had taken his daughter's love away from him. The thought of vengeance comforted him as the morning light tinged the ceiling with the scarlet colour of the summer dawn. He again fell into fitful sleep and he awoke some hour's later feeling elated. He pondered the change of mood and then realised the reason.

Tomorrow I shall have my Kitty back here in this house where she belongs, and the rebel safely in prison.

Williams heard the bell from his master's room clang loudly.

"Good morning, sir."

"Good morning, Williams. I will breakfast in twenty minutes and then I shall speak to you in my study."

"Certainly, sir. I shall come when summoned. Thank you, sir."

He contemplated the transformation once again in his master. It changed from one day to another, he thought.

When finally summoned to the study, Lord Foldsworth discussed the coming of the guests and, satisfied that all was in readiness, he then dismissed his butler. For the remainder of that day Lord Foldsworth did not ring for service. Williams knew that his departure the following day must be timed with great precision. He would quietly leave Oak Hall when the guests had lunched, minimising the risk of his absence being noticed until evening. The planned ambush at the ring fort was to be later that evening and he had no intention of being present to witness the crazed outrage that would follow the failure of the mission.

Lady de Winters would be coming on a fool's errand, despite his master's high hopes and plans for it to be otherwise. Hmm! Wanting Lady Catherine to see 'the folly of her ways' indeed! How ridiculous! Williams found himself wishing the young couple in love every luck in their escape.

That evening, Williams walked throughout the great house recalling his years there and the countless memories it held for him. He looked at the portrait of Lady Edwina. Feelings of sadness engulfed him as he gazed at the beautiful woman dressed in green velvet, with a spray of roses on her lap.

He then considered the uproar that would ensue when his absence at Oak Hall was discovered. He planned on telling the stable lad that he was going to town to enquire of a wine order that had not been delivered. The story was quite feasible, he knew, as only a dozen bottles of claret remained in the cellar. It will buy me time, he thought, as every hour will be vital. He had already put aside some old clothes and a black wig. It would alter his appearance greatly. The sense of adventure welled up within him as he planned the finer details of his journey.

On the mountainside, James and Kitty lay in a warm embrace against the largest stone of the ring fort. Dusk was creeping over the valleys beneath them as the sun deserted them. The ravens wheeled as usual in the sky above them, their loud protests filling the air.

"It will be a long time, Kitty, before we will have such peace again, such freedom," James said, his finger outlining one of her eyebrows. Looking deep into the eyes of the woman he loved, he kissed her tenderly.

"I know, my love. We will miss this mountain very much. Make sure, James de Lacey, that you survive this battle, for you know I could never live without you. It is unthinkable, unbearable; my whole world would be gone. Everything gone."

"Kitty, you know I will be back for you. For it's the thought of you that will make me survive. Besides, you must have more confidence in this rebel who holds you."

She tried to laugh.

"A rebel! It makes you all the more exciting, James, to think of you as a rebel! I sometimes laugh when I think that had I known the truth when we first met, I would have been frantic. Innocent, wasn't I? Then, to think that I almost lost you after mamma's death. I will never forget that day in the church. I was so confused and afraid. Hannah sorted me out, you know. Made me look at the truth. Have you never noticed the rebel in me, James?"

"Yes, I have. I even think that the rebellion you are involved in is greater than my own."

"Really James, I never thought of it like that," she replied.

"Well now you may! You are forsaking, Kitty, what you know, and so clear about what you want. We, on the other hand, are striving towards a place called freedom. Our poets have spoken about it. We dream about it. And we are pursuing a dream, as our reality has been such a hell."

"Yes, it is a hell for them all," she added quietly.

"Tell me, Kitty, when did you first begin to realise the plight of the ordinary people? Was it long before you met me?"

Kitty looked at the flashes her memory presented to her, so many of them events and places past. One incident was somehow clearer than the rest.

"When I was five years old, James, I recall coming home from Jessica Davenport's birthday party. I was in the carriage with mamma. It was a magnificent summer's evening. As the carriage was being driven home at a leisurely pace, I saw a woman with two small children sitting on the side of the road. It was a narrow road, and Philip, who was driving, cracked the whip in warning for the woman and her children to stay clear of the carriage.

"Mamma rebuked him for his harsh action and intolerance and ordered Philip to stop the carriage. The woman was finding it difficult to walk, and we later discovered that she had a very badly infected leg. My mother, having spoken to her, told her to remain where she was and she would have a cart sent which would carry her to the town she was trying to walk to. I remember her thanking my mother profusely. I sat upright and asked my mother, 'Why do those people not have a carriage like we have?'. It was perhaps the first time I actually noticed there was a difference between my family and most people in the area, and I felt confused and wondered why. Then my mother said, 'They are poor people, my darling, and we are not'. That was all she said, no more, no less. Just a simple reply that said everything. I remember thinking that it was wrong somehow. As I grew older, I realised the trap that poverty is. I learned that the people were forbidden education, true freedom of religion, and that the right to property was totally beyond their means and always would be, unless..." and she paused as she surveyed the vast tracts of land now fading in the twilight of the evening. "Unless," she continued, unless they took back what had been theirs initially before Oliver Cromwell came to this land."

James sat up, quite amazed at the honesty of her statement.

"Kitty, since we first met, and even while in France, you never expressed such honest, or should I say heartfelt truth before. Why now?"

"Simple, James. For the first time I have found something I value as real and truthful. A life of privilege can be very empty, very lonely, you know. Did you ever ask yourself, James, how many marriages actually genuinely love? Very few! Our marriages are arranged from the time we are children for the most part. And that is solely to keep land and money within the ascendancy class. Look at it another way, James. Viscount Stewart was born into wealth and privilege. Joe Gilltrap was not! What's the actual difference between both men? One has the social graces that are the trappings of wealth, Joe has not. He simply did not have the opportunity of education and all the other things money can buy."

"Yet Kitty," James said, almost in defence of his friend, "Joe has found love, a wife, a family and contentment."

"Very true, James," Kitty conceded, "but you are forgetting one thing, James, and it is this. Joe Gilltrap can be hanged tomorrow for his beliefs, whereas Viscount Stewart can not!"

It was chilling for James to realise he was in the exact same position, no different.

"Stewart is a very dangerous man, Kitty. I dread to think of him as an administrator of justice!"

"Agreed James, and I dread to think of him as a husband, should my father have his way!"

They lay together as the stars appeared overhead, and made love with a passion and urgency they had not risked since their time in Bordeaux. As they strolled back to the village through the heather, the pungent smell of turf smoke filled the air.

"It has been lovely to live here, James, with our friends chatting every night."

"Yes, I must say I have loved every day of it. I find Mag very fascinating, such wisdom for one who appears almost in her dotage, if one were foolish enough to think it."

They both laughed with a warm affection for the old woman.

"I am frightened about tomorrow, James," Kitty said falteringly.

"I know you are, my love. But we must go through with our plans nonetheless.

It's the only hope we have of diverting your father's attention from the village. Looking at that aspect of it will make it all somehow easier to face."

"It's the meeting of my father, again, James. I have such dreadful memories of that last day in the village when you were arrested. The humiliation of it, the cruelty of it."

They were both silent, recalling the events of that dreadful day for them both.

"Have you ever regretted renouncing him publicly, Kitty? It was such a final step to take, and all the village present to witness it," James said quietly.

"No, I have no regrets, James, absolutely none. Of course I have often thought back on it. I still recall it all vividly. The shame I feel far outweighs my anger and hatred of him. That day I could in no possible way come to terms with the fact that he was actually my father, such was his behaviour. He was a total stranger that day. The father I knew was kind, considerate and understanding. All I could see in his face that day was sheer hate, revenge and a frightening thirst for vengeance. All the things that make monsters of people, that twist them beyond what they once were. If he had truly loved me, he would have reasoned with me. Even to this day his plans are to have me caged like a bird at Oak Hall, only to be forced into a marriage with that detestable Stewart."

James took her in his arms and held her close, stroking her hair lovingly.

"I am so very fortunate to have the love of such a wonderful woman," and they kissed with tenderness from a love that had no limits in either of them.

* * *

Kitty awoke in the early dawn filled with dread. It was the day she feared most somehow, and as she washed and dressed, she attempted to calm the fears that swept through her heart. She talked to herself, attempting to reassure her turbulent mind. Her fears were greater than just the meeting of her father. Far greater. Yet she reasoned it is only a matter of crossing paths for moments, just long enough for him to recognise them before they galloped away in the direction he was meant to believe they were travelling towards.

At breakfast there was little said. Everyone was in subdued form, each thinking their own thoughts and saying little. Mag came in late to join them, and handed James a small pouch.

"Now, James, for the horses' feet. Just rub it in every few hours. And this bottle is for their feed. It will give them the wind they need."

She cast a glance at Kitty, who was eating little, she noticed.

"Thanks, Mag. I will do all you say, and thanks for taking the trouble," was all James managed to say.

Father Doyle blessed them both before they left the table. Hannah was very upset and tried to conceal it, in vain. Nell gave Kitty a parcel of bread and meat and then Marjorie embraced them both.

"You take good care of yourselves now, and don't do anything foolish. We will meet when it's the time," she said philosophically, struggling with her fears.

The morning was overcast and dull, with the early fog not having yet cleared. Joe came down the village with their horses, saddled and ready.

"I've just shod the pair of them, so you should have no worries for a while," he said assuredly, not able to look at either James or Kitty directly. He knew he would miss them both a great deal and felt awkward with goodbyes.

"Thanks Joe," James said, extending his hand to his friend. "Goodbye Joe, Nell and all of you. Don't worry, the next time we meet it will be on the great day itself for Ireland," he said, attempting to smile, swallowing hard.

Kitty embraced Hannah.

"Now Hannah, you must be sensible. You know we will meet soon again and it won't be half as long as before. So cheer up, and have your lacework well finished by then," she said in a calm, matter-of-fact tone.

"Of course I will, Miss Kitty. Just promise me one thing," her old servant asked.

"Anything Hannah, just ask," Kitty said, holding her faithful companion closely.

Hannah stood back from her, looking at her through a mist of tears.

"Just this. Please don't provoke your father, just nod your head or smile or... anything. But say nothing to him, for his fury could provoke him to anything, my dear."

"You need not worry, Hannah. I will be more than careful," Kitty assured her.

They mounted their horses and bid everyone goodbye. Slowly they rode from the village, looking back at the small little group who stood forlornly waving them off. With their gradual descent, the village disappeared from view and they looked at the clouds of fog before them that hadn't as yet lifted. The usual great expanse of the plains beneath them remained obscured from view. Oak Hall should have been visible directly ahead of them, but it, too, remained hidden in the fog. James was the first to speak.

"I hope we will be able to make a vantage point of Oak Hall, Kitty, in order to calculate our distance to meet your father. If we were able to spot him leaving, it would greatly help things. The alternative is more risky in that we would have to hide in a grove on the avenue and wait there. god only knows if there is someone doing patrol duty. Let's hope this fog will lift."

"Well, James, if there are men patrolling, are we not lucky there is this fog? After all, we would be very noticeable if the morning was as clear as all the others we have had!" she said in her usual practical tone.

"Sensible as ever, Lady Catherine," he joked.

Beneath them, however, five men patrolling the area were just out of earshot of them as they made their way to town. The fog indeed was a fortunate gesture of nature.

Lord Foldsworth's horse stood in the stable, saddled and awaiting its rider, who slowly walked down the great stairway of his mansion. He stopped and looked at the portrait of his wife, and smiled wanly as he stood there.

"She is coming home today, Edwina. I know in my heart that it is what you would want. Let us hope she will have the grace to come like the lady you reared her to be!"

Williams met him at the bottom of the stairs by chance.

"Williams, I shall be late for lunch today. So please excuse me to Lady de Winters and the others. I shall join them a little later. Is everything in readiness for this evening?"

"Yes, your lordship. Everything."

"Good. Oh, I trust Lady Catherine's room also?"

"Yes, your lordship. It, too, is ready as you instructed," Williams replied calmly.

"Excellent. So I shall have late lunch, Williams. Kindly remind cook." Lord Foldsworth said, tapping his riding crop on his boot.

"There will be no need to remind cook, your lordship, for it is cold salmon and meats today. So your lordship will have it directly as requested," Williams said, thinking that this minor delay could jeopardise his planned departure.

"Very well, Williams. Then I shan't need you, shall I?"

"Not unless you ring, your lordship, of course," Williams replied, now feeling more anxious.

"Not at all, Williams. I am sure you will be more than busy with the preparations for tonight. Don't forget Justice Stewart will also be here. I did mention that to you, did I not?"

"Yes sir, you did. All will be in readiness, your lordship, as commanded," Williams reassured him.

His employer walked to the front of the house where his horse stood stamping impatiently, held by a stable lad.

"Blasted fog, doesn't do a thing to impress the visitors," murmured Lord Foldsworth.

Mounting, he slowly made his way down the avenue, admiring the rhododendrons in their scarlet blossoms. The beech trees were magnificent in their delicate shade of green and the oaks sturdy-looking in darker colours.

Slowly the sun began to emerge from the thick shroud of fog, while blackbirds filled the air with their shrill tones.

One year ago, he thought, we were all so happy going down this avenue on our journey to Hampshire. What a difference a year makes! My wife seven months dead almost, and my daughter gone with a rebel! What a nightmare! At least Kitty will be back, he consoled himself. Back in her bed this very night, too!

From their outpost, James and Kitty saw him rounding the bend on the avenue and slowly they made their way towards him. The meeting point would be just outside the main gates, where the road some distance south branched north for Dublin and south for the village and then the town.

"Are you ready, Kitty?" James whispered.

"As I ever shall be!" she replied nervously, wishing she could die rather than face her father at that moment.

They halted their horse's yards from the main gates, and stood patiently listening to the approaching hoof beats of the now trotting horse that approached them. Lord Foldsworth looked at the gates ahead of him, making a mental note to have them scraped and painted as soon as possible. Shabby gates always look bad, he thought, can't have that with a wedding approaching! The thought lifted his spirits greatly.

For a moment he thought he was hallucinating. Behold, before him he could plainly see his daughter and rebel lover. He stopped aghast at the sight, thinking every sense in his body had abandoned him. Reality had suddenly disappeared, he thought. This isn't possible or true. But the expression on his daughter's face assured him that it was not so.

"Kitty, Kitty, is that really you?" he said as if he was drunk.

"Yes, it is me... with James, on our way to Dublin to be married..." she replied with a strength that surprised her. She looked at him with derision, and his mouth fell open with this further shock.

"Good morning," James said almost teasingly.

"How dare you even address me, you rebel bastard," Lord Foldsworth replied with the venom that reminded Kitty of their previous encounter. "Dublin to be married, Kitty? So you still persist in this lunacy that will never succeed. You are even sillier than I thought! But you will never see Dublin, either of you. Tonight, my dear, you will be safe in Oak hall, and as for you, you Fenian, you will have the rats of Wexford jail for company."

James laughed and looking at Kitty said, "It's time we were on our way, my love," and without any further comment, they both rode within feet of Lord Foldsworth, heading for the northbound road.

Lord Foldsworth's mind reeled in confusion, helplessness and rage. He did not know what to do. He galloped after them for a mile or more and then stopped suddenly. What am I doing,? he thought, spitting with rage on the ground beneath him. No, I shall go to town and have the militia follow them, head them off. He spurred his confused horse towards the town at breakneck speed.

James and Kitty, aware of his turnabout and the obvious reason for it, slowed their mounts.

"God, James, what a nightmare! He is still raging wild, madder than ever. I should have said nothing about marriage. I don't know what came over me," she said breathlessly.

"No point worrying now, Kitty. We must change route rapidly or we are doomed," he said apprehensively.

They rode some further six miles and then veered sharply where the river came cascading from the mountains. They encountered a herd of cattle and rode amidst them to confuse their hoof marks. After a further half-mile they left the cattle and jumped sharply onto the stony ground of the hillside where they pressed their horses uphill without mercy. They had to, Kitty thought, for their pursuers would be soon on their heels.

The wild mountains of Aughavannagh rose sharply above them as they kept up their steady pace. The pass lay before them, which they would have to go through to be lost from view. The horses panted, but nonetheless they made great ground. An hour had passed now since their encounter with Lord Foldsworth, and they knew he would not be too far behind them. They prayed the patrol would be unable to pick up their tracks, the ground being dry and dusty with the fine weather. They finally dismounted and lay against the giant boulders, breathless and anxious.

The horses were shielded from view lest their profiles betray their location. They looked down to the valley beneath them. From the dizzy height, Kitty thought, the scene was breathtaking.

"Oh God, James, is it not magnificent? I never knew such a wonderful place existed," she said in awe.

"Yes, it is one of the most beautiful places I, too, have ever been in. Look at the waterfalls, Kitty..."

She looked at the silver ribbon of water cascading down the sides of the mountain on the opposite side of the valley.

A fine mist rose from the turbulent waters, where a rainbow shot towards the heavens, its colours clear against the green mountains to the right.

"So beautiful, James. So very lovely," she sighed.

"We are supposed to be looking for our pursuers, Kitty. We must not become lax, my darling. So far there is nothing down there. I am just going to check the horses' feet, and put some of Mag's ointment on them," he said, thinking how fortunate they had been to make such a clean break from Lord Foldsworth. Kitty took out some of the bread and cold meat they had, and placed it on the rock that acted as a table for them.

The horses had suffered no damage, which James deemed very fortunate considering the rough terrain they had just covered.

"No damage to them, Kitty – the horses, that is," he said, looking down at the valley below them.

"Good. Now let's have something to eat while we still can, James. This chicken looks delicious," Kitty said, eating a piece with relish.

"Hmm, you are quite right my love, it is delicious," he replied, without finishing his sentence, for in the distance he heard the loud shouts of men calling one to the other. They both hid behind the larger rock, peering through the narrow gap that led into the valley floor at the base of the mountains.

"Good God," James whispered, "how did they get here so quickly?"

Kitty just looked in shock at the large military following and her heart sank in despair.

"What are we going to do, James?" she asked quietly.

"I don't know, Kitty. The question is, do they know we are up here, for that will decide all for us."

They watched as the group of horsemen gathered together at the bottom of the mountain. Some minutes passed before anything else happened. They seemed to be discussing their position. Then slowly the men beneath them spread out in a long line and began a slow ascent of the mountain.

"Oh Christ," said James, "they know where we are, Kitty. We must act fast. Let me see. Our only chance now is to head back south. They are in no hurry for they know we have little option but to do so. Look at the two men riding out of the valley. See them? Well, they will have a further group approach us now from the south to corner us. Oh God... help us think!"

He pondered their position again.

"If we travel west Kitty, we will go near Glendalough, and perhaps with luck make it to Dublin. Hurry, we must go now."

Hurriedly putting the last of the bread and meat in the saddle pack, they travelled the mountain ridge, hidden from the pursuers beneath them. Slowly they made progress until they came to a lakeshore at the base of the mountain facing west.

"We must cross the lake, Kitty. It is our only hope. It will give us at least an extra hour if we can do so," James said in desperation now.

Without further hesitation they plunged their horses into the cold waters and headed them to the far shoreline.

"What an unexpected bath, James," Kitty laughed.

"Just keep going, Kitty, go with all your might," and their horses lunged through the sometimes deep, sometimes shallow, lake.

Finally they reached the opposite shore and galloped their horses into the nearest wood. There they tethered them and then returned to scan the opposite side of the lake for their pursuers. High on the plateau opposite them the military posse could be clearly seen now. James wondered if they had watched them swim the lake, but they were making no move to descend, he thought.

"I think we may have just about outwitted them, Kitty. I don't think they saw us swim across the lake. We will know for definite, moments from now."

As they sat huddled behind the trees, looking up at the sheer slopes opposite them, the horsemen slowly began to retreat.

Kitty sighed a huge sigh of relief.

"That's one ride I shall not forget, James!" she said, looking at how wet they both were. He lay back on the thick bed of moss and groaned aloud.

"What is it, James?" Kitty asked in alarm.

"It is you, my darling. Look at what I have made you – a fugitive, a common fugitive like myself. We are now the hunted! And what are we going to do now?" he said, looking at their dishevelled appearance.

"A fugitive with a future!" she exclaimed laughing. Her good spirits dispelled his momentary gloom.

"Well then, Mrs de Lacey, let's start working on it," he replied, taking her by the hand and leading her back to their horses.

The swim had refreshed them considerably and they were ready to travel further. Mounting, they slowly made their way through the great oak woods. Their clothes dried in the hot late afternoon sunshine, and they talked little. They rode through dried out riverbeds, attempting to conceal their tracks as much as possible.

"We will have to rest the horses soon James, or they will be of no use tomorrow, I'm afraid," Kitty said, beginning to feel tired herself now.

"Yes, you're right, and we too need to rest, my love. Is there much food left?"

"There should be, James, but I'm afraid it's wet chicken and wet bread! Not a lot, but better than nothing.

They found a clearing where lush grass grew in abundance and they let the horses graze, having unsaddled them. They then sat down and Kitty placed the remainder of the food on the cloth it was wrapped in, spreading it on the grass before them. They ate what was left of it, and lay back in the evening sunshine, tired after the day's hectic pursuit.

"I don't think we were cut out for this life James, somehow. Though as Hannah always said, 'It's surprising what one will do when one has to'. Hannah was always so wise! I wonder what she would say if she saw us now," Kitty said dreamily.

"More importantly still, I hope they didn't go to the village, Kitty. God grant they didn't, that the others may be spared.

There will be great alarm when Marcus reports us missing, not having turned up," he said agitatedly. James did not like plans going wrong. He thought it bad strategy. But then, he reasoned, who would have expected that upwards to sixty men would be in such fast pursuit?

When night came they lit a fire and slept fitfully in each other's arms, waking and talking and then sleeping again.

* * *

Consternation was rampant at Oak Hall. The distinguished guests arrived to be met by a demented scullery maid, who babbled something about Williams having gone off to town and not returning. Lady de Winters looked at Lord Foldsworth and wondered why on earth she had agreed to come to the home of a madman. Being too late to leave, she resigned herself to staying the night.

Lady Attlee thought she had never come upon such a delightful piece of gossip. The butler running away! Lady Catherine absconded into the wilds of the mountains with a rebel lover! Viscount Stewart shouting and raving about not marrying Lady Catherine now or ever! And Lord Foldsworth, drunk and inconsolable in his chair by the fire.

Lord Attlee sat back and took in the scene. He then looked at his wife and whispered: "Who would ever have thought it, dear? Things are so bad at Oak Hall that even the butler fled!"

Lady Attlee felt guilty, for her husband had not wanted to come on this visit. She had insisted, and she now regretted it.

The unfortunate scullery maid had come to the dining room with cold meat and some hot vegetables, to the horror of her master.

"Williams! Another traitor!" he fumed.

"He should be strung up, too," added Justice Stewart. "And who on earth alerted them in the first place, Charles?"

But his host was now snoring loudly, much to Lady Attlee's amusement.

"Poor fellow," she chuckled, "nothing seems to work out for him since poor Edwina died."

"Why did I ever get mixed up with him?" Justice Stewart drawled, having drunk too much brandy.

"Might have been better for him had he died at the hunting accident," Lord Attlee said dourly.

There was a knock on the door and the scullery maid entered the drawing room.

She looked at the sight before her and felt more nervous than she ever thought she could be.

"What is it now, girl?" Lady Attlee asked impatiently.

"More wine, ma'am?" she asked faintly.

"Brandy, girl! It's called brandy, not wine! For heaven's sake go to bed. Go now, girl!" Lady Attlee said, rising from her chair in anger.

"Good heavens, what is it all coming to, Johanna?"

But Joanne de Winters sat back thinking. "Poor Kitty, could one blame her for running from this lunacy, from these men? She wondered. She was quite right, she assured herself. At least she had someone to run with! All my life I have been stuck with stumped up little peacocks! Not a man among them, she thought. Now a rebel! In love with a rebel, Kitty! At least you found love. And she found herself envying her friend. Where are they now? She pondered. Making love passionately in a cave, I hope. Long may it last, yet I doubt it somehow, with warrants for their arrest gone to every town and village in Ireland, accompanied with clear descriptions of them both. It will be a brief honeymoon for them, she realised.

"A ha'penny for your thoughts, my dear," Lady Attlee chirped mischievously.

"Not a lot, I'm afraid. Only where are our rooms and the hope we will not be attacked in the night, Lady Attlee," she replied.

Amidst all the excitement Lady Attlee hadn't thought of an attack on Oak hall and she shrieked in alarm.

"Oh for the love of God, Lady Attlee, please stop your hysterical nonsense," Justice Stewart bellowed.

Lord Attlee stood up instantly.

"How dare you, Stewart, address my wife so! Incredibly bad manners, my man! Come, my dearest, and we shall leave this bad-mannered gentleman to his drinks. We will depart early and breakfast in town. Goodnight, Lady de Winters, and I do hope you will leave with us in the morning," Lord Attlee said softly to her.

Justice Stewart dismissed them without saying goodnight.

"Spoiled brat, always was, that fellow. The damn nerve of him hoping to warm his backside at Oak Hall! Poor Edwina would turn in her grave," Lord Attlee said for his hearing.

"That pair irritate me beyond words – one full of old rattle-tattle, the other one doting, with little sense," Justice Stewart said to Lady de Winter.

"Oh come now, Timothy, you are very poor company tonight! And rude also. You must not let your temper lash at people so," she said calmly.

"Temper? Why wouldn't I have such a foul mood this night? Everything gone wrong once again. Kitty still persisting in her obsession with that rebel, and I still hoping to have her for my wife. I must be quite mad, I am beginning to think. And Foldsworth seems to have lost his grip of things totally to boot!"

He stood up and helped himself to another brandy.

"Then his butler high-tails it off today, with an excuse of going to town to see the wine merchant! Another blasted spy in the camp no doubt. I'll catch up on that fellow sometime and have him transported. That will soon bring him to his spit."

Lady de Winter looked at him, realising that he was as evil-minded now as Charles Foldsworth. She decided that she would leave with the Attlee's early the next morning.

"It's time for me to retire, Timothy. Too tired to join you for another nightcap I'm afraid," she said, walking towards the door.

"Joanna, wait a moment. There is something I would like to ask you," Justice Stewart said seriously.

"What is it, Timothy?" she asked, standing in the centre of the room.

"It's about Kitty. Do you think I stand any chance with her... marrying her, I mean, or is it a pipe dream with me?"

She looked into the eyes of Timothy Stewart before replying.

"Do you want me to tell you the truth, Timothy?"

"Of course I do, Joanna. I'm quite serious, you know!" he said earnestly.

"Well, the truth you shall have. It is obvious that Kitty has found someone she really believes in, and loves. She has abandoned everything for this man, rebel and all though he is! I can't possibly imagine her leaving him easily having gone this far with him and renouncing her father, so I am told," she said, hoping to hear further details of the sketchy story she was told months ago.

"Yes, she renounced him in front of the entire village and he did likewise with her. Must have been some sight, the pair of them. Imagine the Foldsworths arguing like drunks on the street! Good heavens, did we ever think it would come to this with them? Still, I suppose they were both suffering the loss of Edwina. At least we can excuse them on those grounds. So you think my efforts with Kitty futile then?"

"It's not that your efforts are futile, Timothy. Love is something that happens between two people, not just one of them. So you may have strong feelings for her, but what of Kitty for you? Was there ever anything between you in the past?" she asked curiously.

"Not much. We shared a great secret once, and still do I believe. But we were never in love, if that's what you mean. We never had the chance, you see. Odd isn't it, that I love her for her courage. She is such a strong-willed person. There is something else I cannot quite put my finger on, it's elusiveness. Perhaps it's that which fascinates me about her."

"Well, Timothy, it takes a lot more than fascination to keep two people together and while it may develop into a deep love, it still takes time to do so. Believe me, forcing her is the last thing in the world you need to do, for nothing will ever come of it. She would come to hate you in time, not love you. So you must consider the matter well."

He looked at her and knew she was right in what she said.

" Her rebel dead is the only way she will ever look at me again, Joanna."

She looked at him with hidden derision.

"So what you are saying, Timothy, is that you will kill her lover in the hope that she will turn to you?"

"Well, more or less, I suppose, though that fellow is one of the main organisers of this bloody rebellion that is in the boiling pot. Why shouldn't he be executed for it? The others will be when they are caught eventually. It's not solely because he is her lover, though it's a great part of it."

She walked towards the door and turned around again.

"The truth of the matter, Timothy, is that you can't wait to have this rebel captured, just like Charles Foldsworth. You both despise him for the one reason. He has what you both want... Kitty! To think that you are both willing to kill for her return. It makes me quite sick. Did neither of you ever hear the saying, 'He who sows the wind, reaps the whirlwind?' Goodnight Timothy," and she was suddenly gone from the room.

Silly woman, just like the rest of them, thought Viscount Stewart. "Hmm, winds... whirlwinds! Such balderdash! Listening to too much servants' gossip, the trouble with a lot of them today. What the hell would she know of love anyway? Worse to ask her! With luck I shall have that rebel in the next week or two. The reward should see to that! You will always have those who would sell any of you for a couple of miserable pounds! Whit that, he went to his room and lay thinking in his bed how things had once again gone so dreadfully wrong.

Still, he thought, it's just like the fox that outwits the hounds. Some day he simply makes that one mistake. And my rebel lad, you too will do the same!

* * *

Meanwhile, Williams lay in bed at a comfortable Inn. It was warm and clean, he noted. Dinner had been ample and delicious. The staff were very pleasant too, he thought. The landlady was charm personified and her husband a kindly fellow. Nothing too much trouble for him to do for his guests. He felt weary, more from the strain of his escape and the worry of being followed. That's why he had changed his route at the last moment. Dublin was such an obvious choice of route and he knew he could have been pursued, a risk he could not take bearing in mind Lord Foldsworth's encounter that morning with Kitty and James. There had been uproar in the stables, with him looking for several horses to be saddled within moments. The commotion had been dreadful for the lads there, who were not used to such abuse from their employer. No, the Dublin route would have been inviting death, he thought. He blew out his candle and settled to sleep for the first time in over fifty years outside the familiarity of Oak Hall. It was a great feeling, he thought, to be served meals for a change and to go to bed not having to dress in the night if the servant's bell clanged.

Williams tried to keep the anxiety of arrest out of his mind. It was a terrifying prospect! Justice Stewart would revel in him being questioned and interrogated in an attempt to link him with the rebellion. Damn and curse that fellow. How did Lord Foldsworth ever choose him for company, he asked himself. And then to think that he was assuming that I would continue as butler to him! The very idea of it! Eventually he slept, only to toss restlessly with vivid dreams of being chained to a wall, unable to free himself.

James awoke well before dawn, and lighting the fire, he baked some trout he managed to hand fished in the river before it entered the lake. When it was cooked, he woke Kitty, who felt cramped and cold.

"Breakfast, my love, served to you by your faithful servant, which he promises to do for the rest of his life," and he laughed heartily.

"Oh James, you do have a sense of humour this morning! I feel as if I slept on stones all night. My bones ache. Still, it's good to be alive," she said, recalling their experience of the previous day.

"Hmm, this is delicious, James. Trout, baked and fresh. Now if we only had some crusty bread it would be heaven!"

"Well, Kitty, we shall have a sumptuous dinner tonight in Dublin and that I promise you. Now, we will have to travel some miles before sunrise. The horses are well rested and the ground will be far easier on them today."

"I will be ready to join you James when I have washed. You needn't worry, I am not taking a bath!" and she embraced him warmly.

They covered over the smouldering fire remains with clay and stones lest it should be discovered and, mounting their horses, rode through the forest until they came out onto the side of a heather-covered plateau.

"Now, let's see... Dublin is northeast of here, so that means I will have to keep the sun to my right shoulder as much as possible. Great navigator I would have made, Kitty. Don't you agree?"

"I would never question your wonderful judgement, O wise one!" She smiled, as she pushed back her hair that the morning wind tossed.

They rode silently as the early sun finally shed its light across the heather plains before them. As they came to the end of level ground ,there was a steep decline into another valley. They stopped abruptly as they saw a patrol less than a mile down the slope. Fortunately they were not sighted, but James quickly grabbed the reins of Kitty's horse, heading it west with his own. They galloped for three miles at breakneck speed, fear gripping their hearts, until they came to a narrow gap between two hills. Here they stopped and looked back to see if by chance they had been sighted and followed. But there was neither sight nor sound of pursuer.

" That was very nearly being the end of us, Kitty. Obviously they are looking for us everywhere. Stupid of me to think we could travel by daylight. It's at night we should be making ground," he said angrily.

"No point in scolding yourself, James. We will have to be extremely careful, that's all. Now let us clear our heads and plan a little better. We are sitting ducks here, no place to hide, no woods, nothing. What are we to do?" she asked, apprehensive at their vulnerability.

"Well, we can't go back to the wood as that will be discovered soon. We will just have to travel further west and hope we can find somewhere secluded."

And in that hope they rode on. For several miles they encountered nobody. They sat by a stream and allowed their horses to drink. They were both tired now and hungry.

"I think that dinner is going to be another night away somehow, Kitty," James said light-heartedly.

"I think you are right, darling. But we must eventually get some food in a village or whatever. There has to be one ahead sooner or later."

Two miles further lay the village of Baltinglass, which they surveyed from the hillside.

"Now, Kitty, I will go down and buy some food and you remain here in the trees. I will only be an hour or so. Don't move from the seclusion, as a lone woman would look very suspicious."

"Rest assured, James, I will be alright. But be careful, and if you sense any danger forget the food. We can live for another day, you know!" she said, wondering if it was even wise for him to go.

He kissed her, and she stroked his face with her gloved hand.

"Be careful, my love."

"I will, Kitty, and I will be with you as I said in less than an hour, so don't move, promise me?"

"I promise you."

He rode out of the clearing looking about anxiously, but there was nobody in sight. Turning back, he waved to her, but she was hidden from view. Kitty looked after him until he was out of sight. She then tethered her horse and sat beneath one of the giant beech trees. The heat of the sun made her feel tired, not having slept well the previous night. Flies swarmed about her horse, which swished its tail restlessly. Kitty slept and was awoken by the sound of a troop of horsemen who were passing the copse where she had gone unnoticed. She gasped in terror as she saw them ride towards the village where James had gone. A huge sense of helplessness filled her. Oh God protect him, she prayed. If only I had not slept I would have seen them coming and could have dashed to the village to warn him. Oh James, James, she wept.

Then to her horror she saw James ascend the brow, riding directly towards the troop. She almost fainted with fear. She clutched her mare, unsure of what to do. She decided to do exactly what James had told her. Don't move, he had said. In the distance now she saw James encountering the troop and he was singing wildly like a drunken man, and she knew it was a ploy on his behalf. The troop seemed to be questioning him, but all she could hear was his wild laughter and then the singing would start once again.

It was a miracle, she thought. He was left there by the troop, his disguise having fooled them. He slowly made his way towards her, still singing loudly, swaying to and fro on his horse in an unbalanced manner. Oh thank God, she wept, thank God.

James got off his horse and swept her off her feet in his arms.

"My darling, did you ever think you would marry such a drunken man?" and he laughed as he buried his face in her hair.

"James, for a moment I thought it was all over. I am not very good at these close encounters with troops. At one point I was going to dash out there."

"And do what, Kitty? Fill in the picture of what they are looking for? A man and woman riding together, the lady, a member of society. Now that would have been foolish, despite the fact that I can understand why you would have wanted to do so. Always remember, my love, in this sort of situation our heads must rule our hearts."

"Still, James, I feel so unsafe. I wish it were night. We would be safer. Hold me James, hold me, until this dreadful fear leaves me."

He cradled her like a small child until her fear subsided.

"Now, Lady Catherine, will you eat some bread and meat and look, a bottle of wine to take the dust from our throats?"

They ate their meal quickly and rode out of the copse away from the direction of the village. In a lonely glen they found a shepherd's winter shelter. It was a two-roomed stone-built hut with a dome-capped roof. There was a hole in the centre that acted as a chimney, and at the rear there was another small shelter, which was for horses.

"Just what we needed Kitty. We will be well hidden from view at least. No-one would ever think of looking here in the summer months," he said assuredly.

"All I want to do is sleep, James. I feel totally exhausted my love."

And without further ado, Kitty lay down on an old heather-filled bed and was soon sleeping soundly. James looked at her, beginning now to feel guilt. Perhaps I should have sent her on to Dublin separately. She would be there by now, safe and sound. Silly of me to expect her to be able to endure all this worry and fear. He looked out of the door of the hut and surveyed the area every few minutes. No point in being caught the second time in one day, he reasoned. He tried to remain calm, assuring himself that they were safe. He gave the horses water, and then allowed them into the small field to graze as dusk fell.

Kitty awoke feeling a great deal better.

"Oh, that was a wonderful sleep, James. I feel I could jump over the moon," she said as she combed her hair.

"Well, if you could manage to jump over here, my darling, and eat your supper, I would be every bit as happy."

They sat around an old wooden table and chatted happily as they ate the remainder of the food James had bought earlier that day.

"Where are we going to from here, James?"

"We will travel back towards Baltinglass and then ride towards Blessington and then on to Dublin hopefully, Kitty. Sounds a bit ambitious, but then we are ambitious people, are we not?" and he smiled as he brushed the crumbs from his jacket.

"I hope not too ambitious, James, but then we are doing well, all things considered. I feel a great deal better this evening, so you will have a more cheerful travelling companion."

As they rode through the night they only spoke when necessary. The half moon shone from the clear night sky and they could see the outline of the hills in the distance.

"They are the Dublin Mountains, Kitty, and we should make the city by dawn if we have any luck at all."

"That will be wonderful, James. I never thought I would see the day when I would tire of valleys and hills, and horses for that matter too."

As they rode at a steady pace they encountered no one, which James knew was mainly because people were afraid to be outdoors by night. The sky became cloudy and their path less clear, with the moon only appearing occasionally. Thunder rumbled in the distance as a storm approached them. As dawn slowly came, rain fell, and soon the thunder rumbled loudly overhead, the lightening frightening the horses. But they calmed them with reassuring tones. The Dublin mountains were now directly in front of them, and they increased their speed to trotting.

"We must get to the outskirts of the city before morning comes and not be noticed riding together. You will ride ahead of me, and I will follow a half-hour later. Then we will meet at that inn where we said goodbye to Hannah before we boarded for France. Do you think you will be able to find it again, Kitty?"

"Don't worry, James, I shall. But I am worried. I hope you will not be recognised by anybody. Enough gloomy thoughts for now, my love. I shall ride ahead when we get to the top of this next hill, and promise James, you will be careful?"

"Of course I will. Now just remain calm. If you are stopped and questioned, what will you say and who are you?"

"I am from Kildare town and I am going to Dublin to visit my aunt who is ill. I am greatly worried about her. My name is Constance Bellew and I am a governess... So, does that description pass the test, James?"

"Marvellous, Constance... I always wanted to marry a governess," he said teasingly.

"And you shall. And who are you when questioned, James?"

"Oh, I'm a simple country lad going to Dublin to look for work on a big ship, going to Liverpool where my bother awaits me. We are going to America, the two of us, Sergeant, sir..." and Kitty thought this very funny indeed.

They kissed briefly and then parted. Kitty rode ahead briskly now, as James slowed his horse allowing her to ride well ahead of him. Her journey was uneventful and she was neither stopped nor questioned by any patrols. She looked ahead as she rode, ignoring everyone on her route. She hoped James would be as fortunate, for everywhere there seemed to be military, either in groups or individually, watching those entering the city.

* * *

Kitty thought of the countless times she had come to Dublin with her parents. They were such wonderful occasions, she thought sadly. Now I am here, a fugitive from my own father.

She rode her horse through the crowded streets and her mount, unused to such throngs, shied from time to time. Her clothes, though dried out with the hot sun, looked crumpled and almost shabby. All the better, she thought, for her disguise.

However, from a carriage window nearby, to his utter astonishment, Justice Stewart recognised her. He was rendered speechless. He was on his way to Dublin Castle for a Security Council meeting. He ordered his carriage to be halted instantly as he watched her ride by, oblivious to him.

"My, oh my," he said aloud, still finding it difficult to believe what was before his eyes.

He told the driver to wait for him as he stepped out. He watched her ride slowly through the crowd, her blue riding habit dishevelled. Why wouldn't it be? he thought. But where is her rebel lover? Following most likely at a discreet distance! Well, I shall simply have you followed, my lovely, with equal discretion. Going over to one of the police, he pointed Kitty out, instructing him to follow her at a safe distance. His duty was to locate her destination and then have the place surrounded the moment a young, dark-haired man eventually joined her. They were then to arrest them both, and bring them instantly to the nearest jail.

The policeman bowed his head dutifully and began to follow Kitty as she made her way slowly towards the tavern near the quays. Dublin teemed with life. The flower sellers sat with their stalls ablaze with colour, shouting their blossoms for sale. The smell of fresh bread and meats assailed the air, and Kitty felt hungry. She was looking forward to having a decent meal with James when he finally joined her.

Some distance behind her, James, having abandoned his horse, walked through the crowded streets. He felt hot and tired and hungry. Ahead of him, just outside Trinity College, there was a fracas on the street. He walked quickly to see what the source of the disturbance might be.

Two policemen had a youth held by either arm, and what James saw next took him totally by surprise. Justice Stewart alighted from a carriage and went in to the centre of the milieu. James did not wait to see more. He quickly retraced his steps, taking a side street that would lead him to the quays and then to Sackville Street, where he would walk straight down to the tavern to meet Kitty.

His heart pounded. He could hardly believe what he had just seen. What if he had seen Kitty? Neither of them could be sure of that, he realised. No, I must get Kitty out of that tavern somehow without my going in. For it would be far too easy to identify them both in the event that she had been followed. He knew Kitty would never suspect anybody following her, for her mind would be far too preoccupied on finding the tavern.

When James came in sight of the tavern, he stood at a discreet distance and watched the doors. Outside sat a lady selling flowers, dressed in a red, colourful dress. A man with a barrel organ played his melody and tried to sing to the music. He seemed to be either intoxicated or simply out of tune. There was no sight of anyone else other than customers coming and going. Everything appeared normal. For a moment he considered risking going in, but realising that they were now more than likely being followed for arrest, dismissed the idea. He walked back up the quayside slowly, trying to think clearly. Of course, he thought, send someone in for Kitty with a note that would explain his suspicions.

He quickly scribbled out: *"I am outside and have reason to suspect that you have been followed. Leave discreetly and meet me at the top of Sackville Street. J".*

He saw a young boy coming towards him and, calling him aside, told him what to do. He pressed a penny into the youth's hand, telling him to hurry. Delighted with his good fortune, the young boy ran to the tavern and, on entering the door, looked about the crowded room. He walked to the other side and looked carefully for the lady in the blue riding habit, but he could not see her anywhere. He was on the point of leaving when he saw her in a smoke-filled corner. He then waited for one of the tavern staff to come his direction and asked the waitress to give the lady the note. He vanished quickly, not having been noticed, and told James further up the quayside that he had done as he had told him. To his delight he received a further penny, and James walked hastily in the direction of Sackville Street.

Kitty was surprised when the servant girl handed her the note. The man who had been sent to observe her noticed nothing unusual, but Kitty looked around the tavern now, suspicious of everyone. The very thought that someone might have seen her alarmed her. So what now, she asked herself?

Deciding to finish her drink and meat pie that the servant had brought her, she had an idea. The pie half-eater, she called the servant girl to the table.

"Yes, ma'am?" she asked, smiling.

"I am afraid this pie is not to my liking. I wish you to bring me to the cook this instant."

A hush came over the people who were eating and drinking as they stared at her in silence. The observer looked amused as he watched Kitty follow the servant girl to the kitchens.

"Bloody fussy one that," he thought, and continued to drink his ale waiting for her to return. When Kitty entered the steamy kitchens, the servant girl pointed the cook out to her.

"Thank you," Kitty said as she walked directly over to the robust, red-faced woman. The cook looked at her as she approached, rubbing her hands in her apron.

"Yes, my lady?" she asked curiously, amazed at the quality coming into her kitchen.

"I insisted on coming in to say that these pies are simply delicious and I would like the recipe for my cook someday when you are not too busy."

"Most certainly, my lady, perhaps if you called back this evening?"

"Tomorrow evening would suit me better," Kitty replied.

"Very good, my lady. I shall have it written out for you well by then," the cook replied.

"Now tell me cook, I need to leave the back entrance as my chaperone is quite unmannerly. Do you think you could show me out?" Kitty said graciously.

"Well, the cheek of him! Of course I will, my lady. Some don't appreciate a lady when they meet one!" she said, shaking her head disapprovingly.

Kitty thanked her and asked her to say nothing if asked.

"Your ladyship may rest assured my lips are sealed, though nothing would give me greater pleasure than giving him a good telling off!"

Kitty thanked her and made her way through the back lane, deciding to leave her mare in the tavern stable until it was safer to return for her. She ran as fast as possible until she arrived at Sackville Street. Then she walked briskly, trying not to attract attention. She looked behind her from time to time, but it was impossible to know if she was being followed. She then noticed James standing at a corner. When he saw her, he decided to walk ahead of her, and she realised that it was the prudent thing to do. He walked into a small tavern and, stooping to tie her bootlace, she looked back to see if she was being followed. Assured that it was now safe, she walked into the tavern and sat breathless beside James. James immediately told her of his sighting of Viscount Stewart.

"Could one possibly imagine Stewart being in Dublin and seeing me? My God, James, it is a frightening coincidence, to think on the possibility that he may have seen me."

"I know, Kitty, but there is every chance that he did and, besides, it's a risk we can't take to assume he did not!" James said firmly.

"What do you suggest we do now, James? Get out of Dublin?"

"No, not straight away, Kitty. Tomorrow night we will leave and return to Marcus as originally planned. If Justice Stewart has observed you, he will think we are staying in Dublin and have the boats watched. He will think we are leaving the country, which is exactly what we want him to assume. It suits our purpose, Kitty."

They sat in silence and then decided to order dinner, as they were both very hungry. Having eaten, James sat back drinking a glass of ale thinking of their situation.

"Kitty, we must leave tonight. Dublin will be teeming with spies looking for us. Is your mare at the tavern?"

"Yes, I intend to collect at dusk."

"That is wise, for by then there will be different stable lads working for the night and you will not be recognised by any of them. I will have to go to the docks and try and get passage to Arklow on a fishing boat. It's my only hope, for to go by road would be fatal. I would have no chance if stopped and questioned."

Kitty looked at James and felt a sense of hopelessness.

'James, I am at the point of despair almost. Will we ever get out of this dilemma?"

"My darling, on Saturday night we will be able to walk on the slopes of Mount Leinster. Don't you doubt it for a moment, Mrs de Lacey."

It never failed to cheer her spirits when James addressed her so, and for the first time that day she laughed.

"Now Kitty, ride south towards the Great Sugar Loaf mountain, then turn right towards Glendalough and then to the mountains west of Arklow towards Newtown Barry. You know the way to Marcus' home from there. Buy some old clothing and for heaven's sake try and speak more like the people you meet on the roads. I will leave it to your imagination as to your new identity!" And he kissed her.

Dusk was falling as they paid their dinner bill and went outside. The street was almost deserted.

"I will see you at Marcus' home, Kitty, and be careful, my darling." He kissed her again and left her.

She felt despair creep over her like a dark cloud, and walked slowly towards a clothes shop which was still open for business, and a lamp now stood lighting inside the door.

"Good evening, madam." A small man greeted her as she walked inside.

"Good evening, I wish to buy some clothes for my cook. Now let me see, she requires a black cloak and a loose-fitting, black dress. She loves dark clothes... mourning still, I'm afraid." Kitty smiled, congratulating herself on her newfound acting ability.

"Let me see, madam. What size is your cook?" he asked.

"Somewhat similar to myself, perhaps a little more plump," she said, looking at the cloak rack. "Ah, here we are, this looks like the type of thing she wears. And this dress should do excellently for her, poor thing."

Wrapping the clothes carefully, the shopkeeper was delighted with this unexpected evening sale. When Kitty had paid for her purchases, he opened the door and thanked her, and expressed his hope that her cook would be pleased with her choices.

On finding a derelict old building, Kitty checked it out to make sure there were no vagrants there. Satisfied that she was alone, she hastily changed her clothes and, wrapping her blue riding habit into a bundle, she threw it behind a door. Outside once again, she looked at her reflection in a shop window and was impressed with the transformation that made her look many years older. She walked now with purpose, feeling safer in her disguise, and was soon in sight of the tavern where her mare was stabled. She paused at a distance to see if the stables were being observed and, satisfied that all was safe, walked in. A stable lad attended to her and saddled her horse. She paid him and, mounting, rode out onto the street. She sighed with immense relief. The streets were quiet and she rode through side streets until she left the city, now six miles behind. The thought of being pursued still remained with her and from time to time she would stop to reassure herself that all was well.

The moon shone brilliantly from the night sky and in the distance she could see the Great Sugar Loaf Mountain. She remembered the many times she had sat looking at it from the family carriage, never once dreaming how life could change so dramatically. No time for daydreaming now, she reminded herself. She must get to Glendalough as soon as possible and make use of the darkness to travel as far as she could. She encountered many travellers, but to her amazement no patrols. She thought it strange, but then decided not to take it for granted either.

At the base of the great towering mountain, its white quartz shining in the clear moonlight, she turned up the road that James had instructed her to take. It was deserted, the only signs of life being the candlelit cottage windows. She envied the occupants, safe and secure from the night. Realising that it could have been a night of heavy rain, she decided to count her blessings. Her mare was tiring now and she rode at walking pace, patting Misty and thinking how faithful an animal she was.

"All the hunts you brought me to, and safely through!" she said, addressing the mare, who pricked her ears. "Soon you will be in a nice, warm stable, Misty, with lots of oats and a good bed. Not too far now, she assured the animal.

James found a fishing vessel just loaded with coal, about to embark on its return journey to Arklow. Paying the captain generously, he was given a good bunk to sleep in. They would be in Arklow early the next morning, he assured him. James couldn't believe his good fortune. Another hour, he thought, and I would have been too late for this boat. Slowly the boat sailed down to the mouth of Dublin port and turned south, a fair wind behind her. She made steady progress through the night and James slept, utterly exhausted.

On reaching Glendalough, Kitty found a lodging house where the landlady was kind to a fault.

"My goodness, madam, travelling abroad this time of night! You must be on urgent business to take such a risk," she said earnestly.

"Yes, a sad journey I'm afraid, ma'am," Kitty replied, remembering James advice to speak more plainly! "'Tis my poor aunt, ma'am, dying below in Arklow, you know. Poor soul has no one in the world only myself. Oh, 'tis sad indeed, this life of ours, is it not?" Kitty said, rubbing the soles of her feet before the warm fire.

And the landlady talked at length about her own illness of last winter, when all hope had been lost for her.

"But sure, didn't the good Lord decide it otherwise for me," she concluded, as she placed a great plate of boiled chicken before Kitty. "The young fellow will take good care of the mare for you, so get that into you, as I know you must be famished, God love you."

Kitty thanked her and complimented her on the deliciously flavoured meat. The landlady, however, noticed the fine hands and thought "Never knew what work was either, couldn't fool me. But it's her money that I'm interested in." She poured out fresh tea, keeping her thoughts to herself.

"What time would you like your breakfast at, ma'am? Getting up early never bothered me, you know. So whenever you say, I will have it ready for you then."

Kitty thought for a moment.

"Would six o'clock be too early for you, then?"

Taken aback by the early hour, she chuckled.

"Not a bit too early at all, ma'am, for I collect the eggs indeed at that time and will have some lovely fresh ones for your breakfast, I will."

Not wanting to engage in conversation, Kitty went to bed, bidding her hostess goodnight.

She lay awake for some time thinking about James. She worried about him constantly now. Nobody and nowhere is safe anymore.

She eventually slept and was awoken with a sharp knock on her bedroom door after what seemed like only an hour. Sunlight streamed into the small room. It was brightly coloured and very clean, Kitty noticed. Having washed and dressed, she went to the small dining room where a plate of eggs was placed before her. The landlady chatted happily and pondered the fact that the young lady had no baggage. Odd, this one, she thought. Kitty paid her and found the stable lad had her mare ready for her.

"My word, you have brushed her out lovely," she said to him, handing him a penny. He was overjoyed with his unexpected good fortune so early in the day.

Bidding the landlady goodbye, Kitty rode in the silence of the morning. Her route lay through rugged mountain passes, but at least they are safe, she thought and, more importantly still, there should be no military presence. The very thought of being stopped and questioned aroused great fear in her, lest she be recognised. She decided to put aside all negative thought and began to think of Marcus and how surprised and relieved he would be to see them both. Then she thought of James and how long it would take him to arrive from Dublin. Again she prayed for his safety.

James walked quickly through the fishermen's quarters as soon as they docked in Arklow. He knew a friend of Joe's who would either sell him or loan him a horse. He was anxious to leave the town as soon as possible for he knew the morning patrols would be on duty very soon. On reaching the smallholding of Joe's friend, Tom Donoghue, he was heartened to see smoke rising from the cottage chimney and, knocking on the door, was relieved to see it opened by its owner.

"I am a friend of Joe Gilltrap," he began.

"I see, and what can I do for a friend of Joe's then?" the small man before him asked as he looked James up and down.

"I need to buy or take a loan of a horse this very morning," James said anxiously.

"Hmm, how do I know you will ever bring it back then?" Tom asked, smiling.

"You don't," James replied, liking the man instantly.

"Well said. There's a black cob in the field at the back of the house. Take him, but I warn you, he is like the wind. He hasn't been ridden or worked for three weeks!" Tom warned him.

"That won't bother me in the least, Tom. I need something that will fly, so I think he is just exactly what I want."

James was delighted and having had something to eat with Tom they went to the field and eventually caught the black cob. Tom calmed the animal and saddled him.

"I can't be sure, Tom, when I will have him back to you, but I'll do my best! I will tell Joe of your kindness," James said, shaking the man's hand.

"Don't worry about the cob, just get yourself out of this town as quickly as you can, my lad. The cows in the field are looking for you, so be warned."

James had never ridden such a lively animal before and, true to Tom's word, it was as fast as the wind. He rode directly towards Croghan Mountain and then towards Annagh Hill, where he stopped to look at the breathtaking view. The cob grazed leisurely, the edge having gone from him. James patted the animal and smiled.

"That knocked the wild ways off you, my friend."

He knew that if everything went in his favour, he should be at Marcus' home after midnight. He decided not to continue his journey until nightfall. Safety at all times, he reminded himself. Despite the remoteness of the area he knew that it was no guarantee. In the distance he could now see the mountain where their village lay. So much had happened in five days, he thought. He was weary of travelling and he thought of Kitty and how very tired she must now be. He slept for two hours, his cob safely tethered. His body ached when he awoke. Heavy dew was falling on the hillside and he waited a further hour for darkness to fall before resuming his journey.

It is monotonous, riding in the dark, he thought. But then life could be far worse. He thought of the nights he had spent in jail. The smell would always remain with him more than the despair he felt. An owl flew overhead, its great white wings silent in the night. Funny birds, owls. So skilled in the dark, he thought. His cob trotted eagerly on the narrow track, now veering southwest. The piercing sound of a vixen resounded from hill to hill, calling a mate. He loved the sound. It reminded him of when, as a small boy, he would lie in bed listening to it. He felt cold now, and attributed it to fatigue. "Travel on boy, travel on," he said to the cob, which showed no signs of tiredness whatever. He blessed Tom Donohue, assuring himself that he would one day meet him again to say as much.

* * *

Marcus sat by his fireside feeling depressed. He had been looking forward to having James and Kitty come to say, however brief it might be. Now, almost one week later, there was still no sign of them, much less news. He knew that if they had been captured he would have heard. The wind was rising and he knew that rain was not too far distant. He knew it was needed. The potatoes and other crops were parched. The old saying was true: 'A wet and windy May fills the haggard with corn and hay'. Without rain they would face famine, man and beast. The dog stood up from his fireside bed and looked at the door, his ears cocked, alert.

"What is it, Patch?" Marcus asked the dog quietly, as he himself listened to the sounds of the night. The dog growled deep in its throat, then walked back to the fire and lay down again.

Marcus lit his pipe and drew contentedly on the tobacco. His thoughts were never far from the rebellion. Soon now, soon, he sighed. Suddenly, the dog leaped from his bed again and barked loudly at the door. Marcus listened, and this time distinctly heard the sound of an approaching rider. He opened the door and, walking outside with his lantern, could see the mounted figure approach. Small of stature, that much was clear to him.

He walked towards his late visitor and was astonished to discover it was Kitty.

"Oh Marcus, you have no idea how very glad I am to see you. I am utterly spent," Kitty said wearily.

"What a surprise, Kitty! I was just thinking of you and James and wondered where on earth you had both gotten to."

"It's a very long story, Marcus," she said, dismounting, "which I shall tell you when I rest awhile."

"Of course, Kitty. Here, you go inside and I'll look after your mount."

Kitty just slumped into the chair by the fireside, exhaustion overcoming her. When Marcus came back inside, he found her sleeping soundly and was amused when he noticed how she was dressed. One great lady indeed, he thought, as he piled the fire high with wood. Now let me see, she will want something substantial to eat when she awakens. He decided to boil some potatoes and heat the lamb stew he had already cooked for the morrow.

What of James, he wondered. Obviously safe and unharmed or it would have been the first thing Kitty would have told him. Going to the cupboard, he took out a woollen blanket and covered her with it. The dog looked at her, an unusual sight at the fireside.

"You heard her coming, Patch, a long time before I did, you clever fellow." And he threw the dog a large piece of brown bread.

Not being very hungry, the dog took the bread to the fireside and chewed it leisurely. Marcus listened to the sound of the potatoes boiling in the large skillet pot. He loved the familiar sound and the smell that came with the gushes of steam from beneath the shaking lid.

Again the dog looked at the door, ears raised, and then began to bark. Marcus silenced him, for fear of him waking Kitty.

"Another visitor Patch, and no need to ask who it is!" he said excitedly. On going outside, his assumption was correct.

"Well, James de Lacey, your beloved has just arrived an hour ago. Great timing altogether! Marcus said with obvious delight.

"Marcus how is she?" James asked anxiously.

"Tired, weary and now asleep by the fireside, James," he assured him.

"That's a relief, Marcus, and great one too. I was so worried that something might happen to her. We have had a very rough time. I don't know how poor Kitty has managed to stay sane this past week, let alone well!"

On going inside James looked at Kitty sleeping and, like his friend, was highly amused by the clothes she was wearing.

"Did we ever think we would see the day, Marcus, when the Right Honourable Catherine Foldsworth would be dressed as a Dublin flower seller?"

Both men laughed and Kitty moved restlessly, but did not awaken.

"You must be famished, James. Sit down and I will give you a meal you will remember, my man!" Marcus said good-naturedly.

James sat opposite Kitty and looked at the face now tanned from the sun and wind of past days. He wanted to kiss her, but he knew she was exhausted and he did not wish to disturb her.

"Well, James, sit here and have this food and then tell me what on earth ever happened to the pair of you. My God, nobody has an inkling of your whereabouts. They must be worried sick at the village."

James sat at the table and ate the dinner placed before him appreciatively.

"This is the first decent meal I have had in almost a week, Marcus. Always looking over our shoulder," and then, sitting back from the table, he told Marcus in low tones of how their plans had been changed time and again and of his ultimate shock in Dublin to see Justice Stewart.

"There was every possibility he noticed Kitty, Marcus. How many beautiful women ride through the city streets these days? Most of them are in carriages. My instincts tell me that we only barely escaped that fellow's grip. So Kitty rode through the mountains and I came by fishing boat to Arklow. I then rode north of Coolgreany towards Croghan Mountain and sheltered on Annagh hill till darkness fell, and here I am!" James said almost jubilantly.

Kitty awoke with a start.

"Why James," she exclaimed excitedly, rubbing the sleep from her eyes.

He embraced her and she clung to him, still thinking that it was a dream.

"My God, Kitty, I was so relieved to see you here! I had a thousand fears for your safety," James said, caressing her hair.

"And I for you, my darling. How did you finally get here?" she asked him.

He told her of his journey from the time he left her in the Dublin Street. She listened with rapt attention, thinking how fortunate they had both been. Marcus listened intently as he smoked his pipe. He was fascinated how unaware of him they had both now become, so engrossed were they in each other. He did not resent it, only admired their mutual devotion. They have dared to love, he thought, with the odds so much against them.

"You don't think either of us were followed, James, do you?" Kitty asked anxiously.

"Not a chance, Kitty, or at least it's very unlikely," he replied in reassuring tones.

The same thought had occurred to Marcus, though he dared not say as much, seeing how exhausted they both were. They all chatted for a further hour, stopping at intervals to listen to the heavy rain now falling.

"My heavens, I think there must be a storm brewing," Kitty said as she looked at the small windows, the rain lashing against them.

"All needed, Kitty. We will have to harvest you know, after the rebellion, God willing," Marcus said in practical tones.

In the distance a clap of thunder peeled across the sky and lightning lit up the small but cosy room. The dog leaped nervously under Marcus' chair, whining. Kitty patted him reassuringly.

"Nothing to fear, Patch, just the clouds chasing each other across the sky. There's a good fellow." And she smiled at Marcus.

"A brave dog at all times, but when the thunder comes you may say goodbye to him. Many was the day I was bringing sheep home and the thunder would peal, and he would run like wildfire for home! No persuading our Patch when he makes his mind up, Kitty." And they laughed at the picture Marcus conjured up before them.

"Well, I can't speak for you pair, but it's time for me to go to bed," Marcus said, walking to bolt the door. "But make yourselves at home and do as you please for that matter."

The dog followed him to the door and whined.

"Poor Patch, I nearly forgot you. Off you go and do your business," Marcus said, standing aside and letting the dog out. But Patch just stood on the threshold and growled.

"Still afraid of the thunder," Kitty remarked, smiling at the antics of the animal.

Marcus waited a few moments patiently for the dog to decide what it wanted to do.

"Apparently Patch, you don't want to do your ablutions as much as you thought you did," and then he bolted the door securely.

But the dog remained standing at the door, whining.

"I sometimes think he expects the thunder to come through it," Marcus said, laughing.

"Yes, some animals are very odd at times. I remember we had a mare that had a dreadful aversion to snow, above all things. Fell heavily as a yearling and never recovered the fright. Their instincts are so much stronger than our own," Kitty commented, looking at the dog that now lay at the side of the door.

In the distance the thunder faded as it moved across the sea. A great silence then prevailed, but the dog still acted with unease. Marcus wondered now if it was the thunder he had been growling at when he refused to go outside minutes earlier. He was now worried about the dog's behaviour.

"James, I think we had better turn down the lamp and have a look outside.

There is something bothering the dog," he said, trying not to alarm them too much.

"What on earth could it be, Marcus, at this very late hour?" Kitty asked, standing up to join them.

"That's what I mean to find out," Marcus assured her, taking his musket from its place above the chimneybreast.

As they walked into the yard, they looked about, their eyes slowly adjusting to the darkness. Clouds allowed the bright moonlight to penetrate their fleecy lining and the yard cast long shadows. Patch growled and stood riveted to the one spot. Marcus realised that there must be intruders not too far off.

Looking at the laneway that came downhill to his small farm, he saw a troop of horsemen carrying lanterns. Their dimly lit figures became clear as the moonlight shot suddenly through a great gap in the heavens.

"Quickly, go inside James and Kitty," Marcus said in alarm. Once inside he quickly blew out the lamps and outside Patch barked wildly as the horsemen approached.

"Who are they, Marcus?" James asked anxiously.

"I don't know, James, but they are not our friends coming in such numbers at this hour. Quickly, saddle the horses. Get out through the back window. Kitty, get your cloak on. We have to get out of here this minute!" Marcus said with clear urgency.

They climbed out through the small rear window and having only time to bridle the animals, rode silently through the small field at the back of the house. The riders were now in the yard and Marcus could hear them shout his name, ordering him to come out. Patch still barked furiously until a loud shot, and a pitiful yelp, rent the night wind.

They were now under no illusions but that either James or Kitty had been followed. The troops shouted at the silent house and then shots rent the air as they forced their way into the small cottage.

"Ride like the wind, Kitty," James urged, as they fled through the fields onto the hillside.

Looking back, the night sky was illuminated by the cottage burning now, its thatch ablaze, sparks spiralling into the darkness.

"Quickly, quickly," Marcus called. "They don't know our direction yet, but if the sky suddenly clears they will spot us on this bare hillside."

The horses stumbled across the stony ground but were surefooted enough, Kitty thought, as they tried to balance without saddle or stirrup. Their skills stood them well and they were soon on the top of the hill where they dismounted, standing against the great boulders that obscured their silhouettes.

"My God, James, had we been in bed we would all by now be either shot in the yard or in prison by morning. What will we do, James?" he asked, looking for guidance from his friend.

James looked at Kitty, clearly shaken from the experience.

"It will be dawn in another hour. All we can do is find somewhere to hide safely for the coming day. But Kitty, I want you to listen to me. You will now ride back to the village this very instant. Remain there, for they will not think that we would separate."

Suddenly a loud shot from a gun blasted from behind them and Marcus fell to the ground. Kitty screamed in terror as she saw the blood flow from the side of Marcus' mouth as he lay dying.

"Oh God," James shouted, "Hold your fire!"

Kitty ran and clung to him like a frightened child, crying. The band of horsemen emerged from the darkness. Their leader rode towards them, a musket pointing directly at them. The unmistakable voice of Lord Foldsworth filled the air.

"Why, I have never enjoyed a hunt as much as I have this night, my dear Catherine. Did you think we would be so foolish as not to have watched you ride to the cottage? Hmm, well? And then we waited for your lover to come. What an evening we have had. And you came the direction we expected you to." He laughed in hysterical tones of exhilaration, his conquest complete.

Kitty ran to Marcus and cradled his head as he breathed his last breath. She suddenly regained her composure and walked towards her father.

"You are even more insane than I could have ever imagined. Still the raving mad landlord, I see!" she said calmly.

"Out of my way or I will shoot your rebel before your eyes, madam," he hissed.

Before she realised it, James was tied securely and placed on a horse. He knew that resistance was futile.

"Where are you taking him," she demanded of her father.

"To a place where he will finally be secure, my dear. Wexford jail! And your good friend Timothy Stewart will be delighted to be his host finally," he replied icily.

Kitty remained composed and, walking over to James, placed her hand on his arm.

"Don't worry, my love. We will try and have you freed... somehow, James, somehow," and then she cried quietly.

"Kitty, take care of yourself. And don't resist him. It will only make things worse for us both," he told her quietly.

"Take him and make sure you deliver him safely this time. I don't expect that you will encounter any difficulties. The rest of his pack doesn't even know that he is in the vicinity."

The escort, numbering fifteen, surrounded James and slowly moved across the plateau southwards to Wexford and the prison awaiting him. Kitty looked at her father. He smiled cynically.

"My, you do look a sight! Like some woman of the roads. Now be sensible and come back to Oak Hall where we shall try and put this ridiculous episode and all it represents behind us. Be reasonable, Kitty, for your mother's sake if nothing else," he said, almost pleading with her now.

But her hatred of the man welled up within her and she knew that she must try and conceal it somehow. Her thoughts must be for James and a miracle to secure his freedom some way. Deciding to cooperate for the moment in the hope that it would serve her purpose, she looked at her father wearily.

"Yes, perhaps you are right. I am weary and tired. I need a rest despite the fact that I abhor all you are doing. I need not tell you that my stay at Oak Hall will be brief. I will stay just until I regain my strength. Look at that poor man, shot in cold blood by you. No, father, I will go with you this night, but I shall not renounce my future plans... for you, mother, or anyone. Is that quite clear?"

Deciding to make a more conscious effort to win her favour, he simply shook his head slowly.

"The only reason I fight against this militant mob is to try and secure your future, my dear Kitty. I know you will come to your senses after rest and care. Then you will see my point. But for now let there be an end to our dreadful arguments and disagreements. A truce? Just for now, my dear, what?"

Kitty looked at Marcus lying dead on the heather beside her and tears ran freely. He was like a brother to me, she thought.

"What about this man here. He can't be left just like this!" she said, desperately trying to control her anger and hatred of the man she now had to address as father.

"Rest assured I shall send someone to have the body brought to the town for burial, today. Now, come along, Kitty, I am famished and weary," he said, turning his horse slowly.

Kitty could not believe how he could simply ride away as if he had just shot a stag, cold and indifferent. Taking off her cloak, she covered the body of Marcus, now white with the pallor of death.

"Oh, poor Marcus, what a very sad end and such a great man you were, so unselfish and kind. What a brutal end." At that moment she wished she had a pistol to shoot her father. It would not have bothered her, yet she realised that she must remain calm and go along with his plans for now. It could so easily have been James, but she knew that her father wanted to make a public display of James' trial and death. She felt frantic with panic and disbelief.

She rode behind her father, not speaking or wanting to. All hope seemed to have disappeared. Only despondency filled her entire being. Oak Hall stood in the distance, its grand facade lit by the morning sun.

"You must be glad to be home, Kitty," her father said cheerfully, looking back at her. "Don't you want to come and ride alongside?" he asked.

"No, I don't. I am too tired for pretence," she said bluntly.

"Suit yourself! What you need is a good, hot bath and a decent meal. I hope the servants don't notice you coming home dressed so shabbily. Not quite the thing, you know."

She looked at her former home. Not quite the thing, she thought. But quite legitimate to shoot a man down in cold blood. Oh, poor Marcus, lying on a hillside. Suddenly she vomited uncontrollably and fell from her horse. Lord Foldsworth summoned two servants to carry her upstairs, while Kitty groaned in exhaustion and delayed shock.

They put her to bed, drawing the heavy drapes, enclosing the room in darkness, where Kitty fell into a deep sleep. Some hours later she awoke, the morning's nightmare more vivid than ever. She washed hastily and dressed in some fresh clothes. However, on going to the door she discovered it was locked. She banged the door, calling out in anger, but her calling was in vain. She pulled the service bell and after several minutes she heard footsteps approach. From outside an unfamiliar voice spoke.

"Yes, madam, what is it?"

Kitty felt rage and indignation surge through her.

"Open this door at once, whoever you are," she demanded.

"I'm sorry, madam, but we have been instructed not to by his lordship," the faint voice replied.

"Where is my father now?" Kitty asked.

"Gone away for the afternoon, madam," the voice replied.

"Well, I need some food then, and hurry with it," Kitty said, only this time trying to sound a little more calm.

"Certainly madam, I will be back soon with your lunch," and the patter of feet receded from the door.

A hostage now, she thought. I will have to overpower that maid, whoever she is. She sounded quite young too, she reasoned. Kitty waited to hear the sound of the maid returning, and after some time could hear her mounting the stairs. She stood behind the door, waiting for the maid to enter the room.

"Are you there, madam," the timid voice asked.

"Of course I am here. Just enter with the tray please," Kitty said, almost in pleasant tones.

What sounded like a large bunch of keys were rattling now, and the lock in the door creaked slowly before it finally opened. Kitty reached from behind the door and pulled the maid in with a sudden jerk. The tray fell to the floor, only to be followed by a grey-haired elderly woman whom Kitty had never seen before. She was shocked now by what she had done.

"Oh my goodness, you poor woman," she exclaimed, helping the old woman up. "Who on earth are you?" Kitty asked her.

The old woman was now crying from the shock of the encounter and Kitty, taking the keys from her, led her to the side of the bed where they both sat down.

"I'm sorry, madam, 'tis just the master said you were not to be let out and now the trouble I will be in... No job now and he might whip me or anything," she sobbed.

"Who are you? I have never seen you in service here," Kitty said, staring at the frail, old woman.

"Betty, madam. Betty Ryan is my name. You helped my poor son's wife after he died, don't you remember? Pat Ryan. He was my only boy, you know."

Kitty felt great remorse for being so rough, but she had expected a younger woman.

"I am so sorry, Mrs. Ryan, but I did not expect an elderly woman. Now, you must dry your eyes until we sort out some plan for you. Are they expecting you back in the kitchen?"

"Yes, madam, and they will come for me if I am not back there soon. We did not know that it was you, madam that was locked in here believe me. Your poor father must be quite not himself to be doing this," she said, unsure if she should speak so bold.

"He is gone insane, Mrs. Ryan, and that is why I need you to help me. You must!" Kitty said almost imploring her.

"Madam need not worry. You were very kind to my poor Pat's wife and children after he died, so I will now help you madam." And standing up, she straightened her apron and tidied her hair.

"Firstly Mrs. Ryan, I want you to leave this house as soon as you can and take the tray back to the kitchen and tell them I refused to open the door to you. Take this broach." And, going to the drawer, Kitty opened it and took exquisite jewel-embedded broach from it and handed it to the old woman.

"Why, madam, I could never take that from you," she exclaimed.

"Nonsense, Mrs. Ryan, you have earned it. Sell it after the summer has passed and keep the money and do with it as you please. Now, we will lock the door from the outside and I shall hide until evening. Say nothing of all this, or need I caution you?"

"Don't worry, madam. Your secret is safe with me. But will they not plainly see that it was I who let you out of this room?" she asked sensibly.

"Of course they will, but my father isn't fool enough to go hounding down an old woman, is he?" Kitty looked at her and saw what remained of what must have once been a very lovely face. The eyes were bright and the skin a rosy,and tanned colour. Old Mrs. Ryan smiled.

"Lord Foldsworth could do anything madam, saving your presence."

"You are quite right, and that's all the more reason for you to get back to the kitchen and leave as soon as you can. And again, Mrs. Ryan, I apologise for the manner in which I forced you into the room. I do hope you will forgive me."

The old woman reached up and kissed Kitty gently.

"You are a great lady, madam, and I wish you God's speed. Be careful. I am sure we will meet again," and suddenly she was gone.

Kitty walked down the great stairway very gently, hoping that none of the servants would emerge from any one of the many rooms. She went into the drawing room and ate some fruit from the bowl, then drank a glass of wine hurriedly. She then found a heavy cloak and a stout pair of walking boots and went to the basement to wait until dusk. The time passed slowly as she listened for the sound of her father's approaching horse, but it did not come. The windows of the basement, as well as the first floor, were all boarded up. Consequently she would have to leave by one of the doors, unseen. Timing her departure to coincide with the servant's mealtime, she knew that there must now be little time before her father's return. Her anxiety mounted minute by minute, and her breathing came fast.

Slowly she mounted the stairs from the basement as she listened to the servants chatting during their evening meal. She walked carefully, step by step, lest she should make any sound. On reaching the ground floor, she was relieved to see the door open. She walked out into the dusk and looked carefully about the courtyard. All was silence, the only sound being the occasional stamping of a horse in the stables. She walked swiftly towards the shrubbery of overgrown rhododendrons, and followed the path the servants took to the westerly wall of the estate, hence avoiding the long avenue. Darkness fell quickly now as she hastily approached the small gateway. Looking up and down the narrow laneway that led to the road, there was no one in sight. She ran then, until she came to the road and then followed it until she arrived at the smaller fields that stretched out towards the hillside. She knew that she must quickly reach the hillside, lest her father would come riding homewards.

Breathless now, she climbed the stonewall and lay back on the heather gasping. She realised that it was fear that made her feel so tired, rather than exertion. Suddenly her ears picked up on the sound of a trotting horse in the distance, and she crept towards the wall peering through the stone gaps onto the road only two fields distant. In the fast fading dusk she recognised the figure of her father, and he was singing.

Drunk, she thought. His horse slowed now as it came to the incline. Again, she thought, had she a pistol she would use it. He faded from sight; Kitty began the climb that would bring her to the mountain village. James, James. Her heart ached, as she recalled the nightmare of the early morning. Whatever shall I do? She cried silently. Perhaps they will be able to rescue him or bribe the guards, but whatever it took, Kitty decided, no matter what... James must... he must escape. The alternative she simply refused to acknowledge, for it was beyond her comprehension to be without the man she loved, more than life itself. Without stopping to rest she continued her climb upwards, the half moon now shedding some light, the outline of the mountains now clearer.

She sighed with relief as she heard the dogs in the village above her bark at her arrival. She ran, stumbling towards the cottage where the dimly lit windows meant home to her. She cried with relief as she knocked on the locked door. It was opened by old Mag, who looked at her in total surprise.

"Well child alanna! Where have you come from? Mother of God everyone, 'tis Miss Kitty." Immediately everyone rushed to the door.

Kitty sat by the fire and related in detail all that had happened to them in Dublin and finally the events of last night that resulted in the death of Marcus and the capture of James. Sadness and disbelief left them speechless for some moments.

"We must free James, Joe. We must organise his escape first thing tomorrow. Could we bribe the guards? What can we do?" Kitty said, looking about at the faces around the fire.

They looked at each other, thinking the same thoughts. However, they dared not tell her that Wexford jail was an impenetrable fortress, guarded within and without and impossible to escape from. Old Mag realised that life for James was for the most part over. He would be brought to a hasty trial and then executed, all perhaps within a fortnight or maybe less.

"Well," asked Kitty. "Why is nobody answering me? What is it? What are you not telling me? Marjorie, what is it?"

Marjorie looked at her and felt only pity and helplessness.

"Miss Kitty, there is no easy way of telling you this," she began. "But escape from Wexford jail is totally impossible. James will be placed under heavy guard and the very most, my love, that you may achieve, will be a visit. As a rule even that is not permitted."

Kitty screamed, jumping from her chair. They were alarmed as they watched her run through the door and Joe ran after her.

"Poor girl," Nell said, sobbing. "She finally realises that the man she loves so dearly faces only death."

"What are we going to do now?" Marjorie asked, looking at Hannah who sat ashen-faced, the grim reality dawning on her. She followed Joe into the night with a lantern and found him near his forge, an arm around Kitty, slowly guiding her back to the cottage. She was sobbing like a lost child. For indeed, is that not what she now is? Hannah thought. Without mother, father and the man she loves. God, what are we going to do with her? She prayed.

"Come now, Miss Catherine, inside to the fire and we will think of something," Hannah said, trying to comfort her.

"Do you have a plan, Hannah? Oh please say you have," she cried.

Seated once more by the fireside, Mag handed her a glass of dark red liquid.

"Now, my dear, you must drink this. It will help you to think more clearly," she promised, as Kitty drank the potion slowly.

The crackling fire was the only sound in the silent room, each lost in their own thoughts for James and the reality that had to be faced.

"I have an idea," Marjorie began.

"Oh, what is it?" Kitty asked, jumping from her chair.

"Sit down child and be still and I will tell you all," Marjorie said, noting Kitty's anxiety and wondering how long it would take for Mag's potion to calm the young woman.

"I have a cousin in Wexford town. He too owns a tavern. Pat Redmond is his name. Now, if we were to go there and spend a little time enquiring about the jail, its layout, the guards and everything we can learn, perhaps we might be able to do something." It was the best Marjorie could offer Kitty.

"Joe looked at the distraught young lady and knew that it was only a matter of time until her father would come storming into the village searching for her. She would be better gone for many reasons, for she would fret to death.

"I think that's a very good idea," he said, filling his pipe artfully. "Kitty is right. We must do something; make some effort, even though Miss Kitty, the odds are greatly against us in every way. You must realise that, as difficult as this may be for you." He could see the great pain in her face, the reality only slowly dawning on her.

"Yes, I agree Joe. It would be unbearable for me to sit here, or worse still, to be brought back to Oak Hall to be a prisoner again. I would sooner die than sit helplessly while James awaits his trial." And she slumped in the chair, the potion only now having its desired effect.

Mag sighed with relief as Kitty slept soundly at last.

"Would you mind telling me," Hannah asked in hushed tones, "what is going to be achieved by this visit to Wexford, Marjorie?"

"The simple answer, Hannah, is that it may be the only chance Kitty will have to say goodbye to the man she loves. For to arrange his escape would be foolhardy, as Joe rightly said. That jail is too well guarded. However, Kitty must not be told this at all costs. We must try and keep her spirits up by allowing her to think as long as possible that there is some chance of his getting out of there. We can't deprive her of hope, can we?"

They knew it was the only approach that could be taken, and they agreed that Joe, Marjorie and Kitty would leave at first light for Wexford town. Hannah protested at not being included in the party.

"Kitty will need you more when she returns," Nell said calmly and Hannah knew that she spoke the truth.

They carried Kitty to bed and left her sleeping soundly, her mind free of the truth, which she would have to face in the forthcoming days.

Chapter fourteen

James lay in the cell where he had been thrown. He was sore and bruised from the many times he had fallen from the horse on the journey to the jail. When he saw the great stonewalls of the jail that day, he knew escape would be foolish to contemplate. The smell of decay in the cell, the coughing of the other inmates, and the unemptied buckets of excreta made him vomit violently. He longed for the fresh mountain air and knew in his heart that he would never inhale it again. 'Death is staring me in the face,' he thought. The trial would be quick and sentence passed, of death by hanging or, if he was lucky, to be shot. He knew that the authorities would make an example of him as a rebel leader.

They would use the execution to instil fear into the people once again. James prayed that Joe would keep his promise to him, and take care of Kitty. He wondered how she was, and where she was. Not knowing, he thought, is the greatest pain of all. Will I ever see her again? Touch her again? Standing up now, he walked painfully to the window, firmly secured with five iron bars. He looked out across Wexford harbour. The moon shone on the sea, and overhead sea gulls cried out in the darkness. He could smell the salt air and it reminded him of the voyage to France.

'Why didn't we remain there?' he asked himself in reproach. A fool's dream led me home again, and for what? Taking the only chance of happiness that they had known. He cursed the darkness, and his own stupidity. We could have gone to America... what were we thinking of? What was I thinking of? A hero's victory? Glory in battle? And look at the outcome now. Being executed like a common thief, not even the dignity of dying in battle! Oh Christ forgive me for my stupidity. For ruining Kitty's life. For so many foolish decisions. Death! The finality of it all. Darkness.

Or does life continue? He wondered. But what was the point without Kitty? I will never rest without her. He rebuked himself for his selfishness. In time, she would come to terms with his death, and the society she belonged to would enfold her in its world of privilege, forgiving all. He prayed this would happen for her, but in his heart cried out for her nonetheless. Looking into the night sky, he could clearly see the eastern star.

How many times had both he and Kitty gazed at it from the old hill fort as they lay in each other's embrace? Tears came to his eyes as he thought of the hopelessness of his situation. There would be no mercy for him. No reprieve. Not even the option of being transported. That alone would have provided reason to hope to be with her again, for he knew she would have followed him to the ends of the earth. Unfortunately, her father knew it also.

'No. I must begin to accept my fate. Joe will take care of Kitty, and in time she will recover from my death. I will write a long letter to her, and hope she will get it. One guard looks friendly enough. Maybe he would grant me one last wish?'

James then lay down on the straw in the corner. At least it was fresh and smelled of fields and sunshine. He slept then, exhausted from the events of the past week. As he slept, he dreamed of running in a battle charge. They had been victorious, as they now charged on Arklow town. The giant cannons guns roared before them, but miraculously no cannon balls came hissing through the air. Marcus ran beside him, cheering wildly and shouting, "Ireland forever! Ireland forever!" Then Kitty appeared on horseback calling him, "Come back! James, come back!"

He awoke shouting, "Kitty! Kitty!"

"Hey you in there, shut your mouth," the night guard roared at him.

James lay awake, unable to come to terms with the fact that his dream was not real.

"And so foolish too," he murmured.

He tossed and turned and finally stood up, his body aching and his head throbbing in pain. Looking out through the barred window once again, he could see the crimson dawn streaking across the eastern sky. What will the day bring? How many more dawns will I see? His heart raced as he considered his execution. 'God give me strength to die well, he prayed, and to live with hope until that moment comes'.

Some moments later he heard the steps of a guard approaching on the stone passageway. They stopped abruptly outside his cell.

"Are you de Lacey?" he asked coldly.

"I am James de Lacey."

"You are to stand trial today for treason. Do you want something to eat now? It will be a long day for you," the guard said, his voice more sympathetic.

"Yes guard, I would be grateful for some food," James replied, realising the truth of what the guard had said.

"I will return shortly. Can't promise you a lot, but I'll do the best I can for you de Lacey."

As the guard walked back down the passage, James counted his steps. Forty-seven paces to the door, he calculated. He waited and waited for the guard to return, until at least an hour had passed. He lay down on the straw bed, listening to the coughing of the other prisoners. God knows how many of them are here, and some of them may have been here for years, he thought. Consumption coughs, due to lack of food and clean air, meant many would die here. The thought of a life sentence suddenly gave James a new perspective on his situation. What if that is my sentence? Would I be granted even that mercy? He wondered. There would be some hope then of eventual release, if the rebellion succeeded. The thought cheered him somewhat.

He heard the approach of the guard once again, and some of the prisoners shouting abuse at him as he passed their doors.

"Just stand by the wall, de Lacey," he ordered.

"You need not worry, guard. I know how foolish it would be to attempt escape. I won't harm you, if that's your worry," James said, looking at the man before him.

He could only have been twenty-five years of age at the most, James thought. Most likely from a local family in the town. The guard carried a tin tray with a plate of bread and a piece of cheese. There was also a tin mug with milk in it.

"Prison rations de Lacey! The best I'm afraid. You look like a man that was used to better," the guard said, now relaxing more.

"Yes I was, but little point in thinking about that now. I could so easily have been shot yesterday. That and what lies ahead of me worries me more than bread and cheese!" James said, trying to bring a little humour to the situation.

"How do you feel about your trial?" the guard asked him now, his tone more serious.

"What is there to think, other than Justice Stewart has decided my fate months ago. The main problem is not so much that I am a rebel, but rather that the woman I love is the woman he intends to wed." James replied sighing.

His despair was apparent to the guard. He had heard rumours to this effect in relation to James' trial.

"A very sad situation for you and your woman. Who is she, if you don't mind me asking?" the guards curiosity was mounting as James spoke.

"Her full name is the Right Honourable Catherine Lady Foldsworth," James said casually.

"What! A titled lady! My God man you must have been mad. How could you think that such a match would work?" and the guard now sat down on the small wooden stool, totally intrigued.

"You see it did work. Simple as that. We just loved each other from the moment we met, and that was it," James said looking at the guard, who was enthralled by the story. "Would you do me a favour," James asked him directly.

"Oh hold on now. Just because I'm here talking to you..."

James interrupted him.

"No. I'm not trying to take advantage of your kindness, but would you see to it that she gets a letter from me if the worst happens me?"

The guard looked at the prisoner and knew he liked him. There was something almost tragic about him, he thought. One of the prisoners he had seen so many times who are looking death in the face.

"Alright, I'll do as you ask, but mind you, nobody is to know. Is that agreed de Lacey?" he said; now standing up.

"I promise I will say nothing. Would you mind telling me your name?"

"Alan Woodstock," the guard replied, extending his hand much to his own surprise.

"Happy to meet you Alan. Thank you for the conversation and the bread and cheese," James said smiling.

Alan Woodstock laughed, and walked out the cell door.

"I will be back for you de Lacey, in an hour or so. When you return from your trial I will have already put the writing material beneath the straw for you."

"Thanks Alan... very much," James said, feeling a heavy depression come over him.

The guard locked the door and walked back down the stone passageway, banging the outer door and locking it. Odd the way you can hear everything in here, James thought. Doors, locks, coughing. Oh Christ, what a nightmare all this is... poor Kitty, where on earth is she?

He ate the frugal meal, and drank the milk. He hadn't realised how hungry he was, his last meal being at Marcus' home. ' Marcus,!' he thought, then realised if he began to think about Marcus' death, he might not be able to hold on to his sanity.

* * *

On the mountainside the village was deserted, other than the dogs and hens that roamed freely. Some distance away the small population stood as Father Ryan intoned the prayers, and the body of Marcus was lowered gently into the deep peat grave. The people had been shocked when the body had been delivered earlier that morning by some of the townspeople. They saw the deep gash where Marcus had been shot in the back, his flesh rent asunder. Lovingly, Mag and Nell had washed the corpse and wrapped it in a linen sheet provided by Hannah. They had a hasty wake, where all came and paid their respects to what, for them, was the latest murder victim since the market day massacre. Their fear and hatred mounted equally, their anger also, at how another person could be shot down so cruelly.

The sun shone from the cloudless sky, as the soft mountain peat gradually covered the corpse of the young man who died simply because he had sheltered James and Kitty. Nell was glad that Kitty, Joe and Marjorie had left early for Wexford, as they had a greater ordeal ahead of them. The burial of Marcus would have left them utterly distraught and hopeless. They needed what little hope they carried in their hearts.

Mag placed a bunch of wild cowslips and primroses on the fresh grave, and prayed that somehow Marcus would find rest, having left life so violently and suddenly. She sat alone at the graveside now, looking down at the plains beneath her.

"Only a matter of time now for you too, James," she whispered sadly. "Will you rest here too, I wonder, or where? And Lady Catherine? Will she ever be sane again when you are gone? Ireland? God, the curse of this country... so much bloodshed, for what? Nothing ever came of it, nothing other than more violent death. And here I am, having lived so long, and seen so much, and still the call goes out from one generation to the next, 'Die! Die! Die!'" Mag almost shouted this out this last part.

Maybe this time something will come of it all, she thought. It should, with all the bayonets and pikes! Again her thoughts returned to Kitty. She looked down at Oak Hall, shimmering now in the blue haze of the midday heat.

"Bayonets... and ... Lace..." she said audibly.

"What's that you said Mag?" It was the voice of Nell behind her.

"Oh, I'm just sitting here thinking of James and Kitty, and thinking that neither bayonets or lace have anything in common and yet those two found everything together. Life, love, and they risked everything in the finding of it. But I'm wondering Nell about them both. Aye, just wondering. Sometimes out here of a night, years ago, I would lie back and look at the stars after a long day collecting herbs. I would look at the heavens for hours. When the skies were very clear you would see great shooting stars streak across the sky, from one end to the other. Great bright streaks would follow them, and then as suddenly as they appeared they were gone. Gone forever. Somehow I think that is what will happen our James and his lovely lady."

Nell looked at Mag, wondering where she got her odd notions at times. Looking at the night sky for hours! Maybe she was right. Maybe James and Kitty would be unable to live their lives. But that has yet to be seen, she thought.

"Don't go troubling yourself Mag with those sad notions. God spoke first, and remember that!" Nell said with a burst of religious fervour.

"Spoke first indeed! Where was He when Lord Foldsworth shot down young Marcus here? Asleep or what?" Mag said angrily.

"May God forgive you Mag for such blasphemy," said Nell, blessing herself.

"I never believed all that stuff Nell. Oh, I believer in God all right, but the fate of some people can't be changed, whatever way it is. Now, take the likes of Bartley Finnegan and Jerome Hennessy. The pair of them should have been drowned the day they were born!" Mag said vehemently.

"I'll listen to no more of that Mag, now are you coming back for your dinner or what are you going to do?" Nell asked her irritably.

"Oh don't be so fussy with an old woman Nell. I will follow you on in a moment or two. I just want to stay a little longer. The dinner will keep. You're a kind woman, Nell Gilltrap, and a lucky one too," Mag said, smiling up at her.

Nell bent down and kissed the top of her head.

"It's your favourite today, Mag. Rabbit stew!" and Nell walked away smiling.

After some time Mag stood up, complaining of her aching bones, and once again looked down the valley. This time she saw a troop of yeomanry slowly ascending the mountain. Gathering her long skirts she tried to run as fast as she could to give warning of the approaching enemy. She called out as she reached the cottage door, and Nell and Father Ryan rushed out, thinking she must be ill.

"Quickly! The yeomanry are coming. Alert the village!" she gasped.

Father Ryan and Nell quickly went from door to door and within minutes the population of the village was assembled on the narrow thoroughfare.

"To the caves all women and children. We must hurry. Nell, you and Mag remain and detain them as long as possible. Put out all cooking fires and get rid of any remains of the food you were eating. Hurry! You must hurry!" the priest ordered.

Nell watched the approaching yeomanry ascend the last remaining mile. The village was evacuated within minutes. No traces of fires remained on the cottage hearths, only the fowl complacently picking at the potatoes they unexpectedly received.

"Quickly Nell, inside! You must pretend that I am your dying mother. Help me to bed, woman, and leave the cottage door wide open," Mag told her firmly.

In the small bedroom, Mag lay back in the bed, her hair now falling over her shoulders in long grey tangles. She rubbed some green dye, made from tree bark, on her face. She looked dreadful, Nell thought.

"Well, what are you gaping at Nell Gilltrap. Isn't it the fever I have, and make sure you tell them that. Now, pass me that other bottle, and be quick about it," Mag said impatiently.

Taking the cork from the bottle, Mag sprinkled the liquid liberally around the bed and the walls of the room. The smell was appalling, and Nell felt nausea rising within her. Mag chuckled.

"A bad smelling fever too, I have, Nell!" and she cackled loudly in her high-pitched laughter.

They could now hear the sound of the yeomanry; the hoof beats stamping on the dry roadway. Mag waited a little longer, until they were in earshot, then the keening began. Nell stood transfixed as she looked at Mag, thrashing her arms wildly around the bed, and her eyes now rolling from one side of her head to the other. Nell could not believe the transformation before her. Then the recognisable voice of Lord Foldsworth called out.

"You in there! I order you to come out, now I say!" he shouted.

Nell walked out.

"Who is in there woman?" he demanded.

"My mother, dying your honour," Nell answered simply.

"Dying be damned!" he shouted as he dismounted, striding towards the door and pushing Nell roughly aside.

The twenty or more yeomen sat laughing on their horses at the audible groans of Mag within the cottage. Lord Foldsworth walked into the room and was not prepared for the sight that awaited him. Mag, seeing his astonishment, thrashed afresh in the bed. It was then he smelled the noxious air. Taking a linen scented handkerchief from his pocket, he placed it on his nose.

"What the hell is wrong with her?" he demanded of Nell.

"'Its the fever, your honour. She won't last the night God love her," Nell replied, dabbing her eyes with an old rag.

"Fever! Good Christ woman and where is my daughter?" he asked as he walked back, aghast at the sight of Mag.

"All the village have left your honour, yesterday evening. As soon as they saw the marks of the fever on my poor mother they left me, and all alone too."

"Where has my daughter gone?" he shouted.

"With the rest of them, your honour, to the town. Afraid of the fever," Nell replied as she dabbed Mags forehead with a damp cloth.

Mag once more cried out wildly, as if she were on the verge of expiring.

"Bloody banshee..." Lord Foldsworth murmured, "Quick! Out of here. The fever has taken hold," he said to his men, who quickly turned their horses at the mention of the dreaded disease. The cavalcade was gone in minutes.

The two women laughed and laughed, the tears of hilarity flowing down their cheeks.

"Mag you are an incredible woman," Nell said, helping her from the bed.

"Incredible? I don't think that's the right word. Poor Lord Foldsworth! And he stumbling out of the room at the mention of the fever. Thank God he believed it. The others are safe now, which is the main thing, and we are unlikely to be troubled by the yeomanry! Their hasty departure was a great relief," Mag said, exhilarated by her convincing performance.

As Lord Foldsworth and the yeomanry rode south towards the town, he ordered them to turn every house upside-down if necessary to find his daughter, and to question everybody they met. A reward of fifty pounds was to be given to the person who would inform him of her whereabouts.

* * *

Wexford town was a bustle of activity. Tall sailing ships stood by the quayside like great stranded swans, their wares being unloaded, while others sailed out of port to their various destinations. On the hillside, the jail was clearly visible. It was a tall cold-looking building. Sinister, Kitty thought. Their journey had been uneventful, other than the bouncing and rattling of the cart.

None of them had minded the discomfort, as there was so much at stake. Joe thought about the situation, and being honest with himself realised that little hope remained for James. Marjorie had come to the same conclusion, but neither would attempt to say as much to Kitty, who was still convinced that his release could somehow be arranged. They crossed the bridge, where the river Slaney swept beneath them; it's journey ending as it kissed the salt waters of the sea. It passed beneath them darkly, swirling as it met the upcoming tide.

Then they saw a sight that they were ill prepared for. Marjorie was the first to notice it in the distance at the far side of the bridge, nearest the town. At first she thought it was her imagination, but on looking again realised that her eyes were not playing tricks on her.

A man was hanging from the bridge, in plain view for all travellers to the town to see. Kitty cried out in fright.

"Look away, Miss Kitty! You too, Marjorie. It's a gruesome sight for even a man to behold, or any civilized person for that matter," Joe declared, shocked by the sight himself.

Kitty vomited, and Marjorie held her as she retched violently over the opposite side of the cart. There was a sign hanging from the dead man's feet which read:
LET REBELS AND TRAITORS BEWARE
Joe gave the horse a light tap of the whip, so that Kitty, still leaning over the cart, would not have time to read the notice. Having gone some distance, she looked back on the awful sight.

"What was written on the wooden notice, Joe?" she asked.

"Oh, the fellow was a horse thief, Miss. Must have been at it for years for the authorities to do that to him," he replied casually.

Marjorie was grateful for Joe's sensitivity.

"We turn right at the end of the bridge, Joe, and then left. We should be at my cousin's tavern soon. I for one am weary as death, and hungry too," she added.

Kitty felt sorry for Marjorie. Her appreciation of the woman increased hourly.

"Marjorie, both you and Joe are so good to take me here. Be assured I shall not forget your kindness," Kitty said appreciatively.

They felt heartbroken for her, knowing what fate lay ahead of James. They were becoming increasingly more concerned for Kitty's future welfare and wellbeing. Having crossed the bridge they now drove a short distance before turning left, which led them up a small incline.

"Five years since I have last laid eyes on Pat Redmond, Kitty. I hope he recognises his cousin when he sees her!" she exclaimed excitedly.

The streets were thronged with people and soldiers, or so it seemed to Kitty, for the streets of Wexford were renowned for their narrowness. There seemed to be an atmosphere of urgency, Kitty thought. Everyone in a hurry, not like Enniscorthy, where life seemed to move at a more leisurely pace.

At the far end of the street there was a great commotion rising. Joe stopped his horse and cart and stood up to try to see what was happening. All he could see was seven, perhaps eight, red-coated soldiers, and behind them what resembled a great wooden cage on a cart being pulled by two heavy workhorses. Suddenly he realised that it was the prison wagon, obviously taking some prisoners to the jail.

"It's the prison cart, Marjorie. I'd better pull to one side, or there will be trouble in the making," he shouted, trying to explain to her over the rising din.

"A prison cart! What in heavens name is that?" Kitty asked Marjorie, bewildered by the term.

"It's a wooden type of cage, my love, used for moving prisoners to and from the prison. You will see it presently," Marjorie explained.

James lay on the floor of the wooden cage, too exhausted with his ordeal of the day and sore from the beatings ordered by Viscount Stewart. He didn't care now when death came, despite the fact that he was to be hanged in ten days time. The trial had been short, some twenty minutes, during which Justice Timothy Stewart had looked at him with such hate and tangible derision. His mind refused to recall any further details just at that moment. The street was crowded and the cart moved slowly through it. He decided to sit up with his back to the bars for support. It eased the pain that was searing through his stomach and back. Two of his teeth had been dislodged, and the pain seemed to be reaching into his brain.

All about him life bustled. Women and children, laughing and carrying their purchases. A few men singing outside the tavern, where they obviously had spent the greater part of their day drinking. A man stood at a fish stall, the smell of the fresh fish pervading the air as they passed by. James longed for peace, and the thought of lying on the straw of his cell appealed to him for the first time since his incarceration.

Joe, standing on the cart trying to steady his grip on the horse, was the first to notice the prisoner in the cart. He was aghast at the sight of James, who was now almost unrecognisable. Blood seemed to be coming from his mouth, his clothes were torn, and he was completely white-faced as though near death. Joe tried not to panic. He turned to Marjorie and told her to take Kitty into the nearest tavern, lest the horses bolt. But Kitty, overhearing him, jumped to the ground instead.

"You need not worry Joe. I am well used to controlling frightened animals," and she took the carthorse by the head collar and bit, and held him, talking to him gently. Joe beckoned to Marjorie to look at the prison cart.

"Merciful God!" she cried out, the shouting of the approaching soldiers drowning her cry of desperation. Fortunately Kitty stood with her back to the approaching procession as she tried to calm the frightened horse.

"Now, now. You must not be afraid of all this fuss," she said to the animal, which relaxed with her reassuring tones.

Kitty glanced back over her shoulder, and saw that the prison cart was now only some ten yards from where they were waiting. She smiled up at Joe and Marjorie.

"Did I not tell you I would calm her Joe," she called out.

But their gaze was directed beyond her, and their expressions blank. Kitty couldn't understand this fascination with the event.

James jumped upright, for he knew he had heard the unmistakable sound of Kitty's voice. He looked through the crowd, as he stood erect holding the wooden bars with both hands.

"Kitty! Kitty!" he almost screamed, as he saw her holding the frightened carthorse, as Joe and Marjorie stood speechless, looking helplessly on.

Kitty turned around to see the man she loved standing, almost unrecognisable, caged like a wild animal.

"James... is that you?" she screamed out.

He was not able to answer her now for a lump in his throat threatened to choke the very breath from his body. Letting go of the horse, Kitty ran towards the prison cart, clinging wildly to its side.

"Oh James, what have they done to you? What have they done to you?" she screamed out as most of the people on the street stood looking on. Joe jumped down from the cart and ran to her, putting his arms about her in an attempt to pull her away from the attention of the soldiers.

"Let me go Joe! I tell you, let me go!" she cried out.

The soldier nearest came over to her, shouting.

"Out of the way wench, out of the way!" and he pulled her by the cloak, which tore in his hand.

"How dare you touch me, you vermin!" she shouted at him in rage.

"Who the hell do you think you are holding up this prisoner cart? Out of the way now, before I arrest you too," he said to her gruffly.

At that moment a second soldier came from behind James, striking him on the back of the head with the butt of his musket. James fell heavily to the floor of the cart, now unconscious, fresh blood flowing from the wound he had received.

"You bloody animal, how dare you behave like this!" Kitty screamed at the soldier.

Looking at Joe, the soldier nearest him said,

"I'll give you to the count of five to get her out of the way, otherwise she will go in the cart with him. Now, One... Two... Three..."

Joe knew what he had to do now, much as he disliked the idea. Turning Kitty around to face him, he slapped her roughly on the face. Unable to cope with a further shock, Kitty fainted. Joe lifted her and carried her gently back to the cart, placing her tenderly on its straw covered floor.

"Don't feel too bad Joe," Marjorie comforted him, "you had to do it. Just look behind you at who is coming now..."

To add further to his shock, Joe saw Justice Stewart riding down the street towards them. Marjorie quickly threw her cloak over Kitty, who lay almost lifeless on the straw. Joe, leaping from the cart, made his way hastily through the crowd to the nearest tavern. Lord Foldsworth rode directly behind Stewart, and Marjorie almost fainted when she recognised him. She knew she must act quickly. Realising that Kitty may not regain consciousness for some time; she eased herself from the rear of the cart and began to lead the horse forward through the crowds to the opposite side to where Lord Foldsworth would pass. Somehow the horse had now forgotten it's fear, and Marjorie prayed that he would not bolt or become stroppy.

She began to hum a song to the animal, something she had often seen her father do, and she smiled as she noticed that it was her who lost fear, not the animal.

Both men rode by, their heads held high in arrogance. They paid no attention to her or the cart, and relief filled her body.

"Good boy," she said, patting the animal on the neck.

Joe watched Lord Foldsworth and Justice Stewart ride past, and knew that they had achieved their long awaited purpose. They would drink tonight to the death of James, he thought, and on the morrow begin anew their search for

Kitty. As the two men disappeared amidst the throngs of people, Joe walked up the street in the direction Marjorie had taken. It did not take him long to catch up with her, for she stood in a small square waiting for him.

"How is she?" Joe asked, looking at the cloak covered form of Kitty.

"Still in a faint fortunately, the poor girl. What is to become of her? Or of us too, for that matter? My God, we are risking death here, and for what? It's all hopeless, Joe," Marjorie said in despair.

He agreed with her in his heart.

"Come. We have to get to my cousins before dark. There is a curfew here, or so a woman told me." Marjorie went to the rear of the cart to find Kitty stirring beneath the cloak. She lifted Kitty's head and cradled her in her arms.

"It's alright now, Miss Kitty. The danger is past now."

But Kitty just lay in her arms and didn't speak. Speech was beyond her as her mind tried to grapple with the pain and confusion of the past hour.

Arriving at the rear of Redmond's tavern, Joe stabled the horse, now almost on the point of collapse from exhaustion. Kitty stood beside him, listless and silent, as she watched Joe groom the weary animal before feeding it. Marjorie had gone into the tavern to meet her cousin and explain their mission and circumstances.

Presently a young man came to the stables and escorted Kitty and Joe inside. He led them away from the main public rooms and brought them up a long dimly lit stairway, turning abruptly onto a small landing. He opened the door to their right hand side, and Marjorie walked over to Kitty and Joe.

"Pat, I would like you to meet Lady Catherine Foldsworth," she said, "and of course, this is Joe."

"Very pleased to meet you my lady, and good to see you too, Joe. I will have food sent directly, and maybe your ladyship would like to have a bath perhaps," Pat said kindly, looking at Kitty.

"Very kind of you Mr Redmond, but I only long to sleep, if my two friends here will not think me ill-mannered in not joining them for dinner," Kitty replied, her exhaustion apparent.

"Of course not, my love," Marjorie assured her, "I will bring you to your room, if Pat will lead the way?"

Pat Redmond looked at the young lady and wondered how much more suffering could one so young endure! He led them up a further flight of stairs and into a spacious room lit by four lamps. The soft glow gave an almost unreal appearance to the room, Kitty thought. It was warm and comfortable and a great bed stood at the centre of it.

"Lady Catherine, would you like me to bring you a glass of punch. It might help you sleep," Pat asked gently.

"No thank you, Mr Redmond. I don't think I shall have any trouble in that regard. If I could rest for an hour I feel it would do wonders for me," Kitty said softly.

"Well, should you need anything at all, Marjorie here will be in the room next to you," Pat told her reassuringly.

"We will leave you now, Miss Kitty," Marjorie said, kissing her gently on the cheek, "and as Pat said, should you need me at all, do come in."

"You are all so kind, and thank you again," Kitty said; as she tried to conceal her desire just to be alone with her thoughts.

When they had both left her she sat on the side of the large bed and stared blankly at the red carpet on the floor.

"And what of you my love? A cold cell, and old bed, a bruised body. Oh James, James, how will I live without you?" she cried quietly. She recalled the prison cart, and the look of terror and despair in James' eyes, and she heard her own cries of desperation echo in her mind.

Joe and Marjorie ate their late supper by the fireside in the small parlour Pat had brought them into. He sat with them listening to the entire story, and the reality was very clear to him.

"Look Marjorie. God knows, if I thought there was any hope of helping James escape, I would be the first to assist. But in all my years in this town, no such escape has ever been possible. The cells where James is kept are well within the body of the jail, impossible to reach. The windows that look out from their cells are at least sixty feet above ground, in plain view of the courtyard, with soldiers posted there every hour, day and night. It's impossible!

Bribing them is also impossible for the guards know that it's hanging without a trial for them to assist in an escape, even if it's only a thief they assist, much less one charged with treason, such as James is! No. I'm afraid that the very most we can hope for, and mind you I can't promise anything, is that maybe... and again I say maybe... I can arrange for a visit for Kitty to see him one last time. It may take more than a day to accomplish, and money too," Pat finished, looking at Marjorie and Joe.

They sat in further silence trying to grasp the finality of Pat's summary of the situation, even though it matched their own.

"Very well then Pat," Marjorie said standing up slowly, "It is just a matter then of Kitty meeting James for the last time and, as you say Pat, only if it can be arranged. I have money with me, so that at least isn't a problem. The problem is we must not allow Kitty to know that she will not see James again. God love us, were she to know that she would go insane. They live one for the other," she said sadly.

"'Tis true Pat," Joe added, "we will tell her we are working on a plan that will take some weeks to put into action, but that we have arranged for her to visit James for the moment. Then hopefully she will agree to return home with us and await further developments."

"I only hope she believes us!" Marjorie said, "and Pat, if the visit could possibly be arranged as soon as possible, the better it would be for all. This town is dangerous for us, with Justice Stewart and Lord Foldsworth riding the streets. God knows it was only luck that the three of us were not sighted today, or we too would be in jail this night.

Pat Redmond knew well the danger they all faced. He too would be hanged should it be discovered he was harbouring a rebel. He thought of the young woman sleeping upstairs, and of the sacrifice she had made for the man she loved, losing almost everything for that love, and now the apparent futility of it all! It was a tragic end for them both, and they being so young. Life should be only beginning for them, not ending so abruptly.

"What in God's name brought them back to Ireland? What were they thinking of? America is where they belong, not here," Pat said angrily, spitting into the fire.

"They both wanted to return, Pat. Kitty has seen both sides of life here, that of her class and that of us. James loves Ireland and Kitty too. But you're right. Perhaps they should have gone to America" Marjorie wept.

Outside the rain now lashed against the windows, coming from the southeast where a storm was brewing.

"It will be a rough night, and its bed time for me good people," Pat said standing up.

"We are lucky to have you, Pat Redmond," Joe said, shaking hands with his host.

"No, 'tis I am the lucky one to meet people who still believe the country has a future. Tomorrow I will arrange the visit, all going well, and have you all out of this town in a day or two. Meanwhile, keep out of sight of the tavern below, for all types come in here to eat and drink. You wouldn't be quite sure who the hell half of them are."

"You need not worry Pat," Marjorie assured him, "we know only too well that the very walls have ears."

They parted company, each going to their respective rooms. Marjorie paused outside Kitty's room listening for any sound, but all was quiet. Kitty was obviously sound asleep. Marjorie, blowing out her lamp, lay in bed listening to the storm gathering force. She thought of James in prison, and then her thoughts went to the mountain village, and old Mag and Nell and the others. It seemed that everywhere she went there was no peace or security. It was as if everyone was on the edge of a great chasm that was ready to swallow them alive at any moment. The thought frightened her, and she sat up and lit the lamp again. Its soft glow comforted her, as she watched the flickering shadows on the ceiling.

* * *

James lay awake listening to the sound of the sea; it's great waves lashing the quayside in the distance. Rain blew in through the barred window. Earlier he had gathered the straw from the floor and placed it beyond its reach to stay dry. He had managed to wash his wounds with the drinking water that had been left in his cell, and had extracted the two loose teeth. The aching had now subsided, and his thoughts were of Kitty.

It had been like a vision for him to see her, even for the brief moments before he had been knocked senseless. She had looked beautiful despite her anguish, he thought. Imagine her coming this far to try to see me... Oh Kitty... why, oh why did we not take the chance we were given and live far away from all this hell, he wept. He could still see the heartbreak on the face of Joe and Marjorie, so faithful too, he thought, coming to death's door with me.

His mind went back to the trial of that afternoon. The courtroom had been full of people, as he was pushed roughly to take the stand, which was on the right hand side of where Justice Stewart and Lord Foldsworth had sat. They had looked at each other smiling as he was ushered into the courtroom. It was then he had tripped on the chains that were manacled to both ankles. His face had hit the steps and his nose had bled.

"Will you please get that prisoner to stand? We can't sit here all day watching him struggle about the place," Justice Stewart had shouted at the two guards.

Lord Foldsworth had dabbed his nose with his perfumed handkerchief, eyebrows raised, as he watched James being almost thrown into the convicted mans boxlike pulpit.

"Are we finally ready to proceed?" Justice Stewart drawled.

"Ready My Lord," the court clerk replied, then announcing, "The prisoner will stand to respect the court."

But James remained seated.

"Is the prisoner deaf?" Lord Foldsworth shouted.

Immediately a guard gripped one of James' ears, and lifted him to his feet.

"Good, my man. I see you are not deaf at least," Lord Foldsworth said calmly.

"Is your name James de Lacey, previously resident at Oakfort, North Wexford County?" the judge asked.

"Yes," James replied in a casual tone.

"I see. You, the prisoner de Lacey, hereby stand before this court accused of the attempted burning down of Oak Hall, residence of the Foldsworth family. You also stand accused of the consequential death of the Right Honourable Edwina Foldsworth, wife of my revered colleague here on my right. What have you to say of this matter?"

"I did not do it," James replied, knowing the futility of it all.

"So you deny the charges then?" the judge stated plainly.

"Yes I do."

"I see you have not alone the audacity to deny the fire, and the dreadful death of Lady Foldsworth as a result of your fanaticism, but you actually stand there now telling lies! You are also charged with treason, de Lacey. Plotting the downfall of the Government in Ireland. My goodness, looking at the charges one knows not where to begin," Justice Stewart sighted heavily, savouring every moment.

"I believe, de Lacey, that you were responsible for the fire at Oak Hall, and I am reliably informed for a fact that you are a member of the United Irishman's organisation. Now, you tell me the truth! And realise that I have the power of life and death for you my man. If I were you I would begin to consider the very precarious position you find yourself in. Speak up and don't mutter," and with that, Justice Stewart sat back, casting a glance at Lord Foldsworth. Their hour of triumph was upon them.

"I will tell the truth," James said, looking at the two men before him, and looking at the packed courtroom, "and you will also hear the truth. The reason I am here to stand this farcical trial is simple. I fell in love with that man's daughter," he shouted for all to hear clearly, pointing at Lord Foldsworth. "Yes, that's right," he continued, "I did not try to burn Oak Hall. I was working that night in the local tavern. Besides, why would I try and burn the home of the woman I loved?"

The crowd in the courtroom murmured in agreement.

"Yes, the reason I am here on trial is that you both want me dead, out of the way, for the lady I love also loves me truly."

Lord Foldsworth leaped from his seat.

"How dare you tell such blasted lies. You took advantage of a grief stricken young woman who had just lost her beloved mother. Yes! An opportunist of the worst possible kind de Lacey," he bellowed.

Justice Stewart became alarmed at the crowded room, with its occupants now suspicious of the trial and charges. James turned to face the people.

"This isn't a real trial. This has been planned for months on end: my arrest, and my eventual death. Yes, I want Ireland free. I want freedom for all the people, land for them and education. Not endless hunger, ignorance and struggle. The woman also wants the same. She too shares our hopes."

The court erupted into a resounding cheer, and both Lord Foldsworth and Justice Stewart stood up pounding the bench for order. One of the guards struck James in the face with the butt of a long barrel gun, dislodging two teeth. The pain shot through James' face and head as he staggered back, falling against the side of the stand. Lord Foldsworth fired a pistol in the air, and calm was restored instantly.

"Should there be any further disruption I shall have the court cleared and have you all arrested," Justice Stewart shouted, looking down on the crowd before him. "You, de Lacey. I can plainly see you are inciting this lot to violence. Look at my distraught colleague beside me here... you have done enough harm to date! The death of his wife is not enough for you. You wanted his daughter too. What sort of animal are you de Lacey?" he ended in a more hushed tone.

The courtroom was now as silent as a crypt.

"Animal? No. It's you two are the animals in this court, with your trumped up charges. Tell them all here what your own plans are! Go ahead and tell them if you dare. It's you who want the hand of the lady I love, and that's why you will sentence me to death. Out of the way with him is your motto, isn't that simply the truth? No, I tell you all, it is the two of you that stand in judgement of me who are the only liars here today. Well, know this both of you. Lady Catherine Foldsworth would not soil her hands on the likes of a gutless man like you. Has she not disowned her own father? Is that not true? You, Foldsworth, who brought the pitch cap north of the county it was you who shot an old woman in sight of her pitch capped son. The sight of you makes me sick!" James shouted now, realising that he would never again have the chance to speak the truth.

Again the courtroom erupted with shouting and the stamping of feet. This time four soldiers fired shots above the heads of the crowd, plaster falling from the walls like a shower of snow.

"I will have Order! Order! Order!" Justice Stewart shouted.

When calm once more descended on the room, James resumed. Lord Foldsworth realised that if he was forbidden to speak, mayhem would ensue. Better to let him have his say, he thought, and we will have the last word.

"You Stewart. You sit there as a judge! How much did you pay for the position? And you Foldsworth. How would you let your beautiful daughter marry such a fop?"

Both men now sat back, resigned to the folly their court had become. They knew they had little choice. For now.

"You both think that by my death, Kitty will in time resign herself to a loveless marriage? You are even more stupid than I thought. No! She will never marry you Stewart. Never! I know you will sentence me to death. Go ahead. I have no fear of death. But this I will say. Someday... aye... someday, all your deeds will be told to the amazement of the hearers, who will see you as the coward and fool that you are, and your doings will go down in history as abominations. Yes, a day when this country will be free. That day will come, and there will be nothing any of you can do to stop it. The many who die will only hasten it."

Silence prevailed throughout the courtroom and James sat down, exhausted and sore.

"Quite finished our little speech, have we?" Justice Stewart said in mock courtesy.

James did not reply to his cynicism. Lord Foldsworth moved his chair closer to the judge, and they both seemed to be conferring, purely for the benefit of the onlookers. After some time Justice Stewart looked again at James.

"Let the prisoner rise," he said.

James stood up, but looked at the people, the many faces and countless expressions.

"James de Lacey, you have been found guilty on two counts. Guilty of the consequential death of the Right Honourable Edwina, Lady Foldsworth, and guilty of the attempted arson of Oak Hall.

"Having weighed the facts carefully, however much we would like to sentence you to transportation, this is not possible due to the gravity of your crimes.

"Instead, you are sentenced to hang by the neck until dead, on the fourth day of June this year of Our Lord, 1798. May God have mercy on your soul."

The people assembled in the court were speechless, and before they realised it, both Lord Foldsworth and Justice Stewart had vanished silently through a side door. James stood gazing at the empty judicial stand.

Treason, arson, the death of Lady Edwina... quite a list, he thought, and one that had left the crowd dumbfounded, if not convinced of his guilt at this stage.

"You! Get down here," one of the soldiers said, grabbing him by the ankle chains.

James lost his balance and fell down the steps, his ribs taking the heavy impact of the fall. He remained on the floor breathless for some moments before receiving a further kick in the stomach, and as he rolled over, a further kick to his back. He thought he was about to die, and almost hoped he would so intense was his pain.

He was dragged outside and pushed into the prison cart. The great crowd assembled outside stood silently watching the treatment he received, powerless to assist him for the same fate would be allotted to any who might attempt to do so. It was then that James noticed Father Murphy, who nodded to him in recognition. He was dressed as a farmer, heavily disguised, with Matt Ryan beside him. As James looked at them his spirits lifted momentarily. Then, unable to bear the pain anymore, he fainted. His next recollection was the street where he had seen Kitty, Marjorie and Joe.

As James recounted the day's events in his small cold cell, the memory of all the familiar faces somehow kept him from feeling total isolation. They had not forgotten him. Outside the jail the rain had eased, despite the wind that howled in from the harbour. Slowly, his aching body drifted into sleep. He did not dream.

* * *

Williams sat in the sun outside the door of his brother's home, on a garden seat many years old. He wanted to laugh at his own folly, but was unable to do so. Neither was he able to cry. I feel numb, old and foolish, he thought. Why did I think time would stand still, he wondered. Nobody told him his brother had been transported. Nobody had wanted to bring such troublesome news to Wexford and Oak Hall. In one sense he was relieved that at least his brother wasn't dead.

Transported for poaching rabbits! God, the madness of it, he thought. Australia! The far side of the earth. He would never see his brother again. What am I to do, he thought, as he chewed a young dandelion, something he had not done since his youth. The thatch on the roof of the cottage had fallen in, and the place was derelict.

He knew he must face the truth and return to the only place where he had some semblance of family left. The mountain village. There was nowhere else to go. He had been in the village of Stradbally four days now, and it was time to think of travelling south again. Even in the midlands the air reeked of rebellion, and he knew the times were dangerous. Nevertheless, he did not feel any fear. He almost laughed when he thought he could be considered a danger to the authorities.

He returned to the neighbour's house where he had stayed, and leaving them some money discretely, he saddled his horse and began the long ride south to the mountains on the Wicklow and Wexford border. At least Hannah will be there, and Lady Catherine, he sighed with relief. Not all my world is gone.

He stopped outside the old cemetery, tethering his horse. He climbed over the old stile slowly, and made his way through the long summer grasses to find the grave of his parents. He remembered clearly its whereabouts. Finding the grave, he sat down. Wild primroses grew upon it in abundance. It was a lovely sight, he thought. He looked at the gravestone and its simple engravings, now almost covered with lichen.

TO THE MEMORY OF
ANASTASIA WILLIAMS DIED 1749.
HAROLD WILLIAMS HUSBAND OF
THE ABOVE, DIED 1753.
REST IN PEACE FOREVER.

Peace, he thought. Where can it be found? Perhaps only truly in death. Who knows? He felt tired and weary and did not look forward to the journey ahead, but his old sense of discipline prevailed, and having prayed for the souls of his beloved parents, he bid them a final goodbye.

He mounted his horse, and rode through the village, which was quiet in the heat of the afternoon sun. He was surprised at how agile he had become with his recent exercise of long distance riding. He laughed to himself.

"Still full of surprises, this Seymour Williams," he said, addressing his horse.

He rode until sunset, reaching the Carlow border where he went to an inn that seemed quite respectable. There were several soldiers and yeomanry eating at a large table. He paid them little attention, and sitting at a small table near the fire, he ordered some food. As he relaxed he overheard one of the soldiers talking.

"Justice Stewart was the judge in the case... sentenced him to hang June the fourth I hear... tried to burn down a place called Oak Hall..."

Williams was shocked to hear the gruesome news, and felt very uneasy. He called the girl from whom he had ordered his food and arranged for it to be brought to his room, telling her he was extremely tired. She assured him she would bring up the tray the moment it was ready.

He felt more at ease in the small room that overlooked green fields, now fading in the twilight. James de Lacey to hang! Oh what of Lady Catherine! Of Hannah? His apprehension mounted.

After his meal Williams sat at the small bedroom fire. He was still trying to come to terms with the fate of transportation that had been his brother's lot. The people I have worked for all my life, he thought, seem to have turned into monsters. What has happened,? he asked himself repeatedly. Or have I been blind? Closing my eyes to everything about me all these years?

He knew that he had simply lived to serve, from one season to the next, never taking time off other than when the family had gone to England, or some of the other great houses. He had rarely left the estate, other than the occasional trips to the town. No, he admitted to himself, it had always been work in service. It has swallowed my life, he thought, and I allowed it to happen. I am responsible for the way my life has flitted past, like a summers afternoon!

It was a very sobering realisation, and one that affected him greatly. Lady Catherine is right, he thought. Live your life. Find your truth, and then follow it regardless. And Hannah! The one woman he had loved and had not allowed his heart to pursue the dream. Why? Once again the truth struck him like a thunderbolt. Serving! And all for what?

"But maybe it's not too late," he sighed aloud.

As he undressed for bed he speculated on his future. Marry Hannah? Buy a small house? Live out the remainder of our days together? All possibilities, but its only possibilities they are until I talk to Hannah. His heart warmed at the thought of meeting her again, his sense of freedom growing as he realised that he, too, had a life to live.

"And is it not high time?" he mumbled, as he drifted into sleep.

* * *

Kitty awoke feeling a little better than anticipated. The room looked different in the early morning light. A gentle tap on the door, and Marjorie walked in with a breakfast tray, smiling.

"Good morning Kitty, and did you sleep well?" she asked cheerfully.

"Yes Marjorie, all things considered. Oh you are really very thoughtful, to bring my breakfast to me in bed," she said sitting up and forcing a smile.

"Now you eat up, my dear, and remain in bed for another few hours. Rest all you can. You have had a gruelling two weeks. Joe wonders how on earth your strength has held out, as indeed I do myself," Marjorie said seriously.

"It was a question of it having to, Marjorie, and the dreadful thing about all that travelling is that it was so totally in vain. Poor James. I can scarcely think of him, lest I go insane remembering how he looked yesterday."

Marjorie looked at the thin face of the young woman, still beautiful nonetheless.

"Kitty, there are two things you must know. Firstly, Justice Stewart and your father were following a short distance behind the prison cart yesterday. Obviously they had been presiding at James' trial, the outcome of which we do not yet know. Then secondly, my cousin Pat here hopes with some luck that you might be able to visit James. Mind you, he is promising nothing, but as I said, if we are lucky we may get to visit James," Marjorie said, omitting that it would possibly be her final chance to be with the man she loved so much.

"A visit Marjorie! Is that all? What of arranging his escape? Isn't that what we came here for?" Kitty said, almost in desperation.

"Calm yourself Kitty. These things take time you know. Yes they do, and you know what they say, 'slow and easy wins the day'!"

Marjorie was aware that very little would now send Kitty into a bout of hysteria, and she was not prepared for it.

"Yes Marjorie. I know you are right. I am sorry. I shall have to learn to be more patient and less childish. Of course it will take time to arrange his escape. And lest I forget, there is a small bag of sovereigns on the dressing table, and more in my bag. When you think they will prove useful for our purpose, please feel free to use them."

"Very well, Kitty. I will remember that. Now eat your breakfast my dear, and rest. I will be back to you in an hour or so, with some news I hope."

Marjorie left the room feeling only despair and sadness. As she joined Joe for breakfast in the small parlour, she found she could not eat.

"How is she Marjorie?" Joe asked her quietly.

" Joe, all she can think of is James' escape and how we are going to arrange it! She has no idea whatsoever of the impossibility of it all. Sooner or later she is going to learn the truth, and how are we going to pacify her is one great mystery to me. I should have got one of Mag's potions for when the time comes. Silly of me not to think of it, wasn't it?"

"No point in meeting the devil half way..." he replied, not finishing the sentence for, just then, the door opened and Pat Redmond came into the parlour. He stood looking at them both.

"I'm afraid the news of young de Lacey is very bad," he began.

"So he was tried yesterday after all," Joe said standing up slowly.

"Yes he was. There was uproar in the court. Everyone was talking about it downstairs last night. He seems to have told Lord Foldsworth a few home truths, and the judge also. Shots were even fired in the courthouse. However, be that as it may, the final verdict was passed, and he is to be hanged on the fourth of June."

Marjorie almost fainted with shock. The room seemed to turn upside-down for a moment, and beads of perspiration covered her brow.

"My God in heaven; Kitty must not hear of this, or she will lose her mind," Joe said, white in the face now from the dreadful reality they were all finally forced to face. Pat Redmond sat down and poured himself some tea.

"The good news is," he continued, "that I have managed to bribe two of the prison guards this morning who will allow the three of you into the prison tonight. You must be there at six o'clock. You will say that you are the prisoner's parents, and Kitty his sister. You will only be allowed a half hour, for the rest of the prison guards will be back from their supper by then. If you are caught, you will also be jailed, and you know the dreadful fate that would befall you should that occur!" he warned them.

"Furthermore, the town is full of soldiers, with check points on the bridge. I don't think you will be able to pass them without being discovered. They have been told to look out for a young woman bearing Kitty's description. God knows her accent alone would betray her. So I have come up with the following plan for you." Here he paused while Joe resumed his seat.

"Tonight, after your visit to the prison, you are to go directly to the north quay. There a small boat will be waiting for the three of you. The boatman, whose name is Jim, will take you upriver and when you get within four miles of Enniscorthy, he will ferry you to the riverbank. There is an old ruin there, and inside it you will find your horse and cart waiting. I have already sent one of my stable lads there with it this morning. Do you understand all I have told you?" Pat asked earnestly.

"Yes we do," Marjorie assured him.

"You must leave this town without delay, the three of you. I am told that this rebellion is about to unleash its fury at any time. If that happens when you are still here, none of you may ever see your mountain again. Need I say more?" Pat said in a grave tone of voice.

"I can never thank you enough Pat," Marjorie said, as she kissed him on the cheek.

"Indeed you have been very good to us," Joe added gratefully.

"Never mind the thanks, the pair of you. Just get that young woman to see James and then leave this place quickly. I hope we will all meet again in happier circumstances," responded Pat, and then he left, to allow them discuss their plans.

"James hasn't a lot of time left, has he Marjorie?" Joe remarked sadly.

"Very little now, but at least Kitty will be able to see him before it happens. We will have to tell her that his escape is going to take a month or more to organise. Hopefully she will believe us," Marjorie whispered.

"It's important she doesn't lose her grip on herself when she sees James, as from what I could see of him yesterday, he isn't the same looking man that we all knew," Joe added anxiously.

"We must try and be a bit cheerful Joe about the visit, and keep a brave face. I will go up now and tell Kitty the news, and impress upon her the absolute necessity of her remaining calm during the visit. And the consequences should she lose control of herself," Marjorie said adamantly.

Kitty was sitting at the mirror combing her hair when Marjorie came into the room.

"Oh Kitty, what beautiful hair! I have never seen it shine so," Marjorie said, trying to lighten the atmosphere. "And I have a little good news. We are going to the prison this evening to see James, and Kitty, I must warn you that if there is any display of uncontrolled emotion, much as I hate to say this, we will all end up in prison."

Kitty was overjoyed.

"Oh wonderful news Marjorie. I can't wait to see James, and I promise I shall be sensible to the last!"

"We will be visiting under the pretence that you are his sister, and Joe and I his parents. Furthermore Kitty, we must leave Wexford the moment we leave the prison. We are to travel up river by boat to near Enniscorthy. Everywhere there are patrols checking the identity of people entering and leaving the town."

Kitty could scarcely contain her excitement. Obviously there must be some greater plan afoot to release James, and that is why we are leaving town so suddenly, she reasoned silently, hearing Marjorie's voice only in the distance.

"I shall wear my blue riding habit Marjorie. It is James' favourite. I brought it especially as I knew it would remind him of the first time we met at the forge."

"A very good idea, Kitty," Marjorie said, delighted to see her spirits rise, resembling more the lady she had once known.

As evening approached, Joe and Marjorie put on some old clothes that Pat had left out for them. Kitty wore an old cloak, which covered her blue riding habit, and her excitement knew no bounds. At half past five Pat brought them to the rear of his tavern, where a man awaited them. Pat embraced Marjorie.

"You take good care of yourself, Marjorie Bass, and when the rebellion is over go and get that tavern of yours into tip-top shape."

She hugged him tightly.

"For all you have done Pat, many thanks, and you must come and stay with me for a while when you get the chance," she responded sadly.

Shaking hands with Joe, Pat asked him to take good care of the women, and Joe assured him he would guard them with his life.

"And you, Lady Foldsworth. It has been a great pleasure meeting you, and may everything work out for you in time," Pat said, shaking hands with Kitty.

"Thank you for all your assistance, Mr. Redmond. You have been most kind. I look forward to meeting you again, and perhaps you will someday be my guest at Oak Hall! Who knows?" Kitty said optimistically.

"That would be my pleasure, Lady Catherine."

Then Pat spoke quietly to the man waiting to bring them to the prison, asking him to do all in his power to make sure the young lady heard nothing of the impending execution of the man she was about to visit. He nodded in understanding.

Outside, the evening was overcast and warm. They followed the man, who was now walking a little ahead of them as arranged. They went through the narrow side streets with their heads held down. Kitty walked a little behind Joe and Marjorie. They looked like any ordinary parents and daughter, Marjorie thought, trying to keep her fears at bay. As they turned a corner, the prison loomed ahead of them. Kitty's heart sank as she looked at the strong, and clearly well guarded, fortress. Escape would obviously be very difficult for James, she could see, but somehow it would be accomplished. Money and skill, she reasoned, and why not! Wasn't he successfully released before, and the circumstances were also dangerous.

As they approached the prison entrance, six guards stood on duty. Marjorie turned to Kitty.

"Remember what I told you Kitty. Keep very calm, and all will be well. If not, well, this will be our new home!"

Kitty nodded her understanding.

"Halt where you are!" one of the guards shouted. "What is your business here?" he asked the man who had brought them.

"Here to see a prisoner, sir," he told him, handing him a small pouch discreetly. The guard took the pouch and quickly put it in his tunic.

"Open the door, Purcell," he shouted, and the great doors swung open, their hinges protesting from age and the weight they held.

Once inside, the doors clanged behind them with a thud. Another guard, who recognised the man that was leading the small party, was also handed a pouch. The bribe accepted, he walked ahead of them. They went in through a stout oaken door, and then began to climb a narrow stairway. Kitty could smell the stale air, and hear the groans of some of the prisoners. She walked in a daze, trying to persuade herself that of course escape was possible from such a place. Hadn't the guards accepted bribes? Didn't money seem to open all doors?

"Wait there," the guard said plainly, not bothering to ask them any questions.

Joe felt the tension in his body rise, and Marjorie could feel her heart pound in her chest and longed to be at the mountain village. She rebuked herself for her cowardice, knowing that they were unlikely to see James ever again. They stood silently waiting for the guard to return.

"In here, and follow that passage," he said, pointing to the one on the right hand side. The stranger who had accompanied them stood aside and said he would await their return. On either side of them were doors with small grid windows, a face looking through each of them. Some were quite old, Kitty thought, others young, but all with the pallor of death. Lack of fresh air and decent food, Kitty thought. Suddenly a guard, who had a pleasant appearance, stood before them.

"You are here to see James de Lacey, I am told," he said kindly.

"Yes we are," Joe said simply and to the point.

"Follow me please," and he walked slowly ahead of them.

He unlocked a further door and stood side to allow them pass through in front of him. Inside, he locked the door once more, and brought them to a cell at the end of the stone passageway.

"Some visitors for you, James," he said in what was a distinctly friendly voice, Joe observed. They stood aside as Kitty threw the old cloak to the ground and stood looking much her former self. James was speechless as he looked at her.

"My God Kitty! Joe! Marjorie! How ever did you manage to get in here?" and he wept, overjoyed on seeing them.

Kitty ran forward and embraced him tenderly. She was shocked to see him gone so very feeble, and with his two teeth missing. He looked so different. James noticed her observations.

"I can whistle better now," he laughed.

He embraced Marjorie, and then Joe, much to the blacksmith's embarrassment. "This is like a dream for me!" he exclaimed, unable to contain his excitement.

"I'm afraid you all have only half an hour at the most," the guard reminded them.

Joe and Marjorie walked back a discreet distance to allow the young couple some privacy.

"Kitty, you look so lovely. Just like when we first met. Do you remember that day?" James asked her, now holding her close.

"Of course I do. It was the most significant day of my life James. I can't believe you are actually holding me in your arms. Oh, It is a wonderful feeling. And to think that we will have your escape arranged soon, and then we will go directly to America, James," she said, clinging to him.

She doesn't know, he thought, and the pain in his heart seemed to travel to his throat threatening to choke him in his grief. Kitty sensed his tension.

"What is it, my love?" she asked him, standing back a little.

"My back hurts, my darling. Sleeping on the floor never agreed with me," he said, half laughing.

"You poor follow. James, haven't you suffered enough for Ireland? You will come to America, won't you? No more talk of rebellion or meetings. I could never bear living like a hunted criminal, James. I will never forget these past weeks. Never!"

He sat down on the wooden bench with Kitty beside him.

"No Kitty, our days of running are finished. Now, I want you to listen carefully to me. Keep away from the battle when it commences. I don't want you involved in it. Will you promise me that?"

"Of course James. Will we not be safely gone by that time?" she asked curiously.

"Well, perhaps not. Escapes take time to plan you know. It's not always that simple. But I have a further promise I need you to make me. It is the most important one I have ever asked of you," he said sadly.

"What is it James? You know I will do anything you ask," she assured him tenderly.

"I want you to go to the old ring fort each evening and wait for me there. If I am not there by sunset, you must come the next evening, and each evening until I collect you. It is there, Kitty, that we will next meet, believe me," and he held her tightly, kissing her with the old urgency she had missed so much.

"I promise, James. Every evening I shall wait for you. You will come though? You will not disappoint me?" she asked, looking into his deep blue eyes.

"Have I ever disappointed you, my love?"

She clung to him and wept.

"Now, you must be brave, Kitty, and no matter what happens or how long the delays are, I promise you Catherine Foldsworth, that I shall collect you at the old ring fort one evening at sunset. With my life I promise you that," he was hardly able to contain the depth of his sadness.

"Every evening James I shall wait for you, no matter what," she said slowly.

"Yes my love, no matter what takes place I will keep my promise to you. Then we will be together for all time my darling, and no one will ever be able to separate us ever again." He looked at her face and held it in his hands, tracing the line of her eyebrow with his finger. "You look just like you did the day your horse cast it's shoe at the hunt. Do you remember what I said to you that day?" he asked her smiling.

"You said several things to me, James, in that few moments we first met. I think you may remind me," she said teasingly.

"I told you that sometimes things happen to us for a reason, in your case, Misty casting her shoe. Otherwise we would perhaps never have met. Do you remember?"

She thought for a while, remembering the day clearly. The steam and smoke of the forge, Joe sweating as he hammered the horseshoe into shape, the bees on the ivy blossom humming, the happy smiling face of James.

"It's like a lifetime ago, James, isn't' it? So much has happened. So much, my darling."

"I fell in love with you that day, Kitty. Even then, I knew we would be together. I didn't quite know how it would come about, but deep within I knew... and... that's why I want you to come to the old fort each evening. It is a feeling I have beyond any knowing. You will be there Kitty, won't you? And then we will just slip away quietly."

She held him close.

"Of course I shall be there, James. Did I ever miss you before?" she asked him, stroking his hair gently.

"Never. I miss our walks and rides through the mountains Kitty. I miss you. The way you look, the smell and feel of you... Oh God... how much I love you Kitty Foldsworth."

The loud bang on the door brought them back to reality.

"You must be brave now, Kitty. No nonsense, nothing upsetting now. You must keep your promise to me, won't you?" James pleaded with her.

She looked at him and smiled.

"I shall wait, James, and I know you will come for me. You always did."

"Goodbye for a little while, my love. And one last thing! You will be dressed for me just like you are today. I always loved you in blue," he said, holding her in a final embrace.

He wanted to remember how it all felt, and how soft and lovely she was in his arms. Marjorie and Joe now stood waiting to say their final farewells to James. Marjorie embraced him.

"Take care of her for me Marjorie, when the time comes," he whispered.

"Don't worry James, I will look after her as if she was my own daughter. And you my lad, be brave. We will always remember you, James," and she then walked out of the cell without looking back.

Joe shook hands with him.

"Take care of yourself, my lad, won't you," Joe said gently.

"Don't worry Joe, and remember what to do when the time comes, won't you? Your promise... remember?"

"I will do that for you, and hope you forgive me James," he whispered.

Joe remembered the evening that James had made him promise never to let the hangman's noose take his life, but rather a shot from a pistol.

"Kitty my love," James said, walking over to where she stood a short distance from the cell door. She wept quietly as she embraced him one last time.

"James, I am frightened and lonely," she whispered into his ear.

"There is no need to be, my love. Just remember to wait for me," he said, as he held her face between his hands.

He kissed her lightly on the lips, and stood back to look at her, etching her image in his memory for the days and the ordeal that lay before him.

"Time to go now, I'm afraid," the guard, said, as he fingered the large bunch of keys in his hand.

"Until we meet, Kitty," James said, lifting his hand in farewell.

"Oh! I almost forgot to give you this," she said, taking out a small spray of white heather from her bag. "It's from the fairy fort, James, and is supposed to bring good luck."

He looked at the tiny white blooms, and could almost see the hills where it had been plucked.

"Goodbye my darling James, and I will wait, I promise I will."

The guard took her arm and gently led Kitty to where Joe and Marjorie stood waiting for her. They walked through the prison doors and out onto the street, the evening sun now casting long shadows before them. Nobody spoke. Kitty wrapped the old black cloak tightly about her, concealing her blue riding habit.

"We must hurry now," Joe eventually said, with urgency." The tide will be turning soon and we have a lot of travelling to do this night."

When they reached the north quay, Joe walked ahead of both women in search of the boat awaiting them. He noticed a small green vessel with a black sail, and an old man sitting beside it mending a net.

"Are you waiting for two woman and a man?" Joe asked him directly.

"That I am, and if they are here ask them to hurry. There are a lot of soldiers about tonight, and I don't like the smell in the air," he said almost irritably.

Joe beckoned to Kitty and Marjorie, and soon they were safely aboard the boat, Joe at the stern and both women in the centre. The old fisherman pulled the sails into the wind, and then sat with the rudder in one hand and his pipe in the other. The wind coming from the sea gripped the canvas, and with the surge of the incoming tide the boat moved swiftly into the centre of the river Slaney. The old man did not speak, but kept his eye on the river ahead, occasionally glancing at his passengers. He asked no questions. He had no wish to know who they were or where they were bound. He had been well paid by Pat Redmond, and that was all that mattered to him.

The sun was fast sinking in the western sky, the river reflecting the orange and scarlet colours of its death. The Norman tower at Ferrycarrig stood silently watching as the boat and its passengers sailed beneath its shadow. Swans moved swiftly out of the path of the silently approaching vessel. Kitty looked back at Wexford town for the last time as it faded into the twilight. Then they rounded the corner of the river, and it was suddenly gone from view. The reed beds looked golden in the evening light, wafting gently on the breeze. Startled water hens skimmed the river surface. Marjorie held onto the side of the boat nervously. She hated the water, and as she looked at its swirling depths, she hoped the boat would not capsize. Joe smoked his pipe, wondering if the lad had successfully delivered the horse and cart. He looked at the sky as night now approached. There was a sprinkling of stars appearing, scattered across the heaven.

There will be no rain tonight, he thought. We should be back in the village before dawn. He was relieved, as was Marjorie that the visit had gone quite well and without incident. Kitty had kept calm, and he thanked God that she was still unaware of the fate that lay in store for James. As for himself, he knew he would have to come back to Wexford once more, to find a place near the scaffold, and to grant James an honourable death. He dreaded the thought, but knew he must do as James had asked. He had, after all, given his word. Overhead white fleecy clouds raced across the half moon. The wind was rising, and it was in their favour, white river spray splashing the sides of the sailing boat as the sails hungrily grabbed the force and was propelled forward.

"How long now, boatman?" Joe asked.

"Half an hour or less, all going well," the old fisherman replied.

Marjorie felt a little more at ease now, gradually getting used to the motion of the boat.

"Are you alright, Kitty?"

"Yes Marjorie. I feel more at peace about everything somehow. All I have to do is wait for James. I am looking forward to seeing Hannah again and resting. I feel so tired Marjorie," Kitty replied.

"I wouldn't wonder after all you have been through. Plenty of rest and good air, and you won't know yourself after a few days. All I want to do is get out of this boat, Kitty. Never was fond of water, or boats for that matter."

Kitty laughed.

"Just as well then that you didn't come to France, Marjorie, isn't it?"

Marjorie was surprised that indeed Kitty did sound much more herself. She looked across the fields, now plain in the moonlight. She saw what she thought was a great herd of cattle moving across the fields. In a line...! Cattle don't walk in a line, she thought...

"They are men!" she said in a shouted whisper.

"What men, Marjorie?" Kitty asked surprised.

"Look, Kitty! Joe! There! Moving across that brow. Look!"

The moon, now hidden behind a bank of cloud, concealed everything from view for a brief moment. Then the sky suddenly cleared and there, in plain view, was a great column of men marching across the land, moving steadily towards the hill in front of them. Joe stood up in the boat, amazed at the sight. It was a great silent hoard, some horsemen also clearly visible amongst them. It was the fact that they were so silent that gave the scene an eerie feeling.

The boatman said nothing, looking only directly ahead at the river and its meandering course.

"Don't you see them?" Joe asked him excitedly.

"I've been looking at them move alongside us for the past hour man. Haven't you heard? The call to arms went out this morning," the boatman said almost casually.

"Never heard no such thing," Joe said in awe.

"Why do you think we had to move out of Wexford so urgently? Travelling after tonight will be a nightmare by road. You're lucky you still have the night ahead of you," the boatman said bluntly.

The silent army had now come to a halt before the hill, where they seemed to be resting. Preparing their plans more like it, Joe thought. As the boat sailed round the next bend, the sight disappeared from view.

"We are almost there now," the boatman announced.

In the distance there was another Norman Keep, now long deserted. It's gaunt silhouette stood out against the bright night sky. Joe hoped the horse and cart awaited them as promised. Slowly, the boat edged into the tall riverbank reeds, coming to a halt near a great flat stone.

"You are here now. This is as far as I go," the boatman told them, as he slackened the canvas sail.

"We are forever grateful," Joe assured him.

"Well, God speed you the rest of the journey, and take an old man's advice, don't spare the horse. Wherever you are going, I recommend you get there fast, and before dawn," he warned Joe sagely.

"Don't worry. We will make every effort to do as you advise. With the uprising announced the soldiers and military men will be swarming like bees," Joe said in excited tones.

The three of them bid the boatman farewell and watched him sail downriver, the outgoing tide sweeping him into it's current to the sea.

"An odd fellow if ever I met one," Marjorie said, smiling to Kitty and glad to be on dry land.

"Well, he did us proud Marjorie. Here we are safe and sound. Now, we must hurry as the old man said."

Kitty looked to Joe for direction.

"You two wait here, and I will return in a minute or two."

Joe walked briskly in the direction of the Norman tower. True to Pat Redmond's word, the horse and cart awaited them. Joe wasted no time harnessing the horse to the cart, and he drove it out into the clearing, whistling to the two women to signal all was well.

Once all were aboard Joe drove the horse towards the small back road, where the horse trotted briskly forward. Their route would bring them west of Enniscorthy town, avoiding any patrols that could be afoot. The rhythmic clanging of the tackling on the trotting horse almost lulled Kitty and Marjorie to sleep. Nobody was in form for conversation. All that mattered now was to get home safely before dawn, as the fisherman had warned.

Marjorie nodded in and out of sleep. She felt cold in the night air. A sure sign she was getting old, she sighed. During their journey they met several groups of men who passed by, silent in the night. Joe did not speak either, his main concern being soldiers, which so far they had been fortunate enough not to encounter. One by one the blackbirds began the dawn chorus, soon to be followed by a host of other songsters. It was magical, Kitty thought upon waking. She watched the horizon turn from pink to crimson and then present that moment all nature waits for, when the sun rises in the eastern skies.

In the distance the mountains glowed with the first rays, and the mountain village was visible at last. The horse was beginning to tire, and Joe tapped him forward, knowing they must reach the village without Kitty being noticed. Otherwise they would be assured of a visit from her father and there was no telling what that might lead to.

Both women were awake now, rubbing their cramped limbs.

"Oh thank heavens we are almost home," Marjorie said wearily, "I will sleep this day Joe Gilltrap! And how are you Kitty?"

"Much like you, Marjorie. Longing for a decent sleep and knowing Hannah will fuss so when we arrive!"

The horse climbed the old stone road slowly, as the cart trundled over the larger stones. The villagers were still sleeping when they finally came to a standstill, the only ones to greet them being the dogs and the shrill crowing of the roosters.

"Come on, my boy. You have earned a great breakfast and a good grooming," Joe said to the horse as he took off the tackling, leading the horse out from under the shafts of the cart.

Marjorie and Kitty knocked gently on the door of the cottage to be greeted by old Mag, who was already having her morning tea.

"Well glory be to God," she cried out, "if it isn't the good women, and is Joe with you?" she asked, peering over their shoulders.

"Indeed he is Mag, out feeding that good horse that has more than earned its keep this night," Marjorie chuckled.

Hannah and Nell soon arrived into the kitchen, delighted to see them safely home. As they ate a hearty breakfast, Kitty told them of visiting James in prison, and of their awful experience of seeing him in the prison cart. Joe sat silently eating, and wondering whom should he tell of James' impending execution. Old Mag and Nell, he thought. Hannah would be unable to contain the news from

Kitty. When Kitty had finally gone to bed, he called Mag and Nell outside and told them the sorry news.

"Poor James. I knew it wouldn't take them long to pass that sentence on the lad," Mag said angrily.

"And Kitty has no idea Joe?" asked Nell, looking aghast.

"None whatsoever Nell. All he kept saying to her was that she must promise to be at the old fort, where he would come and collect her at sunset," Joe repeated.

"What sunset?" Mag asked with mounting curiosity.

"I don't know Mag, but from what I gather from her she will go to the fort each evening to see if he is there. It's the only thing that will keep her going, and we mustn't take that from the girl. It's all she has left, poor thing," and he looked up at the fort, abandoned and lonely against the morning sky.

Chapter fifteen

Lord Foldsworth and Justice Timothy Stewart ate a hearty breakfast. They felt that their purpose in Wexford had now been achieved and they decided to return to Oak Hall that very day.

"And what of Kitty, Charles?" Justice Stewart asked.

"Oh don't you worry. With the reward money she will very soon be found. You know what they are like, Timothy. They would sell their mother for a guinea. She will be home to us now in a matter of days. I can feel it in my bones," Lord Foldsworth assured him.

Sitting back in his chair, Justice Stewart felt satisfied after his meal.

"Excellent cook here, Charles, don't you agree. My goodness, those kidneys were delicious, were they not?"

"Yes, excellent indeed, though I must confess I would have liked my bacon somewhat more crispy. However, as you say, a good cook indeed."

Rising slowly from his chair, Justice Stewart smiled.

"Well Charles, I will see you out front in the coach in a short while, twenty minutes or thereabouts? I am so looking forward to relaxing at Oak Hall for the week."

"Yes, twenty minutes Timothy. I shall see you there."

Matt Ryan knew what he had to do. The order was quite simple. Shoot to kill. He had quietly found Justice Stewart's bedroom, having entered unseen through the kitchen door downstairs. The kitchen staff had been too busy preparing breakfasts to notice another pass through. He stood waiting now behind the tall screen door. When he heard the approaching footsteps, he was ready. The door opened gently and was closed again.

Timothy Stewart walked to the other side of the room. He sat down on the side of the bed, wishing he could sleep for a further hour. Suddenly a man leaped forward towards him. Justice Stewart did not have time to cry out in alarm. All he heard was, "This is a present from James de Lacey," and a loud blast rent the air. He fell back on the bed grasping his chest where the shot had penetrated deeply. Matt Ryan jumped through the back window, his mission complete, and ran down the narrow street to where his horse was held awaiting him.

The hotel staff and other guests ran upstairs and found Justice Stewart lying on the bed, the sheets scarlet with his blood. Lord Foldsworth dashed into the room, not believing what was happening.

"Quickly! A doctor someone!" he shouted.

"I am afraid a doctor is of no use now, sir. The man is dead," a maid said sombrely.

"He can't be! He must be only wounded," he exclaimed.

But, on closer inspection, he saw the pallor of death settle on the young face of Viscount Timothy Stewart. For a brief moment Lord Foldsworth thought he was going to collapse himself, but instead he sat down in a chair, unable to comprehend what had happened so suddenly and unexpectedly.

The room was now filling with soldiers and police. Someone had handed Lord Foldsworth a glass of brandy, which he drank almost unknown to himself. He was shaking, and was sure he was falling apart as his plans for the future came crashing down about him. Kitty's marriage... the future of Oak Hall... going to Hampshire to live with Glencora. In a mere instant, all was lost to him. He was overwhelmed by a sense of futility and hopelessness.

All around him was confusion and chaos, and despite every effort by two doctors, Timothy Viscount Stewart lay lifeless on the bed opposite him. Lord Foldsworth realised that it was an assassination of reprisal for James de Lacey and his forthcoming execution. The commanding officer, Ronald Digby, came over and sat beside him.

"Dreadful stuff this, sir, and I understand that you also presided at the court case of de Lacey?" he asked the shaken aristocrat in the chair.

Lord Foldsworth looked at him with glassy eyes.

"Yes, that is correct. Only yesterday. He was to be my future son-in-law you know... and now look at him! It is all so unbelievable," he said faintly.

"Well sir, I am advising you to leave this town as soon as possible. I will provide an escort for you to Oak Hall, as I cannot take responsibility for your life in this place. I am afraid you will be their next victim should you remain here," the commanding officer told him without hesitation.

"Here... or at Oak Hall, commander... if they want me, they will get me. Still, I would feel a lot safer at home somehow. Better to die there if that is what lies ahead for me. Good God, this whole blessed affair is a nightmare, commander."

Lord Foldsworth was escorted out of town under protection of twenty soldiers. The commander had insisted that he travel by coach, where he would be less vulnerable, and on arrival at Oak Hall to have his home guarded around the clock. Lord Foldsworth sat back looking at the countryside as it passed the coach window. He was stunned. He thought of Kitty.

What point is there now in her return? He asked himself. She would be in great danger too. Better that she run alongside her newly found friends. At least that way her life might be spared. He thought of home, his brother John, and Glencora..

Perhaps I should leave at once? Yes, it is time to leave this desolate land. Let the government handle it now. After all, they are unable to guarantee our safety. The death of Justice Stewart proves this point adequately. He knew that as news spread of the death of his former friend, there would be two reactions. The rebels would hail it as the beginning of victory., and mayhem would follow.

Yes, I will leave tomorrow, while I still can, he thought. No point in being shot through the window, or in the orchard. There would be no peace for me now. Nowhere would I be safe. Anybody could gain access to my mansion, he thought fearfully. Anybody! And be in my room, or in the drawing room... or on the stairs! No estate is worth it. I could return when law and order has been restored and perhaps bring Glencora and John over to see my home in Ireland. They would love it.

Feeling a lot more cheerful, his mind finally clearing of the morning's events, he slept for a short while. He awoke feeling hot and thirsty. He thought of James. I will be happy when that fellow is hanged. He has done nothing but herald disaster from the outset. He then wondered, had they sentenced him to transportation instead of hanging, would Timothy Stewart be alive this day. Still, what is done is done, and it would be safer for me to be out of the country before his execution, he decided.

In the distance he could see Oak Hall standing proudly amidst the trees. The long avenue, winding its way through the rhododendrons, was beginning to look neglected, he thought. Arriving at the front door, there was no one to meet the coach.

"Commander, you may tell the soldiers to have refreshments in the servants hall, and perhaps you would like to join me in the drawing room?"

The commander ordered the soldiers to dismount and be at ease. They were pleased with the offer of some food, as it had been a long and dusty ride from Wexford. The horses also needed feed and water.

Seated in the drawing room, Lord Foldsworth poured a good measure of whiskey for the commander, and then rang the service bell.

"I am leaving for England tomorrow, commander," he stated matter of factly.

"Really Lord Foldsworth? Perhaps that would be the wisest decision for the moment, until there is some sanity restored here," the commander replied.

"Yes. Sanity! My life hangs on a thread at the moment, as you well know. I presume the remains of Viscount Stewart will be brought to Dublin and then shipped home for burial?"

"Yes, your lordship. Poor fellow. So totally unexpected, a savage act, but rest assured we will find his assassin very quickly. He will of course be executed, without a trial in this case," the commander said adamantly.

"I am not so sure commander that he will ever be found. These rebels have a cunning that is rare. They have managed to hoodwink us all this time, and there is no knowing who is a member of the United Irishman, is there?" Lord Foldsworth asked the young man before him.

The commander was aware of the troubled history of his host, and felt uncomfortable in his presence. He was anxious to be on his way, his duty now accomplished.

"I wish you every safety and future success, Lord Foldsworth. I must now take my leave of you and thank you for your kind hospitality."

"Oh commander, surely you will stay for dinner?" Lord Foldsworth asked him, suddenly feeling the isolation of his predicament.

The commander was aware that nobody had come to the drawing room in answer to the service bell.

"No sir. We must return to Wexford. Matters are quite out of hand there as you realise."

"Why yes of course commander. We are fortunate to have one so conscientious in our army, are we not?" he said, complimenting the young officer.

"Kind of you to say so, sir. Again, I wish you a safe passage Lord Foldsworth. I hope we meet again some day when life is somewhat more peaceful."

Escorting the commander to the front of the house, Lord Foldsworth bid him goodbye. Looking from the drawing room window, he watched the soldiers file down the avenue, where only last week Timothy Stewart had ridden so assured of life and his own future.

"Where is that blasted maid?" he muttered, pulling the service bell once again.

Some minutes later a young woman entered the room, without the customary knock.

"Yes, your honour's worship, what would your honour like for dinner?" she said smiling at him, her front teeth missing.

He glared at her.

"Where are my staff, girl?" he shouted.

"There is only five staff now, your worship. Everyone else has gone," she stood looking at him, still smiling. It irritated him greatly.

"Gone where? Left my service you mean?"

"That's right, your worship."

"You will address me as... sir. Is that clear?" he said, trying to control his temper.

"Whatever you like to be called, sir. Now, what would you like to eat for your dinner... sir?" she asked.

"Oh for heavens sake girl just bring me whatever is already cooked."

"Gladys, sir."

"What? Gladys? Who is Gladys?" he asked puzzled.

"That's me, sir. You can call me Gladys, sir," she said with a broadening smile.

He was about to shout at her to leave the room, but reasoned that the girl must not be quite in her full wits.

"Thank you, Gladys," he said instead, "you may now go."

"I'm delighted you're home, your honours worship... sir," and she walked slowly from the room, a dusting cloth draping the ground from her left hand.

"Good God, what a half-witted maid," he exclaimed to himself.

Half an hour later Gladys appeared in the dining room with a tray. She was humming a tune as she placed the serving dishes on the sideboard.

"Now, your honour will want to eat all his dinner, because Gladys is a very good cook as well as a good maid," she said excitedly.

Lord Foldsworth looked at her in amazement as she sang and waltzed about the dining room. My God, that woman is truly demented, he thought.

"Your honours worship will love my soup. I just know he will," she said, sounding deliriously happy.

Again he looked at her with a side-glance, wondering if she was even safe to have within the house.

"Thank you, Gladys. I will serve myself," he said curtly. "You may go now. I will ring for you if I need you."

She smiled once again, leaning back against the sideboard.

"Will there be a ball soon, your honour?" she asked.

He wondered was he hearing correctly.

"A what?"

"A ball, your honour. You know, the ones where the master of the house dances with the maids," and she leaned back even further on the sideboard.

He looked at her, convinced that she was indeed extremely unstable.

"Yes Gladys, there will be a great ball in two months time, and I should be delighted to dance with the staff when the time comes," he said calmly.

"Gladys is a wonderful dancer," and with that she began to waltz around the table singing some tune he had never heard. "My grandmother was taught to dance by the fairies," she said in shrill tones.

Lord Foldsworth stood up; beginning to think his sanity was also leaving him. He walked to the door and opened it for her.

"That will be all now, Gladys. You may continue your dance in the kitchen, there's a good girl. Go now, I say, go now."

She stopped in the centre of the floor, almost on the verge of tears.

"Oh thank you, your honour. I knew you would love me being here, and I will be back soon with your dessert."

She glided past him, her smile once again portraying her missing teeth. He lay back against the door almost dazed. What has become of me? A half-witted scullery maid almost proposing to me! Dancing about the dining room... her grandmother with the fairies!

Hampshire! I must get there soon, he thought with alarm.

He was pleasantly surprised at how tasty the food actually was, despite the fact that Gladys seemed to be fulfilling several roles. Poor girl, he thought, God only knows what sort of life she has had to live, or where she came from for that matter. He resolved to make an effort to be more tolerant of her odd behaviour. Obviously she has never worked with a family, much less been trained. Just then a knock came to the door. Gladys entered carrying a steaming pudding, with custard flowing over it liberally.

"Your honour, sir, is going to love this pudding. Gladys knows it!" and she placed the dessert before her new employer.

"Looks delicious, Gladys, thank you!"

He looked at her and her smile beamed down on him.

"Now you may go. Thank you again," he repeated.

She curtsied and left him. As he was eating his pudding, Gladys entered yet again, this time without knocking.

"A captain wants to see his honour. Will I put him in the drawing room or where?" she asked as she tidied her hair in front of him.

"Yes Gladys, the drawing room, and I shall be with him presently," Lord Foldsworth told her abruptly.

On entering the drawing room a few moments later, he was more than surprised to see Gladys sitting down entertaining the captain.

"Gladys, please leave us now," he said, noticeably angry.

"Yes your honour. Did you eat all your pudding?" she asked smiling.

Lord Foldsworth walked back to the door, opened it, and left Gladys under no illusion whom he meant to leave the room.

"That girl exasperates me. Has no idea whatsoever of her place here," Lord Foldsworth told the captain.

"Where did she emerge from?" the captain asked.

"I have no earthly idea. The town most likely. Was never in service before, I should think. However captain, I am glad to see you. Now, you will have heard, no doubt, that Justice Stewart was murdered in Wexford this morning and I am lucky to be alive myself. I have good reason to believe they may make an attempt on my life, so I want Oak Hall guarded day and night.

* * *

James awoke early. He sat against the wall of his cell, feeling numb. He tried to pray silently, but this also proved futile. Outside, he could hear the early morning noises of horses and carts trundling towards the town, dogs barking and, somewhere in the distance, a cock crowed only to be answered by another. Normal life, he thought. That which I took so much for granted and is now at an end.

The prison began to come to life with the customary coughing and shouting of some of the prisoners. He pondered the fate of some of them, where they had come from and what had they done, or, more precisely, what had they been accused of doing! To be sentenced here for life would be beyond his endurance. He could understand why some took the decision to end their own lives.

The guard came to his cell door and opened it. He stood there looking at James, feeling great pity for him.

"Anything in particular you would like for breakfast de Lacey?" he asked, as was the custom on the morning prior to execution.

"No. Nothing guard. Only the letter for Kitty. You will see that she gets it, won't you?" he asked quietly.

"I give you my word. I will see to it personally," he assured him.

James trusted him, and knew he was fortunate to have persuaded the guard to deliver the letter into the hands that would eventually bring it to his beloved Kitty. He handed him the letter, and the guard placed it in the inside pocket of his tunic.

"Thank you," James said, now standing up, "thank you for all your kindness to me. I bear you no ill will, if it's any consolation to you."

The guard looked at him and felt only compassion. What a dreadful waste of life, he thought.

"I will be back for you about midday, James. It will be time then," he said, avoiding the prisoner's eyes by looking towards the cell window. Then, turning round abruptly, he walked out, locking the door behind him.

"Poor fellow," James thought aloud, "what an awful job he has."

He felt happy that the letter was now out of his hands and that Kitty would receive it. He sat back down on the straw bedding and thought of his parents. If I am to believe in God, he reasoned, then I will be with them today, and all my forebears. He suddenly felt a nausea sweep over him. He jumped up, panic rising in his heart. He breathed deeply, and the waves of fear soon passed.

In Pat Redmond's tavern, Joe had little appetite for the excellent breakfast, which lay before him. His nerves were raw with anxiety and dread. He thought of having to shoot James, his friend. He had to catch the moment just before the hangman's noose engulfed him in death. He had to afford James a dignified ending, one not perpetrated at the hands of the enemy.

He felt the pistol in the inside pocket of his old coat and wished with all his heart that he was back working in the forge. He realised that such thoughts were foolish. He was tired, having ridden down the previous night under the cover of darkness. That too had been unpleasant, as he feared capture at every turn in the road. It was not himself he had worried about so much as his promise to his friend. At that moment a young man approached his table and sat opposite him.

"Do you mind if I sit here?" the young fellow asked Joe.

"No, I don't mind in the least," Joe replied, struck by the uncanny resemblance this man had to James.

"You don't seem very hungry, if you don't mind my saying so," he said to Joe, who was breaking some bread and dipping it in the egg on his plate.

"Not too hungry, to tell you the truth," Joe replied.

"Same as myself then. Just tea will do me today," he said, looking at the young tavern girl who waited for his order.

"Must be the air in Wexford," Joe said, trying to smile.

The young man said nothing, drinking the tea slowly.

"Are you from these parts?" Joe asked, trying to sound casual.

"No, I'm not. And you? Where do you come from?"

"Oh... north of the county. Just here to do a friend a favour," Joe replied.

The stranger looked about the room slowly and then, looking at Joe, said in a whisper.

"I know who you are Joe. No need to be afraid either. John de Lacey is my name. James my brother is to be executed today. I know why you are here."

Joe looked at him startled. The resemblance bore the truth of the young mans statement.

"It's no wonder, like myself, you have no appetite John. I am pleased to meet you, despite the day that lies before us, not to mention how poor James must be at this time. God give him the strength, is all I can say," Joe said looking at John, feeling equally sorry for him. They sat in silence for some moments.

"We will have to try and get to the steps of the gallows, which will be to the left side of James. At least he will be able to see us as he ascends the stairs," John said, his voice breaking.

Joe was surprised at the sudden expression of emotion.

"Come now, John, don't go upsetting yourself. I know it's a dreadful day for you, apart from myself altogether, but we have to do our duty for James. You are here to support him, and I, to carry out his last wishes."

John recollected himself.

"I know you are right Joe. I'll be okay in a minute or so. It's just when I remember back on our lives together as children... I never dreamed it would end like this for him, poor devil."

They drank what was left of the tea, and went outside. The morning was fresh and clear with the fog now rising from Wexford harbour. Tall sailing ships rode at anchor further out in the bay, waiting the turn of the tide. Seagulls screamed beside the fishing trawlers as they scavenged fish entrails that were thrown over the sides.

James looked out of his cell window at them, and envied their freedom. His hands were now wet from perspiration and fear. Every time the door opened at the end of the long stone passageway, he expected it was the guard coming for him. The sun now cast its beams across the cell floor as it began to climb higher into the June sky. He looked at the mist as it lifted finally, realising he would never see another morning. That same sun will set this evening, he thought, and I will not be here to see it. Strange how much for granted I even took the sun!

Outside, the crowd had begun to gather at the gallows. They watched the hangman as he checked and double-checked the noose on the long rope. The trap door sprang open each time he tested it, greasing it here and there. He stood back against the railings, satisfied that all would go smoothly.

Joe and John slowly made their way through the crowd to the side of the scaffold and the small stairway. Four soldiers, armed, stood in front of the scaffold, and three to the rear. They had been ordered to shoot should there be any attempt to rescue the prisoner. At the rear of the crowd, Matt Ryan and Father Murphy stood, heavily disguised. They watched Joe, who was now standing patiently awaiting his chance. They did not envy him his task.

The prison cart slowly made its way to the scaffold, with an escort of eight soldiers. James was taken from it and roughly pushed forward towards the stairs. John looked at his brother, and at the soldiers who were pushing him forward. He wanted to grab a musket and shoot them as pure hatred filled his heart. Joe grabbed him by the arm, sensing his rising emotions.

"Steady John, or you too will end up on the end of a rope," he whispered.

James looked at them both and attempted to smile. He nodded at Joe, grateful to see him, and then at his brother, who stood ashen-faced with fear. He walked up the small stairway and stood looking down at the scene before him. A sea of faces met his steady gaze, and at the back of the crowd, he could see Father Murphy and Matt Ryan. Father Murphy gestured a blessing, which James was grateful to receive. Then the commanding officer walked to the front of the scaffold and, opening the parchment, read out the sentence to the crowd.

"This man has been found guilty of treason, and also found guilty of other crimes that threaten peace and stability in Ireland. James de Lacey has shown no regrets, nor has he apologised for his misdeeds, hence he is to be hanged for his crimes this day," he concluded.

The crowd hissed and shouted their protest, and instantly a hail of gunfire went over their heads as a warning. Silence then prevailed as the hangman placed the rope over James' head and secured the noose tightly around his throat. The commander walked away from the front of the scaffold and stood looking down at the crowd for signs of revolt. Slowly, Joe took the pistol from his pocket, and took careful aim.

John looked at his brother for the last time and walked away, his eyes brimming with tears. James looked at the sky above him. The seagulls soared on the midday breeze coming in from the sea.

I will be with them in a few moments, he thought, and I will fly along the coast until I can see my mountains. Then I will fly to the old fort, he thought, and Kitty will be there. Oh Kitty, my love, I will soon come for you...

He heard the loud shot and felt the sudden heat in his chest. It burned him momentarily, and then he felt himself sinking slowly as if he was falling through clouds. All around him shouting filled the air, and then it began to fade and he suddenly found himself rising high above them all. He could see the crowd below him, as chaos filled the square.

Joe managed to slip through the crowd unseen. He could scarcely believe his miraculous escape as he hurried towards the river where a youth awaited him with his horse. Behind him he could hear shots being fired into the crowd, and glancing back, could see the body of James, as it lay crumpled on the scaffold. God forgive me, he prayed.

"May you rest in peace, James," he said loudly, as he wiped the tears from his face.

Joe rode slowly through the town until he reached the bank of the river Slaney. He found the track that Pat Redmond had advised him to follow, and then he galloped with all the speed the horse could muster. The tall trees obscured his presence and he knew that if he could maintain the present pace, he would outride the soldiers should they follow him. He could not prevent the final moments beside the scaffold from flashing before him constantly. He had aimed the pistol, and James had looked down at him, nodding his approval. He had fired then, and saw James fall forward, to the astonishment of the commanding officer. Somehow it had seemed to the soldiers that the shot had come from the front of the crowd, and he had dropped the pistol and fled.

His mouth was dry, and his legs felt weak as the horse thundered forward, sure-footed and aware that the rider needed every ounce of its strength just then. Three miles up-river, there was a shallow ford where the current was less violent, as the river spread broadly at that point. Joe urged the horse into the water, and they both swam across the breath of the river. The horse lunged up the bank upon reaching the other side, Joe once again placing his feet in the stirrups.

"Good boy," he said, patting his mount, relieved that they were making good ground.

His path now lay cross-country, and in the distance he could see the outline of the mountains, as they lay enfolded in the heat haze of the June afternoon.

John de Lacey went to the prison with a horse and cart, on which a coffin lay on a thick bed of straw, to collect the body of his brother. Having stated his business, the sentries on duty searched the straw cart and finally opened the great doors to the prison courtyard. John drove the cart slowly across the cobbled yard, where a soldier directed him to what looked like a huge stable. A large lock, attached to a rusty chain, prevented John from going inside. He simply wanted to take his brother's body and leave the place. A prison guard approached him, and taking a large bunch of keys from his pocket, proceeded to open the lock.

"Alan Woodstock is my name," he said, addressing John without looking at him.

"I see," John, replied, unsure of what to say next.

"I have a letter here from your brother. I promised him that I would see to it that it reached the lady to whom it is addressed. Kitty Foldsworth. Will you see that she receives it?"

John was quite taken aback for a moment.

"Yes, I will see that she gets it," he eventually replied, as he followed the guard into what served as a mortuary.

The body of James lay on a wooden table covered with a grey blanket. Slowly, the guard uncovered the body, and James lay still in death. His face looked younger, John thought.

"I washed him myself," said Alan Woodstock, as he stood back to allow John move closer to his brother.

"That was decent of you," was all he could manage to say.

"I liked your brother. We often talked you know," Alan said, feeling awkward as John's body shook with deep sobs.

"Well, he is dead now... my only brother... and he not even thirty years of age," John cried.

"Yes, I know, and I am sorry. You are going to have to get him out of here as soon as possible, because the orders are that his body is to be hung from Wexford Bridge. It's only because I liked him that I am taking the risk of disobeying that order," Alan said matter of factly.

"The bastards! Not alone did they want him dead, but displaying his body on the bridge. How typical of them." John almost shouted with rage.

"If I were you, I would be concentrating on getting out of this town quickly. If you are caught taking this body from here, your brother will be displayed on the bridge and there will be nothing you or I will be able to do to prevent it!" Alan said firmly now.

They lifted the limp body of James into the coffin, and nailed the lid down. Placing the coffin back on the cart, Alan Woodstock walked ahead and shouted for the gates to be opened.

"One last thing, John. When the yeomanry stop you, tell them it's your cousin who died of the fever. That should clear the way for you," Alan said, and then he walked away.

John looked after him and wondered how such a seemingly nice fellow could work in such a dreadful place!

Joe reached the mountain village after sunset. The sky was crimson at the back of the mountains, and the ravens cried out their protest as he rode by the old stone fort. Smoke rose from the cluster of cottages, and he dreaded the thought of having to tell Kitty and the others that James had been executed.

He took several deep breaths before entering the cottage where Kitty, Marjorie and Mag sat by the fireside. Nell was busy putting the children to bed in the loft. Father Ryan sat in a corner alone, reading from his breviary.

"Well Joe, what happened? Is there any news of James?" Kitty said, standing up immediately as Joe came into the room.

"Miss Kitty, this is the worst evening of my life, for the news I have to tell you is tearing my heart asunder," Joe said as he ran his fingers through his hair.

"Whatever has happened Joe?" she asked as she approached him. Marjorie came and took her by the arm gently.

"Well Miss Kitty, they decided to execute James today, and I had to be there for him, along with his brother John."

A loud scream rent the air.

"No! No! No! Oh my darling James dead... no! Never! Never!"

Marjorie held her tightly as Father Ryan came and stood beside her, supporting her sagging body. They helped her to the fireside chair, where she cried out in desperation, pouring her grief uncontrollably into the arms of Marjorie. Mag wept silently, as did Nell, and Hannah made some fresh tea, her face white with fear and dread of what might happen to them all next. Her shock subsided, Kitty looked at Joe.

"Will you tell me what happened Joe? How did he die?" she asked quietly.

Joe went over and sat beside her. Taking her hand in his, he looked at her beautiful face that had known so much suffering.

"Well Miss Kitty, one evening long ago James bid me promise him that should he ever be tried and sentenced to hang that I would do him the honour of giving him a soldiers death. So I went to Wexford, and stood at the side of the scaffold with John. We were right beside where James stood, and he looked very peaceful and brave. Just before they pulled the trap door, I did as he had asked. He died well, Miss Kitty, died bravely, and we hope John will have the body home this night," Joe concluded.

Kitty sat trying to imagine the scene. After some moments she spoke.

"He will come for me, you know. That's what he meant... to wait for him by the stone fort... I know he will come..." she said slowly.

The atmosphere in the house was one of disbelief. Kitty finally fell fast asleep, Mags potion having taken her from her world of pain.

"How was it really, Joe," Marjorie asked.

"Just as I said, Marjorie. The shot was a direct hit and he just fell to the floor of the gallows. He would have felt nothing, poor lad," Joe said solemnly.

"These are dreadful times," Hannah whispered to Mag, who gazed into the fire and said nothing.

Outside a dog barked and Joe knew that someone was approaching. The distinct rattle of a cart could be heard now as it stopped outside the house. On opening the door, Joe was both relieved and glad to see John de Lacey.

"You got here, John, thank God. Come in a minute until you meet everyone."

Joe introduced John to all the company, and each in turn sympathised with him over the death of his brother James. Kitty awoke with the raised voices and came slowly into the room.

"Kitty," Joe began slowly, "Kitty, this is James' brother, John. John has brought the remains home to us for burial."

Immediately Kitty ran forwards towards the door, but Joe restrained her.

"Take it gently now, Miss Kitty. You know this will be a very big shock for you, and indeed for all of us, so wait until we bring the coffin inside, won't you?" Joe said persuasively.

Kitty allowed herself to be led once more to the fireside where Hannah comforted her. Father Ryan, Joe and John went outside and slowly brought the coffin through the narrow door. Marjorie had set out two chairs for it to be rested upon. Kitty looked at the sight and only felt numbness now.

"James in that..." was all she could murmur.

They prised the lid off as gently as they could, and stood it against the wall. Marjorie brought Kitty over slowly to see the body of her beloved James. Kitty looked at the white face, the closed eyes, and the black hair combed back roughly. She caught his hands and wept bitterly, before stooping over to kiss him.

"You are so cold, my love," she said, "so very cold, James. Just like mamma was..."

They all stood around the coffin now as Father Ryan said the prayers for the dead, to be then followed by the rosary. Kitty felt her head spin with the repetition of the prayers, but tried to answer as best she could. As Father Ryan concluded, she felt relieved. The priest now stood beside the coffin, shaking holy water upon the body of James.

"James de Lacey, may you rest in peace, now, forever."

Kitty rent the air with a scream.

"No! Never! James shall never rest without me! He promised me that he would return for me! He said he would collect me at the ring fort! He shall never rest without me!" and she ran through the door calling his name wildly.

Nell ran out after her, following her into the night.

"Lock that door now," Mag ordered.

They looked at her wondering if she too was overcome with grief.

"We have to wash the poor lad and lay him out decently. Joe, follow them and keep them away for a half hour or so until we are finished."

With that, the women set about the age-old ritual of preparing the dead for their wake. Nell and Joe walked with Kitty to the old fort where they sat on the great stones. Kitty continued to weep, sobbing into the night wind.

* * *

Gladys watched Lord Foldsworth ride down the avenue. She knew that he was riding into the town, probably to speak with the new sergeant. The great house was now empty; the old cook having gone home after dinner. The stable lads were probably in one of the lodge's playing cards, and Gladys knew that her time had come.

She carried the two drums of animal fat to the top of the house, spilling them along the passageways and down the great stairway. She moved slowly, listening for any sounds. The great house was silent. She suddenly became aware of the portrait of Lady Edwina. She seemed to be looking directly at her, she thought. Gladys stopped and looked at the beautiful woman with the spray of roses in her hands. 'You were lovely', she thought. 'I am so sorry for what I am about to do, but if you had been here, it would all have been so different maybe. And then, your ladyship, it could also have been a lot worse.' She sighed. As she reached the bottom of the stairs, she knew what she had to do next.

Going to the kitchen, she lit a long taper from the embers of the dying fire and walked with it to the stairs once again. The flame licked the taper hungrily, greedy for more.

"Goodbye Oak Hall... goodbye forever," she said aloud, addressing the portraits of lords and ladies who now seemed to regard her with contempt. "Bad cess to the lot of you," she cried, and threw the taper onto the stairs.

The flames raced up each step, almost with a vengeance she imagined. Soon it reached the top floor. Gladys could now hear the crackling as the fire took hold of the long drapes and carried the flames to the old wooden ceilings. The wood then crackled, and the fire took its grip on the ancient mansion.

Gladys now ran to her room in the basement and collected her few belongings. She hastily threw her cloak over her shoulders and went to the old underground passage, which would lead to the estate wall. She had walked its dank length some evening's prior, making sure that it was clear the full way and that the old wooden door still opened.

"No! Nobody will see Gladys leave Oak Hall," she murmured, as she hastily made her way in the darkness of the old tunnel.

Behind her now, in the distance, she could hear the crashing of wood. The old portraits probably. Well, they had their day the lot of them, she thought with venom. They never spared a thought for the many thousands of homeless families who had stood and watched their own homes burn. Oh no, not them. But Gladys remembered. She remembered how in west Wicklow she had clutched her mother's apron, as they had to watch their home burning to ashes.

On reaching the end of the tunnel, Gladys gulped in the clean fresh air. In the cluster of trees before her a horseman awaited.

"Good job, Gladys," the voice said, adding, "just look back at that for a sight."

Gladys turned around and saw the inferno she had created. She was awestruck by the sight.

"My God, what a fire!" she exclaimed.

"Hurry. Jump up and let's be away from here while we are still safe," he ordered.

As they galloped into the night, Gladys looked back at the blaze of what was once Oak Hall. 'Now your lordship, did you ever imagine foolish and simple Gladys was in your home for this very purpose? How silly of you,' she thought, as she gripped her cloak and pulled it tightly around her body.

On top of the mountainside Joe saw the great blaze in the valley beneath them gather momentum, and at that moment Kitty also noticed the strange sight.

"A fire Joe, and it seems to be... it is Oak Hall Joe! Nell, it's on fire. Oak Hall is burning," she said in an eerily calm voice.

She sat back down on the stone and looked at the huge blaze that, even from a distance, cast a glow towards the mountain.

"My God," Nell exclaimed, "who would do the like of that, Joe? That beautiful place going up in flames," Nell said, overcome with awe.

"He deserves it Nell, every bit of it, that heartless and cruel man," Kitty said, and then she calmly walked back towards the house unaided, not once looking back at the crumbling fiery mass that was once a home, so dear to her.

The entire population of the village stood on the ridge, looking down at the mansion as the flames shot into the night sky. The adults were silent; each with their own thoughts, but no one expressed regret. Not even Father Ryan, Nell noticed. Kitty walked into the house and sat down beside the body of James. She looked at how clean and well dressed he now was.

Mag had dressed him in a high collared white shirt and a green velvet-riding jacket. He looked so well, Kitty thought. Oh James, she wept, if only you would just open your eyes and look at me, or speak to me, she thought. She caressed his face lovingly. But I will wait for you no matter how long it takes James. I shall wait.

"Your ladyship, I am sorry to interrupt you, but I have a message here for you," John said, as he took out the letter from his cloak hanging on the wall.

"What is it, John?" Kitty asked curiously.

"It is a letter from James, your ladyship, given me by the prison guard. He had promised James that he would see to it that you received it, so here it is."

John handed her the letter. She saw its seal was unbroken, and she clutched it to her breast. Standing up, she walked slowly over to the table and sat beside the lamp. She opened the letter and began to read.

My Darling Kitty,

I am writing to you for the last time my words of love for you. The prison guard has promised me that he will see to it that somehow you will receive this letter, and I trust him. He is a good fellow really.

By the time you receive this my darling I will no longer be with you, or any of you for that matter, though my spirit will never be far from you my love.

My trial was quite a sham as you can imagine, and the sentence was death. I was so glad that you did not know this the time you visited me here. You looked so lovely that day, and it reminded me of the many times we rode out together, and of the first time I met you when you had to leave the hunt, your horse having cast it's shoe. I fell in love with you that day, you know, and the love I have for you will never leave me. No! Not even death will take that from me. I want you to know, Kitty, that my time with you was the best time of my life, those days riding in the hills, our journey and time in France, your love for me so lavishly given. You surrendered all for me, my love. Everything you had you let go of, just to be with me. I want you to be strong, Mrs de Lacey. Be brave. You know I will return for you and don't you ever doubt it.

She stopped reading the letter and looked across at James. So still, she thought, and yet I can feel him with me. She resumed reading the letter.

Do you remember the night you came into the Bull's Nose with your father? Oh God, how I wished I could have told him of my love for you. But then how very foolish that would have been! At least we had some time together, and it was wonderful, was it not?

Her mind drifted back to that night in the tavern, and then to the evening when they had met Bartley Finnegan on the road, and how he had sworn vengeance. He had it now! That wicked little man never lived to see it though, she thought. Kitty again resumed the letter, savouring every line.

I know you will miss me my love, as I will miss you, but the wonderful thing that gives me the strength to face death is that we were true to each other, all along the way. Just now I am remembering how we lit the fire beside the lake that evening and ate our fish! And then our journey to Dublin, and then poor Marcus! It was sad how he never got the chance to live his life out either. But then that was the risk we all took to serve our country, was it not. And even you, Kitty, have paid such a very high price for that cause surely?

There is little space left my love only to say that with my dying breath I love you and always will. Don't worry my love. I will come for you, riding on the West wind.

Yours forever lovingly,

James.

She folded the letter and sat looking at James in the coffin. Somehow she felt peace. It is as if he had spoken to me just now, she thought. Deep within her being she now knew for certainty that James would return. He had always kept his promises to her. Always, she thought. She stood up and once again kissed him on the forehead. Then she sat at the fireside beside John.

"Thank you John. That letter has meant everything to me. James was my life, you know. Everything I ever loved meant little to me, once I found him," she said calmly.

"You were his life, your ladyship, and he was a fortunate man to have known your love," John said with a sincerity that impressed her.

Mag looked into the fire and sighed. Young love, she thought. They never think of where it can lead them, do they?

The room was warm with the glow of the fire and Marjorie allowed the neighbours to walk in and pay their respects, on condition they did not disturb her ladyship. Hannah sat beside Kitty, making sure that despite the good will of the people, they did not interrupt her mourning. She need not have worried. They all loved her too much to upset her any more this night.

* * *

Lord Foldsworth rode home at a leisurely pace. He was well satisfied with his meeting with the new sergeant in town. Knows his place, that fellow, he thought with satisfaction, and he had assured him of constant surveillance of the area. Nice whiskey to boot, he smiled, feeling a lot less anxious since the meeting. No, I shall have to wait and see this blasted rebellion through. No point in high-tailing it to Hampshire, much as I'd like to. With de Lacey finally dead, perhaps Kitty will relent somehow.

He rode on through the dim light of the summer's night, and then thought he smelled smoke from a gypsy camp. Becoming more common, that lot. Must be camping in my woods somewhere about, he murmured, resolving to have them removed on the morrow. As he rounded the long bend in the road, he heard the approaching hoof beats of a horse, it's rider obviously in great haste to somewhere or another. He reined in, and waited for the rider to approach. The stable lad, recognising his master's horse, pulled up short.

"Your honour, sir, you must come quickly. It's the house sir. It's been burned down," he stammered nervously.

"What are you talking about lad, what house?"

"Oak Hall, sir. You must hurry," and he rode ahead of his master hastily.

Lord Foldsworth felt his mouth go dry and his breathing become rapid. It was the taste of fear. He rode behind his servant and then, to his horror, saw the orange glow in the night sky. He knew his worst fears had been realised. He looked from the brow of the hill and saw the mass of flames that were leaping wildly into the June night, whipped on with the rising night wind.

"Oh my God!" he shouted. "My beloved home!" and he knew that all was lost.

He dismounted and watched the futile frenzy taking place before him, with stable hands running to and fro with buckets of water. They finally have achieved their ill-conceived desires, he thought, the price of de Lacey's death, a debt now paid. He walked slowly towards the inferno, the air thick with smoke and smuts. He felt helpless and beyond words as he watched his ancestral home crumble and crash before his very eyes. He sat beneath the giant chestnut tree, drinking the remains of the brandy from his hip flask, while his horse grazed nearby oblivious to the commotion in the distance. Poor devils, he thought, as he watched his staff and the yeomanry trying desperately to quench the flames to no avail.

Already the main roof had collapsed, and the fire now raged through what was left of the east wing of Oak Hall. Edwina, he thought. Thank heavens she was spared this appalling nightmare. It would have killed her! And Kitty? Perhaps she is as well with her rebel lot. It would be worse still had she been asleep in the house. And Gladys, what of poor Gladys? Most likely she has perished, poor girl, he thought.

The pain at the base of his head seemed to be getting worse. He felt a slight weakness sweep through his tired body. Too much, all this! Enough to kill a man, he thought as he walked slowly to fetch his horse. He led the animal slowly forward towards the raging ruin Oak Hall had now become. Tom Harris, the head groom, ran towards him.

"We tried, your lordship, did all we could, but as you can see..."

"I know the staff did all in their power, Harris. Nothing to do now but let it take its course. Tell me, did the scullery maid escape. Gladys?" he asked the groom.

"Can't say your lordship. We haven't seen her Sir. Poor girl wouldn't have had a chance," he told him candidly.

"And the horses, Harris? Any losses?"

"None sir. We let them loose in the paddocks first thing, mares and foals included, sir," Harris assured him.

"Very good. Hate to see the poor brutes suffer," Lord Foldsworth said as he walked past Harris in what seemed to the groom to be a daze.

The groom watched his master walk falteringly forward, and considered it best not to intrude lest he make matters worse. Poor man, he thought, how his life has changed and what has he left of it? Nothing. Harris wondered of his own future and those left of the yard staff. It couldn't look worse, he thought, as he stood looking at the roof of the west wing crash to the ground, sending a million sparks into the night sky.

Lord Foldworth stood watching the death of his home and knew there was nothing left here for him anymore. Memories only, he thought. Of the ballroom, the dining room, the many happy events, the portraits, Edwina's beautiful gowns... Oh God, what am I to do? He wept. The fire subsided slowly and he walked down the avenue, deciding to go to the town and rent rooms. What else can I do? he wondered helplessly. The staff came and spoke to him, asking him questions as to what they might do, but he was no longer able to delegate any responsibility.

"See Harris," was all he could say.

The dawn chorus rang out across the park and he thought how ridiculous it sounded. Once his spirits might have soared with this joyful celebration of life, but now there was nothing left to celebrate. He felt increasingly unwell, and his steps began to falter. He stood now leaning against the side of his horse, wishing he were capable of mounting it. The sensation passed once again, and drinking the remains of the brandy, he threw his hip flask on the roadside. In the distance he could see the neat stone house he had given May Ryan when she had been evicted. Good woman that, he thought. No regrets either...

Again the pain shot across the back of his head, this time more intense. He felt his vision leaving him and fear took over. He tried to run, and fell heavily to the ground, where he gazed at the blur of trees above him where the crows protested loudly at the intruder. You will probably eat me; he managed to think, as his arms flailed wildly from side to side. The last thing he thought he saw was a fox standing on the side of the ditch watching him.

Lord Foldsworth then lost consciousness, as the stroke he had just suffered took its grip on his muddled brain. It would be some time before May Ryan would find him lying there.

* * *

The mountain village awoke to two great realities. The death of James, and the burning down of Oak Hall. The people knew that the latter was an act of retaliation for the death of James, and all that day they pondered their fate, knowing it was unlikely the matter would rest there.

Kitty walked to the mountain ledge and gazed down on the charred remains of what had been her home. Smoke still rose from the blackened pile, and she wondered if her father had perished in the fire. The thought did not disturb her. She had sat by the body of James almost the entire night, thinking how her father could have averted so much sorrow and pain had he been more tolerant and reached out to her. But no. He had been adamant from the beginning, despite the fleeting hopes that Kitty had entertained from time to time. Foolish of me, she thought. How could he ever change? Generations before him had not, and neither could he.

Hannah refused to look down upon her former home again. She had sat for some time the previous night looking down on the scene. She felt no sadness or regret as the new day dawned. All her thoughts were for the impending funeral and burial of James, which was to be held that same evening.

The old ruined church where they had met so many times was the place Kitty had chosen for James to rest, amidst the ancient yew trees where they had tethered their horses. They would be his shade, she thought. She had visited the ancient place that morning and it was covered in a mass of bluebells. She could see the cluster of yew trees that concealed the ruin from where she now sat. It was only some two miles away, or less. It nestled snugly at the very foot of the mountains, undisturbed, the only exception being some sheep that might wander onto the sacred ground now and then. As Kitty stood up to walk back to the village, she saw a horseman approach, this time descending the upper slopes above the village. She thought it strange that whoever it might be should choose that route, and she walked in the direction to intercept the visitor.

Upon closer inspection she instantly recognised the rider. It was Williams, she thought in amazement. She ran forward, calling his name, and the old butler was relieved and delighted to see her. The arrival of Williams proved a welcome distraction for the household. Hannah was overjoyed, and it lifted her spirits greatly. However, Williams was shocked beyond words upon seeing James lying in the coffin, and again upon hearing of the burning of Oak Hall. It left him wondering what he had actually come back to.

"Lady Catherine, you are bearing up remarkably well to these dreadful events. I am so sorry to see James here dead, not to mention the destruction of your home!"

"My home is here, now, Williams. Oak Hall would only have proved to be my eventual prison. But as you say, the death of James had been almost beyond bearing," she said, looking at the face of James, now appearing almost whiter than snow, she thought.

"And your father? Has there been any word of him?" the old butler asked anxiously.

"No, none whatsoever. Who is left to come and tell me at this point? I care little, Williams, to be truthful. He was too cruel a man for me to ever care for again. This corpse before you bears ample testimony to that!"

Williams decided to change the subject, as the tension was mounting.

"Well, my visit to my brother's home proved quite a waste of time," he said, looking to Hannah.

"Oh no Seymour. He isn't dead I hope?" she asked, looking anxiously at him.

"No Hannah, not dead, but may as well be. Transported for hunting rabbits on the local estate. I too thought he was dead when I saw the condition of his home, the thatch full of holes and the door swinging off its hinges. It was the first thing I thought also, but no, he's been transported, and what a dreadful fate at his time of life."

Mag looked at the butler.

"So you agree, Mr. Williams, that there is a lot of unfairness the way some were treated then?" she asked him testingly.

"Well yes, you could say that, though I hasten to add that Lord Foldsworth was a kind landlord for many years, before this present state of affairs, if your ladyship will pardon me for saying so," he said, now looking at Kitty.

"Say what you please, Williams. My father... what he does or where he goes... no longer holds any interest whatever for me. I simply could not care less, to be quite frank with you."

Hannah sensed that if the conversation was to continue it would be best if the topic were changed. Or better still; take Williams for an afternoon walk. Having eaten a good meal, Williams accompanied her gladly.

* * *

The arrival of one of May Ryan's daughters looking for Lady Catherine aroused curiosity amongst those in the waking room.

"What is it little one?" Kitty asked her quietly.

"Mammy told me to come and tell you that your father is safe in our house. He is very sick. I have a note for you from mammy," and the child took out the note that she had carried to the mountain village.

"You are a very good girl to come so far with this message, and Nell is going to give you something nice to eat," Kitty said as she kissed the child lightly on the head.

Kitty opened the letter.

Lady Catherine,

Your father is here with me. I found him on the road this morning. He has had the doctor who said that he has suffered a mild stroke. He is still sleeping.
Yours respectfully,

May Ryan.

Kitty felt indifferent to the contents of the letter and handed it to Joe to read. He raised his eyebrows and looked at her.

"Well, at least he didn't die in the fire. I wouldn't wish that on my worst enemy," he said, looking at her directly.

"Kind of you to be able to find such forgiveness, Joe, considering he set your head alight with pitch," Kitty said curtly.

The child looked at her.

"Is there a message for mammy?" she asked innocently.

"Yes, there is," and with that Kitty replied to the letter.

Mrs. Ryan,

Thank you for letting me know that my father is with you. However, I have no interest in seeing him. I will, nevertheless, reimburse you for all your care of him, if you will kindly allow me.

Thank you,

C. Foldsworth.

"Who is the dead man?" the child asked curiously.

"That's James. Do you remember him?" Joe asked her.

"Yes I do. He would sometimes help you in the forge, Mr. Gilltrap," she replied plainly.

Kitty gave her the note and walked with the child to the ledge of the mountain. Taking her by the hand, she looked at the small girl.

"What is your name?" she asked.

"Eileen, your ladyship," the child replied, looking up at her.

"Well Eileen, some day when you are a lovely grown up young woman, you will remember these very sad times. You must promise me that you will place some bluebells every springtime on James' grave, won't you?"

The child was a bit puzzled.

"Will you not be doing that Lady Catherine?"

"No, I don't think so, my little one. But you will remember, won't you?"

As she looked at Eileen, her heart longed for all it had never had the opportunity to experience. This child will grow up, she thought, and fall in love with some local lad, marry him and be happy. So simple and yet denied to me.

"I promise Lady Catherine. I will put primroses on it too," Eileen said, looking up at Kitty with large blue eyes.

Kitty bent down and kissed her on the cheek.

"Now, run along home Eileen and don't lose the letter for your mother."

The child ran down the mountainside, occasionally turning around to wave to her. Kitty felt the tears well up in her eyes, as she looked at the little girl, oblivious to all the pain and chaos in the world about her.

As evening drew near, Kitty knew that they would be descending the mountain for the burial of James. Joe and Father Doyle had thought it would be safer at dusk. With the evening mists descending on the mountains, their movements from the valley beneath them would be obscured. A large group of people moving together could be so easily mistaken for a small marching force. They did not want the soldiers to see them. In the circumstances, they would be shown no mercy.

And so as the sun set behind them, the lid was placed on the coffin and hammered down for the last time. Kitty had embraced James, and held the rigid body, but she was no longer able to cry. All she could feel was a great emptiness that seemed to engulf her.

Slowly the crowd moved in behind the horses that pulled the cart, the coffin covered with wild flowers from the mountainside. Father Doyle walked at the head of the sad cortege. Old Mag walked beside him, answering the prayers, as he would say them. Joe walked beside the team of horses, holding one of them by the head piece.

Kitty was grateful for the heavy mist that shrouded the mountainside. They would be safe from all prying eyes, she thought. From time to time the funeral would come to a halt, so that the older people could rest briefly. There was no sound from the valley beneath them, other than the bark of a dog.

They reached the cemetery where the sweet smell of a myriad of bluebells filled the evening air. Lifting the coffin from the cart, they carried it to the graveside, where it was placed beside the open grave. Kitty looked into the deep hole. She saw that it was lined with moss, and strewn with wild flowers. It had been prepared with love and respect, she thought. As the mountain community gathered around, Father Doyle said the final prayers in Latin.

Slowly the coffin was lowered into the earth, where it came to rest gently on the moss beneath it. The shrill song of the blackbirds filled the air, as Father Doyle gave the final blessing. Kitty just looked at the coffin lid, now strewn with the flowers that had been brought from the mountain. She knew that no sign of a fresh grave must be noticed, or the authorities would exhume the body and have it displayed on Wexford bridge, as had been planned. The very thought of it filled her with fury and hatred. However, this was not the time for such feelings.

Her mind drifted back to the evening she had met James after the hunt. Their courting place was only some feet away, behind the cluster of yew trees. She remembered how he had held her and loved her, and little did they ever imagine that within the year, James would lie here in death.

"My love," she whispered.

Nell was amazed at how calmly Kitty had taken the burial. Mag on the other hand had expected her to be dignified and calm.

"'Tis the way of the quality you know. Never see them lamenting and fainting at a graveside, do you?" she whispered to Nell as they left the grave.

Kitty waited until all were gone and then sat down on the stump of an old tree beside the grave. She looked at the darkness of the hole, and the flowers barely visible with the deepening dusk. She felt a strange peace as she said her final goodbye to James.

"I know I will see you soon, my love. I will be waiting for you," and she slowly stood up and walked towards John de Lacey, who stood waiting for her at a respectable distance.

Though they were never to know it, on the main coach route just then, the body of Viscount Timothy Stewart was being transported to Dublin and was only two miles away from the peace and quiet of the graveyard. The authorities had ordered the removal to be carried out by night. They had received a threat that the body might be intercepted and disposed of. They were not willing to risk this, as should such an event be reported, those in power would think that Ireland was out of control.

The date was, June 9th.1798.

* * *

Charles Foldsworth opened his eyes slowly. The sunlight streamed into the small room, and he saw a child looking at him. He was confused and alarmed. Where am I, he thought. What has happened to me? But his memory failed to function in providing him with the necessary answers.

May Ryan walked into the room carrying a basketful of potatoes. She was surprised to see him awake.

"Good morning Lord Foldsworth. I am happy to see you awake at last," she said quietly.

She waited to see if he had the power of speech, but all that came from her ill guest was a succession of mumbling sounds. She could see how frightened he was, and hastened to comfort him.

"Don't distress yourself sir, you will soon be well again," and she proceeded to tell him how she had found him on the roadside.

He listened attentively, and suddenly the great fire at Oak Hall flashed before his eyes. He reacted with terror, and May guessed correctly what was now occurring in his mind.

"Shhhh. It's alright your lordship. You were very lucky you did not perish in that fire, you know. Nobody did. They thought your maid had, but they found no human remains whatsoever," she assured him.

He turned his head to the wall suddenly feeling very foolish. Of course, he thought with a flash of clarity, it was Gladys who burned the place down. She played the fool so well I believed her. He turned and looked at the woman who sat beside the bed.

"I have sent word to Lady Catherine that you are here, and that the doctor is taking good care of you," she told him, well aware of the poor relationship which now existed between father and daughter.

He smiled faintly, thinking... what difference will that make... she will never come!

"Would you like some food, sir, perhaps a soft boiled egg? They are fresh this morning, Lord Foldsworth?"

But he nodded his decline of the offer.

"Some tea perhaps?" she coaxed.

He nodded his approval of that idea, then, trying to sit up discovered that one of his arms was almost totally lifeless. His distress increased when he realised that there was little movement in his left leg either. May made some weak tea and he took it from her and drank it slowly. He looked about the bright and sweet smelling kitchen. It was spotlessly clean and tidy. It was a good decision, giving her this place, he thought. Her kindness and compassion for him had touched him deeply. Just then, he noticed the four small children peering at him from around the corner, their large eyes betraying their curiosity.

He beckoned them to come closer, but they instantly ran out the door, tripping over each other in turn.

"I have told you before you are not to bother Lord Foldsworth," May called after them.

But he smiled at her, shaking his head slowly, indicating that they were not a nuisance.

"They are quite a handful, your lordship, believe me. Only for your kindness I would never have been able to rear them. My debt to you is a great one, sir."

He could have wept. Kindness? he thought. I was unable to show it to my own daughter. Only hatred and harshness have I shown her. The tears spilled down his face, and May, seeing his distress, guessed the reason.

"Soon you will be well again, your lordship. Perhaps then you will be able to put things to rights, and may your lordship forgive me if I am speaking out of turn, but you are a good man and you must believe that Sir."

He looked at her kind face. There was sincerity in the voice. Perhaps it was not too late after all. Maybe the woman was right. He fell asleep again, and May looked at the tired face and wondered if indeed he would even recover. She wondered how she was going to cope with him, and decided to trust in God. He had never failed her yet, she assured herself.

And so the days passed slowly, with Lord Foldsworth eventually able to sit outside in the afternoon sun. He found the children delightful and watched their little games each day. His mind began to heal slowly and then one morning, to his delight, he found that he could speak a little. May was busy making some bread, and talking to him about her past, which she now had a habit of doing. He listened attentively, and learned a lot about the life of his people.

"Thank you," he said suddenly.

May looked at him in astonishment and clapped her dough-covered hands in delight.

"Oh, thank God you can speak again, your lordship."

"Yes... thank you... Mrs.... Ry... Ryan," he said shakily yet clearly.

"Oh isn't this wonderful news," and the children came running in and sat on his bedside.

"You are all so lovely," he managed to say.

May Ryan looked at the expression of tenderness on his face, and wondered how different Lord Foldsworth could actually be from the man before the stroke. He chatted with the children, but at times his speech would become quite incoherent, and his frustration apparent. The days passed uneventfully as he gradually began to recover under May Ryan's and the doctor's ministrations, but Kitty never came. With time, Lord Foldsworth accepted the fact that perhaps she never would.

Kitty spent her days now visiting the grave of her beloved James each morning, and waiting at the hill fort each evening. The people of the mountain village had become accustomed to her comings and goings, and they nodded their heads sadly. Gone was the dashing young horsewoman they had known , and the one who had always been so full of life. That Kitty no longer existed.

Chapter sixteen

The battle line of ten thousand men marched northwards, clearing the enemy in their path like the sweep of a new broom. Their elation knew no bounds. They knew they were assured of victory! The town of Arklow lay ahead of them and they planned to surround it and overthrow the garrison, then march north towards Dublin and finally take it.

Joe, Father Murphy and Matt Ryan, along with William Byrne of Ballymanus and Anthony Perry of Inch, rode at the head of their army, with their green flags raised high and flapping on the June wind. The men followed with grim determination. It was the morning of June 9th, 1798.

Those ahead of the army rode in splendid and courageous leadership, urging the army forward and assuring them that the bullets of the enemy would never harm them. However, with the sweltering heat of June, and having marched mostly on foot, many called out for rest. Their leaders allowed them to do so, which in turn was to change the course of the battle ahead of them.

The garrison in Arklow had abandoned the town in panic at news of the forthcoming army of rebels. However, General Francis Needham and General Gerard Lake reoccupied the town, and led a force of 1,400 English, Scottish and Irish soldiers. The rebel army was to prove no match for their disciplined troops and sophisticated artillery.

By the time the rebel army approached Arklow, the Durham Fencibles were there to meet them. In this instance, the rebels routed their enemy. Convinced this was an omen of what was to follow, they were encouraged onwards. Father Murphy and Joe were elated beyond words.

I only wish James were here to witness all this, Joe thought as he urged his horse forward. He would have been so proud of our men... so very proud. What a dreadful shame he was not to see it.

While there were casualties, Joe realised that they were not as great as he had expected them to be. However, as they approached the town of Arklow, they were met by the roar and blast of cannon fire, which immediately made it apparent to the rebel army that the tide was turning against them. The thunder of the roaring cannons even vibrated as far away as the mountain village, as the women looked down across the plains towards the town of Arklow. Smoke and dust filled the air surrounding the town, and the hoard of rebels were like a black mass of ants in the distance pressing forward relentlessly. Old Mag, Hannah, Williams, Marjorie and the other women and children of the village stood on the ledge watching the battle, now in full spate.

Kitty sat at the old ring fort, seeing it all beneath her, and she felt no enthusiasm, fear, or any other emotion. There had been no further news of her father's condition, and she was indifferent in this regard also.

Lord Foldsworth paced the small garden to the rear of May Ryan's house, feeling helpless and afraid. The eldest child, Eileen, came running down the road.

"Mammy, mammy, there is a great army of soldiers coming. Come quick and see," the child shouted excitedly.

May came to the bottom of the nearby paddock and, looking across the ditch, saw the several hundred men who were coming in the direction of her home.

"Quickly children, inside. Quickly! A late contingent of the rebel army is coming this way. From what I hear they search the houses and question each of it's members. Quickly, for God's sake, and get to bed Lord Foldsworth. I will say you are my father who has had a bad stroke. Keep your mouth well shut, your lordship, or your fate will be a dreadful one," she said, urging the limping man inside.

He undressed and was in the bed in minutes. He had to follow the orders as his life now lay in the balance.

"Don't say one word, your lordship. Not one. I will say you have lost the power of speech completely," May said with great urgency. "Children, you must tell the army men that this is your grandfather if they ask you, and that he is very sick. Now go and sit by the fire and don't talk unless you are asked a question."

The children sat like frightened rabbits at the great fire, listening to the sound of the tramping feet, as they got closer. May continued to bake bread, kneading the dough slowly. A great pounding struck the door. It was then pushed open and seven or more men walked into the kitchen.

"What do you want here?" May asked.

"To search the place first, and then we want whatever food you can spare us," the leader said.

Two others walked directly into the small bedroom. Lord Foldsworth lay back on the pillows, staring at them.

"Who are you, old man?" one of them asked.

He just looked at them and said nothing in reply.

"Hey woman, come here," the rebel called.

May walked calmly over to him.

"Yes, what is it?" she asked him, looking at the unshaven face of the man before her.

"Who is this fellow here?" he asked her, still staring at Lord Foldsworth.

"My father. He has suffered a stroke of late and is barely keeping body and soul together. I don't think he even recognises me anymore, poor man. Can't even speak now, and he was such a one to talk. 'Oh, the freedom of Ireland', he would say to me morning, noon and night. Isn't that right daddy?" and she walked over and kissed him on the cheek. "Poor man. If he knew you were the rebels he would follow you all on his old stick. Sad too that he wasn't able to see this day! Now, food? Is that what you said you wanted?" She ushered them quickly back to the kitchen. Taking an old sack from the peg on the wall she told the leader to hold it open.

"I'm afraid I am a widow without much, but you're welcome to what I have," she said as she put in three large loaves freshly baked, a large piece of bacon, and a slab of butter. "Well boys, that's all I have for you."

They thanked her, and then the leader walked back to the bedroom where Lord Foldsworth had remained motionless.

"Don't worry, old man. We will have the bloody enemy out in no time. Pray hard for us, do you hear?"

But Charles Foldsworth simply stared at him blankly; hatred filling every fibre of his being as he looked into the face before him.

Soon they were gone. May followed them out to the road and waved them off. Returning inside, she went directly to the bedroom.

"Forgive my familiarity just now, your lordship, but I had to carry the day. Had they the slightest suspicion of who you were, they would have put you to death on the very roadside."

"Mrs. Ryan, it is the second time you have saved my life, and I am grateful to you for doing so," he replied simply.

He slowly got dressed again and returned to the garden. In the distance the roar of the cannon filled the air and he wished with all his might that he were at the heart of the battle.

"Bloody savages," he murmured, as he sat on the wooden bench and chopped the nettles before him with his stick in rage.

The rebel army now made their last great surge forward. It was directed at the right flank of General Needham's troops. Father Murphy led the front column and the rest followed in blind faith, assuring themselves of victory. General Needham, however, had anticipated the manoevour. His reinforcements had made a timely arrival and, despite the gallant efforts of the rebel attack, they were no match for Needham's men.

Matt Ryan fell heavily when his horse was shot beneath him, and then to Joe's horror the animal, writhing in agony, heaved itself across the prone figure of Matt. Leaping from his own mount, Joe beat the wounded animal to one side in desperation, only to find Matt dying, blood spurting from his mouth. Joe lifted him up and propped him against a wall. It was, however, only a matter of seconds until Matt expired, his chest crushed from the weight of the horse. Joe looked about him. All was confusion and death. Men lay on every side of him dead or dying, crying out in their final agony.

The cannons continued to roar as the heavy artillery bombarded them from every side. Horses, now rider less, fled in all directions in terror, and many men tried to limp away only to be crushed under their thundering hooves. Joe knew now that the rebel army was fleeing in retreat, their hopes dashed to pieces.

There were now nine cartloads of wounded to be brought back to Gorey. Joe looked around him and all he could see were battered pitchforks, abandoned pikes, and green flags thrown to the ground as the army left the battleground. Lying on a grass patch to one side, Joe noticed a bayonet, with a piece of lace attached to it. It was crimson with blood. His mind raced in confusion, as he imagined he saw James astride a white horse before him. 'Could it be...?' "James?" he shouted. But as suddenly as the vision had come, it vanished before him.

It was some minutes before he regained his composure, realising the cannon ball had barely missed him.

"We will return!" Joe shouted, "and next time we will wipe the ground with you Needham!"

Finding a stray horse, he mounted and followed the army. Despite asking everyone he met of the whereabouts of Father Murphy, nobody could account for him. Joe rode on, disillusioned and weary. He realised that he was very fortunate not to have been killed or seriously wounded. He looked at the thousands who now travelled before him. Comrades were helping many along the route, some limping, some losing a lot of blood. Some would be dead before nightfall, for lack of proper medical attention.

"It's only a retreat for strategy purposes," many said, encouraging each other good heartedly.

But Joe realised that it was over. 1798, he thought, our year of freedom. Or death? What was achieved? he asked himself. Thousands upon thousands dead now and countless more to die. He felt despair like a torrent within his heart, and he cried out his despair when he looked at the sun declining in the western horizon. Oh James, what did you even die for? For what?

Father Doyle suddenly emerged from the dusty atmosphere about him.

"My God, Joe! Thank God you are alive!" he cried out joyfully. Joe looked at him and shook his head.

"Alive? No Father, I'm all dead inside if you must know. All our comrades! What did they die for today? Well, tell me that Father! For what?"

"Now Joe, it was a great effort. Give them that much at least. We didn't have the training, the cannon, or the guns, but we did have the courage. We did wonders with that. We gave them a run for their money that they won't forget," Father Doyle said, with almost boyish excitement.

Joe looked ahead and said nothing.

"Where are you going now, Joe? On to Gorey?" the priest asked.

"No. Not to Gorey Father. I'm going home, and that's where I intend to stay. It's bloody useless to continue. I'm tired of death, losing friends, pitchcappings... to bloody hell with it all!" and with that he spurred his horse forward, leaving the priest staring after him open mouthed.

From the ledge on the mountain Marjorie and old Mag looked at the retreat and felt the sadness of defeat.

"At least they are not being pursued," Marjorie said, on a more practical note.

"No, they are not. But tomorrow they will be, mark my words. Up this mountain they will come, and God have mercy on us all then," she said, crossing herself.

Those who escaped the bloodbath went either to Gorey, or fled to the mountains. The defeat was a nightmare they had never anticipated. It was unimaginable this time yesterday, Joe thought, as he made the final mile up to the village. He knew what he had to do now.

Nell was overjoyed to see him limp home.

"Oh God Joe, 'tis a miracle you are here with me again," she said, as she bathed his blood spattered face. "And what of Father Murphy? Matt? And the rest of them?"

Joe just shook his head as he collapsed from exhaustion onto the floor.

Most of the men returned later that night some wounded badly, the others very shocked at the sight of such mass slaughter. Kitty seemed less withdrawn than usual, and she helped with the wounded as well as giving words of encouragement to the disillusioned. Later that night, Joe called a meeting. Having waited to no avail for Father Doyle to arrive, he decided to proceed.

"I have called you here tonight to tell you all that this village will be attacked within the next few days. With the reinforcements coming they will sweep across the countryside and scour it for every rebel they can lay their hands on. No need to tell you what will happen to you if you are found here. I am advising every able-bodied man, woman and child to leave at first light and travel deeper into the mountains. It's your only hope if you want to remain alive."

Kitty sat listening to him and knew he was right. The authorities would now show no mercy, but she decided she was staying, despite his well-intentioned warning.

"Mr. Gilltrap is right," she said, standing tall.

There was a hush now, for it had been quite some time since Kitty had made any statement to them as a group. She continued.

"The army will without doubt hunt down every able bodied man, and there will be summery justice. The blameless will hang with the guilty, and that's a certainty. I suggest you waste no time, just as Mr. Gilltrap has advised. Don't worry; you will not be exiles forever. You will be able to return to your homes again and pick up with your lives."

A sense of urgency now gripped the village people, and without further delay they went to their cottages and collected their belongings, and loaded them onto their carts. The children and dogs ran about excitedly, sensing the adventure ahead, oblivious to the dangers that they would face. Many of the people came to bid Kitty farewell, and to thank her for her kindness to them. She kissed the children and watched the village empty. The full moon overhead was a bonus, for it meant that they would have an additional twelve hours start. Their route lay deep into the hinterland of Glenmalure, and some would venture even further to feel safe.

"And you, Marjorie, what do you intend to do?" Kitty asked her, knowing that she would miss her greatly.

"I intend to stay right here, Miss Catherine, and when this nightmare is over, I will go back and reclaim my tavern. Or what's left of it will be more likely the case. No! I am too weary now to travel through mountain country. I will take my chances here," Marjorie said, looking across the dark plains to the sea, glittering in the light of the full moon.

"What about you, Hannah? And you also, Williams? Don't you think its time that you both went, while there is still the chance of having a life together?" Kitty asked them quietly.

"Go! Never! Both Hannah and I intend to remain here and make our home in this vicinity, and here we will stay now. It is, after all, where we have lived most of our lives."

Williams spoke with such determination that their decision seemed irrevocable.

"I see," Kitty said, suspecting their decision was also out of concern for her. "Are you happy Hannah with this decision?"

"Oh, I must do what Williams says now, your ladyship. He is seldom wrong. Besides, I will have to keep an eye on you, and help you to sort out your new life, Miss Catherine, and that's final."

Hannah kissed her mistress, and then held her in her arms.

"I will have to put some flesh back on you, for you have worn away to nothing these past weeks!"

Kitty was touched by her loyalty and concern, but could not share her hopes for the future. Her heart still yearned for the return of James, which she believed with the utmost conviction, was going to happen.

Parting with Nell and Joe and their small family was heartbreaking for all concerned. They wept, and promised to meet again in happier times.

"Now you take good care of her ladyship, Williams," Joe said as he kissed Kitty's hand. "You are one great lady, Kitty, and James would be well proud of you." With that, he went into the house to see old Mag.

"So you are going to stay here, Mag?" he asked her gently.

"Yes, I am going to do just that, Joe. Too old to go traipsing around the mountains, and besides, I'd only be a complete nuisance. I'll go out and see Nell and the children off. Sad night for us all, Joe. I was just here thinking of the many nights when James, Lord rest him, yourself and myself sat in the village tavern, the snow falling outside, and we heating our hands by the great fire. Oh, God be with the days, Joe, for we will never see them again." She walked slowly out into the moonlight and bid Nell and the children a sad farewell.

Within an hour the mountain village was deserted. In the old house, Kitty sat with old Mag, Hannah and Williams by the fireside. Marjorie was busy baking bread.

"They are all gone now," old Mag said sadly.

"Indeed they are, and just as well as there would be wholesale slaughter otherwise. They are not likely to touch the likes of us here," Marjorie added.

I wonder, Williams thought, I really wonder.

Hannah looked at her mistress. She decided to ask her the question that had been on her mind now for some time.

"Miss Kitty, I have been wondering about something and it is bothering me a lot."

"Oh really, Hannah, whatever can it be?"

Kitty looked at her loyal friend and waited to hear what seemed to be so pressing on the old housekeeper's mind.

"Well, it's not very easy to speak of, your ladyship," and Hannah looked at old Mag expecting some help on the matter.

"Why not, Hannah? Come now, you must speak your mind!" Kitty said in her usual direct way.

"It's about your father, your ladyship. It's just that, well, if anything should happen to him, would you not feel remorse for not having forgiven him," and

Hannah felt relieved that she had finally said what had been weighing so heavily upon her.

"Hannah, there are times I imagine I am hearing things and I think this is one of those times! The answer is simply 'no'. Never! That man is beyond forgiving. He has destroyed my whole life and I will never see him again.

With that, Kitty stood up and, taking her shawl, left the house abruptly.

"That wasn't very wise Hannah, was it?" Williams said irritably.

"Wise or not, Seymour Williams, it needed saying! What if we got word that his lordship died this very night and her ladyship cried out for him? Well, would you not feel it should have been our duty, out of loyalty to Lady Edwina, to have at least asked the question?"

Williams thought this over and knew that Hannah was right as usual.

"I hadn't thought of it that way, Hannah," he said by way of apology.

"There's no fear of that fellow," old Mag added with derision, "Lord Foldsworth won't die here. That's all I'll say on the matter."

Marjorie was always intrigued when the old woman spoke with this air of mystery. She wanted to know more.

"Where will he die then, Mag?" she ventured to question.

"I will not be saying more on the matter but this one thing. I saw a great ship in my dreams last night."

"Poppycock!" Williams said, dismissively waving his hand.

"Oh really, Mr. Williams. Is that what you would call it then," she challenged him.

"Yes it is. Any of us could have had such a dream. My heavens, if all my dreams were to come true, what a different life I would have had," he said, laughing.

"Tell me, Mr. Williams, what were your thoughts as you sat by the grave in the small village, before you came back to us here?" old Mag looked at him now, almost jubilantly.

"Well my word!" Williams exclaimed, and said no more, the hair almost standing on his head as a ripple of fear ran through him.

"I take it, then, that Mag isn't talking... poppycock... after all, Williams?" Hannah asked him, smiling.

"I think Mag knows what she is talking about," Williams said, acceding defeat.

"He will soon be gone from us, Lord Foldsworth. To another world completely," old Mag crooned, and soon she fell asleep, her cat purring happily on her lap.

Over at the old stone fort, Kitty wept.

"Where are you James? Will you ever come for me?" she cried.

But only the wind whispered gently, as if wrapping itself around the giant boulders. As if to comfort her.

* * *

Eunice Gainsforth walked home with a greater sense of acceptance. Her husband was now dead four months, and even in that short space, she was learning that time slowly brings the tender threads of life together again. It had been hard watching him die. It had happened so suddenly. His cough had become persistently worse, and he had been forced to discontinue his work at the poorhouse. It had been that wretched place, the doctor had stated, that led to the infection in his lungs.

Finally he had to remain at home, Sunday service being the only time he was permitted to leave his simple sitting room. She missed him dreadfully, and only for the constant support of Glencora and the frequent invitations to Ravenswood Castle, Eunice doubted she would have ever come through the tragic loss to the extent that she now had.

A letter awaited her on the small table in the hall. She recognised the familiar hand of her friend, and she knew instinctively that it was either an invitation, or a request to 'come quickly!'. Eunice smiled at the regularity of her dearest friend's letters. Opening the letter, she was surprised to read the contents.

Ravenswood Castle

My dearest Eunice,

May I come and see you this evening? Your home would be more conducive for the matters at hand to be discussed.

Yours faithfully,

Glencora

Odd, Eunice thought. Very rarely has Glencora requested to come here to chat. Promptly, she dismissed the housekeeper, allowing her the evening off. Privacy would be of the utmost importance, she expected. She thought of the many secrets they had shared over the years, their fears and hopes and joys. It was a strong friendship that had endured so much. Eunice sat in the garden waiting for the sound of the carriage.

The evening was calm and beautiful, and the Hampshire countryside basked in the July sunshine. She looked around the garden at how it reflected the love and care that was lavished upon it. The sound of the bees she loved most of all. There was sense timelessness about it, the promise of a continuity of sorts.

The sound of the carriage jolted her back to the present, and Eunice went inside to tidy her hair and greet her friend at the door. Having instructed the coachman to return in two hours, Glencora walked in hurriedly.

"Oh Eunice, thank heavens you are here this evening," she began.

"Come in, my dear, and we will talk. Tea?" Eunice asked.

"No tea, Eunice. I need advice, urgently too, may I add. I am dreadfully worried, almost beside myself in fact."

Looking at her friend, Eunice could see that whatever was troubling her must indeed be grievous.

"Whatever is the matter Glencora? Is someone suddenly taken ill?"

Having regained her composure, Lady Glencora sat back a little more relaxed.

"Eunice," she began, "for some time now as you know, there has been the most dreadful trouble in Ireland. Henry arrived home from London this afternoon almost at the point of distraction. He met a young lady there, Johanna de Winters. She is a friend of the Foldsworth family, knew Lady Edwina, Charles and young Catherine. She had the most appalling tale to relate. She says that Catherine had absconded with a rebel lover and that he was executed. As a reprisal, Oak Hall was burned to the ground and the entire county has been overcome by these rebels and no account whatsoever of Charles. Oh Eunice, whatever are we to do? Poor Charles may well be dead and our lovely Catherine perhaps even a prisoner."

Eunice was shocked by the revelations, and for a moment did not know quite what to say. Glencora wept, and her pallor was ashen. Eunice went deep into thought for what seemed to Glencora a very long time. It was her habit to do so when confronted with a problem that needed urgent addressing. Eunice pondered on what seemed to her the obvious course of action.

"Henry must go over there," she said suddenly.

"What!" Glencora exclaimed.

"He must go over to Ireland. It is the only possible way forward in this dilemma. There is little point in sitting here worrying day after day as to the fate of Charles and his daughter. Speculation could lead to regret in time, Glencora, and what then? To live with the guilt that would follow, with the usual 'if's' and 'should have's'?"

"But Henry is all that I have, Eunice. I shudder to think of what could happen to him."

Eunice could see the legitimacy of her anxiety. Ireland was indeed an extremely troubled land, and while Henry was intelligent, he was by no means equipped with the cunning he might need to survive such circumstances. Yet, it was the best solution.

"He must go, Glencora. His father and half sister are there. Trust him and encourage him to go. He will be all right. He is, after all, worried himself, from what you say."

"Yes. I must allay my fears and suggest it as a course of action. Knowing

Henry, he will already have thought of the idea himself," Glencora said, feeling less anxious now.

Their discussion was followed by tea in the garden, which in itself gave Glencora the opportunity to raise the next matter, which she was more reluctant to broach. Eunice sensed her hesitation.

"What is it you wish to talk of, Glencora? I think you know me well enough now to relinquish this hesitancy," and she smiled encouragingly at her across the table.

"I feel a little foolish really, Eunice, but if Charles is returned to me safe and well, do you think I should in time marry him?"

"Why not? He is a free man, is he not?"

Glencora thought for a while, admiring her friends simple attitude and approach towards life and it's problems.

"You still love him I take it?"

"More than ever. It is as if our time has finally come, Eunice. I would never have been able to continue the relationship had Edwina lived. I have had time to think, and as much as I love Charles, I know that it would have torn him apart to continue a secret liaison. Secrets can be dangerous. But now we are suddenly free! I am sorry that Edwina died as she did. I little thought I would never see her again."

Eunice looked at her. She is still so beautiful, she thought.

"Let us pray, Glencora, that Charles is well, and that Lady Catherine will see sense! Henry will persuade her, no doubt, to return with him. With her lover now dead, she will only be too delighted to leave that sorrowful land behind her, it's memories included."

Glencora looked across the countryside, and the evening haze that was now descending upon it.

"I don't know, Eunice. Catherine is very headstrong, and a bit like Henry. As an only child, she may tend to be adamant about life. But who would have ever thought of it! Poor Charles must have almost lost his mind with worry. I know that his brother John was rendered speechless when Henry gave him the account, which this woman, Johanna de Winters, had related to him.

Eunice felt irritated.

"I think it is time that families reached a better understanding and perhaps acceptance of their members choice of whom to love, Glencora. Now don't misunderstand me! You yourself have been a victim of this intolerance, have you not? Imagine if there had been no opposition to your relationship with Charles, how very different life would have been! And this rebel fellow that Lady Catherine fell in love with, well, who can say? He may have come from a very good family perhaps, and may have had just cause to be a rebel."

Glencora looked at her shocked.

"Eunice, how on earth can you even think like that!" she exclaimed in surprise.

"Very simple, my dear. Tolerance, I have learned, will be the way of the future for us all. Without it we are all doomed to even duller and more stagnant lives."

This was somehow beyond Glencora. Whatever about religious tolerance between people, the acceptance of a member of the lower classes into ones family was totally out of the question.

"Glencora, you love Henry more than life itself, do you not?"

"You know I do. He is everything to me, and is all I have."

"Well then," Eunice continued, intent on pressing home the point, "supposing one day he brought a young lady home, who was penniless, came from a disadvantaged family, but on the other hand was articulate and beautiful to look upon, and above all, he worshiped her, what then?"

"Heaven forbid that I should be confronted with such a predicament!" her friend replied, afraid almost to allow the suggestion to remain in her mind for any longer than necessary.

Eunice decided to allow the matter to rest with her. Turning her thoughts now to a different issue, she knew it was time for her to tell Glencora of her recent decision.

"I have some news of my own, Glencora, which knowing you, may displease you. I have decided to go and live with my sister in Cornwall next month."

"Absolutely not, Eunice. You will come and live at the castle where there is ample room. You may live your entire life there. I insist. I have been meaning to discuss it with you," Eunice laughed.

"Good heavens, Glencora, I could never do that! But how very kind of you to suggest it. No. Your life is going to change greatly, and you will only really start living, my dear! The new parson arrives in October, and I shall be settled in Cornwall before the winter. But I promise I shall come and holiday with you every June! Will you compromise with that plan?"

Glencora hugged her warmly.

"If there is one thing I have learned about you, Eunice Gainsforth, it is this. Once you have decided your course, nothing will dissuade you. I will miss you, as you have been the sister I never had. I will insist that you come each June, and I know you shall!"

In the distance they could hear the coach approaching to collect Glencora.

"Will you come for lunch tomorrow, Eunice?" Glencora asked, standing up and looking down at her friend.

"That would be delightful," she replied, and linking her friend they both walked out through the small wicker gate, where the bees hummed busily on the honeysuckle that clung to the overhead arch.

As Glencora sat back in the coach she thought how suddenly her life was about to change, and it all now depended on Henry going to Ireland. She felt a chill of fear at the prospect of her son travelling to a land where revolution was rampant. She prayed for his safe journey and return. She knew it was going to be the greatest gamble of her life. Somewhere deep inside, she sensed that all would be well .She hoped she was right.

Yes, she thought, I shall have Goodwin accompany Henry. He is an excellent marksman, and a faithful servant. He would take care of his young master. This idea comforted her, and the entire venture seemed to lose its fear for her. Upon arriving home, she was not surprised to find that Henry had already packed for the journey. He did not object to Goodwin accompanying him. In fact, he took to the idea instantly.

"We will leave at sunrise, mamma. Don't worry, all will be well," he assured her.

He knew her concern was immense, for both Charles and Kitty, and he shared it.

"Henry, speak as little as possible, for your tone of speech will easily betray your origins, and promise me you will be careful?"

Again he tried to reassure his mother, but realised that she would only cease worrying upon his safe return. Henry pondered the account that Lady de Winters had related to him of Kitty's very odd alliance. She had sounded so convinced about it, and no less convinced that Charles Foldsworth was quite out of his mine! He had decided to omit that part of the strange tale when telling both his mother and uncle John. Perhaps the poor man had been unable to cope with the drastic loss of his wife and then this revolution to boot!

Before sleeping he decided that he would do all in his power to persuade his father and half sister to return, for his mother's sake. She would never be at peace otherwise. Early the next morning, Lady Glencora made a point of rising early to speak to Goodwin, and to impress upon him the paramount importance of his master's safe return.

Chapter seventeen

Hannah noticed that her charge seemed to be in much better spirits of late. She said as much to Williams one morning as they sat looking out over the ledge of the mountain.

"Yes, she even looks so much healthier, more colour in her cheeks. Hopefully she will soon stop visiting that old fort, and then we can begin in earnest to try and talk some sense into her. This waiting for James is so absurd, Hannah!"

"Well Williams, whatever you do, never on any account let her hear you refer to her visits there as absurd. Why, she would never forgive you, so sacred is the memory of James to her. But overall I agree with you. She does look much improved. The visits to the graveside have almost ceased. A good sign that, my mother always said."

They were surprised when a moment later Kitty walked over to them, saying that she was going riding for a few hours should they be seeking her whereabouts.

"Be mindful now of any rebels you meet! There are still some going about the hills I'd wager, Lady Catherine," Williams cautioned her.

"No need to worry, Williams. Rest assured I shall return in one piece!" she said cheerily, sounding very much like her old self, Hannah thought.

They were delighted with her initiative to ride out.

"There, Williams. In no time at all we will hear her announce that she intends to go to her friends in Meath or Dublin," Hannah said happily as they both walked back to the house.

They looked at Kitty as she rode out of the village, her mare trotting friskily, and glad to be saddled again.

"It's good to be out again, Misty," she said to the mare, patting it's head good naturedly as she rode down the mountainside.

Her destination was Oak Hall.

She longed to see what was left of her old home, ruin though it now was. As she approached the long avenue, she was shocked to see how overgrown the rhododendrons and other trees had become. She walked her mare slowly up the avenue, trying to absorb the changes that had taken place in such a very short space of time. There was nobody to be seen; only a few mares with foals at foot grazing leisurely on the front lawns. They looked healthy enough, she thought. As she rounded the curve in the avenue, she was not quite prepared for the sight of the great mansion, a charred and blackened heap standing forlornly before her. She pulled up the mare and looked at the ruined splendour of what had once been her home. Memories came flooding back in abundance.

Her first pony, that she had eventually mastered, and how her mother had clapped with delight as she had jumped the poles on the front lawn. Then, the garden parties. The thrilling hunt meets that had assembled for the Stirrup Cup before taking off for those long cross-country chases on crisp autumn mornings. Picnics, and mid-summer night balls.

'Where is it all gone,'? she asked herself.

Slowly she approached the house, and stood at a distance lest part of a wall or some charred timber piece come loose. Then she noticed a young man walk across the stable yard. She approached him tentatively, until he noticed her. He took off his hat, shading his eyes from the summer sunshine.

"Well Miss Catherine, isn't it a great thing to see you," he said respectfully.

It was Tom Woods.

"Good morning Tom. Are you the last of the yard staff now?"

"I'm afraid so, my lady. There's little to be done here now, and I'm sorry for your losses ma'am," he said, turning about and looking at the scene before them.

"Yes, Tom. All is lost I am afraid. Did any of the horses perish in the fire?"

"None, my lady. I did hear it was the new maid who burned the place down. Gladys was her name. Fooled us all, she did," and Kitty knew that he was angry.

"Well Tom, there has been so much damage and loss of life with this rebellion, it leaves us all quite out of place. Has my father been here of late?" she asked cautiously.

"No, my lady, though I did hear he has improved greatly of late. Back walking again, and talking some too!" Tom told her, rubbing both hands together.

She did not reply, which Tom noticed with disappointment.

"It's all quite finished Tom, the life we had here. And it could have been quite different, you know."

The lad said nothing, only wished what she said were true.

"Will your ladyship live here, maybe in one of the lodges? Pardon my asking"

"No Tom, there is no longer anything to stay for. Hannah and Williams will, in time, occupy one of the gate lodges, I am sure. At least that is what I would like them to do. And you Tom? What will you do?"

Tom looked thoughtfully at the mares grazing behind the great beech trees.

"I will look after them, my lady, until the master comes back. He will then tell me what my future will be. I have known nothing else but this place since I was seven years old, my lady. I love those horses, you see."

Kitty looked at him. He was so typical of many of the men and women who had devoted their entire lives to families and estates such as her own.

"You are wonderfully kind, Tom, and I do hope that your future will somehow be part of what is left of the estate. Who knows?" she said, trying to be optimistic.

Suddenly they both heard the approaching sound of horsemen.

"Who ever can that be?" Kitty asked, apprehension rising within her. The thought of meeting her father brought a sense of dread to her heart.

"It seems to be two young men, my lady. Strangers too, for I don't recognise their mounts. They seem a bit unsure of themselves, if I'm not mistaken."

Kitty turned around to face the intruders.

"Perhaps some gombeen men, hoping to purchase the estate at a low price, Tom. Don't worry, I will see them out of here in little doubt as to the foolishness of their schemes, whatever they might be!"

But nothing in the world could have prepared her for the dawning realisation that it was Henry, with a stranger, approaching her. Henry saw Kitty place a gloved hand across her mouth, stifling a cry of surprise. Dismounting, he ran to greet her.

"Oh Catherine! Catherine! I have prayed you were safe!" he exclaimed as he hugged her tightly.

"My God, of all the people in the world Henry! How ever did you find us here? This is like a dream," Kitty said falteringly.

"And your father? Is he well? Is he safe?" Henry asked, holding her now at arms length.

"Yes he is safe, and living not far from here," she assured him. "Come Henry, let us walk."

Slowly they walked arm in arm across the vast lawn, while Goodwin and Tom became acquainted as they led the horses to the stables.

"You have obviously heard of our great difficulties here, Henry. Who informed you?" Kitty asked him curiously.

As they sat beneath the shade of a giant chestnut tree, Henry related his meeting with Lady de Winters, which had happened quite by chance while he was in London on some business.

"Ah yes, the lovely Johanna. What did she tell you Henry?"

Henry hesitated for a moment. Kitty sensed his reluctance.

"You may be perfectly frank with me, Henry. Have we not always been totally honest with each other?" she said, now placing her arm in his.

"You may not like it, Kitty. But as you say, we have always been honest. What worried me most perhaps was the report that you had absconded with a rebel; 'over heels in love with him' was the description she gave! Were you Kitty? Were you in love with this man?"

Silence prevailed for some time, and he noticed she wept quietly.

"Yes Henry, I was and still am. He was everything to me. I can understand your anxiety upon hearing that description, but James was life itself to me."

Then she told him the entire story. How she had met James, and of their courtship. Their travels, and how her father had publicly renounced her. He listened to the long sad story, and gradually the picture grew in his mind. He listened attentively, without interruption. He could now understand her inconsolable loss. The prospect of a forced marriage to Timothy Stewart, her refusal, the trumped-up charges against James, his sham trial and execution.

He looked at the now frail young woman beside him and marvelled at the fact that she was still sane. He put his arm around her and simply held her.

"You must come back with me, Kitty. Back to Hampshire," he said firmly.

"Never, Henry. What would I do there? With father in one wing of the castle and I in the other? It would be like hell for me! No. I shall remain here, and live a simple life," she assured him, thinking it was wiser to omit the promise that James had made to her. He would think her unbalanced.

"How on earth will you survive here, Kitty?" he asked apprehensively.

"Well, I have money, and I also have Hannah and Williams to take care of me. Perhaps in time I will go to Hampshire and purchase a home there. Will you compromise on that, my beloved brother?"

Laughing, he hugged her.

"I have little choice, have I not? But I assure you, I shall be back after the winter and perhaps by then you may have changed your mind?" he said optimistically.

"Perhaps I shall, Henry. But of this one matter I am adamant. I shall never again see father face-to-face, much less ever speak with him again. For me, Henry, that man does not exist. He is presently staying with a woman to whom he once gave a home. She apparently found him on the roadside the morning after the fire. Her name is May Ryan, a pleasant woman, and a widow. She has a kind heart. You will find him there."

"I hope the shock of seeing me will not give him a further stroke! Heaven only knows how he will receive me. He seems to have changed beyond all imaginings Kitty," Henry said, feeling apprehensive about the impending visit.

"Initially he will be surprised, but I think that he will accept your offer of returning to Hampshire. What possible future could he have here? His kind will never again feel secure in this land."

Henry remained silent for a while.

"This mountain village where you live now, Kitty. Are you comfortable there? What can I do for you?" Henry asked her, his heart full of concern.

"You can allow me to continue to remain there Henry, until the time comes when I will decide my own future," she said matter of factly.

"Well, I promise you shall, and if ever you awaken some morning and decide to come back home, I will be only too delighted to have you."

They both stood up at the same time, knowing their understanding of each other had reached its limit.

"Will you go and see father this evening, Henry?"

"No. I have decided I must try and think a little before our encounter. Tomorrow might be best, and if he agrees to return with me, we shall travel immediately."

They walked back to the yard where they found Tom and Goodwin playing cards. They both stood up abruptly and went to the stables to bring out the horses.

"I shall see you again, Kitty? That is, before my departure?" Henry enquired gently.

"No, Henry. I think it best we leave things as they are for now. You will inevitably be persuaded by my father to have me change my mind, and as you realise that can never happen."

He knew she was right, but it was tearing his heart asunder to leave her. He looked at the great mountains beyond where she had pointed out the village. He shuddered at the thought of the coming of the first snows, and how she would have to live there, without the comforts she had been accustomed to all her life.

"Don't worry, Henry, I shall be perfectly alright."

Their parting was simple, with no display of sadness or regret, for Henry believed that in time she would unquestionably change her mind, and rest would heal the great loss to her soul. He rode towards the town, where Kitty had recommended a small guesthouse where he and Goodwin would be safe and comfortable.

When they had departed Kitty's thoughts turned to the small church wherein lay her mother's remains. The churchyard was silent and the ancient headstones leaned like drunken men. She entered the church and stood still, absorbing its timeless sense of calm and peace. Memories of her last visit to her mother's tomb came flooding back to her, how she had so curtly dismissed James that day. Sitting by the tomb Kitty felt the sense of peace enfold her.

" Oh Mama..." she whispered, continuing; "All that has happened. Who would ever believe it? Our world's shattered and broken, you gone forever, our home burned down, and father a stranger to me. You never did approve of James, I think. Perhaps time could have changed all that. I shall never know. But Mamma, I found love and happiness, brief as it was. For that I am so grateful. So very grateful." Standing up Kitty looked at the rows of her ancestors that flanked the sides of the church, at rest within its ancient walls. "I wonder how many of you could have said the same of your lives?" she quietly whispered, but the silence deepened.

Upon her return to the mountain village, Kitty decided to say nothing of her amazing encounter to either Hannah or Williams. She knew that they would attempt, with all their powers of persuasion, to make her return to Hampshire. They would never understand. Never, she thought. *Here I shall remain and await James as I promised.*

That night, Marjorie sensed a strange restlessness in Kitty, and remarked on it to Hannah quietly while the young lady slept soundly.

"She went to Oak Hall, Marjorie, and I'm sure the memories came flooding back to the poor child. But as I keep saying to Williams... or should I say, Seymour... time will heal the girl."

Marjorie was not convinced, but she kept her concerns to herself.

* * *

The following morning dawned overcast, but dry. The cool winds of impending autumn swirled about the house as Hannah lit the morning fire, while Williams laid the table. Marjorie came through the door, carrying a pail of water.

"My God, that wind would peel apples Hannah. I forgot it gets colder in the mountains much earlier than the lowlands," she gasped, as she poured water into the great kettle, which would soon send its steam rising to the ceiling.

"Yes. Williams says the snows will come earlier this year. I don't know what we are to do, Marjorie, but we can't stay here for the winter or we will all die of the cold."

Just then Kitty emerged, wearing her old blue riding habit.

"Good morning all," she said cheerfully.

"Good morning your ladyship," Williams replied.

"Where are you off to, Kitty? Hannah asked.

"Oh, just for some air Hannah. I will wait and have some breakfast though, as I shall be away for a few hours this morning. I love these crispy autumn days. They remind me of so much!" she sighed, as she ate the brown bread slowly.

"Are you not having some eggs, my lady?" Williams asked, adding, "They are lovely and fresh."

"No Williams, but I shall have quite an appetite this evening I imagine, and I promise I shall do justice to whatever Hannah cooks!"

* * *

May Ryan opened the door and looked at the tall stranger who stood before her.

"Mrs. May Ryan?" he asked her, taking off his hat.

"Yes, sir, I am May Ryan," she replied, astonished at the appearance of the visitor.

"I apologise for my intrusion, but I am told that Lord Foldsworth is staying here with you."

"Yes he is, sir, but he is out walking at present. If you would like to come in and wait for him, you are more than welcome."

Henry was deeply impressed by her gentleness of manner and pleasant appearance.

"Perhaps if you were to indicate to me the direction he has taken, I could follow him?" Henry asked her.

"Well, as far as I know he has gone to the oak woods. He likes to take a stroll there before eating his midday meal, sir. Should he return and perhaps miss you on the way, will you call back to see him?" May asked, but not inquisitively.

Assuring her that he would, he smiled and bid his travelling companion await him. May closed the door, and realised instantly that he was the son, or if not the nephew, of his lordships. Why, she thought, they are almost identical. She tidied the house in a frenzy of excitement, and built up the fire. She called the children, and bid them eat their midday meal hastily. They will most likely want to talk in private, she thought, and who knows, his lordships days with me are perhaps at an end!

Henry rode in the direction of the oak woods, and walked his horse through the autumn splendour. In the distance he could now see the figure of an old man sitting on the stump of a tree. He approached him slowly, not wishing to startle him. Lord Foldsworth saw the approaching horseman, and prayed it was not a rebel, who would slay him where he sat. He then rebuked himself for such morbid thoughts, and stood up to greet this stranger, whom he could now see was well dressed. Henry stopped some yards before him.

"Father, it is I, Henry," he said gently.

Lord Foldsworth shielded his eyes from the sun, and walked towards the apparition before him.

"Henry... is it you...?" he said falteringly.

Henry dismounted and ran to embrace the old man.

"Oh dearest father, how I prayed I would find you alive and well," he sobbed.

Lord Foldsworth was overcome with emotion, much to his own embarrassment.

"Henry, this is a miracle. It's almost beyond belief for me, for I was just here contemplating my fate and my future. I simply cannot believe my eyes," he said, the tears still glistening in them.

"Well father, you need contemplate no more. This day you will return with me to Hampshire. Our ship sails tonight, and my mother will be overjoyed to see you, as will your family there," Henry said assuringly.

"Glencora... how is she, Henry?"

"She is worried to death, father," he replied.

Lord Foldsworth felt joy surge within him at being so addressed.

"You have heard, obviously, of all that has happened? Kitty, and all the dreadful nightmare that befell us, Henry?"

"Yes father. I even met Kitty yesterday. I found her at Oak Hall, looking over the place."

"Was she looking for me, Henry? Is she well again?" Lord Foldsworth asked excitedly.

Henry felt sad at the note of pleading in his father's voice, and decided he would have to measure his words carefully.

"She assured me that you were well, which she is very pleased about, but father, it is going to take a lot of time for her to come to terms with all that has happened to her in her young life."

Lord Foldsworth said nothing, only stared at Henry, waiting for him to continue.

"I asked her to come back to Hampshire, and she assures me that she will, but not until next spring, father."

The look of dismay was obvious on his father's face as his spirits sank.

"I have been cruel, Henry. Very cruel to her. There is not a day or night when my conscience does not scream for forgiveness. What can I do? I could never face her again, for she would scorn me. I had no idea, you see... that man... and I admit, yes, I had him falsely charged and executed, may God have mercy on me!"

A long silence prevailed and Lord Foldsworth sensed that Henry's allegiance to Kitty was very strong.

"We will talk no more of the matter, father. It is done with, and just let us hope that in time she will forgive you."

Lord Foldsworth detected the subtle rebuke quietly stated: that he had handled matters wrongly.

"Yes, maybe she will Henry, maybe she will. Tell me, how does she look? Is she well, Henry?"

"Yes father, she is well. A little thin perhaps, but that is to be expected. Now, let us go back and tell Mrs. Ryan that you are leaving today. She seems a very pleasant woman, Mrs. Ryan," Henry said as he led the horse forward.

"I owe her my life, Henry. Only for her kindness, I think I would be dead now. There were a band of rebels here some weeks ago, and had they known my true identity they would undoubtedly have piked me to death. Instead, she told them I was her father. Loyal, beyond question, Henry."

The children saw them approach and ran inside to tell their mother.

"Now, behave well, and no questions mind you. Let the gentlemen see what lovely manners you have, eh?"

May brushed their hair and felt very proud of her daughters. She met her guests at the door and invited Henry to accompany Lord Foldsworth inside.

"Mrs. Ryan, this is my son, Henry," he said simply.

May curtsied.

"Pleased to meet you, sir," May said, looking at the broad smiling face on the young man.

"I owe you a debt of gratitude, Mrs. Ryan, that I can never repay. You saved my father's life on no less than two occasions. We must reimburse you in some way.

"Yes. I have given the matter some thought, Mrs. Ryan, and I have decided that you are to own the twenty acres adjoining this house here. It is the least I can do for you," Lord Foldsworth said smiling.

May was overcome with joy.

"Oh Lord Foldsworth... it's far too much. I could never accept such a gift sir."

"Well Mrs. Ryan, you must accept, and I shall instruct my lawyers in Dublin this very week to transfer it to you freehold, and for all time. Now, that's an end to that."

May could hardly believe her good fortune. Henry was clearly delighted with his father's gesture of generosity.

"Father is quite right, Mrs. Ryan. You deserve it all, and we wish you every happiness and good fortune. Now, I am afraid we are making haste today for home, so if you would be kind enough to pack father's things, we will leave you without further ado."

"Certainly sir. I will have them ready in a minute," and she went into the small room to pack the few garments that were neatly placed in the small drawer.

When she returned to the kitchen, she found Henry chatting happily with the girls.

"Mrs. Ryan, I have one final favour to ask of you," Lord Foldsworth said, drawing her aside.

"Certainly, your lordship, whatever I can do for you, I shall," May told him quietly.

"If I write a letter to my daughter, will you deliver it to her personally today?" he asked.

She could see the desperation in his face, not so much in relation to the request, she thought, but to be reconciled with Kitty.

"Nothing would give me greater pleasure, your lordship. I shall leave with it the moment you have written and sealed it."

Handing him some parchment, Lord Foldsworth sat down at the table and began to write.

My Dearest Kitty,

I have had a long time to think over our recent past, and I stand very sorry and ashamed of my gross unfairness and, yes, cruelty to you.

I do not know what to say to you. Sorry seems such a shallow statement in the light of the loss of the man you loved.

It is only now, no more blinded by hate and fear, that I can see that you loved him and by no small measure. I have taken a great deal from you, obviously more than I will ever be able to replace in two lifetimes even. But I too had my hell. My fears for you were enormous. Your love tie would have isolated you forever from our family and friends, and yet, the fact remains that I have lost you nonetheless.

And for what?

Your mother meant a great deal to me. You also know that Glencora and my love for her was also in my life, but it was not the most important aspect of it. Yes she was there, but for a very long time, she was deep in the recesses of my memory. The hunting accident triggered more than I could cope with.

I love you Kitty and I beg your forgiveness. I am glad you met Henry. He tells me that perhaps in time you might come and live with us in Hampshire. Would it not be a dream come true were you to do so! We could try to be father and daughter once again, be happy again. I would give anything were that to happen. I could ask for nothing more.

I am leaving for home with Henry today.

Until we meet, my darling, I leave the estate in your wise handling.

Please forgive me,
Your loving father.

Sealing the letter, he handed it to May.

"I will go this moment your lordship and hand it to Lady Catherine within the hour," she assured him.

"Thank you Mrs. Ryan. Thank you for everything. I hope you will have a happy life, and a more prosperous one. You deserve it all."

May looked at him. He was a great deal better, and she knew that in time he would make a complete recovery.

"Thank you, Lord Foldsworth. I shall never forget your kindness to me, not just now, but when I needed it most. When my husband died. You will always be remembered by us," and she curtsied.

"Now children, put on your cloaks, for we are going to see Hannah and Lady Catherine," she announced happily.

"Goodbye Mrs. Ryan, and once again, thank you for all you have done for father," Henry said, as he placed a small bag of coins on the table.

May protested vigorously.

"No, no. It is my own present to you, Mrs. Ryan, and let that be an end to it. Use it to buy some stock for the land and perhaps a pony each for your little girls," Henry said, smiling happily.

May stood with her children as she watched them ride away. You were a good man, Lord Foldsworth, she thought. The pity was you let your heart speak too late. We will never see you again... sad to say. The men then rounded the corner, and were gone from view forever.

May hurried towards the mountains, her children playing happily as they ran ahead of her. She opened the small bag and to her amazement counted twenty guineas. She was overjoyed. I will never be poor again, she thought. Never, as long as I live. God bless you Lord Foldsworth, and bless you again. The wind, which had persisted all day, blew hard against her as she walked slowly up the mountainside. She gripped the letter inside her cloak, and the prospect of seeing Lady Catherine and Hannah made the journey seem all the shorter.

The village appeared deserted, even at a distance. No smoke from any of the cottages, except one. It was sad that everyone had left, particularly Nell and Joe. She would miss them a lot, she thought. But someday they will return, and maybe they could be happy again. But for now, it was for the best that they were deeper in the mountains. There had been too much death and grief.

Hannah was overjoyed to see May and her children. Old Mag delighted in the young company and commenced telling the small girls a story, which enthralled them.

"Where is Lady Catherine, Hannah?" May asked, taking the letter from beneath her cloak.

"Need you ask, May? Over at the old fort every evening, as you have probably heard. But I must say, she is more herself these past few days, isn't that right, Seymour?"

"Yes indeed. Out exercising too each day, which is a great bonus to her health," he said cheerily.

Marjorie was busy preparing the evening meal, a task she never tired of. Just then the door opened and Kitty walked in. She was surprised to see May.

"My goodness Mrs. Ryan! This is a pleasant surprise indeed. Hello children!

How very big you have all become. Why, I would hardly recognise you all," Kitty said, picking up the youngest and kissing her.

"Lady Catherine, may I speak with you awhile?" May asked, walking towards one of the side rooms.

Kitty followed her, hoping she was not going to attempt to persuade her to visit her father.

"I have a letter here from your father. He bade me promise him that I would deliver it to you this very day."

May handed the letter to Kitty, and left her alone in the room to read it. Kitty looked at the familiar handwriting and began to read. She read it slowly, and then gazed out of the window. Oh father, she thought, too late now for regrets, for that's all your entire letter contains... and the price I had to pay... no, I shall never forget what you have done to me. Never! Reading it again, it cheered her somewhat that at least she could give Hannah and Williams one of the gate lodges to live in, and Tom at the yard could continue to live there and take care of the horses. Then there was the gardener's cottage. Well, old Mag can live out her life there and be happy with the garden, cultivating her herbs. At least I can see to their happiness a little, and repay them somewhat for all their goodness to me. She smiled contentedly. She put the letter away carefully, and returned to the kitchen.

"Not bad news I hope, Miss Catherine," Williams asked.

"No, not bad news, Williams. All good in fact. My father is going away and he has asked me to take care of the estate. So I have decided that you and Hannah should take over whichever gate lodge you choose. Mag, I wish you to have the gardener's cottage, and Tom may continue to live at the stables."

Williams and Hannah were clearly delighted, and old Mag clapped her hands with joy.

"Imagine a whole garden of herbs. Why, it will be like heaven for me Miss Kitty. Oh, thank you," and her old face beamed with happiness.

"I suggest the sooner the better you all move in and prepare for the winter. And you, Marjorie? Would you occupy a cottage?" Kitty asked her, hoping she would agree to do so.

"No thank you, Miss Catherine. I will go back to my tavern, but Nell and Joe would love one, as they have nowhere to return to," Marjorie said, her practicality to the fore as usual.

"You are so right. Well, that's agreed then once and for all," Kitty, said, as she sat beside old Mag and listened to the remainder of the story that held the children spellbound.

Dinner was a happy event that evening, and as the wind moaned outside, it was decided that May and the children should stay the night.

"That wind seems to be gradually getting stronger," old Mag stated in her mystical tone. "I think tomorrow could be a stormy day. I hope not, for I have to gather roots which I will need for my new garden!"

Kitty smiled. Mags unending enthusiasm for life was wonderful, she thought. Who better to have the gardens of Oak Hall!

Before retiring to bed, Kitty again read the letter from her father. She lay thinking about him for a long time. Before she blew out her candle, she prayed for him. She prayed that he would again find happiness. She smiled, as she realised that it had been a very long time since she had prayed like that.

Yes, she thought, I must be bigger than my hate. As she slept, Kitty dreamed that she was sitting with her mother in the rose garden. Her mother looked beautiful, happy and serene.

"I am delighted you have come home, Kitty," was all her mother said to her, before embracing her.

* * *

Old Mag awoke early. She had not slept well, and she was not sure why. She thought it was the excitement of the new home she had just been given the previous night, and the wonderful garden. But as she dressed slowly, she sensed a heaviness of spirit within her.

"Old age," she murmured.

She opened the door and looked outside. The sky was crimson in the east, and the wind still persisted. Storm brewing somewhere, she thought, as she looked at the sky above her. May and her children presently came into the kitchen, and Hannah had the cooking fire lighting, making some porridge for them all before their journey home.

"Will there be a storm, Mag?" Hannah asked as she poured the gruel out for the children.

"Sure as you have lit that fire, Hannah, but it won't be until this evening I'm thinking. A dry storm too, not any rain, but maybe a hell of a wind. May has no need to worry about her journey home. As I said, it won't come until evening."

With this assurance, May bid them all farewell, with the exception of Kitty who was still sleeping soundly.

"Tired, poor lamb," Marjorie said, as she combed her hair before tying it into a bun.

"Wasn't that great news about Lord Foldsworth giving May the land! 'Tis surely the truth that God works in strange ways," Hannah said to Williams as they tidied the breakfast table.

"He was a good man, his lordship, in many ways, but then even good men come to grief, Hannah. Indeed they do," Williams said philosophically.

"Well, only for him giving Miss Kitty the run of the estate we wouldn't have a home either," Mag, added, as she poured some milk for her cat. The cat lapped the milk gratefully as Mag stroked its silken coat.

"I have to go away for the day today, Hannah. Roots and things I need to collect before the frosts come. Anyway, we won't be here much longer, so I best make use of the whole day. Time enough to be going when I have my smoke though," and Mag proceeded to fill her pipe with brown peat dust, much to Williams's ongoing amazement at her odd habit.

"Did you notice, Hannah, that Miss Kitty never said where she intends to live?" Marjorie asked, as she sat down by the fire.

"That's right," Williams said, gazing out through the window.

"Maybe she will announce her plans to us today, Marjorie," Hannah said, as she buttered some bread at the table, feeling slightly apprehensive.

The prospects of living in the gate lodge delighted Williams. It meant a great deal to him to be able to live on the estate that he had served so well for most of his life. He imagined what life would be like there. He would do some gardening, he thought. Roses, hollyhocks and sweet pea. Yes, doing things that to date I could only dream of! Hannah would be happy making jams and preserves, and visiting old friends. The thought was bliss to him. God bless his lordship, he thought, as he took his morning stroll. He too looked at the sky, and wondered when the storm would break.

Kitty came to breakfast in jovial form. The dream of her mother had made a very strong impact, and she told Hannah as much.

"Well, your mother always loved the rose garden, didn't she?"

"Yes, she would always talk to my father there, if there was anything that was worrying her. They were so happy, Hannah, when I think back over their lives. But then we all were in those carefree days. However, no point in becoming melancholic, Hannah, is there?"

"None, my child. None whatsoever. Now come and eat your breakfast. What are your plans for the day, Miss Kitty?"

Kitty thought for a moment.

"I was wondering if Marjorie would like to go to town and I could help her assert her right to the tavern again. Those soldiers will have to vacate it sooner or later."

Marjorie was delighted with the suggestion.

"That's very kind of you, Miss Kitty. It would give me great support to have you with me when I confront them. I imagine they will not want to leave the place. God knows, it must be in a dreadful state."

And so it was settled.

Marjorie dressed with her heavy cloak, and within the hour they were both riding towards town. The pace was slow, as Marjorie was not quite sure of herself on horseback.

"My goodness, every bone in my body is aching," she complained.

Kitty laughed.

"You need lots of practice, Marjorie, or one soon becomes quite stiffened up."

"I need to lose about two stone of this weight more like. I think that would do wonders for me," Marjorie laughed heartily.

Life was slowly resuming its normal pace, Kitty thought. Or was it? The aftermath of the rebellion was still apparent. The vast number of men, women and children who had died had left almost every family mourning the loss of at least one member. They are beaten to the ground once more, Kitty thought, and said as much to Marjorie.

"Had the French come to this coast, it would have made the greatest difference in the world, Miss Kitty, instead of the west of Ireland. But no. We are still not beaten, for the spirit of the people will rise again another day," Marjorie assured her.

"But don't you feel it was all such a waste, Marjorie. Marcus dead, James, Matt Ryan, and they are just a few that we knew. One shudders to imagine how many thousand have died. It will be some months before we will know the truth of it all, and for what?" Kitty said dejectedly.

"To let them know that we still exist, despite the poverty and dreadful conditions the people have to endure. As far as the government is concerned, we are non-existent as human beings. You saw it yourself, Kitty. It was mere luck that you did not end up the wife of Justice Stewart. You would have had little say in life had you? A mere chattel, that's what we are seen as. When we get to town, I am sure we will be confronted with the same attitude."

The town was a bustle of activity, mostly soldiers and yeomanry. They stood about in groups, laughing, some drunk, despite the fact that it was just midday.

"Marjorie, you must allow me to speak to the commander in charge, if you don't mind. It will make a considerable difference, sad to say. All you must do is to show no surprise, just nod your head in total agreement!"

"I will be only too delighted to, Miss Kitty," Marjorie assured her.

"And Marjorie, just for now I think it would be best if you addressed me formally in front of these soldiers. It will be a lot more convincing for what I am about to say to them."

Marjorie smiled.

"Yes, your ladyship... or should I say... Lady Catherine."

Kitty smiled and then they quickened their pace, Marjorie riding some paces behind as was fitting in the new circumstances. Stopping in front of a group of soldiers, Kitty called one of them forward.

"Where is your commanding officer?" she demanded.

"Well now, ma'am, that would depend on who would be lookin' for 'im," he replied, and then laughed raucously.

Kitty edged her horse closer to him.

"Look here, my man. If you know what's good for you, you will be less insolent. Now, take me to your commander, lest you find yourself confined to barracks for a week!"

The impact was immediate.

"Yes, madam. Just follow me, if you please," he replied respectfully.

The remainder of the soldiers now ceased laughing, and stood aside to allow them pass through. Marjorie, fixing her gaze ahead, did not look at them. Instead she marvelled once again at how Kitty's tone of authority still made men do her bidding. Stopping before a large building that had once been a general warehouse, Kitty dismounted. Marjorie was horrified at how very stiff she was, and Kitty ordered the soldier to assist her. Walking inside, the soldier indicated to them the office of the commander. Ignoring him, Kitty walked through the door and beckoned Marjorie to follow.

The commander, who was studying a wall map, turned around, surprised at the unexpected intrusion.

"Good day, commander," Kitty began.

"Good day, madam," he replied, now realising that the beautiful young woman before him, was obviously from one of the settled families of the land.

"I have come here today, commander, to ask you to vacate the tavern formally known as the Bull's Nose. It belonged to this lady here with me, Marjorie Bass."

Marjorie curtsied, much to Kitty's amusement.

"I see," he replied, looking at the portly woman standing behind his visitor. "And to whom do I have the pleasure of speaking?" he asked courteously.

"Lady Catherine Foldsworth, commander. My father owns the title to Miss Bass's tavern and wishes her to be reinstated, for services rendered to our family during the recent wicked rebellion. I have every confidence you will comply with his wishes."

The commander looked at her. I have heard a lot about you, my lady, he thought. Quite a rebel you were too, if my information is correct. He realised, nonetheless, that it would be very unwise to refer to it, lest the information was incorrect.

"Why has your father not come in person to request this favour?" he asked, a tone of challenge apparent to Kitty.

"My dear commander, I am afraid you are mistaken somewhat. I am not here to request a favour! I am here to request your cooperation in assisting her to reoccupy her home and business."

The commander looked at her in admiration. Not one to be trifled with, he thought. God only knows whom she is connected with.

"Where is Lord Foldsworth, your ladyship?" he asked, intent on not acceding to her request instantly.

"My father, commander, is today returning to England to recuperate. You are possibly well aware that out home was burned to the ground by the rebels. It had a devastating effect on us, needless to add."

"Yes, I was sorry to hear of the arson attack. You do have power of attorney in his absence, Lady Foldsworth, I take it?"

"Yes I have, commander. I have it with me in fact, should you doubt my word," Kitty replied, taking the letter from beneath her cloak, afraid now that he might take it from her and read it.

"No need to produce the document, my lady. I take your word on it without question. The tavern will be vacated today! You have my assurance on the matter and perhaps Miss Bass would like to reoccupy her tavern the following day? We could do with a decent eating house about these parts, Miss Bass."

Marjorie smiled faintly.

"Thank you commander," Marjorie said, curtsying once again.

"You have been very cooperative, commander. I shall see to it that the vice regal hears of your kindness to me," Kitty said, as she put her riding gloves back on.

"My pleasure, Lady Foldsworth. It has been a delight to meet you," and he bowed slightly before her.

"Thank you again commander, and incidentally, would you have the soldiers scrub out the place. I see many of them loitering about the street. Some solid work would be good for their morale! Good morning," and with that Kitty turned about slowly and walked from his office, Marjorie following, her heart thumping wildly in her breast.

Kitty beckoned one of the soldiers to assist Marjorie mount, and they both rode out of the town at a leisurely pace. When they reached the outskirts, Kitty waited for Marjorie to come alongside her.

"Well, Marjorie, you are once again the mistress of the Bull's Nose," and they both laughed.

Nonetheless, Marjorie was under no illusion as to the magnitude of the favour.

"In all seriousness, Miss Kitty, I wish to thank you for what you have just done. All I can say is that you were wonderful to have taken such a risk. I have never met, nor am I likely to meet in the future, a woman of such courage and determination. I am very grateful to you."

"Think no more of it, Marjorie. You were very kind to James on so many occasions. I know he would want me to do this for you. Besides, you have missed the place terribly."

Marjorie agreed with her, and she pondered on how she would settle back after all that had happened.

"It's going to be sad for me in so many ways, Miss Kitty. So many faces that I shall never see coming through my door again! I'd rather not think about it to be honest with you."

Kitty realised the truth of what she said. They were silent for a while. Coming to a corner, Kitty recalled that it was the very place where herself and James had met with Bartley Finnegan that night.

"I still miss James dreadfully, Marjorie. The only thing that keeps my spirits up is the fact that he will come for me," she said, as convinced as ever.

Marjorie's heart sank with despair, for it had been some time now since she had heard Kitty make reference to this sad hope.

"Miss Kitty, would you not let go of the past. I know better than anyone how much you both loved each other, but it grieves me to think you will waste your lovely life on a dream!"

Kitty stopped her horse and looked at the woman whom she knew cared for her.

"Marjorie, it is difficult for me to explain to you, perhaps you will never understand, but I know in my heart... in my very soul... that James will return for me. Yes! You are possibly thinking, 'the poor girls, still disturbed', and so forth. But Marjorie, I know he will come soon, and I hope you will be happy for me. Promise me you will?"

"Whatever you say, my lady," Marjorie said, feeling a lump in her throat.

Nothing will ever change her mind, she thought. She is still in love with him, and who knows, perhaps she is right!

Upon reaching the mountain village, Hannah and Williams were enthralled at Marjorie's account of the restoration of her tavern. Kitty, who was outside grooming her horse, did not hear the many compliments paid to her. Her mind was elsewhere.

Perhaps Marjorie was right. What if it was all an illusion, this waiting and waiting? She sat down on an old trunk, and lay against the old stable wall. They are all sorted now, she thought, homes and a future for them all. What of me? What shall I do? There were two other lodges presently empty, but living alone and with no prospects worth speaking of, the future looked suddenly very bleak.

"Oh what am I to do, Misty?" she whispered to the mare, who looked at her with large curious eyes. "No point worrying tonight, is there," she said, patting the animal.

Kitty returned to the house where everyone was in jovial mood. The restoration of the tavern to Marjorie was the main topic of conversation.

"Where is Mag?" asked Kitty, suddenly noting the old woman's absence.

"Need you ask?" Hannah said chirpily, "Off on her famous herb gathering, and the way that wind is rising, she will be blown home! I wish she would tell us where she goes, and stop being so secretive about her excursions," Hannah continued, voicing her concern.

"How long before meal time," Kitty asked, donning her blue cloak.

"Oh, it will be another hour or so, Miss Kitty," Marjorie said, as she rubbed flour from her hands. "Chicken pie tonight, one of old Mag's favourites."

"Well, I shall go for my evening walk, Hannah, and perhaps I shall meet Mag on my way," Kitty said, smiling at Hannah.

"Where on earth are you going girl in that dreadful wind. Have some sense now and sit by the fire and rest," Hannah said in one of her beseeching tones, Kitty noted.

"Heavens Hannah, I have been abroad in a lot worse, and if old Mag is able to endure the gusts, they will be no problem for a young woman like myself!" Kitty assured her.

Bidding the company goodbye, as was her custom, she left them to their chat.

* * *

Old Mag climbed the side of the mountain slowly, as the wind was against her. 'Confound you for a wind,' she sighed.

"Anyway, I should have more sense at my age than traipsing around the mountains at this time of year," she murmured, feeling tired and breathless.

She sat on a stone to rest, and wrapped her shawl tighter around her frail body. She thanked God that no rain fell. Looking at the mountain now, she could clearly see the old stone fort silhouetted against the evening sky, and the figure of Kitty approaching it. She tried to call out to her, but the ever-increasing wind drowned her feeble voice. She decided to continue her uphill climb, walking slowly and carefully lest the wind would knock her off balance.

"Don't want a broken leg now, do I! That would be a very bad start to my new life in the cottage," she said to her cat, which walked some yards ahead of her.

Kitty sat inside the ring of giant rocks. She wondered where old Mag had gone to, and her concern for her was mounting. She felt suddenly tired, and the sense of helplessness, which she had felt at the stable earlier, now returned in waves. She felt it would engulf her at any moment, and she started to cry. Not the tears of grief and loss, but the cry of a frightened and helpless child. Suddenly a violent gust of wind rushed about the circle of stones, and a great wail ensued.

Kitty felt frightened, then she realised it was only the trapped wind inside the circle, and it reminded her of the evening it had occurred when James had been there with her.

"You promised me, James... you did promise me that you would come for me," she cried, as she lay huddled against the stones.

Mag looked at the sky now, for it had turned a myriad of colours, and the wind seemed to be easing. 'Thanks be to God for that much at least,' she said to herself. But as she began her final ascent towards the great circle, a mist began to descend. That's no ordinary mist, she thought, for there is no such thing as a red and blue mist! She could only see occasional glimpses now of the great stone circle, as the mists swirled downwards from the sky.

"Come quickly cat... let us hurry from here," she whispered to her faithful companion, as she picked the frightened animal up and placed it beneath her shawl.

Kitty was relieved that the wind had abated and, despite the overpowering sense of fatigue, stood up in preparation to leave the old fort. Walking through the giant stones she decided that she was wise to return home. Perhaps old Mag was already there. What a strange mist this is, she thought, as she gripped the side of the largest stone.

As if by magic, the mists parted, drawn back as though by a great hand lifting a veil. The setting sun shone through onto the old stone fort. Kitty looked across at the mountains, and it was then that she saw the horseman riding towards her.

He was waving at her. For one brief moment she thought it was a messenger from the village, but then to her amazement the rider was coming as if riding on the wind.

He approached her slowly now, and she sat back against the stones unable to comprehend what was taking place before her eyes.

Mag, only a short distance away, watched the extraordinary events unfolding, and wept with joy. Kitty stood up slowly, and then recognised him.

"James! Oh James my love! I told them, I told them all you would come for me!"

Slowly she stumbled forward, her steps faltering. He stopped within feet of her and looked at his beloved Kitty.

"Oh James... I can't believe it... you are here at last..." she cried in disbelief.

Reaching out his hand to her, he leaned from his horse.

" My beloved Kitty. Come now, my lovely," he called out to her as he gripped her hand. "I told you I would come my darling, and I know you have waited for me. I had to wait until you were ready," he said, hugging her closely.

Mag watched dumbfounded, unable to move.

"We will go now, my beloved, to be together for all time. I told you once, did I not, that nothing would ever separate us, my beloved, and nothing ever will."

She clung to him, her head buried in his shoulder and her arms enfolding him. He turned his horse and a sudden gush of wind seemed to lift them from the ground. Mag watched, now standing upright. They seemed to ride into the crimson sky. Then she could only hear their laughter as the mist enfolded them in its arms. ' They are gone,' she cried silently, 'gone forever'!.

"Goodbye my James and Kitty, and may the heavens open before you," Mag cried out, waving wildly with joy.

She sat down now, trying to understand the marvel she had just witnessed. As the mists cleared, she attempted to catch a final glimpse of them in the heavens, but all that remained was the vibrant colours of the storm clouds.

* * *

As fast as her feeble legs would allow her, she ran back to the village. Pushing the door open, she fell against the table breathless. Hannah and Marjorie were startled by the sudden entrance, and looked at old Mag open-mouthed. Williams helped her into the fireside chair.

"It's all right, Mag. Calm yourself... just get your breath," he said quietly.

Mag looked at them, trying to find the words.

"He came... he came I tell you. She was right all along, was Miss Kitty. I saw him... picking her up. They are both gone now. James came back for her just as he promised," she gasped.

Marjorie sensed the truth instantly, but Hannah was unable to grasp what was being reported.

"I saw him I tell you," Mag continued. "He appeared in the mists on his horse, and told her he had kept his promise. Then they rode into the sky. Oh it was wonderful to see," Mag cried out jubilantly.

"Where is Miss Kitty Mag," Hannah asked, feeling frightened and confused.

"Have I not told you, Hannah? She is gone with James, I tell you. Wasn't I there to see it all?" Mag stated matter of factly.

Hannah stood up.

"I am going to look for her. Marjorie, will you come with me? You too, Seymour. She is delaying far too long this evening," she persisted.

Marjorie looked at Seymour. They both knew what most likely awaited Hannah.

"Yes, Hannah, we will all go," Williams assured her.

Upon reaching the old stone fort, they found her lying against one of the giant boulders. She wore an expression of complete happiness, Marjorie thought, more beautiful in death almost than in life. Hannah knelt down and cradled Kitty in her arms and cried bitterly.

"Oh my darling little girl, you have left me," she cried.

Williams fought back his own tears and gently lifted Hannah up.

"She is with James at last, Hannah. It is what she was living for, wasn't it?" he said, trying to console her.

"Oh yes, Seymour, it was her hearts desire, I know," she said, becoming more composed.

They carried the body back to the house, where Marjorie and Hannah laid her out in the traditional manner. Old Mag took Hannah's hands in her own.

"Hannah, 'tis not the ramblings of an old woman. I tell you, I saw him take her spirit away, and she was happy beyond words. It would be selfish of us to want her back. The girl is finally happy at last, poor lamb, and she deserves to be after all she went through."

* * *

Two days later, they laid Kitty to rest beside James, the man for whom in life she had given up so much. It was a lovely autumn day, and many people had come from the surrounding area to pay their final respects to a lady who had the courage to be different.

Hannah sensed a great peace when she returned from the old cemetery, and as they sat outside the house in the evening sunshine she said as much to Williams.

"Well, my dear, she is at rest at last. Lady Catherine would never have known peace in this life; for her heart was with the man she loved. We cannot begrudge her that, can we?"

* * *

Their eventual departure from the mountain village was a sad experience for them all, despite the fact that they were to begin new lives. Tom, the stable hand from Oak Hall, brought their belongings in a dray cart, as Marjorie walked beside Hannah on the way down the mountainside. Old Mag sat in a pony and cart driven by Williams, and she gazed up at the old fort.

It was a crisp autumn morning, and the air was cool. High in the sky above the fort and ravens wheeled in a noisy circle, as if to bid them farewell. Hannah stopped to look at the sight, as Williams stayed the pony cart.

"They are disturbed you know," old Mag said in her usual manner.

"Do you really believe that?" Marjorie asked her curiously.

"Yes I do," she replied. "The ravens will always have company there now, you know, for James and Kitty found their happiness in that sacred place. Knowing the two of them as we do, they will only want to be left alone."

From the old fort they heard the neighing of horses, and as the mist descended on the higher peaks, laughter could be heard echoing across the valley.

Mag cradled her cat and smiled.

"I told you so my pet, did I not? They will ride these mountains forever, and forever happy."

Hannah, for the first time ever, believed the old woman.

The End

Epilogue

The French Revolution was one of the sparks that ignited one of the bloodiest and appalling episodes in the History of Ireland: the rebellion of 1798. Yet this sad and gruelling conflict lasted just a mere summer, from May until September of that year.

More men and women died in that season than the combined fatalities of the Northern Ireland Conflict.

Croghan Kinsella is a mountain overlooking north Wexford, spanning part of the southern borders of Wicklow. It is a quiet and majestic landscape of curving hills, overlooking the Bann valley. It lies north of Gorey and west of Arklow, and its gentle terrain echoes yet the whispers of long gone souls whose lives were lived out in this quiet and beautiful corner of Ireland.

James and Kitty were indeed real people and their story is true.

They lie resting now, together in an unmarked grave in Kilninor Graveyard, a mile hence from Croghan and Glenogue. It is indeed an old and sacred place named after the Church of the Nine Alters burned down by Cromwellian Forces.

I have many times sat in that bluebell wooded glade of a May evening, contemplating the lives and fate of James and Kitty ... blackbird song their lullaby. James, the Wexford rebel, and Kitty, daughter of an ascendancy family; a most unlikely match, and in that era, unthinkable.

And yet it happened.

Their love endured onto death and I have no doubt, beyond its narrow confines.

Kitty's remaining days awaiting the promised return of James to *"collect her on the West wind"* were spent in Croghan with a family named Redmond, who later married into the Tallon family. Each evening, irrespective of the weather, would see her climb Glenogue hill awaiting the fulfilment of that promise.

On a quiet September evening 1798, in the aftermath of a storm, the local people set out to find the beautiful young woman who had failed to return.

Indeed, James had kept his promise – and reader, I tell you not an idle tale.

Barry Redmond
bayonetsandlace@gmail.com

Lightning Source UK Ltd.
Milton Keynes UK
UKOW05f0949080514

231325UK00001B/1/P